Attack!

"I don't give a damn what your orders are! I'm going in there!"

The distinctive sounds of a scuffle heralded Ganfrion's arrival.

Mikhyel cast Deymorin an apologetic glance.

{I left an invitation for him to meet us here when he woke. I'd better go clear it up.}

{You could have warned me.} He had set the guards to prevent intrusion. They followed their orders, and admitted no one without authorization.

{I forgot,} Mikhyel said, and sighed as the commotion that echoed in the caverns drew closer. {I've got some explaining to do to him.}

{I've told him most of what I've said,} Deymorin said.

{Everything?} Mikhyel asked.

{Everything he'd accept.}

Mikhyel cast him a look that required no inner elaboration and pulled himself dripping, from the pool, to deal with his gorman.

An instant later Mikhyel cried out and toppled, as Deymorin's head exploded with pain.

JANE FANCHER

Dance of the Rings
RING OF LIGHTNING
RING OF INTRIGUE
RING OF DESTINY
RING OF CHANGE*

*Forthcoming from DAW Books

RING OF DESTINY

Jane S. Fancher

Dance of the Rings: Book Three

DAW BOOKS, INC.
DONALD A. WOLLHEIM, FOUNDER
375 Hudson Street, New York, NY 10014

ELIZABETH R. WOLLHEIM
SHEILA E. GILBERT
PUBLISHERS

First Printing, December 1999
1 2 3 4 5 6 7 8 9

DAW TRADEMARK REGISTERED
U.S. PAT. OFF. AND FOREIGN COUNTRIES
—MARCA REGISTRADA
HECHO EN U.S.A.

PRINTED IN THE U.S.A.

In Loving Memory:
Gary Lansing Fancher
Venus d'my Luv
Dustbunny
Mr. Khym
and
His Blackness, Elrond the Magnificent

Prelude

They made love for the first time on a gilt-edged dream beneath a shadow of doom.

Fingertips extend. Iridescent motes ripple and flow, coalesce as skin touches skin, flare as fingers intertwine.

With separation, even death, an imminent probability, they'd packed a lifetime of experience into one brief night.

Mouths explore, caressing, savoring—remembering.

They'd come to know one another that night, to a depth no poet had ever dared to imagine.

Two Minds brush with a feather's light touch . . .

Her thoughts had smelled of raspberries that night, raspberries dusted with cinnamon and the faintest hint of clove.

. . . then merge into a unified awareness, as two Bodies become one in the most ancient of mortal dances.

That scent—not truly scent at all, but rather some essential radiance that bypassed nose and tongue altogether and plunged straight to his heart—that essence filled him now, heart, mind, and soul. It was indisputable evidence that she was truly, impossibly alive and in his arms, and not some guilt-driven memory come to torment his dreams.

They made love for the second time on a moss-covered hillside, while a new leythium node blossomed deep in the earth beneath them.

They were little more than novices—she a Khoratumin ringdancer, he with a past as black as the hair on his head—but the love they shared transcended fumbling, uncertain hands and shyly diverted eyes, and as they merged, one into the other, experience ceased to have meaning. There was only . . .

Need.
Desire.
Joy.

The glittering false dawn of ley-touched mountain air tingled against their skin. Music born of the crystalline web, steadily evolving in the caves below, filled their minds.

Life emerged in those caverns. The very essence of the earth gained form under the impact of the unbridled energy that bathed this instant in time and this tiny spot of earth. It was energy focused, in part, by the lovers' simple presence.

And as the very ground beneath them surged and receded with slow undulation—as if the mountain itself breathed—they explored those indescribable places, both mental and physical, where Self held no meaning.

Where existence was a deluge of . . .
Anticipation . . .
Sensation . . .
Consummation.

Release.

Mikhyel.
My name is Mikhyel.
Isolation.
She . . . is . . . Temorii.
And the mountain stopped breathing.

SECTION
ONE

Chapter One

Night gave way reluctantly to morning. The glitter in the misty air confused the transition, making ghosts of the rows of field tents, corpses of the blanket-wrapped bodies littering the ground outside the tents.

Assuming, of course, those erstwhile soldiers weren't, in fact, dead and that Ganfrion of No Family and No Node wasn't the only man still living on this hell-blasted mountainside—a mountainside with the unmitigated gall to appear, in dawn's light, as if it were a perfectly ordinary mountain meadow bathed in a perfectly ordinary Khoramali summer morning.

But hellfire *had* filled that deceptively innocent sky last night. Throughout the midnight hours, blasts of energy that owed nothing to the honest blaze of gunpowder or the exhilarating song of steel had blazed an unnatural iridescent web from the northeast to southwest: that was to say, between the cities of Khoratum to Rhomatum, as any man here knew. It had been a battle between node cities, more specifically, a battle between Towers, a battle the likes of which he had never heard, a battle in which these men had had no part, but a battle that, in its aftermath, had rained who-knew-what down on their heads all night, here in the open as they'd slept . . . having been given license by their commanding officer, Deymorin Rhomandi dunMheric, the Rhomandi himself, to leave their underground haven.

License to leave when they damnwell should have been ordered to stay in the limestone caverns nearly encircling the campgrounds until the world was normal again. Why else had they chosen this cave-riddled spot for their semi-permanent base camp all those months ago?

Lightning, a part of him answered his own question. He'd been here when they'd laid out this camp, begun its two permanent structures, the field hospital and the granary. They'd had no idea, not even the slightest suspicion, that they'd need protection against anything other than the wild storms that raged regularly in the Khoramali. They'd set the lines of the camp relative to the caves with those wicked storms in mind, protecting their supplies from deer and lightning, not . . . leythium.

That's what *they* had had in mind, those men who had located and surveyed this site, but he wouldn't hazard a guess as to what the Rhomandi had suspected. Not anymore.

Not after last night.

Ganfrion propped himself against a marker post that proclaimed this block of tents the Aerie of the Seventh Eagle and scanned the rows, seeking any sign of movement, any hint of the sort of stirring that ought to occur among seasoned troops as the sun's first rays gilded the snow-capped tops of the mountains. Never mind most had lain awake watching that web disintegrate into sparkling motes of energy, motes that had drifted down from the sky hovering and darting and floating on a breeze like a billion fireflies on Midsummer's Eve.

And this morning . . . the bodies lay still as death.

The cough that had plagued him since long before the world ended threatened, and he staved it off with a long pull from the flask he carried. Stolen, that flask, or given to him sometime last night before men turned to corpses. He honestly couldn't recall how it had come into his possession. He only recalled wanting a drink, badly, and that flask arriving in his hand in a moment of darkness between one heartbeat and the next—much as he had arrived in this camp last night. One moment, he'd been gasping his last in the middle of the Khoratum Maze, his back braced against a wooden door, the dancer he'd gone to rescue huddled against his side; the next, he'd been here on the leyroad side of the camp, the dancer still at his side and his back to the earthen fortification, his feet hanging in a half-dug trench—a day's ride from that maze under the best of circumstances.

At least, he'd assumed it was the same night. The tower battle had ceased—before or after that final moment in the maze, he couldn't swear to—but the web in the sky had only just begun to disintegrate. The moon was still full. And it was just himself and the dancer, both as immobile as they'd been in the maze. Time had passed; the leythium motes had drenched them, and eventually he'd found the strength to gather himself and the dancer up, to stumble across that waist-high ditch and through the camp to the caves, miraculously alive, and without a clue as to why that was true or how he'd come to be here.

Later, after the stand-down had been ordered, with his precious charge delivered into the proper hands, with every right to a month's rest, with in fact his *liege lord's* direct order to celebrate his unexpected aliveness in that manner—and still no answers to the mysteries surrounding that fact—*he* had refused to so much as lie down as long as the glitter remained in the air. Having cheated Death once that night, in a Khoratumin alleyway and against honest steel, he wasn't about to lie down and passively surrender to this new, insidiously attractive threat. Never mind he'd stood outside the caves watching the spectacle, as mesmerized as all the others by the sheer beauty of the moment. *He'd* recovered. He'd given in once, but had resisted that subsequent effect, that feeling of somnolent well-being that arrived with the glittering rain like a post-orgasmic lethargy. No, he hadn't fallen asleep, and damned if he hadn't cheated those unnamed gods of the Ley and the Lightning yet one more chance at his oft-compromised soul.

Even now, for all he had a tent somewhere in this sea of tents that seemed doubled and even tripled in size since his last time here, he refused to seek out that haven, refused to surrender to the very real exhaustion that made his eyes flicker in and out of focus and his knees turn to liquid. He refused to surrender because even now he had to wonder whether the glitter was gone or simply overpowered by the light of dawn.

Another part of his fractured thinking wondered if perhaps his personal battle was long since moot. Perhaps, considering the flask, still full after so many hours and so many throat-quenching drafts, the gods *had* won. Perhaps he was dead after all, and death, for that compromised soul, was to walk alone, among bodies dreaming the peaceful dreams of the righteous, bone-deep aches in every joint, sharp pains everywhere else, wounds that never healed. Never healing, never dying . . .

With only the flask for company.

He took another swig.

He could live—or not live—with that. He'd made his decisions in life, and he'd die with the consequences.

The precisely aligned field tents rippled, faded, and fluxed back into focus before they disappeared altogether. Caught in mid-stride by this new twist of his singular reality, Ganfrion froze, one foot in the air. But his abused-possibly-dead body betrayed him. Balance went, knees gave, and he staggered. His boot encountered an unexpected lump. The lump produced a curse, and a glancing blow caught Ganfrion's already uncertain knees.

His mercenary blood surged, his vision cleared, and strength returned to his limbs. Battle-honed instincts held him upright, wavering but ready—eager, even—for a fight. A good, honest fight would be a welcome relief after the recent ambiguity of his life.

And proof he wasn't alone in his post-leythium-rain hell.

But the lump ignored him, rolled over and burrowed deeper into its cocoon of blankets, returning to its former corpse-like condition.

Cheated of his fight, Ganfrion responded with the only sensible alternative. He slid down to sit cross-legged next to the lump and offered it a drink. The lump rolled over, produced a heavy-lidded eye that took in the flask, blinked slowly, and a reluctant grin joined the eye above the blanket.

"A bit early, don't you think?"

"Can't be." Ganfrion took a carefully measured sip, then extended the flask again. "Haven't been to bed yet."

The lump's eyes followed his moves, showing a healthy suspicion, a keen analysis. A good border man, like all those other lumps lying about. Grant the Rhomandi that much: luck, good advice, or more sense than Ganfrion had once attributed to him, he'd recruited a good lot for his personal guard. Six—seven hundred, perhaps, encamped here at what amounted to little more than a supply station in the southwest shadow of Mount Khoratum. Large for a personal guard, but the Rhomandi hadn't truly gathered them for his personal protection.

"Maybe you haven't been to bed, but I *have*." The border lump made as if to return to sleep. "I'm in it."

"So?" Ganfrion nudged him with a toe. "Hell, man, first call isn't until midday. The Rhomandi's own order. Breakfast." He shook the flask suggestively. Eyes and grin above the blanket edge developed into a stubbled face atop a hairy chest, then a hand that accepted the flask. The man sniffed and pulled back. "Whew. That stuff'll kill you."

Ganfrion snorted, reclaimed his prize, and gulped a mouthful. "Where'd the Rhomandi pull you from, missy? A Kirish'lani slave market?"

The lump growled and grabbed the flask, coughed as the potent liquid hit his throat, and swallowed again. "Shit, just my luck, the Rhomandi'll call a surprise muster." Which expectation did not stop the lump from helping himself to another hefty sample.

"He won't."

The man snorted and tossed the flask back. "And you, of course, are in his direct counsel."

Ganfrion just lifted a suggestive brow and took a swig that should have emptied the flask. It didn't. But he didn't wonder at that phenomenon any longer. After what he'd witnessed in the past few days, after what he'd *experienced* in the last few hours, he refused to wonder at anything ever again.

"Who *are* you?" the lump asked.

"Ganfrion," he answered, then recalled: "*Captain* Gan-

frion, newly anointed gorMikhyel." As if he could forget.
The flask made another round. "And as your superior, I
order you. It's your sworn duty. For Princeps and Node
and . . . hellsabove, drink to my promotion!"

The lump guffawed, but forced himself to obey the direct
order. The return pass was accompanied by one more of
those Looks. "Captain Ganfrion. Heard of you. You're the
man the Barrister pulled out of Sparingate Prison and the
Rhomandi himself elevated to Captain. *And* gorMikhyel?
Hadn't heard that. The Barrister's sworn man? Should I
be worried?"

"Suit yourself," Ganfrion replied with a frown, and
under cover of his coat, twisted the ring itching and cutting
off circulation to his smallest finger. Damned spider-
fingered pen-scratcher. In one brief moment, Mikhyel dun-
Mheric had saddled him with a ring several sizes too small
and an associated oath that choked his whole gods-be-
damned philosophy of life.

"Heard tell the Rhomandi's brothers showed up in camp
last night. Guess you're proof of that, eh?"

He shrugged, tacitly avoiding the details of that arrival.

A handful of returns later: "What's he like?"

"Hm?" He grunted, forcing his eyes to focus.

"You're shat, man. Better stop."

He growled, and the man raised a warding hand. It was
lack of sleep, not too much drink that slurred his tongue
and made his eyes droop, but damned if he'd explain that
to the lump. "Wha's *who* like?"

"Th' Barrister. Met the kid brother once—never can remember his name."

"Nik—" His voice caught with the stitch in his side. "—
aenor. Nikki."

"Yeah, that's the one. Odd name, to my way of thinking.
Kid visited the Rhomandi on the border back when Deymorin Rhomandi was still Deymio even t' the likes of us.
Solid man, Deymio. Liked what I saw then, liked what I
heard after. City man who looks after somethin' other than
th' Cities. Knows th' value of a fighting man and a farmer,
he does. Proud, I was, when he included me in his special

muster. The kid—hell, he was a kid. But what about this middle brother? As hard as they say?"

What was Mikhyel dunMheric like? Certainly nothing like his brothers. Deymorin Rhomandi, Princeps of Rhomatum and the Rhomandi of House Rhomandi, at least looked the part of a leader. Big man. Solid, as this lump said. The sort that could inspire men to follow and trust just by his presence. A trait that made men like Ganfrion that much more suspicious of him. Still, there was enough substance behind the appearance to warrant this lump's assessment.

Physically and by nature, Rhomandi was a true descendant of Darius, the very image of those who had emigrated from Mauritum three hundred years ago. Nikaenor, youngest of the three, was softer yet still unquestionably the same breed.

Mikhyel dunMheric had been pulled from an entirely different mold. The first time he'd seen him, Ganfrion had mistaken him for a hiller—

No. That had been the second time. The first time, *he'd* been in the High Court sentencing pit and dunMheric had been on the uppermost judgment dais. Mikhyel had seemed . . . taller then.

The second time they'd crossed paths had been in the depths of Sparingate Crypt, prison for the worst and dumbest. *He'd* been there for attempting to assassinate the Rhomandi, never mind he'd been caught because he'd been *stopping* his associate from that precise dastardly deed. The fact was, after tailing Rhomandi long enough to evaluate his worthiness to be dead, he'd gone back on his hire. He'd decided that Rhomandi's loss to the world was not worth the risk to his own well-being should he be caught. And in that refusal to kill Deymorin Rhomandi he'd pissed off the wrong person in the Tower. Since That Person, the brothers' own charming aunt Anheliaa, was now dead, the details of that incarceration were moot.

Besides, over the years he'd acquired ample points on the shady side of the law to offset more than one mistaken ruling.

By the strictest rule of law, *he'd* belonged in the Crypt; the Rhomandi brothers had not, not by any stretch of any law. The Rhomandi brothers had pissed off more than their aunt, and been tossed among the worst element of Rhomatum society for, of all things, impersonating themselves.

Some idiosyncracies of the elite defied even his understanding.

The lump nudged his elbow; Ganfrion ignored him and took another swallow, his mind wandering off, wondering who it was that had wanted them dead—because someone had. Deymorin might have passed unnoticed, save for the normal challenges a strong man faced in establishing crypt-status: of all those in the Crypt, he'd likely been the only one who'd ever *seen* Deymorin Rhomandi before. Nikki was even less well-known.

Mikhyel, on the other hand, was known by each and every scut in that high security level of the prison. Mikhyel, Lord High Justice dunMheric, had sentenced every one of them.

Only chance, in the form of the complete absence of the beard that had been the Barrister's signature for years, had prevented his instant exposure. And it wasn't that it had simply been shaved. In all those long hours the brothers spent in the Crypt, not so much as a shadow had appeared around that deceptively sensual mouth.

Another impatient jab; he handed the flask to the lump.

The crypt-scut had called the unknown inmate pretty, crypt-slang for powerless new meat. The crypt-scut had been in error: Ganfrion doubted Mikhyel dunMheric had ever been powerless. He could imagine Mikhyel dunMheric determining the moment of his own birth from the dark depth of his mother's womb, some twenty-seven years ago.

The flask tapped his elbow. He took it and another swig, ignoring the expectant look on the lump's face.

Twenty-seven. Damned baby. Damned babe who'd been calling the shots for the entire Syndicate of Nodes for ten years.

As he'd called the shots in the Crypt that night. With what he now recognized as typical arrogance, Mikhyel had played to that scutly prejudice, seamlessly slipping into the part of a gutter whore, and subsequently controlling, such as they could be controlled, the majority of the scuts, buying him and his brothers one night of peace, time for them to get free of the Crypt. But arrogance was all that had connected the pale, thin, beardless young hillerman to the man the underworld knew as Hell's Barrister.

A name, so rumor had it, given him by his own brother. That sleek, dark hair and hiller-smooth jaw had thrown them all, including Ganfrion, and *he'd* grown up in the Khoramali, in a hiller village where his large, hairy body had made him as out of place as dunMheric had been in Rhomatum's Crypt.

That beard—so indelibly part of the Barrister image— had just as mysteriously reappeared, much too soon after Mikhyel escaped the Crypt. Ganfrion had assumed, on that first meeting after his release from the Crypt, that the beard was fake, applied to disguise an otherwise embarrassing hiller connection to the first family of Rhomatum . . . would still believe that if he hadn't personally watched Mikhyel's valet, Raulind, trim and shave it on a daily basis.

That beard—was just one more in a long line of the mysteries that surrounded his employer.

What was Mikhyel dunMheric like?

"Lives up to his name," Ganfrion answered at last, then cleared his throat and spat, aiming at a nearby rock.

"Which name?" the lump asked quickly. Too quickly for him this morning.

The damp splotch traced a mostly red path down the stone.

"Take your pick."

His employer was above all else a Rhomandi. Mikhyel lived and breathed for the City named for his ancestor. He was more *the* Rhomandi in that sense than his legally entitled brother had yet proven to be. And he was a dunMheric: definitely a man formed by his cursed father.

And Hell's Barrister? Mikhyel dunMheric was as fair . . . and as ruthless . . . as any man ever birthed.

"I wouldn't cross him, if I were you." Ganfrion drew hard on the flask and passed it again.

"And *you* gave the oath." The raised flask was a silent toast to his perceived daring.

Gave? He wouldn't put the matter that way. He'd had the damned ring thrown at him along with an order to get himself out of hell alive. . . .Where was the honor in that? Where was the choice?

"Since you have the rail in this race, bein' so tight with the Princeps and all, how 'bout explainin' what that was all about last night?"

Explain. Explain what? That the Northern Crescent, fully half of the Syndicate of Nodes, had staged a major coup? That confidence in the Rhomandi Family had shattered at last and that Garetti of Mauritum had been using the Northern Towers to wrest control—however remotely—of Rhomatum Tower out of Rhomandi hands?

That the fact that the Rhomandi had called the stand-down for the troops following last night's atmospheric pyro-technics indicated to him that the coup had failed?

That he himself had serious reservations about what the Rhomandi brothers had done to halt that rebellion?

That he himself had serious reservations about the stand-down here in camp with all the "personal guards" of the Northern Crescent Families encamped just outside of Khor-atum City, only two days' march away? Two days . . . and he'd made the trek in a heartbeat. What was to stop them from the same unexplained trip? What was to stop those troops from landing, armed and ready in the middle of this sleeping camp? Snugged up against a mountain's flank, they *had* no fortifications here—unless you counted that over-sized ditch, the caves and the mountain height, which personally, Ganfrion did not.

A hospital built to handle blisters and dysenteric recruits and a granary to supply trainees' horses didn't qualify as a fort, either, but it was what they had, those and wagonloads of canvas tents. So here they were, come to fight a war that wasn't a war, without an army, plumped down to sleep off the sparkles in the sky in a fort with a half-finished wall, while the Ley bubbled and burbled its discontent underground. The Rhomandi brothers had had a falling out with the ringmaster in Khoratum, men popped up here and there across a map no longer peaceful by means that didn't make sense to a sober man, which he wasn't, nor meant to be any time soon . . . Oh, all was not right with the world.

Not for the first time, Ganfrion regretted having been singled out by some decidedly ill-humored fate to have these insights into the Rhomandi brothers' business.

Actually, it wasn't what he knew, it was what he *didn't* know. He knew the questions but too damned few answers.

He took a hasty, frustrated pull from his flask. Too hasty: the swallow dissolved in a choking cough. The now-constant ache in his side flared to blinding brilliance, and he gripped his elbow tight, holding both cough and pain at bay. The morning light dimmed; the sparkling motes returned, and it seemed to his pain-hazed eyes as if they swirled around him and gathered at his waist—where, beneath his stolen coat, the equally pillaged shirt-turned-field-bandage oozed a sluggish trail down his side.

Saturated—from a wound that by rights should have drained him dry sometime around midnight last night. He should be dead and lying unnoticed and unmourned in a back alley of a mountain node city a good two days' journey away from this camp.

Dead. In Khoratum. Covering Mikhyel dunMheric's escape.

"Captain?"

Yet here he was, still full of liquid . . . just like the bottomless flask.

"*—Captain!*"

The motes disappeared between one blink and the next. The blanket-lump had gained a body and legs, was on its knees now, gripping his shoulders, shaking him. Shouting for help. Loudly.

From the pounding in his head, maybe the haze surrounding him was the alcohol after all.

"Shut up," Ganfrion snarled, and when the lump appeared not to notice: "I said, shut the fuck up. I'm a hell of a way from dead!"

But the damage was done. All around them, other lumps developed arms and legs and loud voices asking questions he didn't want to answer. He staggered to his feet, snatched up the flask, and backed away from the lump's growing suspicion. "That's it. We're finished. See if I ever offer you breakfast in bed again!"

He escaped between tents, wishing he had his old strength, his accustomed skill at vanishing into any convenient shadow, of which there were plenty here. Instead, it was all he could do to maintain an even pace until he was on the edge of the camp, well away from the lump's camp-fire, and even farther from the growing number of permanent structures rising here, structures that included among other things, the infirmary he should, without question, be reporting to even now.

Get himself patched up before the glitter faded altogether and his body . . . and the flask . . . drained at last.

The shouts faded into the distance—or perhaps were just overridden by the pounding in his ears. But a glance backward confirmed that lack of pursuit.

He relented, then, to his body's silent protests, and caught himself against a tree. One of many trees. He'd stumbled his way into a small stand of timber they'd chosen to keep on the inside of the ditch and earth barricade that paralleled the leyroad and funneled honest folk past a guarded gate. From here, had he been so inclined, he could easily make his way up the rocky mountainside, and escape the camp altogether.

Damned sloppy. They should have been all over him. The lump's suspicions were more than enough to detain him for further questioning. And that would mean lying to men who deserved better, which he didn't want to do—or facing the Rhomandi brothers, which he didn't want to do—or landing in the infirmary . . . which might not be a bad idea, excepting the morbid curiosity that had taken him regarding his wounds: he was waiting for them to commit to the task of killing him.

From the shouts, a man would think he'd disappeared right before their eyes. And perhaps he had. Apparitions were inclined to do that. He'd seen dead men walking last night. Perhaps it wasn't these men rising from their beds who had died, but a man called Ganfrion. He'd survived a fight that should have killed him, found a dancer that should be dead, delivered that animated corpse to Mikhyel dunMheric fifty damned miles as the hawks flew from where they all were supposed to be. He had wounds that refused to kill him, a flask that refused to empty, hunters who couldn't find him. . . .

Death was the least improbable of all explanations.

Leythium fire surrounded him again, lit his skin with tingling energy.

Iridescent rain. Leythium fireflies. Motes of pure energy.

Leythium was not humanity's friend, for all that the energy it produced, controlled by the node-based ringtowers, provided humanity with the light and heat for the luxuries of the cities, and power for the steam engines that drove the manufactories. Everyone knew that that energy came at a terrible price to those who controlled it, knew that liquid leythium would eat the flesh right off a man's bones.

Hell, in the Cities, they buried their dead in it and fed it the damned sewage for dessert.

And yet all of them—Rhomandi, soldier, and mercenary alike—had stood in the fallout, gazing up into that lethal wonder like a flock of turkeys staring up into the rain. Drowning in their own stupidity.

An honest man had asked him what had happened. Had asked *him,* gorMikhyel, who should have been in Mikhyel dunMheric's confidence.

What can be done has been done whether I'm here or in Rhomatum.

Mikhyel dunMheric's response when he'd urged his employer to get the hell out of Khoratum, where near-certain imprisonment, if not death, awaited him.

What did you do, Khyel? he thought, and worried anew about how plans had been made at such distance without the use of a ringtower and without his help, he who had been Mikhyel's eyes and ears.

I have my ways, Ganfrion . . . you're not my only source. . . .

"Damn you, Khyel," he whispered aloud. "Why didn't you trust me?"

He clenched his fist until the ring turned his fingertip to ice.

Fools. They were all of them fools.

Perhaps this was death. Perhaps he had died in that Khoratumin alley. Perhaps Khyel had, as well. Perhaps Mikhyel dunMheric's foolhardy dancer had died on the Khoratumin dance rings and they'd all journeyed into death together.

Certainly the celestial pyrotechnics that had greeted him upon his arrival here, the wound that neither healed itself nor destroyed him—the endless torment of a cursed soul— those would fulfill the lightning-blasted, hell-fired image of the next world the True Believers of Maurii had brought into the valley three hundred years ago.

Funny. He'd never imagined he'd spend his time awaiting rebirth among the likes of the Rhomandi brothers.

§   §   §

Deymorin Rhomandi dunMheric, Princeps of Rhomatum and recently appointed Supreme Commander of the Rhomatum Syndicate's (fledgling) Allied Army, included the horse tether lines in his morning rounds not because he doubted the skills of the men in charge of the stock, but because he enjoyed petting a few appreciative equine noses before facing the problems of his own, more demanding, species.

And demands would be high this morning; each of the seven hundred thirty-six men encamped here would be wanting answers, wanting to know what they'd witnessed last night, why a state of high alert had suddenly turned to a stand-down until further notice. He'd sought thinking, independent sorts to be under his direct command, and he paid for that decision with daily inquisitions.

Still, these were fighting men, their curiosity generally short-lived in matters not involving combat. He might yet escape a concerted inquiry.

He'd been dubious last night about giving the order to allow the men to exit the caves at will, despite the strange energy that had filled the air and threatened tempers in the close quarters underground, but Mikhyel had assured him there was no danger. It hadn't even occurred to him to question that knowledge. Mikhyel . . . *knew* things about the Ley, these days.

What *he* knew was that his brother, both the man and the lawyer, would never make that statement if he weren't absolutely convinced . . . no, *certain* beyond any possible doubt that it was safe. So he'd given the order.

The display had faded now to nothing more alarming than the occasional sparkling mote, little different from sun-dazzle in winter—at least to his eyes. From the horses' lack of reaction, and that of the few men on their feet, it would appear that his fellow early risers noted nothing at all unusual about the air they breathed, a realization he found disquieting. He'd grown different enough in recent months without adding daylight hallucinations to the mix.

A solid fence blocked his path, and he ducked between the rails. The horse within the small pen immediately left his morning snack of freshly-scythed mountain grass and trotted over, looking for treats.

"Sorry, lad," he murmured, and stroked the warm neck beneath the flaxen mane. Grass-scented breath snuffled the hair around his ear, assuring him he must be mistaken. Panders-to-No-One wasn't the horse he'd have chosen to bring on this particular venture—the young stallion's attention still inclined more toward the ladies than to his rider's requirements—but next to Ringer, Pander had the most endurance of the Rhomandi stable's stock, a commodity much to be desired these days, when a recall to Rhomatum could come at any given moment.

Pander was at least a well-behaved fellow, for a breeding stallion, and had become a fast favorite with the handlers, as witness the pile of freshly-scythed mountain grass he'd been absently munching.

"You'll get fat at this rate, laddybuck," he said, then laughed as Pander—as if in full understanding—set his chin heavily on Deymorin's shoulder and sighed, boredom in every well-defined muscle. Deymorin scratched the stallion's throat, then pulled the soft ears until they waggled quite ridiculously.

Relaxed, friendly: far different from any of his father's stock. He'd never have dared bring a stallion of Mheric's training on a mission such as this. Mheric had conquered his horses; Deymorin had learned other methods from the Kirish'lani horse traders who had wandered freely among the border patrols, gambling and selling their culls. He'd watched them make their horses dance to a music all their own, and seen those same horses knock a would-be thief's teeth out. He'd braved the traders' camps to ask them how.

They'd thrown him out on his ear.

He'd tried to buy one of those dancing horses; they'd laughed in his face.

So he'd won one in a game of chance—one of the more shameless actions of his youth. The trader had had no sense when the gambling heat was high, and he'd taken full advantage of that weakness. The heartbroken gamester had been more than happy to trade his beloved horse for Deymorin's choice of the yearling stallions—

—and the secrets of their training methods.

It had been a fast lesson, and one steeped in convolutions, the trader's own attempt to salvage his reputation among his peers. But the essence of that skill had proven as natural as breathing to him, and once he'd ridden one of those dancing horses, he'd known he'd never be content with anything less.

Mheric would have been scandalized, but Mheric had been dead three years by then. He'd taken those lessons back to Darhaven, the Rhomandi stud farm, found willing accomplices among the training staff and retired the others, thus eliminating the final vestige of Mheric's influence from the program. Three years later, they were ready to try what they'd learned by trial and error on their existing stock on the first of Pandr'iini's offspring.

The get from that yearling, Pander's own sire, combined with those training methods Deymorin and his staff had developed based on his new insights, had made the Rhomandi stock the most valuable in the Syndicate in a few short years.

But it hadn't taken Pandr'iini to sire the best. Common as a street-rat by birth, Ringer had danced with the best of them.

He rubbed Pander's nose, wondering where in hell Ringer had got to. He hadn't seen the big gelding in over twelve months, not since he'd ridden him into Rhomatum the morning of Nikki's seventeenth birth—

The inner sense tingled in response to thoughts of Nikki. His youngest brother was awake and thinking *horse*.

Actually, Nikki was thinking other, more lascivious thoughts, but with his wife two days' ride distant, his options were limited.

Deymorin could well understand. A similar state of mind and body had had him up with the sun. Kiyrstin, never far from his thoughts, seemed to follow him everywhere this morning. The moment he relaxed his guard, it was as if her hands were inside his clothing, making him tingle from head to foot as only she could do.

Or so he'd believed.

Sparkling motes of color. Insidious energy. No wonder many of the tent flaps had been dropped this morning, for all there were signs of activity within.

And beneath them, a new node gestated. *Let's make a baby*, Mother had said to the Rhomatumin *Tamshi* that had spawned her a geologic age ago.

Procreation. He didn't pretend to understand how it worked for the tamshi, but in a camp full of healthy men, that drive could find any number of releases, some less constructive than others. He made a mental note to warn the sergeants to drill the men to physical exhaustion in the practice field, if nothing else sufficed.

Not the optimum solution: he still couldn't be certain the

Northern Crescent leaders wouldn't come charging down
the leyroad in some mistaken notion of taking hand to hand
what they'd failed to take via the Towers, but the chances
were very limited. They'd been tempted into the rebellion
by the notion that the Rhomandi wouldn't be able to hold
Rhomatum Tower. That notion had been disproved; they
would more likely be slinking home with their tails between
their legs.

Nikki was dressed and headed his way, had made it to
the feed barn that had been their first permanent construction, and was poking about in the dark among grain sacks
seeking equine bribes; the inner sense he shared with his
brothers tracked Nikki's position as surely as if he were
watching from overhead. He searched deliberately across
the camp for Mikhyel's presence, but while he could pinpoint his other brother's location on the hillside where he'd
slept alone, well away from the tents and soldiers, Mikhyel's mind remained as stubbornly opaque as it had been
all night.

Nothing unusual in that, other than the location. Mikhyel
would return, physically or mentally, when Mikhyel was
ready, and not before. Secretive. Alone. That much, at
least, hadn't changed . . .

"Deymorin? Deymorin!" Nikki's eager voice pierced the
morning peace.

. . . Fortunately. If they were all as open as Nikki, they'd
never sort out one brother's thoughts from the others'.

"Good morning to you, too, little brother," Deymorin
said, turning to meet him. "I thought I felt you."

"Shit," Nikki muttered, and then blushed. "Sorry . . ."

An apology that his underlying better sense applied
equally to his language and his mental noise. Sometimes
Nikki's attempts to keep his thoughts quiet proved more
disruptive than the thoughts themselves.

Deymorin chuckled and slapped Nikki's solid arm.
"You're doing very well, Nik. Just a hint at the edge of
my . . ." He fingered the coat encasing that solid arm. *His*
coat. Nikki carried a quarter bucket of sweet feed, and
honeyed grain clung to the fine no-wale corduroy cuffs.

Nikki's blush deepened. "Tonio gave it to me. His wouldn't fit and I didn't have—"

Deymorin laughed aloud. "Stop apologizing, brat. Naturally he did, considering you arrived last night with only the clothes on your back."

City clothes, at that. Clothing designed for the temperature-controlled atmosphere of Rhomatum Tower, and hardly appropriate for a brisk Khoramali morning. It was no wonder Tonio had provided this largesse out of his trunk.

Still, he'd talk to his valet. This particular coat had been a gift from Kiyrstin and it was not something he cared to share with his younger brother.

"At least," he said, to divert them both from the issue that had nothing, really, to do with Nikki, "the Tamshi were rather more generous with you than Anheliaa was with Mikhyel and myself. I'm having a hard enough time explaining my brothers' unannounced arrivals without explaining their bare behinds as well."

"Rings!" Nikki laughed. "I never even *thought* of that. Still—" He gave Deymorin a crossways look. "Still, look what it got you. Maybe if you'd had your clothes on, Kiyrstin would have left you to drown in that pond."

His every nerve flared sensually at the mere mention of her name. He silenced his body with a stern mental reprimand, but not soon enough, from Nikki's widening grin.

"And Mikhyel found Mother," Deymorin retorted. "Not the greatest odds. Besides, whom would you have ensnared last night? And you a married man. For shame!"

That wide grin faded. "No one, I suppose."

The jest had gone decidedly sour. The boy should never have been compelled to accept that marriage with Lidye dunTarec, no matter how well the arrangement ultimately turned out for the Web. Nikki shouldn't have had to— wouldn't have been put to it, if Deymorin had been where he was supposed to be, twelve long months ago.

A senseless argument, it had been, at that. If he'd known Anheliaa had the power to throw him to the ends of the earth with the flick of a finger and a twist of the Rhomatum Rings, he'd never have let her provoke him in her damned tower. Hell, she'd never have gotten him up there in the first place to *be* provoked.

Still, the past was the past. Anheliaa was dead now, and the marriage had not been all bad for Nikki. At times Nikki had been quite infatuated with his doll-pretty wife. Certainly his libido-driven thoughts had been directed that way moments ago. And Lidye had proven capable enough in the Tower. In all probability, their attempts to hold the Web intact last night would have failed without her participation.

Besides, as Nikki had pointed out, if he hadn't had that argument with Anheliaa, he might never have met Kiyrstin, might never have discovered the Mauritumin plot to take over Rhomatum Tower . . .

"Do you suppose that Anheliaa *chose* to do that to you deliberately?" Nikki smoothed the coat sleeve, and Deymorin caught a fleeting image of a roadside near the Boreton Turnout, of Mikhyel lying senseless on a bloodstained canvas . . .

"Which?" he asked, brutally unmoved by the image, refusing to allow his brother to wallow in it either. "Landing us naked as newborns? Or seared like a beefsteak?"

Mikhyel had survived. So had he. Done was done. He held to that thought, and the image from Nikki shivered apart. "Both, I suppose."

"Brother, considering our aunt would have done anything to humiliate me, not to mention her obvious delight in causing anyone pain, I leave nothing beyond her warped capacity, but Khyel seems to think she didn't really know what she was doing when she . . . leyapulted people out of the Tower. As for Khyel—" He paused, recalling a time of shared minds immediately following that journey through hellfire. "Somehow, I don't think Anheliaa had much to do with that. I think that was Mikhyel's own doing, and I somehow doubt he planned any part of it."

Nikki's gaze met his soberly. "Just how powerful is he, Deymio?"

"How can we know? He's . . . changed . . . changed every time I see him. But at the time, he blamed himself for your predicament, and the depth of that guilt might well have played some part in the business."

"Changed," Nikki repeated, and the look he cast outward didn't really appear to take in the mountains' morning beauty. "Aren't we all?"

Point, Nikki. Deymorin tugged a shoulder seam to smooth a wrinkle in *his* coat and drew a return of blinking, blue-eyed awareness. "Tolerably good fit, sprout," he said, the tone light, the sentiment nothing of the kind. "Grow any more and I'll have to borrow your clothes."

Nikki, being seventeen and still self-conscious, blushed. Deymorin laughed and gave him a shove toward Pander.

"Go ahead, brat. Have a nice ride. Just get both of you back intact, hear me?"

"How did you know I wanted—" Nikki frowned, then rolled his eyes. "Of course," he said, and tapped his temple.

"Might as well resign ourselves to it," Deymorin said, then raised his voice to reach two veterans grooming their mounts down the tether line. "*Phendrochi! Darville!* Ride point for my brother!"

Nikki protested loudly as Darville's red head bobbed in acknowledgment, but Deymorin sent his brother a soothing thought and followed the thought with: "Common sense, Nikaenor. Remember who and where we are. Remember what we were involved in last night." And the final reassurance: "*I* wouldn't venture out alone—not today, perhaps never again."

Nikki's lips pressed tight, and *resignation/resentment* flooded past his low barriers, but he nodded agreement.

"Tack's in the lean-to," Deymorin nodded toward the small building adjacent to the feed barn, and without further comment, Nikki was off. "Remember the bit!" Deymorin called after him, and Nikki raised an acknowledging hand. Pander jumped, then shied and danced, reaction to the sudden commotion in his private domain. The horse was coiled spring-tight, as much in need of exercise as Nikki on this morning, when the energy literally saturated the air they breathed.

"You do see it, Nikki?" he asked, when his brother returned carrying his saddle. "Don't you?"

Nikki tilted his head inquisitively, his mind intent on the upcoming gallop, his hands full of leather, and his mouth occupied with a filched apple, a cull, one of the equine delicacies that sometimes appeared tucked in a spare corner of a supply wagon. Deymorin waved his hand through the air, creating currents, sending the motes dancing like dandelion seeds on a spring breeze, and knew a certain relief when Nikki's eyes tracked that ebb and flow and not just his hand.

Nikki bit through, and offered the rest to Pander. "Sure," he answered between chews. "Feels like the ringtower when Lidye's working."

"Really," he said, and thought of those closed tents and wondered that his brother could even visit his wife's office without becoming conjugal.

Nikki's ready blush flared, and he ducked his head. "Not the same that way. Just . . ." He waved his hand through the air, then clipped a lead onto Pander's halter before the young stud shied away. "You know."

"Sorry, Nik." Deymorin chuckled. Nikki just gave him a baleful look and held the lead-rope out expectantly. Deymorin accepted the lowest of grooming positions, while Nikki began to wield curry comb and brush with youthful—and mind-numbing—vigor.

Like the ringtower when Lidye's working.

Deymorin absently fingercombed Pander's fine-haired forelock.

Nikki was accumulating Tower experience with Lidye just as Mikhyel had with Anheliaa, learning to take certain things for granted in the process, and not thinking about it, not questioning.

As Nikki pointed out, they were all changing. Ultimately, he no longer questioned the fact, he'd have to make his own peace with the Tower and its rings. They couldn't be what they were, *do* what they had to do and still cling to the old prejudices.

Pander rooted his chest, seeking his full attention, not

because he wanted anything, but because he was bored.
Another difference between this eager youngster and
Ringer. Ringer had been long on patience, if that lack of
work included a warm spot in the sun and a ready supply
of food.

As first the pad, then the saddle slid into place, he asked,
not really expecting an answer. "Where's Ringer?"

For a moment, Nikki stared at him blankly over the top
of the saddle, the silver Rhomandi crest on the skirt reflecting streaks of sunlight on his cheek. Then his mind
flared with guilt. "Ringer?"

Suddenly, the question ceased to be idle.

"Yes, Nikki, *Ringer*. You know the horse. You helped
train him, dammit! He got me to Rhomatum in time for
your birthday, and I haven't seen him since. Where is he?"

"You disappeared, Deymorin. I thought you'd taken him.
By the time I knew—"

"Knew what?"

Death flared out from Nikki, along with anger, and guilt
and impotence. He jerked a cinch-strap with rather more
force than necessary, and Pander snorted in protest.

Deymorin controlled reactive anger, and grabbed Nikki's
wrist to achieve a deeper link, only to drop it again when
the wave of emotion nearly knocked him to his knees.
"Nikki, stop shouting. I *know* it's not your fault. Just tell
me what happened!"

"Brolucci!" Nikki spat the name out.

Brolucci. Captain of their great-aunt Anheliaa's Tower
Guard, and, like Anheliaa, frustratingly beyond reach of
vengeance. Details filtered through to Deymorin, and he
clarified out of that flow of information: "Brolucci had
him destroyed?"

Nikki nodded.

"At Anheliaa's orders."

Another nod. "To cover your absence after she threw
you out. By the time I realized—"

"Not your fault, brother." Deymorin smothered his own
anger, knowing from experience how his feelings could feed
Nikki's through their link and Nikki's in turn would loop

back to exacerbate his own. "Done is done. Anheliaa's dead, thank the Rings, and Brolucci's mind is gone, so perhaps there is some vague justice in the world." He forced a smile and added: "Go on, brat. Get. Enjoy your ride."

Doubt, depression.

"The minute you're in the saddle, you'll be in the mood again, trust me."

Nikki grinned wryly, shortened the stirrup leather a notch, checked the cinch, and swung up. The instant his weight hit the saddle, Pander erupted.

Deymorin laughed and called, as Nikki pulled the horse back to order: "That'll teach you. Should have walked him out a bit!"

Pander shied and half-reared, threw his head, and started all over again. Nikki swayed easily in the saddle, his delight with the good-natured challenge a sweet shift in his mental flavor. Deymorin smothered the pride he felt in the boy's supple-backed response. He'd taught his brother to ride, but Nikki had a natural seat and hands for which no mere teacher could claim credit.

{Told you,} he sent in that underneath voice, and Nikki answered similarly: {Big Brother always knows best?}

"Get out of here," Deymorin said aloud, swinging the gate open. "And warm him up before you blow him out, hear me?"

{Big Brother always—}

{Out!}

"Enough, old man," Nikki said in a low voice and put a hand on the thick neck. Pander quieted almost immediately, and Nikki cocked an eyebrow at him.

{Show-off.}

Nikki tapped his temple, grinned, and backed smartly out into the open, then jogged off, the two guards falling in behind him.

Chapter Two

Nikki was leaving. Mikhyel noted the fact from behind closed eyelids, as summer-slick hair slid beneath his fingers and warm breath puffed in his ear. Strange how a man could train a half-dozen young horses every year and still have one or two stand out in a lifetime. Ringer had been such a horse; and now Ringer was—

Ringer? Without opening his eyes, Mikhyel disengaged himself from Deymorin's tangled thoughts, gently so as not to alert his brother to his waking presence. They'd earned the right last night to a little peace and isolation this morning. All of them: Deymio, Nikki, four courageous women back in Rhomatum—Temorii, perhaps she, crowned Khoratum's radical dancer and turned fugitive all within an hour, deserved a peaceful morning most of all.

The hard, lean body between his arms stirred in response to his thoughts, and he stilled both with a mental kiss, wondering if his mind would ever be his own again, wondering if he would want it that way.

Hair indeed slid between his fingers, long and silken, not summer-slick horse-pelt. Shaded hair, if he cared to open his eyes to look. Deep sable, near black at the roots, fading to palest fawn on the ends. All of it dusted with rainbow highlights. *Ley-touched*, he'd heard the effect called on the streets of Khoratum. But there it had applied to fruits and vegetables, the occasional flower. Here, the flower was the woman who had captured his heart, a woman who had not only been touched by the Ley, but raised by it and for it. A woman who had relinquished her claim on that mystical heritage—who had risked her very life—to save his.

Twice.

She murmured something and stirred again, her scarred
and callused fingers wandering aimlessly along his skin, beneath his tunic.

Flower, indeed. Like the roses that thrived beneath the
ley-node umbrellas where all other plant life withered and
died. Beautiful, but tough, hard-stemmed, and armed
with—he caught his breath as one of those callused fingers
brushed a nipple—thorns.

Formless thoughts wandered with equal lack of direction—or discretion—through his more thoroughly aroused
mind. With the ley-charged air permeating his lungs, he'd
easily and all too willingly join her in what she called the
dance of love, but she needed sleep, needed to rest muscles
taxed to their limit only hours ago. Before those fingers
helped his body gain equal purpose with his mind, he disengaged them, brought her hand gently free of his clothing,
and turned his thoughts with equal determination toward
those last impressions from Deymorin.

So Anheliaa had ordered one of Deymorin's horses destroyed. He wished he'd known about that at the time. It
was on the order of Anheliaa-induced atrocities in which
he'd been able to intercede with fair success over the years.
But the question was moot. Anheliaa was dead, taking her
cold-blooded whimsy with her.

Dead, and the one great question her passing had left
had been answered definitively last night: the Rhomatum
Web and its associated Syndicate of Satellite Nodes would
continue, strong and united, without her—

{You're a fool, Mikhyel dunMheric. . . .}

Only Temorii's weight across his chest prevented his jerking to his feet, only concern for her peaceful rest kept him
from screaming denial of that voice that whispered in his
head.

Distant. So very faint, but it *was* Anheliaa.

Would she never leave him alone?

{That doesn't even deserve an answer, darling. You lost
*Khoratum. How dare you? After all my sacrifice to secure
it for the Web. . . .}*

{And you had no idea of the forces you were conjuring, Auntie-dearest.} He stifled the retort. She wasn't real. Couldn't be. Not this time.

{Oh, the lad finally shows some modicum of spirit. Would you had when we were together. What we could have accomplished . . .} The voice faded briefly, returned with a sharp: *{What* forces?}

The question bestirred images of Mother in her leythium caves, of her counterpart beneath Rhomatum itself, rising out of a leythium pool, forming out of that energy-filled substance, speaking to his mind with the wisdom gleaned of geologic ages.

Shrill laughter burned his inner ear. *{Tamshi! Oh, my darling child, you've snapped at last. . . .}*

Temorii shivered, and he pulled their single blanket higher, tucked it around her shoulders, doing his best to buffer her mind from the thoughts boiling in his head. His own thoughts, Anheliaa's taunts and criticisms rising from the ashes of memory. Anheliaa's acid tongue had mocked the Tamshi stories he used to read to Nikki.

Anheliaa would do anything to hurt, and that mockery had hurt the child-Nikki badly.

Tamshi, shapeshifter, a creature out of childhood myths but not, as he'd been raised to believe, a creature of fantasy. For want of a better term, Mother, the creature that lived in the leythium caves beneath Khoratum, was a Tamshi. Self-named, or perhaps a name she'd accepted as her own after generations of human worshipers, Mother had indeed been a mother to Temorii after a cave-in killed Temorii's grandmother, leaving her human grandchild alone and imprisoned.

Mother had rescued that child, named her *Dancer*, and taught her far more than Rakshii's legendary Dance. The mindspeaking he and his brothers were still struggling to understand and control, Temorii did as naturally as breathing. Temorii knew the mountains and their whims as well and as intimately as she knew her own body. Temorii had "leythiated" freely between Mother's caverns and the surface world.

Temorii had been as Tamshi as was humanly possible . . . and now Khoratum was lost from the Web forever, along with Temorii's dance rings. It was possible Mother was lost as well, thanks to the new node that was forming beneath them. Gone because that Tamshirin entity didn't want to be ruled by such as Anheliaa and her hand-picked Khoratumin ringmaster, Rhyys.

{Khoratum was lost, fool, because of your incompetence and that of all your . . . allies . . . in Rhomatum. In my Tower! How dare you.}

Better them than Anheliaa. She could haunt his dreams all she liked. She'd never spin the Rings again.

{You're a fool, boy . . .}

So Anheliaa'd told him often enough. The only foolish thing he was doing now was talking to a ghost.

{You should have held the Web, darling, and taken Mauritum. Now . . . what have you but a damaged Web?}

{Go . . . play with a lightning bolt, will you, Auntie?}

Laughter, weak and fading to nothing. In the distance, a flash, a low rumble of thunder. This time, he did jump, half-believing—

But that way lay madness. Anheliaa had nearly driven him there often enough when she was alive. It was only his mind conjuring her memory. His own guilt and fears talking to him, chastising his actions in the words and the damning tone it knew most intimately. And: *Taken Mauritum . . .* Those were his fears of those final days with his aunt given form, that was all. This voice in his head had none of the substance of Anheliaa's former visitations.

Besides, Deymorin had disposed of Anheliaa's decaying corpse, had buried those physical remains like any deceased animal in the dark areas between the leylines, had been forced to take them away when the leythium pool into which they'd buried her had rejected those physical remains as surely as the Web itself had left her spirit adrift, leaving her no more than a fading memory in the crystalline network.

And yet . . .

Doubt shivered in the dark corners of Mikhyel's mind.

Madness loomed. How could he be certain of that? *Something* had animated those remains, something had manifested itself in his room the night of Anheliaa's immersion in the ley pools. He'd seen creatures form out of the Ley, shapeshifting creatures. Thoughts into energy into substance . . . it seemed that what they didn't know about the caves and the leylines that permeated the countryside could, in fact, rise up to haunt them.

It was time he needed . . . time to salvage the Syndicate from the morass into which it had sunk, thanks to this momentary madness. Time for that, yes, but also time to explore those other unknowns and understand the phenomena he'd witnessed—not with the romantic fascination the scholars and dreamers (like Nikki, he thought with loving forbearance) would bring to it, but with a practical eye to the possibilities . . . and very real dangers.

Information. Sound, debatable knowledge: the rational mind's best defense against encroaching insanity.

How could they know, for instance, that Garetti, far off to the West in Mauritum, didn't know more about what was happening in Khoratum even as they lay here resting? He could speak to his brothers' minds over a distance; last night, they'd spoken in much the same way with Garetti and more than a dozen ringmasters throughout the Web. What was to prevent Garetti from gleaning information from some Talent up in Khoratum? The fact that Mauritum was severed from the Web? They had no proof that was enough.

There was so much they didn't know. . . .

But time for gathering knowledge was a commodity in very short supply for him at the moment. After last night's events, his offices in Rhomatum were going to be swamped with the legal and political consequences of last night's battle. Complaints, fears and demands—each one requiring individualized attention. The political contacts he'd spent all spring creating were going to need reassuring, if not complete replacement. They'd won the battle, possibly even the war, but the peace negotiations and the reorganization of the Web and the Syndicate hadn't even begun.

And those very practical and imminent matters would have to take precedence over the admittedly fascinating world of the Ley and all it held. If Garetti had that level of espionage capacity, he'd had it for more years than Mikhyel dunMheric had been alive; they could live with it a while longer.

Mikhyel shifted his arm, easing Temorii higher up on his shoulder. She muttered something unintelligible and dug a fist into his ribs, as if he were a pillow needing realignment. He smiled into the hair that tangled with his beard. Even in sleep, she was singularly self-oriented—rather like the Tamshi who had raised her.

As a Khoratumin ringdancer, such concentration had meant the difference between life and death. She'd stretched her world to include Mikhyel dunMheric and, at least for a time, his wide-flung interests. He had to wonder, now that the impossible had been achieved and they were together in his world, how this fey, mountain-born child would adapt to his city.

A shiver rippled through him as Temorii's chill-fingered touch slid past the folds of his tunic and around his ribs, pushing the fabric aside so that her cheek could pillow against his bare chest.

Hiller clothing, he decided, was far too easily put aside. Proper Rhomatumin dress kept decent layers between lustful bodies, allowed time with each button released and each lace pulled, to reconsider the ramifications of the act about to take place.

He kept his hands still, resisting the temptation to return her caress, kept his thoughts only surface thoughts as well, wanting her to wake or not of her own will, not at his instigation: a small torment, strangely exciting in its own right.

The clothing he—mostly—wore, while his customary black, was rich with embroidery in ley-touched thread. It was her gift, that clothing, and it echoed, in color and design, the dance costume in which she'd competed only hours ago.

Competed, and won. The radical dancer's coronet, which

Mikhyel himself had placed on her head, glinted in the early morning sunlight, a flash of polished silver beyond a moss-covered rock, a small fortune cast aside without a second thought as she'd come into his arms hours earlier.

A subdued glint in the golden morning light, streaked with stains and finger-smears that dulled the sheen. Blood, he thought in a moment's panic. But . . . if the blood was hers, the wound was minor. He'd sense anything else, as he was aware of her exhaustion and the ache in the small of her back. Still, if not hers, then whose?

Pure sensory pleasure flooded through him, his confounding with hers despite his efforts, and he closed his eyes to the multicolored motes lighting the air around them. He lost himself in those responses at once so natural and yet foreign to his nature after a lifetime of—

{You're *thinking* too much again, Khy.} The words filled his head along with a scent of cinnamon and cloves, as a Temorii-shaped shadow eclipsed the world.

Chapter Three

Energy indeed ran high in the camp. Not so much the tempers Deymorin had feared: a handful of arguments erupted, one he felt compelled to break up before serious injury occurred, but for the most part, that energy found outlet in good-natured wrestling matches and groups headed voluntarily for the practice fields—some even forgoing breakfast to ensure their share of time. They were good men.

"M'lord Rhomandi?"

M'lord. Time was, the antiquated form of address was enough to raise his hackles past smoothing. These days . . . These days, Deymorin had other things to worry about. He rolled back on his heel and turned to face the man hailing him.

Nantovi. One of the most experienced men in the camp, a veteran of border patrols who had himself instructed a young Deymorin Rhomandi in proper soldierly etiquette. A man whose only stipulation in agreeing to join Deymorin's guard was that he not be promoted to a desk or even an officer's cloak. Nantovi dealt with men as men, not players on a board, and he dealt well with them.

Behind Nantovi trailed a younger man. Much younger. If those cheeks had felt a razor, it was only in practice against future need.

"Sergeant," Deymorin acknowledged the hail.

"A spectacular morning, sir," Nantovi said, with a nod toward the faintly glimmering sky—a casual opening for any further information that his commanding officer might be inclined to give him.

"Nothing quite like the Khoramali in the Twelfth." Nantovi's commanding officer was not so inclined.

With a look that implied a depth of understanding, Nantovi drew his young companion forward. "Belden dunHikham, sir. Arrived yesterday morning."

DunHikham. Hikham was a major landholder in the Kharatas, the mountain range on the far side of the Rhomatum Valley. Not so long ago, Deymorin had been a guest in Hikham's home for a frustratingly nonproductive visit. Deymorin could well understand why Nantovi, who had been born in the Kharatas and had been part of his entourage at that visit, had brought this particular recruit to his personal attention.

"Belden." Deymorin smiled at the solemn-faced boy. "Hikham's youngest?"

The boy nodded slowly, and the solemn look turned positively cloudy.

"Has your father changed his mind, then?"

An ambiguous dip of his head gained Belden the sergeant's elbow in his ribs.

"Speak up, boy! This is the Princeps of Rhomatum granting you personal attention!"

"N–no, sir." The answer was a barely audible whisper, and Nantovi's eyes narrowed. Deymorin lifted a finger; the sergeant relaxed.

"Best you go home, lad," Deymorin advised. "I'm not inclined to divide the Web more than it already has been."

Earnest brown eyes met his squarely.

"And if I go home now, sir—" That steady gaze swept the nearest camps. "If all these men go home, one day we'll have no home to go to, isn't that what you told my father?"

"And if *I'm* wrong?" Deymorin countered. "If there is no invasion from Mauritum? If Kirish'lan remains content with the new power in Rhomatum? If the Northern Crescent itself is ready to negotiate peacefully?"

"This time. What about the next? What about my children's security?" The boy's voice gained fervor with each sentence. "You told my father that powers in the Web were shifting, that attitudes about Rhomatum Tower and who should control it were all changing. Is peace now any guarantee of peace next year? This base needs to be here. It needs manning."

Deymorin folded his arms. "You quote me well, boy. And for helping me sway the prevailing attitude among your peers in the Syndicate, I'd welcome your advocacy. But have you considered the consequences of you, personally, joining me here?"

"Estrangement from my father," was the unhesitating reply. "But I'm prepared for that. I have options. My mother's family—"

"And beyond yourself?"

"I don't understand."

"Your father has a large holding on the border between Persitum and Barsitum territory. Persitum is Mauritum's most logical mainland base of operations, being a shared node between the Mauritum Web and Rhomatum. Should Mauritum decide to invade Rhomatum, your father would be forced to make a choice of loyalties. Considering that he now feels I—meaning Rhomatum—have stolen his youngest son from his family, how do you think he will swing?"

To the boy's credit, despite the panic that flared in his eyes, he took his time answering. Finally:

"He'd side with Rhomatum, sir," he answered with firm conviction. "No matter what I do."

"Hope, dunHikham?"

"Knowledge of my father, sir. To side with Mauritum would be foolish, economically, and out of character for Father, philosophically. Besides, to admit your arguments could sway me emotionally would reflect on his own training of his sons. He might disown me for my decision, but his pride would never deny that decision's rational validity. He taught me."

Deymorin withheld the smile that threatened. "Nantovi, find him a keeper."

"I can stay, then?" Eager excitement betrayed how uncertain Hikham's son had been of his welcome here.

Deymorin nodded.

"But why . . . ?" The boy's lower lip disappeared between gnawing teeth. "A test?"

"Test?" Deymorin kept his face impassive.

"To see how I'd answer."

Deymorin raised an eyebrow.

"Caution would say Father might side with Mauritum, and therefore I should return home to placate him."

"So why are we still talking? Why aren't you on your way home?"

"Because that's the answer you expected to hear. But it's not the truth."

"And?"

"Saying so would indicate a shallow understanding of my own father, and lack of confidence in my own judgment. You know my father. You know what's the true answer."

The grin broke free. "Watch this one, Nantovi," he advised.

"Personal honor, sir."

Deymorin nodded and continued on his rounds.

Seven hundred thirty-seven.

Hardly the first such familial disagreement his recruitment program had engendered. Generations had split on the question of the current political balance in their isolated corner of the world. Those who had grown old under Anheliaa's domineering control of Rhomatum Tower—her arrogant confidence that no outside force would dare challenge the Rhomandi—could not imagine a serious threat to the Rhomatum Web and would not join him in the field. Those younger, facing a future in their own uncertain self-confidence, could well believe that the Tower, and hence the Web, had become vulnerable now that Anheliaa was dead. The hot-blooded youth wanted to take an active hand in preserving their future.

With any luck, young Belden's father had the right of it. With any luck, all doubt in the minds of their immediate neighbors, both in the Mauritum Web to the west and in the vast Kirish'lan Empire on the mainland side, had been settled last night while this boy slept.

Watch your feet, you clumsy ox!

The camp was waking up.

"Feet? What feet? Where'd they—oops!" A thud accompanied the voices from around a far tent. "*There* they are! Hello, fe—"

"Stick it up y'r—" More thuds, and: "*Damn you!*"

"Too—*hic*—late. Already damned to hell and—"

The slurred and growling response broke off with a grunt, but Deymorin knew that voice all too well. One-time mercenary, one-time inmate of Sparingate Prison, currently Mikhyel's controversial bodyguard.

In camp less than twelve hours, and already Ganfrion was the focus of trouble. Deymorin headed toward the unmistakable sounds of a brawl, hoping to step in before the lout completely compromised the Rhomandi reputation.

As he rounded the tent, a large body rebounded off the stretched canvas and careened into him. Deymorin braced himself to counterbalance, then blocked the fist the ungrateful bastard sent his way. A calculated shoulder to the broad chest, and the big man staggered backward into the arms of three half-awake men in various stages of undress.

Two of the men held Ganfrion; the third went to scrape Ganfrion's erstwhile opponent up off the dirt.

Not that Ganfrion was in much better state. His nose was bleeding and a cut above one eye oozed a slow stream. To judge by his wobbling knees, he should welcome the support of his captors.

"How is he?" Deymorin asked of the fallen man, and the soldier helping the victim sit up scowled across the fire at him. The look quickly shifted past recognition to caution.

"He'll live, sir."

"Take him to the infirmary. Get him patched up." Deymorin caught the eye of another of the men beginning to gather around them. "Give him a hand, will you?"

"Yes, sir," came the single-voiced reply, accompanied by a quick nod, the casual salute his men had adopted at his instigation; and without further ado, the two headed out with the wounded victim stumbling between them.

"Well, well, well—" Ganfrion's distinctive voice was

gravel-rough, veteran of too much black-powder smoke on too many foreign battlefields. "If it's not the unfriend." He had a rep, this man of Mikhyel's, a rep throughout the Web and all along the border that Deymorin's investigators had barely begun to scratch. "Mornin' to you, Deymio-lad!" Ganfrion drooped against his captors' holds in a farce of a courtly bow. They hauled him upright, no small task even for two men.

"You're drunk."

Ganfrion's head jerked, sending filthy shoulder-length hair into the face of the man on his left. His unfocused gaze scanned the ground underfoot, settled at last in the direction of a flask seeping damp into the cleared earth around the campfire.

"By my mother's blessed womb, I believe you're right."

A crowd was gathering, and a murmur that held the word *Rhomandi* filtered outward.

Deymorin stepped closer to the ex-inmate.

"You're making a fool of yourself. Go sleep it off!"

"Fuck you, Rhomandi." Without a hint of the slur, and the eyes that glared up at him were wholly free of alcoholic haze.

The men holding the miscreant growled and twisted his arm. Ganfrion snarled and wrested free, swinging wildly.

Deymorin countered easily and closed. He buried his fists in Ganfrion's coat.

"You may be my brother's man," he hissed into the scarred face, "but that won't stop me from having you thrown in the brig to sleep it off, if you don't pull yourself together."

"Fuck you, and fuck your fancy-talking, dancer-fucking brother."

From the start, the twisted ties binding his brother to the powerful and uncouth Ganfrion had challenged Deymorin's every instinct. Those instincts urged him now to rid his brother forever of this poisonous thorn. But his men were watching him, judging him not as a brother, nor even as a man.

Ganfrion, ten years his senior and a veteran of the borders, *had* a rep, good and bad, to men such as Deymorin had chosen for his·guard. Ganfrion had proven his value several times over in fields of action both overt and covert and with unorthodox methods those same men admired— methods Deymorin himself admired, when he could forget the rest of what Ganfrion was and had been. If he acted on those instincts, and when word got out that the Rhomandi had taken down the very man whose ferreting efforts had made last night's counter-thrust possible . . .

For the first time since he'd accepted the challenge of putting together the army, he was aware of his relative youth and inexperience.

Ganfrion, like a wolf smelling blood, attacked:

"Well, *dunMheric?* What *is* this stuff?" Ganfrion swung a hand through the glittering air, the gesture combined with his deliberate use of Deymorin's fraternal designation rather than his title, a none too-subtle insult. "What was all that fire in the sky last night? Tamshi dust, I heard someone say. That what you're telling them?"

"Not *now!*" Deymorin said through clenched teeth.

"Not? Then when, dunMheric?" The mocking tone turned hard. "Tamshi dust be damned. It's the Ley, any fool can tell that. And leythium *kills*. It *eats* the very flesh off a man's bones. How long before these lads melt away? Why aren't we moving out?"

Surrounding faces began to doubt. Looks were exchanged.

"Shut up, man. For the gods'—"

"Fuck the gods! I was damn-near killed in a Khoratumin alley last night! This morning, I'm halfway down Mount fucking Khoratum." The confident accusation faltered, a quiver of uncertainty entered the tirade. A plea for help to someone prepared to believe a madman's story. "How, in the name of the Mother of the Ley did I get here? Why aren't I still in Khoratum? Why isn't your *brother?* Answer me that—explain *that* to these honest men and then tell me to—"

Damn you, Khyel dunMheric, he thought, wishing his brother would wake up and deal with his own chaff. But

Ganfrion had proven his own worst enemy with that last wild statement. Doubt had grown to pity: pity the poor madman.

He could almost pity Ganfrion himself . . . if he didn't know damn well the man wasn't mad.

"Come with me," Deymorin muttered and, with a nod to Ganfrion's captors, started to haul Mikhyel's problem child away from the growing audience, among whom, he suddenly realized, were Nantovi and young Belden.

"No!" Ganfrion jerked away, twisted, and struck with snakelike accuracy.

This time Deymorin's instincts ruled. He blocked the blow and returned one of his own, putting all the months of suppressed anger toward this man—and *all* those who had twisted his brother to their advantage over the years—behind it.

Ganfrion spun to the ground, rolled and rocked to his knees. He glared up at Deymorin, his nose pouring now, the eye blinded from the cut in the brow.

"Get up," Deymorin snarled.

"You'd like that, wouldn't—" Ganfrion broke off, gave a choked cough and curled over, burying a hand in the front of his coat. Deymorin took a step toward him, but Nantovi was there first, one arm around the bodyguard, dagger in hand.

"Draw a blade, crypt-bait," Deymorin said softly, "and you're a dead man."

Ganfrion froze, curled over as he was, then his shoulders began to shake. Nantovi, with a puzzled look, relaxed his hold. The shakes increased, and a sound somewhere between choking and laughter escaped before Ganfrion swayed, then collapsed into a motionless heap of flesh and bone.

Suspicious, unable to believe that the long-anticipated moment could come and go so quickly, Deymorin moved in, only to have Nantovi again intervene.

"Stay back, m'lord. Please," the sergeant said, and grabbed a handful of Ganfrion's torn and filthy coat. The ex-inmate lolled bonelessly over, eyes closed, mouth hanging slack.

And his limp hand, as it pulled free of his side, was covered in blood.

Chapter Four

The feel of the mountain wind in his hair and a horse pounding the trail beneath him was a rare treat these days for Nikaenor dunMheric. Ever since he'd reached his majority, he'd spent far too much time in Rhomatum and wasted far too much energy worrying about the future and examining himself for character flaws.

Sometimes, a man just needed the freedom to *be*.

They reached an open meadow, and Pander pranced sideways, rattling the bit against his teeth, as anxious as Nikki to end the sedate canter and be off. Without a word to the guardsmen flanking him, Nikki settled his seat deeper in the saddle and gave the signal the horse craved. With the explosive surge of a racer out of a gate, Pander was off.

The meadow's far side arrived all too quickly. Nikki sat back; the horse's momentum eased. A lengthened right leg, a shift of weight, and Pander moved in a clean arc without the slightest falter in the smooth rhythm of his strides. They circumscribed the meadow, swaying back and forth in a rhythmic serpentine pattern, Pander shifting leads as smoothly as if he could read Nikki's mind.

Perhaps he could. Ever since he and his brothers had begun hearing each others' thoughts, Nikki wondered about possibilities like that. Maybe such an ability was the key difference between a merely well-trained horse and one like Pander, who seemed to anticipate his every desire. For a handful of strides, Nikki wondered if he might be able to talk Deymorin out of the stallion, then he recalled Pandorin's Princess, foaled this spring and first of Pander's get, and decided his chances were slim indeed.

Nikki closed his hands on the reins, and Pander dropped smoothly to a walk, his excess energy expended in that wild run.

Besides, he *had* his own horses, fine horses, including the most perfectly matched, beautifully trained harness pair in the Web (and probably the world)—Deymorin's gift. He *had* them; just not here . . . because the means by which he'd arrived in the Khoramali only a few hours before had not involved any such mundane transportation as horses or floater-cabs. One instant, he'd been standing in Rhomatum Tower beside Lidye, the next, he was Outside and at the mouth of a cave which the inner sense had assured him held his brothers.

Mother's doing, Mikhyel had explained. Mother had wanted the Rhomandi brothers all in one place so that she and the Tamshi of Rhomatum could make a new node between Rhomatum and Khoratum. He and his brothers had been, also according to Mikhyel, some sort of focus for Mother and Rhomatum.

According to Mikhyel, without them, it would have taken some sort of major battle between the two nodes to form the new one, the baby node, the offspring.

He wasn't certain he actually understood. But then, he secretly doubted Mikhyel really understood, either, for all he'd sounded so positive last night. Mikhyel was a lawyer and a politician. Mikhyel's greatest talent was sounding convincing, and not even their link mind to mind could disprove Mikhyel's arguments unless he chose to give them that edge. There were times Nikki truly resented the inequity of their gift.

At other times, like this very moment, it really didn't seem to matter. Not all Talents revolved around the ley-lines and ringtowers. He was seventeen. One day, with diligent work on his part, *he* might share at least some of Mikhyel's mental control.

Mikhyel, however, would never share what he felt with Pander. Mikhyel had never even been on a horse. At his advanced age, five minutes in a saddle and he'd be lame for a week.

Nikki circled back past the two guardsmen, whose names he'd forgotten but who looked at him with resigned understanding, and they fell in behind him as he walked Pander quietly for a time, crossing the meadow a second time and starting the next uphill rise.

The two men had tried at the start of their ride to get him to discuss last night's phenomenon, but he had pleaded ignorance and easily assumed the role of rather silly younger brother come from Rhomatum to visit brother Deymorin. It was a convenient thing, sometimes, to be that. It saved tedium and cut off argument.

It was also a bit embarrassing, these days, mostly because the mantle of foolish youngest settled so easily about his shoulders. But then, he thought of the similar role Mikhyel had played for a time and of the way he'd twisted those roles to his own advantage that, provided he recognized it as an act and provided he *could* choose when and how to play the part, it didn't matter what people thought. It only mattered what he knew.

That sounded good today, anyway, especially when riding in the company of older border patrol men it was damned hard to impress under any circumstances.

Without warning, Pander snorted and stepped lightly to one side then the other, his head bent and weaving as if trying to sight on something beyond equine understanding. Something at ground level. Nikki set a hand on the stallion's crest, reminder to the horse he wasn't alone, and scanned the ground beneath the dancing, uneasy hooves that had met water, of all things. The base of the meadow grass was wet here and the ground beneath it growing curiously more so even as he watched, a discrete line of glistening damp between the grass stems that led uphill and into the trees, for all the world (Nikki smiled to himself) as if someone had left a tap open and a sink had overflowed.

But it was more likely a spring on the hill that had gone active. Had it rained in the hills before his arrival? Or was there another, less unremarkable explanation? A great deal

of oddness had gone on last night, wondrous oddness. And
this morning . . . a tap was open.

Excitement shivered down his spine.

He urged Pander forward, letting him pick his own footing, but heading generally toward the apparent source of
that ever more pronounced stream, a sheen of standing
water beyond a thick stand of trees. Unable to ride beneath
the lower branches, he pulled Pander up on a high, relatively dry spot and slid down.

The two guards rushed to join him.

"Stay here," he ordered. "I'm . . . going to walk a while.
Just—" He waved his hand in the direction of the growing
pond. "I won't go out of sight. I promise."

Like a child accounting to his parents, Nikki thought in
some self-disgust. But he hated arguments, and Deymorin
had ordered these two to keep an eye on him. On the one
hand, he supposed he should be grateful that though they
exchanged a dubious glance, they didn't protest when he
handed one of them Pander's reins and started picking his
way through the undergrowth.

On the other hand, he wasn't surprised when the other
of the two men followed him into the woods.

It didn't matter, provided the man didn't try to stop him.
The closer he came to the sparkle of newly released water,
the more determined he was to find its source.

That the mire was spring-fed was almost certain, also that
it was newly erupted, considering the trees and undergrowth with their still-healthy flooded roots, and considering the expanding downhill seepage. If that flood continued,
the water would soon carve itself a narrow channel and
form a true stream. Then these trees would die, and the
pool would establish a clear, clean edge with the proper
vegetation for a pondside.

New—possibly as recently as last night, which would
imply either a connection to last night's events or extreme
coincidence. Springs throughout the Khoramali—and at
one time, according to Darius' accounts, throughout the
Web—were marked with stone altars, artifacts from the
time before the Exodus brought his ancestors to the valley.

Altars that sometimes housed strangely androgynous figurines, Darius had written—before ordering one such shrine and statue destroyed—as other shrines, not connected to springs, housed the hillers' earth goddess and still others, their god of lightning.

The handful of shrines in the hills that had survived Darius' arrival lacked those figures: not surprising, considering Darius' treatment of their valley counterparts.

But perhaps those androgynous and often scaled gods were not water-gods as Darius had believed, but ley-gods. A man who had seen Mother's reptilian form, albeit through his brother's eyes, could easily make that connection. Perhaps there was a connection, the hiller water shrines, with the Ley.

Picking his way along the stone edge, Nikki came at last to the source of the flood: a break in exposed mountain granite where an underground stream had found release. It bubbled energetically into a natural depression, cascading down the stone through a series of irregular pools to the level of the growing pond.

One of those pools was strangely mirror-still, almost mirror opaque, for all that opacity sported rainbow swirls rather than a mirror's silvered surface. Nikki knelt beside it and ran a finger through his reflection. More oddly still, rather than his disrupting the image as ought to happen, the pool reformed behind his finger.

{Neeee . . .} The internal squeal ran like a shock up his arm.

He jerked the finger free and jumped to his feet.

"Master Nikaenor?" the guard's anxious voice echoed across the water. Nikki raised a reassuring hand.

"Sorry," he called back, and flashed a meaningless grin. "Snake."

He let the explanation rest there, exposing his reputation to one more blow without a second thought, the mystery of that voice in his head of far more interest than the opinion of a couple of soldiers he'd never see again.

{Nikki?}

The number of people he knew with the ability was a damned short list.

{Nikki, please hear me . . .}

Decidedly not Deymorin's familiar warmth or Mikhyel's haughty assurances. But other than his brothers, only Lidye and Anheliaa had spoken to him this way, and then, only in the Tower.

{Nikki, I need to talk to you.} The voice grew clearer with each word. {I tried to reach Mikhyel, but . . .}

Lidye, Anheliaa . . . and Mother. The tamshi would be able to touch him, if she wanted. And she had a decided preference for Mikhyel.

{Who . . . ? Mother?} he answered, but whoever it was didn't seem to hear him, which didn't seem likely for Mother.

He glanced about, wondering if the source was nearby, wondering what his "bodyguards" would think if he began searching the woods.

Surprise filtered through to him and curiosity that had him looking more closely at his surroundings . . . as if seeing them for the first time.

{A new node.} A sense of awe, of barely veiled excitement. {It's a new node, isn't it, Nikki? *That's* what Mother's done. How wondrous . . . that explains . . .}

And he realized, then, that he had looked not for himself but for whoever lay at the far side of this exchange. Someone who knew about Mother.

{Where are you?} he tried again, and this time, he was heard:

{Rhomatum . . .}

Rhomatum? Then who . . . ? It wasn't Kiyrstin. Deymorin's lady wouldn't consider using the internal voice— she *couldn't* do it, to his knowledge.

Lidye, more likely, for all the touch had a deep softness he'd never associated with his wife. And, *tried to reach Mikhyel?* He felt a moment's disappointment that his wife would be seeking his brother rather than the husband who had disappeared from her presence the night before. While theirs wasn't precisely a love match, he'd have thought there'd be some concern—

{Nikki!}

As surely as a cuff to his ear, the voice rocked him to attention.

{The pool, Nikki. Look in . . .}

This time, it was not his face the mirror surface reflected, but fawn-colored hair and doe-soft, brown eyes.

{Mirym?}

The image smiled, and relief flooded heart and head.

Mirym! But he shouldn't be surprised, should, in fact, feel foolish. His aunt's servant, his friend and almost-love had been a key player in last night's battle; and according to Mikhyel, Mirym had exchanged thoughts with him on many occasions. It was just hard to think of Mirym as *saying* anything. For two years she'd lived in Rhomandi House, serving Anheliaa, and never spoken a word.

And the only time *he'd* heard her thoughts, she'd been saying hello to Mikhyel through him.

{Where are you?} Nikki asked.

{In the Tower, of course. Lidye thinks to contain me.}

There was a sense of amusement about the thought, a scornful image of guards at the door of a stone room, a cot spread with delicate works of embroidery, in the heart of Rhomatum, two days removed from Deymorin's camp.

Lidye's suspicion *and* the guards, however, he had to think more soberly, were well-earned. Mirym had promised to help them, then defied Lidye's request at a key moment in the battle against—

{I *held* Khoratum! Had I allowed Vandoshin romMaurii through, Lidye would have lost all!}

{Perhaps.} He wondered if he should wait to ask why she had destroyed the Khoratum Ring.

{It was dead already,} her voice whispered, and he realized that in wondering, he had effectively asked. {I simply broke the stalemate between one world and the next.}

{I don't understand.}

{Then I can't explain.}

Nikki swallowed his frustration. It had become obvious

last night that this woman, who had been handmaid to the Ringmaster of Rhomatum for two years, knew more than any of them had suspected. And this morning he knew he had to be cautious, had to avoid pushing her away, at least until Mikhyel had a chance to question her.

Mikhyel.

She'd said she tried to reach Mikhyel and couldn't. *That* was unusual. Of them all, Mikhyel was the most sensitive to this internal communication.

Except . . . he eyed that strange mirror-pool with suspicion.

{To reach you: yes, the ley-source was necessary. For Mikhyel—because of the child I carry, I would have believed I could reach him even at this distance.}

The child she carried. Hers . . . and Mikhyel's, conceived the same night, possibly the same instant as his and Lidye's, Deymorin and Kiyrstin's . . .Three children and only one conceived in love . . .

Objection. Irritation at him for wandering away from what she considered important.

{A child's welcome into the world isn't important?}

{What's important is that I reach your brother. And I did touch him for a moment, but there was a cloud around his mind. . . . No matter. I've reached you and you can tell him.}

{Tell him what?}

{I'm afraid.}

{Of Lidye? She won't harm you. We'll be back soon and—}

{*Lidye?* Not in the least. She far overestimates her power.} Careless contempt of his wife, quickly covered. {Forgive me, Nikaenor. She is your wife and due some respect for that, if not for her treatment of the Ley. No, Nikki, it's not Lidye I'm afraid of, not myself I'm afraid for. It's Mother.}

{Mother?} He tried to pretend ignorance, but her thoughts gently chastised his deception, so he gave that up for a direct challenge, all pretenses dropped. {What do you know about Mother?}

Laughter, light and easy. {Silly, Nikki. I'm here in Rhomatum Tower only because Mother wanted me here. I thought you'd realized that by now.}

{Mother . . . put you there? Mother secreted you in our midst?}

{It was necessary. She wished to gain her freedom from the Tower Anheliaa had placed over her head.}

Mother, the Tamshi of Khoratum Node, Mother, who from under the hill, deep in the ley caverns, had maneuvered and moved and shaken the earth last night, had damned near brought civilization in the southern lands to ruin—

All that, to destroy the Khoratum Ring spinning above Rhomatum and set herself free?

{Not to harm anyone. Certainly not to harm you or your brothers.}

And yet, people had been harmed. Many people.

{Only those who willingly set themselves in harm's way, who willingly gave over their lives to Anheliaa and those of her ilk.}

{Now wait just a minute.} He had never imagined Mother would so resent the ringtowers. He had never suspected her saving them had motives other than a godlike capricious kindness. Tamshi flitted like free spirits through legend. There was nothing of this fire and light across the sky, the lightning raining down on Khoratum. {People are without homes now so that *Mother* could have this . . . mythical freedom.}

{Hardly without homes. Without their cocoon against the world. Heat and light. Everything the Ley gives to your people can be found elsewhere. What Anheliaa destroyed when she capped Khoratum . . . *that* can never be replaced.}

{I don't understand.}

{*Death* surrounds a capped node.} Mirym's thoughts spewed images of desolation, feelings of outrage and helplessness . . . and rose gardens.

And he was reminded of those within the City who would not eat meat because death preceded it, of people who would put the label *unique* and *irreplaceable* on every living creature. Now, Mirym wanted to extend that notion to plants.

{You can't eat roses!} Her mind protested in outrage. {Besides, those are small deaths for the life of the world, hardly the same thing as the destruction Darius brought.}

{I don't understand.}

{You've never looked.}

She mocked him now, and her responses had the flavor of the leyside charlatans who claimed the knowledge of the universe was theirs alone, not to be shared with the unworthy.

{No, Nikki, wait . . . I'm sorry—}

Of course, she was. She'd called *him*, wanting *his* help. She'd called him a fool, she'd fallen into his brother's bed, she'd plotted against the Rhomandi, brought down the Khoratum Ring, and now she wanted him to love her again.

Sometimes he wondered if he truly was the simpleton everyone seemed to think him.

From the corner of his vision, Nikki saw the guardsman working closer to him, suspicion in every step. Wondering, no doubt, why the youngest Rhomandi was spending so long staring at a pool.

{Someone's coming. What was so important to tell me, Mirym? Tell me, quickly. Arguments can wait.}

{It's Mother. I . . . I can't feel her. I haven't been able to for hours. And I don't know—}

—*what she wants me to do* . . . was her unfinished thought, and her mind flared with resentment that he'd picked that up from her.

But what did it matter to him that she let her life revolve around so fickle a creature?

The answer was, it did matter to him. Mirym mattered. She'd been a friend when he needed one badly, or so he'd believed, and he was relieved that her fear for Mother could be so easily solved, whatever the other questions she had raised with her nonsense about rose-gardens and desolation.

{She's been busy 'making a baby'.} He started to gesture toward the lake, stopped himself as he realized she wasn't there to see it and the guard was. {That was the whole point of her bringing me here.}

{No, you don't understand! Mother's *always* with me. Even after the firestorm, when she was at her weakest, I knew she was there. Now . . .}

{It's the new node, that's all. It's between you and Khoratum. It's cut you off.}

{No! I tell you, she's in trouble! Someone must go to Khoratum. Help her!}

He could deny the depth of Mirym's concern no longer. And while Mirym was many things, flighty and inclined toward panic had never numbered among them. He was . . . disturbed. And disturbing news had to go to camp, quickly: {I'll tell Deymorin.}

{*Mikhyel! Tell Mikhyel!*}

Mikhyel. Always Mikhyel, when Mikhyel would only turn around and consult Deymorin and himself.

Or perhaps Mikhyel wouldn't. Perhaps Mikhyel had exchanged an understanding with Mirym, an understanding he'd kept secret. Mirym hadn't exactly earned blind trust last night. And Mikhyel had been secretly involved with a Khoratumin ringdancer. . . .

But he wouldn't let Mirym's innuendo undermine his trust for his brothers.

{We'll *all of us* discuss the matter.}

Mirym had lain quiet in their midst for two years, watching Anheliaa, learning from her . . . if there was anything left for her to learn. She was Mother's pawn . . . his love in thought, Mikhyel's in fact—at least once. If not more often than the one night. *His* wedding night. The night he'd realized, once and for all, he could never truly love the woman he had just married for all the right reasons save one.

Disgust rippled through his mind and disrupted the reflection in the pool. It reflected disgust at him and his carnal thoughts.

{Mirym, I didn't mean it that way!}

{Never mind. It's Mother's safety and Mother's needs

and wishes that matter. And I'll see to *that* myself. —Good-bye, Nikaenor.}

See to it herself? {Mirym, *wait!*}

But Mirym was gone, and a sudden breeze rippled the mirror pool.

Fool! he berated himself. He'd not only lost an opportunity to learn about Mirym's involvement with Mother, he'd lost a perfect opportunity to gain information on the status of the Web and the conditions in Rhomatum. Deymorin would have his hide tacked to his door when he came back with her message, but without that.

And what did she intend to do? He should have played along and kept his hurt pride out of it. She wanted Mikhyel to know, to do something, could not reach him, and now—

{Mirym!} He called and again: {Mirym!}

But there was only silence in his head, and the pool reflected nothing but his wild-eyed self.

Chapter Five

"You bloodsucking bastard of a carpetmaker's whore!"

Ganfrion's bellow rang in Deymorin's ears.

{Mirym!}

And frustration and panic resonated in that area of his head he reserved for his brothers.

"What *is* that? A gods-fucking darning needle?"

{Wait!}

It was a dizzying combination that threatened Deymorin's already sweat-slippery hold on Ganfrion's hairy legs, on a wooden table under a wooden roof by leylight that had returned, with a new alignment, with the dawn. "Damn it, crypt-bait, shut up!" he yelled at the first offender, and at the second: {Nikki, what the hell's going on?}

{Safe, Deymio. On my way back . . .}

Nikki's assurance and deliberate withdrawal solved the one problem; and:

"Let me assure you, Captain, I've far worse in my bag," the surgeon's calm voice anchored Deymorin's mind firmly within the infirmary's cozy wood and stone interior. "Hold him steady, m'lord Rhomandi."

He banished thoughts of Nikki from his mind and reset his grip on Ganfrion's legs, sweat and blood and all, but Mikhyel's bodyguard, for all his noisy complaints, held steady beneath the surgeon's probe, proving Deymorin's presence as unnecessary as it had been for the other, similarly gruesome probes and repairs. The lean, hairy torso, a personal history in old scars, would have several new chapters in the near future.

"Nearly done, Captain," the surgeon murmured, as he

followed the probe with a pair of forceps. "If you hadn't spent all night—"

One of the powerful ankles jerked under Deymorin's hands.

"Sorry, lad," the surgeon continued, which made Ganfrion laugh. "You're all lads to me, Captain. —Hah! Call me a leyside charlatan, I *knew* there was still something in there." He held up a pair of forceps with a bloody sliver of metal trapped between the tines. "Wouldn't have wanted me to leave that inside, now, would you? Now, as I was saying, if you hadn't already pickled your insides, you could have nodded quietly off and come back good as new. Remember that the next time you try to drink away the pain."

By rights, the surgeon's assistants should have been in Deymorin's place. By rights, lacking anesthesia, they should have strapped him down, but Ganfrion had exploded, such as he was able, when they'd tried that, insisting he was no prisoner and damned if they'd treat him like one. Still, someone had had to hold him steady against involuntary reactions, and considering what had escaped Ganfrion's mouth already that morning, Deymorin preferred to keep witnesses at a minimum.

Ganfrion had so far proven as good as his word. For all the numbing solution in which they'd washed the wounds dimmed the worst of the pain, Deymorin had had to endure a similar probe once in his life, and did not envy Ganfrion the five separate assaults the surgeon had made on his body.

The surgeon threaded a new needle with fine silk. "Last time, lad."

Ganfrion pushed himself to his elbow, and the surgeon admonished him to lie still and not cast shadows. Ganfrion ignored the warning and sat up, glaring down his length at Deymorin.

"If you're done gloating, dunMheric, you can get the— *Fuck!*" He swayed heavily, his eyes rolled back and the muscle beneath Deymorin's hands went slack.

"Ah, blessed silence," was the surgeon's comment as he calmly removed the probe and returned to his needle.

"A bit extreme, don't you think?"

"Not particularly."

Calmly stated, as if it was not the first time the surgeon had taken such cold-blooded measures to silence a patient. A strange combination with his earlier compassion. Strange, until one recalled the surgeon was as much a battlefield veteran as the men he worked on.

Deymorin was collecting a vast lot of reminders this morning.

"How bad is he?" Deymorin asked.

"He's lost a great deal of blood." Blunt fingers moved quickly, efficiently, placing neat stitches in the hard thigh. "But he's strong as a Tavernese fighting bull. He'll survive."

Fortunately. He wouldn't have cared to try explaining this particular man's loss to Mikhyel.

"How old are the wounds?" he asked, wondering should he send a search party out to look for bodies.

"Hard to judge. Three, four days."

Not one of his men's doing, then; they were something Ganfrion had acquired in Khoratum.

"The worst appear to have been mostly healed, then re-opened," the surgeon explained almost absently as he placed a sponge oozing green liquid against the newly-stitched seam. A wide *sharuk* leaf, split down the spine and spread flat, followed the wash. It was a border remedy, from the Kirish'lani desert tribes, but a remedy independent of nodes and leylines, unlike so many Rhomatumin solutions, a remedy applied at Ganfrion's specific request. Fortunately, the surgeon, Travendi, had been prepared.

"Quite a trick, actually," the surgeon continued. "No sign of treatment other than that filthy rag, yet he managed not to bleed to death."

Last night, Mikhyel had left Ganfrion facing what he'd termed certain death, but he'd said nothing about his rear-guard being seriously injured heading into the back-alley encounter in question.

Why aren't I still in Khoratum?

Why aren't I dead?

Drunken accusations. An impossible journey. Four-day-old wounds that hadn't existed yesterday evening: only one answer served all questions.

Transportation Tamshi-style. Another of Mother's little games. But was this hairy, obnoxious individual in desperate need of a bath actually Ganfrion, moved about by Mother for Mother's purposes, or had Ganfrion truly died in that alleyway last night? Was this mountain of battered flesh nothing more than Mother herself toying with them again?

He was getting just a tad bit tired of Mother's inexplicable whims.

Travendi turned off the adjustable surgical lamp and pushed its stand away from the bed. The leylights had returned with the dawn, as had the steam units that kept the floor warm. Returned, following the node-making, their Rhomatumin leythium crystal cores still functional, but requiring a complete realignment, slaves now to the new node, to the fragile lines forming beneath them, not the powerful Khoratum leyline that had been. A node city could never function on the trickle of power available, but the lights, and more significantly for a man in shock, the hypocaust of this one building flourished.

The surgeon turned the main lights down, a simple act of adjusting that new alignment, gathered his instruments and blood-stained towels into a steel bowl, then drew a sheet over Ganfrion and followed it with a blanket. Alcohol, blood-loss, exhaustion . . . a normal man would sleep for hours now.

"I want to speak with him." Deymorin headed for the door. "Send for me the moment he—"

"Then drop your balls there, dunMheric." Ganfrion's own irreverent growl interrupted him. "*He's* awake now."

A normal man . . . Deymorin turned to face alcohol-hazed eyes. Deep-set. Dark brown. Without a hint of betraying tamshirin glow.

Which meant exactly nothing: Mother's eyes didn't always glow in her human-shaped appearances, and Ganfrion was not a normal man under the best of conditions.

"If you don't stop staring at me like that, the good doctor

will talk." Ganfrion gave a grunt and struggled to push himself upright. The surgeon pressed him back.

"Lie still, Captain, at least until you're a more presentable shade of green."

Captain. The highest rank Ganfrion had achieved in his checkered career, a rank Deymorin himself, in a moment of weakness, had restored.

Another grunt, a second attempt to rise, and Deymorin grinned tightly across a suggestively raised fist. "Wiggle so much as a fingertip, unfriend, and I'll send you right back to dreamland."

Unfriend. Unsubtle reminder of unfinished business between them. The lines deepened in Ganfrion's scarred face, but he nevertheless sank back into the pillows, apparent obedience that might have been acquiescence—or might simply have been the sudden tremors that threatened to split the meat from his bones, despite the warmth that rose from the floor of the solid stone building.

The surgeon picked up a second blanket, but Deymorin took it from him and jerked his head toward the door.

"Guards?" the surgeon asked.

The last thing Deymorin wanted was witnesses to the interview about to take place. Still . . .

He raised a suggestive brow at Ganfrion.

"Rings, man, what're you worried about? I can hardly lift my head."

"Truth?" Deymorin asked.

Ganfrion shrugged. "Place your bets."

"Planning on going anywhere?"

"Not immediately."

"Planning on attacking me again?"

"Only if you annoy me—again."

Deymorin shook his head at the surgeon, who nodded and slipped out the door, closing it firmly behind him, leaving him alone at last with Mikhyel's bodyguard in the only true stone-walled privacy in the camp. For the following handful of moments, the two of them sized each other like fencers across the length of a salle runway. Then:

"Want your blanket?"

"Not particularly."

Deymorin dropped it at the foot of the cot.

"Since when did the Rhomandi turn nursemaid?"

"Since my brother's prize ferret decided to spill blood and rumor all over the camp. What the *hell* were you thinking of?"

"Men's lives." The scar that pulled Ganfrion's upper lip into a permanent sneer deepened. "Lying, adulterous, baby-faced generals, and their silver-tongued brothers."

"I . . . see."

"I don't pull my punches, Rhomandi."

"I see that as well."

The sneer eased. The man's entire face relaxed. "And I was a fool. Can't even claim it was the drink. I know too much and not enough. It's not a feeling I relish, and I let my anger rule my tongue. For that—" He drew himself up, stiff-backed and proper in his respect, despite the pillows and the bandages and lying flat on his back. "For that, Commander, I deserve whatever punishment you throw at me."

"Don't dodge well, either, do you?" Deymorin asked. "Take it right on the jaw and stand your ground?"

"When I've been a fool. Have to set the lesson."

"Just don't let it knock you out of the fight."

"Hasn't yet."

And there was the greatest truth yet spoken in this tent. This Ganfrion had a strange integrity, an even stranger pride, but he'd lived by those rules and never backed down. A lesser man would have been broken long since.

"So, you tell me. Why *aren't* you dead? That one in the side should have taken you down."

"It did." Ganfrion's scarred upper lip twisted again, this time in what might have been intended as a smile. "I didn't *stay* down."

"My brother said he left you in Khoratum last night about to be gutted by a small army of Rhyys' guardsmen."

That won him a glower and a one-sided shrug. A look gathered about Ganfrion's eyes that might be suspicion and might be fear—and was most likely a bit of both. "Don't be ridiculous. This camp's a good two days' ride out of Khoratum."

"Thought maybe you knew a shortcut."

"Don't *bait* me, Rhomandi. I passed out in the gods-be-damned Khoratum Maze, convinced I'd never see another dawn or drink another drop, and woke up on your back doorstep, fireworks blazing overhead, and a flask in my hand that filled as fast as I could empty it. —Dammit, help me up! I'll *not* lie on my back like some mewling, subservient pup."

Deymorin didn't stop him, now that the surgeon was gone, and shoved the blanket in behind to hold him upright.

"I don't *know* how I got here. I don't even know where 'here' is or if I'm really still alive."

Ganfrion wore a ring on his left hand. It was undersized, even for his smallest finger. He twisted it around the middle joint, then pulled it free with a painful effort and balanced it in one palm, then the other, a flash of silver and gold that Deymorin recognized with a shock: the Rhomandi crest, a filigree of silver rings overlaid with a golden spiderweb. He bore its twin on his own hand.

He'd had no idea the tangle between this man and his brother went that deep.

"When?" he asked pointedly.

"Last night, if you're telling me the truth. He gave me this and an order to get out alive if I could."

"I see you managed to obey."

"Did I?"

"Mikhyel is pleased, I'm sure."

"Is he? Are you?" The ring paused in its hand-to-hand journey, then arced across to Deymorin.

Deymorin caught it, along with the implication. GorMikhyel, Ganfrion was, at least for the moment, meaning Mikhyel trusted him absolutely, meaning Mikhyel assumed all responsibility for his life and his actions.

More importantly it meant that Mikhyel Rhomandi—or, in Mikhyel's absence, the Rhomandi himself—owed gor-

Mikhyel an explanation. As head of Mikhyel's clan, he owed this man everything or nothing.

He told Ganfrion the truth, or the implicit agreement between Ganfrion and Mikhyel was at an end. It was Ganfrion's right. No oaths had been taken or witnessed, only a grand gesture on Mikhyel's part.

A gesture Mikhyel, in all likelihood, had never expected to have to honor.

Of course, once he'd acknowledged that tie, once he had extended to Ganfrion the information he demanded, as head of clan he still had every right to sever the connection—by ordering Ganfrion's death . . . or rather, by taking Ganfrion's life himself. Tradition gave him no other options.

Ganfrion was willing to accept the oath, or so his actions implied, but was challenging the integrity of the offer. Ganfrion was saying that if that offer was regretted, now was the time to end it. And he was setting his price damned high.

"My brother is no military man," Deymorin said, "but he has his own honor."

"Damned right he has, and I'll not have him trapped by that honor—or his damnable pride. As you say, he's no military man. Worse, he's a lawyer and that gods-be-damned ring is about as compatible with his laws as the lightning is with the Ley. I doubt *he* knows his options."

"You may rest assured, *I* do."

"I'm counting on it. If you want me dead, Rhomandi, I die now." And by that statement, the man convinced Deymorin that he was truly dealing with Ganfrion and not some Tamshirin imposter.

Everything . . . or nothing. The very essence of the man described in the reports he'd read.

Deymorin closed his hand around the ring.

"You should ask Mikhyel."

"Then go get him," Ganfrion challenged him.

As if possessed with a life of its own, the ring warmed in his hand—and that was as much of his smooth-talking middle brother as Deymorin cared to have involved in this conversation.

"Do you know what this ring is?" Deymorin asked.

"I can guess. Rhomandi crest, NeoDarian design. Matches the one you're wearing. I also suspect that by rights only you *should* be wearing it. The one Mikhyel gave me is new. I'd wager the one your baby brother wears is just as new, for all he had the original for a time—he *was* Princeps for about a month, wasn't he?—I'd say, you three had problems and needed some sort of symbol to remind yourselves you were a team. I'd say this ring business is a recent development. The man who signed my Sparingate commitment papers had no such ring. The man who hired me did. So what else do you want to know? The cause of the split? The terms of reconciliation? The original—that's the one you *should* be wearing, but aren't—that one's got to be old. Unless I miss my bet, a Mauritumin priest was wearing it when last it saw the light of day, and *he* got it off your baby brother . . . oh, months ago, since none of you were wearing it back in the crypt. —How'm I doing?"

Observant, clever at putting bits of fact together, but he'd known that for a long time. Ganfrion's value as a ferret was never in question.

"The rings are my promise to my brothers. My promise that we're partners. My promise that I'll not use my authority arbitrarily, that they will be privy to my decisions and have every right at all times to question those decisions."

"Foolish of you."

"You think so?"

"Foolish and inefficient. You're a fairly clever man. Certainly more clever than Anheliaa or your father before her. What they did, you could manage. Probably do a better job. One absolute ruler is far more efficient than a committee. Particularly a committee of brothers who haven't agreed on any policy in their entire adult lives."

"My brothers' loyalty and trust are too important to me to risk for the sake of efficiency. And our goals are more in harmony than they were a year ago."

"Mikhyel gor*Deymorin*. Has quite a ring . . . so to say. Wonder how *he* likes it?"

"It's not like that."

"No?"

Deymorin swallowed the retort that rose like bile. The man baited him and had a knack for placing him on the defensive. He didn't like the feeling, liked even less the suspicion that part of Ganfrion's appeal in Mikhyel's eyes was his ability to do just that. He and Mikhyel had spent their lives baiting one another; without doubt, Mikhyel knew the effect Ganfrion had on him.

Damn you, brother.

But he settled his mind to make peace with the man—and only in part to undermine Mikhyel's little joke. "All right, crypt-bait, honesty. Let's say you've got me to rights on the ring's purpose. That means I'm responsible for my brother's actions. I'm empowered to act for him in this matter. I can answer those questions of yours, but first, I'll damn well understand why he gave you that ring."

"Because your brother's a sentimental fool who had no concept of the arena he'd entered. He's a man who spent his entire adult life making rules that good people don't need and bad people don't give shit about, and then condemning those ill-mannered asses to a life he can't even imagine. He found the real world, Rhomandi, and didn't know what to do with it."

"You think you've got him bagged, skinned, and on display, don't you?"

"I think he's a man who puts himself on display by his own ignorance. He's a damned martyr and doesn't even realize it. He's lived by rules and thrown himself on the flames of hypocrisy to protect others for so long, he hasn't any damned notion of his own true place or his own value."

"We're working on it," Deymorin remarked sourly.

The dark-eyed glance betrayed surprise.

"You don't trust me much, do you?" Deymorin observed.

"Does it matter?"

"Not necessarily. But it would help. Do you trust Mikhyel?"

Ganfrion dipped his head toward the hidden ring. "That says I have to, doesn't it?"

"Not necessarily. Says he trusts you. Entirely different."

"Ah. Distinctions only the nobility would recognize."

"Not in my experience."

"Prove it."

"Not yet. I still have my doubts."

"About me?"

"Doubts, Captain. We'll leave it at that for now. My brother said he hired you because he owed you, because you kept him alive in prison."

Ganfrion's expression set in a guarded scowl.

"He said you . . . claimed him. Did you?"

The expression didn't change.

"Damn you, answer me!"

"Think I'm blackmailing your little brother, Rhomandi?"

"Mikhyel would have handed you over to your crypt-friends first. By the time they'd finished getting their own for losing their chance at the Barrister, you wouldn't be telling anyone anything."

"Glad to see you know him at least that well."

"I know my brother, crypt-bait. I knew him before that night in Sparingate and I knew him after, and that night changed him."

Ganfrion's level gaze didn't falter. "We all change, Rhomandi."

Deymorin clenched the ring until it cut into his hand. "Dammit, *did you force yourself on my brother?*"

"Why does it matter?"

The very dispassion in that rough voice nearly proved his undoing. Mockery, he could have accepted. Deymorin drew back the ring-bearing fist, aching to strike that cold challenge off the scarred face, but:

"You'd have done the same, Rhomandi."

"I should kill you for that."

"Only way. You know that."

"I know nothing of the kind."

"Then *learn*, little boy."

The hand that intercepted Deymorin's fist was not that of a man three-quarters dead. Neither was the grip that jerked him off-balance and pulled him close to that scarred face. "Crypt-law, Rhomandi. I kept him alive in hopes of getting out of there. He understood the transaction. There are two kinds of men in a place like that. Wolves and sheep. A wolf is a wolf. Eventually, he plays the part. Whatever that part requires. You, my friend, are no sheep."

"Neither is Mikhyel."

"No, your little brother is a man of principle. Most men of principle use their philosophy as an excuse for being a sheep. Your brother is a fox. Or perhaps—" A bark of laughter that had little of humor about it. "—Perhaps he's a Tamshi. Changable as the weather and just as dangerous. *He* got out alive. *I* very nearly did not. Who, my unfriendly wolf, was the predator in that transaction and who the prey?" Ganfrion released his wrist, and seemed to collapse into the pillows. "Hell, why does it matter? It's over. Done with."

Trust. Deymorin rubbed his wrist and eased his grip on the ring that threatened to burn a hole in his skin. "Truth, Ganfrion. It matters because I have to know whether the judgment of the man who has the power to act in the Princeps' name is compromised where you're concerned. I have to know whether the events of that night have left a gaping hole in my brother's reliability."

Ganfrion studied him from deep-shadowed eyes. Weighing his *truth*, no doubt. Examining the character of the man behind the man who would hold his oath. Finally:

"I have no hold on your brother, Rhomandi, at least that I'm aware of. Our . . . transaction . . . was, I have every reason to believe, understood on both sides to be exactly that. I wanted out of the Crypt. I wanted immunity at least long enough to get outside the Web. I was planning on heading for Kirish'lan—for good, this time. I'm as startled and unhappy with this—" He nodded toward the ring-bearing hand. "—as you are. Possibly more so. I don't *want* that kind of attachment—not just to your brother. To anyone."

"Why not? It assures you of status. Good pay. Legal immunity from any act done in Mikhyel's name—I'd say Mikhyel is the one who should want out of it."

"I don't care for the price."

"Then why'd you accept the ring?"

"Didn't have damn much choice. Couldn't leave the damn thing lying in the street, now could I?"

"Bullshit."

Ganfrion's belligerence faded. "Hell, I didn't expect to survive. Didn't make much difference, did it?"

"And now?"

"Stuck with it, aren't I?"

"No official oath taken and witnessed."

Eyes dropped, hidden in a heavy scowl. "I want answers, Rhomandi."

"No answers. No commitment. I'll help you get to Kirish'lan. Give you cash, references . . . set you up for life, if you want out."

"And your brother?"

"I'll handle my brother. You wouldn't even have to see him again. Just leave. I'll write the letters now."

"I believe you would." With a slow blink, Ganfrion turned his head aside, staring off into some unknowable middle ground. "Rhomandis were born to screw traditions, weren't they?" Eventually, the eyes returned to Deymorin, but not the focus. "Why do I hesitate? Mother of the Ley, what's wrong with me? All sense, common and otherwise, says to accept your offer, yet my gut hesitates."

"Ah, so now we've the truth." Deymorin continued to bait him. "You'll be gorMikhyel as long as it's useful. You'll play the game, get your answers, then sell those answers to the highest bidder."

Ganfrion's scarred face hardened, and his eyes snapped into focus. "Go to your eighteen hells. What have you done to me? What has your brother?"

"Don't be an idiot." And with that final advice, he relented. "Don't you see? You're the man the system was designed for. You *ache* for such an association. You long for the knowledge, the intrigue and power my brothers and I were born to. You want someone who will take you and use you like the weapon you are, and slip you, when not in use, into the elegant, expensive scabbard you'd never afford on your own."

"Fuck you."

"Tell me I'm wrong."

"Damn you . . ." Ganfrion rubbed his hands across his face, then pulled his shoulders back and stared Deymorin in the face. "You left out the most important part. Your damned brother gave me something to believe in, to fight for again."

"Another man of principle," Deymorin murmured.

"Only when I'm caught with my guard down. Give me reasons, Rhomandi, let me understand, and I'll be gorMikhyel until he betrays his own name."

"Is that what happened with Pausri dunHaulpin?"

His heavy jaw bulged beneath its coarse stubble. He looked for a moment as if he would deny the allegation. Then he said, "How'd you find that out?"

"Directly from one of your former fellow guards. Seemed to think you had the right of it."

"Going to tell your brother that one?"

"You mean he doesn't know?"

Ganfrion shrugged. "Doesn't matter. I found out what Pausri was doing to young boys and who was allowing him to get away with it. When he offered to include me . . . I declined the offer and put an end to the practice—at least in his bed."

"You're lucky you're still alive."

"Luck had nothing to do with it."

"I stand corrected."

"Are you going to have me arrested?"

"For what?"

Disbelief. Confusion. And ultimately, suspicion.

"Long time ago now, gorMikhyel, and you didn't, after all, kill the bastard." He opened his hand, rolled the ring in his palm. "I've questioned those who've served with you very thoroughly, gorMikhyel. I understand your personal sense of justice—quite well."

"Perhaps it's best men like us have men like your brother to make the laws."

"Sometimes, I wonder. Tell me what happened last night."

"Your brother hasn't told you?"

"It was, of necessity, an abbreviated account. Besides, I want your version."

"All right, Rhomandi. All right." He jerked his head in the direction of a three-legged stool. "Sit down! You make me nervous, standing there like a damned judge."

Deymorin hooked the stool with his foot and drew it to where he could perch comfortably at eye level. Not that it mattered. Ganfrion's eyes remained fixed on the ring-concealing hand.

"He should never have stayed in Khoratum," Ganfrion began slowly. "We knew—*knew,* dammit—that Rhyys planned to make a scapegoat of him. If Rhyys could rouse the crowd against Khyel—against your brother, he could arrest him openly. That way, if the shutdown went awry—"

"He could blame their actions on the Rhomandi, and have one on hand to placate the rioting masses. I know all that. What I don't understand is *why* Mikhyel stayed there as long as he did. Why he took such a risk."

Ganfrion's brow twitched. "Obligations, so he said."

"Obligations. To the dancer?"

Ganfrion's eyes rose to Deymorin's. "You know about Temorii?"

Deymorin nodded.

"Then you already know the answer to your question."

"The hell I do. Her petition to compete was granted a week ago. There was no problem. My brother didn't have to stay for the competition."

"It wasn't the competition, at least not directly. *Lust* kept him in Khoratum."

"Lust? *Mikhyel?*"

A shadow smile mocked him. "Then you *don't* know about Temorii. —In all fairness, more than lust. He was dousing flames again, trying to save Temorii from a dancer's singular stupidity. He wanted Temorii; she appeared to return his feelings. I tried to convince him to go to bed with her, get it out of his system, but as long as Temorii insisted on competing, your brother was too damned noble to act on that desire, and *not* acting clouded his reason."

"Playing the martyr again."

Ganfrion grunted agreement. "He always said he could get away. Said he had *resources* I didn't know about. Perhaps he did consider it a calculated risk." That dark gaze held his in an unblinking challenge. "He did, after all, get away, didn't he?"

"At the risk of your life."

"That's my job."

"Not if his reasoning was that selfish, that ill-considered."

"No? I see the Rhomandi makes his own rules, just as the Barrister does."

"Why do you call him that?" Deymorin demanded, startled and beyond annoyed to hear his private nickname for his brother coming so freely from this man's mouth.

"Barrister? Hell's Barrister? Doesn't everyone in—" Ganfrion, seeming to sense his anger, was silent a moment, then: "Ah. Family curse, was it? Hate to tell you, Rhomandi, the name's not exactly a secret on the streets. Fits him too well. 'Specially when you've been on the receiving end of one of his sentences."

Deymorin grunted. A man didn't have to stand in the sentencing dock to receive that look.

"The *Rhomandi* believes in equity," he replied, ignoring the rest. "The Rhomandi *believed* the Barrister did as well."

"I think he believed he could get us all out: himself, me—he sent Raulind and the others off before the competition. Hell, I think he figured to get Temorii away."

"Mikhyel said she died on the dance rings—also saving his hide."

"For a lawyer, your brother makes a damned lot of assumptions."

"Assumptions. You mean, she didn't?" Hope swelled. If he could tell Mikhyel his Temorii was still alive . . . "Where is she? Do you know?"

A stifled chuckle escaped. "Last I saw of Temorii, your brother was—"

"She arrived with you, then? She's with Mikhyel now?"

Another dip of the head brought an unexpected release from tension Deymorin hadn't been aware he was carrying. Before Ganfrion's arrival last night, Khyel's thoughts had radiated guilt, even past his attempts to mask them. After Deymorin had sent Ganfrion to him, that guilt and Mikhyel's mind had gone strangely silent. It had been an association Deymorin hadn't cared to consider.

"Where did you find—? No. Just, tell me what happened. From when Mikhyel left you."

"I had my hands full. Five . . . no, six . . . of them, and not bad fighters, considering. I took out two, but by then, one had worked his way behind. I'd taken—" Ganfrion leaned to one side, sought a row of stitches just below the ribs. "That was the deciding stroke, I think. Felt that one leaking all the way to the cobbles. Slipping all over at the last. Damned stupid I was to take it." He shrugged. "Figured my time had come, but I just kept swinging. Gave your brother all the lead on them I could. The world went black; I said my farewells to the Ley Mother, and assumed I'd never wake up."

"Obviously, you were wrong."

"Obviously. When I came to, the alley was empty."

"Bodies?"

"None."

"But you said you killed two?"

"Three, actually. Maybe a fourth." He shrugged. "Thought at first I'd taken one to the head early on and imagined the whole thing. I felt a damned sight better than I had any right to feel, which I figure now for stupidity on my body's part. But my legs still worked, so I headed back for the dance stadium."

"I assume there was ample reason for not simply leaving Khoratum."

"Your brother's wrath."

Meaning, he had to find out what had happened to the dancer or not bother returning at all. Deymorin scarcely recognized his own brother within the narrative Ganfrion gave him. The Mikhyel he knew would never place an individual whim above the fate of Rhomatum. The Mikhyel he knew had braved Anheliaa's wrath more times than any of them would ever know to protect the interests of the city he lived for.

And yet, that same city-bred brother had hired Ganfrion. That same brother had committed himself to a major diplomatic tour that he'd then abandoned, abruptly, to travel incognito to Khoratum on the slimmest of official excuses. Never mind the results had ultimately justified the action: he had gone to Khoratum, jeopardizing his life and theirs for what amounted to personal whim.

He might have done it, given the right provocation. Nikki certainly would. City-born and -bred Mikhyel . . .

And yet, that city-bred brother had *chosen* to spend last night in the open, under that shower of leythium stars. With Temorii.

Trust. Ganfrion. Khoratum. Now Temorii.

His trust for Mikhyel's good sense was taking something of a battering these days.

"Your assessment of this Temorii?" Deymorin asked.

"Guardedly optimistic."

His trust for Ganfrion's sense, on the other hand, was on the rise.

"Meaning?"

"Meaning there was a dancer working for Rhyys. For a time."

"Thyerri. Mikhyel said he defected."

"Possibly."

"Mikhyel also said he's dead now. That he died on the rings during the competition."

Dark eyes stared at him from under heavy brows. "Then your brother lied. Thyerri led us from the stadium and down the back alleys of Khoratum."

"Actually," Deymorin said, ". . . not necessarily."

"Meaning?"

"I'll explain later."

Ganfrion's mouth opened to protest; Deymorin raised his hand.

"Word of the Rhomandi. Explain, first, what Thyerri's allegiances might have to do with Temorii."

There was a long pause while Ganfrion fought some silent, internal war, then: "I'll hold you to that word, Rhomandi. But here it is: Thyerri and Temorii are—were—friends at the very least. Partners . . . probably. My guess is more. Far more."

"Lovers?"

Another pause. A bark of laughter. "*Lovers?* Now, that's a possibility I never considered."

"Then what?"

"Then nothing. They are, in my own mind, unequivocally linked. The actions of one cannot be considered outside the actions of the other."

"You're not going to give me an answer, are you?"

"I've none to give. I won't accuse where I have no evidence."

"Accuse? Dammit, man, is my brother in *danger* from this woman? Is it her intention to hurt him?"

"Ah. *That's* a different issue, now isn't it? In danger, I don't think so. Intentionally hurt him?" Ganfrion's eyes dropped and he continued in a low, expressionless voice. "After the competition, when Rhyys ordered your brother's arrest, Temorii went back onto the rings."

"So Mikhyel said," Deymorin replied coldly, in direct contrast to Ganfrion's tone. "*Distraction,* he said."

Ganfrion's brow tightened. "You might call it that. More like witchcraft. Had the whole place in thrall when I hauled your brother out of the stadium. Even *he* couldn't break free."

"But you could."

"I knew better than to watch."

"Hiller wisdom?" According to the file he had, Ganfrion had been born in a Khoramali hiller village; his mother, at least and for all his size, had *been* hiller, but Ganfrion shook his head.

"Common sense. I saw the effect and used my head. Point is, the competition was over. Temorii was exhausted." Ganfrion shrugged. "Mounting the rings again was infinitely more suicidal than my taking on those six guards, but otherwise . . . No, Rhomandi, Temorii won't hurt your brother. Not knowingly."

"Unknowingly?"

"None of us are proof against that."

"How *did* she survive? Where—how—did you find her?"

"All I know is the street talk I heard on the way back to the stadium. One person said the dancer disappeared off the rings, that it had all been some sort of illusion, another said that the dancer fell and died, another thought they'd seen someone run into the maze with Rhyys' hounds in pursuit. That seemed a logical bolt for a dancer, so I went back to the stadium. Took a while—filched some clothes for myself and her, had to dodge guards—dark as a mother's womb by the time I got there." Ganfrion shuddered. "I'll be honest with you, Rhomandi, I hope I never have to do that again. Damned place is a nest of traps. I wouldn't want to navigate it in the daylight. But I found the radical coronet down an alley, lying in the dirt, and tracker's instinct said Temorii was still there. Eventually, I heard the hounds' wail and followed the sound. I turned a corner, and there she was, with Rhyys' men swarming all over her. I yelled, took them on. Then—" Ganfrion ran his fingers through his hair, combing the sweaty and blood-stained strands back, and looked expectantly at Deymorin. "That's when the fireworks started."

Ganfrion had been their primary source of information within Khoratum. It was through Ganfrion's efforts that they'd known about last night's planned rebellion. Even without his appearing with Mikhyel's ring on his finger, there could be no easy brushing away of *his* curiosity.

"It was the shutdown attempt," Deymorin said shortly.

Ganfrion dipped his head. "And do I assume, from the tenor of this discussion, that you and your brothers succeeded in halting that attempt and are still in control of Rhomatum?"

Deymorin dipped his own head.

"Mauritum?"

"Was involved," Deymorin said, "Isn't now."

"Destroyed?"

That gave him pause. He hadn't even considered the possibility, and he should have. He recalled the moment last night, when Kiyrstin had reached her mind out to her husband, feigning defection from their cause. Garetti had taken that offer, believing he'd won, and the moment their minds had bridged the gap, Lidye had struck. Kiyrstin had held firm as that wave of hatred-laced anger had flowed down the linkage through the shared node tower in Persitum, and on to Mauritum Tower. . . .

And Garetti had vanished, taking with him all vestige of Mauritumin influence over Persitum.

"Destroyed? I don't think so. I damnwell hope not. We don't *need* that level of chaos right on our doorstep."

"Garetti?"

Garetti. High Priest and Ringmaster of Mauritum. Kiyrstin's gods-be-damned husband. If there were justice in the universe, that blast of hatred had freed Kiyrstin and the Web of that particular thorn, but he doubted they could be that fortunate.

"Unknown. At the very least, temporarily no longer interested."

"Shatum?"

Shatum Tower, greatest of the Southern Crescent towers, whose ringmaster, Pasingarim, had been prepared to defect to the rebels at the least sign of weakness in Rhomatum Tower.

"Convinced of the error of their ways," Deymorin answered. "Ready to play nicely again."

"The Northern Crescent?"

"The Towers are under Rhomatum control for now. Thought you might have more specific information for us on the rebel troop situation up in Khoratum."

Ganfrion shook his head. "Nothing. Word on the street was that Rhyys and his visitors retreated into Khoratum Tower, but I've no proof."

"Rhyys and Vandoshin romMaurii manned Khoratum Tower together last night. They were the last to yield."

"RomMaurii? Another Mauritumin was in town? A

priest? How in hell did I miss—" And before Deymorin could explain, awareness dawned on Ganfrion's face. "The scars. Thyerri's gods-be-damned Scarface. I *didn't* miss him. DunGarshin *is* the priest that came in with your woman! That's the one who stole your ring!"

"I'd advise you against calling Kiyrstin that in her presence, but yes. Do you mind telling me how you know about all that?"

"Crypt rumor. Alley scuttlebutt. Some things your brother said. I took it the priest was dead, that a storm from Rhomatum Tower toasted him at the Boreton Turnout."

"That's what *we* thought."

"Your brother didn't recognize him. Was he that changed?"

"Mikhyel never met him."

"Ah."

Silence ruled again as Ganfrion's pain and exhaustion-slowed wits incorporated this newest information.

"The maze?" Deymorin prompted, when he grew tired of waiting. "Rhyys' men?"

"Scattered when the fireworks started."

"Temorii?"

A shake of the disheveled head. "Wouldn't move—might as well not have been there. I think Rhyys had his hounds give chase until there was nothing left. Poor kid just curled on the ground, those big gray eyes staring up at the fireworks. I was bleeding again, figured my time had really come, so I hunkered down, held the kid against the shakes, and watched the sky go black."

"The end of the battle."

"Mine, yes," Ganfrion said, deliberately misreading his words. "I was dying, Rhomandi."

So Deymorin pointed out the obvious fallacy:

"You're here."

Ganfrion's face hardened. "I don't like miracles, Rhomandi. I don't trust them. I know death when she looks me in the face, and she was there twice last night."

"Perhaps you're tougher than you thought."

The snarl that lifted Ganfrion's lip had nothing of humor

in it. "Damn you. Damn *all* the Rhomandi. I wish to *hell* your brother had left me in the Crypt!"

"You'd be dead."

"Death is a natural consequence of life. I don't fear it. I also don't mind avoiding it as long as possible. But *damned* if I'll cheat it!"

"*You* didn't. There are ways . . ." Deymorin opened his fist and rolled the ring on his palm, catching it on his little finger, letting it fall back to his palm. "You know the reputation of Barsitum Node?"

"It's saved my hide more than once."

"You're fortunate. Not all patients are cured."

"You speak from experience?"

"My leg." Deymorin slapped the offending limb. "Broke it years ago."

"Ah. Your brother's seventeenth birthday. His present to you."

Deymorin grimaced, stupidly blindsided by the captain's knowledge. Of course Ganfrion would know. Ganfrion was an information sponge. It was not a day he remembered with any great pride, and just the brand of scandalous event the best will could not have kept from the papers.

"Rumor said your brother tried to kill you."

He frowned at that. "Rumor lied. It was an accident."

"I have no doubt. Even at seventeen, if your brother had wanted you dead, you'd be dead."

That surprised a shout of laughter out of him. "I see you *do* know him. As for the leg, I'm lucky to still have it at all. After the accident, they hauled me to Barsitum and dumped me in the leythium pools, but it didn't do a damn thing. They finally admitted defeat and took me home. I healed, but thanks to good physicians, not leythium magic. To this day, there are times I don't venture to walk without a cane."

Kiyrstin had helped there, as she'd helped him in so many other ways. She had a knack for doing something to his back that somehow made the ache vanish. She'd tried to teach his valet, Tonio, but so far, he hadn't managed. Too long away from her rough-and-ready healing, and his leg gained a fire running down it that seemed, at least, worse than before, though he'd begun to believe he'd simply grown accustomed to it not hurting at all.

The Barsitum pools had done nothing for him; Khyel, on the other hand . . .

"My brother would have died without Barsitum."

"The Barrister?"

Deymorin nodded.

"Maybe he was just tougher than you think."

Echo of his previous rationalization. Deymorin grinned a tight-jawed acknowledgment. "He was thirteen, and indisputably broken. At best, he should have been crippled for life."

"So the leythium pools approve of crypt-bait and barristers, but not principes. Interesting, but what's your point?"

"Would you accuse the Barsitum brothers of cheating death?"

"Hell, no. It's the Ley."

"Exactly. And *you're* alive today because of the Ley."

Ganfrion frowned, then asked, "The fireworks?"

"Fireworks?" Deymorin repeated, startled to realize how deeply into his own argument he'd fallen. He'd been assuming Mother's interference, but perhaps Mother's involvement wasn't a given. That free-drifting ley-energy, energy that even now, he was sure, had Nikki and Pander galloping nonstop along mountain trails, might well have kept Ganfrion alive, and as for Ganfrion's presence here in camp . . .

Mikhyel had returned last night, angry and bitter over the loss of his beloved dancer . . . and his bodyguard. Angry, intent, and highly focused. Could Mikhyel's desires rather than Mother's have affected Ganfrion? Could Ganfrion's and Temorii's presence here be Mikhyel's doing and not Mother at all?

That supposed a hell of a lot of power in his brother. Power to rival Anheliaa's ring-enhanced abilities. Yet Mikhyel had had no rings. All Mikhyel had had was a wish . . . and his brothers. The three of them, Mother kept insisting, formed a node. Mother and Rhomatum had *used* them last night to focus their efforts to beget the new node blossoming beneath them.

Just how powerful is he, Deymio?

That, little brother, is a very good question.

Could Mikhyel be tapping that same source, as naturally as he breathed?

"Rhomandi? Rhomandi!"

Deymorin shook his head, chasing off the chill that rippled down his spine. "Sorry. You . . . posed a possibility I hadn't considered."

"You mean you *don't* know?"

"Precisely, no. I can assure you is that your presence here, alive and mostly healthy, is an explicable phenomenon . . . at least, in as much as anything to do with the Ley can be explained. Someone wants you alive and well—and here. I begin to suspect that someone is my brother."

"Well. Full of surprises, isn't he? A brother of Barsitum, then? No wonder he resisted Temorii's charms for so long." Ganfrion's tone hardened. "Try again, Rhomandi, your brother is no celibate healer."

"Your explanation, not mine."

"A ringspinner? Now, *that,* I could believe. He's got the breeding."

"After a fashion." Neither he nor his brothers knew themselves where the ringmasters' talents ended and theirs began. Their experience had no precedents, at least in Rhomatum's archives. He'd looked.

"So," Ganfrion said, "where are they?"

"What?"

"The Rings."

"In Rhomatum, of course."

"But—" Ganfrion broke off. "And Mikhyel's transport here? Mine and Temorii's? Are the crypt rumors true? Did Anheliaa master that ability? *Was* she throwing people the hell and gone where she liked?"

"*She* didn't master it. But it can be done."

"She didn't master it, but your brother did? Is *that* why he was so damned cocksure of getting out?"

Deymorin allowed his silence to answer for him. It was not a possibility he cared to debate.

"Then why in *hell* didn't he do it sooner? Dammit, why *this?*" Ganfrion swept a hand across his scarred body.

"Settle down. I said it *might* have been Mikhyel. As far as I know, he *knows* no more about how it's done than I do, which is to say, nothing beyond the fact it *can* be done. If, in fact, *his* willing it brought you here, I don't believe it was conscious on his part—beyond the fact that he did want you and the dancer safe. Ley manipulation is still somewhat less than an exact science."

"Oh, that's reassuring. When do I disappear next? Is he going to take offense at my eye color and land me inside a rock somewhere? It would, of course, be an accident, and oh, aren't we sorry, Ganfrion, old man, but, well, he just didn't know what he was doing!"

"It's not that simple—"

"Just tell me who *is* responsible so I can get out of his line of sight."

Deymorin took a deep, settling breath. "Captain, the answer is, you're alive and here because of forces linked to the leylines and the nodes that we're only beginning to understand. Either it was Mikhyel, or it was Mother. Of the two—"

"Mother? Another Rhomandi? I thought your mother was dead. Or did she come back as well? I guess you're going to bring Anheliaa back next."

"Not *my* mother. Mother. Mother is—" He winced, anticipating the pragmatic man's reaction. But there was no avoiding the moment. "Mother is a Tamshi."

"A Tamshi." With a bitter laugh, Ganfrion waved his hand toward the doorflap. "Get out, Rhomandi. And take your crazy brother's ring with you."

Deymorin stood up, half inclined to comply, but having gone too far to just let the man walk free. "Don't you want the rest of your precious truth?"

"I *want* my clothes. I want my clothes. I want a bath. And I want out of here. Khy—your brother treated me as squarely as any employer I've endured so far. I'd as soon get out with the taste in my mouth still sweet."

"You can't. You wanted the truth. Until that truth is no longer volatile information, you're not going anywhere."

"The taste just soured."

"I suggest you hear me out first."

"Damned if I will. Get out! Or run me through, if that's your choice, but I've attained a certain respect for your brother and . . . dammit, your brother *and* you, and I'm damned if I'll go to my grave with my last thought being how great a fool I am for that judgment."

Deymorin deliberately sat back down. "I notice you swear by the Mother of the Ley."

"Damn you for a persistent ass!"

"Yes, I am. And you do."

Ganfrion heaved an exasperated sigh. "It's an *expression*. It doesn't mean—"

"Oh, yes it does. It means a great deal. The Ley Mother is quite real. I've met her. So have you."

"The Princeps of Rhomatum is consulting the Tamshi. I wonder how much your brother will pay me not to take this to the tatter-tabloids in Rhomatum?"

Deymorin, knowing it for meaningless sarcasm, just looked at him, and the sneer faded, with obvious reluctance, into a more thoughtful expression.

"So when did I meet her?"

"Last night. In Khoratum. In an alley, you said."

"Thyerri?"

"Among others. Mother has a talent for mimicry."

"Mimicry . . . Shapeshifter?"

Deymorin nodded again, and Ganfrion ran a hand vigorously over his face.

"It *could* explain . . . You *did* mean Thyerri?"

"At least the Thyerri who led you from the city, according to Mikhyel. He believes the real Thyerri died on the rings."

"And Mikhyel would know."

"If anyone would. He seems to have a special affinity for these creatures, whatever they are."

"Why doesn't that surprise me?" Another eye-scrubbing pass of the hand. "Rings, I need a drink."

"You've had more than enough already."

"Go to hell." Ganfrion grabbed a tent pole and hauled himself to his feet. "I want—"

His face turned gray and he swayed. Deymorin's booted foot against his knee tipped him easily back down.

"Idiot." Deymorin hooked the fallen blankets with his toe, pulled them in reach, and tossed them into Ganfrion's lap. Ganfrion caught them, then sat staring down at the folds.

"You said 'It could explain . . .' " Deymorin prompted.

"Explain what?"

The dark eyes flickered back into focus. "Thyerri, of course."

"Of course. And?"

"And nothing."

"You're holding out on me, Captain. What is it about these ringdancers that raises your suspicions?"

"Dammit, man, I've no proof."

"Then give me suspicions."

"It's your brother's business!"

"My brother's business is mine where it affects the safety of the Syndicate, and my brother's mental acuity definitely falls in that category. I want to know if these ringdancers are compromising his judgment. Captain Ganfrion, I want your report!"

"Your brother saddled me with that damned ring!"

"And you rejected it. Where do your loyalties lie now, Ganfrion of the Khoramali?"

The square jaw clenched beneath heavy stubble, and one large fist ground into the palm of the other hand.

"Ring or no ring, I'm gorMikhyel."

And this was a man who had listed adultery among Deymorin's outstanding faults. Loyalty. Promises. He couldn't say his relationship with Kiyrstine romGaretti, for all he couldn't regret it, didn't bother him as well. For all she was unquestionably estranged, for all the circumstances of that estrangement effectively released her from any moral obligations to her husband, it was not a clean break, and that lack, in the eyes of those who gave their oaths to him, who counted on him to honor those oaths . . . that lack mattered.

Loyalty. Promises. It was the lifeblood of a man like Ganfrion.

Ring or no ring, I'm gorMikhyel. . . .

"I can't argue that." Deymorin flipped the ring back to Ganfrion, and stood up. "Tell my brother to get that thing sized. Better yet, tell him to use his *own* damned crest. That fucking feather of truth suits you both."

But as he turned to leave, Ganfrion's thick-fingered hand stopped him.

"I'm gorMikhyel, and by my money, that means his safety is my business. So sit down."

Chapter Six

"Where do you think you're going with that tray, Kiyr-stine romGaretti?"

Maybe it was the makeup, perhaps the hair. Possibly it was the tone of voice that sometimes sounded so much like Anheliaa's it could send chills down your back.

Maybe it was just the way Lidye romNikaenor picked her teeth, so delicate and proper—right after she'd bitten someone's neck—that raised Kiyrstin's hackles. Whatever the source of that irritation, it took the full experience of fifteen years surviving Garetti's tantrums for Kiyrstin to respond pleasantly:

"Just a bit of breakfast for Mirym."

"She's been fed."

As if the young woman, sitting elsewhere in this huge complex, alone and under guard, were an animal to be tended.

Kiyrstin smiled, warmly, she hoped, since nothing could be gained by further taxing Lidye's already strained temper. Said amiability would have been ever so much easier if her own temper were any less strained. Had she gotten any sleep last night, her curiosity about her current venture might easily outweigh Lidye's petty superiorities.

Unfortunately, sleep had been out of the question. From the moment Nikki had disappeared from the Tower, they'd been deaf and dumb to the brothers' fate, with only the shattered remnants of the Khoratum Ring littering the tower's floor, and the Rings themselves, stable but utterly unresponsive to Lidye's demands, to assure them the night's activities had been real. Until the exhausted messenger had arrived with word from Deymorin less than an hour ago, they'd had no idea that the flaring sky above Rhomatum last night had had any significance beyond causing panic in the city streets.

The City Police had acted quickly and quieted those fears before riots broke out, but she'd been unable to arm those peacekeepers with anything more effective than a generic reassurance and recommendation to people to stay inside until the skies grew quiet, which, thankfully, they had with the rising sun.

A new node, Deymorin's message had explained along with Mikhyel's assurances the glittering rain was harmless. A new node and Khoratum lost from the Web forever. Thanks to Garetti's meddling, both webs were now battling for internal stability.

Garetti's meddling and a young woman's silver needle.

"And what does the girl carry?" Lidye asked, and lifted a finger toward Kiyrstin's maid, Beauvina, hovering in the background.

Beauvina tucked the satchel she bore closer to her chest.

"Just some of Mirym's stitching," Kiyrstin explained. With little to do this morning, armed with that knowledge from Deymorin and a growing curiosity about the young woman they'd all grossly underestimated, she'd sent Vina to find out where Lidye had had Mirym incarcerated and had been headed there when Lidye stopped her.

"I forbid it!" Lidye snapped, and her eyes flared white all around.

"Gently, Lidye," Kiyrstin said soothingly. "Remember your baby."

Furious did not begin to describe Lidye's reaction in those first moments following Nikki's disappearance from the Tower. That fury had settled first and foremost on Mirym, whose final actions, warranted or not, had caused the destruction of the Khoratum/Persitum Ring. It had taken a spasm from Lidye's burgeoning womb to silence her and prevent her lashing out. In terror of losing her child, Lidye had retreated to her room, leaving Nethaalye of Giephaetum to watch the deadlocked rings. Not even news of the message from Deymorin had roused her from her bed.

"You can't keep the girl locked away like some pariah, Lidye," she said. "Mirym was as much a part of last night's victory as any of us. She held the Khoratum line—"

"We *lost* Khoratum because of her!"

"And if she *hadn't* cut it loose, we might have lost the entire Web."

"Nonsense! We *had* them, I tell you."

Kiyrstin pressed her lips tight over the retort that rose. It seemed no matter what she did, she and Lidye were doomed to shout at one another. A few hours without Nikki to mediate with his wife had raised her respect for that young man by several notches.

She wished Nikki were back. Better yet, she wished Deymorin would return to the City. Lidye was not the only increasingly irrational female under the Rhomandi roof. All too often, she felt herself ready to do violence to the smaller woman.

The fate of the Rhomatum Rings and the entire Rhomatum Web left in the hands of four women, three of them pregnant, one a proven traitor, another the sister and daughter of traitors, and the lot of them virtual strangers to the City, its officials and its customs, not to mention each other . . .

It was a situation fraught with dangerous footing, but Kiyrstin had always enjoyed a challenge.

Of all the questions she held, Mirym, this mute servant girl with unexpected and still unclear aspirations and loyalties, was the most intriguing.

"We had them," Lidye persisted, determined, it seemed to start a battle here in the hallway. "How *can* you listen to a word that Khoratumin whore has to say?"

Kiyrstin sensed Beauvina's bristling, and glanced back to calm the pride of the young woman who was in fact and in truth from the most respectable establishment of that nature in Rhomatum.

"Mirym is from Khoratum, that much is true," she acknowledged, adding, "And she knows . . . if not something we don't, certainly more than we suspected she knew. I, for one, would like to know what prompted her to destroy the Khoratum Ring."

"That's simple. She was one of *them*. Had she released the Khoratum line to us as I ordered, we could have *taken* Mauritum! She was helping protect *Garetti*."

"Taken Mauritum?" Astonished, Kiyrstin set the tray on a side table before she dropped it. The Rhomandi mansion, built in the heart of the city of Rhomatum, had a plethora of small tables, as it had a plethora of rooms, statuary, fountains, paintings, hallways—and secrets. "Why would we have taken Mauritum?"

"Why not? Your Garetti tried to take us! We could have shown those Mauritumin fanatics what *true* power is!"

Beyond astonished, Kirystin was appalled. "And what would you have done with it once you had it?"

Lidye's delicately tinted mouth spread in a tight snarl, and the fanatic's gleam shone in her eyes. "Make it pay."

Make, not *made.* The desire hadn't faded with the morning light.

"That's . . . utter nonsense, you know," Kiyrstin said slowly. "That was *never* Deymorin's intent—"

"What care I for Deymorin's intentions? *He* knows nothing of Rhomatum's needs. With Khoratum intact, with Mauritum under our control, who *knows* what we could have accomplished? Last night was our chance. We had Garetti by his religious balls. We could have destroyed him! Instead . . ." She cast her pale eyes toward the Tower. "We have *nothing!*"

"But—"

"*Nothing, I say!* Thanks to that—harlot! And you'll *not* take her any more weapons of chaos!"

Lidye grabbed for the satchel, but Vina ducked back, her round face determinedly set. Kiyrstin caught Lidye's arms from behind and held her easily until her active struggles stopped.

"And you!" Lidye spat over her shoulder. "You're nothing but a harlot as well. Garetti's wife, sleeping with Deymorin! Where does the Rhomandi get *his* . . . intentions?"

Lidye was trembling with a contained anger not unknown to Kiyrstin. She'd seen it often enough in her estranged Maritumin husband, particularly after a long day in *his* tower.

"Calm down, Lidye. Remember the child." She spoke soothingly, ignoring the accusations designed only to inflame her. "You're exhausted. Go back to bed."

Lidye froze, took a deep breath, and Kiyrstin cautiously released her arms and moved to Beauvina's side.

"We've heard from Deymorin," she explained, "and Nikki's fine."

Lidye's face remained unmoved, as if she didn't care at all for a young man trying so hard to be a good husband to her. Kiyrstin's sympathy for Nikki rose to match her respect. "They're *all* fine," she persisted, giving Lidye the news whether she wanted or not. "There's a new node forming between Rhomatum and Khoratum—"

"No! They can't let that happen!" Lidye's false calm shattered completely, leaving her distraught beyond good sense or restraint.

"Done is done, Lidye. And they couldn't have stopped it if they'd tried, from what I read in Deymorin's message. It's all right. They'll be back soon, then and we'll have all the answers."

Lidye stared blankly. "That explains the stasis. The Rings can't shift. They wouldn't dare. The energy must flow smoothly. . . ."

"Go to *bed*, Lidye!"

Those wild blue eyes settled unblinking on her. "And leave you to conspire with that Khoratumin harlot? Stay away from her, Kiyrstine romGaretti!"

"Conspire, no," Kiyrstin said sweetly. "But she seems to have a great deal more knowledge about Anheliaa and the Web than any of you credited her with. It seems to me she should be treated as an asset, not as an enemy."

"She's been given her chance to speak. She chose to remain silent. We shall decide what to do with her when Nikaenor returns. Until then, she'll remain as far from the

Tower as I can keep her and still retain control over her whereabouts, not to mention her *contacts*."

Which meant where she was, in the tiny cell block buried deep within the hill on which the mansion was built, an uncomfortable place Kiyrstin hadn't known existed until Beauvina informed her an hour ago, having charmed the information out of a member of Lidye's Tower Guard.

It was so convenient having a personal servant with all the talents of a Sparingate inmate. Perhaps Mikhyel was on to something with this trend he'd set.

Knowing where Mirym was, however, was not the same as getting there. It was ever so tempting to threaten Lidye's obstruction with retaliation from Deymorin. Deymorin *was* Princeps, for all he'd lost the title momentarily to Lidye's sweet-faced child-husband during Anheliaa's reign of terror.

But Deymorin had had his title back months ago and without an argument, thanks to Nikki's good sense, a fact which had to stick in Lidye's craw, and while Deymorin couldn't give Kiyrstin the title of *wife*, he *had* given her the freedom of Rhomandi House and demanded of the staff and the family that she be treated as if she were his bride in truth.

Another not-insignificant bone in Lidye's craw, she was certain. No way it wouldn't be.

It was tempting to use her power by association for what it was worth . . . but not particularly wise in this case. Instead, she opted for the flattery of a request, and the lure of conspiracy in her tone. "Lidye, it's for the sake of the Tower; give me some time with her. Perhaps Mirym will speak more openly to me. Perhaps I can find out why she did as she did."

"Why should she tell you anything?"

"No particular reason. Just a possibility." And on sudden inspiration. "Like her, I don't belong here."

"Hah! So you admit it!"

"I admit I'm a stranger here, and not a Rhomandi. Yet." Despite the fact it undermined her argument, she couldn't resist adding: "But then neither are you a true Rhomandi."

She was ashamed to admit, the chilling glare that Lidye cast her caught her utterly unprepared.

"I am a Rhomandi in ways you cannot fathom, Kiyrstine *romGaretti.*" And when Lidye took a menacing step forward, Kiyrstin fell back. "Would you know in what way you and *that female* are alike? Harlots, that's obvious. Your ties to the Rhomandi and hers to dunMheric are disgraceful and base. Bastards you bear and bastards they'll be! Harlots and parasites, living off Rhomandi charity, then cutting their throats when your appetites are satisfied."

Lidye paused, her expression eased, and her head tipped—like a bird watching a worm. Kiyrstin said nothing. Lidye's feelings toward her were hardly a surprise; it was the strength and clarity with which she expressed them that had taken her unawares.

"Still," Lidye continued in a lighter tone, as if aware of her victory, "I suppose you have a point. Harlots and parasites that you are, you might well place her at some odd sort of conspiratorial ease. Perhaps, under other circumstances, she might even open up to you. Perhaps in her complaint, something useful would just slip out." Her eyes narrowed; the bird struck. "But the girl doesn't *speak!* She's a mute! Nothing will simply *slip out.* You haven't even the mindspeech that could give you access to her thoughts. I see absolutely no purpose, other than a soft-minded coddling that could only serve to undermine the pressure my current decision is placing on her."

Sarcasm. That was a good sign, as was the subtle relaxation of Lidye's spine. Kiyrstin took her stand quietly, calmly.

"I'm going to try, Lidye, with or without your approval. But I've no wish to . . . undermine your efforts. Think of the needlework as bait, not coddling. Give me two hours, maybe three. If nothing comes of it, I'll admit defeat and leave her until the Rhomandi returns with his brothers, as he promises they will do directly. At that time, carry your complaint of me to Mikhyel and I'll stand by his judgment. Fair enough?"

It didn't take the mindspeech of which Lidye was so arrogantly proud to tell her that Lidye by no means appreciated the option Kiyrstin had presented her, but Lidye was also fully aware of the cards Kiyrstin held in reserve, and from her hesitation, perhaps she wouldn't dare to challenge Deymorin openly. For all Lidye's prideful, problematic insistence on her way, Lidye was still here by marriage, no more born to Rhomatum than she was.

Whatever the reason, Lidye nodded, waved Kiyrstin and Beauvina on their way, and floated down the hall, a trick that had nothing to do with her ringspinning and everything to do with years of walking about with weights on her ankles and braces on her neck, a lady of the aristocracy, brought up in the lap of fashion.

Sometimes Kiyrstin was very glad she'd married early.

"Tell me, Lidye."

The cloud of fabric paused in its retreat.

Kiyrstin asked, "Can you hear my thoughts?"

The pale blonde head turned, the perfectly painted blue eyes assayed her, and a mysterious smile lifted the corners of the pink mouth.

In other words, *no.*

"That's what I thought. —Lead on, Beauvina," Kiyrstin said, and followed the young woman in the opposite direction.

ᔑ   ᔑ   ᔑ

The door swung closed behind Rhomandi's back, silent on its well-greased hinges. Ganfrion twisted the too-small ring around his fingertip, wondering whether or not he'd just done the right thing, whether he had the right to expose his employer's ignorance, to set him up for possible ridicule and almost certain embarrassment.

Not the first time in his life the question had come up.

The difference this time was—he cared.

ᔑ   ᔑ   ᔑ

{*Khy . . .*}

Raspberries, cinnamon, and a hint of clove. Mikhyel

wondered, on the edge of dreams, if that had always been his favorite combination of scents . . .

{Time to wake up, my lazy Khy.}

. . . or was it only since Temorii had tumbled so precipitously into his life?

Sensation returned slowly: sunlight warming his face, the tingle of the leythium mist filling the air, callused fingertips on his cheek, brushing the hair back from his face.

He couldn't remember when he'd first noticed the scent, much less associated it with Temorii. Had it been at Boreton, when she and Mother combined their talents to save his ley-burned hide?

{Khy?}

Or even earlier, when he had been lying in a sickbed, refusing to wake up, trying to die on the hope he could draw Anheliaa into death with him. Temorii had touched his mind then, all the way from the Khoratum caverns. She'd lent him strength and the will, no, the *desire* to live. That had been the first time, but he hadn't known, and the raspberries—

"Dammit, Khyel dunMheric, *wake up!*" The demand was a voiced whisper this time.

He forced himself not to react. Teasing her. Playing games of a sort he hadn't played in over seventeen . . . long . . . years. The games he'd engaged in since his mother died had been . . . quite, quite different.

{As if you could lie to me.}

Besides, if he woke up, he had responsibilities. People counting on him for answers. Deymorin, Nikki . . . Ganfrion. His control wavered. Ganfrion alive and here: as great a miracle as Temorii's presence—greater. Mother, loving Temorii, knowing how much Temorii meant to him, might well, in a moment of charitable whimsy in the aftermath of node-making, have sent her to him. Ganfrion was a greater, unexpected gift. But Temorii understood that miracle. How much was he going to have to explain to Ganfrion?

{Everything. . . .}

Easy for her to say. She didn't have to find the words.

{He's ready to know. . . .}

And there was Raulind, his valet, friend and lifelong advisor, enroute between Khoratum and this camp—Raulind, whom he had entrusted with the safe flight out of Khoratum of a small army, the entourage of guards and footmen and grooms who collectively had kept Mikhyel dunMheric safe and comfortable while he was there.

{Khy . . . }

The warm mouth on his was sheer magic, breathing life into his lungs.

Raulind had no Temorii to awaken him. Raulind hadn't had Mother to spirit him down the mountainside in a heartbeat. Raulind and the rest of Mikhyel's men had had to leave Khoratum by their own efforts, escaping via back roads and in the dark, while Mikhyel was watching Temorii challenge the rings and win and then dance her heart out, giving him the chance to escape. Raulind and the others were riding down the mountain trails like normal men, possibly with enemies at their backs.

{Damn you, Khy!}

Bony knuckles dug into his ribs, but a childhood of Anheliaa's far less restrained training held him still.

Raspberries, cinnamon, and clove. Mother's thoughts smelled of raspberries, Rhomatum's of fire-blossom tea. Anheliaa's fire-blossom tea laced with cloying honey was a scent that had pervaded his life in truth even before he became aware of her thought's essence: she had drunk it every day of her life.

Anheliaa had been indelibly linked with Rhomatum. She'd accepted control of the Rings on the day of her majority, had spent hours in the Tower for years before that. Fire-blossom tea was the smell of Rhomatum, the honey . . . that had been Anheliaa's modification, as Temorii's cinnamon and clove enhanced Mother's raspberry scent.

Deymorin, Nikki . . . he hadn't thought before what their thoughts smelled like . . . it was as if their *essence* as Temorii called it, had been too much a part of him, perhaps for all his life, to be noticed without conscious consideration. But Nikki was freshly baked bread. Steaming, alive with flavor. The basic sustenance of life. Deymorin was . . . a walk in the forest, and hot spiced-cider. Everything of Outside, and nothing ever of fire-blossom tea.

Yet.

Mother and Rhomatum both had implied Deymorin should be ringmaster in Rhomatum. If he accepted that fate, would his scent become tainted with fire-blossom tea?

He hoped not, even as, for the first time, he wondered what scent his own thoughts carried.

{Fine wine and a warm fire, my foolish friend. Wake up, we need to talk.}

Talk? He had no desire to talk. There'd been too much of talk in his life and far to little of . . . whatever activity he was currently engaged in. His brothers were quiet, their minds distant. He liked it that way, and the sooner he roused the sooner the fight for mental autonomy would begin.

And he was tired of fighting. He was twenty-seven years old and he'd already fought a lifetime's worth of battles. In courts, council chambers, and back rooms throughout the Web, in Anheliaa's tower, in his own family's home. Last night, he'd fought a battle in the depths of the earth itself with a creature some might call a god.

The gently searching mouth traced the line of his jaw and down his neck, growing increasingly insistent.

He wanted, just for a while, not to fight . . . anything.

Teeth closed sharply on his earlobe, jerking him into full consciousness.

He hissed, grabbed blindly and dragged his tormentor to the ground beneath him.

{I thought you didn't want to fight.}

He laughed and leaned to kiss her, but Temorii slithered free and launched herself at him in a wrestling attack far more reminiscent of childhood with Deymorin than of last night's tender encounter—and as predictable in its outcome.

"Good morning to you, too," Mikhyel said to the dirt and vegetation poking into his face. "May I get up now?"

The weight on his back shifted and disappeared, the hold on his wrist pulled him over and drew him to his feet in one swift, incontestable motion. Too swift: he overbalanced and came up hard against her.

Or perhaps that had been her intent. She steadied him, held him, her gray eyes drinking in the sight they thought lost to them forever only a few short hours ago. Gray eyes glowing almost green in this ley-touched morning, a finely-trimmed beard and mustache, black, like his hair, hiller-refined features . . .

He blinked, and pulled his mind free of hers, seeing through his own eyes again and conscious of his own near loss rather than hers. He brushed bits of green from her hair and face, felt her fingers in his own hair, and as one, they leaned forward to match lips to lips.

What followed had little to do with thought and everything to do with instinct.

{Khy, please!} If thoughts could gasp, Temorii's gasped. {I've got to talk to you. I must explain—never expected we'd—}

{All the time in the world, my darling dancer.}

"No!" Her thoughts wrenched—painfully—free. "Dammit, dunMheric, you don't understand. I never thought it would come to—"

"*Well*, brother Khyel, are you going to introduce us to your friend?"

Deymorin's presence, a sense of laughter, filled his mind, and images followed swiftly—images of himself, disheveled and half-dressed, arms wrapped around Temorii, hers about him. . . .

Mikhyel gasped and pulled back, vaguely aware of Temorii's sudden distress before Nikki's excited presence filled him, drowning out all other senses, and he was looking uphill, not down, and striding up that same hill, not standing braced against Temorii. Striding with two sets of legs, one young with a jogging spring, the other, with a limp, a painful irregularity . . .

He swayed, dizzied, and felt a blanket settle over him, a blanket woven of thought that shut them all out, Nikki, Deymorin . . . even Temorii.

"Dancer!" In sharp contrast to Temorii's gentle whispers,

Nikki's voice assaulted his eardrums. "Deymorin, it's *Dancer!*"

§ § §

Deymorin caught Nikki's arm as his youngest brother surged forward, and pressed hard in a signal far older than their mental link. He could only hope that the sudden distance he felt from his brothers was mutual; they didn't need that flood of images Nikki was radiating to confuse Mikhyel further.

At the same time that he welcomed the obscuring cloud about his emotions and Nikki's shouting memories, he suspected its source. He was accustomed to Mikhyel's obsessive need for privacy making Mikhyel's mind inaccessible, but this . . .

This was different, more like a headcold in spring, as if his own thoughts were congesting in his head, unable to escape to . . . wherever thoughts went after they were formed.

And he fully suspected the young person standing in the circle of Mikhyel's arms, staring at him with the wide eyes of a startled deer, as the source of that contamination.

A young person who, he had every reason to believe, was a far cry from the hiller woman his brother so obviously believed filled his arms: either Mikhyel's Temorii was indeed the individual they'd all first met in the valley following their first confrontation with Vandoshin romMaurii, as Nikki believed, or enough alike to be Dancer's twin.

With a final quick caress, Mikhyel broke away and pulled his tunic up over his shoulder.

"Deymorin?" Nikki whispered, but Deymorin shook his head.

"Not now," Deymorin said, and began the last stiff climb up to his brother's . . . nesting spot, picking his way slowly, giving himself time to sort his startled thoughts.

The picture, confused enough once Ganfrion's suspicions had been raised, had just taken another twist.

The possibility, as Ganfrion had suggested, that the young hiller to whom Mikhyel had given his heart had been playing a double game with Rhyys had been worrisome and certainly fraught with potential logistical problems, but in the end, the worry was . . . if not moot, certainly less than might have been since both Temorii and Thyerri had proven their loyalties to Mikhyel. Or so it had seemed.

But *Dancer* was *Mother's*. Mother's assistant, and, at Mother's instigation, Mikhyel's savior. Mikhyel hadn't remembered that salvage of his life after the battle at the Boreton Turnout. He hadn't remembered, and *they* hadn't told him, because *Mother* had advised against telling him.

And nothing in Mikhyel's thoughts or words surrounding Temorii had indicated he was aware of that connection to Boreton, certainly not of the even greater hoax that apparently had been played on him personally.

Because Dancer was, to Deymorin's certain and personal knowledge, a man.

Deymorin's thoughts swirled, the congestion grew.

Granted, they'd only met Dancer once, but that meeting had left an indelible image if not in his mind, then certainly in the mind of Nikki, who had not taken his eyes from Mother's graceful assistant from the moment he had appeared, clothed only in a halo of leylight, to the moment he'd disappeared into the woods, draped in a blanket Kiyrstin had placed around his shoulders.

The similarity was too great to be coincidence, and they couldn't afford to even consider that possibility. It was possible they were dealing with twins, which would, at least, simplify matters. So much, so very much could be explained if Thyerri and Dancer were one, and the enchantress in Mikhyel's arms was indeed the Temorii he believed her to be.

And yet, according to the doctors, identical twins always held more in common than their faces: they had to be the same gender. Perhaps they weren't identical, after all, but only very, very much alike.

For Mikhyel's sake . . . he hoped so. For the rest . . .

man or woman, Dancer or Temorii, they were unquestionably Mother's.

And if they *weren't* dealing with twins . . .

Temorii, Thyerri . . . now Dancer. It was a dizzying combination, to say the least. And if Temorii was, as Ganfrion had suggested, also Thyerri, then everything Thyerri had done, all his connections with Rhyys became part of the larger pattern Mother had set.

If they were the same, according to Ganfrion's (by Ganfrion's own admission) pieced together description of the events, Dancer had sought out Mikhyel from the moment Khyel had entered Khoratum, had insinuated himself into Mikhyel's life, had lured him into taking risks, into staying in Khoratum far longer than he should have—then risked death to get him out.

As Mirym had risked death in Rhomatum Tower last night when she'd touched that needle to the Khoratum Ring.

All for the sake of Mother's freedom. *That* was the direction of everything. That drive of Mother's for freedom had manipulated them all, but *none* more than Mikhyel.

Don't tell him, Dancer had said at Boreton, and claimed it was Mother's counsel: *Let him remember, if he will. . . .* And Deymorin, in his ignorance, had agreed. Now, he doubted the wisdom . . . and the motive behind that advice. Keep Mikhyel dunMheric conveniently ignorant? Had that been Mother's plan? She'd insinuated one of her minions into the Tower, the other into Mikhyel's bed. Was she finished yet? Was her freedom all she sought and had she now sent Dancer to Mikhyel only to be rid of them both?

Or was her pattern still changing, and did she send Dancer here to keep them all entangled in it?

Whatever the reasons, while he'd been an unwitting party to that deception in the past, now, at the edge of an encamped army, with the two caught unawares in an embrace, was hardly the convenient time to end it.

As he and Nikki finally reached Mikhyel and his dancer, Deymorin forced a smile and held out his hand in greeting. "You must be Temorii."

"You don't have to pretend, Deymorin," Mikhyel said quietly. "I know you've met. I know all about Mother and Dancer and the Boreton firestorm. Temorii explained everything."

And so the pattern twisted: Mikhyel knew about Boreton now . . . by Dancer's telling. But somehow Deymorin doubted that Mikhyel understood anything at all. He wondered if his brother noticed how *Temorii* took his proffered hand wrist to wrist as a man would, then realized, as his attention shifted to his brother's bewitched face, that Mikhyel noticed nothing beyond what Mikhyel wanted to see.

"Welcome," Deymorin said, turning back to Dancer, and he tightened his grip, testing, as one man would do to another.

Temorii returned that pressure without flinching. But then, so would Kiyrstin accept such a challenge. So would Kiyrstin test a man's assumptions regarding her strengths and limitations.

Anxious eyes met his. Gray eyes rimmed with green. Unusual eyes—Mikhyel's eyes, as in other ways Mikhyel looked to be more closely related to Temorii than to himself or to Nikki.

But that was the Rhomandi hiller blood showing. The Rhomandi line had more than once scandalized the conservative descendants of the Darian Exodus by mingling bloodlines with the natives their arrival had displaced; that lineage came out, overwhelmingly, in Mikhyel.

Doubt rose. His knowledge of hillers was limited. He'd known only a few well in his life and acknowledged his own difficulty at times in telling one casual acquaintance from another. They *were* of a type far more uniform, at least to his eye, than the people of Mauritumin descent who occupied the valley and the node cities. That Mikhyel, who had had no dealings, to his knowledge, with hillers before going into Khoratum, might have overlooked the extreme similarity Ganfrion insisted existed between his Temorii and Thyerri was possible. Ganfrion *had*, according to his own admission that morning, been born in the Khoramali. Ganfrion was, by all legal senses, hiller. Ganfrion insisted he *could* tell minute differences, and Ganfrion also insisted the young gutter-rat he'd followed for Mikhyel *was* Temorii, though even he had been fooled at first, and to this day had been unable to prove his conviction to his own satisfaction, let alone to the rigorous proof Mikhyel would require.

Himself, Deymorin wished he could see this Thyerri lined up with Dancer and Temorii. To see them all at once. To know, in his own mind, their similarities and differ . . .

Through that clasp of Dancer's hand, Deymorin sensed a whisper of raspberries and clove, a scent of fear and hope, a taste of loneliness and love . . . in that moment he knew, somehow, and just as Ganfrion had insisted, that Dancer would not knowingly hurt his brother.

But Mikhyel was being cruelly deceived, regardless of how honest the love Dancer might bear him, and suddenly suspicious of the source of that unprecedented charity, Deymorin raised the mental barrier that he perceived as a massive stone wall, shutting out scent/taste/whisper—and when his mind was again his own, he wasn't surprised to discover his suspicions intact.

He eased that barrier long enough to finish the thought deliberately. Mikhyel was being deceived and in that deceit, Mikhyel was destined to be hurt—badly—whether Dancer willed it or not.

The dancer's eyes narrowed at that rebuff, and his clean-edged chin rose a defiant degree. Clean-edged and beardless, but so were many of the hiller men devoid of beard. Trust Mikhyel to fill even this simplest of human equations with complicating variables.

"Deymorin?" Mikhyel's voice suggested that he'd remained silent too long.

Deymorin eased his grip on the fine-boned, but highly resilient, hand and said, "I understand we have you to thank a second time for the safe return of our brother."

"In all honesty, Deymorin dunMheric—" Dancer's voice was as musical as the one memory provided. "Khy would not have been in danger, if not for me. I could do no less."

"That's ridiculous!" Mikhyel protested, but Deymorin

placed his other hand over the dancer's as a man might to a woman and repeated: "Nonetheless, I thank you. We'd be lost without him—in every sense."

Dancer blushed and turned his head aside, pulled his hand free, and sought Mikhyel's again. Mikhyel smiled gently, and pulled him close.

Nikki just stared.

"Nikki?" Mikhyel's tone implied disappointment.

Nikki blinked, then grinned. "Sorry, Khyel. You didn't warn us, and I'd forgotten how beautiful . . ." Leaving the sentence hanging, Nikki took the dancer's hand and raised it to his lips, in the grandest of courtly gestures. At any other time, with any other person, the abrupt turnabout, the suddenly courtly manner might have been enough to raise Mikhyel's suspicions, but not when it came from Nikki, who historically had a penchant for bad poetry and dramatic gestures.

And not, Deymorin appended uneasily, when Mikhyel's mind was so clouded by love that no amount of adulation could seem extravagant.

"Welcome you are, indeed," Nikki said warmly. "Welcome you'd be, even if you were just *any* dancer, and not, well, *our* dancer."

"Thank you, m'lord dunMheric." Dancer's back relaxed, and he dipped into an equally courtly, equally well-rehearsed curtsy, a move so graceful, Deymorin's mind could supply the swirl of skirts puddling at her feet.

His feet, he reminded his mind sternly. And yet, it was a seamless transition, one behavior to another. Easy to see how a man might mistake reality.

The eyes that flashed up at Nikki were full of mischief. Was that honest amusement at Nikki's thespian approach? Playing Nikki's game for the sheer joy of it?

Or was it mockery?

The clothing Dancer wore gave no clues as to how Dancer expected to be taken. Beneath the several sizes too large hiller tunic, his legs, encased in the body-hugging leggings of a competitor's costume, were lean and hard, ringdancer's legs and independent of what lay at their joining.

"I am *astounded* that Mikhyel discovered *you* out of all the people and all the places he visited," Nikki continued, retaining the dancer's hand. "I had no idea he had such excellent taste. But I'm delighted as well. I've so hoped to meet you again!"

The dancer answered with a throaty chuckle. "I don't think Mikhyel had much choice in the matter. I know that I did not."

"What do you mean?" Deymorin asked, more sharply than he intended. "No choice?"

Dancer pulled his hand free of Nikki, and took a step toward Mikhyel, chin raised defiantly.

"I'm—sorry," Deymorin said, although he was not sorry in the least for the sentiment, or, dammit, the tone. With one questionable ally in Mirym, he hadn't the leisure to indulge in delicate feelings.

"Temorii believes that Mother has had plans for the two of us since Boreton, perhaps since long before." Mikhyel had moved behind his dancer and was idly pulling the shaded hair back, fingercombing it, casual contact from a man who had made keeping physical distance an art form. It was almost, Deymorin thought uncomfortably, as if he *couldn't* keep his hands off her.

Under any other circumstances, he'd be delighted for his brother—Mikhyel had been alone far too long. But these weren't any other circumstances.

"And you, Khyel, do you believe that as well?"

Mikhyel's eyes flickered to him, and a faint smile pulled Mikhyel's mouth. "I'm no one's pawn, Deymorin. Not anymore. Mother makes many claims for herself. I think in reality she's far more limited in her abilities than she will admit."

"Then you're a fool, Mikhyel dunMheric!" Dancer twisted to face Mikhyel, sweeping his hands away, shoving him back with the flat of a hand to his chest. "You've *seen* the World Cave! You've experienced her power—"

"I've seen a cave filled with leythium lace that ebbs and

flows in ways that even *Mother* admits only *mirrors* activity on the surface world. I've not seen that cave *cause* anything."

"The cave does not *cause* things. Mother's wishes do."

"Mother's and yours and mine—and who knows who else affects the Ley?" Mikhyel smiled, a gently indulgent smile, a superior look that could (and had, in the past) tempt even Deymorin, who had seen that look develop over the years, to violence. Now Dancer received it . . . and the tone that accompanied it. "You yourself showed me a pattern that *you* called a node, a flux in the leythium energy flow that *is* the Rhomandi brothers."

"And Dancer, Mikhyel Rhomandi dunMheric," Dancer's voice was a low hiss. "Never forget that *Dancer* was woven into that gods-be-forever-damned node's pattern as well, *by Mother*."

"Are you certain of that?"

"Yes!"

"Well, Mother claims otherwise, my darling," Mikhyel said. He stepped close again, taking the dancer in his arms, swaying gently back and forth, one foot to the other, and Dancer's eyes drifted closed, as if mesmerized by the rhythmic movement. "Perhaps you were drawn to it as we were drawn together," Mikhyel said, seemingly oblivious to all witnesses. "As Deymorin and Kiyrstin were. As man and woman have been attracted to one another since the beginning of time. That's not Mother's doing, that's human nature."

Dancer's mouth tightened, and his eyes flicked open.

"I felt the pattern's call long before I ever met you, Mikhyel Rhomandi dunMheric." He jerked free and spun about to face Mikhyel. "I felt that damned pattern weaving itself into my soul, *forcing* me to care about its fate . . . about *your* fate. I didn't want that, didn't want anything to do with you. I wanted to *dance*. That was all I *ever* wanted. I knew the moment Mother wove me in, and I knew I was going to regret it. That it would endanger *everything* that mattered to me. That I would *lose* everything! Tell me, Mikhyel dunMheric! *Tell* me my fears were not realized!"

"Everything?"

"*Everything.* I didn't know you. Didn't care about you. Everything I wanted then is *gone.*"

The moment had gone too far. In the bond they shared there was precious little privacy, absent or present, one with the other, but this went beyond what the uninvited should witness. Deymorin opened his mouth to intervene, but this time Nikki's hand, a slight twist of Nikki's head, stopped him. He saw then what Nikki must have noticed: Mikhyel's expression had lost the superior look and was intently focused on Dancer's angry scowl, the point-scoring Barrister had given way to his brother.

"Everything? I recall a time, my dearest, my darling dancer, when I lay willing myself to death because I believed that in dying I could rid the world of Anheliaa. I recall a foreign presence invading *my* soul, forcing *me* to want to live. A presence, my love, that tasted of raspberries and cinnamon and clove. A presence that ached with *need* and desire. Mother isn't responsible for our being together. She may have finagled and catalyzed, but she didn't force us to do anything. You wanted more from life than just the Dance. Mother might have realized that. Mother might even have thrown us together, hoping, but Mother *made* nothing happen. That was our own doing!"

The last had become almost a plea for agreement, and Deymorin, knowing how much Mikhyel longed to be normal, could guess how important this distinction was for him.

Evidently Dancer shared that realization—or simply lost the will to fight. Frustration flared, fingers, callused and strong from years of work on the rings, balled into respectable fists—then relaxed.

"Never mind," Dancer said abruptly. "I'm going to find Ganfrion."

"Gan?" Mikhyel shook his head, clearly taken offguard by the abrupt shift in topic. "Why? Leave the poor man in peace. Gods know he's earned it."

"Sometimes, Mikhyel dunMheric, you can be abysmally stupid! He saved my life last night. Saved yours, too, but that's on *your* conscience, not mine. The least I can do is make sure he's all right."

"All right? Why shouldn't he be?"

"Mother!" Dancer breathed the name like a curse, then stretched a foot, and with his toe flipped something from the ground to his waiting hand: a glittering coronet that he thrust into Mikhyel's startled grasp.

Mikhyel twisted it in his hands, his brow furrowed.

The glitter of the silver-on-gold scrollwork was markedly obscured across much of its surface.

"That's not my blood, dunMheric. I don't *know* what happened to him. I only know that Rhyys' hounds had me cornered, there in the labyrinth. I was trapped and resigned to death, had gone away to let it happen, but it never came. I *think* he rescued me. I *think* Mother leythiated us here. But I don't damn well know. All I *know* is that when I decided to live, I woke up here, in the arms of a man I thought was dead. And that man, *my darling,* was not Mikhyel dunMheric. But Ganfrion wasn't dead, though I could tell every breath hurt, and when he got up and left me, all I could do was wait and hope he'd come back, and he did, and then he delivered me to you, and then he left us, and Mother forgive my weakness, I *let* myself forget last night! *Let* myself get lost in being with you! And now, he's gone— who knows where? Maybe dead, for all I know." The breathless tirade ended in a gasp. Then: "Wait, you say? I should have seen to him *hours* ago."

"Rest easy, Temorii," Deymorin stepped into this flow of confirmation of things he'd heard. "The surgeon patched him up first thing this morning."

"Surgeon?" Mikhyel jerked his clothing into place, and seemed finally to take account of their presence. "But I saw him last night. He seemed well enough. Tired, but—"

"He was injured covering your retreat, Mikhyel. He'd lost a great deal of blood—"

But he was talking to empty air.

After that astonishing performance, Mikhyel was on his way down the hillside. Dancer started to follow, turned back as if torn between going with Mikhyel and staying with them, raised a frustrated hand, then darted after Mikhyel.

Before Dancer could catch Mikhyel, Ganfrion himself limped into sight from between the outermost tents.

Mikhyel broke into a run.

"Shit," Nikki breathed beside him. "I didn't know Mikhyel knew *how* to run."

"Y'know, little brother," Deymorin said slowly, as Mikhyel skidded to a stop before his bodyguard and caught the big hand extended to steady his forward momentum, "I'm beginning to think there's a frightening lot we don't know about Mikhyel anymore."

He started to follow downhill, but Nikki's hand on his arm stopped him. And through that touch he sensed Nikki's mind again, the obscuring cloud having followed Mikhyel down the hillside.

"What about this . . . Temorii?" Nikki asked.

"What about her?"

"*Her*? But Khyel admits that's Dancer, and Dancer is—"

"An enigma, Nikki."

"But—" Along with the unfinished protest came an image of Dancer appearing in the woods from a tunnel of light. Nude. Unquestionably human. Unquestionably male.

"And Kiyrstin insisted as adamantly that Dancer was a woman," Deymorin reminded him.

"Mother chastised her for overconfidence."

"And do you recall as clearly Mother's admonitions to you?"

Nikki blushed.

"We can't assume anything where Mother is concerned," Deymorin said. "She shifts shape as easily as breathing."

"Mother's not human," Nikki said.

"And you're certain Dancer is?"

"Mother called him 'human spawn.' Deymio, he's—"

"Mother's assistant. Protégé, perhaps. Dancer leythiated on his own, if you recall."

"But he had to use some kind of— *His*? Damn it, Deymorin, you aren't helping!"

Deymorin gave a shout of laughter, caught by his own

suppositions. "Sorry. We must move cautiously, Nikki. You've shared how deeply Mikhyel feels about Temorii. We witnessed a transformation on this hill. Would you rob him of that happiness?"

"No, of course not. But if Dancer *has* lied to him, has *tricked* him somehow . . . I almost think it might be better if Dancer *isn't* human. Deymio, Khyel's going to be a lot more than hurt when he finds out."

Tone, words, and observation all pointed to a maturity almost as foreign to Nikki as Mikhyel's running was to the brother he'd known a year ago.

"It's the betrayal, Deymorin. I think that's the worst. It's not what Dancer is or isn't. It's the betrayal, the pretense. It's what lay beneath all the anger he carried toward you for years. He's had to learn to trust all over again. He trusts you now. He trusts Dancer, and if Dancer has betrayed that trust . . ." Nikki's voice trailed off uncertainly, and he cast Deymorin a second look. "Are you all right, Deymio? What's wrong?"

"Just thinking how much you've grown, brother."

He didn't know what he expected: the blush and ducked head of earlier that morning, perhaps, but that boyish Nikaenor had slipped away sometime in the last few hours. This steady, tried-in-fire Nikaenor just gave him a rueful smile, a lifted shoulder, and: "High time, don't you think?"

"A good time. We need you. As for Dancer, all we can do is keep the dangers in mind," Deymorin said, thinking of that argument just past, Mikhyel's argument not with him, but with Temorii, and of the heat lurking just beneath the surface. But Nikki laughed and picked his thoughts out of the air.

"Of course they argue, Deymorin. Khyel *loves* to argue. He's a lawyer!"

"Point, Nikaenor. I, for one, am starved. What would you say to breakfast?"

Nikki, being mature this morning but still seventeen, didn't need to be asked twice, and as they headed down the hillside, Deymorin filled Nikki in on his morning with Ganfrion.

Chapter Seven

The small room was a veritable cell: cold and dark, carved out of the stony core of Mount Rhomatum, as all the innermost rooms of Rhomandi House were part of the ancient mountain. The only light was a single candle, one with hour marks on it, a timepiece such as no civilized city had used in centuries.

It was Lidye's reminder, like the cold, unbuffered stone, that Mirym had nothing that Lidye herself did not choose to grant her.

"Bring a lamp immediately," Kiyrstin ordered the guard, still standing in the doorway. "*And* a heater and blankets, for Mauri's own sweet sake! This woman is pregnant! It's cold as—"

{Thank you, Lady Kiyrstin, but no.}

She started, and slowly faced the young woman sitting quietly in her shadowed corner.

{I need nothing. Let her play her little games/think she's won.}

Kiyrstin blinked. Shook her head slightly, wondering if it was her mind playing tricks, as that voice that was both words and concepts whispered in her head.

{No tricks, lady. Send him away.}

"Never mind," she finished without looking at the guard, and motioned Beauvina to leave with him.

{Let her stay, please.}

The voice sounded labored, and carried with it the faint sense that *it* would be easier, if Beauvina remained.

Whatever *it* was.

"Stay, please, Vina," Kiyrstin said, and wondered if she

should be disturbed when Beauvina obeyed without a blink, considering the order went directly counter to their previous agreement. Beauvina, with complete respect for ringspinning aristocrats and their quarrels, eyed that shadow in the corner, but didn't question.

The door closed behind the guard, leaving the room in even greater shadow.

"This is unforgivable," Kiyrstin muttered, seeking the cot that was the only furnishing, besides Mirym's chair and the small table beneath the candle, that she'd noted in that moment of light from the door. As her eyes grew slowly accustomed to the low light, she realized there was a second chair, probably left over from Lidye's visit, and a chamber pot and bowl carved into the wall where the faint gurgle of water indicated at least a modicum of civilized plumbing.

"I've brought you some breakfast," Kiyrstin said and flashed a grin toward the corner as she set the tray on the table next to the candle. Taking on a conspiratorial tone: "I talked the kitchen out of some extra pickled *plinif* and puffed cream pies. I've had such *ridiculous* cravings these days."

She handed one of the tiny pastries to Mirym, who accepted with a faint smile.

And Kiyrstin realized she was able to see that smile, where before there had been just shadow.

More, she realized Mirym's face had a faint greenish glow.

She continued on as if she hadn't noticed anything unusual, popped the puff in her mouth and licked the sugar off her fingers. "Keep this up, and I'll be spending two hours a day in the gymnasium with those cursed trainers Deymorin saddled me with." She rolled her eyes. "I can't believe you people really believe exercise is *good* for this growing stomach of mine."

{Not *my* people, Lady Kiyrstin, though their point is well taken.}

"I stand corrected."

She could see quite clearly now. With the green glow

spreading through the room, the temperature within the room had also increased.

No wonder Mirym had voiced no complaint. Kiyrstin's gaze followed that glow to the stone walls where infinitesimal glowing green tendrils traced the walls like tiny worms, oozing in and around the crevices left by workmen's hammers.

Mirym's attention was all for the satchel Beauvina carried. Beauvina moved silently to her side, and Mirym, with obvious delight, extracted the pieces of the embroidery stand it contained and began assembling it in quick practiced movements. When she had finished, Mirym held her hand out to Beauvina and the servant girl settled soundlessly beside her. Mirym finger-combed the curling tendrils at her temples, and her eyes drifted closed.

"I trust you, Lady Kiyrstin." While the words came out of Beauvina's mouth, Kiyrstin had no illusions regarding the mind behind them.

"Stop it!" Kiyrstin objected, defending her servant. "You don't need her to talk to me! You've already proven that."

"And I have a headache for the effort. The girl has an easy, uncomplicated mind. I won't hurt her. She will be my voice for a few moments and wake up remembering nothing."

The thought of this use of Beauvina sent a chill down Kiyrstin's spine. But it would be the height of hypocrisy to claim shock, considering what she'd seen in the past months. She didn't like using the girl without her knowledge, yet if, in fact, Beauvina was safe, and if, with Beauvina's help, Mirym might be ready to reveal any portion of her secrets . . . she wasn't certain that she could afford to turn down the offer.

"If anything happens to her—" she began, but as if Mirym had already read her concerns:

"Lady?"

A subtle shift in tone. A change in demeanor.

"Vina?"

The girl from the establishment downhill blinked, stumbled to her feet, brushing her skirts down. "What were I doin' down there? 'M sorry, lady. I won't—"

"Vina, listen to me." Kiyrstin grabbed her face with both hands, urging her attention. "How do you feel?"

Beauvina blinked again. "Feel? Fine, lady, why shouldn't I?"

"Vina, do you trust me?"

"O'course. You got me outta Sparingate, now didn' you? *And* give me a nice job 'n all."

"More than that, Vina. I'd like you to help me, but you don't have to. Do you understand that? You don't have to."

A slight frown puckered Beauvina's pretty face. "Sounds like might be you think I wouldn't want to."

"It's going to involve the Ley, Vina. Mirym can't talk, and you're going to help her."

"Will it hurt?"

"She already did it, just a little. Just to show me."

Another blink. "Oh, well, I guess it's all right, then."

So why did she still feel as if she were taking advantage of the girl?

"Lady?" A touch on her arm requested attention. "I know you an' Nikki an' all them have been doin' big things. This has somethin' t' do with that, don' it? T' help th' Web 'n' all?"

"Yes, Vina."

"Then I'm glad there's somethin' I can do to help, too."

"Thank you, Beauvina. I promise you, you'll be safe. —Won't she, Mirym?" She made the last more demand than question and Mirym dipped her head in acknowledgment before extending her hand once again to Beavina, who settled at her side.

"Thank you, Mirym." Kiyrstin acknowledged the gesture and Mirym herself nodded.

But Beauvina's mouth spoke. "You have questions, Lady Kiyrstin?"

"Who are you? *What* are you?"

"Mirym, lady. I was born just outside Khoratum. And I'm quite human, but I've been Mother's since the day I was born."

"Been Mother's? As Dancer is Mother's?"

A slow smile. "No, lady. There is only one Dancer. In the whole of time, Dancer is unique." ·

So . . . Mirym knew about Dancer. There could *not* be two such individuals in the world.

"Are there more . . . like you?"

"Many, lady. Many. At least one from every clan is given to her."

"*Given*—" Kiyrstin bit her lip. "I . . . don't understand."

"I was chosen, lady, taken directly from my birth-mother's womb and placed in the sacred pool. Mother came to me then . . . newborn, yet I remember. That was the first time I saw the caves. . . ."

"The leythium caves, like what we saw last night when Mikhyel faced the Rhomatum creature?"

"The World Cave of Khoratum, but *like* that, yes. And much as Mikhyel went last night, I went . . . I go . . . in essence only. Dancer visited Mother in body." Resentment filtered through the tone. Could Mirym possibly be jealous of Mother's dancer-companion? "Mother taught me, in my dreams . . ."

"To do—what? Control the Ley? Make it glow? Read minds?"

"To become part of the Ley, lady, I have no other words for it. The Ley makes the light because I wish it. The Ley carries your thoughts to me and mine to you, because I ask it to. But I must know the pathway, and some paths are easier than others . . . so much easier. . . ."

Beauvina's voice faded, and Mirym's eyes drooped.

"Mirym? Mirym, please don't leave yet."

"This woman was *with* someone last night. She's wanting sleep and drifted off. Forgive me. I wish to warn you . . ."

"About what?"

"Don't try to retake Khoratum, lady. It would not be wise. Look to the south. Leave the Khoramali alone."

"Why wouldn't you talk to Lidye?"

"She insisted on the mindspeech, insisted on delving more deeply into the source than I cared to allow her. Lidye is . . . not whole, Lady Kiyrstin. There is much there . . . that is not whole."

"I don't understand."

"Neither do I. I don't care to search."

"But you will search, won't you?"

"Why should I? It is . . . a most unpleasant source."

The indifference in the voice Mirym borrowed warned Kiyrstin not to press the issue.

Still, she marked the moment to tell Mikhyel when he returned. Mikhyel had had a special relationship with Anheliaa's companion once . . . a relationship beyond the unborn child she carried, the child's existence being as much a result of Anheliaa's interference in all their lives as anything of Mikhyel's or Mirym's choosing. Hopefully he could capitalize on that history and get her to be more forthcoming.

That she had beliefs, if not knowledge, beyond their own scope was obvious.

"You said look to the south," she said. "You mean the node the Kirish'lani want capped? The one beyond Shatum?"

Ample shoulders shrugged. "Whatever you please. Just—" Beauvina's borrowed voice fell to a hard whisper. *"Just leave the Khoramali to the old ones."*

"Old ones. Hillers?"

"Leave them. They are nothing to you and you are nothing to them, but they have been pushed as far from the source as they will go. The East is dry, and death lurks in the shadows. The sources are hot and angry. We will go no further. Khoratum is ours."

"Is that why you destroyed the Khoratum Ring? To set Khoratum free for the old ones?"

"Mother ordered its death, yessss."

Like a snake, that hiss. A sound to send shivers down a woman's spine. A sound that conjured Mikhyel's descriptions of Mother at her most inhuman, a frighteningly beautiful reptilian creature whose words hissed on the wind.

"Will you explain all this to Deymorin when he returns?"

"If I am here. Perhapssss."

"Why wouldn't you be?"

"I'm tired. Very . . ."

Beauvina's eyes closed and she slumped to the floor.

§ § §

Deymorin's breakfast party included Ganfrion—a surprising invitation considering there had been no love lost between Mikhyel's brother and his bodyguard, when last Mikhyel had heard.

More confusing still to Mikhyel was Deymorin's dismissal of the servants from the tent, and subsequent free, if low-voiced, discussion of Mother and the new node and Nikki's account of his experience at the new mountain spring. Mikhyel tried not to notice, as he sipped his tea and swirled honey into patterns in his steaming oatmeal, that Ganfrion's studiously indifferent gaze drifted with ever-increasing frequency to the face of the man whose ring he wore, asking mute questions.

And that ring cutting off circulation to Ganfrion's little finger certainly would have given Deymorin all the excuse he would have needed to bring Ganfrion into his confidence, if he had, in fact, done so this morning.

There'd been a time when keeping secrets from Ganfrion had been amusing—his bodyguard had been so arrogantly confident in the supposition that without his services, Mikhyel was helpless—but that time was long past. One day ago, two . . . the precise moment that amusement had faded seemed irrelevant, now, but fade it had, and since those final moments in Khoratum, Mikhyel had come to realize that habitual secrecy and personal satisfaction was no excuse for keeping his resources from the man into whose hands and onto whose honor he had cast his personal well-being.

Still, it would have been difficult to admit the depth of his pretense of defenselessness to Ganfrion's face, and he was not sorry if Deymorin had taken that particular decision out of his hands, as Deymorin's behavior would indicate.

He wondered if that lack of willingness to explain to Ganfrion made him a coward and decided that, for once, he didn't really care; the important factor was that Ganfrion was still here, still wearing the Rhomandi ring Mikhyel had practically forced on him last night.

Eventually, of course, the facts about last night's events and even the Rhomandi brothers' mental talents would be common knowledge. Last night's battle had involved every node in both the Rhomatum and Mauritum webs. One way and another, those spinners involved (not the least of whom was Garetti of Mauritum himself) would know the Rhomandi brothers had played an active role in that defense of Rhomatum Tower.

Until that time, however, until the stability of the Web and the Rhomandi control of Rhomatum was assured, the number of individuals privy to the truth was, of necessity and common sense, limited. Suspect all they pleased, the truth would come out under Rhomandi terms.

"Something wrong with your eggs, Khyel?" Deymorin's question startled him out of his reverie, and he shook his head.

"Just full, Deymorin. I never have understood where you two put it all." He lifted the plate to set it aside, caught Temorii's eye and laughed, knowing that look from their days in Khoratum. "Here." He handed the plate to her, and with a contented wiggle, she set it atop her empty plate and began to work her way through the eggs and rather large steak it contained.

Ganfrion was as immune to the phenomenon of Temorii's appetite as he, but his brothers weren't, for all they tried to mask their awe. Not until the final bite was in her mouth did Temorii herself seem to realize she had become the center of attention.

She swallowed quickly and grinned without a hint of self-consciousness. "I didn't eat yesterday. The competition, you know."

"As if that makes a difference," Ganfrion said in an undertone that wasn't, and she laughed aloud and poked him in the ribs on the unwounded side. He protested, and

groaned and fought off her attack. Altogether, they be-
haved like ill-mannered children, and Mikhyel could only
stare at his teacup, wondering what his brothers must be
thinking regarding his choice of intimates.

The fog that had settled about his mind remained, however, sheltering him from those reactions. That fog was
Temorii's doing, he was certain, and from her focused interest in her breakfast, it was a protection mostly reflexive,
now the cloud was in place. She knew how distracting to
him his brothers' thoughts could be, and sought to protect
him. But while he appreciated her efforts in principle, he
wished the fog were gone; he wanted to hear his brothers,
to know beyond doubt that the grins on their faces were
as real, as accepting, as they appeared.

Curious how much he'd come to count on a skill he'd
never dreamed of a year ago.

With the ease of a born father, Deymorin settled the
issue by rising from the table, with a laughing *Enough,
brats!* and shooing them both outside into the fresh morning air, where Temorii burst into activity, dancing within
reach of Ganfrion's long arm, then flitting away in a series
of leaps and twists, her laughter filling the air, along with
a call to Mikhyel to join them.

The look Deymorin gave him as he instead joined his
brothers at the tent door held nothing of contempt, only
amusement. "Don't look so mortified, Khyel," Deymorin
said in an undertone. "We aren't in the Tower now. After
what they've been through, it's good they can still play."
With the words came a look that implied Mikhyel should
try playing a bit himself—it was a look even more familiar
to him than Temorii's *are you going to eat that?* look.

But he'd played too much these past days. It was time
to return to his long-neglected duties.

"About Raulind," Mikhyel began.

Deymorin said, "Consider it handled. Chances are,
they'll run into no trouble. According to the signal mirrors,
the Khoraley road has been clear, and we'll be endeavoring
to keep it that way—if Rhyys' ex-would-be allies want to
fight among themselves, fine, but the roads will stay clear.

Still, I've a detachment headed up to join the Khoratum lookout. I figure, with the Khoratum Rings down and Tower authority highly questionable to say the least, the locals might be in need of some law-keeping assistance up there. We'll start no fights, but we won't allow chaos to reign, either. I'll order another squad to go with them to locate your people and make sure they get here safely."

"Thank you, Deymorin," Mikhyel said, and a great weight lifted from his shoulders.

"Is Raulind coming down via the Khoraley?" Nikki asked him.

"He had intended to, once he was free of the city wall. Why?"

"Just thinking. If I rode with the squad going up there, I could meet Raulind and report to you in half the time, since I'd be on the leyline. If there was trouble, I could let you know that much sooner to send help."

"And what do you think you'd ride, little brother?" Deymorin asked.

"Oh, I'm sure I can find some lazy slug in need of exercise on the line."

And from the look of him, and despite the early morning gallop that had resulted in the discovery of the new spring, Nikki was still very much in need of exercise himself.

"Khyel?" Deymorin asked, and Mikhyel knew a moment's uneasiness as he realized Deymorin deferred to him for his opinion on the unseen and unseeable dangers of the Ley.

"Who can say?" He had no special insight, knew no reason to deny Nikki this simple request except that his gut said it was a foolish risk. Yet, with a veritable cloud of veterans guarding him, it wasn't as if Nikki would be on his own recognizance. . . . And Deymorin had been in active fighting with the Border Guard at Nikki's age.

Of course, Deymorin, at that time, wasn't an equal player in this . . . triumvirate they had become.

Still, to keep Nikki here on these flimsy excuses was to court argument he truly didn't want this morning; more importantly, he refused to live a life governed by unsubstantiated fear, and so he compromised his concerns with Nikki's excess of energy:

"If there *is* a problem, Nikki, you'll turn back immediately, agreed?"

Nikki's internal war, clearly marked on his face, was surprisingly short-lived. "Agreed."

"And if we call you back, you get yourself back, no questions asked."

"Agreed!" Impressively emphatic, that answer, and Mikhyel forced a smile past his own unease.

"Have a good time."

Nikki grinned and headed toward the picket lines at a trot.

"Wait up, brat!" Deymorin called after him, and Nikki stopped, bouncing on his toes impatiently, while Deymorin turned to Mikhyel and said hurriedly: "I'll take him down to the pickets, make certain he's got all he needs. I left those record books out for you in my tent. Anything else you need, just ask Tonio."

"What about the Belisii caravan, Khy?" Temorii asked, appearing at his side, panting from her abortive attempts to goad a limping Ganfrion into action. "Please. I promised them safe passage."

"Caravan?" Deymorin repeated.

"A trading party," Mikhyel explained. "Temorii had arranged with them to get me out of Khoratum. Thanks to Mother, I didn't need them, but she's right. They do deserve what help we can render."

"Were they coming down the Khoraley?"

Temorii stepped between them and stared up at Deymorin. His eyes widened and didn't blink for a long moment, then he shook his head and jerked away. "The old Penremin Trail, then." Deymorin cast a sideways frown at Temorii, a mixture of suspicion and respect. "We'll send a small party to accompany them."

"Thank you, Rhomandi," she said quietly, and he nodded, a quick dip of the head before starting after Nikki.

Temorii stared after them, but somehow Mikhyel didn't think she was seeing them at all.

"What did you just do?" he asked.

"I hadn't the words, don't know what you called it, so I placed the picture of the mountain in his mind." Her voice was distant.

"How?"

"It wasn't difficult. I had his pattern from you . . . long ago . . ." The words drifted from thoughts obviously elsewhere, and the eyes she turned to him held an unexpected hint of panic.

"Come with me, Khy. I want to see this new Source Nikki spoke of, the spring, the pool, and the hill."

"Later, perhaps, Temorii. It'll take too long to walk there, and I've got work to do."

"Now, Khy. *Please.* Perhaps Mother will speak to *me.*" She caught his hand and pulled, and through her touch, he sensed wavering of the cloud in his mind, sensed her contempt for Mirym—for this individual Nikki had spoken of at breakfast, this individual who had spoken to Nikki at a newborn pool, this woman in Rhomatum who claimed intimate knowledge of Mother, and of whom Temorii had never heard.

Mikhyel swallowed hard, and drew her back into the semi-privacy of the Princeps' meal tent and answered her thoughts rather than her words. "Yes, you have heard of her, my darling." And rather than try to explain, he recalled the rooms in Khoratum, a conversation that had begun as an innocent discussion of hiller embroidery and led to questions of children . . . and lovemaking . . . and sent those memories into the fog.

"She's the one, then?" Temorii whispered, without meeting his eyes. "The one you loved, the one who carries your child, was also Mother's?"

"I didn't love her, Temorii. I reproduced with her under Anheliaa's arrogant influence. I respect her. I will give the child such love as I have to offer—"

"That's a great deal of love, Khy."

"I have my doubts. But I'll do my best. As for Mirym herself, I don't know what her connection to Mother is, but she helped us last night. She helped us hold the Rings, and when the war between Mother and Rhomatum reached stalemate, she risked a great deal to destroy the Khoratum Ring and end that stalemate."

"And you admire her for this." Flatly stated. As the emotions that filtered through her touch were flat.

"Yes, Temorii, I do admire her." He would not lie about so simple a thing. He admired Mirym; he didn't necessarily like or trust her.

Temorii scowled, then shrugged. "Then I don't trust her, either, or her words regarding Mother." She pulled again at his hand. {*Come*, Mikhyel. Come feel this new node with me. Come dance to its heartbeat. Let us call Mother to us.}

There was a frantic edge now to her thoughts and in the vigorous pull on his wrist, and he thought perhaps that jealousy now colored her reasoning. She felt threatened, that was all, by this reference to Mirym.

{I can't, Tem. Later.}

{But I need to talk to you *now*. To *explain*—}

"Plenty of time later for explanations, my love." Mikhyel caught her agitated hand in both of his and held it against his lips, wrapping his mind around hers with warmth and love until despite her protests the distress inside her eased. Her eyes closed and she sucked that love in like a dry and hungry sponge.

At times, she seemed so very vulnerable. Long before he'd arrived in her life, she'd needed love, human love. But not sexual love. She'd needed to discover her humanity, not her sexuality.

The gods knew, he wasn't the one to teach either—his own humanity had been compromised long before, and he was convinced she was the only woman to whom he *could* respond in any meaningful fashion—but she had had such need, had been so very alone that it had been far too easy to tip the scale for both of them. He feared at times such as this that he'd taken advantage of that need, that he'd used it to take their relationship where she'd never, on her own, have even thought to go.

But go they had. And it had been more than sex that had grown between them. They'd had long days together wandering the streets of Khoratum and later, from their camp just outside the city, climbing the surrounding hills. They'd been magical times. Times for him to forget being a Rhomandi and, for once, just to be Mikhyel.

But he was not the man she had known in Khoratum. While he could no more deny the essential, gut-deep attraction they had for one another than he could cease breathing, still, he was a creature of lawbooks and committees, of dry, dull offices and favors traded; and she was raspberries and cinnamon and clove: she was fire and she was the dance and she was the open sky. They were, at their core, so very different he had to believe that eventually, perhaps one day soon, she'd find his life and mind far too stifling. She'd find someone more in harmony with her personal needs and move on. Being fire she could do that.

When that time came, he'd have to let her go. He would let her go, because to hold her in his prison was not fair, and because to hold fire in a closed room meant eventually the fire would consume all its fuel and die.

In the meantime, until that inevitable day, the one thing he had to offer her was that rock-solid, stable security of a duty-bound soul she'd lacked all her life. For himself, being rock-solid, he would store up the hours they shared as all they'd have, carve them into that stone soul, admit that was all he would ever have, and one day, when the inevitable happened and she was gone, he'd find contentment in those memories.

Which was a damnsight better store of memories than he'd had before he met her.

He kissed her hands before reluctantly releasing them. "I must go." Duty insisted. "I promise. As soon as we're done." He raised his voice: "Ganfrion?"

The gorman, standing just outside, grunted, listening, no doubt, for all he was staring out across the mountains, pretending otherwise.

"Get us a cart, will you? This afternoon. After I've finished with—"

"*No!*" Temorii said. "You have no appointment with your brother. If we went now, you could have all afternoon, clear into the night, if you needed it with Deymorin. *Please,* Khy. Perhaps—perhaps I can tell you more about this Source. Won't that be something useful to share with Deymorin at this meeting?"

"You heard him. He's left those records for me. He's expecting me. We've been apart for weeks now. We have a great many details to review."

"And Deymorin's wishes, of course, take precedence."

"At the moment, yes. *I have duties, Teymorii!*"

Her fists balled, and her eyes flashed with something between anger and fear. Somehow, the near future he'd foreseen upon waking no longer seemed so idyllic, that eventual parting no longer quite so remote as he had believed even an instant ago.

He attempted reason: he, who had pleaded cases before the Council of Rhomatum. "Temorii, there's nothing you could possibly have to tell me that can't wait an hour or two."

"How do you know, when you don't know what I would say?"

Logic against which the only answer the Barrister, who had a reputation for never losing, could only argue:

"Trust me."

"Why should I?"

"I love you."

"Do you?" She glared, but not at him.

"Would going with you now, ignoring my responsibilities to my city, somehow prove my love?"

"Not your love, Khy. *Your* trust. *Trust* me. It's important that I talk to you right now."

He reached for her mind, intent on negotiation, and felt himself slapped away.

"Trust, dunMheric."

Never ask, boy! Do. When I say. How I say . . .

Anheliaa's rules. He shuddered. And Temorii's eyes widened in horror.

{Khy, *please*, I'm *not* Anheliaa. I'm nothing *like*—}

"Trust goes both ways," he said, stubbornly aloud, realizing her cloud went only one way, that she could hear/sense him while he was deaf to her unless *she* willed otherwise, and with realization came resentment. "We're together now, and safe. Nothing is going to change that basic truth. But our life is different than it was in Khoratum. I've responsibilities I'm not going to ignore for a walk in the woods. That's not the way I am. And I don't jump to orders. Never again. Not yours, not Deymorin's, not spoken and for damnsure not in my mind!"

He had had a lifetime of threats and manipulative assaults on his emotions, worse, on his mind. He found himself wondering, now he had intimate knowledge of the mindspeech, just what Anheliaa had done to his head over the years without his knowing, found himself examining every decision, every opinion with thoughts to that subtle pressure.

Somehow over the years, he *had* knit a protection about himself, had survived first his father and now Anheliaa, and now that she was gone, he wasn't about to start handing the strings to anyone, not his brothers, not even the woman he loved, not even if a parting were *not* inevitable. "I'll see you when I've finished with Deymorin."

"Perhaps you'll see me."

Another threat.

He stopped but didn't face her. There was a sinking feeling in his stomach. He had known. He had had better sense, lifelong.

The only surprise was how much, how very much, it hurt.

"I won't use force to hold you, Tem. I will ask you to hold our secrets. You know as well as anyone how important—"

"Suds, don't be an idiot."

Gan's voice, and Gan himself appeared in the tent door. The bastard had been listening all along, hadn't had the common decency to move out of earshot.

"Stay out of it, Gan."

"And let you two ruin your lives? Fools, the pair of you! Come, little dancer. *I'll* take you to Nikaenor's silly mudpuddle."

Ignoring her protests, Ganfrion pulled her firmly out the

door and down the tree-lined trail, through slanting rays of ley-touched sunlight. Temorii hop-skipped sideways, trying to watch Mikhyel, trying to draw him after them, compelling him with that mental touch.

"Stop it!" he shouted, driven beyond all sense, and swept that invisible touch aside, more angry at her than he would have thought possible. He felt her flinch, felt her mind fall away, and like a physical blow, his brothers' thoughts descended upon him.

He staggered, as the world became three images superimposed, as his ears rang with two different conversations, *neither* of them his own.

And nothing of Temorii remained. She was gone, out the door of the tent, with Ganfrion, away, leaving him with an emptiness the likes of which he'd never even imagined.

He stumbled back into the tent, to one of the breakfast chairs, closing his eyes, gathering his own senses, his own defenses. A cup pressed into his hand. Tea. Hot and bracing. Fire-blossom—with honey. He flung the tea, cup and all, out the door and into the trees and the slanting sun rays, controlling nausea.

Anheliaa's legacy, the tea, the manipulation, the resentment, the outbreak of temper. And always, there were the innocents:

The servant, staring at him in confusion over broken crockery.

Nikki, his need to understand his older brother's moods making him old before his time.

Temorii, whose only crime was love and concern for the only family she knew.

"Forgive me," he said to the appalled servant. "I was . . . startled. Yes, I'd like another cup, thank you, but without the honey, if you please."

The servant poured another while he composed himself. He took it—and as he sipped the fresh cup, the scent of tea filled his mind with the peace of the Rhomatum caverns and the ancient creature dwelling there, the creature who had rejected Anheliaa, making the Rhomatum caverns the one spot, oddly enough, free of her contaminating touch.

And almost without conscious effort, then, the images from Nikki and Deymorin began to sort themselves, his brothers receding to some nether portion of his mind, as if some instinct had been managing them all along.

An instinct evidently bypassed since Temorii had arrived last night.

He'd thought she'd been protecting him. Now that they flooded back into his mind when she left, he had to wonder if she'd been keeping his brothers from him for some other, more personal reasons.

What had they to say that she hadn't wanted him to hear?

Chapter Eight

Deymorin hurried to his tent, certain he was in for a well-deserved lecture, embarrassed to realize that he hadn't warned his guards that Mikhyel would be needing clearance to enter his tent and open the records.

But his concerns proved unfounded. Mikhyel was in his tent, calm, all business, leafing through the records he'd left out for him. Stickler for propriety that he was, Mikhyel would never consider invading the Rhomandi's private papers without such an invitation, never mind he'd had absolute access to those papers for over ten years.

"Either you picked up some tricks from Mother," Deymorin said, as he ducked inside the tent, "or I'm going to have to reprimand my sentry severely."

"Save your reprimands, Deymorin," Mikhyel responded without looking up. "He recognized me. Besides—" Mikhyel did look up then, and the twinkle of latent humor was unmistakable, as if nothing he had seen on the hill was valid. "I've been getting past closed doors for over ten years. Lockouts devised and manned by individuals far more sophisticated than your stout fellows outside."

"So much for Mikhyel dunMheric's obsessive sense of propriety," Deymorin murmured.

Mikhyel's eyebrows rose.

"You'd be singing a different tune if it were *your* private books that had been invaded."

Mikhyel grinned openly. "*No* one gets past Raulind."

"Don't you mean Ganfrion?"

Mikhyel returned to his absorption. "Raulind rules my

privacy, Deymorin, inside Rhomatum and out. Compared to Raulind, Ganfrion is positively accommodating."

"And what does Raulind think of Dancer?" Deymorin asked, casually concentrating on simple things, details of the desk, the books Mikhyel perused, anything to keep his true purpose here submerged, now the mental haze between them was gone.

"Her name is Temorii, Deymorin." It was a quiet rebuke, but the feelings beneath it were suddenly far from quiet. Mikhyel, whose mind previously had been a blank to him under such circumstances, was radiating resentment.

"We were introduced otherwise," Deymorin said, trying to keep the surface of his thoughts. "Adjustments take time."

"Do they?" The tone was absent, cool, remote, attention all for the papers. "Well, this takes a special brand of hubris: dunTroyid of Orenum is requesting a flat fifty percent usage-tax reduction, claiming hardship and inability to make payroll. The orgy he threw in Khoratum last week would not only cover the tax, it would cover his payroll for six months." This, then the whiplash retort: "—Perhaps it's not Temorii at all you're finding difficult to adjust to."

The abrupt shifts of topic were Mikhyel at his most difficult.

"I don't know what you mean."

Mikhyel shot back, "You'll figure it out."

Habit, Deymorin reminded his rising temper. Mikhyel was so accustomed to attack in their exchanges, he knew no other method. "Nikki and I were surprised, that's all," he said, striving to calm that resentment, cool the attack. "From what we'd gotten from you during your time in Khoratum, we had no idea your ringdancer was, well, *our* Dancer, if you will."

"*Your* Dancer. You display your own brand of hubris, brother. You never even mentioned her. Never told me of the sacrifice she made for me. The *obligation* left on my honor." The tone was almost conversational, in stark contrast to the words and seething anger below.

"Ease back, Khyel. Dancer *told* us not to say anything

to you. To let you remember or not on your own. Hi—
Her exact words, brother!"

"And you've always been *so* obedient to arbitrary instructions." The tone slipped, allowed bitterness through:
"Even if you didn't tell me, did you never wonder what
happened to her after she saved my life?"

"We've been just a bit occupied, brother! Mother and
Dancer disappeared. We had no way of—"

Back to the papers, eyes averted, tone detached. "Via-
prini. That name sounds familiar. I think I should consult
Ganfrion on some of these. Does that meet with your approval, Rhomandi?"

"Of course. I —Dammit, Khyel, *stop it*!"

"Mother is one thing. You *knew* Temorii went off alone
at Boreton. A young woman, alone in the woods. Deserted.
You knew that, and did nothing!"

"Kiyrstin tried, but Dancer refused to stay. Didn't *want*
our thanks or our help. We did what we thought best. If
we were wrong— *If* we were wrong, I'm truly sorry. Besides, I *did* try, dammit, as I had time, but Mother and
Dancer disappeared as abruptly as they appeared, and
we had *other concerns*. How were we to foresee the coincidence that would throw you two together again—if it
was coincidence?"

A muscle tensed in Mikhyel's lean jaw, but his gaze remained fixed on the log.

"This is disturbing. This message from Kiyrstin references a packet from Shatum for me that arrived at the
Tower. That might have contained a message from Shamrii.
Help me remember to give Kiyrstin clearance to open such
things in my absence." The muscle jumped again. "Of
course it was coincidence. After Boreton, Mother retreated
to her caverns. The Khoratum line was vastly diminished.
Damaged. Mother was detached from the surface world.
Temorii was deserted. Alone. She returned to Khoratum,
where she survived on her own under unimaginable
conditions."

"Unimaginable to whom? There are hundreds like her
throughout the Web, Barrister."

"Hardly."

"No one is born to live in squalor. Every child begins an innocent. They're all tragic stories."

"She was *Mother's*, for the gods' own sake!"

"They all have mothers, Khyel."

The color rose above Mikhyel's beard, but the gaze that lifted to meet his didn't falter. "I . . . stand corrected. The difference is, none of those other ones saved my life." Mikhyel closed the log with deliberate care and rested his arms on the table. "Mother said Temorii had been with her since she was a small child. That she'd never lived anywhere but in the leythium caverns. You saw the Rhomatum caverns last night when we called on Rhomatum to help. *That's* the world she knew."

"That and Rhyys' court," Deymorin reminded him.

"That and Rhyys' court," Mikhyel conceded. "Still, she had no concept what was waiting for her in Lower Khoratum."

He'd forged ahead against the expectation of explosion. The explosion averted, he pushed another step. "Temorii was far from naive, even at Boreton."

A fact that, from his face and underlying emotion, Mikhyel considered irrelevant. "Quite well-versed, actually. Rhyys made it a point to have all the radical dancer candidates tutored for intelligent conversation. He liked to show them off to visitors. It wasn't knowledge she was lacking; it was her involvement that was limited, until—"

Mikhyel broke off, staring into shadows.

"Until?"

"Until she lived the theoretical. Experience . . . changes a man's perspective—radically—on what's important."

"Who are we talking about? Temorii? Or a more personal experience?"

Mikhyel's eyes flicked back into focus on Deymorin.

"Both."

"How did you meet her?"

Mikhyel opened the book again, found his place, turned a page and took a note, his every move quiet and deliberate—economic to the extreme. "Nikki's got a real talent for allocating resources. He's done an excellent job with the supply plans, and he's still managing to keep that dam project of his moving forward down in the valley. Perhaps I should put him in charge of Alizant's little research project. What do you think?''

"Zandy? His encapsulator? Brother, is there any side trail you won't venture down to avoid an issue?"

"These problems don't take care of themselves, Deymorin. For every problem solved, three wait in the shadows. Alizant's project is on hold pending his reconstruction of the greater encapsulator, which he insists he can do. Once that's finished, I promised him an opportunity to demonstrate to investors. I think Nikki would do well with it, if he's interested.'' A breath. "—She was working in a tavern where I took refuge from a rain storm." Mikhyel glanced up. "Hardly a planned meeting. She was accosted by some customers. She ran. They followed. I followed them.''

"What did you plan to do, talk them out of it?" He meant it as a joke; it came out otherwise.

"No need to remind me of my physical limitations," Mikhyel, accustomed to his jibes, remained cool. "I didn't know what I could do. As it turned out, my mere presence put a halt to the proceedings. They were very minor hoodlums.''

"Even so, an unusual reaction for you."

This time, the gray eyes narrowed, gleamed at him from under lowered brows. Mikhyel's long black hair hung loose, forming a shadowing hood for his lean face.

"If you say so," Mikhyel said, and returned to the records.

On the other hand, a look such as that might well have scared mountain-born troublemakers into more civilized behavior. Deymorin shook off his own spinal chill with a personal reminder that this was his brother, and that they were on the same side.

"What drew your attention to her in the first place?"

"What is this, Deymorin? Interrogation?"

"Just making conversation."

"Like hell. He thinks Tem's the best thing that ever happened to me."

"He? Who? What the—"

"Keep your arguments organized, Rhomandi. Primary rule of effective debate. —Raul. He threatened to leave if I pursued my own suspicions of her. Does that satisfy your curiosity?"

"Maybe. Why'd you notice her?"

Mikhyel scowled.

"Just keeping my arguments organized, Barrister."

"And I should reward your efforts."

"Of course."

A sudden hiss of near silent laughter preceded a pause, during which Deymorin applauded himself for having scored a solid hit. Then:

"Her eyes." Mikhyel's dropped to the table. "I'd seen that look."

"In a mirror."

Mikhyel started, stared unseeing at the papers.

"Temorii's eyes *are* much like yours, Mikhyel."

The eyes in question cast him a frowning glance. "Physically, I suppose. But it was her expression. This . . . determination to survive even though life had taken everything away."

"As I said."

The frown deepened, and Mikhyel's spidery fingers turned another page. "Life took nothing from me, Deymorin."

Cry no tears for Mikhyel, he would say. And in the strictest sense, in Mikhyel's legalese mind, he was right. What his life had lacked, it had never had in the first place.

Thanks to Temorii, one, at least, of those deficiencies had been filled.

And here he was, trying to . . . take that away.

"Likely it was a recollection from Boreton," Deymorin said casually. "When you woke up, you were looking straight at Dancer. Under the circumstances, a memorable impression, I'm sure."

Mikhyel's mouth pulled into a reluctant smile. "Thank you, Deymorin."

"Don't thank me yet. What suspicions?"

The smile vanished. "I have many suspicions."

"You said Raulind would leave if you pursued your suspicions. What suspicions?"

"You're learning."

"Have a good teacher, don't I?"

"There are times I truly wonder. Moot, now. Something Ganfrion said."

"Moot? Even in light of recent developments?"

"Particularly in light of them."

Sensing the subject dangerously near the flash-point, Deymorin changed it even as he ... . kept his arguments organized.

"Nikki's gone," he said quietly. "We should know by nightfall where Raulind and the others are."

"Again, my thanks."

"You're not the only one who's worried."

"Nonetheless, they are my responsibility. Deymorin, why don't you sit down? I'm getting a kink in my neck."

"Sorry." Deymorin threw himself into a chair and crossed his legs. "So, why'd you endanger them all?"

"I didn't. I got them out—"

"At the last possible moment."

"I wouldn't say that."

"No, I imagine you wouldn't. We'd have lost without you."

"And anywhere along the leyline, I could have reached you. Even had Rhyys thrown me in prison. We knew physical proximity wasn't necessary, only that we be on the lines. We'd proven that."

"But you could have cleared out a full day earlier. Guaranteed both your safety and that of your men."

"If I'd left before the competition, Rhyys would have had Temorii killed—or denied her the chance to compete, which would have amounted to the same thing."

"Why? He'd have gained nothing by it."

"Spite? To muddle my thinking? Who knows? Rhyys didn't need reasons. But Gan said—"

"And suppose Ganfrion was right? *Temorii* was responsible for her own life. You did her a favor getting her into the competition."

"Not a favor, Deymorin. She lost her first chance saving my life. I owed her! No favor."

"All right. Your obligations. Still, you got her in before either of you knew the ramifications of your association. She *could* have pulled out with you."

"Dammit, Deymorin, don't discuss what you don't understand! Temorii's a dancer. A Khoratum *radical* dancer! It's taken a merging of souls the likes of which you can't even imagine for me to *begin* to comprehend, so don't tell *me* what her options were!"

"Merging souls? Darius save us, you're sounding more like a Harisham priest every day."

"Don't *mock* me, Deymorin!"

Mikhyel's eyes were flaming, the green rims growing so pronounced they seemed to glow with an inner light. And Mikhyel's anger battered at Deymorin's mind, trying to force understanding.

"Damn you, Mikhyel dunMheric!" Deymorin threw up the internal wall so abruptly that for a moment, he saw the world as solid granite.

When his vision cleared, Mikhyel was sprawled along the side of the tent, his awkwardly twisted body threatening the integrity of the entire canvas structure.

Down, but far from out, as his eyes, gleaming from behind the shadowy curtain of his hair, attested.

Deymorin hauled his brother to his feet, held him there when his knees failed. It was old times with Mikhyel, head to head. He didn't want it, but he had it, and it had never done any good to back away, no matter how he didn't want this confrontation.

"You listen to me, brother Khyel," he hissed softly. "I don't know what your problem is, but you get yourself together and you keep your damned head where it belongs. I don't know what this person has done to you, but—"

Mikhyel wrenched free. "She's turned Hell's Barrister into a man."

"Thinking with your groin makes you a man, does it?"

"Says the man who gave me a whore for my coming of age present."

"Dammit, Khyel, that was ten years ago! Ten fucking years! I made a mistake, all right? A stupid error in judgment for which, I remind you, I've paid handsomely. I'd like to think we've *both* grown up a bit since then."

Mikhyel smoothed his tunic back to order. His hands . . . caressed the fabric. Not exactly a reassuring gesture considering the source of that tunic.

"Ten fucking years." Mikhyel echoed his words slowly, deliberately. "Interesting choice of adjective. And I suppose, for some, accurate. Certainly for you. What was it you told Anheliaa? Two bastards? Affairs of state certainly never interfered with your . . . thought processes."

"I suggest, brother," Deymorin said through clenched teeth, "that you consider very carefully before you continue."

"What's the matter, Rhomandi? Nervous? Worried the Barrister might do something stupid because he has acquired human wants and needs? The Barrister knows that feeling well. The *Barrister* has endured that haunting thought for over seventeen years. The *Barrister* still worries daily about the consequences of the Rhomandi of Rhomatum regularly bedding the wife of High Priest Garetti of Mauritum. Tell me, Rhomandi, who will raise the child she bears? By Mauritumin law, it's Garetti's, you know."

Anger flared, but Deymorin's voice failed, as surely as if Mikhyel's hands were around his throat, and Mikhyel continued without a blink, deadly once the contest turned verbal:

"The *Barrister* is damned embarrassed that his judgment was impaired in Khoratum, but *Mikhyel dunMheric* took a calculated risk for the sake of his soul and his humanity and *Mikhyel dunMheric* isn't one whit sorry for the decisions he's made. The Barrister has covered for Deymorin dunMheric, and endured the consequences of that dissembling for years. If the Rhomandi can't comprehend Mikhyel dunMheric, if the Rhomandi can't simply say *thank the gods we survived the momentary aberration,* then the Rhomandi can go fry in his choice of the eighteen hells above Rhomatum!"

The hold on his voice was gone, but Deymorin seethed behind his own control for some moments before he managed to say, "And if Mikhyel dunMheric is being duped? If he's playing cat's-paw to a Tamshi's whim? Should the Rhomandi remain silent for the sake of Mikhyel dunMheric's delicate sensibilities?"

"How many times must I tell you, Mother's not—"

"I'm not talking about Mother."

"Mother, Rhomatum, what's the difference? *They don't control me!*"

"Does Temorii?"

"Temorii's not Tamshi."

"Are you certain of that?"

"Yes!"

"So adamant, Mikhyel. No doubts? No questions? Totally trusting, are you? The *Barrister* would be more cautious."

"What's the matter with you?" Mikhyel slammed his hands on the small desk; the books jumped. "Haven't I earned a bit of normal happiness?"

"Normal? With Dancer?"

"Why not?"

"Who are you trying to convince, Khyel? Me? Or the Barrister?"

"She's human, I tell you."

"Human be damned, he's a fucking *dancer!*" He caught himself, shuttered his thoughts, but not before Mikhyel intercepted him, word and thought.

"You mean, of course," Mikhyel said coolly, *"she's* a dancer."

"No, dammit, I do not."

"So." Mikhyel rose slowly. "Nikki, too?"

Deymorin nodded.

"Curious." Mikhyel slowly paced the room. "I thought

better of you both, but . . . it's a common enough mistake
in the hills, you know."

"There is no mistake."

"I tell you, there was." He stopped and faced Deymorin.
"Of the two of us, I believe I'm in somewhat the better
position to make such a determination."

"Are you? I saw him stripped bare-ass, brother. Have
you?"

Mikhyel's eyes widened, his color deepened, but he
couldn't hold Deymorin's gaze.

"Rings," Deymorin murmured, "you *haven't.*"

It put yet another twist on the matter. Shapeshifter be
damned, Mikhyel wouldn't be the first gullible fool to fall
for a scheme perpetrated by a clever actor. Deymorin
called up the memories of Boreton, of Dancer emerging
from the forest, clothed only in the golden light of
leythiation.

And he shoved those images into Mikhyel's mind, daring
him to blockade himself against the truth.

"Damn you, *no!*" Mikhyel whirled to face him. "I
haven't seen her, haven't stared like some sex-starved adolescent, but I've *felt* her, brother. From the moment I entered—"

"It can be faked, Khyel. You could have been—"

"What? *Misdirected?* I was in her *mind,* Deymorin. I *felt*
what she felt. Tell me, my oh-so-worldly brother, how did
she *misdirect* that?"

"How did you freeze my words in my throat just now?
Of the evidence you have, Barrister, I'd set *that* as the most
suspect of all! Ask yourself, Barrister, why can we hear
each other now Temorii is gone? *What didn't Temorii want
you to hear?*"

That was a solid hit. Mikhyel *had* wondered, and the
Barrister was making connections Mikhyel dunMheric
couldn't prevent. Mikhyel's face went pale beneath its
newly acquired tan. Temorii's doing, that tan, as Mikhyel's
new-found vitality was Temorii's influence. So many positive things added to Mikhyel's life as a result of his dancer,
and here he was, threatening to destroy it all.

As always when he and Mikhyel faced one another, a simple search for answers had devolved into a pointless verbal war with both sides shooting wide to avoid a resolution that might be more painful to accept than the war was to fight.

"Khyel. —Khyel, listen to me. I had to say something. I don't want you getting—"

"Hurt?" Mikhyel slid into his chair to hold his head in one hand, elbow propped on the table. His long fingers rubbed his temples and pressed their way past his eyes as if he could somehow squeeze the questions out of his mind.

"I've no reason to believe hi—*her* feelings for you are less than sincere—"

"For the love of Darius, Rhomandi, the *words* don't matter. I *know* what you're thinking. Is it so difficult to believe that *you* might be the one mistaken?"

"If it were just me, yes, I could admit that might be the case; I hardly noticed him. I was watching you the entire time. But Nikki was fascinated by Dancer. And Ganfrion—"

"*Ganfrion?* Gods of the Ley protect me from fools. Raul foiled his plans with me, so naturally, the first opportunity he gets, he runs to a higher authority."

"Raulind?"

"Gan's intimations were the source of my own suspicions that nearly lost me Raulind's services. *Raulind* was afraid that if he made those suspicions known to me, I'd somehow be permanently damaged. I've grown just a little tired of people *protecting* my . . . as you put it 'delicate sensibilities.'"

"I shall endeavor to test your mettle at every opportunity, little brother."

Mikhyel's upper lip lifted in a ghostly snarl.

"You don't believe me?" Deymorin asked.

"Why should I? You're the worst of them all." Mikhyel's head dropped again into his supporting hand. "I'm . . . sorry, Deymorin. That was . . . unfair. Ganfrion. Raulind. Now you and Nikki. More than enough to warrant asking her, to hell with Ganfrion's suspicions."

"Is that wise? Ganfrion seems to know—"

"Now that's a new tune for the Rhomandi. *Ganfrion* talks a good story, same as the rest of us. We convince ourselves our concerns are real and think by talking fast enough we can convince the world to agree with us. I'll think of some way to satisfy us all. It's possible . . . she's been trying to get my attention since we woke up this morning. Perhaps . . ." A nearly imperceptible shiver rippled Mikhyel's shoulders. "Deymio, leave me alone, will you?"

Though his exterior was calm, Deymorin knew that underneath Mikhyel seethed. Confused. Hurt.

Angry. Angry at Dancer, at Deymorin, at himself . . . perhaps that most of all. And he recalled that choking hold on his throat, a blow that was no blow that sent his brother sprawling. This damned Talent of theirs was proving increasingly lethal. He had been open in his anger all his life; that toss into the tent wall was likely the extent of his abilities. Mikhyel . . . Mikhyel tended to bottle his feelings up, letting them out in spits and spurts, releasing just enough so that he could stand the pressure. If that choke hold was only the tip of what he could do . . . and if Dancer, who had already tapped into and released so many emotions in his brother now tapped into that anger . . .

Deymorin paused at the doorflap, fearing what he might have just set into motion.

"I haven't handled this well at all, Khyel. Dancer . . . maybe he had his reasons."

"She, Deymorin," Mikhyel corrected softly, seemingly oblivious to the conflict with his earlier request. "Grant me that at least. Until I've proof to the contrary."

Deymorin, finding no comfort in that quiet voice, but out of options, nodded and left Mikhyel to his thoughts.

§   §   §

Could it be true?

As the flap fell on Deymorin's shadow, Mikhyel allowed

the hold he'd maintained to slip, and his fingers clenched into fists.

Had he indeed made a fool of himself, risked his life and the lives of all those who trusted and depended on him for the sake of a man?

No, not just a man. A man who *pretended* otherwise. To take advantage, perhaps, of Mikhyel dunMheric's stupidity.

Mistress? Temorii had mocked his choice of words at their first meeting. Had insisted more than once that she was *no one's* mistress. And she'd thrown his fascination with her in his face often enough. But he'd been struck by love, or what he took for love, for the first time. After only a few hours in her vicinity, he'd desired the Khoratumin ringdancer as he'd never desired anyone, and that gods-be-damned rutting instinct had superseded all good sense.

Even now, male or female, his blood ran hot with the mere recollection of their time together.

He lifted his hands, still clenched, and dug the heels into his eyes, trying to force order into a singularly chaotic set of memories.

There was an admitted androgeny about her, as there had been with all the dance competitors. He'd thought nothing about her lean, hard-muscled body other than in admiration and frustration when he tried to match her pace on a mountain trail.

Dressed in their form-fitting costumes, their long hair flowing in tails down their backs, from the moment they mounted the dance rings, the universally slender and supple dancers were not Man or Woman, but rather the personification of the radical streamer their dance represented.

The radical streamer: that ribbon of pure leythium that simply appeared, rising up from the heart of a node to dart among tower rings the moment the rings began to spin. The radical streamer: a natural, unavoidable addition to the tower rings that added an unknown factor to the rings' pattern, a serendipity to the leythium energy flow that all ringmasters alternately blessed and cursed.

The ring dancers darted among the larger, outdoor dance rings with all the abandon of their leythium counterpart, their moves dictating as much as dictated by those spinning rings.

Dictating and dictated by . . .

And dancers worshiped Rakshi, god of whimsy, of fate, of luck.

A dancer's life depended on lightning-fast reflexes, on reacting to their environment, but also on manipulating those rings to their bidding, to make the dance theirs. Unique. As the radical streamer shifted the rings . . .

Dictating and dictated by . . .

In all their time together, Temorii had rarely instigated anything. She'd followed his lead, then, with a subtle shift of attitude, changed the course of events to her liking.

When they'd roamed Khoratum together, she had slipped smoothly into the role of a young student (male) to Mikhyel's chosen role as tutor.

Perhaps too smoothly.

"Khyel?" Ganfrion's voice had weathered too many battlefields to achieve subtlety, but the attempt was evident in the murmur from outside the tent.

Mikhyel collected his scattered thoughts. "Come."

Standing just inside the doorway, the big mercenary appeared as uncomfortable as Mikhyel had ever seen him.

"Relax, Gan. Did Deymorin send you?"

"No—" The startled answer came just a touch too rapidly; Mikhyel waited for Ganfrion's own conscience to win. "Well, not directly."

"It's all right. I know my brother. Sit."

Ganfrion hesitated, then shrugged and settled into the chair with his customary borderline insolence.

"Nothing I didn't want to air days ago, dunMheric."

"Acknowledged. But Raulind's not here now."

Ganfrion's scowl deepened, and even to his own ears, the statement sounded dangerously close to a child sneaking around behind his parent's disapproving back.

"So—*air*!" Mikhyel snapped.

"I suspect Temorii is not what she seems."

"That's remarkably non-illuminating."

"Stand down, dunMheric, or find your own answers!"

Mikhyel leaned back and waved a hand for him to continue.

"There was a time when I believed that she and Thyerri were the same person."

"But you don't now?"

"You move too fast. My belief was certainly shaken when Thyerri led us out of Khoratum."

"Because Thyerri died on the rings."

"Because *Temorii* was dancing on them. Dammit, Khyel, get those lawyer instincts engaged, will you?"

"Let me worry about my instincts. Your opinion now?"

"Your brother claims it wasn't Thyerri or Temorii, but this Tamshirin creature you all call Mother that led us from the stadium."

"Thyerri died on the rings."

"Did he? And if that was this Tamshi as well? Would it die from so mortal a cause?"

It was an obvious question. One the Barrister damn well should have considered. Mikhyel clenched his jaw, striving to keep his pride in the face of so many flaws in judgment.

"Is there anything else?" he asked.

A momentary battle was waged behind Ganfrion's set expression, a battle that ended with:

"Only remember Thyerri was without question Rhyys' man, and consider carefully how much Rhyys had to gain by your interest in Temorii."

Consider this, consider that. Deymorin and Ganfrion were full of amazingly useless advice and information. What neither of them realized was that far more important than Thyerri's link to Rhyys was Thyerri's possible link to Mother. Mother's will had sent him to Khoratum, and Mother had put him in Khoratum right in front of Thyerri.

And Temorii had insisted all along that Mother had set the pattern that tied them together.

"Where is she?"

"At the pool. She refused to return to camp."

"So you left her there alone?"

"I had to return the horse. But it's not that far, not for

a hiller-born. She wanted to be alone. Your brother has
posted guards all around the lake. She'll be safe."

"Rings, she grew up in the Khoramali. I'm not worried
she'll be hurt."

"Then what are you afraid of?"

That she'll leave, which he dared not say aloud. But Ganfrion knew, had heard the same words he had.

"She won't leave, Khy. Not over that."

He just pushed himself to his feet. "I've a yen to see
this pool."

§   §   §

Khyel was already several strides down the trail by the
time Ganfrion levered himself from the chair and escaped
the tent.

Rhomandi was waiting for him.

"Not now," Ganfrion said. "I've got to follow him."

"No need to kill yourself," Deymorin said. "I feel guilty
enough rousing you out of your sickbed. I've set a couple
of men to tail him. He'll be safe."

"From everything but himself."

"He got himself into this. He's got to get himself out."

But the look that followed Mikhyel's retreating figure
said the Rhomandi wished it were otherwise. *I couldn't tell
him,* Rhomandi had confessed when he woke him up.
Couldn't find the words.

"I couldn't find the words, either," Ganfrion said.

"I know."

"How?"

The Rhomandi tapped his temple. Ganfrion, still not certain he totally believed their mind-reading abilities, just
nodded.

"He's not in a mood to be enlightened." Rhomandi
shook his head slowly. "He's still convinced he made love
to a woman."

Ganfrion felt tired, bone tired now, and he ached. His
bed called; if he was dismissed, he wanted it. But he felt

duty-bound to admit his suspicions, even foreknowing the sharp stare and demand for explanations it would cause. "He probably did."

The stare arrived, and on cue: "What in *hell* are you talking about?"

He propped himself against a tree. "Took the kid up to the mudpuddle after breakfast, now, didn't I?"

"And?"

"Anxious to talk he was. Tried to tell Khyel himself, but Khyel put him off."

"Tell him what?"

"Wouldn't say. Only that he had to tell Khyel himself and never meant it to go this far. But the way he said it . . ." He hesitated, wondering at the last moment if his own mountain-born curiosity was ruling his logic, then decided he was too tired to give a damn. "Ever hear of the Children of Rakshi, Rhomandi?"

"Legends."

"So's your Mother."

That got him a silent stare.

Not often a man like him could silence a man like the Rhomandi of Rhomatum.

"You're sure," Deymorin asked at last, and Ganfrion shrugged and closed burning eyes on the daylight, letting his head fall back against the tree's rough bark.

"Short of stripping him naked and feeling him up, yeah. Tried that the last time I thought I'd found one like him." In Sparingate Crypt, though he didn't think Mikhyel's brother wanted to hear that. He'd cornered a potentially dangerous man that night, a man of power and influence in the outside world, a man with secrets. With thoughts of escape from Sparingate, alive or dead, he'd endeavored to intimidate, humiliate, and gain that hidden knowledge all in one crude act.

He'd failed to accomplish any of those ends. Mikhyel had won that round in every sense. Mikhyel dunMheric had proved to be a man and nothing more. A man with powerful protections against the crude methods he'd employed, and when the Barrister had freed the crypt-bait, it had been in the Barrister's time and under the Barrister's terms.

He shrugged again. "Didn't particularly like the outcome that time, so I'll just stick to my instincts, and you can do the asking."

"What did Dancer say to convince you?"

"Nothing directly; he's a cautious sort, but I had my suspicions. I started talking about the Children, casually, you know. Especially being as he's a dancer and all, I'd've thought he'd know, for all Rhyys' attempts to kill the old ways. But to him, Rakshi means the dance and nothing more. About the physical part—he didn't know, or he's a damn sight better fake than I give him credit for."

"You're talking about the man who has fooled my brother into believing he was a woman for weeks and in the most intimate situations. I'd say he's quite good."

"That's what made me most suspicious. He plays a part well, loves games, but real lies . . . lies you have to stick with day in and day out . . . that have to be there even when you're asleep . . ." Ganfrion shook his head. "I'd swear he didn't know about the legendary Children. He didn't know, but he sure wanted to. Neither man nor woman, but a bit of both, born to dance . . . damn right he wanted to know. Ate it up like a starving kitten, every fantastic detail I could call out of childhood. And if that's the case . . . if he *is* one of the Children . . ."

He let his head fall to the side to hold Rhomandi's eyes.

"If that's the case, you tell me if he lied."

"Rings." That stare returned to the distance, where Mikhyel had climbed aboard a cart and was headed toward the pool. "I wish Kiyrstin were here."

"My, my, Rhomandi, the rumors do have you well and truly pegged."

That pulled Rhomandi's attention free of his brother, and the scowl that turned back to him displayed healthy irritation.

"Not for me, crypt-bait. For my brother. I know of no one better for talking sense into a madman."

"Speaking from personal experience?"

"Speaking from personal experience."

"Then I second the wish, but I suppose we'll just have to make do."

The expression Rhomandi turned on him this time defied analysis, as did the bark of laughter that followed. Ganfrion snorted his disgust, convinced Mikhyel wasn't the only madman in the vicinity, and without another word, collected his aching body and headed back for the tent to which he'd been assigned and the sleep from which the Rhomandi's orders had pulled him. A good tent. A warm tent. Dark, with a decent bedroll.

He'd had his fill of crazies for the day.

Chapter Nine

Mikhyel dunMheric was coming.

Dancer's conscious mind shut out the awareness, but nothing could shut out that internal sensitivity: as a homing-stone pointed always toward the heart of its mother node, one part of Dancer of Khoratum would always and forever know where Mikhyel of Rhomatum was.

Now.

Once, Dancer's essence had been unfettered. Once, Dancer had answered only to the mountain winds and Mother's fickle but infrequent desires. In return, Mother had seen to Dancer's animal needs: food, warmth, even an odd sort of affection, such as she understood how to give. The substance and function of the essence Mother had named Dancer had mattered only to Dancer, and the answers had been very simple. Dancer was a dancer, and Dancer danced. Dancer danced *to* the Music of the mountains, the wind, the rain in the trees, the Ley resonances, and *with* anything that reflected the Music's essence.

There had been a time when the Khoratum dance rings had seemed the ultimate partner, the radical dance the ultimate challenge, intricate, beautiful—and deadly, with its dance that wove patterns within spinning rings. Dancer had never imagined the consequences of leaving Mother's leythium caves to answer the lure of the rings. Dancer hadn't worried when with the dance had come Rhyys and Rhyys' tutors and a knowledge of the world beyond Khoratum. The history and politics of the Rhomatum Web had provided exercises for the mind as the dance had exercised the body, but the knowledge had, in itself, held little significance—

Until the new pattern began to form in the World Cave, a pattern that *was* the Rhomandi brothers and their unique essential union, a pattern that had lured Dancer out of the world of Dance and into the world of Man.

And that contamination had twice robbed Dancer of the rings, once in reluctant forfeit, the second time, in loving sacrifice.

The first loss had left Dancer bitter and alone. In saving Mikhyel dunMheric, Dancer had been . . . misplaced. Mother was gone, the dance was gone, all that remained was survival. A living creature had returned to Khoratum, had found a job at Bharlori's tavern, friends, a name— Thyerri—which meant dancer, but wasn't.

He'd found a place to be, but never to belong—and that was his fault, not the fault of those around him. Because while Thyerri waited tables and even danced for audiences with too little essence and too much money, Dancer had maintained the dream that somehow, someday, the chance to compete would come again and the rings would be his.

Not the puny tower-bound rings that the valley men deemed so important. Those rings merely directed tiny motes of the leythium essence to power human lights and steam engines. The rings Dancer had craved were glorious structures that swept through the mountain air in harmony with the very heartbeat of the world itself. The dream of mastering the dance, becoming part of that heartbeat had been all that kept that soul-dead individual alive for months.

But time had passed and the dream had faded, and Dancer had all but given up hope when Mikhyel dunMheric came to Khoratum and in one day both shattered one life and resurrected another.

It was Thyerri who fell under Mikhyel dunMheric's spell first. Thyerri who saw the poster announcing Mikhyel dunMheric's visit to Khoratum and bearing Mikhyel dunMheric's image.

And it was Thyerri's dreams that image haunted, carrying

with it the intoxicating sense of brotherhood, the strength
of will, the courage that had imprinted itself on Dancer's
essence when Dancer had shared that brief, but intimate,
interlude with the Rhomandi brothers.

Worst of all and without warning, it was Thyerri's growing self-awareness that mingled with that image, besieging
Thyerri's dreams with a world of seething sensation in
which Thyerri's hopes of ever dancing again, even in Bharlori's tavern, vanished as those dreams infused Thyerri's
dance with a deadly carnality.

Thyerri and Mikhyel dunMheric should never have
crossed paths. Mikhyel had been scheduled to visit Upper
Khoratum, the Tower, and the ringmaster, Rhyys dunTarec,
not the oldest tavern still extant in Lower Khoratum. But
Fate—and Mother, who had not spoken to Dancer for
weeks—had determined otherwise. Rather than making the
planned formal entry to Rhyys' court, Mikhyel dunMheric
had arrived in a Khoratumin alley.

Thyerri's alley. His home after his final dance had incited
those who watched to acts of mindless violence, acts that
left Bharlori dead and the tavern in ashes.

DunMheric had arrived between one heartbeat and the
next, leythiated to Thyerri's side directly from Mother's
World Cave. Mother's gift to her neglected child.

Now Khyel had reached the edge of the trees.

Dancer trailed his hand in water that was neither hot nor
cold, merely eminently soothing. There was no essence
here, no personality permeating the very rocks about this
shadowed lake, as Mother permeated Khoratum, but power
resided here, for one ready to feel it. And that power called
to Mikhyel, guiding his footsteps to firm ground, drawing
him to the source, as it had earlier drawn Dancer.

Mikhyel hadn't recognized Dancer in the alley-rat who
greeted him in his first moments in Khoratum, and later,
hadn't seen the alley-rat in the woman he rescued from a
back-alley assault.

Convenient at the time to allow the misconception. Convenient and seemingly safe for one who, unlike Mother,
had no ability to read any of the possible futures. Thyerri

had longed from that first shadowed-alley meeting to sink himself into Mikhyel dunMheric's hot-blooded essence: lustful yearnings, deadly yearnings for any dancer.

But Mikhyel dunMheric had looked upon Dancer and seen a woman, and as Temorii, Dancer had been able to resist his allure—for a time.

When Dancer was Temorii, Mikhyel dunMheric's own nature set a safe distance between them.

When Dancer was Temorii, the remotest chance remained that the dance could still be won.

But the pattern had been too strong; ultimately, Dancer and Mikhyel had had to join, body and mind.

And in loving Mikhyel, Dancer had become whole again—or perhaps for the first time.

Mikhyel stepped from the trees and onto Dancer's rocky oasis, and Dancer raised a double handful of spring water to soothe heated cheeks.

From the time fate had reunited them, Dancer had wanted to tell Mikhyel the truth, but that same fate had intervened, and now Mikhyel had been with his brother, whose suspicions of Dancer had colored the very air between them that morning.

Now the time for explanation was past.

§   §   §

Temorii emerged from the lakeside, a gray-cloaked shadow rising from a mist of shadows. Mikhyel held out his hand, but she made no move to accept his offer.

He let his hand drop.

"Deymorin says you've played me for a fool."

"Deymorin is cruel. You're not a fool."

"My word, not his. I am more honest and less kind. But any man who could lie with another man and believe his partner a woman is missing some essential element. I'd rather be a fool than some of the other words that suggest themselves."

"You're none of those things." A hand emerged from

the shadow, the ley-touched embroidery shimmering about the deceptively slender wrist. "You're a brave, loving—"

"No more!" Mikhyel's voice broke. Embarrassed, he forced control. "No more, Dancer of Khoratum."

The hand clenched and vanished, the shadow seemed to grow taller, drawing in on itself.

"Are you Temorii?"

"Yes."

"Are you Thyerri?"

"Yes."

Too easy. Too glib. Hell's Barrister counseled strongly against acceptance.

"Then tell me how I am not a fool?"

"I . . . don't understand."

Difficult to discount the naivete of the tone, the seemingly genuine confusion. But again, the Barrister knew better than to trust.

"*Are* you a woman?"

This time, the answer was a long time and slow in coming.

"Khy, we've made love. *Surely* you know the answer to that."

"With you inside my head the entire time! How do I *know* what was real and what *you* planted there deliberately?"

"*Your* choice, dunMheric, not mine. I withdrew the Touch. You *begged* me to return!"

"I didn't know then that you were lying to me with every breath, every thought."

"I *wasn't lying*!"

"You don't answer my question. In lieu of contrary input, I must assume Deymorin's evaluation is correct and you're a man. At best you never corrected my valley-blind stupidity. At worst, you reinforced it. I call that lying."

"Rijhili!" *Foreigner*—in the worst possible connotation. The hissed epithet out of the shadowed hood was the back alley of Lower Khoratum all over again. The back alley where he'd kissed her for the first time. She'd kissed him back, echoing his passion—then pretended to be Thyerri and cursed him for ignorant rijhili cruelty, and told him to leave Temorii alone if he didn't want his love to destroy her.

Setting him up for Rhyys and active hatred within Khoratum. Setting him up for ridicule throughout the Syndicate: the princep's brother, the Lord Supreme High Justice of Rhomatum brought to his knees by a hiller dancer. And setting him up for Mother's whims. For self-condemnation—and ultimately near self-destruction.

Pawn. They'd all thought to use him, and he'd obliged them all, simple-minded, rutting animal that he was.

"If being rijhili means I have a problem with spies and cheats and liars, then rijhili I am," he said coldly. "*Why* are you here, Thyerri of Khoratum? Are you eyes and ears for Rhyys even now?"

"I reported to Rhyys." The voice from the hood was tight with anger. "I hadn't much choice, dunMheric, as well you know. I didn't *know* you then. When I did, I turned on him. To my detriment more than yours!"

"Did you? Or are you reporting to him still? Do you speak to his mind as you do to mine? You said we shared minds because we shared love. Have you been his lover as well? Have you ever *loved* anyone but Dancer?"

"Before you and your brothers invaded my essence, I never *knew* anyone but Dancer! I was *alone,* Mikhyel dun-Mheric. And content. *You* destroyed that peace. All Rhyys threatened was my existence, a petty loss in comparison, I assure you!"

"Are you a woman?"

The shadow crossed to his side in three long, solid-footed, anything but feminine strides. Strong, graceful arms spread wide, holding the cloak open, arrogantly inviting his investigation.

"No." In that lay madness. The moment he touched her, she'd be in his mind again, confounding his reason as well as his senses. A small part of his mind mocked his fears: she confounded his reason just standing there.

Strands of shaded hair slipped free of the hood, glinting rainbow colors in a thin shaft of sunlight that pierced the thick canopy of interlaced branches. That hair itself should

have revealed the truth to a rational man. Of all the people
he'd ever met, only Thyerri and Temorii had had such hair.
Thyerri's had been short, raggedly cut, as Temorii's had
been—before Mother restored its silken glory. And after
that, as Ganfrion had so baldly pointed out, the only times
he'd seen Thyerri, it might well have been Mother.

A hand reached for his; a second enfolded it.

"You're cold," she murmured.

"No."

"Inside."

He jerked his hand free, slammed the wall between them
again with force enough to make her flinch. "Are you going
to answer?"

"I— Yes, Mikhyel, Temorii is a woman."

A weight lifted from his back. Illusion. Mother's tricks,
that figure that had so fascinated Nikki at Boreton. Deymorin and Nikki were—

"But . . ."

"But? But, what?"

The arrogance faded from her stance. Her shoulders
drooped.

"I thought . . ." Her voice was a barely audible whisper.
"I thought you knew. I mean . . . how could you not?"

Her eyes glimmered within the hood, brilliant, ley-
touched sparks. Mikhyel fought his hands' desire to sweep
that hood aside, to capture the face between his palms
and—

"Knew what?" That internal battle made his voice cruelly harsh, for which he felt no remorse. He was damned
tired of apologizing for his own human frailties.

The sparks disappeared behind a veil of hair. The cloak,
his cloak, slipped free to form a puddle at her feet. The
overlarge tunic followed, leaving her in her form-fitting
competitor's costume. The costume was of the finest, softest
leather, fitted perfectly to her form and seamless, except for
the buttons, which were of pure leythium crystal. Mother's
creation, that costume, as doubtless was the hiller-dress he
wore, for all Temorii had indicated otherwise, having spoken of her parents' people, and wanting—

Wanting to lay claim to him.

Setting him up, as Mother and Dancer had set him up from the start.

Without the least hint of shame, almost as if he weren't even present, Temorii freed the myriad small buttons and peeled the leather down her arms, revealing herself to the waist. But he'd never had any illusions about her upper body. Like all the dance competitors, she was hard and lean, her breasts virtually nonexistent. He'd understood she represented a type in the hills, and had thought nothing of it. It had been Temorii he loved, not her body.

Not her body.

"Stop it!" He grabbed her hands, which had started tugging at the laces of the protective midriff corset. "Just *tell* me."

Her hands were shaking, her eyes wide and confused, a frightened child out of its depth. He groaned and pulled her into his arms.

"It's not whether you're man or woman, Temorii, it's the *lie*. Can't you understand that?"

"I . . . I don't have the words. I thought you knew, Khy. From the first time, I thought . . . you . . . I'm *Dancer*. I'm not Temorii. Not Thyerri. Those were just words for the moment. Bits of nothing for people to whom *Dancer* was nothing. I'm not man or woman. I'm Dancer. Just . . . Dancer."

She pushed back, and caught his head between fingers powerful enough to pull her easily up the face of a cliff— he'd seen her do it. But with a touch both intimate and gentle, her callused fingers laced through his hair to come to rest tingling against his scalp.

"And *Dancer* loves Khy." Her whisper caressed his thoughts as well as his ears. "Dancer wishes that weren't true, because Mikhyel dunMheric has so many rights and wrongs that confuse his life that Khy might be lost to Dancer forever, and Dancer couldn't hold that against Mikhyel dunMheric, as much as Dancer might want to, and that thought causes Dancer to be more afraid than anything Dancer has ever known."

"But you did lie—" Mikhyel turned to the only part of the narration that made any real sense. "You let me believe—"

"What you wanted to believe, Mikhyel dunMheric. You asked for a name. The person you saw was not Thyerri, who was a fugitive and who loved you. You did not see in the tavern-scut the street-scut into whose alley you appeared. I gave you a name that would protect that part of me from the ache Thyerri felt for you. I should have told you, but *I* held us separate. To tell you was to destroy Temorii's chance and Dancer's."

"What *are* you?" Mikhyel whispered, his own fears growing, unable to see where the question grew so complex. "Are you human?"

"Yes, Mikhyel. Completely."

"Then . . . what?"

"Rakshi's Child?" Her eyes scanned his face, seeking something . . . recognition perhaps. But the term meant nothing to him, except . . .

Rakshi was the Dancer's patron god. A creature of myth. She'd gone mad, and he had driven her there. "Oh, my dear . . ."

She sighed, and shook her head, then turned to the lacing that held the heavier leather corset that provided protection for the soft parts of the body, and to which the dance harness attached.

"Temorii, it doesn't matter." Not any longer.

But she wasn't listening. The lacing had fouled. She cursed and jerked the strings, pulling the knot tighter. Relenting, he brushed her hands aside and patiently worked the knot out. He didn't even recall the process of achieving skin against skin last night, could only marvel now at their mindless dexterity.

Sending his emotions to that protected spot within himself that he'd discovered as a child of Mheric Rhomandi's temper, he slipped the laces free.

I didn't gawk like a sex-starved adolescent . . .

Perhaps you should have.

His hands shook. His internal safe haven faltered.

Never again . . .

It was his fear after their first night come back to haunt him.

"Wait . . ." He murmured and cupping her face between his palms, leaned to kiss her.

"No, Khy." She pulled back. "The Barrister must have his truth, and he must have it without bribery."

Her voice was strong, adamant. She'd found her own internal haven and would stay there until it was safe outside once more.

And Hell's Barrister, cold as a eunuch, helped her slip the leather aside enough to discover—

"So. You lied."

"You judge too soon, Barrister. All the evidence is not yet in."

§   §   §

Ignoring Mikhyel dunMheric's puzzled frown, Dancer sat on a moss-covered mound and began removing the light-weight dance-boots, unwinding the bands at the top, then shaking them loose, impatient to have this moment past.

When he stood to face Mikhyel, free at last of the encumbering clothing, his skin reveled in the ley-touched air. So much energy. So much potential. How could one feel cold? He filled his lungs with that vitality, and tried not to listen to the internal voice that said dunMheric would reject Rhyys' spy, would arrest him in the next few moments and have him sent to a place where the air was dead.

Closing his eyes on the man who held his heart and his fate, Dancer shook back his hair, feeling, for the first time in days, the ripple of the strands against his back and buttocks, knowing, for perhaps the last time, the freedom of life with Mother, where clothing was irrelevant.

For the first time in days and perhaps for the last time: Ganfrion had said the prison authorities had ordered his hair cut for hygienic purposes. But then, a grounded dancer had no need of a radical's tail. A grounded dancer invariably cut it off, to escape the constant reminder of dreams lost.

"What is it you expect of me, Thyerri of Khoratum?"

Thyerri, alone. Not even Dancer. Thus did Mikhyel dun-Mheric declare his judgment and reject Temorii. Dancer shook his head, felt again the living wave, and tried not to let the sensual pleasure distract him.

What did he expect? His breath caught on a painful laugh.

According to his brothers, Mikhyel dunMheric was a prudish old woman—Khyel himself had told Temorii that, and they'd laughed.

But in one respect, his brothers were correct: after that first glance, Mikhyel dunMheric had turned his back to Dancer, had kept his eyes strictly averted. How did one explain to one so determinedly ignorant?

"Make love to me?" He didn't know from what crazed part of his essence the request came, but he knew it was the only answer as soon as he spoke the words.

"Damn you, don't mock me." Mikhyel's voice was a harsh whisper. His head turned slightly, and a silver eye glinted through the veil of sleek, black hair.

"I'm not mocking, Khy." Dancer held out both hands. "Make love to Temorii? Just once more? Without delusions, without darkness, without shame. Honestly?"

"Honestly. How is it you don't *choke* on that word? Temorii is a sham!"

"*Temorii* stands before you, Khy, no different than she was this morning."

The eye disappeared. "Get dressed."

Dancer stepped close to Mikhyel's tense back. "No."

"Damn you!" Mikhyel spun so fast his hair brushed Dancer's skin.

Mikhyel's eyes widened, and he stumbled backward. His foot slipped off the stone edge and Dancer caught his arms and pulled him to solid ground—

And dodged as Mikhyel swung wildly. But Mikhyel was no match for Dancer's speed or Dancer's strength, a fact they both knew well enough. Dancer intercepted Mikhyel's wrist, and held tight, the arm crossed between them, both bridge and barrier.

"Damn you," Mikhyel whispered for the third time. "What have you done to me? I've never struck a woman. Never considered—" His beautiful eyes closed, and his open mouth took a deep shuddering breath. "But then, you aren't, are you? Darius save me, I'm going mad."

Dancer reached his other hand to stoke Mikhyel's angry, tormented face, reveling in the strange but thrilling tingle of the beard, the skin that was so smooth elsewhere. Smooth and soft, angular and hard, the cheek bone lying just below the surface. A core of steel in a velvet casing— the essence of Mikhyel dunMheric.

And the hair. Unwanted tears blurred Dancer's vision as his fingers disappeared among the dark strands, and he recalled the first time he'd seen it, shimmering blue-black in the forest light, the only part of Mikhyel untouched by the Ley's searing fire. Before they'd ever declared their love, Temorii had claimed the duty of combing the long mass. It had been a way to have the contact Thyerri had craved while maintaining the distance Temorii required.

Or so Dancer had rationalized. Likely that evening ritual had been Temorii's undoing. Perhaps without it, Thyerri's cravings would not have crept into Temorii, filling her likewise with—

Audible, deep breaths: Mikhyel's, for all he seemed frozen with confusion. And anger.

And desire. Even granting him the mental isolation he demanded, Dancer could see that the greatest battle Mikhyel fought was not with him but against his own hot blood.

{Please, Khy?} He took a chance, breaking the internal silence with that plea, but he no longer trusted his voice. Mikhyel did not appear to even register the difference.

{Why didn't you just tell me?} his thought whispered in Dancer's head. {At first . . . perhaps you had reason. Later . . . why continue the deception?}

{I thought you knew.}

{About *Thyerri*? Don't lie to me again.}

{I let you believe what your heart wanted/needed to be-

lieve. Had you asked, had you challenged, I'd never have
denied. It was safer for me. I believed it must be the same
for you.}

{*You* believed what you wanted/needed to believe to justify your actions.}

{Perhaps.} Elements of truth, of self-realization of impure
motives. But done was done. He'd never willfully hurt—
anyone.

{But could *you* have loved *Thyerri*? Would you? Now?}

{I . . . I loved Temorii.}

Loved. Dancer blinked the burn away from his eyes before pointing out:

{You kissed Thyerri first.}

{Thinking that he was . . . *you* . . . were . . .} Pain pulled
the flesh around Mikhyel's eyes. "Why did you kiss me,
that first time? Why not reject me there and then? Your
contempt for me was clear enough afterward."

"Not contempt for Mikhyel. Contempt for the *rijhili* Thyerri wanted to believe you to be. Thyerri feared you, feared
what you did to his peace, wanted to drive you off. B–but
Thyerri had l–loved you a long time, Mikhyel. Your gift
was . . . difficult to reject when offered so freely."

"Thyerri. Temorii. *Why* do you persist?"

"Because they are *not* the same person. They did not
learn to love Mikhyel dunMheric at the same moment, in
the same way. Even together, they do not comprise the
whole of Dancer."

"And does Dancer love Mikhyel dunMheric?"

Dancer found himself leaning closer and closer to Mikhyel, until Mikhyel's breath brushed his mouth when he
spoke.

"More than Temorii or Thyerri can comprehend,"
Dancer breathed, mixing his essence with Mikhyel's. "I'm
sorry, Khy. I'm sorry I said nothing. I'm sorry I didn't
tell you."

"This is utter nonsense, you know."

"Are you certain of that, Barrister?"

Lips bridged the final finger's breadth between them, his
doing or Mikhyel's, Dancer didn't know or care. He

groaned and, releasing Mikhyel's wrist, used both arms to draw Mikhyel closer still. And with or without Mikhyel's consent, Mikhyel's arms circled him in turn.

Words vanished into sensation. Together, they sank to the ground and Dancer swept Mikhyel's clothes aside, seeking the touch of his underdeveloped body. They'd begun to change that, Mikhyel and Temorii. Muscle and flexibility had been improving with every passing day.

Dancer ran his fingers along the clearly defined ribs, imagining that body as it could be, the way he'd hoped one day to see it, slick with sweat, healthy and strong. Dancing to the Music at his side. Damp drops hit the smooth skin, making the muscles jump as stomach muscles would, when startled. Stupid, useless tears.

Thyerri's tears. Temorii bent and kissed them away, when Thyerri could not. And with that kiss, the Barrister's resolve was visibly shattered as Mikhyel dunMheric's body stirred to life. Dancer laughed with pure joy and kissed him there as well, cried out in ecstasy as the energy of the new node surged within them both.

Mikhyel gasped and pulled Dancer up, rolled them over, his beloved body hard and ready. The Music filled them, the Dance—

Stopped.

Mikhyel's smooth, valley-man hands slid across Dancer's face, down Dancer's neck, exploring the substance of Dancer as he never had before. Temorii arched under his touch, seeking more, quivered as the silk of his hair tingled across breast and stomach. When the touch brushed his flank, Thyerri sighed in anticipation, responding freely for the first time, trembling with fear and hope.

But fear won. The beloved touch grew tentative, paused, and vanished. Mikhyel gave a broken curse, and rolled away into a curled crouch beside him.

"I can't . . . forgive me, whoever, *whatever* you are, but I just . . ."

Dancer curled around Mikhyel's shoulders. {I love you, Khy. And Temorii is as real as Thyerri.}

Temorii's hands sought the sensitive instrument of loving

that had gone suddenly silent, a gently teasing touch that brought Mikhyel easily back to the Music, and Temorii pressed a bemused, unresisting Mikhyel onto his back. Moments later, he was filling her, his final question answered, if only he had the wit to understand. But questions and answers exploded in a series of rainbow flashes cascading behind her eyelids, as their unison cries filled the air.

Temorii collapsed onto Mikhyel, half-sobbing as spasms continued to ripple through her, while Thyerri embraced Mikhyel for his own sake, quiet and alone for all the leavings of his own passion moistened the skin between them, quiet and alone, knowing he was still unaccepted, knowing that, without him, Dancer would have everything Dancer dreamed of.

"I didn't lie, Khyel," Dancer whispered into Mikhyel's heaving chest, into skin damp with Mikhyel's sweat and Dancer's own tears. "I've never lied to you."

Chapter Ten

I've never lied to you.

That was one way of looking at it, Mikhyel supposed, lying there on a mossy bed with a warm, living blanket draped across his naked body. As he tried to sort out the myriad sensations, he wondered, in a detached way, how many of the guards Deymorin had posted had just witnessed his wanton indiscretion.

Never mind he'd ordered otherwise. The way he and Dancer had been shouting at one another, they might well have drawn unwanted attention from virtuous soldiers who were simply doing their duty.

As for their subsequent performance . . .

He supposed he ought to be concerned over the impression Mikhyel dunMheric was making on men from whom he expected a certain degree of respect.

If the moment were more real to him, he would be concerned. If any of it were more real to him, he'd be on his feet and dressed in an instant. But his existence had become inherently improbable. Mikhyel dunMheric didn't fall in love, not with women, not with men. Mikhyel dunMheric certainly didn't strip naked in the middle of a forest and fornicate like some filthy animal.

But then, what lay draped across him was neither man nor woman. Not even an honest goat.

I have no words . . .

Freak, came to mind. Abomination did.

And does Dancer love Mikhyel dunMheric?

More than Temorii or Thyerri can comprehend . . .

Possibly. He wasn't certain it mattered, under the circumstances. There were only so many lies a man's pride could handle. So many lies. So many betrayals.

Not the least of which had been perpetrated on him by his own body. Just now, with his mind free, believing Thyerri the only truth, believing lies and betrayal, he had still been roused to rut like any animal. Whatever the shape of the body with which he'd just conjoined, Temorii had inflamed true passion in him for the first time in twenty-seven years, and that base, irrational drive was not going to be set easily aside.

But set it aside, he must. Beyond his own dubious rationality, beyond the question of this . . . person's . . . affiliations, he had to wonder what would happen to Mikhyel dunMheric's credibility if he mated on a regular basis with . . . whatever Dancer was.

Was there even a word for it? Were there others like . . . it?

Mikhyel had no intimates among his peers. His was hardly the confidence his acquaintances among the elite of Rhomatum sought—at least on personal matters. But he knew men who were moved only by women. He knew a few others who were moved only by men. Most, as he understood such things, fell somewhere in between, with fate and opportunity being the deciding factor.

He'd never heard of anyone who managed to find both in one body.

Only you, Mikhyel . . .

He could practically hear Deymorin's laughter. Not derisive, oh no. Deymorin never mocked anything to do with fornication. Deymorin would be delighted. Fascinated. Deymorin would demand *details*.

Mikhyel pushed his living blanket aside as gently as he could manage, controlling a shudder as he slid free of Temorii and brushed that other, less beloved, part of . . . him.

Confused didn't begin to cover his state of mind.

He rose on one elbow and forced himself to look at the slender body. Graceful lines of shoulders and ribs led down to the small, but undeniably male organ nestled amidst fine hair that was as shaded as the hair on his head. Lean-bodied, long-muscled—viewed this way and without prejudice, Dancer was an attractive young man of perhaps sixteen or seventeen: past the gawkiness of youth, before the onset of adult mass. Mikhyel wondered, tracing a shoulder's clean curve with his fingertips, if that would change.

Dancer was in his mid-twenties; one would assume not.

And yet, Temorii had had her first mense only weeks ago, if he believed Thyerri's accusations. Perhaps it was not muscle that would come, but the softer, fuller curves of womanhood. He pulled away, clenching his fist to keep from touching again. He'd go insane trying to make sense of it.

Without warning, Dancer stretched, arching, supple as a lizard, and rolled onto his side, a move that emphasized a slight exaggeration of hip that a willing mind could easily round into womanly. From this angle, with one leg drawn up to form an elegant curve, a lock of hair caught under her arm, Dancer became the perfect embodiment of his Temorii.

Dancer had said Thyerri loved him first. Temorii's interest had followed. He didn't pretend to fully understand, but neither could he arbitrarily dismiss what he'd found with Temorii.

I thought you knew . . . And well he should have. Could he hold Dancer responsible for his own blindness?

He loved Temorii. If he had the whole truth at last . . . if Temorii was done with Rhyys, if her deception was unintentioned and regretted, if she was indeed human—with human needs and desires—then surely he could accept Thyerri, if Thyerri was the price of a life with Temorii. Temorii had always been beautiful to him. Thyerri was, recalling his own thoughts, undeniably attractive. Together . . . surely he could accept Dancer without revulsion.

Testing that theory, he lay down again, insinuating his arm under her elbow and around her waist.

It felt natural enough. Comfortable. His gut didn't churn with disgust or uncertainty. Passion did not spontaneously return, not even the instinct to draw her close and wrap himself around her that had come to rule his waking moments, but perhaps, with time, that sweet obsession would return.

He nuzzled her shoulder, burying his nose in her hair, which gained him a warm chuckle that vibrated through both their bodies. She turned slightly, shifting until her profile and a bit more was turned to him.

{So,} he thought, opening his mind, inviting her back in, {who is it I introduce to the Syndicate? Thyerri? Or Temorii?}

A long-lashed, mostly green eye flickered back at him.

"Will Temorii have to wear skirts?" she murmured, and he knew a moment's hurt that she didn't likewise open her thoughts to him.

"I'm afraid so."

She flopped over on her back, cupped her hands behind her head, and grinned. "Thyerri, then. Definitely Thyerri!"

The laugh he sought arrived with surprising ease. He attacked her recklessly exposed ribs, a tickling challenge that quickly turned to wrestling in the way that had become their habit before they'd allowed love to confuse the equation.

And in that subtle shift away from intimacy, Mikhyel discovered a relieved contentment.

SECTION
TWO

Chapter One

Hot baths were an insane decadence for a semipermanent military base, but irresistible once they'd discovered the pools in the lower tier caverns. Honeycomb caves and hot springs were common along any healthy leyline, but Deymorin suspected it was no coincidence that the scouts who had happened to recommend this spot for their base camp had also been the ones who happened next to "find" the ancient waterworks in their first days here . . . thereby gaining tremendous credit with their fellows. A few days of enthusiastic excavation, construction, and repair, and a respectable facility was available for all and sundry who wanted to make use of it.

That long list included, on this afternoon after the world had almost ended, the Rhomandi, who, upon the return (alone) of his decidedly distracted middle brother, commandeered the most private pool of the lot, set a guard out of hearing range, and demanded an explanation.

To his astonishment, Mikhyel matter-of-factly complied with that demand.

"Ganfrion was right, then," Deymorin said, once Mikhyel had finished his conspicuously minimalist explanation. "Temorii *is* one of the Children of Rakshi."

"That's what it calls itself."

Deymorin knew that tone. He gave Mikhyel's comment a moment to settle, then asked:

"Why do I get the feeling we're going to come to blows, if we aren't very careful?"

"I think I'd like an honest fight right about now."

An honest fight . . . Deymorin endeavored to hide his

astonishment, both without and within. Mikhyel's mind was closed to him at the moment—Mikhyel's own doing this time—but that did not mean the privacy was mutual.

An honest fight . . . It was not Mikhyel's ordinary reaction, and yet it was perhaps the most understandable reaction he'd ever heard out of his bookish brother. Equally remarkable, the tension that had radiated from Mikhyel was easing with each steam-filled moment—just as if his younger brother were an ordinary human being without those hidden resources that historically had made him impervious to such relaxation attempts.

He let the matter ride, giving that unexpected weakness in Mikhyel's armor time to take its course. Predictably, Mikhyel sank deeper into the pool, his hair drifting out around him, his head and shoulders barely above the pool's surface. Suddenly:

"Do you believe it?" Mikhyel asked, stiffening his back. "Do you believe that . . . Dancer is human and not some half-breed Tamshi?"

"I don't see any reason to doubt it," he answered calmly, his own mind beginning to drift on the steam-filled air. "It's fascinating, actually. As much a legend in his way as Mother. Everyone's heard rumors, of course, about the Children of Rakshi, but—"

"I haven't." There was a sudden chill, and Mikhyel's flat tone left no doubt that he did not share Deymorin's enthusiasm for the unusual. But between the flickering torchlight, reflections off the small pool's surface, and the steam, reading Mikhyel's face, never a simple task, was momentarily impossible.

"I'm not much interested in legend," Mikhyel said. "This is the wom—pers—*Rings,* I don't even know what to call it!" Mikhyel's brief shudder made ripples in the pool.

"I think you'd better decide, brother, and make your peace with your decision," Deymorin said bluntly, feeling no sympathy. "From what you've said, I don't think it makes a lot of difference to Dancer whether he's 'he' or 'she,' but he's definitely not an 'it'."

Mikhyel trailed a hand through the water, making patterns in a bit of oil soap that skimmed the surface. "I see you've decided."

The pronoun had been unconscious, unthought. Under the circumstances, Mikhyel's taking offense was justifiable . . . if uncomplicated resentment for that small slip was truly all that was going through Mikhyel's mind. Deymorin honestly wished it were that simple and knew damnwell it wasn't. He didn't need to hear the thoughts or even witness the brooding look on Mikhyel's face to know that.

Nothing was ever simple, where it came to Mikhyel's opinions. "Take a stand, brother. You choose, and I'll stand with you. Until that time . . . don't take offense at my choice."

"I don't. Didn't." Mikhyel's shrug sent another ripple across the surface, passive disengagement that both infuriated him and worried him. "Hardly matters, does it?" Mikhyel asked.

"Damn right it matters! Finish your statement. You were going to say this is the woman you love." And at Mikhyel's burning look: "Do you deny it?"

Mikhyel's gaze lowered, found something distant to stare at.

He was almost surprised when that distant something didn't begin to smolder. But at least he'd shaken his brother's unnatural indifference.

"It's not something to be ashamed of, Mikhyel. If you honestly love her—"

A sharp bark of non-laughter mocked him. Caught. Confused.

"All right: *him.* If you love . . . him—"

"But that's the issue, isn't it?" Mikhyel still gazed elsewhere. "Was it honest love I felt or machinated lust?"

"Felt?"

"Darius forgive me, at this precise moment, I feel—nothing. Yesterday . . ." Mikhyel stared into the shadows for a long silent moment, and when he spoke, his words drifted as if from a distance. "You should have seen her, Deymorin . . . Child of Rakshi be damned, she was Rakshi incarnate. She commanded the rings and they sang for her.

When she was done . . ." Mikhyel blinked, and tears mingled with the sweat on his thin cheeks. "Mother's magic is nothing—*nothing* compared with what she did. And after she finished . . . she couldn't move. Rakshi had deserted her, had left her to exit the arena on her own, and it took the love—the worship—of several thousand people to get her on her feet again. And less than an hour later, she was back on the rings, doing it all again."

"For you," Deymorin said, into the longer silence that followed.

"How can I not love, Deymorin? How can I even *think* of deserting that kind of commitment?"

"Are you going to?"

"Going to? I don't know. Thinking about it . . . Darius save me, I'm not *thinking* at all. This morning, the mere thought of her caused a heat in me like nothing I've ever known. Now . . . I'm cold, Deymorin. So . . . very cold."

He'd had enough. More than enough. He saw Mikhyel gathering up his damnable black melancholy, which, once set, wanted no fellowship, no reason, no pity from anyone. And he wouldn't have it, not if he had to hit low and twice. "Rather melodramatic, aren't you? *Something* must have warmed you, up there by the pool."

Mikhyel's lip raised in a self-mocking sneer. "Didn't take long for your guards to pass *that* little piece of information on, did it?"

"My guards said nothing. Your mind was still oozing when you came down."

The sneer deepened. "The Rhomandi blood runs true after all, Deymorin; Mheric would have been proud of me. *Good breeding stallion,* our father'd say, just . . . like . . . *Dammit!*" Mikhyel slammed his fist into the water, sending a shower over the edge.

Finally. *Finally,* the human reaction. Deymorin splashed him back, a good faceful that left him spluttering.

"Ease off, brother," Deymorin advised.

Mikhyel scowled and sank deeper into the pool.

"Is it so hard for you to embrace Thyerri within your

affections? You seemed damned upset about his death last night."

"I was disturbed about several supposed deaths last night. Deaths I felt personally responsible for. *Thyerri's* was not among them."

"You felt nothing when he died?"

"He didn't die."

"You didn't know that!"

"What would you have me say, Deymorin? Yes, I regret the loss of any life worth living, and at the end, Thyerri's was worth living. He was a gifted dancer. He was a proud hiller who got caught up in politics beyond his understanding, who then risked everything to undo the damage . . . he'd . . ."

Something in his own argument had turned a way Mikhyel didn't like. That was unusual.

"Not a bad epitaph, if he were dead," Deymorin said into that drifting silence.

"But he's not dead, is he?" Mikhyel's gaze passed right through him. "And now I can't help but wonder, was there ever any risk to him at all? To any of them? Temorii, Thyerri . . . even Ganfrion? Was it all . . . empty gesture?"

"I can't believe you're following this self-pitying trail, Khyel. Ganfrion knew nothing about Mother. Dancer, by either name, risked everything for you—several times."

"For me? —Or for Mother?"

"What does it matter? You can run that scenario any way you want it for the rest of your life and get a different answer every time, Khyel. Sometimes you, sometimes Mother, half and half. And if Mother manipulated you, she was manipulating Dancer as well, so it was Dancer's life she was playing with, far more than yours. And I hope I don't need to point out, *he* was the one at risk, far more than you. So it *wasn't* Thyerri that 'died' on the rings—it *could* have been. It *could* have been Temorii. It seems to me Dancer deserves your support, not your censure, at least for now. He's here with you. Mother is . . . unavailable. You said you've shared his mind, as we have shared

ours. Do you honestly believe we two could lie to each
other? Can his thoughts lie to you?"

"You were the one who said that was the least reliable
witness of all!"

"And I was *wrong,* wasn't I? Temorii *wasn't* a lie."

"I'm afraid I can't accept that reality quite so mag-
nanimously."

Deymorin stared into the steam, weighing Mikhyel's life
against Mikhyel's pride, the possibility of Dancer's betrayal
against the probability of Dancer's love, and finally asked
slowly, something Mikhyel evidently hadn't gleaned in his
citybound life. "So because a 'tweener escaped the midwife's scissors, you're going to ruin two lives?"

"I don't know what you're talking about."

" 'Tweeners." Mikhyel had asked. Deymorin opened his
mind to Mikhyel on the sudden and right past his guard,
and his brother's eyes widened.

"Do you mean to say there are others like Dancer?"

"Well, I don't know. How complete is he?"

"Deymorin! Rings, such a question. I don't kn—"

Deymorin raised an eyebrow, not believing for a moment
that much prudery. Mikhyel frowned and looked away.

"Very," came Mikhyel's muttered, mortally embarrassed reply.

There was his doggedly celibate brother, and if he
weren't so dumbstruck at the prudery, and if he didn't
know what lay behind that reticence, he might very much
want to laugh Mikhyel out of his embarrassment. He might
want to do it for Mikhyel's own natural good, but a man
really didn't care to weather the storm Mikhyel's reaction
might raise, particularly considering his lack of escape
options.

Instead, a man just said, with straight-faced detachment:

"Interesting. I've never heard of that. Likely it's what
sets Rakshi's get apart from the rest of us normal folk."

"And you've discussed this topic so freely with your
friends."

"Don't be an ass." Deymorin picked up the oilsoap cake
and ran it across his arm, following the application with a

sponge to coax lather out of the film. "The ones J'tarif talked about—"

"Who?"

"J'tarif. The foaling man at Darhaven, when I was thirteen."

"Dancer is not a *horse.*"

"And not all 'tweeners are human. It's not unnatural, Mikhyel. I saw my first that year." Deymorin applied his scraper to his arm. The oilsoap skimmed off into the water and swirled out the drainage channel. "We had a family of hillers helping in the foaling that year and J'tarif was filled with 'tweener stories. Proved more than willing to satisfy my . . . prurient curiosity."

"No doubt," said Mikhyel, who knew exactly what Deymorin had been like at thirteen. "—Turn around, Deymorin. I'll get your back."

Casually suggested, as though they'd performed this service for each other for years.

Brothers usually did, but he'd never have dared even suggest it to Mikhyel.

"Thanks," he said as casually, and turned to lean his folded elbows on the pool's rocky rim, while Mikhyel applied the soap to his shoulders.

"J'tarif said that in the hills, when a 'tweener human child is born, the 'excess flesh' as he called it, is trimmed away, and the child is raised as a girl."

"As a girl. Yes, I suppose that would be—" A pause. The sponge began a course of rhythmic circles across his back. "—the simplest solution. Are they viable?"

With that wall of mental silence back between them, he could only guess at the depth of emotion that leaked out in the slight edge to that question. He twisted to half-face Mikhyel.

"Do you mean, can they conceive?"

A single dip of the head: affirmation.

"Sometimes."

Mikhyel's impassive face gave no clue as to whether or not that information was welcome. "You say this happens in the hills."

"Not just the hills, and not just among the hillers. Diorak confirmed that his niece had performed similar operations on at least two newborns that he knew of, and she's only one of seven midwives in Rhomatum."

Mikhyel's eyes widened ever-so-slightly. "You asked *Diorak*?"

"Naturally."

"That reaction must have been . . . interesting."

The physician in Rhomandi House was a staid fellow. Deymorin grinned and turned back to the rim. "Obviously, Dancer escaped the midwife's mercy."

The hand that skimmed the scraper across his back in a practiced, easy motion, never faltered.

Then water splashed across his back and Mikhyel's hand slapped his shoulder.

"That'll do," Mikhyel said and slid away, sinking down until the water rose to his chin, all the while staring unfocused into the steam.

Deymorin slid down, back to the wall, spreading his arms out to either side along the rim. The water sloshed over the edge and ran in rivulets to cracks in the stone and disappeared. "You wield the scraper quite deftly, brother. Who'd you practice on? Raulind?"

Mikhyel's eyes flickered to life in the torchlight, then stared again into the steam. "Anheliaa."

Well, that was a guaranteed conversation-stopper.

Deymorin raised the soap in silent offering, a movement that drew Mikhyel's distracted gaze. Mikhyel shook his head. "I'm fine. Thanks."

Trying not to feel he'd been part of a very one-sided negotiation, worse, trying not to reckon the particulars of the bargain, Deymorin sank deeper still, realized when he next looked, that his brother was staring at him with eyes to which full awareness had returned.

"Nothing like that, Deymorin," he said. "I was just cold."

"If you say so."

"I say so." A shadow smile softened Mikhyel's mouth. "Later?"

"I might be out of the mood."

With a low chuckle, Mikhyel eased back against the stone, eyes closed. "Never."

Several heartbeats later, Deymorin closed his mouth. For that one word from his prudish brother's mouth, he'd forgive Dancer almost anything.

"Ah, Deymorin, such an image you have of me," Mikhyel murmured.

Instinct threw the stone wall up in his mind. Mikhyel laughed aloud and turned to face the edge, pulling his hair to the side. "Here. Do your worst. And get that left shoulder blade, will you? Feels as if I rolled in a patch of nettles."

Making a final check of his wall to assure his brother's feelings as well as his own were protected, he ran the soap over Mikhyel's narrow shoulders. "Itches, does it?"

"Worse than the burns after Boreton."

The scars from that passage still marred the skin on Mikhyel's back—particularly the shoulder blade in question. Deymorin worked the sponge hard there, and Mikhyel heaved an exaggerated sigh and let his head fall into his crossed arms. In silence, Deymorin maneuvered the scraper across the thin layer of muscle and sharply protruding bones.

"Why didn't I know?" Mikhyel's murmur was barely audible above the sound of the water. "Why have I never heard . . ."

"Diorak claimed that even parents rarely know. That it's been determined kinder to say nothing, and simply . . . repair the defect."

"Determined by whom?"

Deymorin shrugged. At the time, he'd considered it cheating somehow, but beyond a vague curiosity, had never thought of it again, that same prurient interest having deflected his curiosity into other, more immediate realms. "All Diorak said was that the children are kept in hospital for a few days, and by the time they go home, the parents are none the wiser."

Without any real thought, his right hand began to work

on the tight back. When that roused no objection, Deymorin set the scraper in the bowl and went after the knots with greater intent. Mikhyel groaned.

"Rings, where did you learn that?"

"Kiyrstin. She insists on turnabout, so I was forced to learn."

A low chuckle. "I doubt force was involved. You're well-suited. Take care of each other. I envy—"

Fortunately, Mikhyel stopped before he completed the thought. Deymorin was not in a mood to compare relationships. He took the massage deeper and discovered unexpected resiliency. Better conditioned than appearances would indicate.

"Why do you suppose the midwives would do that? Why—lie?" Mikhyel's mind seemed intent on some personal quest for understanding.

"Out of kindness, perhaps. Make the children normal, whatever that means."

"Makes me wonder what else they've kept secret over the years."

"Healthy attitude, I say."

"Still, I can almost understand . . ." Mikhyel ran his fingers across the stone as if memorizing each nook and cranny. "It would be simpler . . ."

"For the gods' own sake, Khyel, you aren't even thinking of having Diorak—of asking Dancer to—"

"No, Deymorin. Not really."

Not really. Deymorin dropped his hands before he acted on the sudden urge to tighten his grip and shake sense into his brother.

As if he'd heard that temptation, Mikhyel slid away and back into the heated water, putting as much distance between them as the pool allowed.

"A message arrived from Rhomatum," Deymorin said, which announcement earned him a satisfyingly startled look from his brother. Diversion accomplished.

"When?" Mikhyel asked. "Why didn't you *say* something?"

"Why didn't you ask?"

Mikhyel's mouth tightened, his brow lowered, and he sank until his chin touched the water.

"Lidye has placed Mirym under house arrest. So far, she's refused to explain anything."

"I doubt she will, at least to Lidye. I expect I'll have better luck with her. The Rings?"

"Are stable. Cycling well-nigh immovable from their orbits, according to Nethaalye. The message lines are functioning, and all the ringmasters have sent their official acceptance of Rhomatum's authority—and their oaths of complete cooperation, pending the signing of diplomatic agreements."

"All the ringmasters. Except Khoratum."

"Except Khoratum. Lidye is livid. Says that line has gone . . . what she calls 'negative.' "

"Anheliaa's term. She means the Khoratum line is drawing power steadily. Hardly surprising, considering what we're seeing here; interesting it can do so with the Khoratum/Persitum Ring down. —And Persitum?"

Persitum was Khoratum's complementary node, the node that had, for years, balanced that line, and the one most vulnerable to Khoratum's loss.

"Has lost the flow from Mauritum as well." A bit of highly significant information that had come via a wildly circuitous routing: Rhomandi men placed in every capped node throughout the Web, including the secondaries and tertiaries could send messages almost as fast as the Towers when they had to.

But the news was devastating for Persitum, which had been a satellite of Mauritum for centuries before it became a satellite of Rhomatum as well. The sole crossroad for the two Webs one day; isolated the next. It was major news, and Mikhyel took that in with a lift of the brows and:

"Interesting. Persitum won't be happy."

"Can you blame them?" Deymorin asked. "With our ring shattered, they're off line. Without Mauritum as well? They've got problems."

"They have company in that." Mikhyel sighed. Understandably. Smoothing those feathers and finding legal answers would fall primarily on Mikhyel's shoulders when they returned to Rhomatum. "But it's the price they pay for dealing with Garetti."

Garetti romMaurii, ringmaster of Mauritum, hub node of the Maurislan Island Web to the west. And Garetti had been the primary instigator of the coup attempt that had started the whole chain of events.

"Garetti's choice to cut them off?" Mikhyel asked. "Or do we know?"

"Rumor has it's Garetti's doing, but after the way we hit him, I'm not so sure he *had* a choice."

"We know for certain he survived the battle?"

Deymorin nodded.

"Rings. There are times I truly wished to take Anheliaa up on her desire to assassinate the man—now being one of them."

"Kiyrstin tried." And for all he wished she'd never been put in that position, had Kiyrstin never been romGaretti, had she never been pushed to an act that was on Garetti's record books as an assassination attempt, she wouldn't be waiting for one Deymorin Rhomandi dunMheric back in Rhomatum at that very moment. Hard to regret such a chain of events.

A ghost smile stretched Mikhyel's lips. "Too bad she didn't succeed. Beware your behavior with that one, brother."

"I'll take her justice over yours any day, Barrister."

It was a snipe from the past and an unfair one, regretted the moment it was uttered . . . and yet, it seemed to fly right past Mikhyel, which in some ways was more troublesome than a good argument.

"Kiyrstin wrote the letter?"

Deymorin nodded.

"Her take on Garetti?"

"Embarrassed, as much as anything, at losing his hand. Possibly taking it out on Persitum, but she's betting ring damage. He needs Persitum too badly. He'll go to ground for a time, pretend it was all some subordinate's fault, but he can't afford to keep Persitum off-line permanently."

"Neither can we. Now that he's dropped them, *we* have the advantage. If we can get a new ring forged and Persitum back on-line before Garetti changes his mind—or repairs his own ring, if that's the crux of his problem—they'll think very differently about the direction their politics has been leading them."

"Takes months to forge a ring," Deymorin reminded him, unnecessarily: a statement of fact against daydreams.

"And damned if I know if it can be added back into the rotation without bringing the lot down to let it start from rest, which means *Lidye* will have to bring them all back up."

"Shit." Deymorin sank lower into the steaming water, trying to avoid the horrifying possibilities that observation raised. Raising and resetting the Rings of a node the size and complexity of Rhomatum's had only been done once in recent memory . . . by Anheliaa. After Nikki had cast a hardwood cane amongst them.

The rings had been brought down that day, but they'd pulverized the cane first. Last night the mere touch of Mirym's embroidery needle had shattered the Khoratum ring. . . .

Mikhyel's eyes flicked toward him. "Disquieting notion, isn't it?"

"You might say that." Personally, Deymorin might call the idea spooky, even horrifying. Still, the two instances were hardly identical. "The ring was under extreme tension, there's that. All of us trying to force it to spin, Rhyys and romMaurii holding it firm—"

"*Mother* holding it firm," Mikhyel corrected him softly.

"All of which definitely changes the scenario. The Rings themselves weren't under assault when Nikki brought them down with my cane, after all. I'd say we should call the mystery of the needle solved and worry about how we're going to get Persitum back into the Syndicate."

"No argument there," Mikhyel said. "In that matter, it would help if we can keep close tabs on Garetti's mood. Have we informants in position in Garetti's court?"

"Mikhyel." This, with a sigh.

"Just making certain, Rhomandi," Mikhyel said. "We were caught flat a year ago."

"We wouldn't have been," Deymorin said, "if our own ringmasters hadn't been operating at cross-purposes with us."

"Point, Deymorin. A moot point, however, if we don't get back and get that ring cast. Damn." Mikhyel rubbed his forehead, pressing fingers to his eyes with the attitude of a man trying desperately to sort out priorities. "Let's hope Darius' records on the original castings are sound. That's one of the largest of the rings. Casting it to match the rest is going to be a nightmare. The balance of leythium within the steel . . . the depth of the coating . . . Rings!"

"A singularly appropriate execration, brother."

Mikhyel chuckled and his hand fell back into the water. "It is, of course, possible that Persitum will simply welcome the isolation and tell Mauritum to go to hell. It's been on the tail end of every power-grabbing tug of war in Rhomatum history."

"Possible that they would tell Garetti go to hell. Hardly probable they'd send the proffered ley-energy to the same destination."

"Ah, Deymorin," Mikhyel sighed, and his head eased back onto the pool's rim. "Must you destroy my every fantasy?"

"Brother, if that's your notion of a pleasant fantasy, we need to have a *serious* talk."

Mistake. He knew it the moment he said it, knew it was too late to rescind, and as the longest silence yet stretched between them, he fully expected Mikhyel to pull away completely.

"To each his own," Mikhyel said at last. "Yes, brother, that *is* the level of my fantasies. I'd love more than anything that a few of these endless crises would simply solve themselves, but they won't, will they? Persitum will have to be won back. The ring will have to be forged and raised. That's the way of my life. Yours as well, if you truly intend to take up the mantle of Princeps."

"Kinder than I deserved for that one, brother."

Mikhyel shrugged. "I took your meaning." And in a smooth shift: "Our primary concerns remain internal."

Meaning internal to the Syndicate and not the Rhomandi Family. Finally.

"You've a good list of all those notables who were taking part in the festivities in Khoratum?" he asked.

"A list, yes, and it's in Raulind's trust. Ganfrion could recite you the details from memory, if you're in a hurry."

"I'll wait for Raulind," he said, and failed utterly to achieve the detached tone he intended.

Mikhyel regarded him sidelong. "You know you'll have to get used to him sometime."

"Ganfrion? I'm used to him. I'm used to him, I just don't like him."

"Get on your nerves, does he?"

"Like a Tower in a thunderstorm," he admitted sourly.

A secretive smile hovered on Mikhyel's lips.

Deymorin shot him a glance. "You hired him just to torment me, didn't you?"

The smile twitched. . . .

"Well, now you've got him under oath, brother. In the family. Ours. Was that sensible?"

. . . . And widened. "I hired him because he's so much *like* you, you idiot."

"*Like me!* He's arrogant, self-righteous, rule-breaking—"

This time, one slim black brow lifted: point proven.

Deymorin reached for Ganfrion's better qualities: "Tough-minded and pragmatic. Intelligent. Worldly."

"Those, too," Mikhyel said.

Deymorin laughed. "Bastard."

"Oh, I don't think so, brother." The smile drifted off Mikhyel's face like the oil-slick skimming off the circulating water. "It's your fault, you know. You said you wished you could be at my back as I visited the nodes. Damned if I wanted you hovering over me, but I saddled myself with one enough like you to drive me almost as crazy. The advantage is, if I order him to shut up, he shuts up."

"Ah, your *lifelong* fantasy."

Mikhyel shook his head slowly. "Not really." The good humor died. "We've a long road ahead, Deymorin."

"Well, that's a bit of non-news."

"Is it?"

"Don't go enigmatic on me, Khyel. Either spout it out or let me in your head."

In your head didn't happen. He felt that exclusion.

But Mikhyel quietly spoke his thoughts. "For the past few months, we've been responding to the emergency of the moment. What we face now, casting the ring, resetting it . . . then rebuilding the Web, let alone the economic structure of the region . . . we're talking years, Deymorin. Are you prepared for that kind of commitment?"

"You've been in my head, brother. How can you ask?"

"I've not been in your heart, Deymorin. You were an Outsider to the City by choice and proud of it. Are you truly prepared to live in Rhomatum?"

"Permanently? No. But that shouldn't be necessary."

Mikhyel only looked at him, accusation without a word.

"What's that stare supposed to mean?" Deymorin asked.

"Rhomatum said you should be spinning the Rhomatum Rings."

"Lidye's doing just fine at it."

"For now. In the long run . . . I don't know how much I trust her. And she's about to have Nikki's child. We've never had a pregnant ringmaster. Considering the timing . . . there's a good chance raising the ring will coincide with the birth of her child, certainly with the most crucial moments of the pregnancy. We might need someone else, in a hurry. With both Persitum and Khoratum gone, the rift between the Northern Crescent and Southern is physical as well as political. Persitum must come back on line. I'm not sure I'd trust her to do it. And if it should come to that, if for one reason or the other she can't, are you prepared? I don't know who else we could trust, and the fact is if you're not prepared to do it—if you're not prepared to deal with the Rings, Deymorin, the Rhomandi should be ready to relinquish control of the Tower, to give over that decision to the Council and let them find someone Rhomatum *can* trust."

The ruling family drop its command of the Tower that was its reason for existence, the Rings that were the center of all the Web? The Rhomandi family give up their prerogatives and responsibilities, retire to estates and raise horses, not mercantile alliances?

A few months ago, the first answer from his lips would have been a simple and uncompromising *damned right*. That *had* been his answer. Now . . .

Now the Tower didn't have Anheliaa, and the power that ran the lights had faltered. Civilization had faltered. If a woman in childbirth, as temperous a woman as Lidye, struck out at the Rings . . . destabilized them . . . if her concentration, in all good will, unexpectedly wavered at the wrong instant . . .

"I'd have to consider it, then, wouldn't I?"

Hope flared from Mikhyel, a white heat of hope that seared Deymorin from the inside out, and on that wave, the whole truth came through.

"You don't trust Lidye?" Deymorin asked, and this time Mikhyel's cynical laugh vibrated inside his head.

"Do *you*?" Mikhyel asked him.

"No," he admitted, when he thought about it. No, he didn't trust her and not simply on the grounds of Lidye's volatile temper. It wasn't even based on the fact that she was not Rhomandi, not even Rhomatumin. It wasn't the fact that while she was family . . . at least she was his brother's wife . . . he could never say Lidye had done right by his brother.

More, there was an underlying inconsistency to her responses, even in the most innocuous of conversations, that hinted at an instability of character and purpose that set his alarms ringing.

All that aside, truth beneath all other truths, he just didn't like her. He wouldn't entrust her with one of his horses, let alone the Rings.

Let—alone—the Rings.

He discovered, to his horror, he cared—not only cared, but cared *passionately* about the fate of the Rhomatum Rings.

When had *that* happened to him?

"*I don't give a damn what your orders are! I'm going in there!*"

The distinctive sounds of a scuffle heralded Ganfrion's arrival.

Mikhyel cast Deymorin an apologetic glance.

{I left an invitation for him to meet us here when he woke. I'd better go clear it up.}

{You could have warned me.} He had set the guards to prevent intrusion. They followed their orders, and admitted no one without authorization.

{I forgot,} Mikhyel said, and sighed as the commotion that echoed in the caverns drew closer. {I've got some explaining to do to him.}

{I've told him most of what I've said,} Deymorin said.

{Everything?} Mikhyel asked.

{Everything he'd accept.}

Mikhyel cast him a look that required no inner elaboration and pulled himself, dripping, from the pool, to deal with his gorman.

An instant later Mikhyel cried out and toppled, as Deymorin's head exploded with pain.

Chapter Two

The deserted campfire held just enough remembrance of flame to harbor some hope of revival. Dancer hunkered down beside it, feeding small bits into the warm coals, wishing it into flames, not flames such as Mother could bring out of nothing, but bending the odds, encouraging, not forcing the fire.

Of course Mother didn't need warmth. She just liked the way fire looked.

He fed larger and larger bits, shivering, cold this far removed from the wild energy of the new source—

And this far from . . . his other source of warmth.

He captured his wayward lower lip in his teeth and bit down hard. Mikhyel was in the caves with his brother, but no depth of stone and no separation could totally mask his presence from Dancer's world sense, for all Mikhyel had wished to cut himself off in that retreat to his brother's side. Thyerri could understand that retreat, Thyerri had severed himself from a union become too painful, there beside the source pool. Mikhyel wanted his freedom; Thyerri would grant him that, as far as he was able.

Whether Dancer would be as kind . . .

Thyerri closed his eyes and wrapped his arms around himself, rocking slowly. His mind had rejected Mikhyel dunMheric long ago, resenting the hold dunMheric had established over his heart, resenting the loss of all that made life worth living—or so he'd believed. His mind had rejected, but his body had failed to follow, and out of that confused morass, Temorii had emerged, safely distanced from dunMheric's effect—until she, too, had fallen under his spell. And now, *Temorii* insisted he was a fool and failed utterly to understand why her Khy denied her his love, after all they had been through.

Temorii's objections ruled the sum that was Dancer, and Dancer reached now, brushed aside Thyerri's objections and sought Mikhyel—

And recoiled from the pain he found.

{Khy!} Dancer shouted, aloud and within, but there was no answer, only white-hot torment.

He leaped to his feet, raced for where his heart said Mikhyel writhed in agony.

Tents intervened; he dodged, jumped tent stakes, eeled past men with restraining hands. He wrenched free of them, bolted from the cacophony of their voices, intent on ending the unspeakable pain that seared through his memory.

"Khy!" he shouted aloud at the cavern entrance. His eyes were blinded by the abrupt change, light to dark. He saw shadows in shadow, but his heart said Mikhyel was—

"What the—" Ganfrion's voice, on a breathless gasp, and in the same moment Ganfrion's large body halted his headlong progress. "Oh, *Temorii*. Bless the Mother— Give us a hand, lass . . ."

Dancer's eyes adjusted to the dark and to the sight of Mikhyel, limp as death and hanging by one arm looped around Ganfrion's neck. A shadowy Deymorin, whose glazed eyes held no real awareness, staggered behind him, supported by two uniformed men.

"Collapsed," Ganfrion explained between hoarse gasps for breath. "Both . . . at once." Ganfrion was wounded, and had no business bearing that weight. "Must get . . . out of sight. Can't let . . . men see . . ."

"I'll take him," Dancer said, taking Mikhyel's arm. "You help with the Rhomandi."

"Girl, you can't possibly—"

"Give him to me!"

With obvious reluctance, Ganfrion released his hold, but remained poised, ready to help. Help such as it might be— from a man whose abused body could barely hold itself upright.

Familiar weight. Less than his own, for all Ganfrion looked askance at his offer to bear Mikhyel's fainting self to privacy. More, Dancer knew the balance and feel of that body as well as he knew his own. He swept the veil of black hair aside to cradle Mikhyel's back and shifted their combined balance smoothly, lifting Mikhyel bodily up into his arms. There were easier ways, but none that wouldn't exacerbate the pounding pressure he sensed growing in Mikhyel's head.

He blocked that connection, even as he desperately wished to ease the pain. If he gave in to that urge, the pain would overwhelm him as well.

A groan escaped Mikhyel's lips. And Mikhyel's arm, as if with a mind of its own, rose to circle Dancer's neck, shifting their combined mass to a more balanced center— an instinctive act: when they touched, their essence joined, and not all Mikhyel's wanting it to be otherwise would change that reality.

"So, my stubborn Khy, you are still awake," Dancer murmured aloud, striving to soothe Mikhyel's heart without adding to the confusion in Mikhyel's head.

Awake, but not truly conscious. The turmoil in Khyel's mind warped perception despite his efforts to shield against it.

Confusion. Pressure. Not as much pain as he'd thought at first. With the added detail that came with touch, he sensed a far more complex assault on Mikhyel's mind than he'd first realized.

"Where shall I take him?" he asked abruptly.

"Rhomandi's tent," was Ganfrion's equally abrupt answer.

Dancer nodded and headed down the hillside, leaving Ganfrion to see to the Rhomandi, wanting to take Mikhyel to some place of safety and rest where he could safely track the assault to its source.

Others tried to intervene in his path, to help and ask questions, others whose names he didn't know and whose essences were even less certain.

He glared and growled, and they backed out of his way

as he sought the Rhomandi's tent. No one prevented him entering.

And in the privacy it offered, past the canvas barriers that separated the sleeping section from the rest, Dancer placed Mikhyel on the lone sleeping cot, leaving Ganfrion to arrange for Mikhyel's brother when they arrived. Steeling his mind, forcing Mikhyel's small remaining defenses aside, he cupped Mikhyel's face in both hands and thrust himself into the middle of that battlefield, found the line of assault and followed it straight to its source.

Nikaenor. The youngest Rhomandi was—

No, not the source. Nikaenor was only the conduit for the attack The source was—

Dancer cried out in denial. "*Mother!*"

But Mother would never be so cruel, would never abuse with so arbitrary and black a punishment the very ones who had served her faithfully.

Yet the source of the attack was indisputably the heart of the Khoratum Node, and the wave of assault carried the scent of raspberries—overripe and fermented, which was not the scent he knew as Mother, but something clearly related to her.

Barring his essence against that pattern, Dancer reached out anew to Nikaenor's mind, seeking simple facts of his circumstances: where he was, how he was, and what he had done to precipitate an attack that rebounded on his brothers.

Images of mountain trails, of Mikhyel's valet, Raulind.

But no, that was response to a scout's report, Nikki's internal image of Raulind, not Raulind's own presence.

Pressure in his head. Pain.

But mild pain compared to what it might be. Say nothing. Endure. Contain.

For Khyel's sake. Khyel needed Raulind.

Pressure growing. Building. Pound pound pound of horse feet, sound and jolt. Each step worse than the one before.

Sudden blast. A warning.

Warding. Collapse. Falling.

Confusion. Hard ground beneath Nikaenor's body; water

flooding Mikhyel's mouth and nose. Brothers bound, sharing panic and . . .

Floating. Horse: gone. Water: gone. Hands: lifting, carrying. Moving uphill to—

"No!" In one burst of imagery Dancer both knew where Nikaenor was and knew the nature of the attack on the brothers. *"Not that way!"* He shouted the warning at Nikki, for all he knew that no one who must hear him *would* hear.

"Temorii? Girl, *what is it*?"

Hands pulled at his wrists, forcing him away from Mikhyel.

It was Ganfrion. Deymorin lay stretched on another pallet, while a man in a plain dark coat knelt at his side, examining him.

"I must go!" Dancer protested, and his voice sounded strange even to his own ears.

"Go? What are you talking about? What the hell was that all about?"

"She doesn't want them! She's fighting to keep him away! Don't you see? They must be stopped! *They're going the wrong way!*"

"Make sense, girl."

Dancer forced his mind the final distance from Mikhyel's. Everything of instinct called on him to protect Mikhyel's mind from the assault, but common sense told him that any such defense here would simply waste precious time and energy, and not end the torment.

"I have to get to Nikki. I have to tell him—tell—whoever's carrying him—to go downhill, not up! Don't you see? They're going closer to the source, and the closer he goes to the source, the stronger the warding! She'll kill them. She'll—" He choked on his own words, his heart unwilling to admit what he knew had to be the truth: that Mother herself was behind the assault, that she *would* kill the brothers before allowing them into Khoratum again. The warding was against them, purposely against the Rhomandi, one and all.

"What *she?*" Ganrion asked, but Ganfrion knew about Mother now. Surely Ganfrion could see . . .

"They're taking Nikaenor closer to the source—to meet with Raulind. He thought it was a headache. He trusts Raulind's medicines, he told the men with him to take him there—to Raulind! But that's—wrong way. He knows now, but too—too far gone to wake, can't tell them now. If he spends the night that close—don't know how much worse . . . They can die. They all will die. . . ."

"I'll get a messenger," Ganfrion said.

"I can go faster!"

"Than a man on horseback? I don't think so."

"Go—straight." Harder and harder to find the words. Hard to pull his mind from the source and that powerful, lethal warding. "No—trail, there. Faster."

"Thyerri—"

The pressure still built, maddening. He sought something he could do now, anything to ease Mikhyel's pain and his own distraction—the only true remedy he knew was to respect the warding and to get Nikaenor off Mother's mountain while he was still alive . . . but as the pain and the pressure built wildly, Dancer was less and less sure any of them could live long enough for him to get to Nikki.

Yet it came not as an outward-running assault, but a powerful warding off of someone within its domain: Nikaenor was the immediate origin and the initial conduit, but Mikhyel's extreme sensitivity to both his brothers was the compounding factor, his sensitivity to the Ley and all its effects that made the assault so dangerous. The pain went in a circle. It built, one brother to the next, and compounded itself in each repeating cycle. Mother herself might be caught in it.

If Mikhyel could be quieted, even partially . . . the endless loop might slow and collapse.

Yet Mikhyel beneath the surface was still aware: heard everything. Felt everything. Endured everything and had had no power to stop it. If only Mikhyel would be weak

for once. If only he would faint . . . if only he could truly,
profoundly, fall unconscious to the Ley—

Asleep.

Dreams. Mother had always said that not all the power
of the Ley could penetrate Dancer's dreams, just before
she kissed him good night.

And after Mother's kiss, his sleep was always deep and
untroubled.

Dancer cupped Mikhyel's face once more and, bending
over, pressed his lips to Mikhyel's.

§   §   §

*A cloud, black and ominous, surrounded Mikhyel, grow-
ing thicker by the moment.*

Or rather, he was moving—into the heart of the cloud.

*There was nothing more he could do for Nikaenor. His
brother had sought to protect his men and misjudged his
enemy, and now his guardians likewise misjudged, carrying
Nikki deeper into the enemy's throat, reacting so efficiently,
so heroically to Nikaenor's requests that the pressure had
overwhelmed his senses before he could tell them to go back
the other way.*

*But the pain was . . . ephemeral. True bodily damage was
minimal. He—they—would survive. He gave that knowledge
to Nikki, shared a fleeting glimpse of what pain he had endured as a child and survived. Not all of it; only sufficient
to put the momentary discomfort in perspective.*

*And leaving his brother's sleeping mind with that dread,
but remote comparison, he moved beyond him and deeper
still into the cloud, seeking the source of the cloud . . . seeking the mind behind the shapeless attack.*

*Thyerri's fleeting presence had cried {Mother}, but Mik-
hyel questioned that identification. Thyerri had not been a
part of the battle for control of the Web. Thyerri had not
tasted that fetid essence ruling the Khoratum Rings.*

*He had. And the taste of this cloud was not unfamiliar
to him.*

Yet not the same, either.

And there, darkest shade within the shadowed cloud, he could see rings spinning. Black and ominous rings, rings damaged in the battle, their essence compromised, but spinning still . . .

He reached, seeking the master, wondering at the delicate touch of the one who could raise such compromised structures into their orbits without destroying them—

But in that moment, sweet breath overwhelmed the fetid raspberries.

Fresh berries and cinnamon and clove was the taste.

"No!" he protested, not yet ready to return, not ready to relinquish the search. But he was not heard. The sweet breath inhaled, taking his breath with it, making his head light.

{Sleep.}

"No." he protested a second time, but more weakly, and knew his battle was lost.

{Sleep, my precious Khy. . . .}

"Damn you," he whispered, as the shadows went all to black.

ᔕ   ᔕ   ᔕ

Spooky, Ganfrion decided as the strain eased eerily from Mikhyel's face. Spooky and getting more macabre by the moment. First the brothers' simultaneous collapse, then Temorii's fortuitous appearance, her possessive, wild-eyed claim on Mikhyel's limp carcass . . .

Now this. A man had to wonder what lay behind those closed eyelids as the dancer's head rose slowly, her lips seemingly reluctant to part from Mikhyel's suddenly lax mouth.

If he'd needed any more evidence to confirm his suspicions, Temorii had just supplied it. She was strong, which he would have expected of a ringdancer. That she could carry her own weight in an emergency was not altogether surprising. That she could carry Mikhyel's all the way from the caverns was on the edge of amazing.

But it was her carriage, the tilt of the chin, the easy shifts of balance as she dodged those men who would interfere with her passage . . . he'd only met one other dancer who was as much fighter as radical, and the name that dancer had given was not Temorii.

Dancer, fighter . . . magician, from the effect of that kiss . . . and what stood at Mikhyel's bedside now, eyes closed, mouth slightly open as the tongue traced the curve of lip, was neither fighter nor dancer, but something elegant, exotic—a creature that could rouse lustful thoughts in any man . . . or woman.

But not in Ganfrion gorMikhyel. Not with Mikhyel dun-Mheric's life in the balance.

"Thyerri!" Ganfrion said sharply.

The dancer's eyes blinked open. "Yes?"

"You *are* Thyerri, aren't you?"

Another blink. "Yes."

"Have you told him?" He pointed with his chin toward Mikhyel, who appeared now to be sleeping quite peacefully . . . as was his older brother, now: change one, change the other.

"Yes," Thyerri said, "I've told him."

"Good!" And, from that passionately possessive reaction on the dancer's face, there at the baths, it was just possible they'd both come through the revelation intact. Perhaps there was hope for dunMheric after all. "So . . ." Ganfrion said, "what did you just do?"

"I gave him sleep. I don't know for how long. I've got to go."

"To find Nikaenor."

"To get him off Mother's mountain before he dies. That's their only hope. —I think it is. I think it's enough."

"You *think.* You figured that out, just by touching him?"

"I followed his mind. His essence reached to Nikaenor, and beyond Nikaenor . . . It's Mother . . . or something that used to be Mother. She wants the Rhomandi brothers gone from her presence." The dancer's voice grew stronger and more positive with each breath. "The warding is building pressure in Nikaenor's head, and for all I know, that pressure is real. Eventually his head will explode . . . or something in it will burst."

"Such a charming image. The brat's not my favorite person, but he's useful. His brother wants him. Besides, it would scare the wildlife." The dancer's grim expression didn't flicker. Ganfrion sighed, and longed for someone who appreciated his humor. "Better get him back."

"I will." There was not a shred of doubt in the dancer's tone.

"How do you know where he is?"

"I know this mountain better than I know the streets of Khoratum." The dancer dropped to one knee and began removing his boots, mountain shoes with good solid soles: Ganfrion had stolen them off one of the guards that had happened in his way. But beneath the soldier's boots were still the lightweight dancer's boots that were little more than a single supple layer of well-tanned leather. "I know his direction. I know the view he had just before he fell off his horse. I can find him."

"I don't suppose there's any sense telling you not to go."

"None."

"You going to . . ." Ganfrion flapped his hands in the air.

Thyerri frowned. "I don't . . . oh, leythiate. I can't *do* that by myself."

"No, I suppose you can't," Ganfrion murmured as Thyerri removed his other boot. "You don't think maybe you should keep those on?"

"I'll be scaling cliffs. I need my grip. Don't much like shoes anyway." He stood up and held the boots out to Ganfrion. "Thank you for letting me use them."

"I'll keep them, and have the tub ready to resurrect your feet when you get back." Something in the look the youngster cast him then hid caused him to add: "You *are* coming back, aren't you?" He envisioned Mikhyel being more than upset at these entire proceedings, and didn't want to explain the loss of the dancer on top of everything else.

The dancer's slanted eyes widened the slightest degree. "You asked me if I told him I'm Thyerri. You didn't ask how he took it. —Farewell, Ganfrion. Please believe me—though I fear he never can—that I have never been, nor ever shall be, his enemy."

That was no reassuring statement.

But by the time it occurred to Ganfrion to wonder whether he should have the boy stopped and held, at least until the Rhomandi woke up, Thyerri was gone.

Chapter Three

"I cannot *believe* you didn't wake me immediately!" Lidye's billowing passage through the halls of Rhomandi House left the maids scrambling, still bent from their curtsies, after numerous objects d'art staggered by her gossamer skirts.

For her part, Kiyrstin, following in her wake and more practically if less fashionably attired in a simple linen maternity gown, kicked and brushed those gossamer folds out of her way, thereby protecting the most delicate antiques.

"You were asleep." Kiyrstin caught a tiny glass fawn and placed it back with its herd before continuing. "Mirym was out cold. So was Beauvina. It's not as if there was anything more to get from her by pressing the matter."

"You had Diorak in?"

"Naturally. She was sleeping normally by then, and *he* said to let you both rest." As they passed the children's library, one of the few spots in the huge house fortified against tantrums, and fortunately empty this morning, Kiyrstin grabbed Lidye's arm and pulled her to a stop. "*Will* you slow down before you destroy the entire house!" Lidye snarled and tried to jerk free. Kiyrstin tightened her grip and her smile. "I wouldn't try that, girl."

"How *dare* you?"

"Easily, I assure you. We've a method of getting information out of this woman that affects my husband and his concerns and I refuse to let you destroy that opportunity in a fit of childish pique."

"Your . . . *husband*?"

"Don't even tempt me into that argument." Kiyrstin

hauled Lidye into the library and closed the door. "Talk to me, girl! Tell me what you really need to know, since you have such strong opinions, and Beauvina and I will try again. But you don't go down there, Lidye, *not you*. Mirym made it very clear she would not deal with you."

Drawing herself up to her full height (which still meant, despite the high-heeled shoes she preferred, that she had to look up at Kiyrstin) Lidye tossed her pale curls back and shook herself free of Kiyrstin's hold. "I intend to discover her accomplices, of course! What do you think? The whereabouts of these *priestesses*. These superstitious *hillers* whose very existence should be repugnant to every educated Citizen in the Web!"

"And do what? Eradicate them? I doubt the Rhomandi will countenance that."

"The Rhoman—" Lidye blinked as if she'd forgotten for a moment she wasn't the absolute power in Rhomatum. It was a lapse in thinking to which the current Ringmaster of Rhomatum was disturbingly prone. Made a woman wonder just what Anheliaa had instilled in her student. "Of course we wouldn't. What the other hillers might do, those of sense, remains to be seen. I certainly believed the Rakshiri had long since been run out."

"The Rakshiri?"

"The most *pernicious* of the old religions." Lidye was wild-eyed, raving almost to herself. Kiyrstin, finding more honesty in the demeanor than the words, ceased trying to recall her attention. Ringmasters seemed prone to talking to the walls and hearing answers no one else heard. Or at least, pretending they heard. "The dance should have been outlawed from the start!" Lidye cried. "Once they interlaced the Dance of Life with the ringdance, they had the perfect cover! And who knows how far their influence permeates the Web now?" Lidye's pale blue eyes sharpened, hardened, then began to flash. "How *dare* she threaten us?"

She began to storm back and forth across the room under Kiyrstin's witness, whipping her skirts one way and the next as if she would rend the fabric, wringing her hands, beside herself with anger. "When I *think* of what we could have accomplished last night, if *only* she had given us Khoratum when I asked—" Lidye let out a scream of frustration, and with an abrupt and vicious swipe of her arm cleared an activity table of its contents. Lamp, puzzles, paper and charcoal—everything went flying. "Damn her to the eighteen winds!"

"Lidye! —Sweet Maurii, *stop it*!" Kiyrstin grabbed her and this time held her as Lidye shook with pure, unadulterated fury. Ringmasters and immaterial conversations be damned. "What is *wrong* with you? Think of the baby, if not yourself!" Her hold slipped. Blood. She grasped wrist and elbow of the arm that had cleared the table and forced it in front of Lidye's face. "Look what you've done to yourself!" A shallow gash dripped a steady, though not dangerous stream, and Lidye stared at it, the tension slowly leaving her body, sanity returning to her face.

"Is it safe to let go now?" Kiyrstin asked, and Lidye nodded. "I'm going to call for Diorak—"

"No!" Lidye said. And in a calmer voice. "No, Kiyrstin. I'm . . . rational now. I've been working . . . too long."

"You must have that arm seen to."

"There's a kit—everything this will require, in that cupboard." Lidye tipped her head toward two large carved doors that comprised half of one wall. "The key is on a ridge along the top. Please, I don't want to explain . . . *Rings,* what's happening to me?" She sank into the one chair large enough for an adult in the room of miniatures, cradling her arm, staring at the wound as if it were on someone else's body. Kiyrstin retrieved the medical kit from the indicated shelf, stifled the curiosity that wondered why Lidye was so intimately familiar with the facilities of this room . . . and knelt beside the chair.

"Give it here." She wasn't feeling much inclined toward sympathy, but she could well understand a desire to keep this most recent performance away from the ears of the household gossips. The stability of the Rings was the economic stability of the City and of the Web; Lidye, who theoretically kept them functional, wasn't seeming at all stable at the moment. She daubed the wound clean, spread an ointment marked for minor wounds on it, then bound it with a linen bandage. "You'll still need to have Diorak take a look."

"I will, I *will*! Leave off! I must think . . ." Lidye sat staring at her shaking hands—thinking, one would assume; one would hope, thinking better of the tantrum just past.

And with that hope, Kiyrstin rose to take the kit back, but Lidye grabbed her wrist, digging her nails in when Kiyrstin tried to shake her off. *"Tell me!"*

"I suggest you extract your claws while you still have them," Kiyrstin said in a low and significant tone, not unshaken, and Lidye released her, with an apology, mumbled and patently insincere. "Tell you *what*?"

"I need to know what's wrong with me." Lidye's voice held a depth of fear Kiyrstin had never heard before. All pretense, all the shrill vixen temper, was missing, so much so she wondered if she was not for the first time meeting the real Lidye dunTarec.

"I fear I'm losing my mind. That must *not* be allowed to happen. What's *happening* to me?"

Well, well, well, Kiyrstin thought, and raised a brow. "Weeping spells? Itching feet that are enough to drive you to the drink none of these folk will let you have? Irritation that turns to tantrum for no reason? Moments of feeling absolutely perfect?" She could not resist it, after all Lidye's airs and pretensions, and added her own most maddening symptom: "The feeling you should just take up permanent residency in the latrine?" She didn't require Lidye's outrage to know she'd hit a mark. "Off hand, I'd say you were pregnant."

"Don't make fun of me!"

"I wouldn't think of it. I fight the same battles daily. Welcome to the glories of Motherhood."

"Rings. I'd never have imagined . . . All these years . . ." A visible shudder set the ruffles at Lidye's neck to fluttering. "I'd thought I was past it all—the sickness, the mood shifts. Now . . . I must not let this . . . bodily aberration rule me." Lidye rocked slowly, her arms wrapped about her waist, and finally, she met Kiyrstin's eyes. "I . . . require your help, Kiyrstine romGaretti."

Aristocrat of aristocrats: as if she'd never contemplated what it took to breed. It didn't take the brothers' Talent to know how painfully those words were uttered. Kiyrstin could never warm to this woman, ever. But Lidye was Nikki's wife, and Ringmaster of Rhomatum. The pregnancy was uncharted territory for a ringmaster. And while on the one hand it was part of a process common to every female creature, what was going on in Lidye's internal conversations didn't indicate anything common.

And a part of Kiyrstin's heart was quite wickedly gratified, despite the threat to the Rhomatum Web that uncommon conflict implied.

"Well, that's a change now isn't it?" In fact, she felt almost cheerful for the first time since Deymorin had brought her back to Rhomatum. "You who are such an integral part of the Rhomandi Family requiring the help of a . . . what was the word you used? Oh, yes, Mauritumin harlot." After all, she'd seen the Mauritum Web weather far greater disturbances than anything Lidye had yet invoked on her own. "Do you suppose the Family can afford such a breach in propriety?"

And as an unstable ringmaster, Lidye was a mere novice.

Lidye's face hardened, but her reply, when it finally came, was amazingly controlled. "I owe you an apology for that. May we say it was the chemicals speaking and not my true feelings?"

"We can say that. You'll understand, I'm certain, when I say fuck you."

Prim and proper lady that she pretended to be, Lidye should have at least made a pretense of shock. Instead, she almost smiled.

"I can hardly blame you, can I? However, Rhomatum cannot afford . . . what my mind threatens. You must help me." A hard, determined swallow. "Please, Kiyrstine, I'm asking, not ordering. I must . . . stay calm."

"No argument from me on that point. What do you want

me to do?'' Kiyrstin asked, and added hopefully: "Carry a club?"

"You try to provoke me."

"Most likely. Don't mistake, I understand your concerns; I'm simply not inclined to hear a request such as this in private only to be countermanded and dressed down in public. If you're serious, yes, I'll try to help—for the sake of the Web as well as the Family. But between us, I think you might have to consider standing down from the Tower, if you can't get yourself under control."

"How dare you even suggest—"

Kiyrstin raised a brow, leaving it silent that Lidye was not the power in Rhomatum, and that when the Rhomandi came back, yes, it might be a question. If anything went wrong with the Rings, he might be back in far shorter order, and Lidye would not *be* ringmaster. Better to limp along with Nethaalye than to have a renegade . . . or even an insane mind in control.

Lidye caught her lip. Her eyes closed and she gave a frustrated growl. "After all I've conquered, I can't believe I can't master a—*yes,* I'll keep that potentiality in mind, damn it!" She rubbed her eyes hard, smearing makeup seemingly without a care. When she lowered her hands, her expression was markedly more serene, if smudged.

"Very good. Shall I take you back to your room now? Maybe a hot bath? Get that arm seen to? The makeup fixed?"

"I must see Mirym. Myself!"

"Lidye . . ."

The blonde woman went to a mirror in that same cabinet, shook her head in obvious disgust and began dabbing at her makeup with a handkerchief dampened on her tongue. A strangely practical solution and one as foreign to the Lidye Kiyrstin thought she knew as the low, resonant voice of reason.

And when Lidye had restored her face, she wrinkled her nose at her reflection and said, "Silly practice. —I believe this is quite clear-headed on my part, Kiyrstine. I have had, since you informed me of this interview with the hiller woman, this most disturbing premonition regarding her fate. I must see her for myself. I must make certain no harm has come to her."

"All right. We'll go down. But I warn you in advance: I won't let you threaten her. And I'm sending Beauvina away when we get to the room."

Lidye drew up short. "Why is that—"

Kiyrstin glared down her nose at the shorter woman, who wisely modified tone and comment.

"And why would your maid be with her?"

"She was feeling ill this morning. She is, after all—" Kiyrstin gave her rounded stomach a light pat, and Lidye shuddered.

"But I'll not have you trying to force Beauvina to speak for her," Kiyrstin said. "If you want Beauvina and me to try tomorrow, fine, but Mirym is as," she almost choked on the word, "delicate as either of us and she's already strained her abilities to tell us as much as she has."

Lidye dipped her head in acquiescence. "If you are still of that opinion when we get to the room, I will not insist."

But as it happened, Kiyrstin's opinion never came into question. When the guard opened the tiny room, Mirym was gone.

ら   ら   ら

Granite rippled in every direction, a vertical sea of frozen whitecaps, a mountain lake frozen in mid-storm and tilted on end.

It was the third such rock face Dancer had climbed since leaving the Rhomandi's camp, the first since leaving the spot on the road where Nikaenor Rhomandi had fallen, and it was by far the most wicked set of switchbacks, seeming at times to curl back on him in ways quite contrary to memory of his first assessment of the climb. It was as if the shape of the mountain warped to delay and confound.

Yet one knew that not even Mother had that ability, not with solid granite. One blamed rather a hazed and battered mind for the confusion of direction. And now, with darkness closing around him and his body aching and numb, he aimed for the next switchback in the leyroad (unless all reality had deserted him and the road had moved) where he intended to check the ground for spoor. From there he trusted he would still see well enough in the world above to judge whether to go forward or back.

A hand slipped, bloodied fingertips losing purchase. Dancer took that as a warning and paused, gathering breath and calming shaken nerves.

He was tired. More tired than he'd hoped was the case before he'd started this climb, but not so tired as he'd feared. He'd danced the dance of his life yesterday—twice. That he was able to contemplate this run at all was due solely to the energizing air above the new node. It was no wonder to him that Ganfrion's wounds had failed to destroy him. The Khoramali welcomed Ganfrion's essence; the new node nurtured him. Ganfrion was *of* the Khoramali as many who had been born and lived their lives here were not, and so the budding node tried to claim his essence, to make him one and well. Had Ganfrion stayed at the birthlake as Dancer had urged, he might well have returned to the camp whole again.

But Ganfrion had left him, insisting it was to return the horse, though they both knew it was out of concern for Mikhyel that he'd gone back to camp.

You are returning, aren't you?

Was he returning to Mikhyel? Would he? Would he willfully entangle his life any further with Mikhyel dunMheric's? If it were just Mikhyel, the answer would be simple. But with Mikhyel came Rhomandi and dunMheric, and with those names, came a sometimes stranger.

The last ray of sunlight vanished, and the short mountain twilight surrounded him. Soon total darkness would rule this moonless night, and strand him on the sea of granite. Before his muscles froze and shivers threatened his grip, he began working his way upward again. He closed his eyes rather than even attempt to see where to put his hands in the now-treacherous light. He felt the shape of the stone, fitting fingers and toes into the crannies, minding the blood that made holds slick and uncertain.

Bare toes, the dancer's boots having shredded long before he began this climb. Once, for the Dancer that had been, it would have made no difference, but Temorii's feet had grown soft in the *rijhili* footware Mikhyel dunMheric had provided her. Boots, shoes, even slippers for inside on smooth floors.

In that one sense, at least, he was more Thyerri now than he was Dancer or Temorii.

And where Mikhyel dunMheric would lead the one he would introduce as Thyerri, far more than footware would change the shape of his life. The town that was Khoratum had been a blemish on Mother's mountain, but at least that town had been in the mountains. The mountain breezes had greeted him every morning, the music of the mountain had lulled him to sleep every night. In valley-bound Rhomatum, they said, the air was all sealed inside the buildings. Pushed about by great compressors that forced it, like the water, underground to human-carved leythium chambers to be purified and warmed—or cooled—before returning to the buildings.

Purified air. As if anything could be more pure than what he drew into his lungs with each gasping breath. He'd heard about it. Rhyys had yearned after such a system for Khoratum Tower; but he hadn't believed until he saw it all inside Mikhyel's head: the compressors, the fans, the huge leythium-lined purification chambers, the leythium-powered heaters. . . .

Fingers sank into a hollow and further, a crag eroded and topped a ledge that accepted a full arm's grip, and signaled the end of the climb. Another few body lengths and he set himself among boulders with increasingly flat pockets of earth and trees clinging grimly to the not-quite cliff, pockets that offered tempting resting spots. He resisted their lure, striking out for the true forest of mossy earth and undergrowth and seasons of fallen leaves and pine needles.

All too soon, his body began to cool in the wind. Sweat chilled his skin, and weariness shook his bones.

A sense of new life, of warmth in the darkness: a tree lay in his path, an ancient defender in its time, its powerful roots providing security for the youth of the forest plants. Fallen now, the defender turned mother, nursing offspring in her decaying substance. The wind was cold, but the essence here was warm, welcoming, and he curled for a moment in a pocket formed by that fallen tree, a nest lined with moss and sweet pine needles, and begged a small portion of her dying warmth for himself.

Life from life. The way of the mountain. The way of the Ley itself.

The humans who had capped and directed the leythium nodes understood that truth after a fashion. They gave their dead and all the detritus that hundreds of thousands of inhabitants (Dancer shivered, the numbers incomprehensible to him) could produce.

But at the same time, they starved their Ley Mothers of that which they needed most. Mother had said it often; she was nothing without her children. When they ceased to believe, Mother would be gone forever.

And Darius, the original Rhomandi, whose dreams had led the Exodus out of Mauritum, the Exodus that had in turn led to the creation of Rhomatum and all her slave nodes, had insisted on the death of true worship. Those who lived in the node cities now regarded the Ley as a commodity. A *thing* to be bought and sold.

Mikhyel and his brothers, despite the evidence of their eyes, still clung to such notions, seeking explanations for Mother and their own node's essence.

Under the Rhomandi, the nodes had starved. Only Khoratum, uncapped for three hundred years, and with all the true believers gathering around her, had remained intact and grown strong. Beneath that mountain, Mother had complained often enough of the foolishness of her siblings, but how could she blame them when those who lived in the surface world denied her existence?

Temorii despised the rijhili for their ignorance. Thyerri

strove, for love of Mikhyel, to understand it, and both, for love of Mother, hoped to help Mikhyel see the truth before it was too late.

It was overall incomprehensible to Dancer, and exhaustion argued that he let the *rijhili* go. That what happened to Nikaenor dunMheric happened and was none of it his fault.

Exhaustion ached in his body. His weariness argued it was too dark, that he had taken too long and might as well give up, that by the time he found the leyroad, it would be impossible to tell had someone passed or not and how recently and in what direction. The ancient tree-turned-mother would be a safe place to spend the night. No one, not even Ganfrion, expected him to make it to Nikaenor, had Ganfrion not said as much? and so why not let them be right? Mikhyel would live. He had assured that before he left.

But Mikhyel's need still haunted him, and the thought of Mikhyel's joy when his brother returned safe ended the battle that raged within and through him.

A battle, Dancer had finally admitted, somewhere along the second cliff face, that must be Mother's doing. Mother wanted her children to return, she wanted no Rhomandi raising the Khoratum Rings again and directing her energy toward senseless tasks.

Mother wanted her children back and safe.

She'd lost Dancer to the Rhomandi; she would lose no more.

Lost Dancer—or sacrificed. She'd needed Mikhyel dunMheric last night, not Dancer, and though every heartbeat cried out against it, Dancer very much feared now that his function all along *had* been to enthrall Mikhyel with the Ley.

That Mother had lost Khoratum to a Rhomandi and so needed to use a Rhomandi to gain back Khoratum had a certain symmetry of pattern.

That Mother had wanted Mikhyel kept in Khoratum until the last moment, and wanted his leaving to cause the maximum disruption also made sense now. She had needed the Towers fighting amongst themselves as much as she'd needed the Rhomandi brothers' presence to provide a focal point for the new node . . . *her* new node, *her* need, *her* making, *her* child.

All aimed at her own escape.

And if, in the process, she granted her once-child Dancer his dream of the dance, perhaps she counted the debt paid.

There were times—Dancer's throat tightened and he swallowed hard, burying his sweat-dampened face in his arm within his safe nook—there were times when Mother's sense of 'equity' reminded one strongly of the Barrister's.

No. He couldn't sleep. Dancer was bound to the Rhomandi's pattern, not Mother's, and part of that pattern could not lie here while other parts shattered.

But exhaustion was right in one sense. He couldn't see the road now, and reason had come to him in his rest. In order to find Nikaenor . . . he hadn't the strength to waste searching, and yet, thinking of the pattern, he could, if he closed his eyes, pinpoint Mikhyel's position back at the camp without the least effort.

He'd never tried to locate anyone else that way. But through Mikhyel, when he looked for Mikhyel's sense of his brothers, he knew the pattern of Nikaenor's thoughts.

And knowing Nikaenor's pattern, being part of the whole, it would seem he should be able to . . .

Like a warning fire blazing on a hilltop, he *knew*.

He pulled himself to his feet, thanked the tree and the leaves for their help, and stumbled downhill toward that flame.

〆　〆　〆

The Rings beat that steady rhythm they had begun last night, that rhythm Lidye so vocally feared to disrupt.

And Lidye sat now, hand clenched on Nethaalye's, trying to draw on Nethaalye's ringspinning Talent as well as her own to force the Rings to her bidding, to help her locate Mirym through the pulse of leyforce that ran throughout the Web.

Personally, Kiyrstin placed more faith in the guards they'd sent to scour the City and block the gates in the old defensive wall.

Which was to say she really didn't think they had a chance in hell of finding the girl.

Which was to say she thought Lidye ran a completely unnecessary risk in using the Rings in this fashion, and if something went wrong, she was going to be here as witness.

And she was here because she'd promised Lidye, and if Lidye appeared to tip over the edge of judgment in the quest for the missing woman, she was honor bound to try and tip her back.

Beauvina sat at Kiyrstin's side the while, shivering, still barely awake, but insisting she be there in case Kiyrstin needed her.

Guilt-ridden, for all the girl could hardly be asked to bear that responsibility. They'd found her asleep in the cell's narrow bed, wearing only her shift and petticoat, which implied Mirym had escaped the cell by impersonating Beauvina. The guard confirmed the maid had left earlier, but considering the vast difference in coloring, not to mention body shape and size, and the fact the guard swore "Beauvina" had spoken to him, it had taken far more than Beauvina's clothing to execute the illusion.

And if Mirym had some of Mother's ability to change her appearance at will, the way Kiyrstin saw it, Mirym would not return to Rhomandi House unless and until Mirym wanted to.

Vina wasn't the only one feeling just a bit guilty. Had it not been for her own interference, Kiyrstin said to herself, Mirym would likely still be under lock and key. In all fairness, any anger at her disappearance should be turned toward her.

In fact, Lidye's anger appeared minimal. Since their meeting in the library, she'd been intensely focused. More, fighting the stubborn Rings for tiny vibrations of information kept Lidye calm and focused.

Still, she'd promised, and so she'd had the stack of mail that had accumulated despite her efforts brought up to the

Tower, and so she sat amidst that same mail strewn in stacks about a dainty writing table here in the glass-encased, uppermost point in the City, watching darkness fall and the lights of the City flicker into life, reflection of the stars flickering into life overhead.

It was the only time and the only venue from which Rhomatum resembled the City in which she'd lived most of her life.

But the letters all had a familiar ring: men of the City and others about the Web who hoped to use her to get the ear of her husband. Never mind Deymorin was not in fact her husband, legally speaking. The point was that those who had met her seemed to think she could influence him . . . which, truth to tell, she could.

Fortunately once they'd met her, the scoundrels among them ceased to cross her path and the power brokers ceased to think they could influence her with anything other than candor and a deserving cause.

There were times she truly enjoyed standing as tall—in every sense—as the average man. And compared to the voices within Garetti's circle or the Maritumin court, most of the Rhomatumin leaders were both charmingly polite and frighteningly naive.

Of all the Rhomatum web node cities, Rhomatum herself was the most insular. Lying as she did at the hub of the Web, virtually all of her direct dealing was with her own satellite nodes; those satellite nodes in turn dealt with the world beyond the Web and had some notion there were other customs.

But none of them, absolutely none of those she had dealt with, had a flea's notion of a cat how to function as a nation. They gloried in their autonomy, frequently exaggerating their differences from their fellow Syndicate members for the sake of being different. Unique.

And terribly inefficient.

And silly. Surface gloss, when underneath, they were all still children of Maurislan. It was all still self-interest, self-interest, self-interest. Altruism for the abstract of the Web had not made its way into Rhomatumin thinking.

Combined with their political autonomy, it meant the Rhomatum Syndicate functioned like a snake with eighteen heads, each trying to go a different direction.

Mikhyel was trying. Maurii love an innocent, he was trying to bring a unified vision to the Syndicate, but he couldn't do it on his own.

She scanned the newest installment from Kharl Varishmondi, head of House Varishmondi, Shatum's shipping magnate. In response to a request from Mikhyel, he was trying to reestablish another shipping line he'd bought out . . . run out of business, if the truth were known: he'd gulped down a small shipper who had had no chance at competing, once Varishmondi decided to take over his routes at a loss.

And once Varishmondi had claimed the rich route between Mosaiidum and Orenum, the one route that had kept the Pobriichi in business at all, he'd dumped the smaller routes cold. The Pobriichi were out, bought out at fire sale prices, and the fishing villages were reduced to overland trade because there was no more shipping service.

Pobriichi himself had committed suicide, his wife had turned prostitute to survive, and his son was in Sparingate Prison following an attempt to murder Varishmondi.

Personally, she didn't blame young Pobriichi in the least, for all it had been foolish: to lose a father to suicide and a mother to prostitution and his own future security to Varishmondi's greed all in a matter of months was enough to push anyone over the edge, let alone a newly married, soon to be a father himself, nineteen-year-old only child.

And neither, once he'd begun to fathom the whole, had the man who'd had to commit the boy to the prison blamed the boy. In the midst of a national crisis Mikhyel had continued his journey to Khoratum, but had sent a letter to her, asking if she would mind looking into the situation. He'd indicated that they'd talk about it when he returned and he'd decide exactly what to do then, but to have the boy housed on the upper levels of Sparingate and to write Varishmondi that the Rhomandi had a serious interest in the matter: that to have those fishing villages go under would devastate the economy of the region.

She'd looked into it, gotten the understanding of the warden, written Varishmondi, and Varishmondi, knowing the whole (and hoping to curry favor with the Rhomandi) had flamboyantly offered to adopt young Pobriichi, to stand for him, and reestablish the shipping routes in question under the Varishmondi banner.

Naturally young Pobriichi, from his relatively comfortable cell, and predictably hard-headed pride, had declined to even consider the offer.

Meanwhile the fishermen were without canvas and netting, long timbers and tar, and Varishmondi's ship cats had a more varied diet than the fishermen's children.

That was the other half of the problem. A man like Varishmondi tried, for admittedly personal reasons, and met a log-jam from the other side. Everyone had an overwhelmingly important reason to have his way, protect his interests—or damnable pride. They had not yet ascended to the concept of favor-trading on the scale of a nation. They had not learned to yield advantages to secure a greater, abstract, and deferred good. They wanted it guaranteed, and in percentages.

And no matter the political philosophy that gave the nodes legal independence, practically, the Syndicate operated as a unified empire. There a former resident of ancient Mauritum had some better notion how an empire functioned. And so Mikhyel turned to her. And so, increasingly, did other players in this strange game into which she'd been dealt.

And so she sat, writing endless letters, treading the delicate path of a woman with insight and connections but no personal power, a person to whom these individuals revealed more than they knew, couching advice in words that encouraged the prideful to believe they'd thought of the notion in the first place, and the timid to believe they had the right to expectations. . . .

Actually, it wasn't that different from her life with Garetti, aside from the fact that these negotiations involved letters rather than bedrooms. The only bedroom involved in this life included a tall and elegantly proportioned man with a glorious mane of hair and even more glorious lust for life. . . .

Sweet Maurii, she missed him.

She missed his big hands that snuck up behind her as she wrote, hands that located and ruthlessly pulverized all the knots that had formed since the last such attack. Not timid, her new man, not missishly frightened of hurting her delicate flesh: he knew his strength and hers and lovingly but effectively tended her needs, not her image.

She missed the sweet scent of the lotion he used, and the warmth of the oil as those same sensitive hands rubbed it into her expanding stomach.

She missed the joy and wonder in his eyes every time he touched that growing mound, a joy that shattered her concerns about her shifting figure, and helped her discover her own joy in the discomforts necessarily connected to maternity.

She pitied Lidye her vanity, in that sense. Lidye, who had banished Nikki from their bedchamber the moment her body began to change. Lidye, who hired dress designers to create garments that would hide those changes. Lidye, who with that isolation set a distance between herself and her young husband. It was a distance, she very much feared, nothing would ever bridge. In some ways, Nikki was very like his oldest brother.

There was, she thought, as she set the seal Deymorin had given her on her response to Varishmondi, a greater war of different worlds here in Rhomatum Tower than anywhere else in the Web.

Nethaalye, Mikhyel's longtime friend, (and, in her quiet way, Mikhyel's coconspirator for a unified future) was Giephaetumin, and yet was here, helping direct the Rhomatum Tower. Granted, that participation stemmed from a marriage proposal that had fallen somewhere by the wayside, but Nethaalye had defied her father to be here, to devote herself to that unified vision.

And Lidye, for all she sought to be viewed as a Rhomandi, was Shatumin, another transplant, a figurehead, if nothing else, for her fellow Shatumin citizens to consider when it came to policy decisions. She stood for their interests; they, for hers. If Lidye, so close to the source of those decisions, supported a proposal coming out of Rhomatum, might not that proposal be, at least in part, a Shatumin proposal, and so, might it not be in their best interests to support it?

On such shallow considerations were world-changing decisions based. Not always, but often enough to tip at least a few scales. Influences were spreading on a practical level. It wanted someone with Mikhyel's organizational thinking, his skills in negotiation, to forge a more stable cooperation. It wanted someone with Deymio's touch to win the hearts of citizens and talk with common folk about their concerns.

And oh, she wished he were back, to deal with Lidye's tempers and Mirym's disappearance and all the rest that threatened hour by hour to come unraveled.

They had the Rings working. They had faced the powers that would challenge the very heart of the Rhomandi influence—and won.

But it was a flawed victory. The fragmented Khoratum Ring, still lying in pieces on the tiled floor, its dust still filling the corners of the chamber, waiting for Deymorin's return . . . that shattered ring warned them all that it was by the skin of their teeth they survived, that things were not now what they had been for all of Anheliaa's long tenure, and that another dawn might see more crises.

They would forge a new ring and raise it—when the Rhomandi was back to oversee the process. Persitum, the connective tissue between the Mauritum and the Rhomatum Webs, was at the moment in a power crisis, having lost Rhomatum thanks to the destruction of the ring and Mauritum in (she would imagine) a temper snit from Garetti. When one of those rings went up, Persitum would have its connection back to a greater web.

But Khoratum was gone. Anheliaa's legacy, the symbol of her unprecedented power over the largest aggregation of node cities in history, gone. And those citizens who had extended their lives into those areas of the extended umbrella, those business interests who had expanded to take advantage of the energy surge, all of those who had thought they'd gambled and won . . .

She picked up another letter, scanned it, and sighed.

. . . were pissed.

She wanted Deymio back, safe, hers. She wanted her hour, amid the rest.

She wanted to give him the letters, and Lidye, and the reports of problems hanging fire and let someone who had the authority to make a decision decide—not console, not comfort, not advise, but settle Lidye's damnable temper and get her away from the Rings, if that was what had to be done.

She didn't like waiting for calamity.

Chapter Four

The pressure in Deymorin's head vanished, without warning and completely.

{*Nikki!*} he called out, fearing the worst, and when that gained him no answer, sent an alarmed silent inquiry toward Mikhyel—

And met head on that deep, near-comatose sleep. That state had characterized Mikhyel's mind ever since late that afternoon, when he'd waked from his own catatonic lapse with a head that felt the size of a freight-hauler's balloon and a body limp as that same balloon deflated.

It was just possible he could move now. He was and had been flat on his back on a borrowed cot in his own tent for what felt like days but was, he knew, only a few hours. His back hurt, his leg throbbed, and his feet itched, and the damned cot was too small. *Mikhyel* had his cot.

Put there, so Ganfrion had informed him, by Dancer before Dancer left, shortly before Deymorin had roused.

Dancer had gone off cross country after Nikki, so Ganfrion had also informed him, and a messenger was dispatched up the line, all to bring Nikki down, away from the source of that pressure . . . knowledge Dancer must have gleaned in link with Mikhyel, because neither Mikhyel nor he had been in any shape to explain verbally what they saw or felt.

So all that could be done had been done, and in the condition he had been in, he'd been utterly useless.

So he'd waited. He waited, and between-times gave way to the more and less of pressure in his head, prepared for a battle that had never quite manifested as he had expected.

He'd been prepared for pain. For an attack such as Anheliaa had perpetrated on him more than once. Or perhaps a recalling, a chasing after a mind hovering on the edge of oblivion, such as he'd once chased after Mikhyel. Or a battle for control, of wits, of sheer power against power . . .

He'd been utterly unprepared for this sudden and total cessation of pressure.

This silence. This ominous light-headed silence.

He pushed himself up off the cot, groaned and slumped back as muscles and nerves, coiled in defense for hours, rebelled.

"Want some help?"

The question floated out of the shadows that memory said held Mikhyel.

"Ganfrion? How's Khyel?"

"The same. Help? Yes or no? Last time I tried, you about sent me through the wall. I've no interest in repeating the experience."

He didn't even remember the moment. "Sorry." He tried to stand up, and his head swam. "Yeah, give me a hand. Rings, I can hardly see straight."

"So stay put."

"I want to see Khyel for myself."

"Suit yourself." A hand under his elbow steadied him, and he crossed the tent to sink into the blanket-cushioned chair still warm from Ganfrion's backside.

By the light of the single oil lamp, he could make out Mikhyel's face.

Peaceful. Evincing none of the tension that made his own body ache from skin to gut. It was Dancer's doing, that peaceful sleep, also according to Ganfrion's earlier report.

But it would help ease his fears now to have Mikhyel back. Mikhyel's was the strongest talent, and Mikhyel had the link to Dancer. He might be able to reach . . . someone. Dancer or even Nikki himself, find out what the hell was happening.

He took Mikhyel's hand, sought his mind with determination, and this time he felt a stirring, a hint of real thought.

{Khyel?} he whispered into that flutter, but as if warned off, the flutter vanished.

"What time is it?" he asked Ganfrion, aside.

"Near dawn," Ganfrion muttered.

"You've been here all night?"

"Where else?"

GorMikhyel indeed.

"You sent out a messenger?"

"Yes."

"Good." Deymorin sighed and closed his eyes, letting his head fall back against the cushioned top rung of the chair back. "I *think* someone has done . . . something." He tried to assume the happiest outcome. "Nikki must be well on his way down . . . from wherever."

{He'll be here in a few hours, Deymorin.}

"Khyel?"

{I'm . . . awake, Deymorin, but don't shout. Please.}

"Rhomandi?"

{He's awake.}

"Rhomandi!"

{Have to *talk* to Gan, Deymio. Words.}

Hint of humor in Mikhyel's mental whisper.

"Rings. —Sorry, Gan—*gorMikhyel.*" He kept his voice low out of deference to his brother's request. He knew the feeling. Intimately. "He's awake. Just not much for talking yet."

"Spooky, the way you just fade out." Ganfrion had moved to the foot of Mikhyel's cot. "I saw him do it once or twice. Thought I was dealing with a damned madman."

Mikhyel murmured, eyes still shut, "I apologize for scaring you, little boy." To which Ganfrion snarled, and Deymorin laughed aloud. "The gift has proven useful, however." Mikhyel resumed inanimate status.

"It's how he always *knew* what you were up to, wasn't it? Damned bastard always left me believing messengers were getting past me."

"Sometimes Mikhyel has an unusual sense of humor."

"You could say that."

{I hear you,} Mikhyel said.

{Of course you do. Going to wake up and defend yourself? Sit up?}

{Cruel.}

But Mikhyel's pale eyes did flicker open, drifted past Deymorin's with a mental acknowledgment; stopped when they reached their object. "Hello, Gan."

"So you're going to live." Ganfrion's was not the tone of a man who had spent the night at Mikhyel's side, but rather that of a dejected man who might have just that instant walked in hoping to discover him otherwise.

And the shadowed uncertainty that crept through the link from Mikhyel implied that Mikhyel, at least, wasn't certain Ganfrion's dejection was jest.

"Thanks to you?" Mikhyel asked, and Ganfrion shrugged.

"Among others. You didn't warn me you were prone to fits."

A low sound escaped Mikhyel. It might have been laughter. "Thought I was over them. What—" His mouth worked a bit, and Deymorin's mouth grew suddenly dry.

"Get him a drink, will you?" Deymorin asked Ganfrion, but the gorman had already fetched pitcher and cup from the small table. The same table also harbored the single camplight, whose soft glow, unshaded now, caught Mikhyel's pale face as he pushed himself up on one elbow to drain the cup. Twice Ganfrion refilled it.

"What happened?" Mikhyel asked again, in a normal, if low voice. "I seem to remember—" His face hardened. *"Where's Thyerri?"*

Thyerri, not Temorii. Deymorin wondered if his brother even realized what he'd revealed to Ganfrion in that seemingly simple question.

"Thank you so much for pointing out the connection, brother. Gan, Thyerri and Temorii are—"

"I know, Khyel. Don't waste your energy."

{That wasn't what I was thinking.} Deymorin thought defensively.

{That's what I choose to hear, all the same. Nikki's safe,

that's what counts. What I think about Dancer, and *where* Dancer may be, and *why* . . . is my own damn business.}

{As you wish.}

"So," Mikhyel said, pushing himself upright and sweeping his hair back, "is someone going to explain what's been going on?"

§ § §

Ganfrion made his report, then retreated to the stool on the outside of the tent door, resolved to leave the brothers to their strange half-conversation. It was as if they forgot whether they spoke aloud or in silence, and if a man tried to follow that thread, he could rapidly be driven to seek out that ley-touched flask still wandering the camp somewhere, creating legends in its wake.

He'd leave altogether, but Mikhyel had requested him stay, so here he sat, out in the cold, wrapped in a borrowed wool cloak and staring out across a hillside dotted with campfires mostly burning low, exchanging occasional quips with the Rhomandi's sentries, who seemed finally to have accepted he wasn't a spy or assassin, while a faint glow to the east and the sounds of wakening wildlife heralded the end of a second seemingly endless night.

The last of the glittering air had finally faded sometime last night, for which he would be thankful, if the aches of his wounds hadn't doubled and a bone deep weariness set in at the same time; he had the notion the magical air had relieved the pain, and he wondered now if that magical flask had run dry at last.

The leyroad, down which dunMheric's party should arrive, and up which he'd sent the messenger, lay just to the north of the camp—invisible from here, now the lights of the predawn camp had gone to their lowest. Thyerri had disappeared into the woods on the southern side of the camp, claiming the faster route began there. And indeed, the leyroad was by no means a direct route, but followed instead the sometimes arbitrary path of the underground leythium river, a river of oozing crystal and pockets of liquid, according to the experts. That underground seepage of leythium kept the roadside clear of concealing undergrowth and incidentally kept the roadside lights aglow on their wooden poles, allowing the safe flow of traffic at all hours. Leyroads were the highroads of the Web, and even in this forsaken place, a lone light burned, miles from its mates.

Not that anyone in their right mind traveled the Khoramali at night, lights or no lights.

He hoped Thyerri had found young dunMheric before darkness set in.

He hoped the elder Rhomandis' current peace of mind meant that Thyerri had accomplished his mission himself, and that the youngest had not turned up simply by the result of the courier's efforts.

He'd had his suspicions about the dancer, still did on certain fronts, but wish him . . . her . . . ill, that he never could, not after all the dancer had done, all he'd risked for Mikhyel's sake, the unmistakable love he radiated for Mikhyel. That Mikhyel didn't trust the dancer any longer was obvious. Mikhyel, sitting stone-faced during his report, had pronounced the dancer gone, returned to Mother or Rhyys or wherever he chose to go, and good riddance.

But as accomplished a liar as the Barrister was, Ganfrion had seen the disbelief on the face of the Rhomandi, who could tap the feelings behind that cold visage and tone.

For that matter, he'd seen the depth of Mikhyel's feelings for Temorii, had himself questioned the effect those feelings were having on Mikhyel's judgment, and strongly doubted Mikhyel's newly professed indifference now that he found out it was Temorii-Thyerri. The lust might have vanished in the flames of betrayal, but anger, suspicion . . . those flared hot and bright on that fuel.

No, an obsession such as Mikhyel's for the Khoratumin ringdancer did not fizzle quietly to indifference. If anything happened to Thyerri—if indeed the dancer did not return, he could be quite certain gorMikhyel's duties would include tracking that elusive creature down.

Not that he'd be reluctant.

For his own part, while he was still curious: *was* the dancer one of the Children? should he call the kid *Thyerri, Temorii,* or something else? what he really wanted were more details regarding the dancer's relationship with Rhyys. He wanted any particulars he/she might have gleaned regarding the former ringmaster of Khoratum— because the Khoratum Ring might be down, the line itself dead, but someone, from the early reports coming down from the Rhomandi's eyes and ears within and without the city, still survived in the Tower itself . . . and that made Rhyys a current, live issue.

Someone, before much time had passed, would have to go back into Khoratum to ferret out the details, and he assumed that someone would also be Ganfrion gorMikhyel.

Anything, he strongly suspected, any excuse to keep gorMikhyel out of Rhomatum, where his previous life would prove a singular embarrassment to his singularly respectable employer. The Rhomandi could be charitable out here. Socially speaking, inside the lily-handed society of the elite, when the Rhomandi was trying to win high-born support for his plans? He was a liability.

Unkind thoughts had to wonder how much of Mikhyel's resentment toward the dancer was rooted in that same obsessive cognizance of *appearances.* Months of close association had given gorMikhyel far too great an understanding of the man who, at a very tender age, had assumed the difficult role of proxy to the highest post in the Syndicate. Mikhyel had fought a long bitter battle against the assumptions of his seniors: assumptions about his young age, about his frail appearance and most of all about his association with Anheliaa . . . he'd fought those notions and won a grudging respect from those hide-bound aristocratic old bluebloods as a voice worth hearing.

Mikhyel had fought and Mikhyel had *been* the Rhomandi, in every sense but legal, until this latest, ill-fated incident, when his brother had sailed back into power, roused up his connections among the nodes, and with little more to endorse him than his title and a winning smile, raised an army.

Mikhyel's pride had taken a thorough beating when he'd found it expedient to play obedient fool to his brother's return to power, because there was no stopping the rush that was Deymorin, and for Mikhyel, pride would ever take second chair to expedience. With Anheliaa dead and Deymorin returned, many had assumed Mikhyel had all along been only a mouthpiece for whoever ruled House Rhomandi. Mikhyel had used that misconception, played it to get what he wanted from the types who reacted well to Deymorin's back-thumping, plain-spoken style.

But while the price to Mikhyel's pride had been high, he'd grown as a man in paying that price—and in getting beyond the safe walls of Rhomatum, if only Mikhyel had the wit to see the growth.

Given time, he had no doubt Mikhyel would have put all that had happened into perspective, had been well on the way to that reconciliation just that morning. It was this second blow to Mikhyel's pride, this weakness in love, that threatened to do the damage. The pride Mikhyel hoped to restore upon his return to Rhomatum in success now had a problem: the very nature of the individual, the ringdancer, who had become indelibly linked to him in gossip and, as of the dance competition, in fact.

The dancer, regardless how deserving of Mikhyel's love, would eventually raise all the questions now churning in Mikhyel dunMheric's gut throughout Rhomatum. Dancer's person would become the prime fodder for gossip mills, law courts and council halls, not only in Rhomatum, but elsewhere. In the minds of all those whose renewed faith and respect he sought, here was Mikhyel the Barrister, who'd fallen in love not only with a ringdancer—which affair had already rippled throughout the Web—but with a Child of Rakshi.

Worse, in that choosing, Mikhyel had given up the hand of Nethaalye dunGiebhaidi, a lady of the utmost respectability, a lady whose father and brother had been key players in the rebellion, who had herself defied her family to side with Mikhyel.

The people of Rhomatum would take any acceptance of

the situation by Nethaalye as evidence of her stirling virtue and dunMheric's vice. And the lady in question *would* accept, graciously and honestly, of that Ganfrion had no doubt. Long before Dancer arrived on the scene, she had given up any claim to Mikhyel's amorous affections or name, giving herself to his cause for belief in the cause and his judgment, not for Mikhyel himself.

She valued, so she'd said to Ganfrion once, Mikhyel's friendship far too much to jeopardize it for the sake of a marriage to which he couldn't commit his heart.

That her heart had been committed, Ganfrion also had no doubt. But it had been, to his observation, a gentle, warm commitment, not the flaring desire that could fuse two hearts into one.

He'd spent several days in Lady Nethaalye's company, escorting her to Rhomatum after she sided with the Rhomandi against her own father and brother, and found her to be a lady of quiet elegance, intelligence, courage, loyalty—

Obviously a woman of taste: she laughed at Ganfrion's jokes—even before he was gorMikhyel.

There was a woman.

Not, however, for the likes of him.

Voices rose inside. Ganfrion advised the guards to sudden deafness and stepped back inside where Mikhyel was sitting on the bed, a lump beneath a swirl of blankets.

"Khyel, I don't like that look, or the rumblings you're letting leak out." Rhomandi's voice carried even at a whisper. At this moment he wasn't whispering.

"Let's just say I'll be curious who all comes down the mountain."

"And if Dancer's not with them?"

"I'll have my answer, won't I?"

"Or your dancer will have killed himself trying to save your hide—again," Ganfrion broke in, and ignoring the gray eyes glaring balefully at him from above those blankets: "You're giving the boys at the door an earful, gentlemen."

"Tell them twenty paces, gorMikhyel," Rhomandi said quietly, and Ganfrion waved the lads in question out of hearing range, then took his own post inside the open flap. The guards by now knew what he was, knew why he stayed in reach of Mikhyel, for good or for ill, when they were moved out of range of the family argument, on the Rhomandi's order.

Ganfrion stood, half in, half out, watching dawn spread over the hillside, and observing the stirring of soldiers, back on their regular schedule.

Inside, Mikhyel said in a much moderated tone: "Thyerri is . . . not dead. I'd know." And the pained, tormented shadow that passed quickly across Mikhyel's face by the camplight roused only a desire to shake sense into Mikhyel's stubborn pride.

But that admission confirmed Ganfrion's suspicion that Thyerri shared the brothers' gift: sharing minds, sharing bodies . . . and those two had made love.

A man whose experience was . . . extensive . . . could only wonder how *that* would be; or how it would affect that stubborn Rhomandi pride when it went sour.

"As for saving my hide," Mikhyel continued stubbornly, "how do we know Dancer wasn't part of some plot that sent Nikki up that mountain into trouble in the first place? Or at least a faction delighted when he chose to go. Making their point fairly clearly, aren't they?"

"You've no reason to believe Dancer's a part of that."

"Haven't I? The last thing *I* recall was Dancer's lips sucking the very life from me. For my own good, you assure me. I'm not so certain. I was well on my way toward tracking whatever was attacking us when he so conveniently put me in that sense-deprived oblivion."

"Try again, brother," Rhomandi said. "You were *out*. And you weren't doing damned much good for yourself *or* Nikki."

Ganfrion, his face aimed again out the door, avoided pointing out that Deymorin had been more out than his brother. Why undermine a good argument with an annoying truth?

"Believe what you want," Mikhyel persisted. "I *know* what happened. The attack was coming out of Khoratum.

Something on that hill was trying to keep Nikki from coming any closer. And the Rings there were *up,* I'd swear to it."

"That's impossible, Khyel," Ganfrion felt compelled to put in. "We've had the early reports, and the Khoratum Tower is down. Blasted."

Rhomandi shot him an accusatory look and he shrugged, turning his back on the brothers again. He'd tried to wake the commander. Got himself tossed across the room for his troubles. The report was on the commander's desk. Damned if he'd bother explaining.

"Doesn't mean they can't raise the Rings, Gan, if the Rings are intact. Rhyys and Vandoshin were both involved last night; they know to beware of us now, and that attack was aimed squarely at Nikki. *Only* at Nikki, in that whole party."

There was a limit to tolerance for self-flagellation.

Ganfrion came into the tent and dropped the flap behind him. "And I suppose, because Rhyys is involved, Thyerri plunging off to save your brother is just more evidence of his duplicity." Ganfrion made no attempt to hide his contempt of Mikhyel's new condemnation of everything the dancer touched, and Rhomandi, from his emphatic nod to continue, quite agreed with him. "You can twist anything to read any way you want, dunMheric. You didn't see the look on the kid's face, not when he commandeered your carcass yesterday, not when he took off up that mountainside."

"And *you* have no idea what instructions he might have been receiving to cause whatever you thought you saw in that look! Loss of his pass into Rhomatum? Recall to Rhyys' loving arms? Possibly being told to stay with me? He views me as the worst kind of rijhili, he's made that plain enough from the start. Only Rhyys' and Mother's wishes could have forced him to ignore his disgust and carry on."

"Step down from that one, Suds. I've seen the bruises Rhyys' 'loving arms' left on him. I saw the look on his face when he exited Rhyys' audience, and damn well felt the bone-deep shakes when he betrayed Rhyys. Hell, yes, I've had my doubts about him. I've had my doubts about Temorii. *Mostly* I've had my doubts about their effect on *your* thinking! If Rhyys was involved last night, hell! worry about Rhyys, not about a kid I watched damn near kill himself getting you out of Khoratum!"

"For *Mother's* sake," Mikhyel said, with that maddening calm. "Mother wanted me out of Khoratum and here with my brothers. Her minion provided the diversion until she could get herself organized to get me out. Mother had her reasons. *Dancer* has no reasons without her."

Dancer: a name as ambiguous as the kid. Appropriate. And because Dancer had shades of gray all about him, Mikhyel was determined to think the worst of him.

"And nothing anyone can say will shake you from that opinion, will it, Suds?" he said out of those thoughts. "You can't handle the notion that someone actually cares about you. Can't handle even the possibility that that brave young kid is so crazy in love with you he'd do anything to save your skinny, arrogant hide? You're determined to free yourself of this burdensome business by any means at your disposal. Well, far be it from *gorMikhyel* to question his lord's precious delusions."

Both the brothers' faces were unreadable masks now.

So, well, likely he'd overstepped his bounds. Likely now he'd be crosswise of the Rhomandi as well. Ganfrion shrugged and turned his attention out the door and back to the camp, where a minor commotion had broken out down one of the rows between the tents.

He hadn't catered to titles in years and a damnable ring on his finger was not going to change the strength of his convictions, nor his method of expression. Hell, no.

Mikhyel broke the silence first, moderately, calmly, reasonably. "We've no evidence he went after Nikki at all, Ganfrion. That's the truth. I can feel Nikki getting closer—he'll be here in an hour or so—but I don't feel—whatever it wants to call itself—at all. And I would if he were near. I can't *escape* feeling her . . . him . . . *it*."

The commotion down the row outside came clear: a cart

had clipped the stake of a misaligned tent, bringing it down on the heads of its occupants, the billowing canvas setting off the mules in the harness. The mules, however, calmed quickly, with the tolerance of animals near exhaustion, and continued on their way, moving steadily toward their end of the camp.

And as the contents of the cart came clear, as the shaded hair of one of the passengers caught a breeze, Ganfrion said, "Make up your mind fast, dunMheric, and be ready to eat your words."

"What are you talking about?"

"You were wrong about the arrival time as well."

Rhomandi grabbed a cloak and threw it around his brother before Mikhyel darted out bare-ass to intercept the wagon that held both their younger brother Nikki and a slender figure with shaded hair.

§   §   §

"Don't touch her, Master Khyel," As it had since childhood, Raulind's calm voice compelled instant obedience.

"Temorii?" Mikhyel whispered to the unnaturally still figure, who sat cross-legged, cradling Nikki's head in his lap, fingers to Nikki's temples. He couldn't even see Thyerri breathing.

"She's been that way for hours," Raulind said. "Ever since we got him settled."

"How's Nikki?" Deymorin's voice asked from behind him.

"I don't know," Mikhyel answered abruptly, and now that the moment had arrived, now that his fears had been proved unfounded and his buried hopes proven true, now that Dancer had returned as well as Nikki . . . he didn't give a damn how Nikki was. The one thing he knew about Nikki's current situation was that he'd *known* he was in trouble and said nothing . . . until it was too late. If Nikki had turned back as he'd promised, none of this would have been necessary.

"Master Nikaenor appears well, Master Deymorin."
Raulind's voice came from beyond Thyerri's head, as Mikhyel widened his attention beyond Thyerri's set face. "His
pulse and color are good. They have been since Mistress
Temorii arrived. Before that, I feared we would lose him,
for all he appeared uninjured."

He'd have to explain to Raulind. Of all people, Raulind
had to know what Thyerri was.

But of all people, a part of him insisted in self-mockery,
Raulind probably already knew.

"You made good time." Deymorin said softly, and Raulind answered:

"We were already in the process of breaking camp when
she arrived. The men who brought Master Nikki to us had
explained how he'd been getting worse, and I thought there
might be a proximity question involved, which Mistress
Temorii confirmed before she herself collapsed. I put her
in the cart with Master Nikki, and she immediately settled
herself as you see, and has been there ever since."

Thyerri's feet and hands were blistered and raw, his face
filthy and scratched, clothing torn, and still, he fought that
silent battle for Nikki's mind, seemingly unaware the need
was over. Mikhyel felt it, felt the calm aura of . . .
nothing . . . that radiated out from the wagon. An aura
that deflected the link, softened it and made Nikki seem
elsewhere than he was.

At least to him. What the aura had done to confound
that black cloud, he couldn't tell.

"I tried to touch her," Raulind said, "to tend her feet
and hands, and she went quite hysterical. I trust you two
might have a suggestion."

Raulind knew all about the link between them. More,
Raulind knew about the battle at the Boreton turnout and
how Deymorin, with Dancer's aid, had pulled him out of
his own mental retreat. Raulind, as only Raulind could, had
accepted that story without question.

What he drew was the logical supposition: what had
helped then could help now, in reverse.

"She's been protecting him, Khyel," Deymorin said.

"Buffering against whatever it was you felt—still is, do you feel it? That's why you thought Nikki was farther away than he actually was. Is this enough? *Now* will you trust her?"

"Not now, Deymorin! We've got to separate them."

"We, together? She knows you. She trusts you."

Touch her? Alone? Without Deymorin's stabilizing force? Knowing what the slightest touch of her hand could do to his common sense?

"I . . ." He nodded. "You're right. Let me try first. Alone."

There was a silence in the air. A retreat. A distant: "You know where to find me."

{Thyerri?} Mikhyel called, and used the name he somehow felt Dancer preferred.

And he was startled to discover nothing of raspberries or cinnamon, only that freshly baked bread that was Nikki.

Second try: second name: {Dancer?}

Blue-veined eyelids twitched, the eyes beneath shifted. His heart skipped a beat. The theoretical possibility of reaching him had ceased to be theory. The cloak slipped, his knees gave, that burst of energy that had carried him to the cart depleted now.

Don't touch her, Master Khyel . . .

So, he should stand here and fall on his . . . he'd never make it up onto the cart on his own. He swallowed what little pride remained and murmured:

"Help me up, Deymorin?"

Deymorin hoisted him bodily into the cart. He landed amidst a padding of blankets and pillows, doubtless Raulind's arrangement, and eased over to kneel beside Dancer. Pulling the cloak tight around him, he called again, closing his eyes, reaching deliberately for the raspberries, cinnamon, and clove.

He found nothing.

He conjured scent and taste, the feel of Dancer's skin beneath his fingers, the image of Dancer darting and flowing among the towering dance rings.

And sensed movement, a shrinking away: shadow within shadow within shadow.

{Dancer!}

Dancer: name, concept, essential state of being; not Temorii or Thyerri, which were mere sounds for smaller subpatterns.

The sum that was {Dancer} had caused that flicker of self-awareness.

{Dancer!} he called a third time: a shout, within this shadow realm, and the shadows fled, all but one, a black shadow . . . edged with rainbows.

Mikhyel chased after the shadow that was Dancer, and it seemed as if the shadow wished to be caught—or that he wished to catch more than Dancer wished to avoid, for he began to close in, which he could never do in the real world. Two steps away. One. He reached—

Suddenly the dance rings filled this world of shadows and the rainbow-edged figure darted in among them, hooked a passing arch and spun into the pattern. The shadow flew among the spinning rings, became a fluid ripple, a gossamer ribbon dancing among the spinning silver, like the radical streamer of the tower rings, the namesake of the radical dancer.

The essence of Rakshi. Of chance. Of whimsy. Life . . . and death.

Follow, the figure challenged him. Mocking him. Daring him to enter this most treasured sanctum. The launch tower manifested, that mundane means by which normal mortals mounted the rings. All Mikhyel needed do was climb it, fling himself among the rings—and then catch Dancer.

Easier to catch the wind.

It was madness. He was no dancer. And the dance was deadly even to the most skilled. Substance was fluid in this strange inner world, but death, the death of what Dancer called the essence, was real, of that he was certain. Nothing else would do. Not for Dancer. The dance without the risk was no dance at all.

Yet the challenge continued, that slender figure darting

with joyous abandon among rings accelerated now to a blur.

He ran for the launch tower.

The first ring caught him in the midsection. Not a honed edge, luck favored him at least in that much. It changed direction and flung him free. A second ring passed; he snagged it reflexively, and for a moment, was lost in the sheer exhilaration, as his body flew through the air behind the ring; the streamer-shadow passed, laughing, a sound that filled the air with a flute's pure tone: joy, unadulterated and free to all who would share. No mockery. No anger. No illusion. Just an invitation to the dance—to life—and for a moment and a lifetime, Mikhyel followed that streamer, realized the weightless existence that allowed the impossible to be possible, and added his own variations, caught in the rapture.

Caught. Here. Forever. An eternity of adrenaline thrills, as much a trap as his own internal sanctum of peaceful fires and books and fine wine.

{Dancer!} He fought now to catch that figure, solid weight once more as the rapture fled his essence, grabbing for the next ring, and the next. But luck denied him: a razor-sharpened edge sliced through his fingers and he was falling—

{Dancer!}

He called out, desperate, knowing, somehow, that if he struck the ground, that laughing, mocking figure would be lost forever, whether or not he survived.

A waft of air slowed his descent . . . and vanished.

{And would that not be better, Mikhyel dunMheric?}

{Dancer!}

Another waft. A hint of wine, of old books . . . and fire-blossom tea.

{Perhaps Dancer. Perhaps not. Kinder to let the dancer go.}

{Not like this! —*Dancer!*}

Another waft, slowing his descent. He would touch down safely. Alone. With Nikki and Dancer still held captive by good intentions.

{Kill one, the other goes free.}

{Not an option. You're not Dancer. —*Dancer, where are you? Dancer, help me! Help me release you!*}

This time, solid flesh, not the wind, stopped his descent. Toes touched solid ground and he held tight to the shadow that was shadow no longer.

{I'm here, Khy.}

The rings vanished. The shadow Dancer took Mikhyel's hand and as they touched, he found himself surrounded by masses of iridescent leythium web. Delicate draperies billowed apart to let them pass. The mouth-watering scent of fresh bread filled the air.

And the shadow vanished.

Mikhyel surged forward, following that scent, searching desperately for any hint of raspberries, cinnamon, and clove. The web grew thicker, formed a pattern that began to point to a common center, a center where all threads converged, and wove together into a man-sized chrysalis.

An end drifted free. He touched it, and it clung to his finger, releasing the faintest hint of clove.

"Thyerri," he whispered, and lifted the thread toward his lips. It broke and fluttered away, dissipating on the breeze.

Raspberries, cinnamon, and clove burst free, overpowering even the scent of bread. The clove was strong and vital now, where before it had been little more than an occasional hint, a side of Dancer held at a distance by the cinnamon.

Thyerri, something whispered and in his heart, he knew that was true.

He lifted the threads of that cocoon, strand by strand, from Nikki's peaceful mind. And each as it was freed, dissipated on the breeze, tiny wafts of air that caught the threads and turned them to shadows.

And Dancer's scent grew faint.

{Dancer? *Dancer!*}

{Farewell, gentle Khy.}

Gentle? He was far from gentle. He was cruel and rude and suspicious and he was damned if Dancer would die because of his character shortcomings.

The flute's laughter filled his head.

{Die? I'm not dying.}

{Your essence is fading.}

{Escaping. I'm free at last. I bound myself too fully to you—to your brother. I meant only to shunt the ward to an unknown pattern, to protect without alerting the warder. I did not know the danger past. Would not know now, but for your coming. You promised to set me free. Set me free, Khy.}

{But—} And his mind filled with the time after Boreton, of his sanctuary, his retreat, his wish to free his brothers—and himself—of the burden of his life.

{I'm not Mheric's son, Khy. I need no escape. That is my essence. I go there to live, not to die. To think, not to escape. You shouldn't fear your inner world.}

{Then of what should I free you?}

{Mother's changing. I must go to her, battle the fermentation. How can I do that when your pattern holds me here?}

His hand shook with the next thread. Dancer meant he should release his essence. Let the scent fade from his mind. Yet even as Dancer asked for freedom, the next sweet-scented thread wound around Mikhyel's hand, danced up his arm and brushed his face before turning to shadow, belying that wish.

Regret came on the next strand. Regret of humanity lost if Mikhyel set him free. Regret that they would never dance the heights again, never love. Never—he had to smile—argue. And a vision of himself, of eyes alight with competitive fire, a dance of words in which Dancer was the student and Mikhyel the teacher.

Determination on the next, that Mikhyel would be free, his mind at ease, resolve that humanity lost was a small price to pay for peace.

One strand remained. It wrapped around Mikhyel's finger, forming, in this place of shadows, the Rhomandi ring he lacked here and in the real world.

{I . . . can't. Dancer, I can't.}

{Yes, you can. Release me. Be free.}

{Free? Of what? Love?}

{Fear.}

{I'm not afraid.}

{Then let me go.}

The final thread turned to shadow and drifted free. But at the last moment, as it shimmered in the air:

{I can't . . .} and he cupped his hands about the shadow-mist as he would about a rose and inhaled . . . and the scent of raspberries, cinnamon, and clove filled his world.

". . . I love you," he finished on a whisper.

And Dancer gave a gasping sob and crumpled into Mikhyel's waiting arms.

Chapter Five

Bacon. *Pepper* bacon. And eggs.

Without opening his eyes, Nikki sighed deeply, and inhaled again. Biscuits. Ham, and oatmeal. . . . He loved morning.

Beyond half-mast lids, morning sun filtered through canvas, and he wondered why he was in a tent, and why he didn't recall pounding the stakes, which was even more strange, because pounding in the stakes was *his* job ever since the first time he and Deymorin . . .

Ringing song of steel on the air: shit. The army camp. How did he get back here? He'd been headed up the mountain in search of Raulind. He'd *fallen* off the horse . . . Rings! Deymio would never let him live that one down.

But how had he gotten back?

And what time—what *day* was it?

He flung the blanket back, got a blast of cold air, and snuggled back into his cocoon for another few moments of warmth while his head sorted what his senses reported.

"Aren't you awake *yet*, Shitnik?" A loud whisper asked from beyond the canvas flap.

Shitnik? Only one person in the world dared call him that, and *he* hadn't in years.

"Shit. I was sure the bacon would do the trick." That, in a muttered undertone.

"Jerrik? *Jerri*, is that you?" Nikki kicked free of the blanket and stumbled to the door, and flung it back, to find his best friend leaning against a nearby tree, grinning. The next moment, they were hugging and pounding each other as if they hadn't seen each other for months instead of a mere couple of days.

"How?" he asked on a back-thumped breath, and Jerri shrugged.

"Word came down from the Tower you'd disappeared. Best bet was, this was where you landed, so here I came. Figured you'd be wanting clothes."

"Oh, you had that right. My brothers?"

"Asleep. Raulind, too." Which meant, *They're fine, don't worry, and ask them when they wake up because that's all I know.*

Which was fine by him. More than fine considering the smell from the campfire. "Is that bacon for me? *Please* say it is! Rings, I'm *starving*!"

"All for you, buddy. Brought it along, too."

"You are a prince among men!" Nikki sandwiched Jerri's face between his hands and kissed him loudly. Jerri retaliated with a cuff to his ear that set his head ringing, and for a time, even bacon was forgotten as the primary goal became to see who could land the next solid blow.

They dodged in and about the tent and its neighbors, stumbled over ropes, and knocked over a cookpot, until an exasperated sergeant grabbed a handful of Nikki's hair in one hand and Jerri's shirttail in the other and brought them to a panting, laughing halt.

"Damned school brats. Wot 'n 'ell's the old man thinkin'? Where'd 'e dig you two up? Wot's yer names, soldiers, so's I know wot t' put 'n yer obit?"

Nikki choked his laughter down, tried to explain, caught Jerri's eye, and was off again.

Jerri sobered first. "Sorry, sir," he said to the sergeant, who scowled.

"It's all right, sergeant," Nikki gasped. "We're . . . I'm—"

"Princeps of Rhomatum!" Jerri sang out.

Nikki slammed an elbow in his ribs, and hissed: "Shut the fuck up!"

The indulgent look the sergeant cast him had become all too familiar in this place of serious adults and adult matters.

"Ye'd be th' old man's kid bro, then? Heard ye was here; din't know I 'ad me such a 'lustrus neighbor. Master Nikki, isn't it? Sorry to break up yer fun, but this's a workin' man's camp, ye know."

"I do, sergeant, and I do apologize. This is Jerrik dun-Daleri, my . . . manservant." He and Jerri had come up with that excuse three years ago to keep constantly together, Jerri having been born and raised in Darhaven, where Nikki only visited and infrequently. "He's up from Rhomatum as well. I assure you, we are not always so . . . out of control."

"Not my place t' say, now is't, m'lord."

He winced. "Yes, sergeant, it is. I *give* the right to you, if necessary. But we'll behave now, I promise."

A sizing up that he hoped to all the gods he passed. He did *not* want this to get back to Deymio. "Heard tell th' ol' man had th' rearin' of ye."

"Deymorin and Mikhyel both," he said, "But don't blame—"

"Good job, they did. Move well, got sense . . . Make a soldier of ye, if so's ye wanted."

Nikki relaxed and grinned. "I'd like that very much, sergeant, but I'm afraid I've got duties elsewhere."

"S'pose ye do. Wot 'bout 'im?" The sergeant jerked his head toward Jerri. " 'E as smart as you?"

"Smarter," Jerri piped in. "And *he* needs me to wipe the drool from his chin in the morning."

The sergeant snorted. "Get on with ye, then, afore the lads commandeer that bacon yer fillin' th' air with."

Nikki grinned, and snapped a salute, shoved Jerri toward the fire and the imperiled bacon, raised a warning hand when Jerri would have continued the scuffle. " 'Nough, Jer. Let's eat."

The eggs were beyond salvage, the ham edible, the biscuits perfect . . . and even charred, the bacon was a gift from the gods.

Raulind, his eyes heavy with too little sleep, appeared out of Mikhyel's tent long enough to explain how they'd all come to be back in camp, and that they once again appeared to owe their lives to Dancer. Raulind couldn't explain all that had happened—Nikki imagined only Mikhyel and Dancer could do that—but he did say that his brothers were resting quietly, and that they shouldn't be disturbed, unless it was very, very important.

Which translated to a free day, with just him and Jerri . . . and a camp full of soldierly activities.

§ § §

Pale eyes, green-rimmed and black-lashed, flickered close, expanding shapeshifting to an all-consuming haze of mist and spring-green.

There was a warmth, a presence at Thyerri's back: welcome ease for muscles aching from long hours twisting and turning through crowded rooms, from laden trays held high, above harm's way.

Thyerri sighed and stretched, curling slightly about his pillow, exposing his lower back more fully to that friendly warmth.

Silken strands slithered over his shoulder and across his chest to tangle under his arm and downward, like a spiderweb. The tendrils gained bone and muscle, became long fingers that stroked his chin and down his neck, where they intercepted moist warmth nuzzling his shoulder, then threaded delicate patterns down his breast and across his ribs.

Thyerri sighed again, and buried his face in the pillow, too tired to object, even when the fingertips flattened into heated palms that pressed upward, crossing over his stomach and chest, drawing him closer to the unknown presence at his back.

Though helpless in sleep's lassitude, he wasn't frightened. A response occurred, deep, deep within. Recognition, yearning, a sense of . . . need, of . . . desire. Those palms stroked downward in a clean thrust that veered at the last moment around his groin, to tickle his inner thighs with a light, fingertip brush.

He groaned and shifted. But those fingers shifted with him, teasing, tempting, then drawing back, building the tension within until his pulse pounded.

The presence at his back began to move, lifting him with it, leading, falling away and leading again, until their two bodies danced as one. . . .

It was the old dream, the first dream, the dream that had plagued Thyerri's nights and perverted his dance, the dream begun when Mikhyel dunMheric had reentered his shattered existence. Only this time, the dream was alive, was warm arms holding him close, warm body molded to his back. Gentle hands that cradled him through the fabric of soft hiller clothes.

I love you . . . Mikhyel's essence had whispered in that otherworld in which he'd drifted, having bound himself too closely to Nikaenor's essence to know the threat had passed. And that Love had been Truth, Mikhyel's essence whispering to the essence of Dancer, so the essence of Dancer had been unable to find purpose in denial, and so fell once again under Mikhyel dunMheric's spell. But Mikhyel's essence and his mind did not always agree, and how long this truth would last and what guided that hand's deliberate caress might hold less of Love than of Obligation, and might even be nothing more than reflection of the Dream.

I love you . . . said one to another. Who had said and who had loved hardly mattered. They were bound, one to another, and that binding could only cause . . .

Obligation. Duty.

Mikhyel's primary overriding motivation in life.

The dancer had saved Nikaenor's life. Therefore Mikhyel must set aside his revulsion to satisfy the dancer's needs, whatever those might be.

Revulsion for the *freak*, the *abomination*. Dancer had never been so aware of his differences, hadn't even known the words until he gained them along with the horrified and horrifying associations from Mikhyel's mind. Mother had raised him to believe his body was a gift, special in every way, had named him Dancer and in his name, he had found pride of accomplishment, but no shame. With the loss of the dance, lacking the strict regime of the dancer-in-training, surrounded every day with the carnal thoughts of the common folk, his body had betrayed him and the Dream had begun to haunt him. But all the time he'd resented the change, he'd never felt he was anything unnatural.

It had taken Mikhyel dunMheric to make him think he was that.

He felt ill, swallowed the bile, and buried his face in the pillow.

Pillows. Blankets smelling of rose petals.

And when he opened his eyes, it was to the tapestry hangings that formed the interior of Mikhyel's tent.

Raulind made certain his City-bred master dwelt in comfort. It was a comfort Dancer knew from their time together . . . before. Before, when they were Temorii and Khy, not lovers, not even truly friends, but just two people out to seek justice for Khoratum. Or rather, Mikhyel had sought justice, and saw in Temorii one means of achieving that end.

Temorii had sought the dance, single-minded in her goal, passionless, in her way, as every other competitor.

And that which made a Rakshi dancer different was *passion,* Dancer understood that, though Temorii hadn't at the time. Dancer knew now that without that which Mikhyel had brought to her, Temorii's dance would have been little different from all the others, technically awesome but without the essence that bridged the worlds of dancer and spectator.

You practice conservatism: Mother's words, from a lifetime ago. *Not art. Tradition, not inspiration; rules, not faith. The radical factor in the Ley is rarely conservative. The radical dances to the most unusual flux and designs its own rules, challenging the universe to join it. Until you gain that courage to laugh in the face of the judges and dance as you were born to dance, you've no right to win. . . .*

To share of oneself. To love. To hate. To challenge. To hazard. That was the essence of the Dance, that which lay beyond the substance, which anyone could learn. Dancer had danced better than the competition, and so Dancer, wanting the dance, had chosen not to Dance, but merely dance as all others danced. Better for Dancer's Dance that he had *not* competed that day. That first time. The day he'd been drawn to Mikhyel's near-death side.

Better for his Dance that he had learned the meaning of challenge and hazard—and love.

Better for the Dance, but better for Dancer? Better for Mikhyel?

Mikhyel's finger hold eased, his hands slid across Thyerri's flank, pressing him close, as he molded himself to Thyerri's back, his body more honest than his mind, which was itself foggy with sleep and likely caught up in the backwash of the Dream. Thyerri held still, his mind distant now from the sensations and the Dream.

"Temorii?"

Not asleep, then. But Thyerri wasn't called and Dancer didn't answer. Wouldn't answer to that name ever again. *Temorii* contained too much of denial, of lies and subterfuge. Thyerri was more honest. Thyerri had come first. Temorii was made for Dancer's needs, not Mikhyel's, and it was Dancer's right to say when Temorii had grown superfluous.

That which was Temorii screamed in protest. Dancer was more than Thyerri alone. Temorii loved Mikhyel as thoroughly as Thyerri loved. Temorii throbbed and ached to be filled with the love and the flesh that was Mikhyel, and for Dancer to ignore that was to die half a death.

And Dancer shuddered with the internal conflict. Tears filled Dancer's eyes, then dried, sucked away in determined insistence. There would be no half death and no half love. If Mikhyel could not love Thyerri, Mikhyel could not love Dancer. And as long as Temorii was there, Mikhyel would love the half while professing to love the whole.

"Time to wake up, love." Mikhyel's hands brushed his hair back and Mikhyel's lips nipped his ear and his neck. "Come, little pretender, supper's getting cold."

Impossible to ignore the gentle teasing, impossible to keep his perverse body from responding. Dancer groaned and rolled over, intercepting that kiss. He raised his hands to push Mikhyel back, to take control of the kiss and of himself, then cried out as pain lanced through his body.

{Be careful, my precious idiot.} Mikhyel caught his hands and held them still for him to see the bandages that had turned them to awkward paddles. {You were not kind to your fingers in your race to save my brother.}

But it was Dancer's back that screamed in unimaginable agony, not his hands, not even his feet, though every finger and every toe stung with surface cuts and cramping muscles. And while Mikhyel murmured soothing nonsense interspersed with even more nonsensical endearments, Dancer ignored him, taking poll of his limbs, trying to sort the cause from the pain. Nothing he'd ever done could account for the way he felt, which was not the healthy ache of well-challenged muscle, nor the sharp pain of damaged tissue.

{Perhaps I can help . . .} Mikhyel kissed his neck and urged him onto his stomach. {Relax, darling.}

He wished Mikhyel would cease using those words that meant nothing, words that served only to bypass the problem of Names, as if by using them he could make those nothing words mean Something. But as Mikhyel's fingers pressed into his back and began easing those aches away, finding the pressure points with such assurance that Dancer began to doubt the efficacy of the barrier he'd constructed between their minds, he ceased to care what Mikhyel said or thought, as long as he kept rubbing.

"I don't . . ." Dancer's voice was hoarse and dry. He swallowed and tried again ". . . I don't understand. What did I do?"

"Ganfrion says that run you made should have been impossible."

"Gan exaggerates. Besides, it's not just that. I feel . . . I feel as if each muscle is shattering when I move. As if I'm made of stone."

Mikhyel pulled at his tunic and Dancer let him work it off over his arms, then tried not to shiver as Mikhyel leaned over him again and Mikhyel's hair brushed along his bare skin. But with the mere touch of skin to skin, Mikhyel's warm, long-fingered hands began to turn stone back to pliable flesh, and Dancer sighed in relief.

"You *were* sitting still as a statue in the back of a cart for hours holding my brother's head."

"Ah." Memory returned in a rush, of sitting in the back of the cart. Of drawing that blond head into his lap . . . then: nothing. "Is . . . Is Nikaenor well?"

"I heard him wake quite naturally this morning. Not even a headache. Doesn't know there was anything wrong with him."

Would that he could say the same. In another of those prescient moves, Mikhyel's fingertips penetrated to the throb in his temples and the base of his neck, breaking up the tiny knife-points, sending them flying.

"That help?" Mikhyel murmured.

"Do you need to ask?"

"You're keeping me out, Temorii, I won't—"

"Temorii's dead." Dancer pulled free and sat up to face Mikhyel, though his image wavered in time with the throb in his head and to the rhythm of Temorii's objections. "I'm not certain she ever existed for anyone outside this tent. Accept that, Mikhyel dunMheric, or leave me and grant me peace."

Mikhyel recoiled, his face, normally so controlled, naked in its pain. Mikhyel was vulnerable now. More vulnerable than Dancer had realized. The dream of the dance, the threads . . . was not a dream.

I love you . . . What must that admission mean to Mikhyel dunMheric, who gave meaningless words like *normal* and *abomination* power over his heart?

{Khy, I}

"Temorii's dead," Mikhyel conceded quietly, and gathered Dancer back into the living haven of his warm arms.

§ § §

Parry, thrust, fall back, pivot, bring up the left blade—

"Thus! Very good, young lord. Again. Faster."

Nikki fell into the unfamiliar stance more easily this time than the time before, the balance coming more naturally with each pass. The double-bladed fighting of the Drus of Eastern Kirish'lan was an art form that had fascinated Nikki since he'd first seen it in a circus almost ten years ago. Unfortunately, his primary fencing instructor was less fascinated, declaring it ideally situated in a circus.

But on this fine Khoramali morning, with that instructor gone back to his bed after two sleepless nights, and his other brother likewise absent, caring for the dancer, a man who had slept soundly through the night thanks to that dancer's efforts was free to roam the camp, watching the activities which heretofore had been only references on requisition sheets.

Parry, thrust, pivot—Nantovi changed the pattern, and Nikki laughed and countered. Nantovi's eyes flashed, a grin flickered and vanished—and he returned to the pattern.

On one of the practice fields, he and Jerri had found a man he recognized as one of Deymorin's instructors from his border patrol days, instructing a young fellow, about Nikki's own age, in that very double-bladed style he'd always craved. The young man (whom Nantovi called dun-Hikham, which meant he must be Hikham's youngest, Belden, which meant Hikham must have declared for Rhomatum, which was nice) attacked the lesson with more sincerity than skill.

Nantovi called an early end to his session, leaving Belden red-faced and panting, and Nikki dancing from one foot to the other, wishing he dared ask—

"Touché, lad," Nantovi's low tone held laughter, and his two blades made a cross at Nikki's neck. "You're wandering, boy."

Laughter, from more than just Nantovi and Belden; several of the men who had been practicing here, stripped to the waist, heads dripping from a ducking in the cooling tub, had gathered along the perimeter—to watch the commander's little brother make a fool of himself, no doubt. Among them were Phendrochi and Darville, the two who had accompanied him to the new lake just yesterday morning.

Nikki felt the heat rise in his face and ducked his head, but Nantovi's blades turned to tap his cheeks with the flat.

"None of that, now. You did very well. Too well. That," Nantovi said with a nod to the grinning audience, "is pure jealousy. Are you certain you've never done this before?"

"No, sir. —I mean, *yes,* I'm sure. Deymorin doesn't like it."

"Ha! He taught you, then? That explains much. Good balance to both sides. You match left to right?"

Nikki nodded.

"That's your brother. Time to quit now."

"But I'm not tired! I'll pay attention, I promise."

"Patience, lad. You were improvising at the last, for all your thoughts were elsewhere. Your mind has accepted the patterns and the logic of the blades. Your muscles, the balance and timing. Let them discuss the matter for a time."

Time. For him, that time might be months or even years. His life was Rhomatum, not this world of fighting men. Still, the sergeant was right.

Reluctantly, Nikki acknowledged the wisdom behind the order and returned the slightly curved blades to the stand, where a man waited to clean and inspect them. He'd as soon have done that himself, it being part of the ritual instilled in him by his brother, but the practice field had its protocols, the weapons-groom his own pride, and a man didn't step on those protocols for the sake of the feel of polished steel beneath his fingertips.

He was just glad Nantovi hadn't had the option, in this group of veterans, of using practice weapons rather than true steel.

Jerri was waiting patiently on the sidelines. If it didn't involve arrows, bullets, or gunpowder, Jerri wasn't much interested. And with a curved sword, he was downright hopeless. But he was grinning widely as he helped Nikki strip off the protective pads.

As the other men had done, Nikki pulled his sweat-soaked shirt off, tossed it to Jerri, and ducked head and shoulders into the barrel of water. An unexpected blow to his backside brought him up spluttering inhaled water, ready to skin Jerri alive. But the laughter that met him this time was accompanied by hands slapping his shoulders, and fists jabbing his back, testing muscle and resilience. He gasped after air, as the comments flowed regarding fighting men hiding behind City flowers. Even Phendrochi, who had openly scorned him, swept him a theatrical salute and retracted his earlier comments, which grew to truly insulting in the retelling, which only made the retraction that much more dramatic.

Truth to tell, Nikki didn't much care. He reveled in a camaraderie of a sort he'd only dreamed of. Deymorin had always wanted to send him to the border, but Mikhyel, for reasons of Mikhyel's own, which Nikki now understood but nonetheless resented, then and now, Mikhyel had vetoed those plans time and again.

But these were men who saw the muscle in his back and knew he'd stacked hay every year since he was twelve. These men saw the scars from the past year, and knew him for a man of doing, not of sitting. They'd seen him wield the swords with the authority of a man ready to use them, not . . . a City flower, and this ex-City flower just grinned foolishly and laughed with them.

Best of all was Nantovi's hand on his arm, the quiet *Good job, lad,* just as Nikki had seen him do once to Deymorin.

And Belden, shyly introducing himself, had a look of longing that Nikki suddenly recognized: just so must he have looked that long-ago day, and he said to Belden, "Maybe we can practice together sometime." Belden's face glowed, but Nantovi's did not; Nikki qualified quickly: "Not the double-blade . . . yet," with a sideways glance at Nantovi. "But have you learned to match left to right? *That* I can help you with."

Nantovi just shook his head, but a secret grin tweaked the edges of his tight mouth, so Nikki knew he'd get his time with Belden, who truly did seem his only peer in this camp of veterans.

And that made him wonder how in the world Belden came to be here. But Belden disappeared with Nantovi, and Jerri was there with a towel and a fresh shirt, and the information that he thought Nikki might want to get over to Deymorin's tent right away.

More than that, he would not explain, so Nikki said farewell to his new friends and headed off with Jerri. A man was waiting with the guards outside the tent when he arrived, a man who looked ridden hard and put away wet: the report from Khoratum, so the guards said.

"What's he doing out here? " Nikki demanded of the guards. "The man's dead on his feet."

"Waiting for the Rhomandi, sir."

Evidently they'd been given orders not to waken Deymorin except in emergency.

"Captain Owiin?" Nikki asked, naming Deymorin's second-in-command.

"Cap'n told me to report only to the Rhomandi himself, beggin' your pardon, sir," the exhausted man said.

Nikki chewed his lip in uncertainty. "You can give it to me. I'll judge whether or not to rouse the Rhomandi."

The guards protested, the courier said: "Sir, that I can't."

Uncertainty vanished in a heartbeat, in the face of opposition, and as the mantle of responsibility settled as easily on his shoulders as had the mask of feckless younger brother, he asked:

"What's your name, soldier?"

"Sergeant Biilim, sir."

"Well, Sergeant Biilim—" Nikki raised his hand, clearly displaying the Rhomandi ring he wore to all three. "This says you not only can, but *will*."

The guards exchanged a glance, and as one, their bodies subtly straightened, a fact Nikki acknowledged with a nod before he led the way inside to the tent's main room. Deymorin's quiet snore drifted from behind a double separation of canvas, and the link informed Nikki that his brother was sleeping soundly.

"Wait outside, will you, Jerri?" he asked, and Jerri stared at him a moment, then, with a shrug, slipped out.

He'd never asked Jerri to leave. If Jerri happened to be with him, Jerri heard; but not this time. This was a military man who deserved to have the security of the message with which he had been charged respected. Chances were, it was a simple report, and he *would* tell Jerri all about it; but it might not be. *Things* were happening up in Khoratum, and until he knew what those things were, Jerri just had to stay outside.

It was, he decided, the hardest part yet about growing up.

But he'd run the City when Deymorin and Mikhyel had been out making deals and building armies; he had stood in Rhomatum Tower during the contest with Khoratum; he could damned well handle a dispatch from the camp Deymio had set up outside Khoratum and give the report to Deymorin when he woke.

He *wanted* to do that, to prove something to himself, perhaps, something of the nature the matter with Belden had proved to the weapons-master. And if, in proving that to himself, he could relieve his hard-working brother of a mundane administrative report, so much the better.

"Sit before you fall," he said, settling into the chair behind the desk, and waving to another, and when the messenger had sunk into the offered seat on a camp-stool: "Let's hear your report. And keep it low. Wake *him* up and I *will* let you face him—alone."

But before he had heard it all out, he knew there was reason to wake Deymio.

Chapter Six

"When the Kaithnarum delegation demanded to see rom-Maurii, the Khoratumins threw his body out of the Tower and shut the door." Face to face with a Deymorin just roused from sleep, Sergeant Biilim paused to clear his throat. "All red and shriveled, he was. Don't know how they could tell it was him, but the leader of that lot, he seemed sure."

A Kaithnarum delegation in Khoratum, Deymorin thought. *That* had been an interesting bit of information that had arrived with Sergeant Biilim, and worth the wake-up. Kaithnarum was a Mauritumin satellite. Not even Mikhyel's Ganfrion had known about their arrival across the straits, and they hadn't gotten there overnight. Obviously, someone had been sheltering them within their umbrella of influence.

{Bhartog of Orenum, Deymorin,} Mikhyel whispered underneath, suddenly aware of the exchange, his name having surfaced in his brother's head. With it came intimations Mikhyel was not alone. But the flow of information continued: Mikhyel had that ability to track two threads at once. {His daughter recently married Ylenissii, who is partner to Polundrii of Kaithnarum. . . .}

He wondered, sometimes, how his brother kept the catalog of players straight in his head under normal circumstances.

{They were in Khoratum and at the competition, ostensibly on post-nuptial holiday. Gan said he'd lay odds they weren't there alone, but couldn't prove anything. I would have said something. Should have, anyway. Sorry.}

{Can't see where it would have made much difference, Khy. Let it go. *Interesting,* however.}

And, to the sergeant, Deymorin said, "You were there in Khoratum? Witnessed this transaction personally?"

The man nodded. "My job to watch the Tower, Commander. That was why the cap'n sent me down-country with the rest o' th' writ reports what was coming back. Thought you might want a first-hand accountin'." Overall, the sergeant had a well-spoken manner, hence his posting in Upper Khoratum, but in his uncertainty, his accent began to slip. "M'lord."

"Captain Aiilanor was certainly right in that."

The man sent a worried look at Nikki, sitting on Deymorin's right. "I'm right sorry t' wake you, sir."

"On the contrary. Nikaenor was correct. Your efforts were not wasted, sergeant."

He knew the gist of the rest of the man's report already, having half-heard the tail of it before Nikki's mind waked him fully.

And he knew Mikhyel was on his way now, the short distance between their two tents.

"The Persitumin delegation took Vandoshin romMaurii's body, then?" Deymorin asked quietly.

"Yessir. Heard those nearest talking deals with the High Priest. Fearful of Garetti's anger and free with their tongues, they were, head to heel. Nothin' secret, if one can say from their goings-on. Figuring to reinstate Persitum, he was, and now Khoratum down as well."

"Khoratum Tower itself?"

"Under repair before daylight came, sir. But no lights yet, leastways not before I headed downhill."

"Rumors on the status of the Web?"

"Full range of opinion: the Rings are down for good, no, they'll be up within the week . . . that Rhyys dunTarec has gone completely mad seems the most popular. Certainly most of the foreign visitors are packing. All the foreigners residing on the Hill have pulled out at least to the camps Outside the wall. —Your lordship."

Mikhyel had ducked into the tent, and the surprise on

the sergeant's face was not all for his rumpled hair and open shirt.

"And Rhyys' support?" Mikhyel asked, all business despite his appearance.

"Without romMaurii, with no proof of yr lordship's fate," the sergeant had half-risen, gave a nod toward Mikhyel as he settled into the chair. "Without the priest, Rhyys' support is fleeing. —And glad I am to see you well, sir."

Mikhyel returned the nod and asked: "Word on the street?"

"Rhyys would have it he has you still, m'lord." Which could account for the fact Biliim looked like a man talking to a ghost. "Like to blame the shutdown on you and stave off the Khoratumin-folk's panic and anger. No one knows what to believe. We all feared you was dead for sure, at th' camp. Rumor has it you escaped into the hills. Another rumor that you disappeared from the middle of the street. Another that you were a Tamshi come to dispossess Rhyys. There's a great deal of hope underground for that 'un, sir. Folk's watching corners for your return."

{Becoming something of a legend, little brother. A myth in your own time.}

Amusement tempered Mikhyel's mental disgust, but: {Deymorin, if you've nothing more to ask him immediately, I think we should discuss some of this.}

Deymorin nodded. "Sergeant, well done. I'll send you back upcountry tomorrow. —Stay sober, in case we have more questions for you; but get some rest. And a good meal and a soak in the springs."

"Yes, Commander. Thank 'ee, sir."

As soon as he'd cleared the room, Mikhyel said:

{Rhyys *has* raised the Rings.}

{Impossible. It took the combined forces of the Web to cap it before.}

"Deymorin, Khyel," Nikki spoke up, "Could we please speak aloud? I still just get a buzz sometimes, and I don't think this is the time to practice."

"Sorry, Nik," Deymorin said, and Mikhyel continued smoothly:

"I told you I *saw* the Rings spinning. They're . . . not right. Damaged, perhaps. They looked black, but—"

"Khyel, please," Nikki pleaded again. "When did you see them? What do you mean, 'damaged.' "

"Last night, Nikki. When you—we—were under attack, I traced the source of that attack to its center. It was as if you were entering a cloud. And at its heart, I saw the Rings. Spinning. And it damnwell *wasn't* my imagination." *That* to himself. Deymorin shrugged, and Mikhyel continued: "He wouldn't be capping a part of Rhomatum now. Khoratum is independent. I don't know how he's done it, but it's the fact that Rhyys appears to have done it that I find surprising. I find it hard to believe there was enough sound mind left after the ocarshi smoking to manage such a feat, but he must have. I *know* what I saw. But I could have sworn it must have been romMaurii—he is . . . was . . . after all, one of Garetti's men. He was sent here on the assumption that he might even be able to wrest control of Rhomatum from Anheliaa. The man had to have had a great deal of Talent. But if he's dead and Rhyys is in control of the Tower . . . I must have misjudged him."

"I can't believe Mother would allow that to happen," Nikki said.

"If she had any say in the matter," Mikhyel answered.

"I don't understand."

"Think about it, Nik. What have we actually seen these Tamshi *do*?"

"You mean other than save your hide and leyapult you all over the map?"

"I mean where the Rings are concerned. Mother complains—vehemently—about the Rings and who controls them, yet seems helpless to do anything about it. She wanted her freedom, but she couldn't obtain it until Rhyys and romMaurii's efforts, backed by the entire Northern Crescent, to take control of Rhomatum ended in stalemate."

"Perhaps they can't take action at all, except as we direct them," Deymorin said thoughtfully.

Mikhyel tipped his head and the underneath current encouraged him to expand:

"*You* set Rhomatum into the battle. It was *your* will, not his, that broke the stalemate."

"Actually," Nikki reminded them both quietly, "It was Mirym's needle that broke it."

{We stand corrected, Nikki.} Mikhyel's thoughts or his own, Deymorin couldn't have said for certain, but Nikki was right. They'd been at a standoff, all of the Web except Khoratum under absolute Rhomatumin control. In Rhomatum Tower, the Khoratum ring would not spin. Mother's doing, or so they'd assumed. Mother, working through Rhyys and romMaurii. The unified efforts of the satellites to take over the Rhomatum Rings had given her the leverage she lacked on her own. Leverage to penetrate Rhomatum's umbrella, leverage to hold the Khoratum ring and force it offline, but not enough leverage to destroy it.

How long that stalemate might have continued would never be resolved. In the end, the Khoratum/Persitum ring, under unimaginable stress, caught as it was between two opposing wills, had shattered at the touch of a silver embroidery needle, wielded by a slip of a girl who had been a trusted retainer in Rhomatum Tower for two years. At that same moment, all the rings in the Khoratum Tower had gone down, fallen or destroyed, they hadn't known for certain—until this most current report—but certainly they'd gone inert, no longer transmitting power.

"The very structure of the ring must have been under tremendous strain," Mikhyel said. "But Mother . . . she *needed* Rhyys and romMaurii and all the rest to affect the Rings at all."

And Nikki: "And she needed Mirym in Rhomatum Tower."

"Let's be careful not to condemn before we have more information," Mikhyel, the barrister, cautioned. "We don't know that Mirym is Mother's agent. Her actions might well have saved the rest of the Web. Between us, we might have destroyed all the Rhomatum Rings."

"Let's be careful not to read too much into any of this," Deymorin added to that caution. "But it certainly does seem that what you traced last night, Mikhyel, actually *is* Khoratum back on line—at least in some sense."

"A very warped sense. What I felt, what I saw was . . . not healthy, Deymorin."

"Hard to think it could affect the Rhomatum Web, not isolated as it is, but if Rhyys thinks to make a separate power base and if Mother thinks to oppose Rhyys . . ." Deymorin frowned. So much speculation, in all they did these days. "At the very least, we'll need a close watch on the Tower. Someone with authority to act, more than the captain. Someone with at least some concept of what we're dealing with."

"Ganfrion would return."

"Let's keep him in reserve for a time yet, Khyel. We just don't know how many battle fronts are still active. Damn, I wish I knew what was waiting for us back in Rhomatum."

"One of us at least had best get back home and soon. It's maddening, waiting for couriers."

"I'll go," Nikki said. "I can even leave you your horse, Deymio. Jerrik brought Tandy up with him. They'll be rested enough by tomorrow, and—"

"Are you sure you're well enough?" Deymorin asked.

"I feel fine. I don't know what Dancer did, but I feel as if nothing at all happened."

"There is no justice," Deymorin moaned, his head still aching, his neck stiff from those hours of tension. "But it *is* best if I stay here at the base for a time, at least until we know how civilized a retreat this is going to be. Khyel, you'd probably best get back to Rhomatum, with Nikki. There will be feathers to smooth for . . . Khyel?" His brother had gone strangely silent, within and without. "What's bothering you?"

"It's . . . Dancer." Mikhyel's eyes dropped. He gave a slight shrug. "He's awake."

"Ah. Tell him to join us."

"He's . . . perturbed. I asked Raulind to prepare the

traveling tub for him, and he wants to meet us in the baths.''

"Sounds fine to me. What's the problem?"

"Deymorin, would you invite Kiyrstin to bathe with your brothers? Possibly a dozen other men just passing through?"

"And have the lot of you gawking? Of course not."

"Exactly."

"To anyone meeting him, he'd just be Thyerri. . . . He certainly fooled us at Boreton."

"He wasn't trying to fool anyone. And . . . you *do* know."

"We wouldn't gawk! Rings, brother, what do you take us for?"

But Nikki was blushing. Deeply. And the underneath side of Nikki's thoughts was filled with curiosity, embarrassment, and apology. Mikhyel stood and placed a hand on Nikki's shoulder.

"No need to apologize, Nikki. It's only human to be curious. And nothing . . . nothing your honest curiosity could do to hurt him can compare with what I've already done. I—" {Forgive me, Nikki, but . . . would you leave us alone? Please?}

It was a break in Mikhyel's control, and what followed was all emotion, raw and unfocused, but left no doubt as to Mikhyel's need to talk to Deymorin alone, not knowing how to ask without hurting.

Nikki stood up, without even a flicker of resentment— though maybe a little sadness—and faced Mikhyel. "Sometimes I'm still your little brother, I know that, Khyel, but I wish I *could* help. I'll keep my head to myself, best I can. But . . . but I'd like to say, Dancer . . . maybe he left some of himself in me. It's going away, but—he loves you, Khyel, in a way . . . in a way I envy. Greatly. Promise me you won't endanger that."

Control wavered right on the edge.

"I'm trying, Nikki. By all the gods, I'm doing the best I can."

"Then it'll turn out all right. Never tell the Barrister 'can't.' Right?"

"Right. Thanks, Nik."

When he was gone, Deymorin just waited for Mikhyel
to collect himself and speak. And waited.

"You know, we'd never have pulled it off without
Nikki," Mikhyel said at last. "He directed the whole thing,
not Lidye. Her temper . . . she'd have ruined everything,
but Nikki kept her out, let you and Kiyrstin reach Mauritum and cut off Garetti, let *me* reach Khoratum . . . He's
really—"

Words seemed to fail him; Deymorin supplied: "—a
good man?"

Mikhyel gave a slow nod.

"That's not, however, what's on your mind."

"No."

"What is?"

"I don't know what to do, Deymorin. Surely you see how
it is. I couldn't ask Dancer to endure being with the rest
of us. Not here in camp. Not in Rhomatum. He insists on
being addressed as Thyerri. Insists Temorii never existed
except as a buffer between Dancer and Thyerri's feelings."

"So let him be Thyerri. Khyel, what's your problem?
Afraid you'll be fighting the ladies for his attention?"

Mikhyel looked startled, as if the thought hadn't remotely occurred to him. "I . . . no. But, I suppose . . . I
suppose he expects to live in Rhomatum. I suppose he
wants to go on with the relationship, in public . . . might
want . . . a child, but if he wants that . . . Deymorin, what
if he becomes pregnant? I'm at a loss here, brother. If I
tell the world what he truly is, he'll become an object of
curiosity. You know the attitude about the hillers . . . possibly even a point of contention throughout the Web. Bad
enough that it's going to appear that the Rhomandi have
been keeping their own ley-Talents a secret, but that the
Barrister is living with a—"

He was sure Mikhyel was searching for a decent, polite,
uncharged word. He set it in bluntest terms: "A freak?"

"That's not my word, Deymorin," Mikhyel said, then
amended: "At least it's not what I think now."

"But a word he'll have to deal with?"

"Inevitably. My . . . *affair* with the dancer was too

damned public. A female dancer. If he shows up at my side . . . Ultimately, there will be questions, Deymio. Ultimately, the truth will come out. I don't blame him for wanting to live as Thyerri, but, *gods!* it complicates everything!"

"Is that his choice?"

"Yes."

"And what's your choice, Khyel?"

That tipped-headed questioning look returned.

"You've said what you suppose Thyerri wants; what is it *you* want?"

Mikhyel only stared at him.

"I'll only ask this once, Khyel. Are you ashamed of him?"

"I . . . don't know, Deymio. I can't be more honest with you than that. I don't *want* to be, but . . . I think . . . I think, perhaps, I'm frightened for both of us. We've so much at stake. My reputation . . . gods, what reputation? Have I *any* left? Between our brotherly tantrums in Shatum, my behavior in Khoratum—rings, I even purposely encouraged that one! How can I possibly be ashamed of him when I've shamed myself so thoroughly?"

"You're wallowing, brother."

A blink shattered the stare at last. "You're probably right. Still, I wonder, sometimes, what I was thinking."

"Expedience. They weren't about to give you a choice, so you turned their own blind ignorance to your advantage. You know that, when you're thinking clearly."

"Perhaps. Nonetheless, in the next few weeks, I must face these men and women in the Council and across the negotiating table and win, not with web-spinning but with sound arguments. I *can't* have them speculating on my bedroom activities rather than the future of the Syndicate."

It was, Deymorin had to admit, by no means an easy question. Had it been he who had gotten involved, they'd have weathered the storm with little trouble: he'd flaunted custom all his life, continued to do so in his open relationship with Garetti's exiled wife.

Mikhyel—Mikhyel's entire life, both publicly and privately, had been balanced on a different scale. That scale had shifted, and none of them could know, yet, what the effect of that shift might be.

Mikhyel, by his face and the underlying emotions, didn't really expect an answer. Only understanding . . . that for all he loved Dancer, it could not be easy loyalty. Feelings might be held hostage. Personal matters made public. Neither side of the relationship might survive that assault unmarred. Rhomatum's social fabric might not survive it unmarred.

{Never mind.} Mikhyel sighed, and his hand pressed Deymorin's shoulder. {One day at a time, Deymorin. One day at a time.}

His hand stopped Mikhyel before he could remove that touch. {I'll think about it, Khyel. I promise you, we'll come up with something. If nothing else, hell, if Dancer starts breeding, we'll pack you both off to Darhaven. Force you to take a vacation.}

{I can think of worse fates. I'd best get back to my tent. Thyerri and Raulind will be waiting.}

§ § §

Thyerri and Raulind will be waiting. Well, he was half right.

"When did he leave?" Mikhyel asked Raulind, and idly stirred the water in the tub.

The empty tub.

"While I was arranging the water delivery. I'm sorry, Master Mikhyel, I had no idea there had been any disagreement between you."

Disagreement? He wouldn't exactly call it a disagreement. Thyerri had simply announced he was not a shrimp to be dipped in a boiling pot of water, and severed the connection.

He had no such reservations. Letting his clothing fall to the floor, he stepped into the steaming tub, catching the sides with his hands and sliding his feet into the lowest chamber, to ease down on the seat.

As the water rose to his neck, Raulind gathered and folded the scattered clothing into arcane piles destined for fates he didn't need to think about and so did not. He had far more than enough else to think about, all of which he endeavored to drive from his mind as the heat soaked into his chilled body.

"Did you have a chance to look at his hands?" Mikhyel asked from behind closed lids.

"He rejected my efforts, Master Khyel. But he'd pulled the bandages off. I do hope he's careful of infection."

"Stubborn."

"And he is, of course, alone in that characteristic."

A reluctant chuckle escaped him.

Soft sounds of Raulind's movement about the tent, effecting those invisible changes that made the difference between an ordered existence and one filled with chaos, sounds that congregated at his back. The weight of his hair eased and warm water drenched his scalp: start of a daily ritual that was yet another brick in that wall against encroaching chaos.

"It's possible he's gone to the Belisii camp."

The Belisii, the caravan of traders who had agreed to help him escape, his numb mind remembered that much.

"They're here?"

"They followed us down the leyroad. They arrived a few hours ago and set their camp north of the line."

He was glad for that. Temorii—Thyerri—would be relieved.

"It's possible," he said from behind closed eyes, "though I got the impression they were philosophical and political allies rather than personal acquaintances."

"Curious." Raulind's kneading fingers paused in their attack on his scalp. "I got quite a different impression. Still, I suspect he'll want to see Sakhithe, if not the others."

"Sakhithe? Who's that?"

"Master Khyel . . ." A hint of disapproval. A name he should know. He wracked his memory, pulled a face, an association. . . .

"The parade of the radicals," he said, considering that

recollection a small personal triumph. "The night before the competition. Rhyys' servant. The one Thyerri smiled at . . ."

"They knew each other. She was in training with Master Thyerri. There was an accident; she had to leave the program. Later, when he was released from the program—"

"Released. You mean, after Boreton. After he lost his chance to compete because of me."

"Then, yes, though you do yourself and those around you no favor to dwell upon unsubstantiated obligations, Master Khyel."

"I stand corrected."

Those soapy hands fingercombed his hair in gentle absolution, a reassurance as old as their association.

"Upon his return to Khoratum," Raulind continued calmly, "Master Thyerri evidently survived in the streets until she found him and got him a job at the establishment where she worked."

"The one that burned down." Memory flashed detail in bits and pieces. "Bharlori's."

"Bharlori's," Raulind affirmed. "There's a bond between them. I believe she once harbored notions for something more than friendship from him."

Jealousy flared, hot and unexpected. "And he's gone to her now?"

"Her hopes in that direction are gone, Master Khyel. Rinse, now, sir. Keep your eyes closed, please."

The rushing flood of water provided a welcome respite. When the rinse water had been removed and the toweling began, Mikhyel said, "Perhaps I should send a messenger. See if he's there."

"I don't think that would be wise, Master Khyel. He is free to move about, is he not?"

Free? With what he knew, with what he could do, with the situation up in Khoratum in such question? Dared they let him wander at will?

And gone to a woman who had had *hopes*. Another dancer. A life long City-man could only imagine, as he shifted his bony behind to a more comfortable angle on the ceramic seat, how two such honed bodies might dance in bed. A man who had found both man and woman in one body now found himself wondering about the nature of all dancers and whether this Sakhithe was like Dancer in more ways than fitness . . .

Spiraling thoughts that gave new meaning to the term inadequate.

He glowered and sank farther into the tub, getting his equally bony shoulders completely immersed.

"The water is chilling," he said, while knowing the chill was not in the water and furious at his own failing. "Turn up the heater, will you, Raul?"

"Perhaps you should get out now," Raulind suggested quietly. The sun is still warm; your hair will dry more quickly outside."

"I don't care to go outside at the moment, Raulind. Turn up the heater, please."

Without further comment, Raulind lit the heating unit beneath the tub. Oil, not leythium, based, it was a unit independent of leythium flux.

Like a shrimp indeed. As the temperature of the water increased, he wondered, sourly, where mountain-born Dancer had gotten such a concept. Mother, no doubt. Mother who seemed at times to think with her tastebuds, and whose knowledge far outstripped the boundaries of her mountain node.

As Raulind returned the lighter to its stand, and resumed toweling his hair, Mikhyel asked, "What do you think. *Dare* I trust him?"

"Why wouldn't you? It appears to me that he's proven his devotion to you quite unequivocally."

"But that devotion is divided, is it not? Mother has at least as great a hold on him. The lies . . . even if I accept the . . . devotion . . . as real, can I afford to simply overlook the lies? His opposing loyalties—past if not current in nature? How can I know the hooks such associations have left in him?"

Raulind did not answer immediately. Only after the

towel was folded and set aside, only after the gentle tug of
the comb began did he say:

"We all have 'associations,' Master Khyel. Once he was
free to choose, he came to you. As for the lies, I see no
reason to condemn his survival tactics. He is certainly not
the first young person I've known to be guilty of a bit
of obfuscation."

"Obfuscation." Raulind never chose words by accident.
"He didn't have to *obfuscate* to me in order to survive. At
first, maybe, but once . . . once we'd grown to be friends.
How can I trust when he didn't trust me enough to tell
me?"

"Ah. And did you tell him all about yourself? Have you
revealed all there is to know about Mikhyel dunMheric?"

"It's not the same thing."

"No? We all carry our secrets, my friend. And I knew a
youth who used a person's own assumptions about him to
carry the day more than once, unknowing, and as an adult,
does it every day, quite knowingly."

Mikhyel had no doubt who the youth in question was.
"Not to those I care about, Raulind."

"No? I suppose you see it that way. The instinct is set,
my friend. You share your true self with no one. Not even
yourself. Until you can, I find it just a bit ironic that the
Rhomandi family barrister begrudges an opponent a gentle
lie." It was as close to censure as Raulind ever came. The
tangles were free. The comb slipped smoothly through the
strands. "The small heater is working. I think, perhaps,
you'd like to sit beside it and dry?"

Which was Raulind's way of saying he'd had the last
word and perhaps Mikhyel would like to think for a while
before continuing on the track down which he was headed.

But time and meditation failed utterly to clarify his thinking, and as the afternoon descended into evening, and as
Raulind without comment prepared a simple but elegant
meal for two to which only one attended, he began to wonder if he hadn't made a terrible mistake in not sending
Ganfrion out after Thyerri the instant he'd disappeared.

When he sent for Ganfrion only to discover Ganfrion had himself vanished, he knew he had.

Raulind counseled him to reserve judgment. To wait, and both Thyerri and Ganfrion would return in their own time.

Mikhyel did not share his valet's confidence. Calling with that internal voice until his head pounded and his eyes were bloodshot with the effort had roused no answer, not even a hint of raspberries. Dancer was gone. Without a word. Without regret.

So much for Mikhyel dunMheric's taste in lovers.

And by all evidence, Dancer had taken Ganfrion with him. At least Ganfrion had been seen leaving camp with him, and Ganfrion, too, had failed to report.

So much for Mikhyel dunMheric's taste in liegemen.

Unless, of course, Ganfrion had followed Dancer out of suspicion. But Mikhyel's instincts argued against that.

Of course, those same instincts had urged him to hire Ganfrion in the first place, and to give him the Rhomandi ring.

And damned if he'd give Deymio the satisfaction of sending out a search party for either of his younger brother's mistakes in judgment.

His brothers assumed he was dining with Thyerri, and cheerfully kept their distance, in every sense, as they'd assumed all day that he'd been with his newly restored lover. Perhaps by morning he could come up with an . . . obfuscation to explain the disappearance of that lover, one that would survive even the test of their ever-strengthening mental link.

He extinguished all but one oil lamp, and wasn't certain why he left it alight. Leythium motes drifted into the tent through the slightest opening, whirled and danced in the darkness, adding the sense of light, if not the reality. He didn't need light, didn't need to see what lay outside himself tonight.

If it weren't for the distraction of unanswered questions and the real danger of having their knowledge of his and Rhomatum's affairs running about unchecked in the diverse persons of a ringdancer and a scoundrel, he could almost hope they were both gone forever. He'd managed most of his life without the interference of personal entanglements—other than his brothers—and his assessment of his own actions over the past weeks led him to believe he was just as well off without them.

And what does Mikhyel want?

Deymorin had posed the question for which he'd had no answer. . . . At least, not one he could admit, either to himself or his brother. He feared that what he truly wanted was to have loved . . . and lost. He'd found faith in his journey to Khoratum. Faith in himself, as a man and as a lover—faith in the notion that he was more than just the Barrister. But for Mikhyel dunMheric to do what Mikhyel dunMheric was born to do, he had to leave the source of that self-revelation behind, to take what he'd learned about himself and move on with his true life.

He feared that what he truly wished for was that tragic, fatal—poetic ending to his transcendence. For the one perfect night where he discovered he *could* make love, gently and passionately, to be all there was for him and his impossible love. In a perfect world, Dancer and Ganfrion would find happines and freedom in their beloved Khoramali and Mikhyel dunMeric would return to Rhomatum, to renew his contract with Nethaalye, secure in the knowledge he could, at last, be a true husband to her.

His first responsibility was still for Rhomatum. Deymorin's *Barrister* was tired of Mikhyel dunMheric's wandering attention, and wanted Mikhyel dunMheric *back* in Rhomatum with his damned noisy libido silenced. The Rhomandi brothers, the Barrister insisted, had business that needed seeing to.

Rhomatum was the core, the strength of the Web, and at the moment, the woman standing unchallenged at Rhomatum's helm was Rhomatumin by marriage alone, and a damned tenuous marriage at that. Lidye's Shatumin Family associations continued to hold her loyalty—and that was only the start of their problems.

By Lidye's actions the night of the coup, her collapse under stress, he couldn't even trust her ability to handle the Rings without Nikki's aid, yet she was there, alone, with only Nethaalye to temper her actions. Not that the Rings could take much more than a steadying hand, with the Khoratum/Persitum ring gone missing.

The knowledge that the reestablishment of the Khoratum/Persitum ring hung on such tenuous ability should be foremost in his thoughts and his concerns—that and the knowledge that his recent actions, both necessary and otherwise, had compromised, if not destroyed beyond resurrection, the work of a lifetime.

The Rhomandi brothers had to get back to Rhomatum as soon as they could, they'd agreed on that indisputable reality.

Nikki was going, doubtless riding as fast as courier relay mounts would carry him. Deymorin and he would follow their breakneck brother at the more leisurely pace demanded by their respective entourages . . . and his disinclination for riding. He'd have a sedate trip—apparently alone—by carriage.

Within a week, he'd be back in his own offices, with his own staff and a mountain of solid, recognizable problems to be solved. Problems which would not, apparently, include explaining his love life.

He wished that realization left him more relieved.

The eighteen—seventeen, without Khoratum—satellite nodes would require individual and intricate negotiation. But, thanks to his tour, however truncated it had been by his diversion to Khoratum, he now had a good notion of precisely which leaders to call to Rhomatum. He'd seen them in action with their peers and, more significantly, met their staffs. He knew who could get the job done. He'd met the dissidents and learned who had remained loyal, some by their absence from the gathering, others by their guarded speech and pointed questions.

Most importantly, he knew, as the plans and goals began to crystalize and his mind slipped comfortably into the old, analytic patterns, that *he* could get the job done. He could play the social part, as needed. He could push the past few weeks into a box and shut the lid. Especially with Dancer gone. He'd arrive in Rhomatum alone, as he'd always been. That in itself would silence most rumors.

Mikhyel dunMheric had bowed to the Barrister's greater significance for years. He could damnwell do so again.

Yet even that thought was not free of Dancer's contaminating influence. If he could consider himself as two separate entities for the convenience of explaining his personally aberrant actions over the past weeks and even months . . . if he could accept that, then why did he find it so difficult to comprehend Dancer's dual nature?

Was it—

He caught himself diving in the looped thinking that led to nothing concrete, only hours of leaping from one ring to the next—

"Dammit!"

A single sweep of his arm cleared the table before him. He set his elbows firmly and pressed his fists to his temples and repeated:

Rhomatum Rhomatum Rhomatum Rhomatum.

Rhomatum was his first love. His true love. His life's work.

Rhomatum was honest, with a city's solid needs, not some fickle human whim.

Rhomatum needed him now. Needed the Barrister, clear-headed and ready to deal with embarrassed, cowed, but still belligerent ex-rebel node-city leaders.

Ganfrion had been his eyes and his ears in Khoratum, while he had provided the diversion. Ganfrion knew which of those leaders had been most deeply entrenched with Rhyys, might well have heard details about those who had remained aloof from the conspiracy, those powerful individuals who might be the keys to reconstructing faith with the Northern Crescent. Tomorrow, he'd sit down with Gan—

But he *couldn't*. Ganfrion was gone.

He groaned and let his head fall into crossed arms.

There were written lists. Raulind would have them, and Raulind knew the code they were written in, having created it.

Provided Raulind didn't choose to leave him as well if Dancer didn't return.

It was a sudden, painful realization that he had become so dependent upon a select few associates, and how utterly alone he would be should they leave.

"Khy?"

Music on a breath of air, like the morning breeze through humming grass.

A touch on his back; he jumped despite Anheliaa's years of training. He steadied his nerves, and raised his head to stare into the lamp flame.

"So you came back."

"I never left."

{Lie.}

But there was no response to his challenge. The hand moved to his hair, smoothing it back from his face. That familiar touch was back. But Dancer's mind, his essence . . . wasn't. He was still . . . alone. A loneliness such as nothing in his life had prepared him for.

"Where have you been?" he asked the lamp flame.

"The source lake. I went there to heal."

A hand left his hair and extended into view over his shoulder: a stranger's hand, pink skinned, uncallused, without even the dancer's scars he was so accustomed to note.

"I couldn't find you."

"I was immersed."

"Gan go with you?"

Slightest hesitation.

"I needed his help, Khy."

"I could have helped you." The unexpected constriction in his throat nearly smothered the objection.

"I didn't want your help."

"Is that why your mind is blank to me?"

"That needed healing as well. I needed to find my essence again, to free you from me."

"I thought we'd covered that. I don't want to be free."

"To free myself, then."

Mikhyel inhaled deeply. "I see."

"Do you?"

Thyerri glided into view, a slender form, only vaguely human in his dark green, hooded cloak. A cloak of hiller styling. A cloak that hadn't come from his own stock, of that he was certain. A hand emerged from the folds and brushed the second chair clear of the contents of Mikhyel's plate before the cloaked form settled in the seat. As always, Thyerri's every move was full of strength, grace, and beauty. And pride. That heavy cloak masked whatever residual human awkwardness might have remained—

As a similarly cut, though far more ragged, cloak had obscured the real Thyerri the first time they'd met in Khoratum.

Thyerri had been all cocky resentment that night: bitterness, Mikhyel now understood, toward the rijhili who had singlehandedly ruined his young life. A rijhili, Dancer would have him believe, Thyerri had loved as much as he hated.

In their next encounter, only Mikhyel's own supposition had stood between them. He had been moved to ease a hiller woman's too-heavy burden, and in that moment of foolish chivalry and missed perception, he knew now he had set the pattern for their current dilemma.

Because he'd seen a woman . . . and a stranger—instead of the man from the alley . . . and instead of the dancer who had sacrificed his dream to save a stranger, he had set a distance between them. A distance Dancer had snatched and spun to his own purpose as deftly as he'd manipulated the swing of the dance rings.

"*Was* it to punish me?" he asked out of that overlong silence.

"That I went to the pool? No, Khy, not at—" A pause, then: "In truth, perhaps it was. I was angry that you wanted to hide me from even your brothers."

More honest than he'd expected, though not the answer to the question he'd intended. "I meant *Temorii*. Did you create Temorii to punish me? Did you think I noticed her only because she was a woman? out of lust?" There'd been no lust. He'd noticed her *because* he'd sensed that same battered but stubbornly intact pride that he'd seen in that cloaked alley-rat. The same pride, the resentment . . . and the fascinating grace, the strength, the cocky self-assurance. "I tried, that first night, to help Thyerri, but he—you—ran away. The second time, when you said nothing, *how was I to know?*"

The pride, the resentment, but not, also according to Dancer, the love, at least, not then. *Because they are not the same person. They did not learn to love Mikhyel dun-Mheric at the same moment, in the same way.*

Dancer set his elbows on the table, leaned forward to rest his chin in a cradle of thumbs and forefingers. "I don't know how to answer that. I acted . . . without thought. You were not the first to see Temorii; it was not the first time I'd used the name. But before . . . before, it was just the name, a name without essence, used out of spite, I fear, for the blind rijhili assumptions. The name, and your assumptions, gave Dancer a buffer between Thyerri and the object of his obsession . . . for a time, at least. But Dancer's love for Mikhyel was too deeply rooted, and Temorii gained more than a name. Dancer had found one refuge in Thyerri, a second in Temorii. Ultimately, both succumbed to Dancer's feelings for you."

Even together, they do not comprise the whole of Dancer.

"I don't understand. *How* could Dancer feel anything for me? *How?*"

"Dancer knew Mikhyel's pattern for a long time before they met. Dancer was entranced by the pattern, and Dancer loved what Dancer found in Khyel when Dancer joined Khyel's mind there at Boreton. Dancer found a part of Dancer's pattern that had been missing, and that pattern was a bud off the pattern of Mikhyel and his brothers."

There was a pause, a search for words, perhaps, or perhaps just a moment for Mikhyel to respond. But if the latter, it was in vain. Mikhyel had lost the capacity to reason. He could only listen and wait for the words to make sense.

Came a sigh from the shadowed hood, and the lilting voice continued. "Dancer learned that day what it meant to be a part of a whole. Dancer began to understand words like *brother* and *family* and *human*. Dancer began to understand what had been absent in Dancer's essence. And so, when Dancer returned to Khoratum to find abandonment from the only one who knew Dancer, Dancer floundered in uncertainty, floating in a sea of essence without any anchor to the World. To find an anchor, Dancer assumed a name for the men and women of Khoratum, a name Mikhyel would have chosen for himself, were Mikhyel a fallen dancer, not one like Sakhithe."

"I don't understand." His voice emerged a hoarse whisper.

"Sakhithe is a woman's name. Mikhyel would not choose a woman's name."

Mikhyel closed his eyes, thinking, hoping, fearing he began to understand. Male, not female. Dancer had been born both, had not seen Dancer as anything other than Dancer until Dancer merged into *his* mind. It was *his* . . . essence, that had helped Dancer *create* Thyerri.

Dancer's next words confirmed. "Dancer presented Thyerri to the world and found a human anchor in that name and strength in the name's association with Mikhyel and Mikhyel's strength. And when the rijhili failed to see that strength, when they saw instead a vulnerable woman, Thyerri mocked them with Temorii, who was woman but far from vulnerable. When Mikhyel saw Temorii and not Thyerri or Dancer, I was, I think, disappointed. Hurt, perhaps. And perhaps I even hated. But if I hated, I hated what I thought you were or had become . . . or perhaps, what you'd come to represent to me. It's possible I wished to punish—or perhaps to test. Not just you, but my own vision of you."

The cloaked shoulders lifted in a graceful shrug.

As if the reasons didn't matter, Mikhyel thought with his own measure of resentment.

Another shrug. "I don't really remember why I did all that I did. I've only just learned to consider those reasons, as I've never before felt the need to explain them. *I* understand my reasons. That others understand doesn't matter. That *you* understand . . . I realize now it is only fair that

I try to explain, but you must seek your own pattern and find how Dancer's reasons affect Mikhyel. I can say this: *if I hated, it was only at the very first. After a time, only a day or two, it became . . . a game. It was fun waiting to see if you would find out. Or, if you did know, when you would call my bluff. If . . . when . . . how."*

Fun.

But this was, he reminded himself, the person whose greatest joy in life was to leap among rings sharp enough to decapitate. Dancer did not live in half measures.

Even together, they do not comprise the whole of Dancer.

"I didn't mean to hurt you, Mikhyel. I didn't know I had the means to hurt you. I was sure Ganfrion knew the truth, at least about Temorii and Thyerri, so I thought you must know. Ultimately, I was caught in my own lie and Rhyys' trap and promises to you, to Rhyys and to Mother. I . . . had no answer for what to do, and so I did nothing. I thought . . . I thought I'd never see you again after the competition and so it wouldn't matter anyway."

Wouldn't matter. And thinking of it that way, perhaps it wouldn't have mattered. Mikhyel could have lived his fantasy forever.

"And then, after we . . . the night before the competition, I was certain you knew the rest, yet your thoughts were still only of Temorii, and I thought that was because Temorii was all you desired. Thyerri accepted that as a condition of being near you." Dancer shook his head. "I just . . . didn't know. So much I didn't know. I never expected this moment would come. Never dared hope there was anything beyond the competition—at least for us, and so I took what I could, and in doing so, I've hurt you. For that one thing, I'm sorry. I'm truly sorry."

And hadn't he done the same? One night together, once Mother dispelled the myth of the danger to a dancer who loved. One night where he'd endeavored to pack a lifetime of nights into one. *He'd have the memory . . .* One night when their minds had so meshed he couldn't have told afterward which body or what sensations were Mikhyel and which were . . . Dancer.

That night. That wondrous night when so many of his fears about himself had been laid to gentle rest. What of that sensory mix had been *his* response and which of those responses had been . . . Thyerri?

Anger flared, unexpected and startling. Resentment did. Was he *jealous*? Jealous of Thyerri's unfathomable intrusion into that perfect night? A night the memory of which, a kaleidoscope of sensation, was burned into his heart. And those myriad sensations had been a magical mix of Temorii and Mikhyel . . . until Dancer's revelations about Thyerri.

A man who mistrusted his very nature had to wonder if Mikhyel had entered that equation at all that night. A man who was honest with himself recognized the foolishness of that question and tried to smother the doubts. But the doubts remained, for all an honest man tried to ignore them.

If only Thyerri hadn't run off that first night. If only he'd explained the moment Mikhyel called him "mistress" rather than deride his rijhili perceptions.

If only Mother hadn't confused the issue beyond recognition the night before the competition by impersonating Thyerri in the parade of radicals.

If that even had been Mother and not Dancer himself deliberately confusing the issue—*for fun.*

That hurt.

"Was that Mother?" he asked, out of that thought, and from the confusion on Thyerri's face, he had no doubt that the barrier between their minds was complete. "The night before the competition. At the presentation banquet. Both Thyerri and Temorii danced there as well. Was that Mother impersonating Thyerri?"

Dancer drew up defensively, hands retreating from the table and coming to rest in his lap. "Perhaps Mother was impersonating *Temorii* all along. Perhaps it was Mother to whom you made such passionate love, Mikhyel dunMheric. Does that set your mind at rest?"

Another doubt cast on that once-perfect moment in his life. Mikhyel reached for the decanter, poured himself another glass, his shaking aim missing the cup as often as it hit, then, out of inflexible, civilized manners, poured a less wasteful second cup for Thyerri.

Thyerri pushed it aside.

"So," Mikhyel continued, "It's all in the past, is it? Over and done with? Accept blindly or not, and damn the truth?"

"I think you demand too much truth, Mikhyel. Reassurances I don't know how to give you."

"Or won't."

"Or can't."

"Which is it?"

"Take your pick."

Mikhyel's frustration escaped in a hiss. "Rhyys knew, didn't he?"

"Knew?"

"About you. Your double game. —*My* half-witted blindness."

"Your words, dunMheric, not mine." Dancer shrugged. "Difficult to say what Rhyys knew one day to the next, especially toward the end. Scarface certainly knew—about my double game."

Scarface. Thyerri's name for Vandoshin romMaurii.

"Then why did Thyerri have to appear at the presentation banquet? To mock us all? To confuse us?"

"All competitors attended. Thyerri appeared as Dancer wished to appear, and Temorii could not."

Cocky. Mocking. In hiller leathers and a feathered hat. Temorii had arrived and danced in a gown of pure leythium lace, that flowed and rippled as if with a life of its own.

And Thyerri was Dancer's choice.

Will I have to wear a dress?

"When Temorii entered the room," Mikhyel said in low-voiced rebellion, "I thought I'd never seen anything so beautiful."

"The gown was beauty incarnate."

"I wasn't thinking of the gown."

"Then I'm very disappointed. The gown formed the dance. Through *Thyerri's* dance, Dancer spoke to all viewers; Dancer created the leythium-webbed beauty for Mikhyel alone. *By my choice*, Mikhyel. It was a fine dance, a joy to make part of me, a greater joy to give to you. It was meant to be special. It was meant for you. *Thyerri's* dance was for the rest, to remind them *this* dance was of the hills, not Mauritum or Rhomatum or any other rijhili node."

As if his dance were an entity apart from his own body. Mikhyel doubted he'd ever truly understand the symbiotic relationship between Dancer's mind and his body.

"Is it too much to ask which times Temorii was real? Which times you were?"

"I? You mean Thyerri?"

"Thyerri."

"But when Mother was Thyerri, Mother *was* Thyerri. Dancer wished to dance many times and in many ways. There was a great chance Dancer would never dance again after that day. Rhyys' plans made a second Dance possible. When Thyerri danced, Dancer danced, and when Temorii danced, that was Dancer as well."

"Either it was Mother, or it was you."

"Where does Mother end and Dancer begin? I can't answer that, Mikhyel."

"Is Mother here now?"

"Only in my source."

"I don't understand."

"Where does Mikhyel end and Dancer begin? Where is the division between Mikhyel and Deymorin? Nikaenor is warded off Mother's mountain, and Deymorin and Mikhyel collapse."

"You're saying you experienced the dance through Mother, as I sometimes share sensation with my brothers."

"Like and not. Mother is both far more and much less than any of us."

"Will you stop handing me riddles?"

"I say things the only way I know, Mikhyel dunMheric. If you disapprove of the answers, I suggest you cease to ask the questions."

"You told me once you were human. I ask you again, are you human?"

"Yes."

"Can you mother a child?"

"I don't know, and I never thought about it."

"Can you father a child?"

"Rakshi was said to be both mother and father of dancers."

"You don't need me at all, then, do you?"

"If that is all you want of me, rijhili, look elsewhere."

They were back in the alley of Khoratum. Thyerri's cloak hid his face in shadow, as it had then. The mocking voice challenged rijhili prejudices—after his shadowed hiller mouth had taken Mikhyel's rijhili breath away.

"It's . . . not all," Mikhyel whispered, breathless in the wake of that memory.

"What else?"

"If I knew that, I wouldn't be throwing my dinner on the floor!"

Dancer laughed, a ringing, uninhibited sound. He leaned forward, the hood fell back, and his face was all light and freedom from the tension that churned Mikhyel's stomach. His hand reached out, inviting Mikhyel's to join it, an invitation Mikhyel's hand accepted before Mikhyel's mind could stop it.

Dancer's fingers closed around his, warm and strong.

"Don't starve yourself, my friend." His voice trailed off, and his eyes widened as his fingers tightened on Mikhyel's. "You *are* my friend, aren't you?"

Mikhyel's mouth went dry. "If that's all you want of me, hiller," he whispered, "I suggest *you* look elsewhere."

Thyerri shuddered, and the formal façade that had kept a safe distance between them since he'd appeared cracked. "Don't do this to us, Khy. Not again."

"What are you saying? *Is* that all you want?"

"Sakhithe says it would be best. At least for now."

"Sakhithe." So, Raulind had had the right of it: Thyerri *had* gone and visited the ex-dancer, ex-servant, ex-almost-lover, and came back wearing a hiller cloak, a cloak that masked him from Mikhyel's eyes, that armored him against Mikhyel's touch. "And you listened to her? *Went* to her? Why? Anger? Spite?"

"I went to see a friend, Mikhyel dunMheric. To wish her well and ask advice, such as she had to give, and which, in the past, has been very sound and helpful. She saved me from the gutters of Khoratum . . . and from other, deeper pits. She was taken by Rhyys' men because of me. Now she's safe, thanks to you."

"And she loves you. Wants you."

"She . . . I think, once, she might have harbored hopes for herself and Thyerri. I didn't realize that when we were together before, but there was much I didn't understand then."

"And now this Sakhithe is encouraging you to forget what we've shared and join her in the Beliisi camp." Mikhyel swallowed wine against the bitterness suddenly filling his mouth.

"No. Only to slow the pace and give myself room." The warmth left his hand, and Dancer's arms disappeared under the cloak, and Dancer's shoulders hunched as if he hugged himself, seeking warmth, protection: Mikhyel wished the move didn't feel so damned familiar. "This morning, I tried to kill myself."

Mikhyel surged forward in his chair, reaching, but a hand appeared from under the cloak, raised in reassurance.

"Half of myself. The half you weren't already trying to kill."

Temorii is dead . . . Hope surged, plunged, and surged again.

"I cannot live half measures, Mikhyel. I thought Temorii was less because she appeared second, but she is as much a part of me as Thyerri. I thought Thyerri needed your love more. I was wrong. As I can't let you see only part of the whole, neither can I deny my own nature. I went to Sakhi because Sakhi could be friend to the whole."

"As I can't be."

Dancer didn't answer, but then it hadn't been a question.

"Why her?" Mikhyel asked.

"Because she, of the few people I know, might understand."

"Because she's like you?"

"Like? . . . She was a dancer, yes."

"I mean . . . physicially."

"Oh. No. At least, I don't think so. I know of no others. Not for certain."

"Raulind says she loves you."

"Yes."

He closed his eyes, striving to control the black jealousy that would not go away.

"But I don't believe she loves that way any longer—at least about me. I think, perhaps, she has transferred those feelings to your Raulind."

That startled his eyes open. "*Raulind?* She'll find no luck there."

"Really? I was certain she said they'd spent the last two nights together."

"But—" He bit off his protest. Raulind wasn't a Barsitumin priest any longer. Hadn't been for years. But—*damn it.* First Thyerri. Now Raulind? His world was skewing beyond all recognition.

"I don't think it's a true pairing," Thyerri said. "I think . . . I think they were frightened for the future, and lonely and found solace in each other in time of need."

"And is that what she thinks happened to *us*? Do *you* believe that's why we came together?"

"You have several times denied my explanation for our 'coming together.' Sakhi merely told me that dancers who fall from the path frequently fall with overwhelming intensity, and that such intensity fades quickly. She says it's because we deny ourselves and our nature so long." He held Mikhyel's eyes firmly. "I'm not the only one here who denied those feelings overlong, Mikhyel. I think we would be wise to do nothing rash or with permanency until we are more certain of our feelings and our futures."

It was only sensible, what Dancer's Sakhi advised. But deny his feelings? Deny the urge that pulled him out of his chair and around to Dancer's back, away from that calming gaze? Deny that the mere scent of the hair was enough to drive him mad with desire?

Keep his hand from sweeping the shaded locks aside and stroking the strong, slender neck with his thumb?

And did Dancer's soft moan denote feelings in doubt? Did the tilt of the head that put cheek and jaw in reach of his thumb?

Did the hand that rose to clasp his?

Temorii was still here. He closed his eyes and lifted those silken strands, inhaled her scent and pressed his lips—

Thyerri twisted out of the chair and faced him, hands up and flat on his chest, pushing him back.

"Not now, Mikhyel. I won't live by halves. *Can't* and still be Dancer. I won't have you loving me today, only to have you hating me tomorrow." He backed toward the door. "I'll go and stay with the Belisii. They entertain for spare coin, and could use a dancer."

His throat spasmed. He swallowed hard. "You'll go with them and I'll never see you again. How can that help us?"

"They're bound for Rhomatum. They hope for trade agreements for their village wares. If not this visit, the next or the next. We must bide our time, Mikhyel. If we're meant to be patterned lifelong, the needs will not fade."

"They'll have their trade agreements. I can arrange it."

"They want no Rhomandi charity. They believe in the value of what they would sell; they will negotiate fairly." Dancer raised his hood again. "I think I should leave now."

"No!"

The hooded figure drew up, tall and defensive; Mikhyel drew in a breath, fighting for common sense that suggested Thyerri had the right of it, fighting the uncommon sense that whispered this time was the last; this time, Dancer wouldn't return.

"Please, Thyerri." He was unaccustomed to begging. Demands and concessions had been the way of his life. Pleading had brought only ridicule, in his experience. Still, he pleaded with all his heart, cast with words and inner voice: "Go to them tomorrow? I—concede your point. Time apart is—I'm sure you're right, it would be wise. But—if I'm to lose you . . . Can't we at least have tonight? One night, in full understanding. Or . . . do you in fact feel nothing? Have you rejected everything we had already?"

The shadows beneath the hood revealed nothing. That

shared essence was equally void of color and scent: a rejection more painful than any of the ridicule experience had brought. Mikhyel drew himself in, felt his own back tense, as still and quiet as the cloaked man.

"So. Well, I won't force you to stay." He hoped the pain and bitterness behind the words he forced himself to utter had the good sense to remain silent. "Goodbye, Radical of Khoratum, and . . . fare well."

Gray-cloaked shoulders fell; hope surged.

{Please, Dancer.} He sent the plea on a mental whisper: either Dancer would hear willingly or he would not hear at all.

The cloak drifted to the floor. Without looking up, Dancer stepped free of the folds and over to Mikhyel. When his face lifted, the naked desire took Mikhyel's breath away.

And the chill hint of fear that accompanied his touch vanished quickly in the fires of passion.

Chapter Seven

Pale eyes, green-rimmed and black-lashed . . .

It was the Dream, but with one exhilarating difference: it was no dream.

Khy's mouth brushed his in a lazy, breathy kiss, then fell away, his essence shimmering with sated pleasure. {Nothing left, my darling chameleon, no more.}

Chameleon. It was only a word, but a word, a mental flavor that accepted all that she was in all his variations; a word so different, so exquisitely different from those words Khy had earlier used to bypass the issue of what to call his dancer. Love, precious, darling . . . those were rijhili words. Chameleon . . . that was Dancer's Word, and s/he cherished it, held it to him/her, made it part of his/her pattern.

Dancer sighed and nuzzled the sweaty chest heaving in front of his nose. {Lazy, lazy, Khy,} he whispered, then snugged his head in under Mikhyel's chin as Mikhyel pulled the blanket up over their shoulders: guard against the chill certain to set in now the dance was over.

The Dream incarnate, except the lassitude now had nothing to do with Bharlori's bar or work of any kind. Only the dance of love. The warm presence was no longer a mystery, but Mikhyel dunMheric's arms surrounding him.

Silken strands slithered over his shoulder and across his chest like a spiderweb. His hair and Mikhyel's, ley-touched and blue-black, entangled and entangling.

The tendrils gained bone and muscle, became long fingers that stroked his chin and down his neck, where they intercepted moist warmth nuzzling his shoulder, then tread delicate patterns down his breast and across his ribs. . . .

Thyerri shivered at the mere memory. Mikhyel's mind had not flinched, his touch had not faltered. Mikhyel had called him Dancer in his mind and Thyerri with his mouth, and there had been nothing of rejection in his mind as they explored each other freely and intimately and shared their pleasure, until Mikhyel had . . . nothing left.

Temorii sighed again, shifted and wiggled, filled even now with the energy of the pool, not quite satisfied, even with all that had passed. Earlier, as Dancer and Ganfrion had drifted in the water, Ganfrion had spoken with great candor, had listened to the Dream and answered her questions freely, had told him things about her Khy . . . his silly, frightened Khy, whose cooling nipples tightened into hard nubs begging for a warm mouth's touch—

Mikhyel groaned and rolled away, curling himself into a protective ball. Thyerri laughed and pursued those aching nubs, became the warm presence at Mikhyel's back, became the fingers that stroked down Mikhyel's chin and neck, his the mouth that nuzzled Mikhyel's shoulder.

Leylight filled the air: motes rising from the floor, flowing through the fabric of the tent, eager to join with them in the dance of life. Energizing motes that tingled in his spine and gave added life to his desire.

As if he needed more. He filled his head with the Dream, knowing Mikhyel's sensitive mind would revel in it with him.

He groaned and shifted. But those fingers shifted with him, teasing, tempting, then drawing back, building the tension within until his pulse pounded with the rhythm of life.

{I knew you weren't done, my Khy.} He brought his touch back, delighting in the thrust of bony hip, the developing muscles of the buttocks, thrilling to Mikhyel's shiver as his fingertips rounded into the dark warmth between. And with that tour, the Dream began to expand, to incorporate the wisdom Ganfrion had shared, there in the pool of life. The Dream, Dancer now knew, that wasn't only Thyerri's, but was the union Thyerri and Temorii shared.

That had been Ganfrion's wisdom as well. It was the

union, Ganfrion had suggested on a deep laugh, between Dancer and Mikhyel that would exclude no one.

But Dancer hadn't laughed. Dancer had known from the moment Ganfrion explained that *that* was the culmination of the Dream. *That* was what he wanted from Mikhyel.

Show him the way, Ganfrion had suggested, *and he will follow.*

The leylight swirled about them, filled his lungs and fed his Need, and the Dream consumed him. He withdrew his hands from between them and pressed himself tight to Mikhyel's back, cradling Mikhyel's awakening flesh—

The presence at his back began to move, lifting him with it, leading, falling away and leading again. . . .

Mikhyel's back arched, Body following Mind, following Dream. Only in this Dream, Mikhyel was Thyerii, and Dancer the warmth at Mikhyel's back.

He is afraid, Ganfrion had said, *Show him the way. Show him there's nothing to fear and you'll have what you want. . . .*

Mikhyel's hand, following the Dream, reached back, seeking Dancer's buttock, fingers biting into heated flesh. The excited motes spun a whirlpool of rainbow colors around them, and Dancer's body sought the warm cocoon that was Mikhyel. Pressed gently, seeking access. . . .

"*No!*" The whirlpool exploded into a million pieces. Mikhyel's mind thrust him out, and Mikhyel's body fought for freedom. Mikhyel swung away and pushed himself upright, hunched over his knees.

"Khy, I'm sorry." He scrambled across the pallet and wrapped his arms around Mikhyel's shoulders, hugging him, but Mikhyel flinched away and snarled, and Dancer curled his hands back to himself. "What did I do wrong?"

"Where—where did you get . . . that?" Mikhyel's voice was strained, harsh.

"That? What?"

"Whatever you just brought into bed with us!"

"The Dream, Khy. It's just the Dream. I've told you about it."

"The hell it was. I've shared your dream before. That wasn't it."

"My essence is not so ignorant as it once was. I know what I want."

"Well, you won't get it from me! *No* one fucks me. Never again! *No* one, do you hear me?"

"Yes, Khy. So, I imagine, did half the camp." Dancer sat back into the pillows and crossed his arms, thrusting away the guilt along with the flare of sympathy that threatened. Ganfrion had warned; now he saw the truth behind that warning: Khy's own lies, his own shadows that rose between them. "I had no idea you viewed our . . . activities . . . in that fashion." Mikhyel's glower did not ease; Dancer continued matter-of-factly: "*I* love you, Khy. I love the feelings we share. I love the dance of love and every variation. I want to share them all with you. I want to feel me inside you, and you inside me—especially that, perhaps, because it's the oldest want, a want both Thyerri and Temorii share. I love it when you make love to Temorii, but it's Thyerri who has wanted you the longest, Thyerri who has had to dream the longest."

"You're still *living* in a dream world. It's not like that image you were so free with. It's filth and blood, and pain and humiliation." And the leythium motes screamed a raw and dark red.

{I don't believe that,} he said into the breach in Mikhyel's barrier.

{I don't believe, I *know*.}

{I'm not a child and you're not Hausri dunHaulpin.}

"Ganfrion has been talking too damn much."

"I asked for advice, for knowledge. To understand the dream."

"Rings, have you *no* shame?"

"There is nothing shameful in knowledge. And Ganfrion's words made a great deal clear to me. He says what I desire is not unnatural. He says that you're frightened, but very brave and I should help you past your fear."

"And Ganfrion can stay the fuck out of our bed!"

"I'll agree to that. I'm not inclined to share you with anyone."

Mikhyel turned to him slowly, his mouth slightly open. And a breath of suspicion touched with amusement drifted across his mind, an image of darkness and great massive rock overhead like Mother's caverns, but not. Of fear and humiliation, and a brother's laughter to ease the tension.

. . . I don't think Kiyrstin would be inclined to share . . .

And a fleeting thought that of all the pairings he'd seen, none were more natural than the one between his brother and the Mauritumin woman.

Natural. Mikhyel wanted to be natural. Normal. But Mikhyel would never be either of those things. Long before Mother or Thyerri, Mikhyel had passed much too far into the realm of Special: even with his limited experience, Dancer could see that.

"I don't want to talk about Ganfrion," Mikhyel whispered, and the anger was gone, leaving only a hint of desperation shining in the back of those gray and green eyes. Tamshi eyes, Zelin had called them, and said there were others like Thyerri where he came from. Thyerri had thought, once, to leave Khoratum and to seek out that distant kin. Had thought that, until Mikhyel's picture changed his needs and his life.

Until that distant kin to all that was significant appeared in the alleyway practically atop his half-frozen body.

{Anything you want, Dancer.} And that other self he had found was frightened now, the terror of loss more powerful than the fear of the past. And that fear of loss, not desire, made that concession, and so, for now, Thyerri, out of love, relinquished that portion of the Dream which so terrified that other self.

{Only when you want me as much as I want to have you, my Khy.} And he opened his mind with all the subtext of that promise and that desire, and tried not to mind when Mikhyel's relief flooded their united essence.

Part, he was willing to relinquish for Mikhyel's peace, but not all. *This one night*, Mikhyel had said, *with no lies between us.* This one night . . . because *Mikhyel* needed his peace.

Well, Thyerri needed his peace, too.

"Love me?" Thyerri asked and held out his hands, and Mikhyel's hands answered for him, bringing life once again to Thyerri's body. Mikhyel brought him to the brink and over, but when Mikhyel sought release, he found it within that inner space that Mikhyel thought of still as Temorii, and even as Temorii writhed with pleasure, in his heart, Dancer felt patronized and indulged.

The Ley swirled, feeding that need created by the Dream, a need that filled the essence and the nature of which Khy could not have mistaken.

Khy couldn't mistake, therefore Khy chose to ignore.

{No!} He pulled free, struggling to his knees. {I was Thyerri first. I'm Thyerri more. You love Thyerri or you don't love me.}

Mikhyel's eyes glowed green in the leylight. His need, and Thyerri's growing frustration filled them both.

{You said you'd wait.} Panic/anger/betrayal, all those and more came through.

{For *you.* You know what Thyerri wants. *Feel* what Thyerri needs.}

{You push too hard, Dancer.} And it was the totality of Dancer's pattern he used, but even that was a lie, Dancer now knew, a Barrister's pretense. Word games played by a master. The Barrister would claim that that internal acceptance should somehow be enough. Temorii was a proper vessel for Mikhyel's physical essence, the Barrister would further argue.

But it wasn't enough. It *wasn't.*

Dancer was shaking, Dancer knew he *was* pushing, and still he couldn't stop.

{If I want to live a dream, you want to live a lie!} He shot back, as outclassed in these games of words as Mikhyel was in the physical games between them. {You can lie to yourself, but you *can't* lie to me, and I won't live my life waiting for you to see *me*, and not just what you *want* to see.}

The dance of life rippled deep in the earth below, and found echoes in the surface world, in every living creature, large and small. For all *he* understood the source of that tension, knowledge was not proof against it, not with Khyel's need as well as his own adding to the strain. He should have left, but he hadn't had the strength. Mikhyel should never have asked him to stay, but Mikhyel hadn't the wisdom.

The Dance, once begun, must be seen through to the end.

"You tell your brothers not to coddle you," he said aloud, not trusting the inner voice, his thoughts had become that convolute, the meanings too layered. "You insist you're not afraid of me, not repulsed. Well, *live* with me, Mikhyel dunMheric! *Dance* with me now! Challenge your fears and let us lay them to rest at last!"

"No! I tell you, I won't do it! *Can't,* Thyerri."

{Can't? Do I hear can't, child of Darius?} It was Mother's challenge, lifelong. It had never failed to rouse the pride necessary to overcome fear.

Until now.

{Can't, child of the Khoramali.} And the heat, the *need* that had accompanied Mikhyel's essence vanished, vanquished by some unknown hidden resource.

And so the final movement came: stay, and be Temorii in Mikhyel's heart and mind forever, or take advantage of this reprieve and leave.

He couldn't win, but he could end it before he lost.

"Then we have our answer, don't we, Mikhyel dun-Mheric?"

Dancer pushed to his feet, and stepped from the pad, but the Ley swirled around him and pulled at his feet like deep mud, objecting to his leaving; the heartbeat of the node ripped through him, set his blood to pounding in concert with Mikhyel's heart as Mikhyel's control slipped.

Mikhyel *wanted* and that Want permeated the air, overriding fear, overriding anger, and all the other colors of thought.

Mikhyel's hand on his ankle tripped him, and Mikhyel pulled him back onto the pad, forcing a wrestling match

Dancer could have won, had he wanted to, though not as easily as once she had. Instead, she laughed and matched strength against strength, challenging Mikhyel to greater exertion leading to greater passion, and when their mutual need became overwhelming, he let Mikhyel win, let Mikhyel pin him on his back. Let Mikhyel's mouth devour his—

And then twisted, open challenge in his mind and body, open plea.

{Damn you.} Even Mikhyel's mind seemed breathless, but his curse tasted of concession. Thyerri waited, trembling with anticipation—

—and cried out in protest as Mikhyel pressed against Temorii.

{Shush.} Mikhyel's mind soothed as well as his hands. {Grant me this small wisdom.}

And in Mikhyel's thoughts, there followed a confusion of Temorii first, Thyerri later, which only meant that once again, Mikhyel would have *nothing left,* and Thyerri would be conveniently forgotten.

"No!"

"Dammit, Thyerri, I only want—"

"*I* want Temorii *gone* from your mind!" He filled the link with the Dream and all it encompassed, sensed a surge in Mikhyel's body to match that in his own, and pushed harder against the wall Mikhyel raised against his thoughts.

{Damn you.}

{Once, Khy! That's all I'm asking! Is that so much?}

{Yes-s-s-s . . .} A hiss, like Mother's sibilance and not.

Doubt threatened, cooling Dancer's ardor, and she reached for Mikhyel's mind, seeking reassurance . . .

That never came. And just before Mikhyel's mind closed off, it hinted of Rhomatum's fire-blossom tea—laced with the sickly sweet scent of honey.

§ § §

Release came, ugly and tainted.

Repelled by what he'd done, desiring only escape, Mikhyel pulled free before the final throbs ceased, still swollen, causing them both more pain.

Unnecessary pain, as it had all been so damned unnecessary.

Thyerri's breath came ragged and deep, but he was conscious; Mikhyel felt his mind reaching, trying to draw Mikhyel in, to share this experience as they had shared all the others.

Well, he damnwell wasn't interested. Mikhyel slapped the attempt aside. Whatever had made the dancer so damned insistent, he had his answers now, every vile, disgusting, painful answer. The vile, disgusting Truth behind Mikhyel dunMheric.

And Dancer had his wish: Temorii was gone from Mikhyel dunMheric's mind, not just for tonight, but forever, taking with her that purity and beauty, that hope for something approximating a normal man's existence.

He staggered to his feet and stared down at the sweat-slick back, the rounded buttocks where leythium motes coalesced. Drawn to blood, no doubt, healing, as the Ley was prone to do for Thyerri.

Most living tissue, the Ley would as soon consume.

Thyerri rolled to his side and stared up at Mikhyel, his eyes luminous in the leylight motes that danced in the air, revealing not a hint of proper horror. And again, Mikhyel felt Thyerri's mind trying to draw Mikhyel back. Back to Thyerri's mind. Back to Thyerri's bed. Trying to—

"No!" His own voice was as ragged, and the fingers of his left hand were bound in a webwork of hair. Thyerri's hair. Broken off as he—

And now Thyerri wanted more. Called him back.

For more.

And Darius forgive his descendants for what they'd become, a part of him *wanted* to answer that call, to lie beside this poor creature and take all that it would give him. Its draw was so powerful, he was on his knees beside it before he was aware he'd moved.

And somewhere, Anheliaa laughed.

Thyerri hadn't moved, had waited. Eyes wide. Anticipating. This child of Rakshi with its seemingly endless capacity for rutting—this creature of the Ley, whose body healed with miraculous swiftness, had drawn Mikhyel dunMheric into the very pit of his own black nature that he had deflected all his life.

Some might call them the perfect match: he could hurt it endlessly, and it would return for more, healing almost as quickly as his anger could destroy.

But one day, it wouldn't heal enough. One day, the anger would win.

Anger. His hands were shaking with it. He'd controlled it all his life, had found refuge in the law, where *rules,* not revenge, ruled.

And Darius forgive him, he wanted revenge. He seethed with the desire for revenge. He wanted Anheliaa's repulsive neck between his fingers one last time. He wanted to squeeze the life out of her. He wanted to divest dunHaulpin of his offensive organ and feed it to him one dainty bite at a time. He wanted to bankrupt all the officious, narrow-minded, money-grubbing bastards in the Web, who couldn't see past their own stuffed pocket book to the people dying in the streets around them.

And he wanted to push Thyerri down before him and take him again, and again, until he cried for him to stop and admitted he was—

The Dancer would die first.

As *he* had died, half a life-time ago.

But he hadn't begged dunHaulpin. He'd never begged for anything—until tonight, when he'd begged Dancer not to leave, and in that one stroke, had signed the death warrant on whatever scrap of humanity had remained in him.

The delicate strands rippled and flowed across his palms, turned blood red and dripped a trail across his naked thigh.

And somewhere, Pausri dunHaulpin declared his own twisted victory.

{Khy?} Gentle thought. Reassurance. A mental hand reaching to comfort. But along with the comfort came Desire. And the Dream. Even now.

And his blood surged.

"What have you done to me?" he whispered and then regretted. Dancer had done nothing. He was, as he had always feared, Anheliaa's creation. Anheliaa, dunHaulpin . . . Mheric: they'd all had a hand in his forging.

Thyerri hadn't died on the rings. Temorii hadn't. Mikhyel dunMheric had murdered them both. Tonight.

Dancer had left the dance and come to rescue Mikhyel dunMheric, had shared his mind as no human was meant to do, and the dark pit that held the worst of Mikhyel dunMheric had tainted that gentle, free, loving spirit and warped it into a living need. A need against which he had no defense. A need that would destroy them both—if it hadn't already.

"I'm sorry. I'm—gods, Dancer, I'm so sorry."

It was too late for him.

He stumbled away from the pad, gathering his robe and what clothing and undergarments found their way into his hands . . .

He could only hope it wasn't too late for Dancer.

. . . and without a backward glance fled to the darkness beyond the tent's doorflap.

§ § §

Raulind was awake and reading when Dancer entered his tent. He looked up, set the book aside, and held his hand out silently, seeming to sense without necessity of words, that everything had gone wrong.

But Dancer ignored that invitation. He'd come for only one reason.

"What happened with Pausri dunHaulpin?"

Raulind's hand withdrew, quietly and without censure.

"It started before I came to Rhomatum, before I even knew Mikhyel dunMheric existed. What I know is what I've pieced together from bits and pieces he has let slip. He talks freely, you must realize, to no one about it."

Dancer waited.

"Mikhyel's father used his son shamefully, of that I'm

certain. Regarding the precise nature of those acts, I know very little before the Pausri dunHaulpin incident."

It was an opening for questions; Dancer didn't take it. How and why Raulind knew things was irrelevant. That he knew was all that mattered.

Raulind nodded and continued, "Mheric Rhomandi sought dunHaulpin's endorsement on a project the nature of which is irrelevant. DunHaulpin set Mheric's son as his price. Mheric agreed, on the stipulation that he wait for the child's thirteenth birthday."

"Why?"

"Legal reasons."

Dancer waved his hand, not caring in the least for legalities, accepting what was.

"Khyel objected. An argument that escalated and left him very badly injured, locked in a closet and awaiting a father who never returned."

All this he knew, in one form or another.

"Ganfrion claims Mikhyel went to dunHaulpin of his own will."

"Later. To achieve a similar end for Anheliaa. To establish himself as a valuable resource."

"She knew?"

Raulind shook his head. "She wanted dunHaulpin's signature; Mikhyel got it for her. *That* was the sum total of her interest in the proceedings."

"What happened?"

"Details? I don't know. He was gone a week. He left a somber, silent child. He returned a cold, bitter, and angry young man. But he contained that anger, directed it toward becoming Anheliaa's bridge to the Syndicate."

"He never returned to dunHaulpin?"

Again, Raulind shook his head. "He would have. There came another arranged meeting, but it never came about." Secret humor tweaked Raulind's mouth. "Ganfrion didn't explain?"

"No."

"Ganfrion was gorPausri, then."

"No!" he refused to believe it of Ganfrion.

"A mistake, he admits. He didn't know of dunHaulpin's propensities when he took the oath. Afterward, he betrayed that oath and took steps to make certain dunHaulpin never did to another young boy what he'd done to Master Khyel, for all he had no idea at the time the identity of the boy he saved."

"And Mikhyel's second meeting never took place."

"Thanks to Ganfrion."

"And now Ganfrion is gorMikhyel."

"And lucky Master Khyel is to have such a man at his back."

Luck . . . "Rakshi's whim . . ." he whispered, but Raulind shrugged.

"Hardly pure coincidence. A man who does such a thing once does not limit his underground fight for justice to one incident. That Gan's deeds should ultimately intersect a man with the power and character to absolve his legal guilt, in that, yes, your Rakshi might well have had a hand."

Dancer stared across the tent, in his mind was the black guilt, the anger that had characterized his last touch with Mikhyel.

"And so, because of what this rijhili did to him, Mikhyel feels himself . . ." He sought the word that had flitted through Mikhyel's essence. "Tainted?"

"Very likely. But he's more and less than that. Anheliaa was equally destructive to him. As was Mheric. Mikhyel harbors deep passions and deep anger, and has never learned how to release them. I've tried to teach him, but I fear I've not been entirely successful."

"You have. He just doesn't realize it yet. He thinks he hurt me. He thinks his anger ruled his body. He thinks Anheliaa's touch drove him." Dancer met Raulind's eyes at last. "Sometimes, he thinks too much. —Good night, Raulind."

Chapter Eight

"What do you mean, Khyel's going with me?" Nikki couldn't believe he'd heard correctly. "He's never even been on a horse!"

"Actually, Nikki, we used to ride together quite a lot, before you came along." Deymorin pulled the girth snug, but not tight, and left the gelding he'd personally chosen for Mikhyel's mount to join Nikki. "He was quite good. Not your seat, of course—"

"He was seven years old. And riding a pony. How could you tell anything at that age?"

"I knew you would be the best rider I'd ever seen, so back down, brother. Mikhyel is set on this course, and I expect you to help him out."

"He'll only slow us. Let him follow in a carriage."

"Keep this up, and you'll be the one traveling by wheel, or bouncing down the mountain by the toe of my boot!"

Nikki pulled Tandy's girth a notch. "All right, Deymorin, but you know as well as I, he won't make it."

"Let him try. His mind's closed tight this morning, but he had some sort of falling out with Thyerri last night. He's overloaded. He needs to get back to his routine—"

"He's running away."

"Haven't we all? But you know Khyel. He'll deal with it as soon as he's able."

"If he doesn't kill himself first. Deymio, you know I'm planning on going straight through, using the courier relay stock. You *know* what a ride like that can do to the innards of a man used to it. Khyel will be all over the saddle. By the time we reach Rhomatum—Rings, Deymio, I don't even want to think about it."

"No, I *didn't* know you planned a straight-through. That's completely unnecessary. Make good time, yes, but at the very least, stop at the Raven's Nest."

"I'd rather not, unless I have to. But with Mikhyel, I damn sure won't have the option."

{That's why Gan is coming with us.} Mikhyel's voice in his head preceded his brother's arrival along with his gor-man. They were both dressed for riding, though Mikhyel's oversized clothing was obviously not his own.

And following that brief brush of his conscious thoughts, Mikhyel's mind vanished from the link. "If I can't keep up, he'll drop back with me, and we'll continue at whatever pace I can hold."

"Khyel, this is foolish. You don't ride. . . ." His voice caught as he got the first good look at his brother. Mik-hyel's hair, always meticulously braided when he appeared in public, hung free—and ended just below his shoulder blades, not much longer than his gorman's prison-hacked hair.

Mikhyel's chin rose. "And?"

"And *he's* wounded!" Nikki finished defiantly, with a side glance at Ganfrion. *Let* his brother pretend everything was normal. *Let* him pretend he wouldn't be the talk of Rhomatum with that radical style. He'd be lucky if the Syndicate didn't impeach him on grounds of insanity, once they got a look at it.

"Half dead, I can keep pace with the likes of you, boy," the big man growled.

"This time yesterday, you weren't the picture of health yourself, Nikaenor," Mikhyel said quietly. "You should temper your pace accordingly. Perhaps with me along, you'll do what's best for yourself as well." And underneath the words:

{He went with Dancer and soaked in the pool yesterday, Nikki.} Mikhyel whispered. {Says he's doing quite well and insists on going. He's of your own mind regarding my abil-ity to maintain the pace and assumes the two of you together can out-argue me. But it won't require that. Nikki, give me a few hours on the road—two—and we'll discuss the matter. I promise you, I won't hold you back. I have Gan with me.}

Nikki shook his head, not believing for a moment he'd last even that long, but he waved a hand toward the gelding. "Up you go, then. Let's see if you can even stay in the saddle."

"Nikki," Jerri began to protest, and he shook his head. He wouldn't point out to Mikhyel that the girth was still at standing tension, and if Mikhyel wanted that bit of information out of his mind, he'd have to dig past a great deal of extremely unflattering imagery to find it, so Nikki very much doubted that he would bother.

Deymorin looked at him suspiciously, but said nothing: and Nikki maintained a dead calm: this was *his* party, *his* call, and nobody on the road was going to be in a position to babysit his elder brother. He'd rather learn the extent of Mikhyel's ignorance here than halfway down the mountain.

Mikhyel gathered the reins, carefully positioning them—as a child would—and worked his foot into the stirrup a bit awkwardly, but then, so would any man his size be a bit awkward with the tall horse Deymorin had chosen for him. By the gelding's well-sloped shoulder, he'd have a smooth ride, but he'd have to get up there first.

Two hopping, aborted attempts to mount text-book correctly later, he set his mouth and gripped the saddle, front and back, and hauled himself upward.

Predictably, saddle and foot arrived in a tangle nearly under the horse's belly.

The gelding danced aside, Mikhyel hopped, got his foot free and brought the horse under control even before Ganfrion caught the horse's head.

Foolish, but not badly done. Nikki exchanged a look with Deymorin, while Mikhyel freed the saddle, but he refused to help: Mikhyel's choice, Mikhyel's duty.

His confidence wavered when Deymorin frowned at him and stepped in to reset the saddle. And when Deymorin said, "Nikki's an ass," loud enough for everyone to hear, he set his mouth and fought the heat rising in his face. But:

"Nikki was right to say nothing," Mikhyel answered, his voice low, but still loud enough to be heard by those that mattered. "I should have checked. I won't forget."

In response to which, Deymorin shot Mikhyel his biggest grin. "That's what you said the last time."

And received a faint, dead-eyed smile in return. "Slow learner, I guess."

"Twenty years is a long time to remember."

Twenty years. Deymio referenced events that had happened before he'd even been born. Nikki shifted in his saddle, anxious to be off.

"Twenty-one is longer," Mikhyel answered. "Time I got used to it again."

"There are easier ways."

"I'll manage."

"Maybe. But you never were very good at this part." Deymorin snugged the cinch tight this time, double checked it, then bent over with his hand cupped. "Leg up?"

Mikhyel set his toe in Deymorin's hands and Deymorin tossed him aboard as easily as he would a child. Mikhyel, Nikki had to admit, landed lightly in the seat, catching his weight with his off-hand before he hit the saddle so that the gelding seemed scarcely to notice his arrival. Once settled, Mikhyel set his stirrups with quiet competency, if not a particularly deft touch.

Sometimes he wondered if Mikhyel had ever done anything truly graceless in his life.

Mikhyel glanced over at him, and he regretted that thought, but in truth, horses had been the part of his life he shared exclusively with Deymorin. In truth, pettily perhaps, he didn't *want* Mikhyel to do well.

{Watch that, Nik,} arrived from Deymorin, who must have caught the thought. {He needs more confidence, not less.}

Deymorin's thoughts held hints of all that had gone wrong with the link, of the ways in which expectations found ways of manifesting in outward actions, and he acknowledged his brother's wisdom. {I'll try. —Sorry, Mikhyel.}

If Mikhyel had been privy to the exchange, Mikhyel, thought and voice, failed to acknowledge it. Mikhyel, in fact, was discussing something in a low voice with his gorman.

Ganfrion's horse had arrived with the rest of Mikhyel's entourage last night, a fine, solid animal built for endurance. The big man swung aboard without need of stirrup, his hands and seat as easy and natural as Deymorin's. Nikki did likewise, and settled in for Tandy's nonsense.

But if he'd thought to impress Ganfrion, he was mistaken. When he finally touched Tandy's shoulder to calm his dance, he found Ganfrion leaning on his horse's neck, man and horse looking equally bored.

"Don't suppose you'd care to direct some of that energy toward Rhomatum?"

§   §   §

{Take care of yourselves—} Deymorin aimed the thought at his brothers' diminishing backsides, and received something that might have been reassurance from Nikki, but Mikhyel's mind had receded, untouchable as he'd been all morning.

They were learning, the three of them, through simple self-preservation, if nothing else, to control their link. As long as they stayed on the leyroad, Nikki would be able to reach him, if worse came to worst.

Yet, because they were sticking to the leyroad, they'd be lucky if that resentment Nikki was radiating didn't knock Mikhyel off the horse at the first opportunity. Two hours, Mikhyel had said, and Nikki was right; he'd be surprised if Mikhyel lasted that long, even without Nikki's unconscious challenge.

Another part of him almost hoped Mikhyel would stay the course. Two days dealing intimately with Ganfrion might do Nikki some good.

And that hair . . . that . . . suggested Mikhyel's staying here in camp was not a good choice.

A man worried about his image and his reputation did not declare, in so public a fashion, a change in his attitudes. That decision, made on impulse and in anger would be with him for years to come. He could ill-afford any more slips.

Deymorin grew aware of a presence at his elbow, deliberate betrayal, he was quite certain. The dancer oozed across the ground quiet as a shadow when he wished.

"Are you all right?" he asked. He owed that to the dancer, no matter his loyalties. He knew Mikhyel's darknesses, knew them as a brother.

"Mikhyel thinks himself more cruel than he is," the dancer said.

"Did he hurt you?"

"Only when he left me alone. But I hurt him. More than I could have guessed. I pushed too hard. We should have waited."

Sex. Need. The air vibrated with it still.

A bad combination with two people already in complicated love.

{Thank you.} That musical voice sang in his head. {I only hope he realizes as much. He was far more gentle than she would have had him.}

{She?}

{Anheliaa.}

"Anheliaa's dead."

"Not in Mikhyel's essence."

There was an unwelcome revelation. But not unbelievable. Far from unbelievable.

"Then we'll have to drive her out."

"*We* can't."

Painful truth. There were indeed things a brother couldn't do.

"So what now?" Deymorin asked. "He said you would be joining the Belisii."

"I think not. The Belisii are bound for Rhomatum; Mikhyel and I need time well apart. I think I'll return to Khoratum. Ganfrion said you have left men to watch. I know the city. I'll find out what I can and send word."

"It could be dangerous. No matter the garrison."

"Most things worth attempting are dangerous. I'm quite certain this is. Something is happening in Khoratum. When I traced the warding, I saw . . . rings. Like they always were, but . . . black."

"Mikhyel said the same. Vandoshin's doing, he thought, until word came that Vandoshin had died. He felt Rhyys wouldn't have the talent."

"Mikhyel sensed that?"

"Before you put him to sleep."

"I had no idea . . ." The oblique-set eyes followed the rapidly disappearing riders. "He's even better than Mother said."

"Suspicious by nature, that's all. He doesn't *know* anything, from what I picked up from his head. —Don't risk it, Thyerri. You owe us nothing. Quite the contrary. Come with us to Rhomatum, and I'll make certain you have anything and everything you want."

"There's only one thing I truly wanted once the dance was gone, and that's lost to me as well, at least for now. No, that's not fair. I *drove* it away. I should have controlled the need. I saw what the Ley was doing to us both, and I let it. I had only need. He had fear and hatred. It was not . . . an equitable situation. This way, I can at least serve his cause. I have none of my own now, except to find out, if I can, what has happened to Mother, and that answer lies in Khoratum as well."

Mother. At once so much a part of the Ley that she should be considered with every issue, and yet was constantly forgotten—at least by him. Thyerri, obviously, never forgot.

Mother, and rings raised, in Khoratum. A situation seething with questions about the Ley and the Rings and all that would report to him as it stood now was the ley-blind captain of the garrison. The dancer, if he chose, could prove an invaluable asset. How Mikhyel would feel about his precious dancer throwing himself into this maze was an issue, but one Mikhyel would have to face, whether he accepted Thyerri's offer or not.

"You'll have what you need," Deymorin said.

A dip of the shaded head acknowledged, but didn't ask details. He doubted if Thyerri really cared about those details, but he'd make certain those details were covered before leaving for Rhomatum.

"When he asks . . . *if* he asks, you'll know where to find me," Thyerri said.

"Will you come to Rhomatum . . . if he asks?"

A long, slow breath, a lengthy consideration he could well appreciate.

"Truth, Rhomandi. It will depend. Change is . . . in the air."

True enough—for all of them.

"You seem to be making a habit of wandering in and out of our lives, Thyerri of Khoratum."

"After disrupting them beyond repair."

He couldn't claim the statement was unfounded. The dancer had made choices that had, in fact, disrupted their lives. Greatly. Whether or not that disruption was beyond repair . . .

"Only if my brother is a greater fool than I believe him to be. Take care of yourself, Thyerri."

"Dancer."

A world of revelation in that one word. He wondered if Mikhyel understood even now.

"Dancer, then. Take care of yourself and wander back to us as soon as you can. I have a feeling Mikhyel is going to regret his decision very soon."

"Truth, Rhomandi," Dancer said, but with a glint of suppressed humor in his gray-green eyes. "I suspect he regrets it already."

ॐ ॐ ॐ

It was a good thing Dancer wouldn't need him, if ever Dancer cared to procreate. Even if Dancer was still speaking to him after last night, following this particular piece of folly, the chances of his ever siring another child were only slightly lower than the chances of his flying to the greater moon for a Transition Day picnic.

Mikhyel clung grimly to reins and saddle, his knees already shaking and numb. The moment they'd hit the ley-road proper, Nikki had set them at a ground covering, running trot that was surely one of the nine greatest torments of hell.

He felt Nikki's eyes on him constantly, felt Nikki's doubts and frustration niggling at the corners of his mind, but he said nothing, avoided Nikki's gaze and blocked himself against Nikki's thoughts. Two hours, he'd asked for. After that, he could back down. He could fall back, letting Nikki forge ahead, and travel on to Rhomatum at a sensible pace with Ganfrion, free of both his brothers and their natural curiosity.

Free of Dancer, whose mere presence was enough to drive him mad, and whose raw needs had brought out all the darkness he'd feared lurked within him, darkness that even now, despite the pain—or worse, perhaps in part because of it—tightened his groin with desire.

Mheric, dunHaulpin, Anheliaa . . . their creation had come into his own last night.

Or had he? Last night, Dancer's Dream, however misguided, had invaded his mind with thoughts of pleasure and need that confounded the truth experience had brought, that forced him in the cold light of dawn to admit to the worst of the nightmare dunHaulpin had given him, the horror that with the pain, even in spite of the humiliation, sometimes there came pleasure.

Was it possible to have one without the other? Surely Dancer believed that. Ganfrion did. But—

Of a sudden, the gelding he rode, Boski, Deymorin had said his name was, stumbled, throwing him forward, then steadied back into the relentless two-beat rhythm. Mikhyel groaned, forced his knees to straighten, holding his no-longer-tight groin clear of the saddle for a handful of strides.

Two hours, he'd asked for; surely ten had passed.

The downhill grade leveled, and Nikki broke into a canter. The other horses followed. Childhood memory said this should be a relaxing gait after the bone-jarring trot, but to bruises and blisters, it was all the same nightmare. It was all Mikhyel could do not to cry out in relief when Nikki, without warning, eased the pace to a walk.

Mikhyel gratefully sat back, wondering, as Nikki consulted with the guide Deymorin had assigned to them, if his two hours were up and he could now gracefully back down. But, while the two faces held a measuring expression when they landed on Mikhyel, they didn't look as if they expected to quietly part company.

And indeed, when he worked his watch free of the layers of borrowed, unfamiliar coat, it was only to stifle another groan when he realized barely an hour had passed.

Nikki rode up to his side and said, in a low voice, "There's a side trail ahead that will take us off the major line for a few miles, but will cut off a large switchback. Khyel, I know we agreed with Deymorin to hold to the leyroad, but this will mean slower travel for a time and still get us to Rhomatum faster. I think it'll be easier on . . . all of us."

"Deftly fielded, Nikki." Mikhyel stood in his stirrups and stretched his legs, biting his lip against a scream of sheer, unadulterated agony. "I think if I have any chance at all, that could make a real difference. Let's try it."

"Are you certain, Khyel?" Nikki asked, and Nikki's face had gone quite pale.

"Sorry. Picked that up did you?"

Nikki nodded.

"Temorii always said—Dancer said I was lazy, and would regret not working harder." He closed his eyes and stretched again trying to push his heels to the ground the way Mheric had insisted, while trying to forget the methods Mheric had used to insure those heels stayed down.

When he opened his eyes, Nikki was staring.

"He didn't really do that, did he, Khyel?"

"Special boots. Strap from the toe to the top of the boot.

Shortened every day. Stretch that tendon and keep that heel down, and if it cripples the boy, serves him right for disobeying his father. Yes, Nikki, he did. Trained his horses the same way. Vicious brutes. Do you wonder, still, that I've not touched a horse since he died?"

Or that Mheric's second son, trained in a similar fashion, had become similarly vicious? Similarly brutish?

Mikhyel laid a hand on the warm neck before him, a creature innocent of his father's actions, kinder than any his father had trained, but forever linked in his own mind with fear and anger and resentment.

Almost as unfair, honesty forced him to realize, as his own assessment of himself. He had no reason to associate this morning's rudely interrupted arousal to the cruelty of last night; for weeks, *any* thought of Temorii had caused much the same reaction.

"You've done better than I expected, Khyel. Good balance, don't mess with the horse's mouth. I . . . I admit to pushing harder than I would have on my own, but I had to know. You must have learned something."

You must have learned something.

And therein lay his fears. No reason to make the link, but on the chance it had been made, for his soul as well as Dancer's well-being he had to rend himself from temptation. Of necessity or in anger, he had been cruel in his life; he'd never enjoyed it . . . and he didn't intend to start now.

Mikhyel pulled himself up and gathered his reins. "I'd rather not talk about it, Nikki. If I remember enough to get me to Rhomatum, that's all I ask. You'll not change my feelings about riding."

"I'm sorry for that, Khyel, I truly am."

"All I want is a hot bath and my own bed, Nikki. Get us there as fast as you can."

Two miles later, he was of a very different opinion, as the horses picked their way along a trail barely wide enough for a goat, with what Ganfrion casually termed a meaningful descent on one side. Personally, *he'd* call it a cliff. Stare straight ahead, Nikki had said, and: Trust the horse to place its feet.

Leap for the next ring and trust in the spirit of Rakshi. He swallowed hard, gripped the reins, and closed his eyes.

A moment later, the world fell out from under him, and a heartbeat after that, his mind went blank.

("Cut it."
("Sir . . ."
("Cut it, Raul."
(Shock. Dismay. "Khyel, be sensible. . . ."
("Enough for decency, then, but I want it gone.")
{Come, Khyel, dance with me!}
follow the streaming tail of hair, the dancer's own radical streamer. Float on the wind. Feel the currents in the streamer—
("I'm no dancer, Raul. Our ancestors chose a vanity and ignored the essence. I want no part of it!)
{Come, Khyel. Dance with me.}
But the call was weak, his resistance strong. He felt the currents no longer. He was in the room with the books and the fire and the wine, his hair falling free about his face.
The rings were gone . . .
And Dancer's voice was silent.

{Khyel?}
He was in the safe haven in his mind, the spot with the fire and the portrait of the family of his dreams and all the books he could ever desire. *{Khyel! Can you hear me?}*

{Nikki?} He yawned and stretched. He must have fallen asleep . . . but no, this wasn't real. Had never been real.

"Look out, boy."

A sharp slap to his cheek that was definitely not part of the haven and a protest from Nikki were enough to make him force his eyes open.

"What in . . ." He shook his head, expected pain and got nothing more than the aches he'd earned already. "What happened?"

"The trail collapsed under you. I—Khyel, I didn't know

what to do. I was afraid. I think . . ." Nikki glanced at the guards they'd brought with them. {Can you hear me, Khy?}

{Yes. Curious . . .}

{I thought you would. The Ley must be here as well. Mother said there were tributaries everywhere . . .}

"Nikki!"

{I . . . I took you over, Khy. At least, I think that's what I did.}

And the images came in a blur. A cloud of dust and dirt churning in the updraft, himself, a hazy figure on a brown horse, and then, it was his own hands, as if through his eyes, slipping from the mane, catching a better hold, his body leaning forward, swaying with the lunges as the horse scrambled back to safety . . .

{It was like . . . like I was me and you, and I—you—were holding on as the horse got himself back on the trail. I was afraid you'd fall, Khy. I'm sorry.}

{Sorry?} The possibilities flooded his mind, and without giving himself time to consider the consequences: {Nikki, I have only one question—two actually: can you do it again, and how long can you keep it up?}

The next time he emerged fully from the fire-lit room, he was in Rhomatum, and the Rhomandi physician, Diorak, was leaning over him telling him he was eighteen kinds of a fool.

Fool, perhaps, but he was alive, warm from a hot bath, and in his own bed at last. A bed that, for the first time in his adult life, felt strangely large. Cold, despite the carefully controlled temperature of his room.

Empty.

SECTION
THREE

Chapter One

Mikhyel delicately moved the lever, filled the pen and wiped the tip, all without a stain on his fingers . . . a precise instrument, a precise ritual at his desk, the fine-line nib worn to his hand to a glassy smooth flow, as nibs did rapidly wear to his hand after a month in his possession. He was home again, in the office that was more *home* to him than any room in Rhomandi House, home with his books, his records, his shelves—his life—all in order.

And he had his notes. Most importantly, he had his notes, though by now, some three months after he'd written them down, most of those had been ticked off as accomplished or underway. He had his notes and the final few sheets of a good ream of smooth rag paper.

The balance of that ream lay in the safe behind his desk, the contents of those originals having been copied a dozen, a hundred, and in some cases thousands of times over by his own army of clerks and the Syndicate print shop.

In those sheets—the future of Rhomatum. Treaties, trade agreements, waiver of liabilities, and dissolution of old agreements in favor of new ones, right down to the market strategy and the import quotas. A plan, complete and elegant, wanting only the endless details. In pursuit of those details, his life had become a steady stream of private meetings and open debates, of long nights without sleep and drugs to quiet his mind when his body collapsed.

And he had no dreams.

He'd ridden back to Rhomatum, a passenger in his own body, and the moment he'd awakened from his self-imposed exile, he knew he'd mortified that body enough to bring his *mind* back to the business of Rhomatum.

Sometime during those hours, the lingering memory of his personal failures had merged with that hellish ride down-country, and he'd realized precisely what he needed to do—what he needed to do in the office once he could move and sit in a chair again, and what he needed to do in Council, once he could get his peers to listen.

The hardest task had been getting those plans outlined before his mind lost the details.

He'd had his notes to take ... desperately had his notes to take. Diorak, hadn't liked it in the least, but he was a Rhomandi man, and Diorak had supplied the powerful drugs he'd demanded to keep his body and mind functional and awake for three successive days without sleep. He'd taken those notes, and set agents to collecting information, dictated letters, memoranda, and directions to a rotation of clerks—all from his bed, since Diorak had refused to let him up.

He'd finished. Then he'd slept. To this day, he didn't know for how long.

By the time Deymorin had arrived in Rhomatum with Raulind and the rest of Mikhyel's staff, he'd been ready to return to his office and to put that same staff to work writing the proposals and directing the campaign to reorganize the post-Khoratum, post-Anheliaa Web.

Everything he'd planned in that silent inner room of his mind on the wild ride down, while Nikki's waking mind controlled his body, and everything he'd dictated during his recovery, while Diorak's drugs helped control his pain and (more importantly) keep him awake, was in his notes, and those notes now, day by day, were flowing into reality, in diplomatic letters to node cities, in proposals and treaty drafts, and in private letters to individuals he'd met throughout the Web who shared his dream and were just waiting his cue and direction to take action.

And when the image grew muddled, when one too many new factors entered the equation, well, he and Nikki just went riding again ... to Nikki's clear amazement. A trip to Armayel and back, a turn about the Barsiley forests, a crazed gallop across country . . . to which dangers he remained blissfully ignorant, thanks to Nikki . . . and he had just about enough time in that inner room to revise his plan to accommodate the new elements that came in with daily messages.

Because the crash of the Khoratum Rings was not the only disaster. In Persitum, Khoratum's delicately balanced reciprocal node, the tower rings had likewise crashed— three times now. Ringmaster dunDrison was becoming something of a master's master at resetting. Even when Persitum's Rings spun, with her link to Mauritum cut off for reasons still under debate, and without the Khoratum/ Persitum ring spinning in ley-link inside Rhomatum Tower, Persitum's power was drastically reduced, barely enough to cover the true emergency needs of hospitals and food storage units. For the luxuries of heat and light, Persitum's citizens were resorting to firewood and oil lamps.

It was a situation unprecedented in living memory.

Under Deymorin's respectful supervision, the master craftsmen of Rhomatum were recasting the Khoratum/Persitum ring according to the exact specifications recorded by Darius three centuries before, which would make it second largest of all the node rings, third in diameter counting the Cardinal.

Of course, no one knew whether or not those specifications were any longer valid. Darius had made the calculations on an established node with eighteen established satellites, all according to theories still under debate. For as long as he could remember, scientists and philosophers alike had debated whether a leythium web *could* change . . . a question now somewhat moot.

How that new node would affect the balance of the umbrella or whether the ring being cast would be appropriate for the task . . . only time would tell. All the ringmasters seemed to agree that it was a sensible place to start, that only the ringmaster bringing the ring up would be able to tell if the line could hold it stable.

Besides, as Deymorin had rather cheerfully pointed out

over the dinner table only a month ago, if the entire lot crashed . . . well, that *had* happened before. The Web would just have to be prepared for that eventuality.

Lidye had nearly choked on her soup.

The task of restoring full function would be easier if Lidye and Nethaalye hadn't agreed that the Shatum/Giephaetum ring needed to be replaced as well. The Shatum/Giephaetum ring was outermost of the node rings and had been damaged when the Khoratum/Persitum ring shattered.

At least the new node that had broken forth lay directly on the Khoratum line, opposite Persitum. That simple geographical reality at least saved them the danger and the benefit of an entirely new leyline opening up, with its reciprocal sure to follow . . . danger, because Rhomatum already tested the limit of the number of leylines a Tower or a ringmaster could manage, and they no longer had Anheliaa as ringmaster.

They had Lidye dunTarec. Nikki's Lidye. And Mikhyel, when he spared a worry for the Rings at all, had his doubts whether it was truly Mirym's action that had shattered the Khoratum ring or whether it was the Ley itself slipping the less expert hands of Lidye dunTarec.

Anheliaa had been an inescapable force in his life. She'd been ruthless and single-minded in her ambition, but she'd been a legendary ringmaster. No one could question that the Rhomatum Rings had spun to her bidding. At times, even the radical streamer had seemed her personal pet. Her assistants, who had watched the Tower when of necessity she had left it, had been little more than conduits through which she monitored the Rings. The assistants would say that even when she slept, they could feel her working through them.

At least, they'd admit to it now Anheliaa was dead and in response to questions from a member of what had become known as the Rhomandi Triumvirate. Before, they'd been Anheliaa's closemouthed minions, that silent communication a secret they shared with the Ringmaster of Rhomatum.

Of Lidye's comparative command, those assistants were

judiciously ambiguous in their comments, though from the looks they'd shared as they answered his questions, he had to wonder if they were simply assuming he was picking the details from their thoughts, details they dared not voice.

He couldn't, but he hadn't revealed that deficiency, had acted instead on what years of interrogating far more devious individuals had taught him to notice in human behavior and consequently startled many a look of fear and reluctant nods from them.

Their reports only confirmed what he'd suspected from the start, that much went on in the Tower of which Lidye was completely unaware. Since his return, her control appeared to have diminished even from what it was. She appeared utterly deaf to the Rings, except when physically in the Tower, a weakness which did not help the confidence of the man accustomed to making agreements based on the Rings' reliable performance.

It was not, however, a point he wished to raise . . . yet. That same weakness worked very well for Deymorin, who for the first time in his life and of his own volition had quietly set himself to learn the routine management of the Rings as the Rhomandi birthright and duty. Thanks to Lidye's apparent obliviousness, he could slip in and work unnoticed. With Nethaalye as his willing accomplice, he was in the Tower daily, when he was in the City.

Deymorin felt he could achieve some moderate skill in controlling the Rings, he had certainly shown the talent, and the day Deymorin felt truly confident he could control them if Lidye failed, Deymorin's brother would be very much relieved.

Ring casting, ring management . . . ring mastery—overall, Mikhyel was very happy to relinquish that particular headache of the House Rhomandi legacy. Mikhyel by his own choice no longer had anything whatsoever to do with the Rings, Mother, or the Rhomatum ley-creature—if that creature had ever truly existed, a matter he sometimes questioned in the confused memories of those turbulent days. The wall of pain had set at a distance all that had preceded that ride, and Rhomatum's manifestation was part of that welcome haze.

Deymorin had tried to reach the Rhomatum-creature; Nikki had; once Mikhyel had reluctantly joined his brothers in a joint attempt, but all to no avail. If the ley-creature still existed, he drowsed under Rhomatum now, engaged (so Deymorin liked to quip) in a post-coital nap.

For himself, it was enough that his nights were quiet. He wanted no more distractions, was more than happy to entrust all matters of the Khoratum line to Deymorin, and trust his brother would tell him should anything occur that might impact on his current negotiations. He knew a permanent garrison was going in at the new node. He knew Deymorin had allowed a group of hillers to move in and settle beside Nikki's pond that had now become, from all reports, a picturesque lake.

He knew that whatever was happening in Khoratum was not reaching his offices in Rhomatum, and beyond that, he didn't care. Couldn't *afford* to care. He had to proceed with his life as if there had never been a disruption; he had to proceed with the City's business as if the Rings were as stable as ever and as if there would never be another power crisis. He had to deal with Persitum as if that ring would rise and normalcy would return. For his sanity's sake he had to do the one and for the survival of the Rhomatum web he had to do the other.

Six months ago, he had persuaded himself that he had charted the course of the City so ably that his subordinates could run it. He had persuaded himself he could leave this office and hare off across the countryside, that the Rings would run themselves, that Lidye was adequate for the job, and that he could, by going out into the country, settle the last-gasp resistence of certain moneyed interests in the Web to dealing with each other in honest good sense.

He had gone so far as to think he could leave his post— so far as to delude himself that he was made for anything other than what he did here, in this office, and did better than anyone.

But he saw now and clearly, in the fall of the Ring and

the disaster that followed, that he had been part and parcel of that disaster. His leaving had caused it, if indirectly. His presence here could heal it—directly. He was the last of Anheliaa's administration in power. She had taught him to wield the civil power that came with the Rhomandi name, and when Anheliaa had grown too distracted and too ill to think of anything beyond the Rings and her own ambitions, he had used the secrets she'd taught him, the contacts she'd given him, to mold her policies to his vision of the Syndicate. She had, in her way, relied on him, and his actions had made the City rely on him.

He could save his vision of the Web . . . if he had a ringmaster capable of raising the downed ring. Perhaps one day they'd cap the new-born node, but that was years, perhaps centuries away. They were back to the power levels of the pre-Khoratum years, which was a blow, but hardly a fatal one: even before Anheliaa had capped the high-mountain node, last of the Rhomatum web's satellite nodes, Rhomatum had been largest node city in the world. In a world of two, one had to be greater, the other lesser. Mauritum had the same number of satellites, but the number of functional, capped tertiaries in Rhomatum far outstripped the island web.

The greatest number of nodes, the largest rings, all to link eighteen cities in a mutually dependent, albeit uneasy alliance. But the Web would not be what it had been until those rings cooling in the temperature-controlled depths beneath the Tower were up and spinning, and on the day that happened, that alliance would stabilize. He was as certain of that as he was that the sun would rise in the east.

But the new rings had to spin first. He feared Lidye was not up to the task, but who was he, after all, to complain of Lidye's performance to date? Lidye had to get those rings up, had to supply the power for the Web's industry, for light in the cities and heat in the homes; he had to restore the diplomatic stability that his personal faults had damned near ruined. He could *not* lose himself, not again.

Lidye was Deymorin's problem.

He wrote. He cradled a large *paciimi* mug in one hand

and sipped the dark brew, tempering its bitterness with a liberal dose of heavy cream. Paulis had gifted him with the cup itself . . . and a crockery brewing pot . . . on Transition Day last. Much to his personal secretary's dismay, he'd rarely touched the drink prior to his tour; now it seemed the mug rarely left his hand. In some ways, the bitter drink was as potent as Diorak's semi-legal drugs.

And Paulis was his willing supplier of a variety of specialty roasts and flavors . . . all of which boiled down to two simple virtues: they kept his fingers warm and his mind awake.

Which raised the question of whether or not the import of the beans from which the drink was brewed ought to be controlled. Lawyer thoughts, a ridiculous notion that raised a chuckle as he finished his letter draft, set the mug aside, and picked up the first of the day's petitions: ban paciimi?

In a matter of a few years, paciimi had become damned near as important as the Ley itself to every office on the Hill; if they prohibited the drink now, the entire government of Rhomatum would collapse in nervous prostration. Murders would proliferate. The black market would rule the economy of the City.

It was a southern vice. It seemed destined to spread north. If it produced tranquillity in City offices, he had no desire to stop it.

Topmost on the stack of folders was the monthly listing of civil requests for official authorization. A cargo-hauler's request to enlarge his stable on the Orenum line, a couple and a widower asking for a third-party extension on the marriage, a second twin requesting a change in birthdate . . .

People did change official birthdates, for symbolic reasons. Usually, as in this case, it was to establish clearly a separate festivity from a twin. Less often, it served to sever the person in question from an unpleasant association—a reason he well understood, having taken the step himself ten years ago when he came of age.

It was a series of prescreened, near-automatic signatures and seals and—

"Paulis!" he shouted, and from his private secretary's

office, just off his own, came the scrape of a chair and scuffle of feet. The bespectacled young man appeared a moment later.

"Sir!"

He held up a birthdate-change application. His hand shook. He had not intended that his hand shake. He had not intended to have a fit of temper. He was working hard at getting those under control. But this, in his previous train of thought, was a cap to a string of events starting with the damnable mess in the ringtower. "How did this get in here?"

Paulis frowned and ventured closer. "What is it, sir?"

"Another demand, this time in the standard form, on the ordinary blank, from my sister-in-law, to change her birthdate to the Ringmaster's Day."

"Sir, I didn't know."

"Has she been in here?"

"No, sir."

"Any of her ferrets?"

"No, sir—none that I—wait. *Dammit!* Your pardon, sir. A man was in early this morning. To fix a leak in the window, he said. He had a signed work order. I kept an eye on him, but not, I fear, a particularly diligent one. He was a workman. I'm sure he was a workman. He fixed the window."

Paulis at times had a naive view of the social order. They had maintained the highest security on his notes and his work, knowing that his return to this office had threatened certain interests just as surely as his presence in Khoratum had turned over rocks and exposed the crawling life underneath to light.

He had not intentionally included his sister-in-law in that number of conspirators, but damn! she had become tenacious on this point. She'd invaded his sickroom and his drugged concentration on his work to urge her damned birthday change, she'd confronted him again on the stairs in the dining hall with a written request, and considering what had happened, with Mirym flown from the Tower and a ring shattered, he was not in a mood to coddle Lidye.

"Damn the woman anyway! She *knew* I was coming in late today. She must have gotten one of her men to slip this into the stack."

"I should have been more careful."

"Not should have been, Paulis, but *will be* from now on. No workmen I don't pass. What did the woman think? That I wouldn't *read* what I was signing? Third damned time she's made this request."

Paulis was red-faced, hands behind him. But he lingered and absorbed the instruction; and he was not a stupid man. "With all due respect, sir, could she be plaguing you in this one fashion to catch you unawares in another? You know she wants this change of birthdays very badly. Perhaps she thinks to do something more subtle—like slip the 'news' to Lorianthe dunHustrip, that Rhomatum's Transition Day parade will formally welcome the new Ringmaster of Rhomatum to office."

Transition Day was the first day of the intercalary days' festival that reconciled Darius' calendar year with the seasonal, and the only recognized state holiday. It also, and not coincidentally, happened to be Ringmaster's Day, the traditional birthday of the Ringmaster of Rhomatum.

And *damned* if he'd let Lidye have it until she'd proven she deserved it.

"Of course," Paulis continued, blinking behind his spectacles and rocking on his heels, "it would be foolish indeed for the *Internode's* society page to print such an announcement without gaining confirmation from the man who signs the papers."

Mikhyel let out a shout of laughter. "And you wonder why I keep you around, Paulis. Out with you, now. I've got work to do."

"Aye, sir."

He hadn't intended to lose his temper with Paulis. Lidye was pressing for official endorsement; and had fastened on this means to force the issue. Damn Darius the Third for an absent-minded fool anyway. It was *his* inability to remember his own birthday that had led to the whole tradition.

Never mind he'd made the change of birthdays himself,

the day he turned seventeen, changing his official birthdate away from midwinter, away from a day that held such bitter memories, to a date in the late spring, well past the final freeze, to a time when the earth was renewing. Many people did, for sentimental reasons, even business reasons.

But no one, absolutely no one, ever *asked* for Ringmaster's Day.

He rubbed eyes gone tired and blurred, and located his reading glasses from among the stacks, feeling suddenly very much older than twenty-seven. His choice of birthdates hadn't worked out any better than the one he'd been born to.

Maybe he should let Lidye have her whim and hope it went as sour.

But *dammit,* Anheliaa's choice of Lidye as her successor notwithstanding, Lidye *hadn't* proven herself worthy of that title or that day. Not yet. Not until she raised the Khoratum/Persitum ring and had it stay.

Maybe not even then. Damned if he'd even set a private goal for this particular decision.

"Sir?"

He looked up over the half-glasses' rims. "Yes, Paulis?"

"A note for you, from gorMikhyel . . ."

He blinked, his mind overall so far removed from Ganfrion's activities these days that it took a moment for Paulis' announcement to register. And then he recalled that, for once, Ganfrion had been engaged on *his* business rather than Deymorin's.

"He's back from Giephaetum, then?"

"I'm not certain, sir. This was delivered from the front office along with a notice of a packet. I'll have to go sign for it at the guard station."

Mikhyel received the folded missive, slid a nail under the seal, found a simple scrawled: **Sorry, Suds. Details later. Bed's calling.**

A curse died unuttered.

Failure, then.

Nothing they hadn't expected. Ganfrion, who had been running back and forth to New Khoratum all summer, helping his chief antagonist *Deymorin,* of all people, set up the permanent military post there, had asked to be the one to look into the death of Giephaetum's former ringmaster, Ioniia.

They'd been hoping to find evidence pointing at someone other than at Nethaalye's own brother, Verti dunErrif. Ioniia had opposed the rebellion and the conspiracy that had brought the consortium of anti-Rhomatum interests to meet with Rhyys in Khoratum, all of these types hoping to use Mauritumin help to gain their independence. Verti dunErrif had been one of those most keen to break free, a key factor in pushing Errif himself into the conspiracy; he was a self-centered if gifted scoundrel, and so far everything they knew pointed toward him as, at the very least, the instigator of the lady's death, whose demise had left Verti himself in charge of the Giephaetum tower.

Sorry, Suds.

He discovered himself twisting the ring he wore, the copy of the Rhomandi ring that had come back to him before he'd risen from his bed. Ganfrion had one of his own now, fitted to his finger, made on an order he'd carried with him from New Khoratum. Deymorin's order.

The original . . . that had been on the hand of the corpse carried from Khoratum Tower three months ago. The corpse of the man at the hub of the conspiracy. A man who had more than once used that ring to sway otherwise right-minded people, as he'd discovered in the past three months. People who believed they were backing Deymorin, the rightful Princeps, against a power play orchestrated by the second Rhomandi brother.

So convolute the picture had become; so many the concessions for equity's sake.

Verti was not, evidently, one of those innocents.

He was sorry. He was sorry for Nethaalye and what it meant to her. Damn, damn, and damn. He was sorry he had to do justice. He was sorry he couldn't work a miracle for a woman he otherwise owed profoundly.

He had hoped. He had very much hoped he was wrong.

"Go get the packet now, if you please," he said to Paulis.

"I'll just have time to scan it before my luncheon meeting with the Giephaetumin delegation. It might contain news I should take with me."

"I hope so, sir, for everyone's sake."

"Thank you, Paulis."

Small chance of that. Had there been anything significant of hope to him, Gan would have brought the information in person.

Sorry, Suds.

Damn!

He'd never met Verti dunErrif, and nothing he knew of the man's character gave him reason to regret the findings personally. But for Nethaalye's sake, he was more than sorry. For her sake . . . and his own.

He'd asked her two days ago, in the one private meeting they'd managed to work in since his return, to renew their previous marriage engagement and make it permanent before winter. Of course she hadn't given him any personal reason for refusing him; she'd simply said she couldn't marry him.

It hadn't surprised him.

She'd said . . . her words . . . she couldn't do it to him and not to herself, and he'd tried not think about it since.

Likely she'd heard about Dancer. He'd been afraid of that before he asked her. Kiyrstin knew, he was certain. Kiyrstin had met Dancer. Deymorin would have explained to her. Deymorin would have explained *everything* to Kiyrstin, and Kiyrstin and Nethaalye talked daily.

Of course, the simple fact Mirym carried his child was reason enough for Nethaalye to reject him, for all she'd said forthrightly that she considered such dalliance with a servant quite unexceptional in a man of his stature, and the existence of the child to be an act of Anheliaa's, not the gods or Mirym or himself.

But even if that was true, and Nethaalye had never lied to him, it was not how the world beyond Rhomandi House would view the situation, and she would bear the brunt of all such ill-considered rumor.

It took a special talent for a once dedicated celibate to

accumulate such a bewildering tangle of scandal in so short a period of time. If he were Nethaalye, he'd look elsewhere, too. He was a fool, he supposed, for even considering pursuing the marriage their parents had planned, but he'd thought—hoped—gratitude might dispose her to renew the engagement, if only he could have cleared her brother.

Now Gan's report made it certain he had to do something that could only widen the breach between them.

Not that she held any illusions about Verti. Nethaalye was, among many other sterling qualities, honest with herself. Honest, honorable, intelligent—all the qualities a man could want in his life's companion, and talented with the Rings, as well. She was an asset to the Rhomandi house, if only he could keep her.

Her brother's treason might be overlooked by the social set under the wide-spread banner of amnesty that had been required following the coup attempt, but the charge of murder besides was certain to be hard on her family. Dutiful daughter that she was, Nethaalye might well choose to go home, though what sort of welcome she might get remained to be seen. Her father, one of Rhyys' major supporters in the rebellion, had not been so foolish as to reject publicly the daughter who had sided with the Rhomandi, but privately he was by no means a tolerant man.

Mikhyel didn't want to see Thaalye hurt. He didn't want to see her leave, either, under any circumstances. He by no means wanted that. The Rhomatum tower needed her.

And he needed a solid marriage for the sake of the Syndicate. The Syndicate wanted stability and normalcy in its leaders, and he had to regain the reputation his Khoratum performance had nearly destroyed.

In the wake of that fateful night, no one had dared mention his ringdancer to his face . . . yet. But he was certain it was there, lurking behind the pleasant faces and amiable manners he met. He kept waiting for it.

Now, to cap all, there might be a question about Nethaalye's family's stability. The rock of probity on which he had hoped to rebuild his own reputation . . . might turn to sand. It might not be to his advantage, politically, to have that engagement.

But the truer truth, the Truth he discovered in the moment of discovering Nethaalye's weakness as a possible bride . . . he didn't want a marriage only for his reputation's sake. He wanted the marriage to Thaalye for himself. He wanted peace of mind—about himself. There was a void in his life now, a massive need a Khoratumin dancer had first created, then sensibly escaped before it went very wrong. Passion . . . was not his nature. He had had an iron control on his emotions lifelong and having met the darkness lurking within that passion he now knew why; he burned inside, and anyone who touched that fire would ultimately be consumed.

For that same reason, Nethaalye, a friend he trusted, was his safety, the refuge he dared take, if only she would offer it. He regarded her highly, had no passion toward her, nothing that could ever ignite that internal fire. He respected her. He was sure, as he was sure of sunrise, that he would never raise a hand to her. If she would have him, she could cool the anger, damp his inclinations . . . turn him toward normalcy and, above all, rescue him from what being Mikhyel Rhomandi dunMheric had made of him.

But she'd refused marriage with him. He couldn't complain of that refusal, but he suffered in it.

He had come to realize he was, in one very basic sense, normal. He wanted someone to care for, and who would care for him, physically, mentally . . . sexually. But he had seen how dangerous that last normal need could be in him. Mheric had bent and Anheliaa had twisted, and his own nature, that need to care, had broken. He saw it all too clearly in cases that crossed his desk: jealousy, assault . . . murder.

The business with Mirym should have warned him, should have warned them all. She'd been an innocent, a servant sitting watch at her employer's sickbed, and he'd been so easily caught up in Anheliaa's ring-directed rutting instinct, he'd roused out of that collapse and forced himself on her. They all, Mirym included, laid the blame on Anheliaa, but perhaps they should have looked closer at the one who'd done the harm.

And now Mirym would bear his child; wherever she had run, she bore that small bit of him with her. He hoped, for that unborn child's sake, that what Anheliaa had done to him, what she'd done to them all, had not already begun the process of turning the child toward the same dark and lonely path he had walked all his life.

It was a strange sense. He'd never imagined himself with children. That Deymorin would have offspring was a foregone conclusion—Deymorin loved children almost as much as he loved making them. That Nikki would have children, in the midst of a normal, perfect marriage, had been his own dream, if not one Nikki himself had yet evolved. That *he* found himself a father as well was an inescapable reality now, but the darker truth was . . . having done what he did in passion, the fact of the child contained no emotional component at all.

He'd have offered the protection of his name and association with the Family to Mirym as well, as a titled second wife, could they have found her—that was only justice, but they hadn't found her. She had gone, and a part of him wished they could afford to allow Mirym her own desired freedom.

It was possible, even, that she had recognized what was surfacing in him and run for her life, as he had run from Dancer and all Dancer roused in him, though Raulind would chastise him for over-dramatizing the facts.

It was fact, however, that thanks to a situation he hadn't in the least helped, Mirym had become a serious concern to the Rhomandi family and the Web. With her knowledge about their current situation and her unmonitored ability to manipulate the Ley, she posed a potential problem wandering unchecked anywhere . . . inside the Syndicate or among its neighboring countries.

She was a weakness in their armor that few knew about . . . yet.

And so, the Family searched for her; his guilt worried

about her; but instinct whispered to him that her interests were so far removed from Rhomatum that the knowledge she took away could not be in safer hands. And, perhaps based on some attitude lingering from Dancer, his rational mind was tempted to accept instinct *in this case* and move on.

But rational thought was all he had to hold the darkness within him at bay, and so he sought to substantiate that instinct with logic.

There was a faction in the hills, small pockets of people who still held to the truly old ways, the traditions and beliefs that had ruled here before the Darian Exodus. And those folk tapped the Ley, in their own fashion, had been doing so since long before any rings spun in the world. Official records held they'd been wiped out in the first century after the Exodus; after his handful of weeks in lower Khoratum and his time with Dancer in all Dancer's attitudinal aspects, he had begun to suspect that official judgment. He took the possible existence of that community now for likely, and the hopeful answer of where Mirym had gone.

Sorry, Suds.

Yes, Ganfrion, there was a great deal they might now regret, but none of it, *none* of it, would be allowed to touch the Syndicate. Not during his tenure here.

He had a narrow, footed vase on his desk, next to the sealing wax, a bronze vessel, lacking flowers. Occasionally it served as other than a receptacle for bits of broken seal. He touched Gan's letter to the heater of the wax-jack, and curled it neatly into the vase before it flared.

As it did.

Flames shot up briefly, passionate and possibly needless destruction, an act of danger in an office full of papers and dust, but he left no tag end of use to anyone who wished to manipulate him.

Nethaalye. Dancer. Mirym. Those were the losses.

He had his City. He had his brothers. He had Ganfrion and he had his staff. . . .

He had his notes, his pen, and a ream of paper that held the future of them all. . . .

Worse might have happened to him.

₰   ₰   ₰

"Deymorin!" Nikki called down the hall after his brother and hurried to catch him before he headed up the stairs to the Tower. "When did you get here? Did Kiyrstin come with you?"

Deymorin paused at his hail, one foot on the stair, a grin on his face. "She's gone to 'freshen up,' which means she'll still be soaking when I get through. Heard Lidye was resting and thought I'd catch a few minutes with Thaalye. Almost had something the last time."

"That's good." Nikki plucked a stray bit of hay from Deymorin's shoulder, and recalling *why* Deymorin had been Outside at their Armayel estate, he asked: "How's Deyma?"

Deymaluv was his brother's favorite broodmare. Deymorin had been gone for two weeks, up to Darhaven in the hills, to fetch her down to Armayel so she could be near him for her foaling.

"Holding her own. Going long as usual, I'd wager. Could even hold out until your birthday. Damn, I wish she'd stayed put last year. She's too old for this nonsense."

"Nonsense, is it?" Nikki grinned, knowing full well—and sharing—his brother's love of baby horses.

"For her, yes. She's twenty-five now, Nik. Almost as old as I am, and deserving of a peaceful old age."

Not to mention the foal was dangerously off-season. The grain was ripening fast at Armayel, and Deymorin thought she might not drop the foal before Nikki's birthday. His eighteenth birthday.

Less than a year since Deymorin had disappeared.

His hand slid along the door frame. Newly refinished, that door, as the stairs to the Tower had been reopened. The centrally located lift that had become the exclusive entrance during Anheliaa's tenure, was rarely even accessed these days.

And Deymorin practically lived in the City now . . . it was why he had brought the mare to an estate only hours outside the City limits.

"A lot of changes in just a year," Deymorin said, as if out of his own thought, though he hadn't felt his brother's mind. They actively avoided the link as much as possible, here in the City, and right above Rhomatum Node. Avoided it because once engaged, it occasionally took a sledge hammer to get *Mikhyel* disengaged.

"Good changes," Deymorin elaborated, seeking, Nikki knew, a reaction.

"Overall, yes." But a brother's enthusiasm was not what Deymorin had expected, he could tell with or without the link. He stared at the floor, traced a pattern in the rug with his toe, thinking how pleasant it must be at Armayel right now, and wishing he were there waiting for a late foal rather than here tracking down the lost load of wheat flour bound for Fort Mariidi, or researching the history of the Gorthaani land disputes for Mikhyel.

Even better, he'd like to be out with the Princeps' Guard at New Khoratum. He'd been back once since his return to Rhomatum, and they had permanent barracks now, and a thriving hiller village had grown up beside the lake. He'd even gotten a couple of arms-practice sessions in with Belden. He'd had the advantage in those matches, still, of greater skill, but Belden had outlasted him. Easily. Getting soft, he was. . . .

Hell, he'd never been hard. Not really. Not like Belden would be in another month with the Guard.

"How are your rides with Khyel going?" Deymorin asked into the uncommonly awkward silence, and Nikki shrugged.

"Fine. We go out about twice a week. The exercise is good for both of us . . ." But not, he sometimes thought, healthy. It wasn't right, how Mikhyel went off into that inner world. It wasn't right, how he courted something that had given him such pain. But Mikhyel had grown more able. And he didn't want to bring that up with Deymorin. To give up those rides . . . without them, he'd do nothing but sit and write requisitions all day and become as City-bound as Khyel had used to be.

"I know that look, fry," Deymorin voice interjected into his thoughts. "What's wrong?"

He sighed. "Nothing. At least, nothing that you can do anything about." He met Deymorin's eyes and forced a smile. "I just heard Lidye was ill again, and went to see her. To make sure she was all right."

"And?"

"I got a flying slipper in my gut for my trouble. She just doesn't want me around. Ever." He shrugged, trying not to think about the very different reception he'd gotten with the Guard, trying very hard not to resent the family posturing that had kept him from joining the border patrol two years ago, even for a single season. Deymorin had been all for it, Mikhyel had been all against it—and as usual, Mikhyel had won. Mikhyel, the lawyer, had always been able to think up more reasons to support his position than anyone opposing him. It wasn't fair.

And if he'd just left in that year, as Belden had done, it wouldn't be Nikaenor dunMheric who suffered, it would have been his brothers, as his leaving would have estranged them even further. So that would have been his fault, too, though no one would ever say that, no. Nikki was never to feel guilty. No one would ever accuse Nikki so that he could face his mistake and move on.

"Nikki?"

And as a consequence Nikaenor dunMheric was stuck permanently in Rhomatum with a wife who hated him, a child he'd more than likely never be allowed near, and two brothers now so close to each other, nothing short of death would separate them. But he wasn't in the partnership. He was the commodity they still managed, and he couldn't get around them.

If it weren't for Jerrik, he'd have no one—and even Jerri was busy these days courting a young woman in Lower Rhomatum.

He sighed again. "As I said, Deymio, nothing you can do. Nothing anybody can do."

"Maybe it's just the baby. Kiyrstin says *she's* on the edge of tears half the time and for no reason. And that's this week. Last week, it was giggles. It's driving her to distraction. Lidye will probably settle down after the baby comes."

"I hope so. I just wish she'd confide in me. Just a bit, you know? Dammit, I'm not a child, I'm her husband, the *father* of the child she carries. There must be *something* I can do."

Deymorin smiled wryly. "Yeah, Nik. I do understand. If Kiyrstin kept me at such distance . . ." His brow puckered. Then, he said, emphatically: "Oil. That's what you need."

"Oil?"

"That scented kind. Kiyrstin loves it when I rub that glop into her stomach."

He didn't even want to think of Lidye's reaction, should he suggest such a thing: Lidye hadn't let him see her, let alone touch her since the baby had started showing.

"Nikki?"

"Kiyrstin would love it if you rubbed anything anywhere, as long as it was on her." He gave Deymorin a shove before his own distraction became an issue. "Get on upstairs. I'll see you at dinner."

Deymorin grabbed his shoulder and gave it a sympathetic squeeze. "I know it hurts, Nik. Nothing I can say, except that. Be patient, and hope she's better after the baby arrives."

He nodded. "Good luck—" He cast his eyes toward the Tower. "Up there."

"Thanks." Deymorin was halfway around the first turn when Nikki realized there *was* something he wanted. He had one brother to ride with, even if he said nothing on the rides. The other . . .

"Deymio?" He called and stepped into the stairwell.

Deymorin stopped and looked down.

"I want to start working again. The salle. The gym. And all the decent armsmasters are gone—assigned to the army. Except *one* . . ."

He gave his brother his best hopeful look, and Deymorin laughed.

"Okay, Nik. Maybe next week, after I—" Deymorin began, then broke off and stared at him. "Let me rephrase that, Nikki. Damn right. I could use it, too. About time I started testing this thing." He slapped his leg. "Haven't needed the cane in a month. How about we start tomorrow morning? Before breakfast."

Nikki grinned, happier than he'd been in months, and Deymorin, with a cheerful wink, was off up the stairs.

The grin still on his face, Nikki started slowly back down the hall, headed for his office, where stacks of requisitions awaited him, and, of far more interest, a report on the status of the dam under construction up in the northeast section of the valley. That was his project. His idea, his plan, his to execute.

But even the dam failed to excite him today. Lidye's dizzy spells came with increasing frequency. Beyond the problems this presented to Nethaalye and the Rings, this was his wife and his child at issue.

And dammit, he was worried.

He could hold his own against the Princeps' armsmaster and his own wife could run him out with a slipper?

Turning about, he headed back for the stairs that would take him up to the ringmaster's suite, the rooms he'd thought they would share. Instead, his living arrangements had remained virtually unchanged following his wedding. He still had the suite he'd been moved into the day he left the nursery. In fact, after their fateful wedding night, the number of times he and Lidye had been together wouldn't constitute a satisfactory honeymoon.

Not at all what he'd planned, but it was all he had at the moment. All he had, but not all he had to settle for.

He took the stairs two and three at a time, reached her door breathless, but determined. As he raised his hand to knock, however, the door opened and—

Kiyrstin came out.

She saw him immediately, raised a finger to her mouth to keep him silent, and half-turned to say back into the room, "I'll explain to him, Lidye." She paused for a quiet murmur from within, then, a bit impatiently: "Trust me."

She closed the door and still silent, gestured him to follow.

Down the length of the hall to the main stairwell and halfway down the stairs, Nikki stuttered, "Wh–what was that all about?"

"I came as soon as I heard she had taken to her room."

"But . . ." He bit his lip. Half the time, these two women weren't even speaking to one another.

"I know." Kiyrstin gave him a wry grin very like Dey-morin's. "It is strange, isn't it? Something of a woman-to-woman arrangement. I'm not quite certain how it happened myself. But . . . the main thing is, she says she feels terrible about how she's been treating you. I promised her I'd tell you."

"She *says* she feels?" The careful qualification was not lost on him.

"I'm not sure what she actually feels and what she says for the sake of peace. I'm not sure she knows. In this case, I think it is, at least in part, genuine."

"And how do I know you're not just saying that to make me feel better, just as she could have said it to placate me?"

"Because I don't lie, curly-top. I tell you when you're being an ass."

"I hate it when you call me that."

She grinned. "Which?" She sobered then. "I think it's time we had a talk, Nikki."

"What about?" Suspicion flared. Kiyrstin had never tried to talk to him before. For all she and Mikhyel spent hours together, at least before Mikhyel had left the City, talking, he'd supposed, about Mauritum and trade possibilities and Garetti—except for a handful of moments in the Tower, when they'd all come together for a single purpose, she'd rarely even addressed him in public, let alone sought private conversation with him.

"Your wife, for one," Kiyrstin said. "I think you deserve to know some of what she's going through, and I don't think she'll ever tell you."

"Did she tell you not to?"

"Do you mean, am I betraying a promise? No. I don't do that. Is there a tacit agreement for discretion? Naturally. I trust you won't betray your wife to the gossip columns."

"You said, Lidye . . . for one. What else?"

She tipped her head and studied him a moment. She was tall for a woman. And no slender willow. Overall, a good physical match for his brother, if a bit intimidating to a lesser man—and he'd never be his brother's equal, in any sense.

"I can tell you that now. I was wrong about you, Nikki."

He took a step back, hands raised in mock horror. Except it wasn't all sham. She'd startled him.

She frowned. "Oh, stop it. I hate it when you go all cute on me."

"Cute." He dropped his hands. "I'll try to remember that."

"You mean that, don't you?"

"Of course."

"You try to figure what everyone wants of you and then comply. You'll be 'cute' around Deymorin because he wants his little brother, but you'll drop 'cute' around me because it drives me to homicidal rages."

"I . . . well . . ." Of course he did. He tried to make people happy. It helped avoid arguments. He stared past her, knowing she hated him . . . that he drove her to homicidal rages, which didn't seem like a good thing to do, and dammit, he was tired of this place that used to house An-heliaa, who was curious, but cruel, and arguments between his brothers and now arguments between Lidye and everyone else. And he knew she was right: only a moment ago, he'd used his *best hopeful look* to mortify his brother into fulfilling his request.

A sudden stinging blow to his cheek. He snapped to attention, and caught her hand, thinking for all the world if she weren't Deymorin's woman, he'd strike her back for such an unprovoked attack.

"*That's* what I saw in the Tower!" she grinned at him— *up* at him as he realized for the first time he was taller than she. "*Good* lad. Think about how your face feels right now, Nikki, and try it *again* some time."

He blinked.

"What?"

"You're a good lad, Nikki. Maybe even a good man. I saw backbone in the Tower the night we practiced. I saw it again the night of the shutdown. Lidye would have lost the whole damned thing without you. Remember that. I felt privileged to know you that night. And I liked the feeling. I just thought you should know that."

He blinked again, feeling foolishly like grinning.

She grinned back. A wide, honest, engaging grin that made him realize why Deymorin found her beautiful. "What do you say, Nikki? Have you time?"

Impossible to resist that honest welcome. Nikki held out his arm, she tucked her hand in it and he asked: "Where would you like to go, madam?"

"Oh, let's make it your room." She winked at him. "Make the neighbors talk, shall we?"

He swallowed hard and wondered if it was too late to retract his arm.

Chapter Two

"Deymorin?"

That was a voice out of place in his bedroom. He ignored it, concentrated instead on that green-eyed gaze slanting up at him.

"Deymorin, please, wake up."

A gaze that could make a corpse's blood run hot.

"Come, Rag'n'bones, snap out of it."

Right voice, wrong tone. And a stinging slap to his cheeks confirmed his suspicion that he was no longer in his bedroom in Armayel. A hum that penetrated to his bones confirmed the memory that placed him in the Rhomatum ring chamber.

A second stinging slap roused a faint protest that came out on a yawn, and the third came as a laughter-accompanied pat on his cheek.

"He'll survive, Nethaalye," Kiyrstin's voice said. And Deymorin blinked his eyes open to her laughing green eyes. He yawned again and sat up, swinging his legs to one side of the couch to face her.

"H'lo, lovie," he said, grabbing her chin and giving her a quick kiss. "What're you doing here?"

"Raising you from the dead." She rubbed her hand. "Between you and your brother, I'm going to demand a piece of that vaunted Rhomatumin disability insurance."

"Beating Nikki, were you? What'd he do?"

"Never you mind. He and I have an exquisite understanding now. Having a lovely gossip which *you* just interrupted. I may just dump you for him. What's all this?" She waved a hand at the couch, large, adjustable; Mheric had built it especially for Anheliaa when Deymorin was a child. Too large to conveniently remove from the ringchamber, it provided now, according to Nethaalye, a place for comfortable meditation on the Rings which were in her charge at the moment.

Too comfortable. He'd fallen asleep. Had a dream instead of the revelation he'd come here to find. Three months back from the base in the hills, a quick vacation to bring Deyma down into the valley. Two nights sitting watch to make sure the trip hadn't induced labor on a foal not yet shifted, and the arrival of a letter from Nethaalye reporting an anomaly in the Rings and a request for his immediate return. A fast drive back to Rhomatum . . .

Such was his current life.

After a quarter hour in the ringchamber meditating on the couch, with the hum of the Rings on one side and the soft scritching of Nethaalye's pencils on the other, he'd not felt the anomaly, he'd not even felt the couch: he'd slipped back to Armayel.

And from the look on the white face a step behind Kiyrstin, and Kiyrstin's unexpected presence here, he'd scared Nethaalye thoroughly.

"What is this?" He slapped the couch's deep cushion. "Supposedly helping me to concentrate. Sorry, Thaalye," he said, as he stood up and stretched. "I've begun to think quiet contemplation isn't the answer."

Kiyrstin laughed. "I could have told you that. You want his attention, Thaalye? Put him on a horse. Deymio, you're still half-asleep. No wonder after the last few nights. Why don't you let it go for today?"

"Lidye's being 'delicate.' She doesn't know I've arrived back from Armayel, and it just seemed a perfect window for us to try this. I hate to let it go completely. I *think* I'm right on the edge of feeling the currents Nethaalye keeps describing, which means she's probably right: it's easier to feel when something's wrong than when everything's in proper balance."

"Well, I doubt you'll find them snoring away."

He yawned again. "Maybe I should call for some of Mikhyel's precious pachiimi."

Nethaalye bit her lip, hugged her sketchpad to her breast. "I don't think that would be wise, Rhomandi. The one time I tried to operate the Rings under the influence, they, um, well, it wasn't a solution, but rather added to the problem. Greatly."

"No pachiimi, then," Deymorin agreed.

"I'm not certain what else to try," Nethaalye said. "Anheliaa insisted that releasing oneself from one's body was the key to following the currents. I find it in this." She lifted the sketchbook. "I find that if I let the pencils drive my thoughts, I find the currents." She shook her head. "But Anheliaa called it a crutch. Said it was why I'd never be a master. For Deymorin . . . I just don't know what to suggest next."

"Well, he won't find anything if he falls asleep. Why don't you shed your coat and stretch the kinks out, JD? Get your blood moving with that thing you do in the morning when civilized people are ignoring the sun."

It was a thought. Possibly a good one. The *thing* she referenced was an exercise routine he and his armsmaster had worked out years ago after the accident that nearly crippled him. It involved a great deal of stretching and twisting—but was hardly something he cared to perform for an audience.

"I'll go order some tea," Nethaalye said, reading either his face or his mind, neither seemed out of the question these days. "Perhaps that will help."

"Diplomatic as always," Kiyrstin murmured as Nethaalye slipped from the chamber, then she turned to him and grabbed his chin to deliver her own, not quite so quick kiss. She released him with a pat on his cheek, then helped him shed his coat. "Don't fall asleep again, laddybuck. You don't want to go to dinner smelling like the barn."

"I won't forget. C'mere."

Free of the coat, he took her into his arms just to remind himself of the feel of her against him. But even as he rested his chin on her head, the Rings beyond her beckoned. Nine rings, one for each complementary pair of nodes, and the outermost Cardinal that was Rhomatum's own. There should be ten. One day soon, the tenth, cooling in the caverns below, would return. At their center, a viewing sphere that was not even real but rather a by-product of the Rings' spinning.

And darting one way and another among the rings, the streamer of pure leythium that rose from the ground—or perhaps formed from the air itself: accounts varied—the moment the rings were properly aligned. The radical: a random element to the Rings' actions that all ringmasters alternately cursed and praised.

It paused now, and drew back, facing him, like a cobra poised to strike: accusation. Guilt, in the form of a flitting ribbon of rainbows.

He kissed Kiyrstin soundly, then shoved her gently toward the door. "Get out of here. You're more distracting than sleep."

She grinned and deliberately swayed her way out of the room, reminding him just how distracting she could be, which thoroughly roused him, though not in the way he needed.

To shift his thoughts away from that swaying backside, he paged through Nethaalye's sketchbook, feeling, as always, a bit intrusive as he did so, particularly since she wasn't there to monitor his perusal. But she had suggested he start each session that way—after his first polite request to look had discovered in him a curious resonance to the imagery.

Nethaalye had a talent for capturing a likeness, a talent that went beyond features to the essential qualities behind the physical. That sensitivity extended into her image of the Web and its energy flow. Her depictions were always of faces and human figures, sometimes blooming with health, at others, stretched and warped to near unrecognizable. Sometimes hundreds of faces in a single piece, sometimes only one. But sprinkled throughout those images of the Web were sketches of himself and Nikki, Kiyrstin and Lidye, at all stages of their pregnancies, many, many of Mikhyel, some even of Ganfrion's scar-twisted face. Delicate images, sensitive to all the strain and joy hiding within. It was in those sketches that he most felt he didn't belong, and yet, the depictions were compelling.

He turned the pages back to her current piece, one of the many-faced, straining pieces, and propped it up before him as he began to follow Kiyrstin's suggestion and flex and move.

Minutes into the familiar routine, he knew his lady-love's advice to be as sound as always: she had a knack for knowing what would work with him. He could feel his mind falling into place along with each joint and muscle. He increased the pace and even the hum from the Rings achieved a cadence to match the beat of his heart. As his arm stretched to the south, he could almost hear the Shatumin ringmaster speaking to his assistant. And as that same arm arced over his head—Giephaetum touched his fingertips.

It was not illusion.

His prior contact with the Rings, in Anheliaa's tenure, had had no such understanding. He'd entered this room no more than a handful of times and always, *always*, felt nothing but a vague unease, a tingling of nerves that led invariably to temper.

Except when he'd come with Mikhyel as a child, the day he'd reset the Rings and never even known. He'd been in command that day, as he was in command today. Other times, Anheliaa had been trying to use the Rings to command him. Other times, since Anheliaa had died, Nethaalye had been there, urging him to find his own path, yet unconsciously directing his thoughts to her perceptions of the Web.

For the first time since that long ago day with Mikhyel in the room, he was able to feel the Ley for what it was, not what others in this room tried to make of it.

The feel of the air, the scent that drifted up his fingertips, was different for each leyline. Currents, like the flow of blood, signals like a touch of a nerve ending, but more than that. The give and take of a horse's sensitive mouth on the far end of the reins, each line unique just as every horse, no matter how similarly trained, was a bit different.

Then he felt the flow from multiple directions.

And he could tell, through those signals, the health of the line. That one labored, like a fish gasping for air, another was bloated. Relieve the one with the other, place one arm there, the other, thus, and send the flow from feast to famine.

Resistance. Antipathy.

Nonsense, he responded, and insisted calmly and repeatedly, as he would with a recalcitrant young horse. Central to the Web, he held the invisible reins: a thousand individual lines to a thousand individual demands, some needing steadying, others urging. And slowly, the dam between the lines dissipated, the bloat eased, bringing a palpable sense of relief—like the mouth of that same horse relaxing and giving in to the bit. . . .

This, he thought reluctantly, this could be fun.

᭜   ᭜   ᭜

A sense of triumph sailed past Mikhyel's barriers. He raised his pen and smiled at no one and nothing: Deymorin had had some sort of success in the Tower.

He hadn't even known his brother was back in the City. If he had, he might have been more prepared and less vulnerable to the link, but under the circumstances . . . not a bad hello. He sent a congratulatory thought Deymorin's way as subtly as he could, and closed off the connection to Deymorin, relieved when it severed smoothly and easily.

It would be convenient, if Deymorin could actually come into his own as a spinner. From what the Rhomatum-creature had implied, in his hazed memories, Deymorin *should* be master. And if that were the case, if Deymorin *was* the stuff of which great ringmasters were made (Deymorin would not settle for being mediocre at anything), his own job became ever so much easier. He would not have to negotiate with Lidye every time Lidye's refusal to cooperate became a potent threat.

He'd had enough of that with Anheliaa.

And when it came to raising the Khoratum/Persitum ring, he'd feel a damn sight more secure if Deymorin as well as Nethaalye could be available to back up Lidye's efforts.

Welcome as the news was, the interruption had effectively destroyed his train of thought. The letter had been, of necessity, "folksy" in tone, not the best developed of his pen's voices, and he couldn't even remember the gender of the offspring he was about to reference, let alone said offspring's name.

Besides, he had to leave soon for the luncheon he had scheduled with the Giephaetumin delegation.

He set the unfinished letter to the side and stretched his arms over his head, trying to relieve the persistent kink in his right shoulder. Raulind would have something to say to him tonight for propping himself on his elbow while he wrote. Sometimes it was prop or fall face down in the stacks of paper.

The paciimi called. He sipped, then stretched again. Let his head fall back into the chair cushion which had, over the years, formed itself perfectly . . . to a head with twice as much hair. For all the irrationality of the decision to cut his hair, it had been, as things turned out, a good one. When necessary—which was virtually every day now—his morning ritual could be cut down to a handful of minutes instead of the better part of an hour.

He didn't know why he hadn't had Raulind cut it years ago. If he could only have back the time wasted drying a length that, when loose, would reach below his waist . . . But the past was definitively out of reach. One simply endeavored to use one's new-found freedom to its best advantage.

And then one remembered this same morning, when—for the first time in weeks and thanks to the upcoming luncheon with the highly conservative Giephaetumin—Mikhyel dunMheric had truly allowed time to prepare for the day, and in the process had sat still under Raulind's ministrations. In contemplation of that hour, despite his desire to get his day moving, he realized how much Mikhyel dun-

Mheric had missed the good counsel that had invariably accompanied that ritual grooming.

And one decided that, for the sake of Mikhyel dunMheric's character, it was probably a good thing that the length of his hair had forced him, all his life, to sit quietly each day, to think and to ponder under that wise guidance before heading out into the world.

But even as one acknowledged the personal benefit of the counsel, one began to wonder at the origins of such an impractical tradition of extreme fashion among the descendants of the Darian Exodus. Mauritumin men wore their hair short, as did the Kirish'lani, though some factions among that huge empire let small sections of hair grow to great lengths which they then braided according to some internal social code. But the long hair, virtually uncut from childhood—that was a hiller notion, and even among the hillers, these days, the extreme length was the mark of a radical dancer, meant to simulate the radical streamer that flowed and rippled among the tower rings.

Or so they now claimed. It was a tradition older, far older, than the ringdance, a fact those who would blend in the Rhomatum tended to overlook.

It was an extreme of the fashion which he alone of all his generation of the Rhomandi Family had affected. Deymorin, being too clever to encumber himself with such an unwieldy mass, had kept it short around his face and just long enough in back for respectability, and Nikki's curls had become impossible to manage past a certain length. But his hadn't been cut since his thirteenth birthday, had, in fact, been carefully nurtured as a deliberate reminder to the council of who he was . . . *that* had been Anheliaa's notion, one he'd never thought to argue—

Until it became too much a reminder to himself of what he'd had and lost *because* of who and what he was.

The fashion itself could be traced to his own ancestor Darius and the wife of Darius' old age, the child bride born of a hiller woman and notoriously entranced with all things Tamshi. Darius' fascination with his young wife had led him down many strange paths, not the least of which had been the hair Darius suddenly, at age fifty-five, had begun to let grow. Hair that had grown so rapidly, one unkind account openly accused the founder of the City of wearing a wig.

But he'd seen hair grow that rapidly before: shaded, ley-touched hair, hacked short in a moment of passion—

He emptied and cleaned his pen, using that most mundane of acts to free his mind from *that* danger-riddled track.

So, Deymorin was spinning the Rings in the Tower. He hoped that was what he had felt a moment ago. Not that the ability was any real surprise to him; he'd seen Deymorin reset the Rings when as children they had gone into the Forbidden Territory and his own incurable curiosity in the form of a fingertip had fouled the Rings' balanced orbits. He could still see his hand, child-sized and filthy with the dirt of the underground tunnels, reaching toward the radical streamer flitting among the spinning rings, irresistibly drawn to the colorful sparkling band. He could still feel the sickening drop in his stomach when the alarms had gone off.

Deymorin had grabbed that filthy hand and hauled him off behind a table, told him to be quiet or he'd thump him, then stared out at the Rings, his young mouth set, his eyes determined.

And the alarms had stopped.

Remarkable enough that he had touched the streamer and come away with all his fingers.

More remarkable that Deymorin had stared the Rings into obedience.

But a year ago, Deymorin's antipathy for Anheliaa had so colored all his feelings about the Tower and the City, Mikhyel had despaired of ever ridding himself of the mantle of proxy to his brother as head of house. That Deymorin, their wild, outdoor spirit, would even consider Tower work had been unthinkable.

And now, Deymorin had not only assumed those reins of office that Mikhyel so wished to relinquish, he had thrown himself quite enthusiastically, if quietly, into the ringchamber as well. Lidye was his motivation, so he said.

He learned the workings of the Rings so he could keep a general, knowledgeable eye on Lidye, no different than he'd kept an eye on Mikhyel's proxy decisions over the years.

If Mikhyel knew his brother and Lidye, *that* was a situation that would not survive, if, indeed, Deymorin had the Talent to properly control the Rhomatum Rings. He knew now that if, over the years, Deymorin had ever truly disapproved of his proxy decisions, Mikhyel dunMheric would have found himself thrown out of this office in a heartbeat.

And Deymorin did not approve of Lidye. He most decidedly did not.

For all Mikhyel had eliminated himself from the entire ringmaster equation, he couldn't help but wonder what the Rhomatum creature thought of this new development, if think it did.

It remained quiescent in the caverns below, and considering the condition of the Rings and the ringmaster he supposed he was relieved it kept so quiet . . . not that he feared the confrontation; he'd faced both Mother and the creature he thought of simply as Rhomatum at their most obstinate, and while he remained curious about their precise nature and abilities . . . they were ultimately controllable phenomena.

That was the entire point of the Exodus: that rational rather than supernatural explanations existed for the Ley. That ringmasters were just people with a talent no different in singularity than the ability to write music or design a bridge.

And if the eruption of a new node had broken Khoratum out of the Web, that new node was still . . . ultimately . . . a controllable phenomenon.

Rather, it was his control over his own nature he held suspect, the other side of the darkness, that fascination with knowledge which became, in his hands, power. And power had mattered to him in Anheliaa's regime. Power to construct his own vision. Power to subvert hers. Power to create the reality in which he personally lived. When he waked, he worked. When he worked, there were no memories. When he dreamed, however . . .

Diorak had refused him more sleeping pills, and now the caverns brushed his nights, when the drugs wore thin, touching his sleeping essence with their billowing drapes of leythium lace, the tinkling chandeliers of leythium crystal and swirling iridescent pools of liquid leythium. Rhomatum had whispered to him in a dream last night, or so his sleeping mind had conjured the creature, beckoning him to enter the World Cave, offering anew the secrets they held.

Truth or his own wishes, those were temptations to which he hadn't even considered exposing himself while working on those all-important agreements . . . he had prevailed on Diorak that far, without saying why. Distracting enough in themselves, those billowing clouds inevitably evoked associated memories.

And those memories and emotions he'd worked very hard to sublimate, since returning to Rhomatum—to submerge them as effectively he'd submerged his childhood, since they refused to be eliminated completely.

But it was probable, he finally admitted, to himself if no other, that he'd have to go down there and expose himself to the creature's influence—eventually. He'd be irresponsible not to, Dancer's lurking memory notwithstanding. The syndicate's economy revolved around the leythium web. Anything that expanded their understanding of the forces involved could not be overlooked.

If Deymorin couldn't reach Rhomatum, if Nikki couldn't . . . he might have to.

Among their most immediate concerns, it was likely that Rhomatum could succeed in locating Mirym where Lidye had failed. But even together, they'd failed to rouse the creature to helpfulness, so to think that he alone could rouse it, let alone deal with it, as unstable as he had been—

{*I've miss-ss-ss-ssed you, child . . .*}

"Rhomatum?" he whispered, then repeated: {Rhomatum? Or Mother?}

"Sir?"

{Rhomatum!} he shouted inside his head, but the whisper, if it had ever been there, was gone. The presence burst like a bubble.

"Sir, I've got the packet—"

He pulled his mind fully into his office, discovered he occupied a body in the throes of panic . . . eyes wide, heart racing. Rapidly, he fought for control.

"Yes, Paulis?" he said, and his secretary, standing cautiously in the doorway, lifted the brown-wrapped packet he held. Mikhyel nodded to his desktop, and Paulis set it there, then bravely met his eyes.

"Are you all right, sir?"

"Fine, Paulis."

"You do remember the luncheon?"

"Yes, Paulis." The package cording gave to the slightest touch of his razor-sharp penknife. "Thank you, Paulis."

Paulis nodded and backed out of the room, keeping his eye to what he undoubtedly assumed to be a manic employer, armed with a knife and dangerous.

Mikhyel carefully set the penknife aside, and folded the waterproof cloth back.

{Come, child of Darius-s-s-s.}

The packet disappeared from his fingertips.

The scent of fire-blossom tea and the billowing drapes of the Rhomatum World Cave surrounded him, enveloped him, first in his doubting mind, then with solid reality, and Rhomatum was emerging, forming out of a pool to glide over to his side, the scales on his long reptilian body glittering in the leylight that filled the cavern. The creature was bare of clothing, as Mikhyel himself was, and Mikhyel's hair, free of braid and clip, brushed against his shoulders, fluttering in response to the energy that flowed like wind currents in this place.

"I've miss-ss-ss-ed you, child," the creature repeated, his sibilant, audible hiss a concession to Mikhyel's stubbornly human attitudes during his previous visits here.

"It's only been a few months," Mikhyel answered, wondering how a being that counted time in geological eras could even notice such a time span.

"M-m-months-s-s-s. Years. Yes. Recalling . . ." The pronounced, reptilian jaw stretched in a yawn, then the faceted eyes brightened in awareness, and the voice quickened and solidified. "Well, you're here now. Come, sit with me. How's that silly bud of mine doing?"

Bud, as the Ley reproduced by budding. *Mother,* he meant, who was his daughter in some sense. And mother of his newest offspring-node. "I don't know," he answered the creature. "I'm sorry. But I can't stay here. I must return—"

"You questioned. You sought. What did you seek, child of Darius?"

Sadness filled him, his own or the creature's; either was possible. He hadn't wanted this, not now, not yet, but he knew what had drawn him here, and damned if he'd squander the opportunity. "It's Mirym—"

"What is *Mirym*?"

He formed the woman's image in his mind, and as a part of that image, the thought of his child that she carried.

"Bud?" Rhomatum's mouth stretched in joy, baring sharp teeth. "Child of Darius having child? Beauty. *Continuity.*"

"She's gone. I want to find her."

"Then look." A powerful arm glittering with scales swept through the air.

"Look? Where?"

"Find her pattern, child of Darius. *Look to the lace.*"

"How can I know her pattern?"

"You shared her mind. You budded within her depths. Her pattern is part of you, now. You are part of hers. Look for yourself. Look for your bud."

He ceased to listen, having come to accept that most of the Tamshi's speech was nonsense, particularly where it intersected human biology and human needs. That this World Cave, like Mother's below Khoratum, reflected the surface world, that he could accept. That the strands of lace and billowing fabric and glowing chandeliers bore any recognizable resemblance to that surface world was patent nonsense.

That centralized, constantly metamorphosing mass—the most dominant feature in the cavern—one would assume that was Rhomatum itself. Eighteen rays of light—he knew there were eighteen—thrust out from the core, pulsing down what appeared to be tunnels to varicolored lights at the far end—until one looked more closely. And then those tunnels became bottomless pits that drew one's very self deeper and deeper and—

Mikhyel cried out and staggered, fighting that lure. Solid stone met his back, surrounded him, held him firmly in Rhomatum.

{Demanding buds. My apologies, bud of Darius.} Thoughts from the stone that had engulfed and now re- leased him. *{Listen to the lace . . .}*

Listen. He closed his eyes, shutting out the haunting beauty of the place, fought the instinct to make visual sense of the patterns. And one spot did draw him, as a node stone was drawn to its mother Tower.

His hand lifted without conscious thought, and he felt the brush of lace against his fingertips, smelled rich wine and fresh bread and new-mown hay. That was *his* pattern, himself and his brothers, Nikki, and Deymorin. And from that pattern, his own—

He thought of Mirym, of the quiet, rather mousy individ- ual who had bravely attended Anheliaa in his aunt's final years. Small, unassuming, yet magnificent in her defiance, first of Anheliaa, then of Lidye.

{The budding, child of Darius, think of the budding.}

He'd much rather not.

{And therein lies your wall, foolish child.}

It had been a humiliating night. A night ruled by Anheli- aa's whim, not their own honest desires. Anheliaa wanted an heir—the child Lidye now bore—and had taken steps to make certain an innocent and reluctant Nikki performed his husbandly duties. But in her determination, she had overshot herself, had caught Deymorin and himself in that web of reproductive instincts—as well as a host of others throughout the City. The last week of the second month had become a notoriously popular prediction among Rho- matumin midwives.

Deymorin had been with Kiyrstin that night, a right and

inevitable pairing. He had been with Mirym, whose only involvement had been nursing her employer's sick nephew.

A gentle, kind young woman—yet not shying away from his near-mindless advances. Enigmatic. At that thought, an image divorced from the quiet little mouse, an image laced with mystery and danger, a hint of darkness—a woman, he realized suddenly, with her own agenda, who claimed the child as hers and none other's. Mirym's desire for a child of her own—a ley-touched child—might have exceeded even Anheliaa's.

She was hiller.

A spot in the lace glowed with iridescent fire. He sought the glow, or his mind did, and he was with her, knew her, knew she was safe. She sensed him, tried to strike him away, but he released his hold on the glow and on her, sending peace/security/silence/trust on the final thread of light.

He hoped she received it. She *was* safe, at least from Lidye, so long as she remained where she was: at the new node, in the village of hill-folk forming there by the new lake, under Deymorin's express protection, to nourish the new spring of power.

[She heard you . . .]

So certain the creature was, reassuring him about exactly what he wanted to believe.

Which might have been coincidence and might not. As the months had passed, and he'd had time to ponder their actions, he'd grown increasingly suspicious that the Tamshi were little more than human desires given shape, here in this world; that just as a single individual, through the rings, could shape the energy of the ley, so could countless minds of varying Talent in concert over generations create Mother and Rhomatum to be exactly what humanity wanted them to be.

If that was the case, what they did and said was more desire than reality, and if *that* were the case, Rhomatum's reassuring answer meant exactly—

"Sir?"

Paulis' voice called him this time, echoed, first in the cavern, and then off the walls of his own office.

"Please, sir, wake up! You're late!"

Chapter Three

When it was over, they had to admit the old lady could have done it all without them. For all the help she needed, she could have dropped the off-season foal in the pastures of Darhaven. But Deymorin was not inclined to take unnecessary chances with any broodmare, particularly not this one, and the high pastures of Darhaven had been known to be several inches under snow by this time of the year.

Besides, if they'd left her in the Rhomandi stud farm in the foothills rather than bring her here to Armayel in the Valley, he and Kiyrstin would have missed all the fun. This way, he'd been able to continue working in Rhomatum, and yet was still able to come on a moment's notice when Deymaluv's time came.

True to form, Deyma waited until just after midnight to start her serious contractions, then delayed dropping the foal until she had collected a goodly audience about the stall to admire her accomplishments. She'd had him worried just for a moment, when she went down and seemed ready to quit, but then, just after Kiyrstin arrived in the barn, yawning, the mare proceeded to bring the little filly into the world without breaking a sweat. She'd licked it and talked to it, and nipped it until it was on its feet and sucking on the proper spigot . . . proving to the lot of them they might just as well have stayed in bed.

But Deymorin had discovered the day Deyma was born that keeping his hands off a horse of any age wasn't natural, and a newborn just begged to be rubbed and hugged and talked to; he'd decided that picking its little hoofs up while its balance was still unsteady set a pattern of trust for that

back-breaking necessity of domestic horse life. His father
had maintained it was best to leave dam and foal alone in
those first hours, to allow them to bond without human
intervention. Perhaps he fooled himself, but he liked to
think his horses ended up just a bit more clever, a bit more
willing than most, and that it was due, at least in part, to
this early handling.

His father on the other hand had claimed all his son's
horses were willful and spoiled—which Deymorin conceded
likely was right. Before he'd learned the trader's training
tricks, he'd spent almost as much time of a morning getting
the adult horse's attention as his father had spent 'topping
off' his horses.

The truth was, he'd do it time after time, even if he did
have to untrain the results later. He wanted that foal to
know his voice and his touch as well as it knew its own
mother's.

Jealousy, perhaps, of the mother's biological advantage.

But this time his wasn't the only touch the filly would
know. Zandy was there from the start, had been sleeping
right outside the stall for a week—just in case—and his
hands were ready and willing to follow each suggestion
from Deymorin. Kiyrstin stood quietly outside the foaling
stall, watching. Deymorin glanced up, now and again, to
make certain she'd noted some particular, defining moment—the foal's first nose-clearing sneeze of a snort, the
mother's resonant whuffle, the cross-legged attempts to
stand. They were moments that never lost their wonder for
him and that she was witnessing for the first time.

When the foal was dry and nursing, he motioned Kiyrstin
to come in. She hesitated, a strange, rather quizzical expression on her face, but before he could ask, the look disappeared and she slid into the stall, easing her own round
belly through the gate. She was dressed practically, as always, in a simple wool dress, warm against the fall evening,
but nonbinding on her blooming figure. More importantly,
the gown's heavy folds hung quietly, minimizing flapping
distractions, for all the old mare was utterly imperturbable.

Kiyrstin paused at the mare's head, speaking softly, com-

plimenting her on the performance and the appearance of
her offspring. Kiyrstin had the low-pitched voice horses
tended to like, and Deyma, after a seemly interval to make
certain Kiyrstin did not consider her an easy conquest, graciously accepted the gifts of hand and voice, returning to
Kiyrstin the ultimate compliment of using her back as a
scratching post for her head.

Kiyrstin chuckled, and endured for a moment, then gave
the old girl a slap on the neck, and told her she'd had
enough.

Just before the horse stopped on her own.

Just the way he'd taught her.

"Good girl," he murmured—to Kiyrstin.

"Stuff it, Rags," Kiyrstin responded in the same, even
tone.

Alizant grabbed her elbow and pulled her to where she
could better see *his* accomplishment, pointing out the filly's
multitudinous perfections, speculating on her future until
he had her winning the Indrecon Derby, the Tridicci
Crown, and the dam of the year award before she was
weaned.

"*Whose* horse did you say this was?" Kiyrstin whispered
as Zandy released her elbow to continue his infinitely more
important task of coddling the baby.

Deymorin laughed and wrapped his arms around her
waist, letting his hands rest where they would, which just
happened to be where they were most likely to intercept
the impact of another baby's kick.

"He's come a long way, JD," Kiyrstin murmured when
he rested his chin on her shoulder, and indeed physically
Alizant was far from the undersized street-rat Deymorin
had met last spring in a camp full of brigands, including
(he squeezed Kiyrstin lightly) the future mother of his
child. Zandy would never be a tall man, but thanks to regular feeding (and a great deal of it) the waif now looked the
proper fifteen-year-old, gangly and a bit out at the wrists
despite the efforts of the Armayel housekeeper to keep
him in clothing.

But the boy who extolled the virtues of his filly-foal with

enthusiastic, idealistic extravagance was the same gutsy
chemist's scut-boy who had traded his future security, such
as it was, for the sake of an outlawed machine, a machine
he'd helped his master build, then rescued from that same
master's hand—all for the sake of a dream he'd believed
in and his master had given up. He'd dared the wrath of a
ringmaster, challenged Garetti himself to see that dream
fulfilled, but in all Mauritum only Garetti's wife would hear
him out. Garetti himself hadn't even spared the effort to
have the boy arrested and the machine confiscated . . . well,
to be charitable, Garetti had been occupied with a painful
wound and the disappearance of his wife.

Kiyrstin had taken to the road for her freedom, Zandy
for his dream, and thanks to this scut-boy's courage and
vision, that ringmaster's wife had gone swimming in a Persitumin mountain lake just in time to save the hide and capture the heart of one Deymorin Rhomandi dunMheric.

Deymorin would say that alone earned the lad a good
horse and a new suit of clothes. It was Zandy's own keen
mind that justified the private tutor Deymorin had hired.

The old mare, having accepted the boy as a proper baby-
sitter, settled into the straw, her large brown eyes at half-
mast. For a time, the baby stood next to her, taking full
hedonistic advantage of the human hands scratching her
withers and lipped her mam's forelock in childish mimicry
of her own first bath.

But soon the foal's legs began to shake, and she was
faced with the second monumental mystery of life: lying
down. Alizant looked at Deymorin in dismay, but he motioned the boy back. "Just watch," Deymorin said softly,
and with a grin.

The canny old mare heaved a sigh and lurched up, snuffled the filly, then settled again, deliberately, almost as if
demonstrating the technique. Over the next few minutes,
she repeated this exercise twice, until the filly seemed to
get the idea, though the babe's performance was still a
qualified collapse.

Alizant laughed delightedly, then knelt beside the filly,
praising her cleverness.

Kiyrstin frowned dubiously. "Did the mare do that on purpose?"

Deymorin chuckled and swayed her gently side to side. "I have no idea. For all I know, she simply has some instinct that won't let her settle until her foal does, but I've seen that act for—oh, what is it, Deyma? Ten foals now?"

"Ten! How old is she?"

"Old enough to retire from motherhood. She was supposed to this year, but she snuck through the fence for a final fling. So here we are."

Kiyrstin's rich chuckle vibrated clear through her, until it felt as if the babe itself was giggling against his fingers. "Can't say as I blame her for the fling."

Alizant yawned and shifted, half-leaning against Deyma, who took no offense. Both mother and babe sniffed and rubbed him, marking him, he suspected, as one of their own.

"I'm thinking of adopting the boy," Deymorin said, in a low voice, directly into her ear.

"That should be fodder for familial fireworks." Her murmur was equally private.

"Rings, I hadn't thought of that!"

"Not very smart, sometimes, Rags."

"I think Nikki's grown out of his jealousy. He's got his own family to think of now." He sniffed exaggeratedly. "I thought you'd be pleased."

"I knew you would do it."

"I'm that transparent?"

"You're that kind-hearted."

"You mean I'm not even going to get a hug out of this?"

"You want my answer now? Or later?"

He bent his head to meet that teasing mouth, to cover it with his own. Their breath mingled—

"Deymio?" Gareg's voice. The last person he cared to talk to at the moment was the Armayel overseer: Geri's arrival always harbored a problem.

"Go away, Geri," he said, against Kiyrstin's lips.

"Sorry, boss. Message from your brother."

"Shit," he muttered and Kiyrstin chuckled, then tipped her head and bit his nose. "Down, laddybuck."

He sighed and freed her, accepted the message with reluctance. Reluctance that vanished the moment he slit the seal and began to read.

"JD?" Kiyrstin murmured, her patience, never overlong, strained to the utmost, waiting for enlightenment.

"The Rings are ready," he said.

"And?"

He looked up, met those calm, wise eyes that held his world in their green depths.

"*Lidye* plans to raise them on Nikki's birthday. Loudly and with an audience. A gift for her husband, so she claims."

"Sweet Maurii. And if she fails, if you step in, if your brothers do . . . everyone will know."

"Not *if* she fails, my dearest shepherdess, but when."

"And if you don't step in . . ."

"The Web is in a shitload of trouble."

Chapter Four

"And Brodiin of the *Internode* will sit here. That way, he can see everything . . ." Lidye tapped her front teeth with a polished nail, contemplating the arrangement, her face the picture of a debutante planning the seating arrangements of her coming-out party. "And Papa will sit here . . . I do wish Mama might have come as well. . . ."

Nikki shuddered. It was unthinkable. Anheliaa never let anyone extraneous in her tower, particularly when she was performing delicate maneuvers, and nothing could be more delicate than slipping into orbit those two rings lying, still within their moving crate, on the floor next to the gently spinning rings.

Tonight, after all the preparations of the room were complete, those crates would be removed, leaving the two concentric rings on the tiled floor, awaiting tomorrow's . . . spectacle.

It was, Nikki decided, the ultimate insult, her choosing his birthday, the façade of loving gesture, to force Mikhyel into acknowledging her as Anheliaa's true heir and Ringmaster of Rhomatum. She was risking everything, inviting the elite . . . and the press . . . into the Tower for this attempt, and he and Mikhyel, to their chagrin, had been caught flat-footed.

But Mikhyel, who until last night had been for the simplest solution, who had wanted to forewarn the entire Web that power would be temporarily interrupted, and then simply bring the Rings down completely to reconstitute the order before raising them again, had decided to let her have her show. If she succeeded, she'd made her point. If she failed, it was Shatumin pride that was at stake, not Rhomandi, and the Web would survive both the moment down . . . and the embarrassment of Lidye.

That was what Mikhyel had said to Lidye, last night, when she'd blithely announced her plans.

Then Mikhyel had gone back to his room and sent a special courier to Armayel to inform Deymorin of the sudden addition to tomorrow's festivities, and followed that courier with another carrying his own, private invitation to the Rhomatum editor of the *Source of the Syndicate*, the newly established, factual-based competitor sheet to the scandal-laden *Internode*. The raising of the Khoratum ring and exclusive interviews with the Rhomandi Triumvirate would, Mikhyel had pointed out in his letter, make an impressive lead story for their first-ever intercity edition.

What Mikhyel hadn't addressed in his response to Lidye, in fact what Mikhyel had markedly avoided mentioning was Lidye's husband's embarrassment. Nikki was appalled that she'd managed to slip her own invitations in with the invitations to his party, but since those invitations made it clear that it was Lidye romNikaenor's moment, he was inclined to agree with Mikhyel: let her sink or swim—on any other day.

A man could grow to resent having his birthday become the official sparring day of his family.

But the plans were moving apace, regardless of his wishes. The ringchamber glistened as the morning light shimmered through glass walls . . . walls that were virtually invisible, even the outsides having been scrubbed for the occasion. Sunbeams glanced off the newly polished wood and crystal furnishings. And Lidye, who had grown increasingly fragile in these final months of her pregnancy, was glowing with health and positively giggling with enthusiasm.

She had, Darius forgive him, returned to the simpering woman he'd married.

He shuddered . . .

And left the debutante to plan her next scheduled appearance.

᠖   ᠖   ᠖

Mikhyel closed the document case and rested a moment, hands flat on the lid, reviewing the contents in his mind a last time before tucking them away. The next time they'd be opened would be in the presence of the combined houses of the Syndicate.

A year's worth of work was in there. A year's work and more accomplished in less than a third that time. Transition festival come and gone. The damned birthday-change . . . he had *not* granted his sister-in-law.

Kiyrstin and Lidye become round as full moons as autumn deepened.

The rings recast. And Nikki's eighteenth birthday.

And Lidye's damnable ambition threatening it all—again.

Well, he'd advised Deymorin; he'd alerted all the businesses he could reach to declare a holiday, if they cared about their employees, with the intimation power might be unstable today. It was the best he could do. When there was an advertised adjustment to the Rings of Rhomatum, rare as it was, the prudent did not rely on an uninterrupted power supply . . . there'd been the recent consequences of the Khoratum ring shattering to advise them of the hazards, an incident still green in memory. And the rumors were on the streets and in every shop, that the Khoratum ring was about to rise. The restoration of a higher level of power to the City was not a matter of small interest.

If all of them were there, especially if Deymorin was there, Lidye might have some hope of success. If she faltered, it was possible they could quietly back her without that cursed audience Lidye had arranged ever knowing the fact.

He'd *let* Lidye win her acclaim rather than have the Rings crash. Let her have her public victory; *she* would forever know the truth, if Deymorin had to save her display.

And knowing that, she would have to loosen her hold on the Rings . . . would have to relinquish the Rings, ultimately. No ringmaster survived a blow of that magnitude.

Confidence to the point of supreme arrogance—absolute confidence in their ability to succeed—was too intrinsic to their success.

He knew that much, after years of dealing with history's greatest ringspinner . . . and an egotist and autocrat of the first water . . . just not one who'd known, always, what he was doing in the Council.

Without his consciously willing it, his fingers caressed the tooled leather. Through all the confusion of the autumn— and in some measure throughout his tenure as Deymorin's proxy under Anheliaa's rule—he'd worked on the contents of this document case. Whatever Lidye did today, even if that new ring shattered and sent them back to the forge . . . this at least offered ways to hold the Web together for another attempt.

Did so much come down to such a small package?

Only one more major hurdle, and the task was done.

A waxing strip pulled from the wax-jack and bent around the packet's leading edge, sealed with his mark, secured that packet as surely as a lock—old-fashioned, but effective; and his own seal, set in that wax, would mark the content as coming indisputably from this office. It would be opened and read into the record at a meeting of the combined representatives of all the nodes of the Rhomatum Web.

Paulis slipped into the doorway. "Sir. A young man." Paulis cleared his throat. "A very young man, to see you. A Master Alizand . . ."

"Alizant." *Deymorin.* Bless the rings, he'd come already. "Is my brother with him?"

"Master Nikaenor?"

"My other brother."

"No, sir." Paulis was decidedly more respectful of the young visitor now. "Shall I show him in?"

Alizant alone. Deymorin had come to the City. Mikhyel was sure of it, vastly relieved . . . and wondering what brought the young scamp to his office without supervision.

He remembered now a letter somewhere in the stack, a letter which, in the press of other business, he had not attended. He was chagrined. He had the affairs of the City in good order, but he could not say the same about family business.

He held up a finger to Paulis. "Quarter hour. Then let him in."

"Yes, sir."

Paulis withdrew, doubtless to test his skills at entertaining the young.

Mikhyel searched the folders for a neglected piece of business, a letter scripted with elegance, but a letter which lacked the grammatical polish of his usual correspondents.

> To the honorable Mikhyel dun'Mheric, High Councilor of Rhomatum,
>
> Sir,
>
> It is with great pleasure and pride that I am informing you that the Greater Encapsulator is done and working bettern ever. I and it are ready whenever you are. I hope you don't mind me remembering to you your promise, but, sir, I am not getting any younger-like, and I truly don't have no notion to live on Rhomandi charity for ever, no matter what Deymio says about owing me and all. Not that I am not inordinately grateful, sir, for all you and your brother has have(?!?) done for me, what with the clothes and Randi and the puppies and all.
>
> Oh, and just in case you're wondern, Baggarrat's doing real good, sir. Best nose in five years, so Gari says! Though, do you suppose he's only just sayn that?
>
> Well, sir, I know you're real busy and all, and Randi's going to come in any minute now and he said not to bothur you, so don't figure you even need to keep reading this, but if it wood make things easier-like, I cood bring it into the City. Not inside the walls, sir, I know that. But the Petroki building in the old expansion ring, it was abandoned and has a big court yard that would work, and with Koratum down now, it should be safe there, shouldn't it? I cood wire all the old ley lamps with kopper, but that wood take a while. I've made seven bulbs so far, well, Blakis made them, cuz I don't blow glass, now do I? And that wood be enuf to show the investors, woodn't it?

Well, I said I woodn't bothur you.
If it pleases your honorship.
Your Servant,
Alizant

It was laughable on the one hand.

But not inconsequential to the Web . . . ultimately. He'd postponed and postponed it because the letter did not pose the flight of fancy it seemed on the surface.

The boy's grammar was getting better . . . on the surface. The first of these formal petitions had required the efforts of both Deymorin and Kiyrstin to translate for him, but it was no young fool he had to deal with.

Mikhyel soberly refolded the letter along its precisely measured folds, wondering how Randoril dunTressan managed to pull the boy away from his precious lightning generator and his puppies long enough to teach him his letters, let alone teach an illiterate waif well enough to let him assemble such a missive . . . and such a daring proposal . . . as this.

Inordinately. Even spelled right. That must have been the Word for the Day.

And the generator was already done. That was a wonder itself. It appeared *his honorship Mikhyel dunMheric* and his clerks weren't the only ones in the Rhomatum Web working overtime these past months.

Remembering to you your promise . . . Alizant could be a very literal, very stubborn young man—and he *had* promised the boy that if he got his encapsulator gadget ready he'd have his chance to convince the cream of Rhomatum's investors. He had simply assumed it would take the boy at least until next spring to reinvent his former master's machine . . . if anyone could.

A promise of patronage, a moment of weakness . . . when the current threat to the Web hadn't existed, when this packet of papers hadn't existed, when the Plan hadn't existed.

A more innocent time, in all senses.

But even in his present plans, the device itself might have

extraordinary implications, and it might have application, now that he thought of it in that context, to shake the node's ruling monetary interests into attention.

Ley energy didn't like lightning. The power umbrella of the node cities didn't like lightning, not in the least, to the extent that, in the Towers, ringspinners were forbidden any clothing that might carry static.

The boy had had a working lightning-concentrator, generator, encapsulator, whatever one might call it—before it and the Ley had met.

And the device was working "bettern ever." From what Deymorin had said, the original device had been impressive enough.

He hadn't seen it himself, but its sheer existence had been sufficient to galvanize Anheliaa into her most aggressive posture.

And that was more than sufficient to pique the interest of at least one gentleman speculator he knew: the old notion of light and heat for areas outside the leylines, for those who didn't mind the risk of being blown to hell.

And yet the recent outgrowth of a new leyline into virgin countryside ought to give pause to anyone who thought seriously about a vast network of such encapsulators.

It might provoke the hillers, who had their own opinions about the Ley.

And Mother had said the Ley was everywhere. It was possible that such a network, one rivaling the Web itself in usage, would result in open elemental warfare that would make the Khoratum battle for freedom look as tame as the Transition Day fireworks display at Armayel.

On the other hand, for more conservative investors, the original encapsulator's destruction might well have proven a blessing in disguise. This way, it took time, and this way, no one could question that the boy had the knowledge to reproduce the results. If one took the letter at face value, Alizant had clearly done it on his own, and might make his fortune and be set for life before the negative consequences came due and burned the speculators . . . in whatever sense that might happen. In certain places, the remote country-

side, away from leylines, the technology had possibilities;
at sea, where leylines did not extend their power, and
where boats relied on sails and the wind, it had real possibilities, sailing contrary to the wind or even without the
wind.

Commercial applications, however remote from
Rhomatum . . . rings, once he let his mind consider the
notion, the possibilities became endless.

And the boy said this thing was done.

He hoped to the several hells that the boy hadn't brought
it with him—but of course he wouldn't. He wouldn't be
here without Deymorin, and Deymio would never allow
him to bring it into the City.

As far as the boy's legal right to profit from the technology was concerned, every specialist he'd queried had confirmed his belief that the patent was indeed fair game for
anyone daring enough to develop it. Others had tried to
encapsulate the lightning, and failed, not, as he understood
the matter, through a flaw in the concept, but rather having
been blown up like the predecessor to Alizant's machine, or
intimidated—or bought out—by self-interested ringspinners
who didn't want competition . . . or (more charitably) the
danger to their cities.

Alizant's master had been the latest inventor of this
often-rumored technology. Maybe he'd been out to get a
payment to destroy the device. Maybe he'd really believed
in the dream that drove Alizant. Whatever the reason, he'd
lost his nerve, folded to the will of the spinners in Mauritum, notably Garetti, and given the machine to Alizant.
Alizant, with the pure faith of youth, had dared Garetti's
lair . . . and won Kiyrstin's if not Garetti's goodwill.

So now that goodwill and circumstances had landed him
in Deymorin's hands, and no less than the Rhomandi of
Rhomatum was inclined to support the endeavor.

Well, Zandy's perseverance seemed more than enough
to validate his right to profit, under the circumstances.

He slipped the petition back in its envelope and set it on
the stack that would end up in Nikki's office. The logistical
problem was right down his younger brother's line of ex-

pertise, and it would do Nikki good to shepherd someone younger than himself.

"Khyel? I mean, Justice dunMheric? Excuse me, sir."

A blink, and he saw, for a split instant, a stranger—until he looked past the new suit, a summer's growth, and the neatly braided hair.

"Alizant!"

"Yes, sir, it's me. Uh, I."

"Well, so what are you doing here?"

"Came with Master Deymio, sir. For the birthday party tomorrow."

"Of course. Please, sit down."

Alizant settled on the edge of the cushion, hat in hand, shoulders rigid beneath the new coat.

"I've read the petition," he said, into the ensuing silence. "I'll have Nikki start looking into the details of the demonstration immediately."

"Sir, I'm not sure . . ." Alizant's voice squeaked. He gave a tiny cough behind a rapidly raised fist, then continued: "Maybe you should wait to talk to Master Nikaenor about it."

"Why is that? You're ready, aren't you?"

"Uh . . . yes, but, um . . . I'm not here about that, sir, it's about Dey—Master Deymorin."

"Of a sudden formal, are we?"

"No, sir. I mean, yes, sir. I mean—It's not about th' encapsulator." The boy looked miserable, twisting his new hat nervously. "It's—I don't know what I mean."

He dealt with politicians and lawyers, adults of the most difficult sort, malefactors and litigants. He hadn't known how to deal with a youngster like Alizant when he was Alizant's age. He certainly couldn't now. He would, in fact, give a great deal to have his own hat to twist.

"Alizant, where *is* Deymorin? You came into Rhomatum with him, didn't you?"

"Yes, sir. He's stayin' in town, doncha know? Wants not to tip th' boat and ruin Master Nikaenor's party afore it starts."

"Ah. Wise of him."

"Yes, sir. I thought so, sir. But he and Mistress Kiyrstin were goin' shoppin' an' I don' gives a . . . I mean, I din't really care t' go with'm, and I wanted to talk with you before he—" The cap flipped from his hands; he gave a swallowed curse, scooped it up, and said in a rush: "Sir, if Master Deymorin were to do somethin' . . . legal-like, you'd have to do the papers, wouldn't you? If it's Family stuff?"

"Probably." Caution was always wise when dealing with Alizant. "What kind of . . . 'Family stuff?' "

"A-doption?"

"Ah."

"Yes, sir."

"You?"

"Yes, sir."

He could certainly appreciate a young lad's feeling of being cornered in a situation. And could appreciate his courage in coming to deal with it. "Don't you *want* to be adopted?"

"Yes, sir. I mean, no, sir. I mean—"

"You mean, how could a lad such as yourself *not* be tempted, eh? Is it Deymorin? Do you not want to be his son?"

"Yes, sir. More than anything, sir. It'd be . . . wonderful, sir. But it ain't right, sir. Him feeling obligated and all. He's a good sort, and real generous, but he already give me the clothes and Baggarat and Miikho—"

"Who's Miikho?"

"The filly, sir. Born last night?"

"Ah. Indeed, generous of him." Now the Barrister knew what to do with the case and how to think. "But perhaps it's not gratitude that drives his decision."

"What else, beggin' yer pardon, zur?" Zandy's speech floundered in his fight to explain. "Already has a son, now don't he? Acknowledged an' everythin'. An' I likes 'im, don' get me wrong. I ain't jealous er nothin'. Wouldn't want ye t' think it. But he's *got* Kherdy—"

He almost asked *who's Kherdy*, but caught himself in time.

"—An' another son on th' way, most like, if not 'nother girl, and likely more eventually, with Mistress Kiyrstin."

It was Deymorin's two illegitimate children. The two whose mothers, or so Deymorin had informed Anheliaa, were *married now, and doing fine.*

He'd never met them. Never heard their names. Obviously, Alizant had.

"And for friends," Alizant was arguing earnestly, "he's give me a place to stay, now hain't he? I'm th' one owin' *him.* And if he 'dopts me, I'll be that much more beholden. And then, with th' encapsulator, th' investors and all, those gennulmen won't dare say no, cuz I'll be *his,* don' ye see? Son of the Princeps, and so they'll be fighting to get in good with him by givin' me money for the gens, not cuz it's a good idea and all, an— Well, damn, sir, —'scuse me— but I want to make it myself, I do. I don't want to be beholden any more than I already am, don't ye see?"

He did indeed see—finally. No little relieved about the situation, he asked:

"Tell me, Alizant, if the encapsulator were not involved, if Deymorin was just Deymio, Lord of Armayel still, but not Princeps of Rhomatum, how would you feel then about his offer?"

The boy chewed his lip and dropped his eyes. And when he spoke again, the gutter-panic had left his voice. "You ain't reckoned the biggest problem, sir, an' the reason I think you should ought to think again 'bout havin' Master Nikaenor in charge of the demo. Master Nikaenor, he already thinks mebbe Deymorin should drown me, er somethin' like. I don't want to be no cause o' trouble between you all, when you been fightin' so hard t' be a family again and all."

"I see." Alizant had been at Armayel with them during the convalescence after Boreton, and heard far more than young ears should hear. Mikhyel let the wild spate of revelation hang in the room a calculated number of heartbeats, then offered: "Well, Alizant of Mauritum, allow me to inform you that what you've done today only confirms my belief in my elder brother's good sense in adopting you."

Dark eyes flickered up, startled and puzzled.

"Deymorin already talked to me about this," Mikhyel continued, "and he wants very badly to adopt you. You're beholden to him, yes, and he to you, on a number of accounts, but he's also very fond of you for your own sake. He wants to give you the protection—and the Family association—that goes with his name. He feels very strongly you not only deserve it, but have earned it."

"But, sir—"

Mikhyel raised his hand. "As for my younger brother, you met him first at a very difficult time. We've all discussed the matter, and, yes, he's dubious—justifiably. He was very much afraid that you might try to take advantage of our good-natured brother. What you've just done in coming to me this way should more than allay any objections he might remotely have harbored, and I promise you, he *will* see it that way. My own feeling is, if you have it in you to love and honor my brother as a son should a father, it would be not only a fair and just option, it would be a very happy one for all parties, including Deymorin's lady and his upcoming children. —*If*, however, you do not harbor those tender feelings for him, if you hurt or disappoint him in any *significant* way, I promise you, you'll answer to both Nikaenor and myself."

A faint smile greeted his words. "I'd have to answer to Mistress Kiyrstin first, by your leave, sir, and by y'r leave, she scares me more n' any of you."

He laughed in spite of himself. "Good point. So, should I draw up the papers?"

The frown hadn't completely disappeared. "But the investors?"

Pride. He appreciated that. "Hmm. . . . Good point again. I might draw up the papers, sign them to be legally binding, should the need arise, but we Rhomandis might agree to keep it quiet until, say, you come of age? Another, what? Two years? That would give you time to prove yourself on your own merits, don't you think?"

Hope lit up behind shadowed eyes. "Well . . ."

"Think about it." Mikhyel stood up and walked around

the desk, his hand again out, this time in leavetaking. "I'll stall Deymorin until you tell me one way or the other. And while I won't tell him about this meeting, he'll likely find out eventually. I hope you realize that."

Alizant tapped his skull by way of question, and Mikhyel nodded that, yes, there were very few secrets possible for him and his brothers.

"Spooky, that must be," the boy said.

"Sometimes. It makes it hard not to understand each other, doubly hard to disappoint one another. That's the sort of family you're getting into. I hope your answer is yes, I'll say that up front, but you make it an unqualified yes before you do anything, you hear me?"

"I hear you, sir. And thank you, sir." Alizant headed for the door.

"Alizant?"

The boy turned.

"I'd be proud to have a son like you."

Alizant blushed deeply, and ducked out the door.

§ § §

The deep plush velvet caressed Kiyrstin's fingertips, and a part of her longed to fling herself in a suitably sultry sprawl across that wine-red expanse. The other part could see that reflection in the mirrored wall even before she flung, and not even Deymorin would be able to avoid laughing.

So instead, she settled herself comfortably on the edge of the bed and smiled at the famous establishment's voluptuous ruler.

"It's lovely, Tirise. Thank you. Thank you very much."

Deymorin, having been delayed at the door with the porter carrying the day's gleanings, came up behind Tirise and set his arms around the woman's waist, then grinned provocatively at Kiyrstin over the madam's shoulder. "What did I tell you, Tess? And you were worried."

"Still am, m'lord Dee." Tirese brushed his hands away and admonished him to behave, and Kiyrstin laughed.

"Don't worry, Tirise. He's told me all about you and how *much* he owes you. And I, for one, am very grateful for the job you did housebreaking him."

The madam looked from one to the other of them, in some wonder, obviously at an unfamiliar loss for words.

"C'mere, laddybuck," Kiyrstin leaned forward and grabbed Deymorin's hand. "Quit embarrassing the nice lady." She tugged, and Deymorin quite obligingly settled on the bed beside her and transferred that cuddling hold to her. "When Zandy returns, Madame Tirise, will you send him on up? I'll control his lordship here until we're sure he's safely ensconced."

"I'll bring the lad up myself, Lady Kiyrstin. I'd wager he's not as old as he acts, and some of the girls have already taken a bit of a shine to him, and you don't need that complicatin' your stay."

Deymorin's low chuckle vibrated against Kiyrstin's ear. "Always take good care of your boys, don't you, Tess?"

"And how d' you think I've stayed in business all these years? Know the law, I do, and not inclined to forget. Not with Mikhyel dunMheric's brother a paying customer all that time. And not knowing when the lad's comin' back, if you'd like me to, I'll make sure he's taken care of proper so's a mother could approve, and you can just enjoy yourselves. There's a bath through that door, big enough for two, and won't cramp your little third, if you're careful."

Trying not to reveal her own, very strong inclinations, Kiyrstin said: "Your call, JD."

He leaned to the side and caught her chin to turn it toward him. He smiled, and kissed her lips lightly. "Thanks, Tess. We accept. How's the hot water supply?"

"Deymio," Tirise's tone chastised gently as she slipped out. Then, as if on a sudden afterthought, her face reappeared. "Just you remember, not too hot! Not with the babe." And before Kiyrstin could respond, she dipped her head so hard the feathers bobbed, then disappeared, this time closing the door behind her.

As the latch clicked into place, Deymorin turned Kiyrstin full toward him, his big hands gentle on her shoulders.

"Are you sure you don't mind this?"

"What? A lukewarm bath? Not the first time—"

He growled and stopped her with a brief kiss. "You know what I mean. If it bothers you to stay here, we'll go find a proper hotel, or say to hell with Lidye and go on up to Rhomandi House with guns blazing and swords flashing."

"And what about your plans for tonight?"

"I'll take my chances tomorrow along with my brothers. It's probably a silly notion anyway."

"Is that why you won't let me come with you to the Tower?"

"And if something *does* go wrong? I don't want you there. I don't want the distraction. I don't want the concern for your safety."

Her safety. As if his didn't matter.

It wasn't a silly plan. It was, in fact, a fairly sound plan . . . if he stuck to it. Deymorin's sources within the Tower had assured him that Lidye had taken to her bed and would stay there until the fateful hour, meditating and *fortifying* herself for the moment.

Tonight, thanks to the quiet weather of recent months and the nearly unshakable stability of the Rings, Nethaalye was getting her own rest before the party. The Tower would be held by three monitors . . . two in the Tower, one in Lidye's room *listening* to the other two, assistants who could wake Lidye on the instant, should that be necessary. With his unquestioned access to the Tower, Deymorin planned gently to displace those monitors from the ring-chamber, and to see, just *see* (or so he insisted) if he could budge those rings. He wanted some idea, before the fateful moment, exactly what they might be up against.

Unfortunately, she knew her Just Deymio, and if the rings did move, she couldn't see him stopping there. And neither did he. *That* was why he wanted her to stay away. He'd admit that possibility if she challenged him, but there was no point. He knew that she saw right through him, trusted her to know him that well.

And trusted her to trust his basic good sense. If he hadn't the skill, he wouldn't try.

He also trusted her to tell him truthfully if her staying here in the City's best whorehouse would in any way disturb her. Not one to take his concern lightly, Kiyrstin queried her gut, and found herself not the least unnerved by the warm and gentle intimacy between these two, which might have been something of a concern, at one point, for a woman whose hold on Deymorin was in truth no more legitimate as the law saw matters than was the madam's. She'd been a bit jealous, perhaps, but not of Tirise herself, who turned out to be an immensely likable woman. She couldn't claim superiority: Deymorin had the likes of Tirise in his past, an honest madam . . . and she had . . . Garetti.

And a variety of other men, as Deymorin had known several other women besides Tirise. She liked to think of it as having studied her options, she'd chosen the best available with a clear head. Which was laughable; considering the gymnastics her stomach still went through every time she saw him, there was small chance she'd chosen on logic alone.

But then, while her stomach leaped, his eyes burned with a fire that had only grown along with her stomach.

She sprawled across that velvet bed, her full belly as silly in the mirrored reflection as she'd imagined, and Deymorin's hoarse *Gods, you're gorgeous* . . . as gratifying as only the reaction of a man crazy-blind with love could be.

"Mind?" she repeated. "I think it was a brilliant notion. I've always dreamed of spending a night in a brothel with the man of my dreams." She held out her arms. "C'mere, Rags."

§   §   §

I'd be proud to have a son like you. . . .

Mikhyel had surprised himself with that one, but it was the truth. Alizant was a good-natured, scrupulously honorable young man—for all he had the thespian soul of a leyside charlatan. If Deymorin hadn't taken the step, it wasn't out of the question he'd have done it himself. It would have been another issue of debts repaid, but not grudgingly.

Strange how much easier it was to imagine being father to a grown lad such as Alizant than father to the unknown entity growing in Mirym's womb that truly was of his own making. Possibly the difference he felt was nothing more significant than the comfort of dealing with a known quantity; or he simply had a hard time connecting himself to the events that had culminated in his own child.

It had been different with Temorii. For a brief few hours, he'd actually imagined a life that included—among so much else—children. . . .

And that had been the greatest fantasy of all. Good that he'd been cured of such reckless thoughts before he'd actually condemned a soul to a life with himself as father. A child. That, with his damnable black temper, with Mheric's heritage, and Anheliaa's teachings . . . was the last aspect of family he should contemplate.

Besides, he had it on the best authority, Temorii was dead: there would be no child, ever, no life from the joining of Dancer and Khy. And that was beyond question a good thing, because there would be reminders enough over the next years in the form of nieces and nephews growing up happy and secure in their fathers: he didn't need his own mistakes to prove his inadequacy to himself and the world.

Mirym, lying secure up in New Khoratum, had been wiser perhaps than she knew to escape his well-meaning but ill-fated aid. He could be a fair brother, probably an indulgent uncle . . . but never a father.

He shut that thought down, quietly, solidly, as he'd learned to do these past months. It was harder to wall out extraneous matters today, with the seal on that report. So many strands of the pattern in which he'd been absorbed for so long being now tied off left empty rooms in his mind . . . and leisure to think reminded him, with too unexpected an immediacy, of unfinished business.

How had he swung back to thinking of Temorii? He hadn't consciously done it.

Still, he should ask Ganfrion if he'd heard anything about the dancer. That he'd gone back to his beloved mountain was a foregone conclusion, once the Belisii arrived without a dancer. The Belisii had arrived midsummer, had gained their supporters and their trade routes and become a standard notification that crossed his desk bimonthly.

That Dancer might possibly have found entrance once again to Mother's caverns . . . for that much desired fortune, a man who had once cared very deeply—too deeply— for Temorii could profoundly hope. That would settle everything, in the best possible way.

But if he had not, if Dancer had found shelter: a home, a calling, perhaps even a lover who could care for him as he so fervently had wished—if Dancer had found that contentment somewhere in the mountains, possibly even in the hiller village at New Khoratum itself, Ganfrion would be able to find that out, if he didn't already know.

Ganfrion, who had a knack for choosing ferrets almost as slippery as himself, and who managed somehow to always be where he needed to be to pass information to whoever needed to hear it, had slipped without fanfare into the role of information-gatherer and chief spy for both Deymorin and himself, on one side of the Web and the other, over a course of months.

The fact that Mikhyel had heard nothing about Dancer did not necessarily mean Ganfrion knew nothing, only that he knew nothing that he thought Mikhyel needed to know.

And Mikhyel hadn't asked, damn sure he hadn't asked. The fire inside him had been quiet, protected in his ignorance.

If he knew . . . if he *knew,* nothing would ensure Thyerri's safety; that was the true curse of his new ability. He could avoid actively pursuing, could avoid *trying* to find Dancer, but knowing where he was, given anything, any hint where or how to locate Dancer as he had Mirym in the world pattern of Rhomatum, he knew he would be curious. He would think about it. And thinking would threaten that blessed isolation they now had.

He couldn't do that. Not to Thyerri, not to himself. Because thinking would lead to finding and finding to touching and touching to burning and burning to destruction.

He knew folly when he stared it in the face. Keeping busy was a damned lot safer.

He took that sealed, official report and placed it in his safe, together with the official copies of the treaties, then gathered his coat and hat and gloves . . . it grew chilly in the evenings this time of year, even within the Tower's energy umbrella. Chilly: more so this year than ever before, a man didn't need the official reports to know that. But he'd discovered, during his time in the Khoramali, that he liked the chill air. And so he dressed accordingly, and walked home, even though the cabbies would grant him priority in any request for transportation and have him home in minutes.

He said good night to his diligent staff, reminded Paulis to turn down the lights and lock up, and headed out.

Tomorrow, perhaps, he'd take a cab. Tomorrow, he wouldn't want to risk being late. Tomorrow: Nikki's party and Lidye's damned sideshow.

Chapter Five

It was ridiculously simple to sneak into the Tower of Rhomatum . . . when your name happened to be Deymorin Rhomandi. No one questioned his late arrival, or his orders not to announce his presence, now or in the morning. A simple *I want to surprise my brother* . . . more than sufficed to quiet the guards' well-trained curiosity.

And in the Tower itself, at his request, the monitors simply left the Tower for their bedrooms on the second floor, where they would await his summons to return.

For the second time in his life, it was just him and the Rings in the Tower. No Nethaalye, no Anheliaa, no Khyel. . . .

And the ringchamber felt . . . different.

Forcing his attention away from the Rings, an increasingly difficult task, and one he meant to master tonight, he discovered a room that bore little resemblance to the ringchamber he'd known all his life. Chairs had been brought in. Row upon concentric rows of seating for tomorrow's public spectacle. He'd never felt the size of the place until he saw how many seats of ordinary scale it could contain. All Anheliaa's sparse furniture had been either of massive scale, or so delicately diminutive a man his size didn't dare touch it let alone sit on it.

And there was *bunting* obscuring half the view.

The walls were windows, full circle. A ringmaster had to see the weather . . . in every direction. Or so he'd always believed. Now . . . he'd felt the wind in the Rings, sensed the number and density of clouds, the areas of the sky where opposing forces met: wind, pressure, temperature.

Why would a master need to see what he could already feel?

However, no one could argue that it did allow for an unparalleled view of the City, and perhaps that was its true value. To a ringmaster too caught up in the Rings that sight could serve as a reminder of why the Tower existed at all.

At the moment, in the dark, predawn hours, it was a city of stars. The primary constellations were the silver street lights that radiated out in every direction, terminating, eventually and after a hundred miles or more of solitary splendor, in another node city. Between the lines and within the radius of the power umbrella, the houselights glimmered, eclipsed, on occasion, by a passing body, even at this late hour. Fewer of those now than there would have been earlier, hence his other reason for scheduling his experiment for this hour. Should his test somehow disrupt the energy flow, the number of people affected should be minimal.

Better than having the energy flow stop altogether and stay stopped for a long interval, which would be the case if Lidye tried to raise those two rings, he was certain of it. Why he should be so positive of that disaster, he didn't stop to question: his conviction of its probability was that strong.

Arrogance on his part? Possibly. It did seem to run in the Family.

He worked his way through the rows of seating that filled every spare section of floor, appalled at the number. What in hell was the woman thinking? Had she invited the press as well?

Taking a front row seat, he gazed at the Rings aloft in their slow, apparently random beat, contemplated the two newly cast that lay on the bare stone floor, their leythium coating gleaming in the Tower's soft light, and began to assess the extent of the problem facing him, matching reality to the plan he'd practiced a dozen times in his head—in just the past hour.

Assuming the rings moved at all to his asking, the inner rings would pose little or no problem. Fortunately, if fortune could be said to have worked at all in this business, the two secondary node rings involved in the recasting were the two outermost. The real trick would be bringing those two rings up past the Cardinal and slipping them into the continually revolving set of eight others without disrupting either the Cardinal or the existing Giephaetum/Shatum ring.

Or, Darius have pity on a fool, without touching the radical streamer dancing so crazily about the rings. But the radical, he suspected, simply required his healthy conviction that it *would* be a problem to stay out of his way. It had seemed to him that the radical, rather than being a random factor, was simply a contrary one, generally choosing to do the exact opposite of what the spinner expected.

The Ley's own humility factor.

The Cardinal ring was both the greatest obstacle and the most reliable factor in the entire operation. Unlike the axes of the secondary rings, the Cardinal's axis, perpendicular to the floor, never varied. Therefore, while it prevented him simply raising the rings from a center point, it at least meant that tilting them up and dropping them around the center rings and into orbit should be possible.

And to that end, the two replacement rings had not been left directly beneath the spinning rings, but rather off to one side.

The other problem was the Giephaetum/Shatum ring, the damaged one he'd have to replace, hopefully slipping the new one in without disrupting the orbit of the old Giephaetum/Shatum ring that was up and spinning at the time.

If he raised them both at once, tilted them up and around and in, synchronizing both of their orbits with the damaged ring . . .

He leaned forward, propping his elbows on his knees and his chin in his hands, visualizing the entire operation, focusing on the central imaging sphere as his reference point. He found himself nodding in time to the Cardinal's rhythmic orbit, his foot taking up a counterpoint to the G/S ring's passage past his chosen referent, thinking it would probably be best to use the rings' own momentum rather than to try to control its passage altogether, to set it in

motion . . . now—two, three, four—tilt—two three—arc . . .
and swing—

He stared. Blinked. Rubbed his eyes and stared again.
Finally, he murmured:

"Well, I'll be damned . . ."

§ § §

{Khyel, could you please come to the Tower?}

A soft voice filtered into Mikhyel's dreams. A request
that his half-formed thoughts said should come from Anheliaa, but neither tone nor request held Anheliaa's autocratic
stamp . . . so his half-waking mind grew curious and came
full awake to find out.

{Deymorin?}

{Yes-s-s-s.}

A very distracted Deymorin. And in the Tower. At 5:00
in the damn morning. And wanting secrecy, that much was
obvious. But there was no sense of panic or emergency,
just mystification.

Mikhyel drew his robe on and headed bare-foot silent
for the Tower.

When he arrived, his brother was alone in the ringchamber, sitting in a chair, legs crossed, chin propped in
his hand, staring at the Rings. Mikhyel followed that bemused gaze . . .

And saw the new Rings spinning quietly in tandem with
the old Giephaetum/Shatum ring.

"It was so easy," Deymorin whispered. "So . . . damned
easy. I just thought . . . and there they were. If she knew . . .
no wonder she was so confident."

"*You* did that, Deymio?" Mikhyel asked, and Deymorin's shoulder lifted in a half shrug.

"Must've. I don't know . . . I just thought about how it
should happen, what I was *going* to do, and . . . there
it was."

"The energy flow is quiet?"

Deymorin nodded.

But there were two Giephaetum/Shatum rings, spinning as one, and the next smaller, the Khoratum/Persitum ring, moved within as if attached.

"How will you remove the old Giephaetum/Shatum ring?" Mikhyel asked softly, and Deymorin, still watching the Rings, stretched a smile.

"Blow it up, I sup—"

The radical flitted around and tapped the old Giephaetum/Shatum ring. With a little popping sound, the ring vanished.

Mikhyel jumped; Deymorin said:

"Shit . . ." An almost thoughtful expletive. Then a whispered: "So much power. . . . Gods, so *much*!"

"Deymorin?" He grew worried at his brother's intent distraction. {Deymio?}

{I'm all right, Khyel. It's a bit overwhelming. But I know . . . Persitum must come back on line, but if I shift the orbit . . .} And past the verbalization, came the worries of surges, of industry heaters left aligned for maximum draw, and suddenly glutted and overheating in a power rise endangering buildings and businesses . . .

"Can you control the flow?"

Deymorin's head dipped; Mikhyel took it for affirmation. Deymorin's mind seemed . . . otherwise occupied, his head-tipped stare a familiar one.

He'd known, all those years ago, that his brother had to have ability, if not extraordinary Talent for ringspinning. But this . . . it went beyond his wildest imaginings. A handful of sessions with Nethaalye, and—

{Oh, rather more than that, brother.} Humor drifted through the link. {Every time Nikki came near them, I might as well have been here, conscious link or not.}

He—they—together recalled the night of the uprising, at the last, when Nikki, not Lidye, had directed their efforts. Interesting. If Nikki could be Deymorin's remote assistant, and if those two could, as Deymorin implied, maintain that level of link without Mikhyel's at least conscious involvement, that linkage opened many possibilities for Deymorin's ability to maintain some portion of the Outside lifestyle he loved and still keep direct control of the Rings.

Though how much of that thought was his and how much Deymorin's was a question that had more of curiosity than significance under present circumstance. They were far ahead of reality represented by this sea of chairs. Still, it might reconcile his active brother to the increasingly obvious facts.

"I told you before, I was prepared for that possibility," Deymorin said.

"Any physical reaction? Any sign of Anheliaa's decay in the joints?" He couldn't imagine his active brother living with that particular consequence.

Deymorin shook his head. "On the contrary. Feeling better than I have in my life."

"Even the leg?"

"Even the leg."

"Maybe Rhomatum likes you."

"Maybe I like sitting on my ass. I'm not happy with it, Khyel, but even that . . . I'd live with it. *I will* live with it. In point of fact, I don't think I've much choice."

Mikhyel didn't like the sound of that. He didn't at all like the notion that the Ley controlled the options they had with any power other than the appeal of a life of convenience, a power they themselves granted it. That they might live lives challenged by it, shaped by it, ultimately sacrificing their lives to it as Anheliaa had done . . . that was a damned grim thought.

Deymorin grinned, still without looking at him. "Hardly my point, brother. Call it childish selfishness. I've found, in the past few hours, that I don't *like* sharing the Rings. At least, not with Lidye."

That was hardly reassuring. Whence this sudden possessiveness? Not so long ago, his independent brother had been ready to consign the Towers to the first taker. How did this new notion take over? When?

"Time was," Deymorin said, "the Tower meant Anheliaa. The place reeked of her ambitions. Damned right I hated it. It's . . . different now."

Mikhyel frowned and consciously strengthened his barriers, resenting the invasion of thoughts not yet formed, far from comforted: it made his brother feel too much like Anheliaa, who had, he'd come to suspect once he and his brothers had developed the ability, manipulated his mind all his life.

Deymorin's eyes flickered to him at last, a brief apology, and then returned to the Rings. "Sorry, brother. Hard not to hear at the moment."

Which made him wonder if Anheliaa had been listening to his thoughts as well as manipulating him all these years he'd spent in the Tower with her. He'd never heard her thoughts, except toward the end, but that didn't mean—

A second glance from Deymorin. "I doubt it, brother. She'd have found out about your machinations with her proposals and ended your career before it ever got started."

"Dammit, Deymorin! Stay out of my head!"

His brother only shrugged abstractedly. "Sorry. Give me time. I'll try to figure out how to stop it. At the moment, I've other things . . ."

Deymorin's brow tightened, that concentrated stare grew fierce. The air rippled with leythium motes coalescing around the Khoratum/Persitum ring . . . then the tingling energy dissipated and Deymorin's face relaxed.

"Damn! It just won't move."

"It might be better to wait anyway," Mikhyel suggested. "Anheliaa used to have to rest, after a major effort, and while you say raising them was easy—"

"Gods, brothers," Nikki's horror-stricken voice arrived unexpectedly from the stair landing. *"What have you done?"*

Ꮆ   Ꮆ   Ꮆ

It was a foregone conclusion, Nikki decided, that when Deymorin decided to become a ringspinner, he'd not only conquer the Rings, he'd conquer them spectacularly—neither of his brothers ever did anything halfway.

That Deymorin's victory came with comparative ease was also not surprising. Deymorin had never really had to work at anything, not even reconciling with Mikhyel, once he'd put his mind to it. Not that it was Deymio's fault. He didn't ask to be perfect.

That Deymorin should accomplish this milestone on Nikki's birthday and draw the attention away from Nikki and to himself was also part of the pattern of their lives. Nikki's birthday was the one day of the year the entire family could reliably be found in the same room—and when the Rhomandi Family got together, sparks flew, generally centering on the strong and independent Deymorin.

That Deymio had called Mikhyel alone to share his victory might seem, to someone outside the Family, to be cruel and exclusionary. But Deymorin had imagined him sleeping soundly, needing his rest on the morning before the big party . . . hadn't even remotely intended a disturbance. Hadn't wanted to put him in the position of knowing until he had some solution to offer.

Deymio had only called to Mikhyel, Deymio explained as the sun rose behind the Khoramali, seeking advice to help him decide what to do now. Deymorin had not intended to raise the rings, only to test his ability. Deymio didn't want to cause a furor on Nikki's birthday, but it did seem foolish to risk bringing that ring down now only so Lidye could have her show in a handful of hours.

Besides, the old Giephaetum/Shatum ring was gone, vaporized—so a wide-eyed Mikhyel had explained, inviting him after the fact to share in the adventure—so he couldn't take it down anyway. The Giephaetum/Shatum line would collapse.

All this to console him and make him feel, belatedly, part of their plans.

Now he'd so inconveniently arrived.

He'd awakened early, excited, as celebrations of all sorts always made him, and worried about tonight's showcase for Lidye. —Or so he'd thought. He knew now, it had been Deymorin's startled call to Mikhyel that had snuck into his dreams and alerted him, a fact he'd realized as he dressed, as his brothers' thoughts had buzzed on the edges of his mind.

Now he was here; now the endless explanations began.

Sometimes, he wished they would stop making excuses, that Deymorin would just say *I snuck in in the middle of the night because I didn't want to make a fool of myself in front of an audience—especially you and Mikhyel—and when I fucked up, I thought of Mikhyel and not of you . . . Sorry, old man, but that's how it was. . . .*

Instead, to make *him* somehow feel better, they both rattled out a dozen reasons that would make him feel like a cad if he came back with *Apology accepted, but dammit, Deymorin, pride or no pride, birthday or no birthday, you were damnwell wrong not to warn us, not to consult us about something this potentially explosive, but you didn't, so let's all admit we're damned lucky to have escaped disaster, try to learn from our mistakes, and move on.*

That was the crux of their problem: they still, in some senses, could not move on. And damned if he could see how to change that pattern today.

Deymorin had not intended to become the center of the universe on Nikki's birthday, but Deymorin had, and now in good grace *he* had to fall into the familiar position of mopping up, placating the family tempers, keeping the peace, and deciding what to do about it before the feuds tore all their lives apart.

Suddenly, he realized the excuses had stopped. His brothers were staring at him.

"Sorry, old man," Deymio said softly, "but that's how it was . . ."

Nikki's startlement lasted only a moment. "Apology accepted, big brother. So . . . what *do* we do now?"

"Let Lidye explain to them," was Mikhyel's solution. "The damned show was her idea."

Which on the one hand was only justice, but on the other . . . *he* had to live with her. And on that dismal thought, he said, "I want to tell her."

"I can't ask you to do that," Deymorin said. "I caused this mixup; the least I can do is weather her storm."

Oh, he knew how successful that would be—as did Deymorin. Deymorin knew he would say:

"I'd like to try and avert that storm." Nikki strove to

remain calm. "I believe that I can." He was accustomed to resort to humor to make his way with his brothers; there was damned little available in this. He simply plowed ahead. "But it will be in my own way and my own time."

"We don't *have* time, Nikki," Deymorin said.

"For the love of Darius, brother, give me the chance! She's my wife."

"All right," Deymorin's agreement was not exactly enthusiastic—it never was. "But I'll stick close."

Said the man who had just been up all night and on whom the safety of the Rings now squarely resided. While his brothers gave lip service to his efforts, their actions rarely implied confidence, which made it damned hard to have any confidence in himself.

It had taken Kiyrstin to give him that, and fragile though that confidence still was and because this time he *knew* he was right, he dared to say:

"I'd prefer otherwise, Deymorin. Where are you staying? In the Tower?" He hadn't heard Deymio come in. There'd been no stir among the servants.

"Tirise's."

And he'd have brought Kiyrstin and Alizant with him. Only Deymorin would think of housing his wife-and-son-to-be in the fanciest brothel in Rhomatum. And yet, knowing Kiyrstin a bit better now, he could almost imagine her exchanging tips with the madam.

"I think I'd prefer it if you went back there," Nikki said. "I can reach you there, if needs be, but if you're not in reach to hear, Lidye is far more amenable to reason."

"Your call, Nik. Tirise's it is." Deymorin yawned widely. "And I have to admit, I won't be sorry. I'd like to be awake for your party tonight. You might, however, point out to Lidye that I haven't been able to set the Khoratum/Persitum ring. That should make her happy."

Which only proved how blind Deymorin was to Lidye's tempers.

"And if she wants to try and set it beforehand?" Mikhyel asked.

"Hell, if she wants to try and do it at the party, with all

of us there, I wouldn't argue, but I think she risks making a fool of herself. I don't think she'll get it to budge—not with all the distractions she'll have. I think it might require the lot of us to get it out of sync with the Giephaetum/ Shatum ring, but I've got to think about it. Meanwhile, and this I'm firm on—she doesn't come near the Tower, Nikki. Do I make myself clear?"

"That doesn't give me a lot to negotiate with."

"That's the condition. For her own safety. And the child's. And the Web's."

"That rather well goes without saying, Deymorin," Nikki said quietly, to which Deymorin at least had the good grace to apologize for the necessity, if not the decision.

Or would have, if Nikki hadn't interrupted him. "Never mind. Khyel, I know you meant to spend the morning at the office. I think you should go; I think we should continue with today's plans as if this hasn't happened. I don't want her to find out by walking in here; I also don't want her worrying about why everyone's suddenly changed plans without telling her."

"I agree." Mikhyel stood and wrapped his silk robe more tightly about his body. "The house will be rousing, Deymorin. If you hope to escape unremarked, you'd best get going."

"Don't worry." Deymorin grinned. "I can get out."

"I imagine you can," Mikhyel murmured, then pulled the cord that would alert the monitors to return to the Tower. "Nikki, you're decidedly better covered than I. Will you wait for them?"

Nikki nodded, and as his brothers left together, moved to the window to watch the sun rise.

Lidye's calm reception of his revelation exceeded Nikki's wildest hopes. Seated in her elegant chambers, she heard him out without speaking. Then: "He raised both together? You're certain of that?"

"I saw it myself. They spin as if connected."

Her fine shoulders twitched beneath the frills of her dressing robe. She rose and went to her mirrored dressing table to dab at her makeup, but the hand that attempted to apply the lip gloss began to shake so that she had to set it down. She turned, and leaned back against the table, hands resting on either side, mouth stretched into a smile.

"Together." She repeated, and laughed aloud. "Oh, Nikki . . . the *fool!*"

"I don't understand."

"Why should you? You haven't the least notion . . . the lot of you. Ignorant as babes. Nikki, they'll *never* be separated now. The rings *must* be lifted one at a time."

His stomach dropped. "You're certain."

"Of course I am. The only possible solution now is to bring the lot down, and raise them one at a time. Stupid, novice trick . . . Well, nothing to be done now. The party must go on. We shall let them see the Rings, praise your brother's accomplishment, then make a show of trying to set the Khoratum ring. Then, when I fail, as I must, I'll simply apologize, explain the problem, and plan the day to bring them all down. I'm sorry, Nikaenor, but thanks to your brother's hubris, your birthday is not to be the time of celebration I'd hoped."

"Don't be angry, Lidye. Deymorin didn't mean to make the problem worse."

"Of course he didn't. But he's arrogant, Nikaenor, *arrogant;* and that arrogance will prove his undoing. Still," she said with a shrug, "we'll work it out. Mikhyel will smooth all the ruffled feathers, as he does so well. We'll have our public showing today, then set a day, bring the Rings down in an orderly fashion, raise them properly, and all will be well. It's only you, once again, who will suffer from your brothers' assumptions. Thanks to Deymorin's arrogance, your special day is ruined."

She drifted over to him and cupped a smooth hand beneath his chin, to tip his head up. "Poor Nikaenor," she murmured, and leaned over to brush his lips in a light kiss.

He rose from his chair and turned away, no longer the gullible fool he'd been only that spring. "I'll survive, my lady wife, I assure you." He ducked past her and headed for the door. "Thank you for taking it so well, Lidye. I'll be meeting my brothers for a private toast before the party. I'll explain to them at that time what you plan to do."

He hadn't had to explain she wasn't to visit the Tower. She'd no intention of doing it. She'd been, for whatever reason, civilized.

But as he closed the door between them, a final glance intercepted a secret smile that chilled him to the core.

Chapter Six

"She's up to something, Deymio, I know it. I just don't know what." Nikki paced the floor of the Blue Salon like a penned stallion in breeding season; the glass in his hand sloshed perilously at each turn, threatening the carpet with the carbonated, overly-sweet horror that was all the rage among the younger set.

Deymorin swirled the wine in his glass, acknowledging the validity of Nikki's concern, still not convinced Lidye had the right of it. No doubt it was easier to bring the rings up one at a time. He could even believe traditional wisdom held that it *had* to be done that way, and Anheliaa, knowing (also without doubt) Lidye's limitations, had likely told her that was the only way.

But that they'd have to bring the lot down? That he didn't believe. He'd almost gotten the damned thing free that morning, tired as he was. A part of him wanted to head up to the Tower even now to prove the woman wrong.

Nikki paused, glanced at the door that remained stubbornly closed, said, under his breath: "Dammit, Khyel, what's keeping you?"

"He was waiting for some courier when I went past his office before coming home. I imagine that's the core of the problem. Relax, Nikki. Whatever comes, whatever Lidye tries, we'll take care of it when it happens. As Khyel has pointed out so often we're making this up as we go along. Lidye can't know what we can do because *we* don't know yet. She'd be foolish to challenge us over something so vital to her very existence."

"Not to mention ours." Nikki grunted, and continued

staring at the door, then, with a deep breath and shake of the head: "Late courier, you say?" Blue eyes flickered up . . . "I hope that's all it is." . . . blue eyes returned to the carpet: Nikki had something other than Lidye's actions on his mind.

"Any reason to think otherwise?"

A one-sided shrug said: plenty of reason, but all Nikki said was: "Khyel and I went riding yesterday morning."

"You've *gone* riding every week since your return to the City."

"Rather farther and harder than I realized. I was . . . I was frustrated with Lidye, and didn't really want to come back. But Khyel . . . he could hardly walk on the way back to the Tower. He joked about it, but . . . I haven't seen him that bad since . . ." He gave another shrug, an awkward, self-conscious twitch of the shoulder.

Deymorin stifled a laugh; obviously this was not humorous to Nikki. "I wouldn't worry overmuch about it. He seemed fine this morning. I doubt his delay has anything to do with that."

"You're probably right. Still . . ." Nikki took a sip, then stared at his glass with a concentrated frown. "I wish you'd go with us sometimes, Deymorin."

Somehow Deymorin did not think Nikki was frowning at that obnoxious substance in the glass for the same reason he would. Nikki's concern went far beyond Mikhyel's sore backside.

And what did any of it have to do with Lidye's self-aggrandizing pride?

He really hated mazes.

"Be happy to, Nik," he said, lightly skipping over the maze. "I just wasn't asked, in point of fact. Never thought about it. Thanks to our sessions in the salle and the necessary running about, I've been getting my exercise. I assumed you were giving him lessons and neither of you wanted an audience. I was all for anything that got you out of the Tower and him out of that damned office."

Nikki continued counting bubbles a moment, then asked:

"Do you suppose we'll ever really understand the link? That it will ever stop surprising us?"

"Understand it?" He shrugged, as the maze gained another layer. Let Nikki's thoughts trail as they might, he decided, eventually they'd circle back. "Probably not. Cease to be surprised, that's something else. Personally, I'm just glad we can all be here in Rhomatum without driving each other insane."

Nikki grinned at that, a private grin that raised his suspicions and made him ask, dutifully: "What's that mean?"

"We didn't *need* the link to drive one another insane."

That much was true. A year ago, before they'd been perpetually inside each other's heads, Nikki had held a stack of IOUs over his head to make him promise to stay around long enough to mend his fences with Mikhyel.

Only to have Anheliaa leythiate him out of Rhomatum before that debt had been cleared.

"What, do you say, Nik. IOUs paid in full yet?"

A blink, awareness, on a gentle smile: "Long time ago, Deymio, long ago."

The relief that assurance brought surprised him: he'd been carrying more guilt in his heart than he realized. "This last year—I guess it's all been worth it, then."

"I suppose."

But Nikki didn't sound at all convinced, and doubt returned in Deymorin as well.

"What's bothering you, Nikki? What's it got to do with you and Mikhyel riding?"

Seeming to come to a decision, Nikki threw himself down in the chair next to Deymorin, and leaned toward him, elbows on his knees.

"We aren't . . . I'm not really giving him lessons. When we go riding, he's *not*. Riding, I mean. He gives his body over to me, and he goes into that little room inside his head—you know the one."

Too well. Last spring, when Mikhyel lay near death—a death more of the soul than the body—Deymorin had followed his brother to that room and convinced him to live.

"Damn. I thought he was over that. Is it Dancer?"

Nikki looked startled. "Dancer?"

"He hasn't even asked about Dancer. Not since I came back. Is he escaping?"

"Escaping what?"

"How the hell should I know. Guilt? Desire?"

"No. At least, I don't think so. He goes into his own thoughts to work things out, or so he says, but I don't think it has anything at all to do with Dancer. And he always comes out cheerful and ready to return to his offices, but . . ."

"But?"

"I think—I think I shouldn't do it anymore. He . . . forgets. He . . . goes into that make-believe room and starts planning and I, Darius save me, I don't call him back anymore. I just keep riding, even though a part of me knows we should stop. Yesterday . . . I really went too far. We were jumping fences high enough to make *my* teeth rattle."

"This began on the ride down from New Khoratum?" Deymorin asked, and Nikki nodded. He'd had no idea, but now that he did, it made a great deal of rather crazed sense for why Mikhyel had pressed on, and Nikki had pressed on and the end result had been Mikhyel in bed for a week. It had been a bad time. He'd received strong indications Mikhyel didn't want to discuss anything about it: Mikhyel had reacted by taking enthusiastically to riding. Hell, how should he have known there was something going on besides a determination to recover his skill at riding?

On the other hand, in the silence, perhaps there had been clues.

Knowing his brothers, Nikki might well have reason to be concerned. And Nikki, knowing both his brothers to be absorbed in their own all-consuming duties, had tried to resolve those concerns himself—evidently without success. "Care to talk about it?"

Nikki leaned forward, elbows on his knees, staring into the past. "It was—*is*—thrilling, Deymorin. It's . . . I don't quite know how to describe it. You're riding two horses at once, but not. There's *my* body, just moving with the horse like always. I mean, I don't have to think about it anymore, do I? And then, there's Khyel's."

The glass in his hand tilted precariously. Forgotten. Deymorin liberated it and set it on the side table between them. Nikki continued, as if he hadn't even noticed.

"He's so . . . *different*. His weight and strength, even the way his hands work. I have to think about every move for him, find different options, but the balance is there—quite good, actually—and the muscles do what I command, and it's . . . it's just intoxicating. A whole different challenge."

"And meanwhile *he* goes off into that imaginary room."

Nikki nodded. "It . . . scares me, Deymorin. I found out . . . when I'm in him, I haven't got the normal checks a body needs to protect itself. When we were coming down the mountain, I—I never felt anything. Only the ride. Only the thrill. I never got tired. I was fully conscious of the horses' needs—we stopped twice on the way to change them out—but mine, Mikhyel's—the men . . . I thought they were just going soft on me. Darius forgive me, I gave Ganfrion a terrible time when he and Oerden had to drop out. Gan was furious at me—justifiably, I've realized since. I'm surprised he's still speaking to me."

Ganfrion had dropped out. That, he hadn't known. On the other hand, Ganfrion had taken a bad wound at Khoratum. It was understandable Ganfrion wasn't riding with as much endurance as he might.

But under any circumstances, Ganfrion was as tough, body and mind, as men came. That Nikki could outlast him . . . that *Mikhyel's* body could . . . that was significant.

"I'm sure Mikhyel explained to him."

Nikki shook his head. "He shouldn't have had to . . . I knew how long we had ridden, I know from experience what I *should* have been feeling, and I should have been damned suspicious, and called a halt. It wasn't just Ganfrion. Jerri thought I'd lost my mind, and I wouldn't listen, not even to him. Jerri and the others fell asleep right there in the barn when we got here, and I felt . . . nothing. When we got down, and I let Mikhyel go—" Nikki's face was pale, but his voice held steady. "I thought he was dead,

Deymorin. I honestly thought he was dead and that I had killed him."

And Nikki had been holding all this inside for months. How could he not have suspected? Deymorin asked himself, even as Nikki shook his head in despair.

"Deymorin, I don't know what to do. He keeps asking to go out . . . more frequently the last few weeks. I should have stopped—hell, I should never have let it get started. He was more than ready to ride on his own. But I didn't, and he hasn't asked me to stop. I think, maybe, I shouldn't ride with him at all anymore."

"And yet, it's good for you both to get out."

"No, Deymorin, it's not good. Not this way. It's—" Nikki's eyes dropped. "It's too tempting. For both of us. I'll wait to say anything—he's so close to being done with this plan of his, I hate to shift his mental rings off orbit, but he's got the papers, got everything written down. It's over, all but the presentation. I think we've got to stop."

There was little to say when the young man who sought your counsel had already found his own answers. Finally, he said simply: "Y'know, Nikaenor Rhomandi dunMheric? There are times I'm extremely proud to call you brother."

And from the way Nikki's eyes widened, it was, perhaps, the best answer he'd ever given. It was, perhaps, a good thing for them both that before Nikki had time to do more than blush, the door swung wide, and their third brother blew into the room in a swirl of black coattails and loose, sable hair.

A thick sheaf of papers hit the table with a thud that rattled the glassware.

"There they are, brothers, signed, sealed and delivered, properly constructed for each idiosyncratic twist of every node's legal system." Mikhyel's eyes gleamed with pride as he leaned one hand on the table and tapped the stack with the free forefinger. "Every last one of the nodes—satellite, secondary, tertiary—they've all come around. Rhomatum in general and the Rhomandi in particular have been relieved of Anheliaa's original contract. All affected companies will send semi-annual accounting to a central office here in Rhomatum. Assessment to be made and taxes adjusted accordingly. That office will be under my direct supervision, but will have advisors from every node. All have agreed that the growth in profits after the addition of Khoratum more than covers damages now, with those affected least by the collapse agreeing to help those destroyed."

Mikhyel threw himself down in the vacant chair across from them, raised the waiting wine glass and, with the widest smile Deymorin had ever witnessed on his face exclaimed: "Happy birthday, Nikki!"

§ § §

Before their glasses touched in toast, Nikki paused to savor the moment.

Was it worth it? Was this moment worth the events of the last year? Was it worth the embarrassment of having his seventeen-year-old self-centered thoughts echoing in the minds of the very people he wanted to impress with his maturity? Was it worth nearly losing first Deymorin, then Mikhyel to the searing flames of leyapulting? Was it worth a life with Lidye and playing research librarian to his two more dynamic brothers? Was it worth the loss of seventeen-year-old dreams of personal glory?

Was it worth the constant worries that they might somehow, in their blind arrogance misuse their newfound abilities?

A year ago, his coming of age birthday had been like every other, remarkable only for the mounds of presents from people he'd never met. As every other birthday before it, the evening had been endless sniping between the people he loved most in the world. It had been pulling every string he had in his hands to force even an attempt at an intimate family gathering such as this. His true family. These days, such interludes happened on a near daily basis, not because he begged, but because it was right and natural that they share their daily experiences. Just them. Not Kiyrstin, not Ganfrion or Raulind, not even Jerrik. Just the three Rhomandi brothers, working out those problems, finding right and just solutions to the mistakes they made.

"Was it worth it, Deymorin?" Deeming it his right on this day and worth the risk, he reached out to his brothers' minds even as their glass rims touched, and filled the link with those images, past and present. "Absolutely. Every minute of it."

The moment lasted an instant and a lifetime. Then, Nikki's stomach gurgled a protest into that sharing and the link dissolved easily, naturally, rather like a burst of Kirish-'lani fireworks—or laughter.

"Well, Khyel?" Deymorin tapped the pile of papers that had been the silent fourth, and Mikhyel raised his glass in another toast.

"We're done, brothers."

"I thought you said at least two more months."

"The opposition wasn't there. I thought Giephaetum would be more emphatic, but they've folded. There are some details still to be finalized, but they're details only, negotiations between private parties that I've agreed to mediate. The treaties and trade agreements are ready for ratification and entry into the lists whenever we can convene a General Session."

"Amazing what a threat to their Towers can accomplish," Deymorin said dryly, and Mikhyel chuckled.

"I had that in reserve, naturally, but for the most part, enlightened self-interest if not common sense proved sufficient. These—" Mikhyel tapped the stack of papers, "—are far from arbitrary arrangements. They are aimed toward the future and flexibility. I think, brothers, that we're actually going to pull this off."

"Provided Lidye doesn't foul all our orbits," Nikki said quietly, and at Mikhyel's querying look, went on to explain what he'd already explained to Deymorin, what Lidye had said about bringing the rings up separately.

When he was done, Mikhyel turned to Deymorin and asked, "What do you think? Bring them down? Play it safe?"

Deymorin shrugged. "Don't really know. Can't, now can I? What would a crash do to that?" He nodded toward the stack of papers.

"Accounted for. We're clear of liability unless we can be

proven to have been willfully reckless in our use of the Rings or negligent in their care."

"Then I'd like to try. I'd wager next year's foal crop that we three could get the Khoratum/Persitum free and aligned, if I can't manage it myself. If we could reach the Rhomatum-creature, I'd call her bluff for certain. I . . . doubt much of what Lidye has been claiming. She maintains nothing *significant* can be done for the next several years, and yet the pulse I sensed in the Ley felt steady and strong, once I cleared the blockage between Shatum and Giephaetum."

He paused, and into the soft link that still existed among them, there came a sense of that day, now several weeks past, when he'd first made real contact with the Rings. "I wonder, thinking about it now, how much that blockage was a product of damage to the Web and how much a reflection of the two women in primary contact with the Rings. I was still in contact with the Rings myself after Lidye came in, and I could *feel* every time they so much as looked at one another." He blinked and shook his head. "It's very strange. All that time I spent in the Tower, all Nethaalye could do was describe the desired end result. After that, it was trying one thing and the next to see if I could . . . connect." He shook his head again. "It's no wonder Anheliaa had such a hard time finding a replacement. It all seems unnecessarily haphazard to me."

"Perhaps it's time someone tried to make it less so," Mikhyel said in that quiet way that invariably captured the attention of everyone in hearing distance.

"Someone," Nikki repeated. "Meaning Deymorin?"

"Meaning all of us, ultimately, I suppose."

"And what makes you think we can discover what a thousand years and more of ringspinners haven't?" Deymorin asked, and Mikhyel's mouth twitched in conjunction with a sardonically raised eyebrow.

"Hubris?"

Which made Deymorin laugh, and left Nikki conscious of some past exchange to which he hadn't been privy.

"Don't tempt me," Deymorin said, "And your real reasons?"

"Actually, most would say that *is* the real reason. However, as I see it, we truly do have a unique perspective on the issue. The ringmasters I've met have all been fiercely egocentric. They hold great stock in their . . . unique qualities, and that tendency not only colors all their decisions, it affects their dealings with other people, makes them secretive and superior."

"Nethaalye's not like that at all," Deymorin protested.

"And I suspect that's one reason Anheliaa chose Lidye, and why Nethaalye herself feels her potential as a master is limited. I don't know if they start out this way, or if it's a by-product of ringspinning, but at the moment, and I trust this will not change, Deymorin is able to share what he learns with us, and while we might not be potential spinners, we do have some unique perspectives to bring to the analysis."

"You aren't just talking about spinning, are you?" Nikki asked.

"Obviously. If Anheliaa knew about the creatures like Mother and Rhomatum, she certainly didn't pass that information on to Lidye. And Lidye, by her own admission to you, has read most of the private literature in the ringmaster suite, so I must assume it's not common knowledge."

"You do realize you're beginning to sound like those self-important spinners, Khyel," Deymorin said pointedly. "Mys-ter-y. Answers to the universe to which only you have the keys."

"Hubris, brother. I warned you. However, you can't deny we do have . . . unusual resources. And I, at least, have no intention of keeping what we learn secret, at least not without serious debate among those who have been necessarily privy to the information from the start."

"Resources." Nikki repeated. "Rhomatum?"

"Among others."

"Think you can reach him?" Deymorin asked.

Mikhyel took a sip of wine, and, eyes suddenly averted, said, "I know I can."

Which tone and positive statement said: *I have.*

"When?" Deymorin asked, and Nikki noted the sudden set of Deymorin's jaw without surprise, knowing the agreement between his brothers on this very issue, knowing Deymorin's fear that Mikhyel would be sucked into communion with the Rhomatum-creature and never escape.

"The day *you* made connection with the Rings," Mikhyel answered without a blink. "I've wondered, since, if the two events might not have been related. Whether or not we two . . . woke him up."

So long ago. Weeks. And Mikhyel had said nothing.

"Dammit, Khyel, you promised—"

"Not to try on my own? I know. I wasn't trying. I just thought about it, and I was there." He lifted a black brow mockingly. "Rather like the man who slid the rings into place."

"Point, Khyel," Deymorin acknowledged the hit.

For himself, Nikki wondered if his brothers were as concerned as he was at the ease with which near miracles appeared to be occurring. It seemed as if all they needed do was *want* something to happen, and if it was in their ability at all, it happened. And while those miracles appeared confined to his brothers, he found himself suddenly inclined to examine the changes in himself more closely.

"However, it only happened the one time, or I'd have said something, I assure you. And only my mind went—at least, that's what I think. Paulis woke me in my chair." He met Deymorin's eyes squarely. "But I will go down to that chamber again, physically."

"Not without us."

"Not without you. I've a healthy fear of the process, Deymio, trust that if not my word."

"You just make sure that creature knows I'll kick his ass into the nearest thunderstorm, if he tries to hold you there."

Mikhyel shrugged. "In truth, I think the Tamshi are the least of what bears investigation. Mirym's references to the old ones, her actions . . . all would indicate a body of knowledge we'd do well to understand at least enough not to insult those 'true believers' more than we can help doing. More, it seems obvious she's tapping resources in ways that might help us to understand what *we're* doing."

"All well and good," Nikki said, "but we don't know where she is."

It was, Nikki had to admit, a failure he did take personally. She'd been his friend, and fear of his wife, he was certain, had driven her off. He'd tried to find her, had set it as his task, with both brothers otherwise occupied, and all his efforts had come up empty.

Mikhyel's eyes dropped to his wine glass. "I do."

"What?" Nikki jerked upright in his chair, feeling . . . betrayed. "How?"

"I found her through Rhomatum himself. It was the thought that he might help us locate her that drew me down to him."

"And you said nothing?" Nikki said, anger was waiting behind the betrayal. "*Did* . . . nothing?"

Mikhyel leaned back in his chair. "I saw no reason to *do* anything, Nikki. The fact is, she's not lost; she's been right under our noses, up with the hillers at New Khoratum. What little I got from her was fear that she'd be taken away from the village. I tried to assure her otherwise, seeing no real reason to bother her."

"You knew, and you didn't tell us! You *knew* I was searching for her and didn't tell *me?*"

There was a heartbeat's pause, and a second, and Mikhyel's eyebrows twitched, hinting of real disturbance. "No, Nikki, and I was wrong not to have done so. I don't really know why I didn't. I went off to a meeting, and I've . . . hardly even thought about it since." Another contemplative pause, and the lines between his brows vanished. "Which omission is in itself curious. I think, perhaps, we should keep that silence in mind while we deal with her. What doesn't happen with the Ley is perhaps as significant as what does."

"You think she's responsible for your *not* mentioning it before now?" Deymorin asked.

"Or are you just looking for somewhere to shift the blame?" Nikki muttered, and immediately regretted, but which accusation Mikhyel seemed to accept without rancor.

"That is a possibility, certainly," Mikhyel acknowledged. "And for that possibility, I apologize. I do think we should be careful. Because I also believe we must contact her, and in such a way as to make her feel safe and accommodative.

I doubt she'll be willing at first, but if we persist with clear intentions of respect and solid legal protections, she might come around. It is, after all, for the good of everyone, not to mention the Ley itself. If, as you suggested, Deymorin, opposition between minds attempting to manipulate the Ley is reflected in the Web, it can't be advantageous to have the hillers pulling one way and Rhomatum another."

Deymorin stared into his wine, then caught and held Mikhyel's eyes. "You haven't mentioned your most obvious source."

To do him credit, Mikhyel didn't even pretend not to understand.

"It would be asking a lot of him."

"He can always refuse."

"I don't know where he is."

Deymorin's mouth pressed tight, and Nikki sensed the temptation to inform Mikhyel then and there that Dancer had never been out of touch—which was a far greater omission of information than Mikhyel not telling about Mirym—and so Nikki, who truly did not want that specter to rise now, on top of all the rest, interjected quickly: "You found Mirym. You could look for Dancer the same way, couldn't you?"

"Not if he doesn't want to be found. In some ways, he's far more facile then the rest of us combined. I doubt he even has to think of keeping me from his mind." A distant look entered Mikhyel's eyes. "If I knew *where* he was, as I know *where* Mirym is, that . . . might well be different."

"Still, you could try."

That distant look vanished into hard practicality. "I could try. And will, if the time comes. Right now, my greatest concern is more immediate. Tell me, Deymorin, when all is said and done, when the Rings are fully functional again, do you think you'll be able to control them? Or, more to the point—and forgive me, Nikki—if we were to lose Lidye, could you hold them? *Would* you?"

"Lose Lidye? Why should that even be an issue?"

"I doubt that it will prove to be. But I might need the leverage of the threat, the possibility of her replacement."

What's this all about, little brother?"

Mikhyel stood up from the table and went over to stand by the window, staring out toward the mountains.

"I've one more trip to make before the snow flies," Mikhyel said.

"Trip?" Deymorin echoed, and his voice sounded none too pleased; this roundabout speaking was the side of Mikhyel he most abhorred. "To where? I thought you said the matter was settled. The contracts signed."

"This is not about the Syndicate. At least, not directly."

Silence surrounded them, as he and Deymorin waited for Mikhyel to explain. When he didn't, Deymorin reached with his mind, pressing for contact—

And Mikhyel struck his probe aside.

"Just trying to help, brother," Deymorin said. "You seemed a bit tongue-tied."

"Like hell."

"Then explain yourself. Trip to where? Why?"

Mikhyel half turned, but his face remained primarily in shadow.

"Persitum."

Deymorin blinked. Confusion driving out the growing irritation on his face: Persitum was not an answer he was expecting. "Why Persitum? Are they backing out of their deal? Why the mystery?"

But Nikki wasn't surprised.

"It's not Persitum at all, is it, Khyel?" he asked quietly.

"No? And why do you suppose I plan to go to Persitum again, Nikaenor?"

And for a moment, they were cast back to old times. Ever since he could remember, Mikhyel had rarely answered his questions directly, but had chosen rather to tempt and tease him into finding the answer himself.

But Nikki said, "It's no game, Mikhyel. Not this time."

"Did I say it was?"

"You're going to meet with Garetti, aren't you?"

Mikhyel stepped back to the table, and his face was calm, controlled as he took an elegant sip of wine.

"High time, don't you think?"

Chapter Seven

The guards the Tower set were lazy and paid more attention to autumn ale than to the comings and goings of countryfolk. Fall leaves blew through the streets of a town mostly uninhabited, over which a tower presided, but a shattered tower, its summit like a snaggled tooth above a city with few intact roofs remaining.

Thyerri found the crumbling wall of the old compound extending northeast from that tower an easy conquest. He perched outside the window that had had no shutters or glass even when he'd slept here and with a glance at the cold gray sky, drank in the tree-covered mountains disappearing into the evening mist, a view that had been his solace after many an evening of performing for Rhyys' guests.

Not dancing for those guests, no; nothing so rewarding. The dancers-in-training had been elegant window dressing, primped and coached and tutored for engaging and polite conversation at the tables. Thyerri had never been very good at that part, had been sent back to this room frequently as punishment—particularly after he'd figured out precisely what to say and to whom to accomplish that blessed escape.

He'd been Dancer then. Dancer 13 to those in Rhyys' halls, and just Dancer to himself and to Mother. No one else had mattered. These days, he was Thyerri more and more, being *Thyerri* to the Rhomandi's men and *Thyerri* since the time before Mikhyel to his contacts among the remaining few residents of Khoratum.

And so he became more Thyerri to himself because Thyerri had lived in the Khoratum streets and because to remember Temorii was to remember Mikhyel and to remember Dancer was to remember Mother and Mikhyel and all that had been.

Time was that from this room with the unglassed window, he could leythiate into Mother's caverns, or sneak out through the hidden pathways that had riddled the ground beneath the Tower, legacy of the compound's original owners, to run the hills in freedom.

Those tunnels, such as he'd checked in the rubble for his old bolt-holes, were gone. Filled in, either from the wounds of battle or the reconstruction done by the survivors, the moving and rebuilding of fallen stone, a process which had restored a handful of the buildings to some semblance of habitability, but which had so radically changed the outward appearance of the main complex he wouldn't have recognized it . . . but for this nearly forgotten wing.

This wing, oldest and virtually unused even when he'd lived here, notorious among the servants for hauntings and cave-ins, had yet to be touched, either in reconstruction or as a resource by the stone-gatherers and the masons.

From behind and above him, a glow within the Tower proved to all who might wonder that Rhyys had successfully repositioned the Rings in the newly restored structure. A glow confined to the Tower itself, for all the energy generated made Thyerri's skin crawl even in the hills.

Whoever ruled the Rings, they did not want light. They wanted power for something far different.

Rhyys, as rumor claimed that spinner to be, had required that ringtower to be constructed around the rubble above which he'd set the Rings spinning after the battles with Rhomatum—or so rumor said. Before the walls went up, canvas had obscured the site.

Spinning in the open mountain air . . . like miniature versions of the dance rings, for the lizards and squirrels to dance among.

That Rhyys had accomplished that minor miracle of raising the Rings, Thyerri's own senses had told him months ago. That he'd accomplished so extremely provocative an act without opposition from Mother seemed the greater mystery.

And his cause for continued concern.

He had not found a way to Mother. Had not felt her or heard from her since his return to Khoratum.

And Mother's scent, always a part of his world, especially here directly above her caverns, continued to carry that slightly rancid quality he had first noticed during that attack on the Rhomandi brothers, a hint of something dark and fermenting where once had been the freshness of mountain raspberries. He'd waited in the hills during the summer, skirted the ruins, calling softly, hoping she'd answer.

But there'd been nothing.

Hence his visit here, with fall's chill in the air, to his former dormitory, where he hadn't ventured since the morning of the day of his disastrous first competition. During his time spent in the complex with Mikhyel prior to the second competition, he'd been denied access. Rhyys had gone so far as to place a guard specifically on the room to prevent his carrying off any of the precious robes he'd been required to wear to those precious gatherings.

As if he would want such heavy, uncomfortable garments.

He wasn't looking for robes, wasn't seeking anything of Rhyys' provision. He was looking for a single object, a jar that contained his other means of entry into Mother's realm, a means which required no help from her. He had gathered his courage to make this venture, to tempt that fetid source to notice him, and in the wake of Mother's months' long silence, he made this desperate effort, into the domain of a hostile ringmaster who might . . . might . . . gather some awareness of him.

It was like venturing onto a bridge of leythium lace, knowing it could crumble at any moment.

A quick glance inside confirmed the room's vacancy; he slipped through the window, and dropped lightly to the floor, crouching amid in the wreckage of what had been his surface world residence for some four years, listening.

Silence, save for the swirl and swish of the mountain breeze. Dust was everywhere, thick and vermin-tracked on the floor. The wardrobe, overthrown, lay on its side, spilling its contents, those precious robes, to be washed by rain and fouled by dust and dry leaves. Part of the wooden sheathing on the stone had buckled in splinters and lay amid a heap of stone. If the rest of the wing was as badly hit, he was amazed that anyone had been persuaded to sleep here, and yet, from his observation, at least two rooms were currently occupied.

Crazy, as Thyerri had been crazy to live in this old, ramshackle end of the compound, when newer, better quarters had been available . . . for the compliant. But he hadn't been exiled here, he'd chosen this room and he'd have endured far worse than cold drafts at night for that wondrous view that stretched unblemished by human interference.

But this room was not livable by anyone any longer, not even him. Bare ground would be preferable to wondering when the next plank would fall from the ceiling.

Thyerri stretched out belly-down on the floor beside the rotting, rope-slung bed, anxious to retrieve his prize and be . . . elsewhere. With only that thought, he reached under the frame into the darkness, past dripping tendrils of rotting fabric—

Rope-shaped, soft, pliable . . . he swallowed hard and sent {Safe—safe—safe} down that arm. A *tsii't'pic*, one of the ley-loving serpents, which thrived on the ley-energy itself, had coiled itself there. No other serpent that size should survive in this chill section of the Tower.

And such a snake should respond to the mental signal and leave quietly.

It should retreat from disturbance.

He'd almost died once when one had not.

Mother and the Ley had saved him that time. This time, there would be no Mother, no leythium pool to counteract the venom. He held his breath, as the rope uncoiled and slithered around his wrist and up his arm. Not a particularly large one of its kind, but size meant nothing to the potency of the venom, and he didn't breathe easily until the creature slithered its way along the base of the wall beyond the bed and retreated through a rat-sized hole between stones, escaping to prey on some tastier morsel than himself.

The next time he breached that darkness beneath the bed, he preceded his hand with his essence—a precaution he had once practiced as reflexively as breathing in this domain of ley-attracted lizards, insects, and serpents with no fear of anyone. He had gone lamentably careless in the land of headblind men, living outside the rich Ley-presence.

His essence encountered nothing living. He reached again with his hand, still cautious, and found—

Nothing—except a forgotten hair clip.

He flung the clip out the window, and reached again beneath the bed, felt all up and down, encountering shattered bits of stone, rotten bedding and a great deal of dirt and leaves blown in from the window . . . but no leythium jar.

He slumped flat to the floor, burying his face in his arm, wondering when and how and into whose hands that irreplaceable container had fallen. The oil it contained, like liquid leythium, but not, was a gift from Mother. It had made his solo transfer into her realm possible; to anyone else, only the pot had value. But to him . . . the silvery content of that jar was the object of a summer of dreams and trepidations.

He should have come here sooner . . . if it had not been too late the moment the Rings fell, in those first few days, when he had been, instead, with Mikhyel, and looters had had the run of Khoratum.

Even here.

Pushing himself up off the floor and swinging about, he propped his back against the bed and drew his knees up to support his crossed arms. The rubble littering the room, legacy of Mother's battle for freedom, created a miniature mountainscape across the dust in the evening glow. From the shattered wardrobe, chief of that mountain range, the fine clothes he'd worn to Rhyys' fancy affairs spilled out.

Dead leaves chased one another across the floor.

He rested his chin on crossed arms, contemplating the ruin of cloth on which beading still glittered in the fading

light. Not that he particularly cared about the clothes—
they'd been Rhyys' property, not his—but it was hard to
imagine a thief who would take his pot and leave the infinitely more valuable (to anyone else) clothing to follow the
course of the rotting mattress.

Frustrated, and in growing desperation, he surged to his
feet, kicked one of those fine robes along the base of the
door, and by patient fussing with the wick, managed to light
the residue in the oil lamp.

With that small light he began to search the room in
earnest, reckless of anyone questioning a light from the
window or a crack of light from under the door. In faint
hope some looter might have flung it aside, he sifted
through the rubble, finding only broken rouge pots and
mouse-nibbled kohl sticks, remnant of his personal goods—
more of Rhyys' provision for "proper appearances." He
saw a gleam of silver . . . a mirror, dusty-faced yet miraculously intact but for a single crack across its center.

He found everything he'd left behind except the leythium pot.

Returning the small mirror to its proper hook on a
cracked stone wall, concession to its stubborn survival, he
started sifting disconsolately through the last pile, and when
it proved fallow, stood in numb helplessness, perplexed,
aimless now his long-postponed search had proven fruitless.

He even wondered if Mother herself might have reclaimed the pot, unable to imagine why she would do such
a thing. He'd imagined finding it, he'd imagined attempting
her caves in vain. He'd imagined glorious success and
Mother's love soothing, if not filling, the emptiness Mikhyel
had left in him.

He'd never imagined leaving here without that jar.

Six months . . . all summer and into fall, he'd waited.
He'd done the Rhomandi's bidding, lived close to the earth
and quietly, reported to Ganfrion when Ganfrion came to
the appointed place, others of the Rhomandi's men when
Ganfrion did not . . . all the while he'd moved to the Rhomandi's orders, not daring his own plans.

Now he imagined Ganfrion's anger at him, provided he

got out of here alive. He'd risked the Rhomandi's eyes and ears in Khoratum without clearance and, it now appeared, without reward.

Too late, from the very night of his escape, he feared. With all it meant. Even then, even with Mikhyel he'd been cut off from Mother and hadn't known it. All this time, he'd thought he could go back, all that time with Mikhyel, a time that, even yet, was so vivid to him, those days so fraught with fear and hope . . . he'd believed utterly that he had other choices.

In the fermenting rot of raspberries he'd waited for Mother's recuperation from creating the new node. He'd waited for her to overcome whatever contaminated her essence and call him to her, but that stench had refused to go away and Mother had not called.

Only in his dreams could he escape the scent, and he did dream, from time to time, of raspberries and cinnamon and clove, of warm fires and complex wines. If he didn't know better, he'd think his other self, down in the valley, was thinking about him at such times.

But Ganfrion, who came and went from Deymorin, in secret, and who was his only source of news of Mikhyel, Ganfrion only said that Mikhyel was absorbed in his work, and no, not doing as well as he might be, but that he hadn't asked after Thyerri, and that the strain he showed might well be due to the long hours at his desk.

And then, Ganfrion would advise him to find someone else, would shake his head and say Mikhyel dunMheric was determined to be unhappy and that they couldn't fight that much stubborn pride . . . and all the while, Ganfrion's eyes would be saying he hoped Thyerri would do no such thing, that he hoped Mikhyel would come to his senses, once this crisis was over.

But there'd only be another crisis after that, and another, and another. If he could, he would accept one of the offers he'd been extended. There were at least two exceedingly pleasant young women who fed him the local gossip, who had made it quite clear his presence in their bed would be quite welcome—singly or both at once.

He'd been rather taken aback by their candor on the subject, and in that surprise had somehow strengthened the women's desire. It was all quite puzzling to him, yet not a puzzle he cared to pursue. The reality was, only Mikhyel dunMheric, in all his flaring vitality and frustrating obstinance, could rouse the Dream, and only Mikhyel could quench the flames within him.

At least for now. Time, Ganfrion insisted, would change things, if he wanted things changed.

For now, without Mikhyel, he had only Mother. He'd sought her every waking hour of the days past, and yet heard nothing. It might be a stubborn silence . . . it might be a wounded one; but coupled with the renewed activity in the ringtower, *he* knew the Rhomandi neither dared intrude on nor ignore the changes taking place here, even if Mikhyel did not.

The changes. The dire and constant unraveling of Mother's domain here.

Mother might supply the answers, but he had to get her attention first. The oil had been his only means of independently penetrating her underground domain. Without it, without her help, the transition would burn the flesh from his bones. He hadn't told Ganfrion about the oil, hadn't told Ganfrion about his plan to use it to reach Mother. That was his hope, his future, and Ganfrion would try to talk him out of it.

Ganfrion would have had no idea where he had gone— or had no idea that he had gone; but once he knew, then where . . . where he had gone ought to be within Ganfrion's power to guess. And if it was not in Ganfrion's, certainly it was within Mikhyel's, whose desire to know was the only desire that mattered.

And Mikhyel, so Ganfrion implied, wouldn't care that Dancer had gone.

Back to where he had been.

Back to where he'd begun, before a green-eyed rijhili had seduced him from the Dance that Rakshi had formed him from the womb to dance.

He wandered back to the window, staring across his

mountains, calling to Mother with his heart, but not his essence . . . for the very whisper he had sent out to the serpent, from this close proximity to the Tower, might alert Rhyys to his presence: a cry to Mother would rend the peace of this hilltop.

Being heard was not a concern he'd ever had before, but his association with the Rhomandi brothers had sensitized him to the noise that individuals such as they could make in the world. One learned, dealing with Mother, to keep one's head quiet and to keep random outside thoughts at a distance . . . and never, never to shout. That someone with the mindspeak would not be so inclined toward silence, or unable to keep that buffering distance, had been inconceivable—until he met Mikhyel dunMheric and his brothers. And now he knew he was capable of a shout to bring the lightning of hell down on his head.

Or Rhyys down from his tower in bloody vengeance.

And yet either fate would eliminate a great deal of turmoil within the Ley, turmoil that was nothing more than Dancer's own confused thinking.

Leaning his head against the stone, Thyerri closed his eyes to the brightening stars and to all thought of such a foolish end. Rhyys—or whoever had raised the Khoratum Rings, had much for which to hate the new Khoratum radical dancer, but the still unproven ringspinner had to find him first, and as long as he'd stayed on the edges of the umbrella, there'd been little chance of discovery.

He should never have come this far in—wouldn't have, had cold hard sense ruled his actions. While he was worried about Mother, and while that concern had been pushing him toward this moment, it wasn't *only* concern for Mother that had driven him to act precipitously on this precise day.

Mikhyel had been too much in his thoughts of late—most particularly in the last few hours—and the risk of the venture had turned his mind from those thoughts . . . at least for a time. Now that the venture faltered, those thoughts reared afresh.

That intrusion might be momentary personal weakness, or perhaps, just perhaps, he'd been unable to get Mikhyel's image out of his mind because Mikhyel's own thoughts *were* turning for once to the dancer he'd loved, then deserted.

It was possible. It was Mikhyel's brother's birthday, a time of remembrance.

Of course, it might not be Mikhyel's thinking at all, but rather Dancer's own wishes that Mikhyel *might* think about him and end this exile.

He frowned and closed his eyes, his brain a mishmash of such thoughts, questions about why and how and by whom that he'd never considered before Mikhyel. *He* was thinking about Mikhyel because he still loved, still wanted, that was all. Mikhyel hadn't called to him; for all Mikhyel knew Ganfrion served the Rhomandi here, close to Khoratum, Mikhyel hadn't even asked about him: if he had, Ganfrion would have said so.

He knew his waiting might be doomed to failure, knew it wiser to let the dream vanish, wished that he could, and yet, with the mountain breeze whipping his hair and tickling his nose, he could almost feel Mikhyel in this room with him.

He should have known he couldn't escape his own thoughts, should have known that thoughts of Mikhyel would even now distract him from the job he'd come here to do.

As they had distracted him all summer.

He should have tried to find the oil months ago, but he'd expected a decrease over time in the tension and security about the Tower, not an increase. The mood about Lower Khoratum, all that remained of the former node city, had grown more and more ominous since midsummer, as goods—and people—disappeared into the Tower. Orders came from the kitchens and the repair crews up on the tower hill; payment arrived, so coin and gold still existed, the lights worked, if fitfully and only those closest to the Tower, now in this street and now in that . . . but the normal daily traffic from the inhabitants of the Tower had ended abruptly that day in spring, when unbridled lightning had destroyed the Tower and most of the surrounding buildings.

A whisper of sound: air across stone or footstep. He spun about.

And gray eyes rimmed with green gleamed from the shadows.

{Khy!} His mind cried out from desire, and in a heart-beat, he knew that for impossible, and in the next heart-beat, knew that gleam for his own lamplit reflection in that stubborn, dusty, crack-faced mirror.

He sighed and approached the broken reflection, past, present, and empty future welling up about him in this cra-dle of memories. That mistaken impression was just his own distracting need playing tricks on him: their features were of a type, but Mikhyel's hair was raven wing's black, his own dark sable at best . . . darker now than he'd ever known it, untouched by the Ley for months, where once daily contact had silvered the ends.

And his face, softer-edged, would certainly never reflect that hawklike intensity that commanded both respect and fear from men twice Mikhyel's age. He was not born to Mikhyel's authority, not by breeding, not by circumstance.

And yet, that same face, stripped of the beard, had been ever so different to his eyes and to his memory. He had seen that face vulnerable in sleep, naked to the emotions that seethed beneath Mikhyel's cool, calm surface.

Perhaps it was the beard that made the difference, the beard with all the *rijhili* traits that went with it.

Perhaps, if *he* could somehow grow a beard, he might command some of that same respect from their ilk.

Certainly, if he'd had a beard last spring, his life would have gone very differently.

If he'd had a beard, Mikhyel would never have seen Thy-erri one time and Temorii the next.

He would not have deceived Mikhyel, would not have been tempted. And he'd never have driven him away in anger . . . for that shifting of true and true again was the source of Mikhyel's anger.

Could he be one thing, like the *rijhili*?

Or half of what he was?

Was one a lie, and the other true? Or could he pretend, if his happiness depended on it?

He picked up a kohl stick, and scribbled a facsimile of Mikhyel's mouth-framing beard on his reflection, paused at the startling result and began applying the kohl directly to his jaw and with greater care.

With each stroke, the likeness grew. The oblique, gray-green eyes, thin face, dark hair and beard . . . he stepped back from the mirror, pulled his hair tight and struck a typical Barrister pose. Not good enough for someone who knew either of them even casually, but in chancy lighting, for distraction, possibly even a decoy—

"Dammit!" He swept aside that image that wasn't Khy and was even less Dancer, then stared in horror at the splintered remains of the mirror, glittering shards scattered across the floor.

It had been his. It had reflected a different life. Had shown him himself, once upon a different world. Now he sank to his knees, cradled one of those remnants from the sole survivor of Mother's battle with Rhomatum between his hands and closed his eyes on the fragmented face it held. "Leave me alone," he whispered to the empty air, then in frustration screamed at the walls, *wanting* the kohl-bearded image gone, *wanting* that jar and his freedom back.

{*Mother!*} he shouted, at the insensate earth.

Wind whipped through the room, setting leaves to swirling, and was as quickly gone. Before his eyes cleared of the dirt, he felt damp spread between his fingers. He slowly opened his fist, found the mirror shard stained with his own blood.

And between the streaks, behind his reflected self, was an iridescent glint beneath the shattered boards of the old wall paneling.

He rose to his feet, let the glass shard fall free, ill-liking the sense of his blood dripping to the dusty floorboards of this abandoned room . . . liking even less the fact that he'd found the jar at last, after he knew he had searched every hand's-width of the place.

After paying for it with his blood.

He drew it out, opened the stopper, found it full, which he hadn't remembered it being, but then, he'd often suspected the oil of reproducing when he wasn't watching.

Why shouldn't the jar?

For he had to wonder, as the vessel cupped between his hands warmed with his touch, and as the familiar feeling of ley-healing tingled on his bleeding fingers, whether this was, indeed, his leythium pot, or whether Mother, for whatever reason, had sent him another.

Or perhaps not a gift. Hadn't he just paid for it with his blood dripped into the dust, as blood fell in the arena, as dancers fell, when they failed the rings?

He shivered, but tucked the container safely into his belt pouch. However acquired, he'd be a fool to leave it. Perhaps a greater fool to trust it, all things equal, but that—

". . . pompous old goat, join us. Liipipsi won't mind, will you darlin'?"

Thyerri doused the lamp and flattened himself against the wall beside the door.

"Old is the key word, Batokh. I'm for bed—and sleep, thanks all the same."

Recognition came on a handful of words. Thyerri's throat tightened painfully. He knew that voice.

"We'll pour a glass on the floor for you, Zelin."

Confirmation, although he didn't need it.

"May the Mother smile on you, children, and grant you endurance."

Somehow, the old soldier Zelin had survived the fire at Bharlori's tavern . . . and that knowledge took at least one more death off Thyerri's conscience.

Survived the fire only to end up, as the ex-dancer Sakhithe had, in Rhyys' employ, employment from which there would be no escape—not without outside help.

The voices faded as the celebrants meandered down the hall. Doors thudded shut at some distance.

To follow Zelin's voice, or not . . .

An ally within the Tower would be useful, and one such as Zelin, an ex-warrior who could defend himself, possibly escape should the situation require . . . he would be invaluable. It was a tempting—very tempting—touch of fortune, but temptation made it suspect: Rakshi's gifts were never simple.

Still he trusted Zelin more than anyone else he knew in Khoratum as the city was or as it had become. And should Zelin himself want help to win free of whatever service he had found here in Rhyys' tower compound, Zelin deserved what help the Rhomandi's local ferret could give him. An ex-dancer could fault no one who had taken Rhyys' coin for his daily bread and a roof to shelter him. And he owed this man, who had taught him to defend himself, owed him and would welcome his good sense as well as his knowledge of this place that was not the Tower Dancer had known.

Setting the darkened lamp aside, he cracked the door open to a completely black hallway, not even a glow from under the doors to indicate which room held his old friend.

From his observations, he knew two rooms at least were occupied. But there were fewer doors inside than windows outside and how those doors corresponded to those two lighted windows, he didn't know the wing well enough to say. He'd slept here; he hadn't lived here.

Inside the stone walls, his options were limited. Outside . . . he shut the door and went to the window, eased onto the sill and headed for those rooms, the same way he had gotten in, for the stone wall, even where the masonry was intact, provided him markedly easier passage than the mountain cliffs he once scaled regularly, and his fingers and soft-soled boots found easy purchase.

The first two windows he passed were empty, the next, from the sound, haven to the generous, noisily amorous couple—he dropped below that window. The fourth, the one which in the past had been lit, was dark, the room empty. By the fifth window, he began to fear Zelin had chosen one of the several internal rooms, strange as that choice would be in one who had come to Khoratum to be near the mountains of his ancestors.

He assumed otherwise and kept going, determined to find this man whose lessons in self-defense had kept him alive more than once, even before his current occupation. At the sixth window, he heard an eerie melody from one of the windows he had passed . . . the darkened fourth window, as it proved. It sounded like a pipe of some kind.

Backtracking quickly, Thyerri clung to the stone just outside that darkened window.

"Z'lin?" he whispered, as the melody came to an end and his fingers started to cramp in their grip on the stonework. "Z'lin, can you hear me?"

A murmur from within had the cadence of a prayer. He moved to the verge of the unshuttered window, catching his weight with his forearms on the sill. "Z'lin, please hear me."

This time he augmented that whisper with an internal call, a tactic he'd learned could get a head-blind person's attention, even if they couldn't hear the words. But when the prayer continued, he lost hope and his arms began to shake.

Sudden light blinded his night-accustomed eyes. He gasped and clutched at the sill.

"Give it up, hiller." Zelin's voice whispered. "Khoratum is lost! Get your sorry ass out of my window, and I'll forget I saw you."

His hold slipped, his arms gone numb in shock. He'd expected recognition . . . welcome from a man he'd trusted, whom he thought had trusted him.

"Z'lin, let me in!" He reached toward the figure beyond that blinding light.

"Sweet Mother . . . *What* did you call me?" The light moved closer still.

"Z'lin! Z'lin, Z'lin, Z'lin—in the *name* of the Mother, it's me!"

"Thyerri, boy!" Welcome laughter filled his ears, and the light jumped aside. Strong hands grasped his shaking arms, hauled him through the window, then thick arms surrounded him in an exuberant hug. "I heard you died on the rings!"

"Long story, Z'lin," he said on a gasp as his ribs gained breath.

"I've got time. But what is this?" Zelin's short-fingered hand grasped his chin, a finger swept its length, came away black in the lamplight: the kohl-beard he'd utterly forgotten.

"Disguise?" Thyerri suggested, mortally ashamed, and felt his face flush hot when Zelin just laughed.

"Pretty damn sad one, lad."

"Fooled you."

"Hardly." Zelin grabbed a towel and tossed it to him, waving him toward the basin and pitcher in the corner as he gathered up the light, an oil lamp like the one Dancer had had. Even before the current power crisis this section of the Tower hadn't been allowed leylight. Zelin set the lamp on a table, revealing a room better than the wreckage of his, but by no means luxurious. A huge crack ran across the wall, stonework considerably offset by a fracture. It cast a shadow in the single light source. "You want a beard to hide behind, lad, there are better ways."

"Undoubtedly." Thyerri willingly scrubbed the damning kohl away, then rubbed his face dry on a towel worn smooth with age. "You said Khoratum is lost? Hiller, you said. Who did you think I was?"

"Rebel hillers try the Tower regularly, lad, knives in hand. Those whose lives have been ruined, one way and another, looking to free Khoratum for good and all. They creep in, just as you did—although . . ." He leaned out the window and stared down. "Although normally they take a somewhat more earthly route. Like doors. What did you do, fly?"

Thyerri studied his raw fingertips, thinking he'd have to make a more regular practice of cliff-walking. "Flying might have been easier. Looters?"

"Assassins. Would-be assassins, at any rate. Trying to rid themselves of Rhyys and all he represents. Mostly, they end their troubles by ending themselves."

"Can you blame them?" Thyerri asked.

"Not till it's my door they're at," Zelin retorted, which was the Zelin he remembered, and he felt his back relax.

"The battle among the Syndicate nodes severed Khoratum permanently from the Web," Thyerri felt compelled to point out. "We *should* be free of the valley."

"We?"

Thyerri shrugged. "I admit freely, I don't like what I see happening here. We should be free of Rhomatum and the Rings. Instead, the Tower goes on. Rumor on the street has Rhyys taking over minds and sacrificing children. People are more frightened than ever."

"Not that bad, but close. Sounds as if you're one of them."

"In spirit, perhaps. Not that I bring any knives. Never against you."

"So what *are* you doing here?"

Thyerri patted his pouch, where the leythium pot hung. "Reclaiming property. My departure from the ranks was abrupt. When I lived here, my room was just down the hall. I was leaving when I heard your voice, and I had to see if it was truly you."

"Most of the old crew from Bharlori's place got swept up by the watch following the fire. We thought you were dead. Sakhithe was here, but she disappeared after the Radical Parade banquet. We heard the second Rhomandi brother took a fancy to her and claimed her along with his other pets, but we never really knew."

His other pets . . . And thus, even Zelin looked on Mikhyel—and Temorii.

"Not claimed," Thyerri said in a low voice. "Rescued. Had he known about the rest of you, you'd be free as well."

Zelin's life-wise gaze studied him across that dim lamplit room. "And just how would you know that for a fact?"

"He took her in because she was my friend and I was frightened for her. Because I felt guilty for what happened to her."

"That *was* you she saw, then."

"After a fashion."

"The Rhomandi rescue friends of yours, and you don't intend to give me the explanation."

"Someday I may explain. Not now. It's . . . complicated."

"You can at least tell me why a Rhomandi would give a damn about Thyerri of no family's feelings."

"Because he'd already rescued me. It was he who got me back into the competition."

"You and his Tamshi witch, both, eh? What's the man's obsession with dancers?"

"His—*what?*"

"His Tamshi witch. That's what they're calling her, all through the Tower. They say she held the entire stadium crowd in thrall with some magical dance while dunMheric escaped, and then disappeared. Vanished right off the rings."

"That's . . . not quite how it happened," Thyerri stared down at the towel in his hands, not wanting to lie to Zelin, not knowing how to explain, either.

Silence filled the room as he searched for the means, and as he searched, Zelin's eyes widened, his head went back, as if for longer vantage, and then: "That Tamshi witch . . . that was *you*, wasn't it?"

"I . . . yes, theoretically, I'm the—" Thyerri felt a rueful grin steal onto his face. "Theoretically, I'm the reigning Radical. I don't think I'll be dancing any time soon, however. The stadium is, well . . . quite thoroughly destroyed, and the last time I encountered Rhyys' men, my health was not a high priority for them."

"It's a shame, lad. From what I've heard of that dance, your blood runs truer even than I knew. No wonder you were so quick to learn."

"I'd rather not discuss it, if you don't mind."

Zelin squeezed his shoulder, then let his hand drop. "But if you were Rhomandi's dancer, then who was that other Thyerri? The one Sakhi saw—the one who died on the rings?"

"That was me, too, after a fashion."

"You look lively for a corpse."

Thyerri just shrugged.

"You're not going to explain, are you?"

"Perhaps. Someday."

"Oh, lad, what *have* you gotten yourself into?"

"Nothing that hasn't been part of me from the start."

Zelin gripped his chin, turned his face to the light.

"You and your Tamshi eyes." Zelin released his chin and turned away to throw the dirty water out the window. "I don't think I want to know more."

"Probably not."

"Just tell me," with an over the shoulder glance, "has the alley-rat learned to fight?"

"You taught him. You should know."

Zelin turned full to face him, a careful, comfortable distance between them now.

"And does he still trust his teacher?" Zelin asked.

"He wants to trust him."

"So. Why *are* you here? You didn't risk that climb just for a visit."

"Actually, I did risk it to reach my room. I had no idea you were here. The fact that you are is an unexpected bonus."

"What happened to you? After Bharlori's burned?"

"You do know that was my fault. Sakhithe told you."

"I know it was an accident, lad. I heard all the accusations, and Rhyys certainly tried to put it on your head along with a bounty, but Sakhi told me the real story. You defended yourself and lamps fell. Rhyys' damned fancy drapes were far more at fault. Let it go. Let Bharlo's death go. Another accident for which he was at fault as well. He should never have subjected you and the girls to that monstrous farce."

"Done is done," Thyerri repeated, and went to the window, wondering should he just leave now, and let the past—all the past—be the past.

"Who are you spying for, Thyerri?"

He started, and turned. And told this man the truth. "The Rhomandi."

"Last I heard, you were consigning all Darius' descendants to the cloudy heights of their own lightning-blasted hell."

"I've learned to make exceptions."

"For love of the younger Rhomandi? This rijhili who'd rescue your friends?"

"For politics. Deymorin Rhomandi's plans for the Web are far more reasonable than his predecessors', not all we want, but more than we have. I was on the streets a time, surviving as I could, then . . . that's when Mikhyel dun-Mheric found me and took me in."

"And you work for him now?"

He shook his head. "I report to the Rhomandi."

"You work for the elder, then, not the middle?"

A small pause while he sought the words. He had to say it aloud, the truth he didn't want to hear. "My association with Mikhyel dunMheric is over."

And surely the pain came through his voice, for all he tried to swallow it. "I'm sorry," Zelin said after a moment.

"Nothing to be sorry for."

"Just business, then?" Zelin's look said he didn't believe that for an instant, and Thyerri saw no reason to lie.

"I didn't say that. Done is done. Good and bad. We met, we grew, we parted. That doesn't change the needs of the world. The Rhomandi needed to know what was happening here in Khoratum. I'm acquainted with them, I'm intimately familiar with Khoratum. I was the logical choice to get them that information."

Zelin looked thoughtful. "Paying you, is he?"

"Well. Very well." He paused, then asked, not truly what he had come to offer this man, but because the money might be a need he could supply. "Would you like in on it?"

"Tempting, lad. Very tempting. But too dangerous."

"For *you?* I find that hard to believe."

"You don't know what it's like these past months, lad. It's a risk just talking to you."

"Then come away with me now!" He fell back to the plan that had brought him to this room. "I'll get you to Rhomandi's men and—"

But Zelin was shaking his head. "You don't understand. He's got us all marked. Says he'll know our minds, he'll hear us if we try to escape. There's no avoiding him."

"Rhyys?"

Zelin nodded.

He snorted his disgust. "I know that act. Mauls your naked body and says he 'knows' you. But it's all nonsense." Rhyys had not had the mindtouch . . . not truly. His mind had mauled with much the same finesse as his hands.

Again Zelin shook his head. "Might've been his way with the dancers, but ugly ol' mountain goats like m'self just got our heads squeezed. Felt like those damned nails of his sliced right through my skull, then sent worms crawling around my innards, but at least I got to keep my shirt on, thank you."

Zelin's words sent an unexpected shiver down his spine.

(. . . *I think that you will do this, because I think you want, above all else, to live* . . .

(Fingers growing through his skull, sending tendrils throughout his body; he couldn't move, couldn't escape that invasion . . .)

"I've seen too many try to flee this place get carried back screaming with pain from wounds you can't see." Zelin continued. "If they come back to work, they're . . . different. It's not something I'm ready to chance, lad. Not yet."

But those invasive fingers hadn't belonged to Rhyys. They'd belonged to Scarface—the priest, Vandoshin romMaurii.

"Zelin." The words came with difficulty past those sudden and ongoing shivers. But he could not go back, now, without knowing. He could not sleep again at night, without knowing. "I want to see Rhyys. If they bring in people from the town, I want to see how he does this . . . marking. Up close. Is it possible?"

"You're mad, boy!"

"Probably. But I have to try."

Chapter Eight

A well-bred lady like Nethaalye dunErrif seated on the couch of the Blue Salon less than an hour before guests were scheduled to begin arriving—sketching—was a clear indicator of the tension that had been building within House Rhomandi all day. It was certainly not the ordinary way a lady prepared for guests.

It was the ordinary way Nethaalye ignored Lidye.

"That bad, Thaalye?" Mikhyel asked as he entered, and she looked up with her serene smile.

"Not really," she said, "Just waiting for someone else to arrive." And she began to gather her pencils. The little area she'd staked out as her own in the salon was pleasantly cluttered—a state he rarely associated with her.

"Please don't stop for my sake. I haven't seen your work in . . . rings, years. May I?"

"Of course."

Wine was breathing on a side table. He nodded toward it with a questioning look.

"Please," she answered the unspoken question.

In a smaller tray beside the wine tray, lay an envelope addressed to him and sealed with his official seal, the one with two notches rather than one, the one Paulis used. He smiled and tucked the envelope into his breast pocket: a gift, but not for Nikki. Not this one. His gift to Nikki resided in the reception area with all the others that had arrived over the past few days; this gift he planned to slip quietly into Kiyrstin's possession at the first opportunity.

As he raised the carafe, the Blue Salon doors swung wide

and Lidye stormed into the room. "Compromise with Mauritum? *Make peace with Garetti?* Insanity! I forbid it!"

Mikhyel froze, wine goblet and carafe in hand, and half-turned to face Lidye. Beyond her, a chagrined Nikki waved the servants away from the doors and closed them, securing their privacy. Moments before the guests were scheduled to begin arriving, the lot of them primped and primed for a fancy party . . . naturally, Lidye had to throw a tantrum.

Mikhyel finished pouring the wine and handed the glass to Nethaalye, who accepted it with a sympathetic smile, set it on the table next to her pencils, and returned to her sketching.

He poured a second for himself.

Sipped.

Waited as the wine traced its slow path across tongue and palate, leaving evidence of its year and point of origin as well as a promise of future calm in its wake. Only when the handful of drops cleared his throat did he address his seething sister-in-law, still dramatically posed just inside the door, awaiting his answer.

"You—forbid. Do you care to rephrase that opening, madam?"

"Mikhyel, I'm sorry," Nikki said, slipping between them. "I thought I could explain the situation so that you wouldn't have to. I'm afraid I didn't do very well."

"The apologies are traveling between the wrong two points, Nikki," he said. "You had every right to speak with your wife about so significant an opportunity for the City's future. How could you anticipate such a rude, uncaring, and self-serving reaction on the part of your wife?"

"Mikhyel dunMheric, I protest!"

"Protest all you like, madam, I merely state the facts as I see them. For weeks now, you've sought a way to focus this day around yourself for reasons I fail to comprehend— unless it's simply to lay claim to the first Rhomandi House party in nearly twenty years, and I'd hate to think anyone so petty and shallow, let alone my brother's wife, so I assume there is some advantage I'm missing here. Be that as it may, Deymorin's precipitous action fouled the orbits quite literally on your first attempt—a situation, I must say, in which you not only might have had some legitimate say, but also some legitimate pique. However, you chose to take that situation as an adult, and seek a mutually beneficial result. I . . . respected you for that response. But I find that respect misplaced, since now with Nikki's party guests arriving in less than half an hour, you attempt to instigate a singularly unpleasant scene on a foreign policy question in which you have little to no voice at all. I'd say my brother deserves an apology, but possibly I mistake the matter."

She drew herself up, bosom heaving. "You mock me sir."

"Not at all. I say I might well be mistaken."

"Of *course* you are mistaken. I have a great deal to say!"

"I have no doubt. The question is, do I need, let alone *want* to hear it?"

"Your *needs* and *wants* are irrelevant. I am the Ringmaster of Rhomatum, and you *will* listen!"

Next she'd call him *boy,* in exactly Anheliaa's tone, for all he was three years her senior. Another of Anheliaa's damned legacies. His aunt had gone to great pains to imprint her style on this very willing, if not particularly adept, subject, and Lidye consciously echoed that high-handed style as if it were her right, even down to direct quotes she seemed to think had particular potency. He had never loved Anheliaa, far from it; but he had respected her Talent and her intellect, though he wondered, at times . . . *frequently* of late . . . what she'd seen in Lidye—beyond Lidye's fertility and her convenient attachment to Shatum. For a time, he'd kept thinking there *had* to be something in Anheliaa's choice he was overlooking. A strength of character, of Talent, but he'd never seen it, and damned if he'd act in fear of suspicions of suspicions.

"Ringmaster or not," he said, calmly, plainly—provocatively, "Mauritumin trade agreements are *not* your business."

"The *Tower* is my business, and all that affects the Web! Therefore *Garetti* is *always* my business!"

Mikhyel pressed his lips tight on the retort that rose.

This confrontation had been brewing for months; it was infuriating that it should break loose tonight. And yet, with those two rings spinning up in the Tower, could he really be surprised that she chose now to make a scene on any available topic?

He met Nikki's eyes apologetically, got a slow, supportive nod, but no attempt to bridge their mutually intact barriers. None of them cared to risk the link snapping tight tonight, particularly not now. They couldn't risk exhausting themselves trying to break it. Not with the upcoming party, particularly not with Lidye's damned show looming later in the evening.

"This summit is at Garetti's request, but I have no reason to believe Garetti will be directly involved at this time," Mikhyel said to Lidye, keeping his tone even. "Garetti cut Persitum out of the Mauritum Web. There is no power link. Our relationship with Mauritum now is strictly trade economics. This meeting will be between Minister of State Paurini and myself."

"It doesn't matter *who* you talk to, you'll be *dealing* with Garetti!"

"Nonetheless, agreement, on any issue coming out of this meeting, will be dependent on the Syndicate and Council. On the other hand, *if* all goes well, I do hope to arrange a meeting with Garetti after the spring thaws. *He* wants it, *I* want it, and both Webs require it. That meeting *will* happen, Lidye."

Lidye seethed. "I warn you, Mikhyel dunMheric. I am the ringmaster in Rhomatum Tower. I control the power flow you barter. Don't forget what I can do."

"Never, madam. As you would do well never to forget what will happen to you personally should you employ any obstructive tactics to gain your way. Need I remind you that you are *not* Anheliaa?"

"You have *no idea* what or who I am, Mikhyel dunMheric!"

"I know you are not Anheliaa—not in reality, not in my eyes, most definitely not in the eyes of the citizens of the

Web. I know you have yet to prove yourself as anything more than a mediocre spinner."

"I took control of the whole damned Web—"

"On the contrary, madam, *we* took control. While you may have directed the energy, *Nikki* was the anchor, and *Deymorin* the power. I repeat, a mediocre spinner. I also know that since once the Khoratum/Persitum ring is aligned, the only thing required of you for the next decade and possibly more will be the relatively mundane task of keeping the Rings aligned and the power flow even, you will not have an opportunity to adjust that image. I think that you are, in a word, expendable; the child you carry is not. You're in the Rhomatum tower by the grace of the Rhomandi family. We're grateful for your aid. We carry responsibility for the actions of our aunt who brought you here under pretenses and promises she had no right to make—but you are *not* by any means going to dictate the actions of this family. Do you understand me?"

"You *dare*—"

"I most certainly do." Mikhyel drew a deep, steadying breath. "You had, in Anheliaa, a flawed example of a ringmaster, and your imitation of her is utterly ridiculous, if you must know. I'd suggest you seek your own style, if I had any confidence there was a style to be had."

"How dare you!"

"Easily. Let me enlighten you, since you seem to have missed the point. Anheliaa had established not only a history of intimidation, but a record of *performance* before any of us were born, and those dual attributes gave her name a power in the Council and Syndicate no amount of reason could withstand. But it was not a legislative power. And it did not set policy. Anheliaa was not, was never even remotely, the Rhomandi. That is not, madam, an empty title, and *I was* the Rhomandi—by proxy, but not as a puppet *of anyone*. I routinely moderated Anheliaa's more outrageous demands before presenting them, at times for fear the awestruck representatives would vote them into law before even considering the consequences, at times because they would justifiably horrify any rational person. *I* ran foreign and domestic policy under Anheliaa and will continue to do so until *the Rhomandi* requests otherwise. Don't ever expect to change that."

"You moderated . . . How dare you? *Which* demands?"

"Those issues were between my aunt and myself. They don't concern you—except, perhaps, that you might want to bear in mind that *I* wrote the marriage contract you signed, and you might want to read it again and think carefully before you try to wield your still-shaky title too enthusiastically. The fact is, where it regards the office of ringmaster I find I must justify your presence in the Tower to someone nearly every day. You do not have Anheliaa's reputation. You're dangerously close to gaining quite a different one. Those are the facts of the situation. If you can't handle them—" He sipped his wine and continued. "Once the child is born, if you can't handle those facts, you will be free to renegotiate that marriage contract. Even to go home, if you wish . . . leaving us the requisite heir."

"These are *my* rings! This is *my* home! You'll never force me out! *Nikki* won't let you!"

Silence. He let it sit heavily in the room, allowing ample time for Nikki's silence to make its point.

"Your rings," he replied at last. "Your home. And not a word of the child?" Not that he was in any way surprised. She merely confirmed his belief that she harbored none of those maternal feelings mothers were supposed to experience.

Her possessiveness of the Rings also came as no surprise. Considering Deymorin's example, that attitude came with the job.

"I *won't* leave!" Lidye screeched. "And I *must* know what you changed! Anheliaa—Anheliaa taught me dependent upon her understanding. If you *dared* change that situation without telling me—"

"You threaten us, madam?"

An openmouthed heartbeat, then, in a somewhat calmer, even pleading tone: "Not threaten, no. But you must understand: I rely on what she taught me, on what she *knew*. I thought I could depend on that." Painted lips trembled.

Her delicate face acquired a singularly annoying vulnerability: one of her less endearing tactics, to his way of thinking, but one that had undoubtedly worked well over the years, considering the frequency with which she resorted to it. "I . . . I haven't meant to say anything, because . . . it's so . . . but Anheliaa and I—shared minds, as you and your brothers do . . . to give me the patterns of the Rings, you know. Surely you understand. I can't have you changing that which she believed to be true. You of all people should understand the confusion that creates! Sometimes I . . ." She shrugged delicately. Pitifully. "But all of that aside, those patterns depend in part on what she believed to be true. How am I to know what you've done to all the plans?"

A link between Lidye and Anheliaa? It was possible, if a somewhat repulsive notion to equate what he had with his brothers . . . what he'd *had* with his lover . . . to some connection between his aunt and this woman.

"If it's truly that significant, you might try asking."

"Asking? *Me?* Ask for something I should never have to even *think* about? It's too much. I can't deal with so many possibilities! You must give me a list of these things you've changed. I need to know!"

A touch of his sleeve drew his attention to Nethaalye. "Yes, my dear?" he asked without taking his eyes from Lidye.

"What do you think?"

A confusion later, he realized she spoke of the drawing in her lap. "Thaalye, do you truly think—"

"I'd *truly* like to know, Khyel,"

Frowning in barely controlled exasperation, he looked at the tablet she held up, an attempt, he thought, to divert them from an irritating, but perhaps essential, argument.

Exasperation vanished. In an area blocked for shading, fine letters said: **She's lying. Anheliaa made us seek the patterns ourselves. There was no sharing of minds.**

He traced the final words with a forefinger, not quite touching. "You're certain of this line?"

Tilting her head as if to study her sketch at a different angle, she wrote:

Warned us against "true love" <u>because</u> our "personal patterns with the Rings" could thus be compromised.

"Ah," he said, and a man whose *personal pattern* had been forever warped by *true love* could well believe that to be Anheliaa's position on the matter. "I think you have it now."

She took her stub and smeared through the lettering, then deepened the shadow until no trace of the exchange remained.

In the meanwhile, Lidye blotted at her eyes with a lacy sleeve handkerchief.

"All right, Lidye," Mikhyel said more moderately, at ease in the knowledge of the depth of her deception. "I grant you leeway for a disturbing connection. And if you want to know, your knowing is certainly no problem. The legislation is available for anyone who wants to read it. I'll have Paulis prepare a summary listing of all Anheliaa's proposals for the last ten years and the reference numbers for the actual legislation passed. At your leisure, you can look up the references."

Which kept Paulis' extra work to a minimum and assured hours of occupation on her part, sorting through legal language she was ill-prepared to comprehend.

"And if I have objections to that legislation?"

"I said your *knowing* is no problem."

"I have opinions to voice!"

"About the legislation? Put it in writing and submit it to my office. It's your right as a citizen and will be considered in due time. About Garetti?" He shrugged. "Have your say. I'm listening."

He thought, for a moment, he'd stopped her cold; he should have known better.

"The man organized a coup against House Rhomandi," she spat out, "and now you want to go to bed with him. Is that supposed to give me confidence in you?"

"Garetti is still solidly in power in Mauritum and we haven't the power, nor the inclination to depose him."

"Then *we* are an idiot."

"Tell me then, Lidye, what would you do with Garetti, keeping in mind he's cut Persitum off and so severed our connection to Mauritum?"

"The ring is still up. He'd not be such a total fool as to drop it entirely, and if we destroyed it that night, we'd have known it. Align the Satellites, use that link of yours—which is, when you put your minds to it, damned potent—to run up his ass and force Garetti's Persitum ring back into orbit. Strike fast, strike hard, and you've got him! With Persitum down, he's got a whole line down. He's wide open."

"And do what with him once we've got him, madam? Defend yet another front? *Govern?* We don't need Mauritum. We don't know the people or their needs or anything about them. But Mauritumin leaders know the strength of the Rhomandi Triumvirate now. *Garetti* from the tone of his letters, fears we intend to do exactly as you suggest. With proper negotiations, we can use that same leverage to seal a long-term agreement and to undo the damage Darius' isolationist policy created in what might have been a profitable neighbor."

"You're a dreamer. Worse than ever Nikki was. This is *no* time to be negotiating with that religious fanatic. We should be pressing our advantages, legal and moral! The man should be run out of power, not . . . indulged."

A muscle in his brow twitched involuntarily. "Morally— that's for his people to decide. They seem content with him, according to Kiyrstin and our own informants. Legally—we have no more law to stand on than he does. We *have* no legally binding agreements; that's the problem. We need that trade agreement more than ever, and now is the time to get that agreement, while he's still demoralized by his associates' failure to bring down the Rhomandi. He's lost Persitum. He wants to bring Persitum back into his web, but he's waited too long. Our Khoratum/Persitum ring is up. If he wants to bring Persitum back in, he's got to reconcile with us, he's got to deal with us, and if we have Persitum's loyalty—"

"Loyalty? Those *barbarians?*"

"*Yes*, loyalty." He held his tongue with an effort. "If we

bring Persitum back on line, restore the power that was lost *due to Garetti's actions* while Garetti himself *willfully* withholds that power, damned right we win Persitumin loyalty. We're dealing with businessmen now, madam, not politicians. We'll have *their* support, and we'll be on Garetti's threshold, face to face with him in a way he can't ignore ever again, provided we don't betray the trust we're hoping to establish with Persitum. Brishukh dunIliis of Persitum has offered us as neutral a meeting ground as we could hope for. When the time comes, *damned right,* I'll go to Persitum and meet with Garetti, and *damned right,* this upcoming summit meeting will include laying the groundwork for that next one, but that is by no means its total function."

"You'll go alone?"

"Mauritum is naturally suspicious of the Triumvirate and wants only one of us there."

"I'm not surprised, considering the wild rumors you've spread."

Again, Mikhyel held his tongue. The rumors regarding the Triumvirate were not of his making . . . though he'd done little to counteract them. "The important thing is, at the moment, they have no means of knowing that the Triumvirate's ability is independent of Towers and even proximity; I don't intend to clarify those erroneous notions. I had assumed I would go; my brothers have endorsed that assumption. My brothers and I have discussed the matter and we are in agreement as to where the Rhomandi Triumvirate stands. It is not an issue up for further debate. Would you care for a glass of wine?"

He held his out to her, catching her eyes, daring her to protest again. She bared her teeth in a most unladylike snarl, but took the glass—and drained it. She held it out for a refill. He obliged, adding, "You seem thirsty. Should I ring for water, or do you prefer to greet the guests from a day bed?"

She lifted the glass in a mocking toast and whirled about, sending her skirts swirling across his legs, to sink gracefully into the window seat. She was very close to her time now, yet she remained deceptively slender (due in part to the services of an extremely expensive dressmaker who had designed a whole new line just for the "Mother-Lady of the Tower," and her condition rarely showed in her actions—the carriage and exaggerated care of movement seemingly designed to disguise this stage of a woman's life.

He poured wine for Nikki and himself, then settled next to Nethaalye on the couch, leaving Nikki his pick of the chairs.

Nikki, brave young fool that he was, chose the seat nearest Lidye, and tried to distract her.

Nethaalye smiled and showed him the sketch she'd been working on: quick, free-flowing, yet obviously portraying him as he poured the wine. She was an accomplished artist, and had used him as a model since they were children.

"I think, as always, you are too kind to your subject matter," he said, and meaning far more than the sketch, "Thank you."

She smiled and pressed his hand, then returned to the sketch, attacking a recalcitrant perspective.

He'd been glad, very glad, when the news of her brother's incarceration had failed to pull her away. For all she adamantly maintained her distance from a marriage bed, they'd been friends as children and adolescents, a quiet sort of friendship that had flourished despite the tension their arranged betrothal had placed on them.

"You *can't* deal with Garetti." Lidye was back at it, with Nikki the one now under attack. Mikhyel stifled a groan. "You can't trust him. *Who* you're meeting is irrelevant. You'll be *dealing* with Garetti."

"Not entirely true, Lidye." Kiyrstin's voice preceded her into the room and Mikhyel welcomed her with relief: she'd had a surprisingly calming effect on Lidye these past months—not to mention Kiyrstin had a proven ability to temper his own argumentative nature. "Hello, Thaalye. Khyel. Nikaenor. Deymorin said there was a discussion going on that I should be part of . . . having lived with Garetti for fifteen years."

"Which argues why you should *not* be in this discussion!"

Lidye said, and Deymorin, who had entered in Kiyrstin's wake, bristled.

Kiyrstin merely smiled and reached a hand to Deymorin to help her ease into a chair. In sharp contrast to Lidye, Kiyrstin, round as a full moon, simply laughed at her condition, and groaned, and begged Deymorin for assistance—mainly because he so obviously loved obliging her . . . not that she couldn't maneuver perfectly well on her own when he was not available.

Of the two, he vastly preferred Kiyrstin's style.

"Lidye," Kiyrstin said pointedly, "you're being entirely unreasonable."

The magic words. Mikhyel noted Lidye's shift in expression hopefully. But:

"My father conspired with Garetti, Lidye," Nethaalye interjected quietly. "Does that mean I must leave as well?"

Well meaning, but ill-timed. Lidye's frown returned. "Don't be ridiculous. The issue is whether or not we are going to allow Mikhyel to negotiate some placating compromise with Mauritum over this most recent insult. Conspiracy, in our own Web! I say we make our demands and they accept them, or we shut them down! They're in no position to argue!"

"What makes you think I won't?" Fool that he was, he sought to end this once and for all.

"Because you're too damned cowardly to take a stand, regardless of the strength of your position. You *hide* behind philosophical points of fair play. You *have* him, dunMheric. He's frightened. You and your brothers represent an entirely new quantity, one he can't predict. Force him to his knees. *Rule* Mauritum."

"And I say we can scarcely hold our own web, madam. What do we need with another? We profit by their stability, not their taxes."

"Who gave you this advice? Rings, you've lost what little backbone you had."

"Use your common sense, Lidye, not Anheliaa's obsessions. There's more to controlling Mauritum than controlling their Rings. What would you do, should the people object? Invade them with our poor half-trained troops? To what purpose? They didn't create the discontent within the Northern Crescent. That already existed, thanks to our own dealings, thanks to Anheliaa's high-handed actions, among others. Our job lies here, healing our own internal differences.''

"*You* changed the policies, but it's *Anheliaa's* fault! Such convenient twists you put into your arguments, Barrister. I'll tell you what we should *not* do and that is cater to a tyrant with delusions of godhood!''

"Oh, come now, Lidye," Kiyrstin drawled. "I assure you, Garetti is too lazy for tyranny. Certainly for godhood. Why don't we rant on demagoguery instead?''

"How dare you!''

So much for Kiyrstin's mollifying capacity.

"Lidye," Mikhyel began.

Deymorin broke in, saying, "For the love of Darius, this is Nikki's night. We don't need a tantrum in the house.''

And all the time, Nikki sat, stone-faced, sipping his wine.

"It's Mikhyel's doing!" Lidye wailed. "How *dare* he spring this on me now as an accomplished fact, right before Nikki's big party, when he *knows* I have no time to organize an argument? This isn't a debate, it's an assassination!''

"I didn't bring it up," Mikhyel reminded her. "Nikki did, when you insisted. Personally, I find trade agreements to be fascinating, but I really don't expect others to share that interest, particularly this evening.''

"And when *did* you plan to tell me?''

"You, madam? I assure you, discussing this trip with you never entered my plans at all.''

"Damn you, Mikhyel, the goal was to bring the priests down, not fly the welcome banner! The northerners are a superstitious lot, no matter how hard we try to educate them. Bad enough the rumors that are already flying through the scandal sheets about you three. Let Garetti and his blind followers in—''

"I would appreciate it," Kiyrstin said, speaking with slow deliberation, "If you would cease denouncing people about whose faults you know absolutely nothing.''

Lidye's upper lip raised in a tiny snarl. "You're all against me. I see that. I was wrong ever to rely on you." Her hands spread out over her extended belly almost in a self-caress. "Do what you like. He will prevail, and deal with Mauritum. I shall see to that."

Nikki's blue eyes blazed at that. "You, madam, will see to nothing of the sort. Our child will be taught love and tolerance and intelligent statesmanship, not obsession and certainly not hatred!"

Lidye froze. Blinked. And then smiled tremulously at Nikki, almost tenderly. "Of course, of course he will be. Or she. Oh, Nikki. They hate me. Why do they hate me? Why do they hate our baby? Don't let them talk like this to us."

And she held her arms out toward Nikki, urging him to her. There was hesitation, and knowing how badly Nikki wanted his little family, knowing how Nikki had waited for just such a gesture from her, Mikhyel couldn't say he was surprised when Nikki responded by standing and raising her into his arms.

But just as her face disappeared into his shoulder, the calculated and calculating expression made Mikhyel's skin crawl.

"You're just tired, Lidye," Nikki said. "It's the baby. Kiyrstin explained everything—"

Lidye jerked free, shot Kiyrstin a scathing look.

"Only enough to understand, Lidye," Kiyrstin said, unruffled. "You'd have lost him utterly if I hadn't."

"And I'm very glad she did, Lidye. I'm so glad she's been here for you. We've been lucky to have her, as we've been fortunate to have Nethaalye to spell you in the Tower. And now with Deymorin able to take over—"

"Never!" She was determined not to be placated, and Mikhyel glanced uneasily at the clock. The first guests were undoubtedly already at the door.

"I don't recall asking you," Deymorin said.

"You're not fit! Not chosen—"

"Rhomatum himself indicated otherwise." Mikhyel pointed out, hoping to bring an end to it.

"That's terribly convenient for you, isn't it? No one to

verify your claims that this *creature* said anything of the sort. Well, I won't give the Rings to you! *I* am the master of Rhomatum Tower."

"Be careful what you say, Lidye," Mikhyel said. "We've just eliminated one tyrant from the Tower. We won't have another."

"No? And what are *you*, if not a tyrant?"

"Smart enough to never set foot in Rhomatum Tower again."

"That's right. You don't need the Rings, do you, Mikhyel darling? Not content to be a tyrant in Rhomatum Tower, you intend to control the *world* from its source. You'll visit the caverns like some seer and come back with dictums from these gods of yours!"

"You're welcome to go down in my stead. But I forgot, you can't, can you?"

Her brow lowered. "You're a cruel man, Mikhyel dun-Mheric."

"Madam, you don't know the meaning of the word."

"Would you care to lay a wager on that?"

Of a sudden, it was as if the others in the room had ceased to exist. She hit a nerve. That question, delivered in that tone, had haunted his existence for years . . . because he'd never known how much Anheliaa knew and how much she guessed of what he did. She'd known his darkest, nonpolitical fears and taunted him daily. And despite Neth-aalye's reassurance to the contrary, he could almost believe this witch with the face of a pansy *had* shared minds with Anheliaa and knew things about him he never wanted known, all the shameful scenes he and Anheliaa had shared, all Anheliaa knew of his father . . . this chit of a girl who simpered her way into the Tower and now proved her predecessor's aptest pupil.

Common sense, however, hoped that Nethaalye was right and that there'd been no secret sessions about which Neth-aalye did not know. Common sense warned him to assume that what she knew she'd learned from Anheliaa in the ordinary manner: observation.

Most of all, he'd be damned if he'd let himself give in

to those old reflexes and flinch at a lucky, perhaps accidental, quote.

"I'll not cross swords with you on this, Lidye. Not tonight. Rumors about the Triumvirate's talent are running wild. If one of us can be established as a ringmaster—better yet, if Deymorin actually excels at it—that will go far toward restoring Syndic confidence. Also, those spinners in the other Towers will be far more reconciled if we can eliminate some of the mystique around the Rhomatum Rings and present a more understandable face."

"That's foolish. Keep them off-guard."

"I said 'some,' Lidye. I'm quite well versed in negotiation, and in the value of exclusive knowledge. Now, I suggest we let the matter drop. This is still Nikki's birthday and the guests—"

A discreet tap on the door interrupted him.

"Yes?" Deymorin said, and the door opened cautiously to Alizant's thin face.

"Excuse me, but Cap'n Gan said for me to tell you if you didn't want him being the official host to . . . um . . ."

"Get ourselves out there?" Deymorin finished for him.

"Yes, sir. Something like."

"Then best we . . . get ourselves out there," Nikki said quietly, and Mikhyel's heart ached for the dignity with which his little brother held out his arm for his wife.

{Sorry, Nik.} He chanced making contact enough to send him, and received back a sense of resignation that held nothing of self-pity, only a wish that they'd get past such time-wasting arguments, and a suggestion that they get in to the festivities in front of the guests, where good behavior was more assured.

With a backward glance, Nikki said, "Relax, Khyel. I got a quick preview of the ballroom and dining hall. And nothing, absolutely nothing, is going to ruin this night."

Mikhyel couldn't help but think of that upcoming presentation of Lidye's, the question of setting the Rings, and the antagonism now in the air and could only hope Nikki's optimism would rule.

Deymorin had assisted Kiyrstin to her feet. Time was

slipping away, the occasion for a gift untainted by the stresses of the night already fled.

But thinking they all needed something to salve the stings of Lidye's temper, he slipped the envelope into Kiyrstin's hand as she passed. Kiyrstin paused and looked at him curiously. So did Deymorin.

So, in the doorway, did Lidye. And Nikki, and Alizant. The whole room had come to a halt.

"When Garetti approached me about the meeting, I sent a counterproposal," Mikhyel said, in a low voice. "Naturally he turned it down. I sent another he couldn't refuse."

She broke the seal with a fingertip, unfolded the paper. Her face lit. And to his complete consternation, she flung her arms about his neck and kissed him soundly on the cheek.

"What's this?" Deymorin asked.

Kiyrstin transferred her affections to Deymorin, hugged him hard. "Rhomandi?" she whispered in his ear, "Will you marry me?"

"He didn't!" Deymorin said, and cast a questioning look at Mikhyel, who hoped his appearance was unruffled.

"He did!" Kiyrstin crowed, though softly, conscious, as were they all, of stealing this day from Nikki, yet unable to contain her joy. "I'm free, love."

Deymorin cast a second look his way. "Khyel, I—"

"Don't say it, brother. She's the best thing that ever happened to you. I'm pleased I could help. Write that baby's name down as Rhomandi."

Nikki, in his honest heart, beamed, and came and congratulated his prospective sister-in-law. Nethaalye hugged Kiyrstin with warm formality.

Lidye stood in the doorway with a scowl unbecoming a flowerlike face, but for once, she held her peace, acknowledging, perhaps, that this round had been lost.

Mikhyel was not such a fool as to believe the war itself was over.

Chapter Nine

The formal dining hall had assumed a fanciful mask for Nikki's birthday. A huge buffet along the back wall centered on a fountain of sparkling water that cascaded down glass lily pads into a small pool in which tiny leythium-crystal lilies floated, shimmering with a ghostly iridescence. From that pool, and following a route of a delicate glass riverbed, the water complete with lilies then wended about the table, past plates of cleverly carved fruits and breads and colorful pools of sauces, carrying sparks of light with them in constantly shifting fashion, cascading safely down tiny falls to the next level of platters and bowls, until by a miracle of engineering beneath the lily pads, the glass flowers reemerged above, to retrace their descent.

Crystal sparkled.

Roses and flowers of every description from the Armayel greenhouses decorated every niche.

The guests marveled at the traveling lights.

The kitchen and indeed the entire Rhomandi House staff had been planning this event for three months. It was the first large party to be held in Rhomandi House since Mheric's death and creative talents once stifled by Anheliaa's misanthropic ways had run wild, with Deymorin's shameless endorsement.

The guest list was . . . mind-numbing. In addition to Lidye's hand-picked list of notables, who would ascend later to the ringchamber for her announcement, Jerrik and Deymorin had conspired to bring together everyone from Nikki's past and present, a presumption of preferred company that Mikhyel would never have dared.

But Mikhyel had to admit that the look of unadulterated delight on Nikki's face when he entered the room and began enthusiastically greeting one guest after another dispelled any doubts he might have had.

Anheliaa would have been scandalized . . . which was the greatest endorsement he could think of.

As the dancing commenced in the Lynthaliam Ball Room, Mikhyel did his duty by Nethaalye and several other women of prominence, then pulled the handful of wallflowers into positions of prominence by first singling them out and then presenting them to eligible partners—his duty alone in the house, now his brothers were both permanently out of the marriage market.

It was one of the few social tasks that he had enjoyed over the years, but with each intricate set of steps, each touch of his partner's hand, his enthusiasm waned. Though he'd never danced with Temorii, his body *knew* how Temorii would have moved; he'd sway with the music anticipating a counterbalance—that wasn't there. His partners were all graceful women, all well-trained in the steps, but there was an essential element missing for him now.

It provoked memories, too, too keenly, and he was glad to retreat to the observational sidelines to fetch refreshments for the older ladies who had settled in for a quiet gossip.

As he sipped his own glass of punch, he noticed Ganfrion at the far end of the hall, standing just outside the door to the gaming room, holding two glasses of punch and watching the dancers. He hadn't seen his gorman for weeks, not since Ganfrion had returned from his luckless mission to Giephaetum on the matter of Nethaalye's brother, and he hadn't expected to see him here tonight.

Deftly evading the looks of more willing ladies, he worked his way over to Ganfrion and said, by way of greeting, "I thought you were up in New Khoratum."

"With this many young fools all gathered together for fleecing?" Ganfrion said without looking at him. "How could I turn down such an opportunity?"

"And yet you stand outside the room, holding someone else's drink. Such a sad disappointment that must be."

Ganfrion's dark eyes flickered toward him, then back to the dancers. "Not really."

So, not the gamers at all. He grinned. "Who's the target this time?"

A frown pulled Ganfrion's scarred mouth into a sneer. Not a handsome man, even a rough man from the outside, but he had the knack for fitting seamlessly into any company, and formal ball or dockside tavern, was generally very successful with the women of his choosing.

"Just doing a favor for a friend, Suds." And his voice gave no invitation to pursue the matter further.

"My apologies." He changed the subject. "Hard trip back?"

"Delayed too long." His dark eyes continued to follow the dancers—or rather, one specific couple. "You never told me how Lady Nethaalye took the news."

"She wasn't surprised. She knows her brother."

"I didn't think she would be. But I think she hoped . . ." Ganfrion shrugged and looked down at the glasses he held. "Doesn't make it any easier—for any of us." His deepset eyes rose to meet Mikhyel's. "Has she come up to the bar yet on the engagement?"

He shook his head. "I don't think she will, either. I wish it were otherwise."

"You don't love her."

"Actually, I do. In my own way."

"Bullshit. You run away from love. She deserves better."

"Better." Mikhyel stared out at the dancers, refusing the visual confrontation Ganfrion would most certainly win. "A burning in your gut that makes it impossible to eat? A need that blinds you to the needs of all those around you? I'd spare her that. I have a great deal of affection for her, and I'd rather make her happy."

"You'd make the both of you miserable. *She*, at least, has the sense to see that."

Startled, he turned in spite of his better judgment. "She told you that?"

"She'd never betray your trust, Suds. Even you must see that." To his surprise, Ganfrion did not take advantage of the moment. To his surprise, it was Ganfrion who avoided the visual confrontation. And in a voice so low he almost didn't hear, added, "I only wish she'd trust me that much."

Removing any question about *which* couple Ganfrion had been watching, and what friend he favored.

"Ganfrion, I—"

"So, Khyel, what *do* you think we should do about Khoratum?"

He jumped, glanced over his shoulder to verify that low murmurous voice emanated from his brother, not his head.

"Rings, Deymio, you just aged me ten years. You're getting better. I didn't even hear you coming."

"Must be all the noise." And Deymorin's glance held a hint of concern. "You *do* hear them, don't you?"

He dipped his head. Six months ago, he only had to worry about his brothers' thoughts. These days, rooms full of people such as this created a mental hum rather like running water, or the soft whisper of circulating air.

"And Khoratum?" Deymorin repeated, which persistence puzzled Mikhyel. Khoratum was a dead issue. Why raise it here?

"Khoratum is gone. We've been burned. Badly. Best to let it go."

Deymorin turned to stare accusingly at his gorman. "You haven't told him."

"Told me *what?*" And even as he wondered, impressions surfaced out of the mental hum, associations calculated to shake him out of his carefully cultivated calm.

Ganfrion shrugged. "He hasn't asked." His dark gaze flickered toward Mikhyel. "*Rhomatumin kisswi.*"

Once again, he found refuge in the swirling skirts and colors. But this time, his heart raced underneath, and Deymorin, damn him, knew full well.

"Khoratum is a dead issue," he said firmly. "We've insulation against her—it. Let it go!"

"Just because you've got your head buried in the sand

doesn't mean your ass isn't going to be someone's lunch, brother."

A second glance revealed Deymorin's attention similarly directed outward, as his tone likewise remained low and private.

"I don't need you to explain my gorman's insults, *brother*."

"Could've fooled me. Khoratum's far from dead, and I think you'd better get your gorman's report and make a decision now."

"This is hardly the venue—"

Both of his self-appointed consciences just stared at him.

"All right!" he hissed. "GorMikhyel! Report!"

"Not that much to report," Ganfrion said, at his most off-hand, which tone signaled Mikhyel to be at his most wary. Deymorin's expression didn't help at all, and his mind was a stone wall. "The Tower's not dead," Ganfrion continued, "but you knew that. Rebuilding is taking place. Mother's scent grows—"

"*Mother's scent? Who* do you have in there?"

"Three. Fopelti and Ulinar are good, but Thyerri's the natural. —Hello, Lady Nethaalye."

Thyerri's the natural. He said that and then left it hanging, as though nothing else were necessary. Damn him! And Deymorin had known all along. Wait for Mikhyel to ask about Dancer, wait for Mikhyel to ask about Khoratum. And the music had ended, the dance was over, and here was Nethaalye, full of lively greetings, a bit breathless, reclaiming the glass she'd left with Ganfrion, who raised the second glass now, and asked her, with a mocking frown:

"Where's the man who stole you and left me with this?"

As if he'd not just cast a lightning bolt into the heart of his employer.

Nethaalye sighed and swept her hand around in an exaggerated gesture. "Gone. Left me for another."

"Foolish man." Ganfrion said with a mock frown. "Still, his idiocy is my good fortune." He raised the second glass to her, then drained it. She laughed and followed suit, though with somewhat daintier sips.

"So," Deymorin asked pointedly, "are you going to ask the pretty lady to dance?"

"Come, Gan, it'll be fun," Nethaalye said with a wistful tone, that hinted of previous refusals. And Ganfrion, snarled, more at Deymorin than at her:

"Dammit, girl, it's not right!"

"Not right?" Mikhyel repeated, and recalled, suddenly, another night, not far from Nethaalye's home node: *You've no damn business invading my world. . . .*

Ganfrion's words to him. Ganfrion, who openly sneered at social differences, who challenged daily Mikhyel's right to give him orders, and yet remained fiercely protective of his underground world, found himself caught in his own Web. He wouldn't demean the Giephaetumin lady by appearing on the dance floor with her.

No matter how much he wanted to go there.

"You're my gorman," he said firmly. "The Rhomandi himself suggested the partnership. You don't get any more proper than that, Gan. Get out and dance with the lady."

Still protesting, Ganfrion let her pull him out onto the floor.

ဢ ဢ ဢ

He'd made a mistake, coming up on Mikhyel and his man as he had, Deymorin thought, as he was left alone with his quietly seething brother. Deymorin had been for waiting until after the party to tell Mikhyel about the request from Dancer. Ganfrion had said, when he had given him that request earlier in the evening, that if the Rhomandi didn't, *he* would at the earliest opportunity, party or no party. Ganfrion had said to him that Thyerri was not the sort to wait long, once he'd set his mind to a thing, and that one of his men's safety—Ganfrion put Dancer in that category—should not wait on social foolishness.

So he'd assumed, when he saw them together, and with such sober expressions, that Ganfrion had made good his threat. He hadn't tried to confirm that suspicion through the link. It was too inclined to snap tight here above Rho-matum Node, and there was no need to ruin Nikki's night as well as Mikhyel's with this news Ganfrion had walked in with.

Instead, *he'd* walked straight in—into a wasp's nest—and potentially created another incident on another of Nikki's ill-starred birthdays. He was determined not to have it ex-plode. He was determined not to do this to Nikki, not again.

The problem was, when the Rhomandi clan gathered, be it for birthdays or funerals, issues walked through the doors right along with the participants.

"Obviously, Thyerri did not go with the Belisii caravan." Mikhyel said to the air in front of him, once Ganfrion was gone. Mikhyel's Barrister face was fully in evidence.

"Obviously," Deymorin admitted.

"He went back to Khoratum."

"Obviously, also."

"And he's been spying there. *For you.*"

"Don't be an idiot!" That was not the politic word; per-versely, he used it anyway. "He's doing nothing for me."

"To find Mother, then. Poor Mother, who didn't answer his call."

"Let's be just. Neither did you answer him."

"He never called."

Never called. All right. There it was, the opening he'd wanted for months. He kept his voice down with an effort. "No, you damned stiff-necked idiot! He's been waiting for you to make the first move. The Belisii held nothing for him. He went to Khoratum to help Mother, yes, but he also went to help *you,* to be useful while waiting for you to come to your senses."

"You had no right to involve him."

"He had a right to involve himself! And damned lucky we've been to have him. The details don't matter. My im-mediate concern is that he's sent word he wants to infiltrate the Tower itself. There's something in there he needs to get. He says if he can get to his old room, he might be able to get to Mother's caverns and confront her directly, and through her discover what's contaminating the node. But he's *asking leave to try*, Khyel. He's trying not to do anything to undermine our operations."

Mikhyel stared bleakly at the dancers. "Dangerous to go in?"

Stupid question. "How can you ask?"

"Who controls the Tower? Do we know that?"

"Rhyys. We think. No one who's gone in has come back out to verify."

"So, naturally, Thyerri wants to try. And you want to let him."

"His idea."

"Rings, the man's an idiot with a death wish!"

"He's a damned clever infiltrator who has unusual insight into the problems he might face. He's our best hope. I want to let him go in, 'Khyel."

There was a small silence. "Then let him. He wants to go. You think it useful. Let him go."

"That's *it*? What if he doesn't come back?"

"Then tell him no. It's your call."

"It's not my damned call! I'm asking you!"

"I don't want him on my conscience. If it's my call, keep him out of it. We'll find out some other way or deal with it when it blows. *If* it blows."

There was another silence through another evolution of the dance, a complex set of turns. He could be silent, could let Mikhyel slide away unchallenged on the point.

He could, and wouldn't.

"And if I'd said *Temorii* wanted to go in? Would you be as indifferent?"

Mikhyel's mouth tightened to a thin line within the frame of beard and mustache.

"Have you nothing more to say? No feelings left for him at all?"

"Feelings? Of course I have *feelings*. But feelings are a luxury I can't afford, especially in this case, as you should know better than anyone. Easier if you'd never told me. Easier now if you pulled *Dancer* out, but do as you will. I'll cope with my *feelings*."

Mikhyel didn't make it any easier. *Cope with his feelings*, if they lost Dancer, if *he* lost a man, which he never took as a matter of course.

What they might lose Dancer *to*, that was another question. What they might lose a town . . . an entire mountain to . . . that was also a consideration, the lives and welfare of multiple thousands of people. Someone had to make the hard call, and do what was necessary. He'd hoped for Mikhyel to beg him off, to supply him that better choice, to use his head and get better sense out of Dancer.

Or better yet, make himself available for fast communication with Dancer. With Dancer inside and Mikhyel outside, they had a good chance of finding out why their other spies *hadn't* returned.

"I think we need someone who can tell us what's going on in that ruin."

Mikhyel sipped absently at the dregs in the cup he now held for Nethaalye.

"How many is that?" He didn't know when he'd seen Mikhyel drunk, but his brother was heading for it, his eyes on Ganfrion and Nethaalye.

"None, that I've had a chance to finish." But the bright look in his eyes made Deymorin wonder about how many half-finished glasses resided about the house. "Covering his lie well, isn't he?" Mikhyel said, as Ganfrion's steps faltered, then quickly recovered.

"Lie?"

"He dances better than most of the people out there."

"So why'd he lie?"

"How should I know? To spare her feelings?" Mikhyel's chin raised a notch, challenging a direct hit. "Perhaps to end an inappropriate relationship with her before it gets out of hand. Perhaps he's learned from his employer's mistakes."

Deymorin dipped his head in defeat. "I'll deal with Thyerri, Mikhyel. Forget, if you can, I even raised the issue. Ease off the wine."

That pugnacious pose relaxed, and Mikhyel said quietly: "I will. You're right, we need our wits about us tonight.

Compromise? Let him go in. He's shown he knows ways in and out. He can do it. Tell him to get whatever he needs. Tell him to find out what he can without physically contacting anyone inside, and we'll go from there."

It sounded like sensible analysis.

"But he's not to speak to anyone in there. Make certain he understands that. Regardless how well he thinks he knows them."

Mikhyel had been on the inside himself. And might know things he hadn't said.

"Why so adamant on that score?"

"Feelings, Deymorin. Just a feeling." And Mikhyel seemed to be looking right through the dancers now. "Every contact creates a Web, and Webs bind the essence to the source. And that source is . . . contaminated. Mother . . . is contaminated."

"You could tell him faster than any courier."

"Possibly." Mikhyel's eyes shifted to him, hard and clear. "But I won't. He knows if anyone knows, and I'm not a messenger service. I'm not even certain it would work, trying to speak to him, and I have no desire to find out if it will. I've broken free of that Web, Deymorin; I'm not inclined to risk respinning it. Besides, we don't know who might hear. Now, if you'll excuse me . . ."

He handed Deymorin Nethaalye's glass and left the room.

§   §   §

Roses were a given in a node-city garden; roses were the only plant that thrived above a capped node. No one knew why. Priests of every faith had their rationale; chemists and botanists had long since given up. A handful of varieties of ivy, a select few herbs that only grew around the nodes, a few intensely poisonous berries, and two or three small plants that varied according to each node might add to the design, but overall, roses, of every height, growth pattern, shape and color, provided the landscapers' options.

Rhomandi House topped what the residents laughingly called Mount Rhomatum. And once it might well have been an impressive peak—a geologic once ago, just as Khoratum and Giephaetum were said to be mountains now.

Since Kiyrstin had never actually been to either of those node cities, she had to take their magnificence on Deymorin's word. A deficiency in her experience about which—she decided as she followed Mikhyel's slender shadow along the crushed marble rockways of a moonlit garden—she'd have to talk to her soon-to-be husband.

But all that remained these days of Rhomatum's peak was a steep-sided mound in the center of the Rhomatum power umbrella. Rhomatum Tower and the surrounding Rhomandi House dominated that mound, the lesser government buildings followed a spiraling path down to the valley floor where the City itself radiated out along the leylines.

Mikhyel's garden refuge was all pastels, pale blues and lavenders that carried an internal glow the likes of which Kiyrstin hadn't seen outside Rhomatum. It was even possible the varieties would only grow here—or grow a different color if planted above another node: another of those mysteries that plagued the nodes' botonists. Pale roses, the stone all white marble. It was obviously designed to be viewed at night, preferably by the full moon, as tonight's was just short of full. In that icy cold light, the entire garden glowed as if inhabited by ghostly spirits.

But one ghost was quite solid, a black shade beside a glittering pool between fey creatures of white marble down which trickles of water flowed, making their delicate features sparkle in the moonlight.

"Was she very beautiful?" Kiyrstin asked, and Mikhyel started, unusual reaction in a man tempered by Anheliaa's harsh methods.

"She?" he repeated without turning.

"The dancer who gave such grace to your three-step."

"Kiyrstin, I don't think this is the time—"

"When is it the time?"

Still, he didn't face her, and tension rippled the air be-

tween them. She retreated and tried a different approach
to the citadel.

"I haven't had a chance to thank you properly. You gave
me an incredible gift tonight. I owe you more than I can
ever repay."

"You owe me nothing." His tone was harsh. Abrupt.

He didn't want to talk. Patently wanted to be left alone.
But Mikhyel dunMheric had been indulged too often in
that desire, to her way of thinking, and Kiyrstine no-longer-
romGaretti had never been one to back down.

She shifted until she could see more than just his profile.

"You used to talk to me, Khyel. Have I changed so much
in five months?"

His jaw tightened. He stared elsewhere.

"All right, so I'm a bit more rotund. I've lost my girlish
appeal. Is that it? Or is it the third party? I'll cover his
ears, will that help?" She pressed her hands to her belly.
"Hmm, not there. That's a foot. Shush, brat." She shifted
her hands. "Maybe . . . not there either." And again.
"Maybe— Sweet Maurii, I think he's got four legs!"

His profiled mouth twitched.

"Well, that will just have to do."

The stiff back relaxed, and his face, pale as the moonlit
marble, turned to her at last. The twitch steadied into a
reluctant smile, and he pulled her hands away from her
belly and kissed them. "You're quite mad, you know."

"Naturally. I'd have to be to love the lot of you—though
I wouldn't put it past a son of Deymorin's to have four
legs. And we won't discuss the possibility of a tail.—Won't
you tell me about it, Khyel?"

"You mean he hasn't?"

She shook her head. "Insisted it was yours to tell, if you
cared to. He's trying not to interfere, Khyel, but he's very
worried."

He rested a leg on the rim of the fountain and trailed
his hand in the pool. Night-feeding fish rose to nibble at
his fingertips, flickering bits of moonlight reaching out to
touch god. "This is my favorite of all the House gardens.
Possibly of all the gardens in the City. I come here often."

"I'm not surprised. It's very like you."

She supposed the bitter tone to Mikhyel's responding laugh shouldn't have surprised her, but it did.

"Pale and insubstantial?" he asked.

"No, Khyel. Elegant, mysterious, best experienced in the shadows of life, not the bright daylight."

"You make me sound such a . . . cheery sort."

"And do you see yourself as cheery?"

"Hardly."

"Then why should others? I meant it as a compliment, my dear friend. My savior."

He twitched at that. Objecting, no doubt, to her putting any such label on an act he was determined to take as just another tick off of his duty list. Aloud, he simply said, "Then I shall take it as such and endeavor not to speculate further on its meaning."

"Ha!" she said, tiring of the game. "I know you better."

"Meaning?"

"You'll keep worrying at it, wondering what in your eighteen hells I meant, until it drives you mad, or you come to some exceedingly nasty interpretation of it, totally irrelevant to my original thought. I'm sorry I said anything."

She sniffed. Loudly.

He laughed. "All right, my not-quite-sister. Your point is made." He held out his hand. "Peace?"

She placed hers in it and squeezed, then, without letting him go: "Peace. What's your favorite spot? Preferably one with a place for a fat lady to sit down."

"Your wish, my not-the-least-bit-fat lady, is my pleasure." He led her, then, through a maze of marble and roses to a nook where the maze towered behind them, shielding their view of the house. The city lights stretched to the northeast, bright and vigorous along the Orenurn line, markedly subdued along the Khoratum line.

And there was, indeed, a bench of carved marble, in the form of some fantasy beast, shaped for comfort as well as whimsy.

"How long have you been coming here?"

"This spot? Probably since . . ." His brow tightened in

thought. "Since I was a child. I don't remember the first time. When we were in the City, if Mheric turned particularly unreasonable, I could avoid him here. But any of the gardens would suffice; he hated roses."

"Probably because he associated them with the City, and the City with Anheliaa."

"Most likely." But his voice indicated indifference, his eyes, pale as the moon itself, stared beyond the roses, beyond the City, to Khoratum's snow-covered cap glowing eerily in the moonlight. The mountain seemed to float above the shadowed foothills.

"And did Khoratum call to you even then?"

With a shuddering twitch, he was back with her. "Call? I don't understand."

"No?"

Try as he would to match her eye to eye, his gaze dropped first. "Possibly. I don't know that it calls me now, only that . . ."

"I ask again, my dear friend, the man in whom I would confide anything—was she very beautiful?"

From the silence that followed, she feared she had moved too soon, that not even his haunted garden would induce this strangely haunted man to open to her, then:

"I . . . can't answer that honestly. To me— I've never seen anything more— Was?" His eyes widened a bit. "What do you mean, was?"

"She died on the rings, didn't she?"

The panic disappeared behind a shadowed mask. "You mean Deymorin hasn't told you even that?"

"Deymorin said it was for you to explain. I was waiting, assuming when the time was right, you'd tell me. But the look on your face in there . . . I had to ask."

"Rings. Was it that obvious?"

"It was to me. I can't account for others." And when he didn't answer, she said quietly. "When the rumors came that Mikhyel dunMheric was making a fool of himself over a Khoratumin ringdancer, I was both thrilled and sad for you."

"Pity the poor fool," he said bitterly, and she let that hang heavily between them a moment before saying:

"I don't deserve that, Khyel."

He blinked. "No. No you don't."

His head bowed, a few strands of hair, slipped free of his braid, brushed his cheek, starkly black in the moonlight. Finally, his head lifted.

"I suppose you have a right to know." Another long pause as again those moonglow eyes drank in the distant mountain peak. "Temorii didn't die . . . at least not on the rings."

This man could pack more into what he didn't say by what he did than anyone she'd ever met.

"Yet you were surprised when I used the past tense. Did she die . . . some other way?"

"You could say, I killed her."

"Well I won't. Don't go dramatic on me, Khyel."

He blinked, broke away from the mountain and looked at her. "Fair enough. You asked was Dancer lovely. You've met her; you tell me."

"Dancer? *Mother's* Dancer? *That* was your Temorii?"

A single dip of his bearded chin.

"Oh, my . . ." It did add a twist. "I can well understand the attraction, then. She was quite distractingly lovely. It must have been quite the romantic reunion when you met again."

"I suppose it could have been, had I remembered anything about Boreton. But I didn't know about Dancer when I met . . . Temorii. I didn't find out about the connection with Boreton and Mother until—until well after I . . ."

"Fell in love with her?"

He didn't answer that, and his Barrister face was less revealing than the marble statues among the roses. "Until after I agreed to help her compete. Once in Khoratum, my infatuation with her proved a useful rumor."

"You're saying you didn't love her?"

"I perpetuated the rumor."

"In other words, you loved her." Which earned her an exasperated look. She shrugged. "I'm sorry, brother-to-be.

You can't have it both ways. You have to *know* what passion feels like before you can pretend to have it. When you left, you didn't know. When you returned, you did."

"You're very sure of yourself."

"It's obvious to anyone who knows you. Why do *you* think Thaalye continues to resist you?"

"She has more than reason enough."

"Only one reason that matters."

His pale eyes flickered, a flash of green odd in the cool moonlight.

"All *right,* Kiyrstin. I admit I loved her. I loved her to total distraction, to my own detriment, and to her death. *Now* are you happy?"

She shook her head slowly. "Not happy, no. But content that we can move on without the Barrister standing between us."

"What happened in Khoratum . . . it is the stuff of bad romance. We fell in love, resisted to the last moment. Made . . ." His throat worked in a hard swallow. "Made love the night before the competition." He shook his head. "I never meant it to happen. *Should* never have let it happen. I knew there could be no happy ending for us, that nothing could come of it—even if it didn't destroy her dance, even if I didn't plan to leave the moment she finished dancing."

"Without her?"

"Without her. We *couldn't* have a future. We were too different."

"Because she's a hiller?" She couldn't believe that of him. He was not so class conscious as that.

He shook his head. "Because . . . because above all, I'm the Barrister." Without giving her time to sort that out, he continued. "The rest . . . the rest rumor has pretty much right. Dancer competed and won. There really *was* no contest, even without the voting being rigged. But it was rigged, as we'd known all along, and a setup, and I waited too long to get out. I was trapped by my own stupidity. Dancer went back on the rings and . . . spun some magic the likes of which I can't describe. The audience, my guards . . . everyone, including myself, were frozen. Except Ganfrion—I swear, nothing shakes him. After Ganfrion got me out of the arena, Dancer escaped into the maze. Later, Gan found him there, saved him from Rhyys' men. Just before the final battle between Mother and Rhomatum, Mother leyapulted them out of the maze and into our camp. Or I did, if you believe Deymorin."

"Him?" Kiyrstin repeated, and recalling Mother's admonishment: *you would do well, Kiyrstine romGaretti, to question your own senses before you ridicule those of others. . . .*

But before she could speculate further:

"Or her. It seems you're free to take your pick. Tell me, Kiyrstin, does the term *Child of Rakshi* mean anything to you? Or is there someone else in this world as incredibly ignorant as myself?"

"Child of . . . oh my! Khyel, if it helps at all, it wouldn't have meant anything a year ago. Not even six months ago."

"Meaning Deymorin has been prepping you for this conversation."

"So it appears."

"I just wish he'd told you the rest of it."

"He's trying not to interfere, Khyel."

Mikhyel shrugged and stared back at the mountain.

"You said . . . he . . . Dancer . . . arrived in camp. Yet he didn't come to Rhomatum. Did you have a falling out?"

"Please, Kiyrstin," he said, his voice hoarse, "ask my brother. I don't *care* if you know, but don't ask me to explain it. It's . . . hard enough dealing with my own shortcomings. It's nothing to do with him. Only me."

"Oh, I'm certain on that point."

"How inspiring that my reputation is so solidly upheld," he said bitterly.

"Reputation, hell. You'll *hold* yourself responsible for everything bad that happens around you. Next, you'll be taking the blame for the ache in my back."

The muscle in his jaw jumped. She could practically hear his teeth grinding.

"Possibly," he acknowledged in no good grace. "But this

time the harm *was* my doing, *my* weakness alone. I had to leave. I couldn't run the risk of staying around him, of doing again to him what—"

"What Mheric did to you?" She had saved that knowledge, given to her in a moment of fear on Deymorin's part—fear for his brother's sanity. She'd held it back, let it loose now in the hope the violation of confidence wouldn't create a breach that never would heal.

His eyes closed, opened again with great deliberation.

"Not Mheric," he said in the continuing silence, "no."

"Care to talk about it?" she asked, sensing the point of danger had been passed.

"Not really."

"It worries Deymorin, you know."

"Rings, tell him to let it the hell go! *I* have. It's over and done with. Tell him— Tell him . . ." His whole body seemed to droop. "Tell him he has too vivid an imagination." He drew himself up and continued in a cold voice. "Tell him Mheric sought only to frighten and humiliate me . . . to break the willful streak he'd decided I'd inherited from Mother."

There was a silence, and while she let him remember, she wondered how any man who had raised Deymorin could consider Mikhyel willful. But Deymorin would have laughed in his father's face and done whatever he wanted. Mikhyel . . . Mikhyel would have argued his brother's right to do it. A man of action might well find such a child . . . willful.

"I remember . . ." Mikhyel continued softly, "One of the first things I remember was Mheric holding me upside down by one foot out the nursery window." And in a stronger, more pragmatic voice: "That was rather more thrilling than I wanted. I'd said no. He didn't like that word. As for Deymorin's rather obvious suspicions . . ." He shook his head. "He truly does worry too much. Mheric required me to perform for his friends on occasion—in a variety of ways. But I was never . . ." His jaw tightened and his gaze flickered toward her and as quickly away. "Mheric wanted certain high-stakes agreements—badly; dunHaulpin wanted me—badly." He paused, and then, as if he were a witness giving sworn testament clarified: "Actually, he wanted Nikki badly. He agreed to compromise with my inferior self."

"*Nikki?* Nikki would have been, what? Four years old!"

"He was as large for his age as I was undersized. And he was fresh. Untouched." Mikhyel's voice vibrated with bitter anger. "Mheric put him on display regularly—just . . . brought him out to play—to remind me, I suppose, of my agreement, and what would happen to Nikki should I give him trouble." His eyes caught and held hers this time. "For the love of your own sweet Maurii, you asked and I'm trusting you. *Don't* tell Deymorin that. *Ever.* There's no one left. No one for his vengeance. Even dunHaulpin has paid for his sins . . . quite equitably."

"I promise, Khyel. I do promise. But I warn you it's no more than he suspects."

"Then I'm amazed at his restraint." The Barrister returned in full. "The long and short of it is that dunHaulpin signed the agreement for Mheric and I was to fulfill Mheric's side of the bargain on my thirteenth birthday. I'd be officially out of the nursery, then, you see, and legally able to agree to such a proceeding. Naturally, Mheric would make certain I agreed."

"And that's when you fought your father and he nearly killed you."

"Instead he died."

"Of a fall from a horse he'd trained. And because of that beating, you went to Barsitum and gained Raulind. There does seem a sort of symmetry of justice in that, doesn't there, Barrister?"

A faint smile rewarded her. "You do have a way of cutting to the heart of a matter, Shepherdess."

"Don't answer that!" She waited, and when he failed to continue, prompted: "Justice, you say."

"With my father gone, the agreement fell through. Later that year—after I'd recovered—Anheliaa wanted dunHaulpin's support on a different matter. So I got it for her."

"Sweet Maurii." Her breath deserted her for a moment.

"I was . . . rather naive to make the agreement. I didn't think it mattered. Couldn't imagine anything worse than Mheric."

Naive, indeed, for all his innocence had been shattered years before. Yet she hadn't been much older than thirteen when she'd been handed over to Garetti. She'd been innocent, but hardly naive. Mauritumin children of her status were raised to understand matters of both state and reproduction.

"I thought I was over it." The Barrister remained coldly in control, and the hand she touched was warm and relaxed. "I even thought—when Temorii and I came together, I thought perhaps I had a chance to be a normal, loving man after all. But I learned . . . things from my life I'd rather not have known. And later, with Anheliaa's help, I discovered—I discovered I'm capable of great cruelty, Kiyrstin. Mindless, selfish cruelty. I . . . I hurt Dancer that final night in camp."

"Physically?"

He nodded, and his eyes were distant. "There was blood . . . gods, there was blood everywhere." He blinked, and was back with her. "That's an exaggeration. Forgive me. But yes, I hurt him. He made me angry. He sees himself as Thyerri, wants me to love Thyerri—is quite aggressively insistent that I both accept Thyerri and reject Temorii. The damnable truth is, a part of me loved that aggression of his. A part of me, if I'm honest, loved that trait in Temorii as well. But . . . with Temorii, something *tempered* my worst side. If I'm around *him*, if *Thyerri* insists again, rings, Kiyrstin, I'll hurt him again. I can't face that."

It was difficult to argue such a heartfelt notion.

"You said Dancer insisted you both accept Thyerri and reject Temorii," she said slowly, feeling her way carefully. "Were I Dancer, I'd insist rather that you accept *both* Thyerri and Temorii."

He twitched; she'd hit a live nerve with that and followed quickly with, "And yet you were the one who ran, not Dancer."

"And if, the next time I don't? *Can't?* I could have killed him. Would have, to get him to admit defeat."

"I don't believe that."

"I do. My leaving gave him his chance to exit gracefully. He took it."

"And not a day goes by that you don't regret it."

"Not a day goes by that I haven't feared he'd call me back, that I'd lack the strength to resist, and finish the destruction of us both. Tonight—" He looked again out toward that distant peak. "Tonight, I learned that Dancer has been working with Ganfrion. He hasn't left. He never left." Another of those painfully hard swallows. "Tonight Deymorin told me where he is. I very much fear that's the most dangerous piece of information I've ever . . ." He held up his hand, and his eyes acquired that distraction she knew meant he was in contact with one or both of his brothers. "It's time. Lidye is gathering her 'special attendees.' We have to go in."

Damn, she thought. Lidye's cursed timing. He had come that close.

And fear filled those moonglow eyes.

§ § §

Without Zelin as guide, Thyerri would have been lost in a handful of turns: it was not the Khoratum Tower Dancer had known. Even in the areas untouched by the battle, all the reliable signposts had vanished. Gone were the trinkets in every nook and cranny, stolen, Zelin said, in the looting aftermath of the battle; gone were the garish tapestries depicting fantastical Kirish'lani tales, ripped down, Zelin said, and destroyed, on Rhyys' own order, without thought for the months of labor involved in their making, without a reference to the tantrums Rhyys had thrown if a face was poorly depicted or a hair color wrong.

And the design, the mathematically rigid placement of rooms, all dictated by Anheliaa at the time of the building of the complex, a placement held in near religious awe by the Rhyys he had known, was gone. In its place, Zelin and the other workmen had created a warren of rooms nearly as convoluted as the radical dance maze. Hiller workmen's doing, not Rhyys'. This Rhyys hadn't cared.

That observation alone should have been enough evidence to take to Ganfrion, Thyerri thought, as he followed Zelin deeper into the building. Regardless of who rumor thought ruled here, it was not the Rhyys who had ruled before that fateful night. Scarface, perhaps. Perhaps that charred body that had been tossed from the Tower had not been Scarface, but Rhyys. For all he knew, a Mauritumin priest's Talent might well extend to tricks of the eye.

Or perhaps it was the shell of Rhyys that lived and ruled here, but not the essence; perhaps Rhyys' mind had been damaged that night and the stench that permeated the node was a reflection of that damaged, but still Talented essence.

If that were credibly the case, he should leave immediately, should get that truth to Rhomandi before he walked into something he couldn't walk out of. But somehow he could not follow that sensible path. Zelin was willing to help him tonight; tomorrow he might not be, because Zelin was mortally frightened of this Rhyys, and that, too, was not within the proper pattern.

And so, he followed Zelin deeper and deeper into this maze of tunnels and rooms and hallways, learning the lay of the new corridors with a mind trained to hold not only the convolutions of the dancer's maze, but the shifting patterns of Mother's caverns as well. That was all he sought at this time: knowledge so that he might come here on his own and observe this non-Rhyys at some leisure and with a better chance to plan.

Whatever, or whoever, the man passing as Rhyys really was, he had no desire to be brought to the attention of any ringmaster.

For all it was late and the tower complex silent and dark, for all Zelin insisted there were guards only at Rhyys' own door and in the chamber deep below where an entire new set of rings lay cooling, Thyerri moved cautiously, avoiding so much as eye contact with anyone they met. Over the course of four years, he'd spent many months in and around the Tower, and while the apprentice dancers tended to dwell in limbo, revered but not obeyed, neither servant nor master . . . while he doubted even the longtime residents of the Tower, such as were left, would be able to lay name to him . . . the luck that would let him pass those longtime residents completely unnoticed would take more of Rakshi's favor than he cared to test.

In company with Zelin, however, and dressed in Zelin's spare uniform, with his provocative hair hidden beneath Zelin's cap, he moved with fair anonymity, particularly as the handful of servants still about were interested only in completing their tasks and getting to bed.

As they passed from room to room, Zelin said nothing, asked nothing, confining his role to trail-guide. It was, so Zelin claimed, Zelin's way of helping without helping. What Zelin didn't know, he couldn't reveal.

And by that admission, Zelin revealed the depth of his fear and the conditions he had accepted to survive here.

They were headed for the source of that fear: that room where Rhyys habitually gathered the staff to observe whatever disciplinary actions he'd decided were necessary.

They'd moved into a part of the complex cut into the mountain itself, a part Thyerri did know, intimately, though he'd never physically been here, for he'd felt it from Mother's cavern often enough. The Ley reached physical strands toward the surface here . . . capillaries rising to touch the light of the sun, or perhaps toward the stars. One never knew with the Ley.

The walls here were irregular, partly human-hewn, partly natural, for capillaries of the Ley regenerated quickly, built, and vanished on a whim. He could just see them, in the darkest shadows. He followed one of those shadows deeper into the hill, pressed his hands to the faint green strands and closed his eyes, stretching his essence along those strands. And he smelled . . .

"Thyerri?"

"This one goes all the way to the surface," he whispered back.

"How . . ."

"I smell the night air."

"Lad, you're a strange one. C'mon."

They passed other strands he suspected might lead out, but when he tried to stop and check, Zelin pulled him on.

"You want to go cave-walking, do it on your own time. I hate this place. The lamps just aren't enough."

Thyerri smiled into the dark that was less and less dark to him. The Ley was weak, very weak, here, but its warmth and energy seeped in through his very pores, nonetheless. He fed back that energy, encouraging the strands to greater effort, warming them with his own essence, and the glow increased, the soft golden glow of fall, easing the shadows, even for Zelin—

—who stopped short.

"What in—" Zelin cast a suspicious glance back at him. "That better be your doing!"

Thyerri grinned.

Zelin muttered something about Tamshi eyes, and hurried down the passage.

"Here." Zelin stopped beside a door, and, with a quick glance about, tried the bolt. It moved, silently, easily, swung just wide enough for them to slip through.

And in that instant Thyerri knew they'd made a deadly mistake.

In that instant, the walls about them began to glow, seething a green and sickly brown where it should be golden at this time of year.

"Get out!"

"What?" Zelin asked, dumbfounded.

The walls reached palpable tendrils toward his essence. "Out!" he shouted, and shoved Zelin back out the way they'd come.

But at the first branching, he grabbed Zelin's arm and pulled him deeper into the mountain.

"Thyerri, for the love of the Mother, that's the wrong—"

But that way, Zelin's way, lay the source of those tendrils. He pulled harder, racing into the dark, Zelin protesting all the way, but keeping pace now. Thyerri poured his energy into the Ley, begging for light, knew himself for a fool when those vile tendrils used that need to wind their way into his mind.

A branching: one way dead-ended in a cavern, the other still smelled of the outside. He sped toward the outside and on to another branching that had possibilities, and another and another. They ran until they could run no farther, until they both had to stop to ease their heaving lungs.

Still that putrid essence followed. And others came now: Rhyys' human hounds. Just as they'd chased him in the radical maze.

Panic threatened. He shoved fear aside, then risked everything, throwing his essence into the Ley, and seeking—

"This way." He pulled Zelin into the darkest tunnel, down through a hole that dropped them a body-length and more straight down onto uneven surface. He staggered with the landing, steadied Zelin, then poured himself into those capillaries, seeking the surface, isolating a route, then begging for light.

"Go!" he said to Zelin. "This leads to the surface." He hoped it did, hoped the light here went all the way. If it did not, he sent Zelin to his death.

Better that than what waited behind them.

"Thyerri, I can't leave you—"

"You must! You must go!" He could scarcely form the words past the tendrils' choking touch. Fear such as he'd never known filled his mind, as whatever dwelled in that sickened essence reached for him. "He *knows* I'm here, but I don't think he's noticed you yet. He's distracted, for the moment. I'll keep him that way." Panic flared through his nerves, sending waves of red and orange through the nearby capillaries. "The ley threads will glow for you as far as I can feel, but I don't know for how long. You can *smell* the night from the end. Follow it!"

"I'm not leaving you!"

"Don't be a fool! He's coming after me, and he *will* find me." The tendrils of foreign, putrescent ley-stuff wove deeper, contracting, choking, drawing him. "Please, Zelin—

go! Get to the Rhomandi. Tell him—tell him the Barrister's Child of Rakshi sent you, and Rhyys is not Rhyys."

"Not—? Who—"

. . . back. Back to the Room. Back to—

"*Scarface.* Tell him remember Mother and not to trust his eyes or his ears. Tell him Rhyys died, not romMaurii. Now, in the name of the Mother—*go!*"

"I'm sorry, Thyerri-lad. I'll do everything I can . . ."

He heard the sounds now of running feet, or felt them through the now-living stone.

"*Go!*"

Zelin gripped his arm in friendship, then disappeared down that glowing corridor. Thyerri followed a different track a handful of heartbeats later, fighting now for each stride. A gap in the glow showed him a side tunnel, dark, not on Zelin's line to the surface. He took that offered path, pouring more and more into the Ley to light it, to draw Scarface's men after him.

And with each touch of his feet on the stone, his essence spun down the tendrils, flowing toward that vile essence. There was the source, he now realized, of Mother's pollution. Vision failed. Stone slammed into his face. The narrow tunnel walls held him upright. Ley fingers found purchase and hauled. Escape was any gain against that pull.

And then there was nothing. Only the pull.

No stone. No glow. No tunnel. And he was tumbling free, flying among the rings, even while the pull drew him back.

After that fall there was only darkness.

Chapter Ten

"And so, ladies and gentlemen, as you can see, the difficult part has been done." Lidye's most perfect smile rested gently on her face, and Deymorin felt Nikki, standing next to him in the north window bay of the ringchamber, tense. "My brother-in-law, the Princeps, has come into his own at last. Once again, Rhomatum will be blessed with a true Rhomandi, Ringmaster and Princeps in one. I hope you will all join me in wishing him well, indeed."

And she began to clap, fingertips to fingertips, so delicate, so perfect . . . she made Deymorin's teeth ache. And the others seated in the concentric rows of chairs, those whose faces held the look of ill-contained reverence, joined her, a rhythmic applause which she ceased to lead in order to hold her hand out in invitation.

"Deymorin?"

It was not his choice to be here in the first place, less to be put on display by Lidye in such a fashion, but he could hardly politely deny that hand and maintain the façade of household tranquillity on Nikki's night. He could hardly keep her from slipping it through his arm, and pressing lightly against his shoulder, the very image of familial equanimity.

They'd left the majority of the guests dancing, left to knowing cheers of well-wishing: Lidye had made no secret of her plans for the evening. Neither had she bothered to clarify that those plans were no longer as advertised in the invitation. She had simply, at the appointed hour, made the announcement in the ballroom, and led the parade of the Chosen up to the Tower.

The anger left unresolved before the party started had clearly festered in her. He could feel it here in the ring-chamber, as clearly if she shouted it to him.

Nikki had been right to worry; she planned something.

"And now, ladies and gentlemen, our final surprise for the evening." She tightened her hold on his arm. He seethed at her, even as he knew that to pull free would be to cause more comment than he cared to raise.

{Hold,} Khyel's voice whispered, and Nikki's joined them. The link snapped into place, strong and vital, here at the heart of the power umbrella.

Lidye's hand jerked. She'd caught that linkage. But her fair demeanor didn't waver; she made a grand gesture to the invited press and social elite. "My dear brother-in-law, your Princeps, has chosen this moment to stake his claim to the Rings. He raised the new rings last night, because he feared for the safety of those assembled here should he make a misstep. As you can see, an unwarranted fear, under the circumstances. But now . . . Ladies and gentlemen, your ringmaster."

She released him, then, and stepped back, the look on her face challenging him to deny her words, to make public to all these influential people their private disagreements.

{Deymorin?} Mikhyel asked, and the unspoken thought wondered what he wanted to do.

{Not surprised, are you, Barrister? She was bound to try and humiliate me, and this is the obvious tactic. She doesn't think I can do it.}

{So?}

{I think . . . let's give it a try. First, let's take her punch away.} He continued aloud. "My friends, what my dear sister-in-law has failed to tell you is that, in my attempt to raise the rings in the most rational manner, she informs me that I unwittingly performed a beginner's mistake." The last thing Lidye would expect was candor. "You see, according to custom, these two rings should have gone up separately. Now that I've allowed the Khoratum/Persitum ring to stabilize in an orbit not its own, it's just possible that we might have to bring the lot down in a controlled fashion in order to raise them again."

A dismayed murmur rippled about the seated guests. Deymorin raised a soothing hand.

"I said it's possible. One of the things that any spinner can tell you, if they would be so honest, is that everything they do is based on gut instinct. Frightening, after a fashion, isn't it?"

He grinned. Lidye was horrified. But he'd never liked the subterfuge about the Towers: Khyel had said it was time for the knowledge to become more general—

{Not *this* way, brother!}

He grinned across the room at his lawyer brother. "If not now, brother, when?"

As one, heads turned toward Mikhyel, who had his Barrister's face well and firmly set, then attention veered anxiously back to him.

And the rumors about the Triumvirate most clearly took another twist.

Deymorin propped himself comfortably against Anheliaa's movable chair and continued. "But don't let it worry you. There's nothing different about the process now than what it's been for the last three hundred years, and a thousand before that in Mauritum. The only reason I bring it up to you is because *my* instincts said to raise those two rings together. I was inclined to trust those instincts. And since my sister-in-law, in a fit of humor, has elected to put me in this position in view of you all, I'm inclined to put those instincts to the test again. I make no promises, but . . . hell, why not? —Brothers?"

And at the same moment, he reached out to them, he raised his arms high above his head, stretching, seeking that flow with his fingertips. He could almost feel . . . almost, but not quite—

{Kiyrstin?} he called and Mikhyel's thought came: {Aloud, Deymorin.}

He reached a hand blindly for where she'd been, knew the instant she rose and moved toward him, seeming to know . . .

"Kiyrsti," he whispered, the moment she took his hand, and he felt her lean close. "Pull me to Mauritum . . ."

"JD. I don't . . ."

"Stand on his west side, Kiyrstin," Mikhyel's voice said, and he felt himself twisted, felt her connection to that Place in the World drawing him. {Deymorin!}

And Mikhyel had his other hand, and Mikhyel instinctively pulled toward Khoratum, toward a pattern that held . . . affinity for him.

{Yes-s-s-s-s . . .} He felt the flow, subtle, but true, regular as a heartbeat, a heartbeat unique to that line.

And he felt Nikki behind him, without needing to touch, holding his base here in Rhomatum, providing the pivotal point. His own Cardinal . . .

The ring had to go . . . there and there. One . . . Two . . . One . . . Two . . . But the beat of the Shatum/Giephaetum line overpowered that beat, caught his heart and tried to impose it on the Khoratum/Persitum line.

The ring would not move. He felt Lidye's burning disbelief. Felt Lidye's scorn. Knew Lidye had come up to him and physically laid a hand on his chest. She was driving doubt and uncertainty into him the way a syringe filled a blood vein with mind-warping drugs.

"Ganfrion!" Mikhyel's voice called. "The lady Lidye looks pale. Please remove her."

The hand left, the doubts left Deymorin's mind.

And still the ring wouldn't move. There was about that refusal a hint of fire-blossom tea. And honey.

Anheliaa's damned legacy. He was fighting Anheliaa's damned wishes that everything be done *her* way.

"Dammit!" Deymorin shouted, then: {Rhomatum! Dammit, Rhomatum, help us out here!}

In the next beat, Mikhyel's call joined his.

In the next after that, he was falling.

The ground arrived suddenly, but not painfully.

Deymorin stumbled to his feet, wondering, as he stood buck naked among the leythium-lace draperies, if he was indeed here, physically in the caverns, or only here in some dream sense. Wondered if he'd return to the Tower to stand among those stolid citizens in this rather humbling lack of—

{Welcome, son of . . .}

Puzzlement. That struck him before he spun toward the slight swish of tail against earth and stone.

Long and elegant, beautiful in its shimmering, exotic way, scales that glittered in the leylight emanating from the bubbling pools. Fanged jaws, hands and feet webbed and clawed, a long tail that rippled with a life all its own . . . though he'd seen it before, the creature that was Rhomatum incarnate still had the ability to take his breath away.

{You're not the one who called. Where is-s-s-s he?}

Mikhyel. Mikhyel whom these ley-creatures seemed determined to consume wholesale. Mikhyel, who was with him now, but who had not been with him all summer . . . Mikhyel, who had actively and by his own admission, *not* wanted to make contact with the Ley . . . not until he'd wanted the creature's help to find Mirym.

"My brother's busy," he answered Rhomatum abruptly. He felt little awe, none of Mikhyel's fascination, the fascination which more than once had threatened to hold his brother here timeless and thoughtless in the depths of the world.

He wanted one thing only from this creature—power.

{But I don't want you,} Rhomatum informed him.

Mikhyel had argued eloquently with the creature. He hadn't Mikhyel's way with words. He had never had Mikhyel's way with words, and damned if he'd worry about achieving Mikhyel's way with words now.

"We're trying to set that damned ring, Ley Father. Lidye's stopping us. You said I should be commanding them. Well, so, I'm trying, but she's got just a bit of practice on me. It's now or never, Rhomatum, so unless you *like* the taste of Lidye, unless you want her calling the shots up there, I suggest you help us, no matter which flavor of Rhomandi you prefer."

Instantly power was all about him, raw and intoxicating. He'd felt it flowing through Nikki the night of the rebellion.

And he could sense a trickle of ley-stuff rising to oppose it even now, a trickle that smelled faintly of honey.

Fire-blossom tea and honey: according to Mikhyel, the scent of Anheliaa within the Web. Yet he suspected Lidye as the instigator of that honey-scented trickle. He suspected Lidye drew on the power now to hold the one misset ring in its incorrect orbit. But hers was a minor draw: she needed very little help to hold one ring in a stable, safe orbit that, at the moment, it preferred to maintain.

She fought to counter his efforts. He needed to match her efforts to break that hold, plus provide the energy necessary to the rings to shift that orbit, and *then* he needed to convince the damned ring it would rather be elsewhere.

To do that, he needed power. He wanted the power to break that hold, and to shift that orbit, and he was going to get that power from Rhomatum.

{Will you, now?} Rhomatum asked.

"Damned right, I will."

{Then take it,} Rhomatum said, with a fluid shrug.

"Just like that."

{I told you before, I have nothing to do with the rings. I do not control them, they do not control me. You desire power to move them . . . take it. And then leave me in peace. I want none of you.}

Which might well explain how Lidye could be drawing now, as he sensed she was, without knowing the creatures.

"Yet you helped Mikhyel."

{To move rings? No. Mikhyel wanted. Mikhyel took. I followed. My argument was with my bud.}

"Fine." Great help. Mikhyel wanted. Mikhyel took.

Deymorin dropped to his knees beside a pool, felt the radiant energy filling his pores.

Liquid leythium ate the flesh off a man's bones: that was common knowledge. Yet he'd seen his brother healed by the Barsitumin pools, had seen Mikhyel plunge his hand into the hypogeum pools of Rhomatum with impunity.

And from then on, Mikhyel had been . . . connected to the Ley.

He looked up, met the creature's enigmatic gaze. As cold as the Barrister's, it was.

{Deymorin?} Mikhyel's voice queried, and Nikki's followed, and he realized he'd walled them out, that barrier of his, solid as stone.

{Here.}

A moment's confusion, then confirmation: bodily, he was still in the Tower; in another sense, he was a thousand feet below it.

And, holding the creature's gaze, he thrust his hand into the pool.

{No!} Protests from first one brother, then the next.

Searing pain.

Rejection.

{Brothers,} he called calmly, shutting that pain out of his mind, continuing to hold that facet-eyed gaze: {set that damned ring now, if you please.}

And he felt the draw, knew both his brothers—no, it was *Nikki* who took that energy and channeled it toward that ring. Through Nikki's eyes, or perhaps even his own, he watched the ring begin to glow, to shimmer and shake, saw the radical whip through and rear back, like a cobra—

Somewhere, Lidye screamed . . . and the resistance ended.

{Nikki, the radical! Fill the radical!} Deymorin shouted past the pain he could no longer keep confined. Nikki's mind recoiled from that raw agony, filled with concern for him—and Mikhyel ignored them both and took control of the flow.

A subtle twist, a redirection smooth as thought. The shimmer left the Khoratum/Persitum ring, and the radical began to glow.

{It's yours now, Deymio,} Mikhyel whispered, and Mikhyel's cool mind slipped around his and cut him off from the pain of his hand. {You're right. The radical is the key to change. The ring itself isn't.} Confirming it, there came flashes from Mikhyel, of times with Anheliaa, of passing comments making sense. {It's like a child, Deymio. A recalcitrant, mischievous child, that plays with life and death daily.} More flashes. Of another radical. Human, but still filled with that dangerous playfulness.

And there were two ways to deal with a radical, Mikhyel's mind knew but didn't say. Try to force it into the mold you desired . . . that was Anheliaa's way. Set it free . . . that was Mikhyel's desired choice.

Or, dammit, Deymorin thought, you could let go and play its game.

And looking out through Mikhyel's eyes, Deymorin saw that flitting, mocking radical, and thought toward it, supreme nonchalance, {You know, I don't really give a damn if that ring shifts or not. Let Lidye win and see how long the Rings keep spinning.}

The radical reared back . . . he could almost imagine serpent eyes on the front end of that ribbon. Then it swirled back on itself and coiled around the Khoratum/Persitum ring. Deymorin caught the heartbeat of the Khoratum/Persitum line again, found the angle toward the distant towns, and said to it,

{Now would probably be a good time, but I really don't give a shit.}

And the ring shifted, smooth as butter, into the new orbit.

§   §   §

"Deymorin?" Mikhyel's smooth voice was the first—human—sound Kiyrstin had heard in the room since Lidye's removal, and Kiyrstin, taking her cue from Deymorin's brother, murmured: "JD?"

The audience sat in stunned silence.

The energy that had filled the room only moments ago was gone now. The radical streamer had slipped free of the Khoratum/Persitum ring and begun its usual, free-spirited flitting.

And still Deymorin's mind seemed locked in the heights—or more likely in this case, the depths—of whatever hell he'd entered to force that ring into the orbit it now so calmly pursued; beyond the one expletive, he'd said nothing, only gripped Kiyrstin's hand to the point of pain. His set expression had revealed nothing to her, but that painful grip told her a different story. Mikhyel's face, more revealing under the circumstances, had implied concern, but confidence, and on that evidence, she had based her trust.

Certainly the manifestations of whatever battle the brothers had fought had been sufficiently impressive for the assembled audience.

But now Mikhyel, at least, and Nikki, whose hand appeared on Deymorin's shoulder, were free of that trance into which they'd fallen.

"Khyel?" she murmured urgently, alone among strangers, and he looked at her, his expression puzzled, as if he expected a response he wasn't getting. "Speak to me, Khyel."

He shook his head, not in denial, but as if to clear it. "Forgive me, Kiyrstin. He's still down there. He's . . . reluctant to pull his hand from the pool."

As if that should make sense to her. But it would soon enough. And if Mikhyel's arguments wouldn't pull her Deymorin free of the leythium morass, she had arguments to try.

She laid her free hand on Deymorin's cheek, still smooth from his pre-party grooming. His head turned easily, but his eyes stared far beyond anything in this room.

She leaned forward and kissed him, lightly at first, then harder as his mouth opened and his sudden inhalation took her breath away. His hand freed hers, and his strong arm wrapped around her, drawing her into a desperate hug that threatened her ribs.

And laughter rippled through the audience, a much needed release of tension.

"'Ware Junior," she whispered against Deymorin's mouth, and after a brief delay that revealed to her in more than words how far his mind still wandered, his hold eased.

One hand left her completely, and she leaned back to find him staring at that hand in disbelief.

"I was sure I'd lost it," he whispered, and Mikhyel's touch descended on his back, cautioning.

"Ladies and gentlemen," Mikhyel announced. "As you can see, the attempt was quite outstandingly successful, if rather more spectacular than we anticipated. We have just discovered there are forces even now willing us not to succeed." He set his hand openly on Deymorin's shoulder. "They have been reminded, once again, that the Triumvirate is a force to be reckoned with and that Deymorin Rhomandi dunMheric is indeed the proper master of Rhomatum Tower."

"Oh, stuff it, Barrister." Deymorin stood up, and stretched. "Done is done. The damned thing's going, so let's get out of here. There's a party going on downstairs, and I, for one, want to get back to it. —Happy birthday, brother." He turned and held his hand out to Nikki . . .

Then froze, staring at his own hand as he had when he first woke up. He stared until Nikki grasped it, wrist to wrist, and broke him free of whatever image that sight had conjured.

ଚ୍ଚ ଚ୍ଚ ଚ୍ଚ

Spirits were high as Mikhyel shepherded the guests out of the ringchamber, Deymorin's own casual, even jocular acceptance of his accomplishment apparently striking a willing resonance in the minds of those still trying to sort out what they'd witnessed . . . and not wishing to believe they had ever been in any personal danger.

Lidye had invited them . . . and been invited out.

And it was not, Mikhyel knew, an assumed nonchalance on Deymorin's part. Deymorin truly did feel he'd done nothing particularly noteworthy. Deymorin accepted gladly the fact that he'd not, as he'd feared, lost his hand as a result of his actions, but he'd sunk it into the ley pool prepared for that possibility. It had been a necessary baptism for a ringmaster, was the way Deymorin thought of it.

For the rest, Deymorin had accepted responsibility for

the Rings, and getting the damned things spinning was part of that job.

Mikhyel could believe that in his brother. Deymorin had never held Anheliaa in awe, had never considered ringspinning any greater a talent (and perhaps less of a talent) than horse-training. And that very lack of reverence had been transmitted quite clearly to all and sundry tonight.

Including—or perhaps, most particularly—the radical streamer.

But if Deymorin lacked reverence, he did *not* lack respect for the job he'd assumed, and Mikhyel had every reason to trust that his brother would now pursue his spinning with the same dogged determination, the same desire for perfection, with which he had pursued the training of his horses.

And with the same confidence that his way was the true and right way.

He noted Deymorin's quiet conference with the monitors who would be sitting in the Tower for the balance of the night, and registered the startled relief on the lead monitor's face when he felt his brother reach to her mind and make a gentle contact.

"If it doesn't maintain once I'm out of the room," he heard Deymorin murmur, "I'll come back. I'm quite certain it's a healthy orbit, but I'm not expecting you to shoulder the responsibility for my over-confidence."

"I trust that won't be necessary. It feels very good, very stable, m'lord Rhomandi."

Deymorin gave a wry grin. He did so hate the honorifics that came his way. "Nonetheless, I'll keep in touch."

So casually said. The contact so casually made. They all of them had passed some boundary of comprehension, were beginning to use their abilities without thought—a realization that was, in itself, enough to cause Mikhyel some concern. The power they wielded could never be taken casually.

He held back, playing host to the last out the door, while his brothers mingled in the midst of the procession back to the ball room.

But there was a major piece of business left at loose ends. When he followed, he turned at the first landing and headed not for the ballroom but upstairs instead, to Lidye's room.

ெ   ெ   ெ

Ganfrion was waiting for Mikhyel outside Lidye's door, along with two armed guards.

"I take it you got the ring spinning," was Ganfrion's observation, and Mikhyel nodded. "She's been noisy in there. Then she shut up real fast, half an hour or so ago."

The scream . . . just before the rings had gone into secure orbits. "I'm not surprised."

"Fighting with you, was she?"

He nodded, first in acknowledgment, then toward the door. "Locked?"

Ganfrion nodded.

He tapped on the door. "Lidye, unlock the door, please."

"Go away!"

"Not likely. You know that. We can do this the easy way, or we can call talkative workmen and have the locks removed. Either way, you will talk to me tonight, and without the door between us."

A curse, then the thud of the bolt being thrown. The door swung open.

"Come in, then, you arrogant bastard." She flung herself about, her jeweled party dress a glittering swirl in the leylight.

He stepped through; Ganfrion made as if to follow, and Mikhyel shook his head. "Not yet. The door will remain unlocked, and I'll call if I need you."

It was not a happy gorMikhyel, but a resigned one. Ganfrion dipped his head, but muttered, "Just don't wait until too late, hear me, Suds? And *don't* drink the wine."

"I hear you. On the other hand, I don't think she's about to try anything tonight. Unless I miss my bet, she has one hell of a headache."

Ganfrion nodded and closed the door behind him.

"Well, dunMheric?" Lidye was in true voice tonight, low and angry, and he saw no reason to play word games with her.

"You do realize you have just abdicated any right ever to enter the ringchamber again."

"You wouldn't dare."

"You haven't the power, madam, to back any threats, as we have just proven, so I suggest you cease right now to make them."

Her very lack of rejoinder confirmed that she did, indeed, realize her deficiencies had been revealed. She settled on a vanity stool, to all appearances calmly accepting the reality.

He was not such a fool as to believe appearances.

"So, dunMheric, what now?"

"You lost up there. You lost the Rings, you lost completely the high-powered support you sought. It was a gamble, and a big one. It depended on Deymorin failing. You did your best to convince him that he must fail: you and I both know how much controlling the Rings depends upon the utter confidence that one *can* do something. Unfortunately for you, all you did was reveal how ignorant you are of Deymorin's character."

"Am I ignorant?"

A hint of fire-blossom tea and honey brushed his mind; he swept it aside with repugnance and consciously blocked out that attempt to use the Rings to unnerve *him* with one of the few things that ran along his nerves. "It won't work on me, either. Not with Deymorin, not with myself. So now you have a choice, madam. You may pull back, become a model wife to Nikki, go back downstairs with the guests and play the social game. More, you can acknowledge your actions upstairs were ill-considered and apologize profusely to everyone you meet—"

"Never!"

"Or you are welcome to go into seclusion here. Permanently. Either way, you will not be allowed near the Tower ever again."

The heat that flared from her corner, this time definitely

ring-carried, momentarily blinded his inner eye. She called on the power quite well, it seemed, once the Rings were up, a fair-weather ringmaster but *not* one that would stand in storm. She had, in fact, failed under assault in the Tower, and again here, as he slapped that attempt aside.

"My *father* will have something to say about this," she hissed. "Mine is a marriage of alliance, of state . . ."

"If you want to enter into that arena, best you think again, remembering again who drafted the agreement. Your performance upstairs has put your already shaky public image into a spinning plummet. I lack the evidence to bring criminal charges against you—your crimes are of such a nature, the law has never addressed them. But they were witnessed. Civilly, I have more than sufficient grounds to annul that marriage contract and disgrace you *and* your family, which would not be to the disadvantage of your numerous political rivals in Shatum. I don't want to do that, but believe me, I will not hesitate to do so, should you push me to it."

"Oh, I do believe you. Anheliaa trained you very well, and left me to reap the benefits."

"I remind you: Anheliaa trained you as well. *I'm* not willing to be Anheliaa's posthumous puppet, certainly not for a ringmaster who can't deal with the Rings. What you make of your reputation henceforward is for you to decide." He gave that a few moments to sink in, then: "Well? Which will it be? Exile? Or public apology?"

She rose smoothly to her feet. "Hardly a choice, is it?"

He stood back and let her precede him to the door.

Chapter Eleven

The party was over, the guests either gone home or bedded down somewhere in the vast Rhomandi House, and his glowing youngest brother had last been seen staggering down a hallway, singing at the top of his lungs.

In the privacy of the Princeps' bath, steam rose from the smaller of the two pools, water warm enough for comfort, but tempered to a near-term mother's comfort and safety. Himself, Deymorin was for the exhilarating chill of the larger pool.

He hung his robe on a hook and made for the pool's edge.

"So, tell me, JD," Kiyrstin said as she hung her robe beside his. "Now that you've proven you're the master here, when are you going to call Dancer to Rhomatum and put an end to the rest of this nonsense?"

Having already committed, Deymorin finished his dive into the bath, before spluttering:

"Wonderful sense of timing, Shepherdess."

"Naturally. Going to answer? Or avoid the question?"

"It's none of my business, Kiyrstin. I hope I've learned that much."

"And your timing couldn't be— Oh, my . . ." Kiyrstin left the insult hanging on a sigh as she lowered her body into the swirling, heated water of the sitting pool, "My, my, my. You Rhomatumin are a hedonistic lot."

Deymorin chuckled and stroked his way to the barrier between the pools, felt the shock of changing temperatures as he slithered over the barrier, then ducked under to come up face to her belly. He nuzzled his way to the surface air,

running his palms up her sides, over her full breasts and
along her arms to clasp her hands and hold them prisoner
against the tiles, while he found and held her mouth for a
breathless moment.

"Don't let the secret out," he whispered, and transferred
his attention to her neck, laying his body against hers, riding the current's ebb and flow, letting the water do the
hard work, reminding her just how hedonistic this particular
Rhomatumin was.

"Hmm . . ." Her hum vibrated against his mouth as she
relaxed beneath him, "Wouldn't dream of it."

He chuckled and bit her ear, she retaliated with a knee
applied gently to flesh drifting rather farther below the water's surface. They'd worked out how to enjoy one another
despite the third party necessarily sharing the procedure. It
had become an ongoing challenge to the game that was
such a pleasant addition to their love. Hedonistic, indeed,
but their love was more than sex and gained nuances with
each passing day. He released her hands, and they slithered
around his neck to draw him close.

He was ready for a snuggle—now. After they'd left the
ringchamber, it had been quite another story; he'd been
overflowing with energy. He'd requested one lively country
dance after another, pausing between each only long
enough to kiss Kiyrstin and seek a fresh partner.

Not bad for a man supposedly crippled for life.

It had set a tone for the rest of the evening, a tone that
had made it obvious to the most hidebound socialite and
the least savory scandal-monger alike that he had no desire
to discuss the events just past, certainly no desire to make
more of the feat than it had been.

For those with the wit to realize what they'd observed,
the biggest problem Anheliaa had left them had been
Lidye. Clearly Anheliaa hadn't intended to die and leave
her in charge. Clearly Anheliaa had intended to maintain
her grip another twenty years or so and had strung the
Shatumin ringspinner along, had promised Lidye the moon
all to gain a child conceived of a skilled spinner *in* the
Tower . . . an ambition, he stroked the full belly beside

him, that had resulted in pregnancies more than Lidye's, to his everlasting delight.

Lidye had assumed of course that the importance of her child was her importance as well; how little she had known Anheliaa. Lidye had taken Anheliaa's endorsement to heart . . . far too much to heart . . . and assumed that Anheliaa's mentally-declining reliance on her was due to her own brilliance.

With each passing day, he was increasingly convinced Anheliaa had chosen Lidye precisely *because* she was Talented enough to stabilize the Rings, conveniently connected politically—and fool enough to be another of Anheliaa's pawns.

Anheliaa had failed, perhaps, to appreciate the draw of the Rings themselves. A man whose possessive instincts flared greater with each session with the Rings could hardly be surprised at Lidye's battle to maintain control of them.

But Lidye was out, and Deymorin was in . . . in fact and in the minds of everyone in that ringchamber tonight. Afterward, as he'd danced, those bemused witnesses had gathered in confabs throughout the party, passing on who knew what to those invited to the party but not the Event.

Another unexpected benefit of the evening—his performance on the dance floor had effectively shattered any temptation to compare him to the reclusive and physically impaired Anheliaa. The limp that had plagued him off and on over the past ten years hadn't manifested tonight. These were Nikki's peers, overall, ten years his juniors. And he'd danced the babies into the ground . . . satisfaction, for a man who'd missed no few years of dancing.

That was another miracle no doubt under discussion in those multitudinous shadowed corners and behind raised fans. *Deymorin the cripple* the cruelest among them had termed their Princeps.

Well, Deymorin wasn't crippled now. Between Kiyrstin's hands and the effect the Ley seemed to be having on him, he'd never felt so . . . rejuvenated, as he had this night.

Said shepherdess leaned elbows on the side of the pool and gazed at him with:

"He loves Dancer, you know."

Khyel. Again. You'd think, just once, he'd get to be the hero of the night without sharing his glow with one or the other of his brothers.

He should have known something was coming. He'd seen Kiyrstin disappear into the garden after his brother, and could well imagine the interview that had taken place. He also knew his Kiyrstin had a romantic streak as wide as her heart was generous, one that could put Nikki's poetry spouting soul to shame, and Kiyrstin had this particular bit in her teeth for certain.

"And Dancer loves him," he acknowledged, then begged: "It's *their* problem, Kiyrstin." He was far more interested in the wet neck in front of his mouth than in one more night-long replay of his brother's unbudgeable attitudes.

"And was it their problem when Khyel risked his life and all your plans staying in Khoratum? This obsession of his is not going to go away."

He kissed her nose; it wrinkled at him.

"His mind is at peace now. The gods know, he's thinking clearly. *Look* what he's accomplished since he got back."

"And now he's done? Several glasses of wine while you court me and Nikki tries to make a silk purse out of Lidye."

It had been a worry. "You noticed that."

"Takes a lot of energy put somewhere to wipe that much love out of your head. But it goes beyond the love." Her fingers played idly with the strands of his hair floating along the surface of the water. "The fact is, Deymorin, I'm worried about him. He's close to some breaking point, and now the pressure's off virtually everywhere else in his life, that built-up steam is all going to that one spot of personal weakness. I've seen it happen before; I've seen good men shatter under the pressure."

He didn't doubt her words for a moment. Kiyrstin had been Garetti's number one deal-making commodity, from what he'd gathered. Many of those Garetti would choose to manipulate, he'd also gathered from between the lines of her stories, had been the best and brightest of Mauritum.

That they'd come to his clever lady for more than sex did not surprise him in the least.

"You think he's close to shattering?" he asked, and knew some relief when she shook her head slowly.

"I doubt it. He's very strong. But that one spot has some crazy notions about himself that will never be laid to rest if Dancer dies up there in Khoratum. Notions that *will* color his life and his decisions."

"Speaking from your own experience, Shepherdess?"

"Only my experience with people, love. My situation with Garetti was much different. I never had any illusions about what was expected of me, or that any of it had anything to do with something wrong inside me."

He gave her neck a final nuzzle, then pulled back in favor of serious talk. "And what if there *is* something wrong with Mikhyel?"

"You're not serious."

"Anheliaa twisted him, Kiyrsti. Mheric did. Maybe—and I pose it as hypothesis only—he's right to be concerned."

"What did he tell you about that night that he bolted from camp?"

"*He* told me nothing. Thyerri said Mikhyel thought he was more cruel than he was, and that he pushed too hard."

"In-trust-in'." She quoted their favorite Zandy-ism and stared past him . . . not, he suspected, taking in the patterns in the steam. "Pushed too hard. Like horses over fences?"

Unpleasant association. Mheric, and a fatal jump. "His words, not mine. I didn't ask details."

Her green eyes flickered back to him. "I did."

"Why am I not surprised?" he said, but it was one of the things he loved most about her. She didn't hide behind façades and didn't let those around her hide, either.

"We talked. He didn't say much about that night, but from what little I did get out of him, there was nothing 'wrong' with what he did. He said he hurt Thyerri, and talked about blood being everywhere . . . which he revised. I imagine the conversation was just pulling up bad memories. Practically speaking, I suspect he simply entered too fast, even for a seasoned lover. He has no concept of technique, Deymio-luvie. You should talk to him."

"*I* should talk to him? You're joking, right?"

"Not at all." She smiled and patted his cheek. "You're quite good, m'love."

"I *know*, but—"

"And modest, too. Such a paragon."

He growled; she laughed, and for a moment, they were both distracted, discovering variations on techniques. Then, just when he thought he'd escaped that uncomfortable territory, she murmured: "So, you'll talk to him?"

He growled again and burrowed into her neck. She pushed him back.

"Dammit, Kiyrsti, I *tried* that once and only made whatever problem he had worse."

"Ten years ago, JD. You didn't mean to add to his problem. You didn't even know he had one. But he did and you did, and it's time to put that part to rest for good."

She knew full well what she asked: there was very little she hadn't heard about the family, and especially the long and convoluted history between Mikhyel and himself, history which more often than not revolved around the events of Mikhyel's seventeenth birthday, events that had started with his gift to Mikhyel: Tirise awaiting him in his bed, and ended with the accident that had left Deymorin crumpled on the ground of the Sunrise Garden, his leg a shattered mess beneath him.

That night was his own, unwitting addition to Mikhyel's current dilemma, and Kiyrstin was suggesting that, as the only perpetrator available to rectify his actions, he should get off his behind and start rectifying.

"Not as if I haven't tried in the past, Kiyrsti," he said, feeling a bit on the defensive.

"But you're different now, both of you. You know more; he does. He's found passion; he could use a practical approach to sex."

She had a point. Considering the conversation he and Mikhyel had been able to have up in New Khoratum, this time he might actually get somewhere in those efforts.

"No façades," he said, with a wry grin. She tipped her head in inquiry, awaiting agreement. He finger-combed a strand of wet hair from her eyes and kissed the vacated spot. "Never mind, Shepherdess. You're right. I'll talk to him."

"Good. And you'll get Dancer back here?"

"Tell you what. You hatch, then *you* can go pull Dancer out of Khoratum. I don't think anyone else could."

"Mikhyel could."

"One point to the pretty divorcée. We'll discuss it tomorrow. I promise. And I'm now officially throwing my brother out of my bath and my bedroom for the night." He slithered about, coming to rest on the ledge beside her, keeping one hand on her the entire time, leaving it pressed flat to her stomach. "Hah! That was a good one. In a hurry to swim, the fry is."

"Going to be waiting a bit, old man," Kiyrstin murmured. "At least one more of your silly little months yet, according to the good doctors."

"I can hope, can't I?" he answered, and cradled his head into her crooked elbow, leaving his hand right where it was until a breast, impossibly perfect in supportive water drew his undivided attention. Having paid the left globe proper homage, he moved to its sister, teasing until it heaved with Kiyrstin's lazy sighs.

"You know," she said, "I thought at first I'd truly resent it."

"It?" His question bubbled into the water, and when she patted her stomach: *"Why?"*

"I'd avoided this situation quite deftly in Mauritum. I thought, just on general principals, I didn't want to carry a child."

Thinking perhaps air deprivation was addling his thinking, he surfaced and bobbed in front of her. "Obviously, you have the good sense to see the superior value in my bloodline."

"Not really. Quality had nothing to do with it. You'd best understand, I would never set out to *get* pregnant, not even with your obviously superior seed. But now that I am . . . I'm not inclined to do anything about it. Wasn't even really tempted, even at the start."

. . . not inclined to do anything about it . . . He drifted back to the submerged ledge.

"All right," he said lightly, trying to hide the revulsion her words roused in him. "I'll swallow the wiggler. Why?"

"Hush!" She twisted around and punched his shoulder. "I'm ruminating."

He decided she'd spoken metaphorically, and returned to nibbling—beginning with the fist he'd intercepted.

"I find I'm quite content—"

"Ha!"

Which nearly got him a bruised lip. He bit her knuckle. She ignored him. He nibbled again, and she rather absently caressed his jaw with the knuckle's neighboring thumb.

"But I'm content not because I'm particularly anxious to be a mother. Not because you'll make a particularly outstanding father—"

"Speak for yourself!" He began nibbling his way up to her shoulder.

"Boy or girl, you'll spoil it. Just look at Nikki."

"I'd rather look at you." And back down throat and chest to the gently bobbing breast. "Besides, I learn from my mistakes."

"Nikki isn't a mistake. —Oh, that's lovely, Rags. —Nikki is what happens when you grow up safe and loved. And now that his big brothers have quit protecting him, he's grown quite admirable."

"But—"

"*But* we'll manage. We're intelligent, resourceful individuals, and thanks to your ancestors, money and a roof over our baby's head will certainly never be a problem; parents have been doing it for thousands of years without nearly that much in their favor. But I'm not talking about parenting. I'm not really talking about the sprout, here." She patted her stomach. "Whatever it turns out, I'll love it, I'll throw all my mental and physical resources into caring for it—well, those left over after taking care of you—because

I love you, and that's all part of the equation, and I know you'll be doing the same thing."

He lifted his head to look up at her. "Then what are we talking about?"

"It's just . . . I always thought I'd feel less, somehow. That carrying a baby would prove the man I was with had the balance of power on his side, that all things being equal, nature could still force me to take time out of my life to bear the inevitable results of our conjugation. That, in the end, I was little more than a glorified chick incubator. I must admit, JD, the realization did *not* reconcile me to my femininity."

Suddenly, the bobbing flesh changed flavor. Deymorin sat back, puzzled, and what had been a pleasantly escalating passion dissipated with the swirling waters.

"Kiyrstin, I . . ."

"Don't look so distressed, Rags. I said that's what I thought. I foresaw—and quite correctly—several months of growing fat, which I hate, being fussed over, which I hate even more, and pain before, during, and after, which I truly detest. And then, there's been the inexplicable cravings, the swollen feet—gods! the swollen feet!—emotional swings that have had me saying and doing all manner of things I hate myself for after."

"Sounds—" Deymorin swallowed hard. "Wonderful."

Her teeth sparked in a lip-lifted snarl.

"What do you want me to say, Shepherdess? I'm not damnwell sorry."

"Neither am I."

"Huh?"

"How eloquent, my love. Our offspring will be an orator, I'm certain. It was all going according to expectations. My only reconciliation with my fate was the fact the child was yours and not Garetti's. Then, the other night, the night the foal came, I suddenly realized . . . I suddenly realized . . . it was power, a power I'm not certain I care to have."

"I don't understand."

"I get to feel this creature growing inside. I get to hold it in my arms when it's born, knowing it knows me in a

way it can never know another living being. All you can
do is imagine. All you can do is watch. You can hold it,
you can wash and dry it, you can . . . tickle its feet—but
that's all after the fact."

"Is that what's bothering you?" Relieved, he smiled and
kissed her hands, one at a time. "I promise you, my imagination is pretty good in that department."

"Is it? I've seen you, Deymorin, with those pregnant
mares. I saw your face that night, when I came into the
barn and you thought Deyma was giving up. When her
head lifted and she started in again, you had tears in your
eyes, tears that didn't really go away until that babe was
nursing. You dried the babe with towels, you talked to it
constantly, it will grow up knowing your voice and your
touch . . . but you'll never have that sense of belonging the
mother and babe share."

There was nothing he could say. It was all true, but that
was the way of the world. He couldn't see the problem.

"You should see your face when you lie there at night
and rub oil into my stomach. It cuts clear through me. That
is both the wonder, and the singular power my sex grants
me, and while I'm not certain I'd choose that, given an
option, I'm not certain I'd choose to be you. The fact I have
this chance, with you here to ease the unpleasant parts . . ."

She shrugged, apparently at an uncharacteristic loss for
words.

A most unpleasant quiver occurred, deep in Deymorin's
belly, and he found he couldn't look at her. "Kiyrstin, I—
I can't promise I will be here. You talk about Khyel and I
don't want to talk about it . . . the truth is, something *could*
happen. I might have to leave. Khyel might need me to go
to Persitum with him, and we could be delayed too long."

It was a point, though she wasn't sure that Persitum was
the likeliest destination.

"Feeling guilty, Rags?"

He opened his mouth to deny it, but:

"Yes. And dammit—"

"Don't bother. I know you might not be here physically.
I know you have duties—rings, man, you're the Ringmaster

of Rhomatum now in addition to Princeps. That's not what I meant." She paused, and her brows knit in concentration, and when they returned to his, they were filled with something utterly indecipherable. "But I had you, didn't I? Guilt. Hurt."

He scowled.

"Not consciously, Deymorin. Not damnwell willingly."

She drifted about, spreading her legs to straddle his lap facing him, bobbing with the water's movement, her skin slipping lightly across his, that beautiful, wondrous globe beneath her breasts filling the space between them. She smoothed his hair back from his face with manicured fingernails that were a far cry from the ragged, dirty paws that had caught and pulled the strands the first time they'd made love. And with every touch of her flesh, every whisper of her voice, every inhaled scent, his excitement returned.

He fought his own nature. She was obviously concerned. She was following some thought to its conclusion. He didn't want to cheapen her revelation. Didn't want it to turn into the lovemaking they so easily and eagerly expressed, even now, with her so near her time, and lose this insight into her heart she was trying to give him.

"Kiyrstin, tell me, what's wrong? What do you want of me?"

"Not you, my darling JD. Me. It's the most frightening power I've ever wielded over another human being." Her voice dropped to a whisper, and her brows were pulled together. "I don't want to hurt you, Deymorin. Not when you can't fight back."

"Rings," he said, and let his head fall back on the pool's edge, closing out her sight and scent, thinking only of the words, and of the heart of the woman who could say them.

Without opening his eyes, he pulled her close and buried his face in her neck.

Chapter Twelve

Silver eyes in a green mist. Thrilling, tingling hands. Mind rich in thought, essence rich in emotion. Why/because. When/if. Love/hate. Fear/courage. Need/nurture.

Complexity upon complexity, ever in flux. Endless possibility.

Morning fog filled Thyerri's mind. Clouds come down to greet the earth, bringing with them the Dream in its ever-increasing detail, detail he'd been spared in his innocent ignorance only a few months ago. Detail which would now and forever set the benchmark for the Need the Dream had created within him.

Too high. Too high the goal. Khy was lost and no other could match the challenge of his pattern, the exhilaration of his dance through life. Reject the Need, reject that Dance, that Dream—

His body rejected that conclusion. His body sighed and strained toward the Dream as the dream-Khy captured his hands and held them tight over his head as the dream-Khy's kisses devoured Thyerri's body and the dream-Khy's mind devoured Thyerri's essence.

{Sweet, sweet chameleon,} dream-Khy whispered, dream-voice with dream-essence, which made Thyerri laugh and cry. Khy had called him that only once before, a name which accepted all that Dancer was and didn't dwell on whys and what ifs. It was a name from Before, a name from Might-have-been.

Khy's dream-body pressed his to hard stone wall, Khy's dream-hands held his captive, stroked his cheek, cradled his hardening sex.

All at once. Too many hands. He laughed again. Khy as

Chameleon. Shapeshifter, as Mother could shift shape to accommodate her desire of the moment.

But this was not a Good Dream. He wanted his hands free to touch back. To love in return.

{Let me in, Chameleon, and you'll have them.} And Khy's mind reached for his, seeking entrance, which it should have had easily. He sought to bridge the gap, found mountains between his pattern and Khy's and cried out in frustration.

And still he felt the dream-mind probing at his, begging for union.

He protested, wanting free, and again Khy laughed. He reached for Khy's pattern, and Khy eluded him.

His mind asked *why*? Khy whispered {Come . . . Join . . .} He fought that order. Fought the too-real dream. Memory flowed back to his half-awake mind. Slowly. With great effort. Pushing constantly against that need to join.

Running. Tunnels. The Call to return. Blackness.

{Soon, Chameleon . . .}

Restraint. Confusion. Pain. A not-Khy not-dream-pattern that chased him into waking. He reached frantically, seeking truth, threw all his effort into bridging the mountains and breaching Mikhyel's defenses—

And Mikhyel's essence was there, intangible arms reaching for him, an essence foggy with sleep. Sad. Cold.

Alone. Filled with need that sensed him . . . touched him . . .

{So that's your secret. Even better. Yes . . . Hold him . . . Give me the pattern—} And rancid raspberries filled him, flowed through him, reaching toward that foggily defenseless essence.

"No!" Dancer shouted aloud and thrust the lonely cold away, slamming the mountain back down, leaving Mikhyel on one side, on the other. . . .

§   §   §

"Thyerri!" Mikhyel shouted into the darkness of his bedroom, and then sent the name flying across that other dark-

ness, seeking that pain-wracked, terrified essence, and
found . . . nothing. Not dead, of that he was certain; walled
off from him, that was also without question. And by Dancer's own touch, none other. None other *could* divide them.
Not now.

But . . . why?

He rolled upright, then sat hunched with the blankets
drawn up against the icy chill filling him, in his own
bedroom.

{Thyerri!} he called, because it had been *Thyerri's* Dream
that had gone sour. {Thyerri!} and again: {Thyerri!} But
there was nothing. Only his brothers' startled, waking
minds, as his frantic search snapped the link into place.

{Hold me!} he shouted to his brothers, and dived into
the heart of Rhomatum-below-the-Tower. {Rhomatum!
Damn it, come to me!}

{Rude, Child of Darius.}

{Manners be damned! I need your help!}

*{Child of Darius needs nothing. The power is yours.
Seek yourself.}*

Tamshirin obfuscation. He was sick of it and wasted no
energy or precious time deciphering this newest example.
Here, in the heart of the node, what Thyerri called his
essence burned fiercely, hot, cold, sweet, bitter. The crystalline leythium surrounding him radiated blinding white. Energy, pure and unadulterated. Power incarnate.

The power is yours. He gathered that light, swept it into
himself, and cast it into the black emptiness between himself and that dream-invasion. The light fizzled into oblivion.
He cast again. A third attempt touched—

{Mirym,} he whispered, and her mind acknowledged.
{Help me . . .}

But she turned from him, declared his need none of hers,
and slipped from his awareness.

He cast again. And again and again, touching startled
minds, striking nothing but fear in the recipients. Sleeping
minds.

Defenseless minds that would account their midnight encounter as nightmares in the morning.

{*Shooting blind, Child of Darius. Look to the pattern.
Look to the pattern within . . .}*

Not the pattern in the Ley: not Thyerri's pattern, not
Temorii's. *Dancer's* pattern. The inner shrine, the rings that
were Dancer's haven, the sensation of diving free, of cheating death. He held that image tight to him, wrapped it
around him like a cloak, made it contiguous with his own
and cast again, closing his mind to all other thoughts, calling to his brothers to lend him their strength.

The essential light winked out, and as darkness engulfed
his outer awareness, a gasp of sheer agony engulfed the
inner.

Dancer's pain, not his, that seeking bolt more effective
than he could have known.

{I'm sorry . . .} He sent healing and strength across the
link that throbbed red in the darkness, stabilizing the touch
with each passing heartbeat. The red cooled to blue and
then began to glimmer with the myriad colors he associated
with health.

And past the healing, he sensed Dancer's regret, a wish
that this last dance had ended differently—

And in that instant, against imminent sense of loss, he
knew:

{Last? *Ended?* Nothing's over, unless you want it to be
over.}

Hunger. Longing. Reaching.

He clutched that essence to him. *Wanting* Dancer. *Wanting* to be near him. To hold him. To ride the mountain
winds . . .

And with that wanting, his sense of the solid world
around him dissipated. Bed and sheets in one world, the
leythium cavern in another. And more real than both: stone
beneath his feet, the stench of oil torches, walls that flowed
with sickly green-brown threads of light . . .

And fetid raspberries oozed black along that bridge of
light, seeking . . .

Him.

Realization on the face that filled his mind's eye.

{No, Khy! Go back! Don't—}

Wanting . . .

{Come, child of Darius . . .}

. . . Him.

A new Voice, an essence drawing him to that diseased room where the fetid essence said Dancer waited, where corruption promised a glorious reunion painfully at odds with the image beyond that beloved face, images of chains and shackles, of blood and terror . . .

{Khy, *please*! Go! Get out while you still—}

{Come . . .}

{Khyel! Dammit, Barrister, get back here!} Deymorin's mind enveloped his, shuttering the light, severing the bridge to Thyerri.

§ § §

Dancer drifted in a sea of non. Non-sight. Non-sound. Touch, taste . . . even his essence had vanished. Thought was all that remained. And Thought wondered, was this death? Had Dancer died and was this . . . eternity?

Where the essence? Where those gone before? Where even the lightning blasts of the hells Darius' descendants swore by?

It lacked . . . Symmetry. Equity.

Justice.

Non-voice cursed. Non-essence added its protest.

There was, of course, no answer in this sea of Non.

What, Thought wondered, with nothing else to occupy an excess of eternity, had happened? That which had been Dancer had been running down a tunnel beneath Khoratum, had been running from Rhyys-who-was-not-Rhyys' men, with Rhyys-who-was-not-Rhyys' mind trying to force him back to the room of corruption.

The mind calling him had belonged, Thought insisted, to the scarfaced one. But the essence remembered the touch of Scarface's essence and this Touch had not matched that Touch. The same but . . . different.

Rhyys-but-not-Rhyys.

Scarface, but different.

And seeking Khy's pattern. Seeking Khy through the Dream. Through Dancer-who-was-one-with-Khy.

But not at first. At first, Scarface/Rhyys was seeking the Chameleon. Seeking to gather the Chameleon in. To make the Chameleon one with the pattern that was not Rhyys and was not—

"Wake up."

A shimmering in the Non.

"I *said* wake up, you curst mistake of nature."

Fireworks exploded in his head and he was adrift no longer, but swinging free, suspended by wrists that dripped damp warmth. Blood.

And the pain that rippled out from his knotted shoulders implied his Dream struggles had been . . . quite real.

Struggles to reach Khy, to repair his personal pattern, then struggles to push Mikhyel away, to save Mikhyel from That-which-held-him. Struggles to stop that essence from absorbing Mikhyel, and finally the battering from the far side of the mountains as Deymorin's powerful essence demolished the bridge.

That bridge in the pattern neither he nor Mikhyel, alone or together, could have broken, it had grown that strong.

"Revive him."

Cold. Wet. He was melting, like dead flesh on a leythium sea. Soon his wrists would disappear, his bones would part and he'd be free. Without hands, but free . . .

"Wake up."

Dead, but free. And no longer able to supply that bridge to Khy.

His head rocked, and the lights in his head were without as well. Smoking, noxious torches, not the restorative glow of leylight. And one of those torches swung close enough to singe his skin, had he not been dripping wet. Sweat, water—

"I said, wake up!"

—blood . . . the copper taste was strong in his mouth as the next blow split his lip open. He squeezed his eyes shut against the smoke and against the image awaiting him beyond that torch.

"My lord, please, take care." A new voice touched the air, breathless and light, as a new essence, gentle and artless, brushed that other realm. "I think he's awake."

"Of course he is." Rhyys-but-not-Rhyys. Rhyys' voice, but not Rhyys' tone. That velvet evil belonged to Scarface, as did the deceptively gentle touch that made patterns in the sweat on his chest with Rhyys' sharpened, enameled talons.

"Poor thing, you did work hard, didn't you?"

"Please, m'lord," the light voice spoke again, "May I . . . ?"

May I . . . what? Thyerri wondered, and shivering set in, spasms in muscles already strained to their limit. Hadn't they done enough?

More water. A great deal of water, but this was warm, and smelled of mountain herbs, and arrived on a gentle touch of sponge, and he stifled the cry that threatened before it escaped. The gentle touch dabbed the blood from his face and squeezed the sponge over his head, rinsing his scalp and setting his hair to dripping, then proceeded to the rest of him, lingering over his chest and genitals. But it was a respectful touch, and the essence held a sense of awe, and of fascination.

And to his horror, his body, exhausted as it was, responded, as the Dream threatened the edges of his world.

"So, Child of Rakshi, that's your secret." Velvet voice returned along with those talons. "You prove as base as your disgusting cousin."

That momentary response vanished. He opened his eyes to that familiar-yet-not face, but it was another between them. A delicate hiller face, with wide Tamshi eyes.

"Don't tease him, m'lord," the hiller said, and smiled faintly. "It's a natural response . . ." the Tamshi eyes flickered toward Rhyys, and the tone turned gently teasing. "As well you know."

And the raised eyebrow, the chuckle that acknowledged a hit, held nothing at all of Rhyys, for all they came from Rhyys' body.

Rhyys would have had this gentle hiller flogged for such impertinence.

Warm water sluiced the sweat away, but the chill remained. The shivers increased. There was stone beneath his feet, but he didn't even try to hold himself upright on knees certain to give, and his eyes drifted shut out of sheer exhaustion.

"Enough, Mheltirin." Impatience colored the velvet yellow, and with a murmured apology, the sponge disappeared, only to be replaced by a soft, warmed towel. "Give it to me." And the towel returned accompanied by the occasional brush of nails. Casual contact as the towel patted his skin, then enwrapped him against the chill. One fist held the towel in place, the other gripped his jaw. "Open."

He clenched his jaw and squeezed his eyes tightly closed.

"Have it your way."

The hand tightened, and somehow, his jaw went numb. Something hard was forced between his teeth, prying his mouth open, and holding it open as a tube was shoved in.

"Swallow the pill, or swallow the tube. I wonder which it will be?"

Just as his jaw began to quiver, nerves twitching involuntarily, tube and bar were removed.

"Well?"

He forced his head up and his eyes to focus.

"You . . ." His voice faltered, his throat dry. "You've made your point."

"Good."

He opened his mouth for the pill, tried to drink the good spring water from the cup held to his shaking mouth, and prayed to the power of the Ley that it was not poison.

The power of the Ley only . . . for Mother's aid was no longer to be trusted.

"Very good." Rhyys' ocarshi-tainted breath brushed Thyerri's mouth; he jerked his head away as far as he could, but could not escape the damp tongue that licked a spilled drop from his chin. Another warm towel pressed gently, absorbing the rest of the overflow. "So suspicious, Rakshi-dancer. I hate to disappoint you, but it will only help, not hurt. You'll feel better very soon. Quite well, in fact. More than able to answer all my questions."

Hands brushed his shoulders above the towel, and Thyerri turned his head away, closed his burning eyes on a room that insisted on spinning behind the almost familiar face.

"Such a lovely shell. Hard to imagine it bears any relation to this one."

Shell. As if . . . Thyerri swallowed hard. As if Rhyys' body were a suit of clothing to be donned at will.

"It's the Dance that formed you, isn't it? In every way. Live, eat, sleep the Dance. That obsession formed your shell . . . as it formed this one. Rhyys was obsessed with the Dance, too, did you know that? Rhyys' shell was inadequate, so he controlled the dancers and flew among the rings on the wings of ocarshi smoke."

Thyerri shivered as those fingers traced his collarbone and down his back.

"But it's not the Dance that drives you now, is it? You want him. Sweet, sweet Maurii, you want him so badly it twists your very soul." A smile that held nothing of Rhyys stretched that almost-familiar face. "And he rejected you, did he? Foolish of him."

Rejected? Hardly, though he'd believed as much once. Now, too late, he knew differently. If only he had called sooner . . .

{Khy . . .} His essence cried once, and Thyerri forced silence on it. To call would be to draw Mikhyel to this creature who had casually donned Rhyys' "shell" and seemed now to regret that decision.

"What is it like, to be so attracted to one person?" Scarface's velvet tones caressed his ear. "What is it you get from him that makes it worth such loyalty for so little reward?"

It was a question he'd asked himself often enough over the past months. But as much as he had given, as much as he had changed for Mikhyel dunMheric's sake, Mikhyel dunMheric had given and changed for the sake of a dancer

who challenged his very essence. Because he'd pushed un-
wisely, they had been parted.

Loyalty? It wasn't loyalty that had held him to this task,
it was self-interest.

And it was faith. Faith in Mikhyel dunMheric's sense of
fairness, and in Mikhyel dunMheric's ability to sort out
Truth, given time.

And, he remembered, that trust had been vindicated. The
love that had flowed across that bridge could not have
been contrived.

If only he hadn't misjudged his timing. He'd leaped too
late; the ring had passed.

"Let us draw him here, Rakshi."

Velvet tones. Gentle hands.

"Give me the pattern of his mind. We'll call him here
together."

All the more vile for their hypocrisy.

"You've a strong mind, Child of Rakshi. Talent, yes, and
the knowledge of it, unlike Mheltirin and the rest of these
folk about here. Where, I wonder, did you learn it?"

All the while he spoke the tendrils fluttered at the edge
of Thyerri's awareness, seeking to snatch any stray thought/
image/emotion. He followed those tendrils, hardly hearing
the velvet voice.

"I think, perhaps, it's best to leave you untouched. For
the moment, at least. Let us concentrate instead on—what
was your thought? Completing . . . no, repairing your pattern. Such a quaint notion."

The towel dropped away. Hands began to bring his body
alive again.

{Chameleon, he called you. But *toski* would be more ap-
ropos, don't you think? A ley-loving lizard that leaps from
male to female and back again. So many possibilities, little
toski.} And the scarred mind brought images now, teased
him with them.

{Forever, radical dancer of Khoratum. You could dance
this dance forever. Bring him to us. His revulsion will be
gone. You'll be one.}

The voice went on and on as the hands touched and the images lured him in.

His mind began supplying images of its own. Thyerri, Temorii, and back again. One ring to the next. His world became a world of dreams and hopes, of possibilities he'd never imagined, of sensations . . . and the voice promised to fulfill those dreams, urged him to seek Mikhyel's mind, to bring him here to—

To give him to Scarface.

Like a dive into glacial-melt, Dancer's body froze. The intimately probing hands clenched, and his vision blurred, but it was real sight, not those insidiously sweet images, that failed. And now he felt the drug, blurring the aches in his body, blurring his mind, opening him to that insidious world the velvet voice suggested.

Dancer called on the pain in his shoulders as the reality of his world, used that pain to reject the drug and the velvet voice.

"Damn it!"

Dancer's head rocked backward, slammed stone and re-bounded into waiting fingers that bit into his jaw and forced him to look at a too-close face.

"Get him *back,* damn you!"

With the curse came spittle that dripped down his cheek, breath that held the faintest taint of ocarshi, the sour scent of a tooth gone bad. Physically the creature before him was indeed Rhyys.

"I *want* that pattern!"

The tendrils that permeated his essence, contaminating him with malignant raspberries, were not. More than Rhyys and less. More and less than Scarface. Not a woven pattern. Not interlaced. Separate strands of essence tied in a jumble.

The tendrils wanted to reach Mikhyel, wanted Mikhyel's pattern. But Rhyys-who-was-not-Rhyys *had* Mikhyel's pattern, had *all* the Rhomandi at its mercy. Had warded Mother's mountain against them—

"Idiot!" Another blow. "Surface features. The recognition of battle opponents. Useless. I need the complete pattern. Mine to his. Get him back, I say."

And he began to understand, as he'd never considered the matter: there were thoughts that were mutable, there was essence that was not, and there was pattern that grew and shifted with the tides of life.

And this one wanted Mikhyel's pattern. Wanted to reach that pattern through Dancer's pattern. To reach and then to create its own bridge to That-which-was-Mikhyel.

Not from him. He'd never give Mikhyel to this pattern-less creature.

A heaving sigh; an easing of the finger-grip. The tendrils withdrew, but Thyerri could still sense them, could practically see the collection of wits, the cooling of temper.

"And are you so certain you have a choice, radical dancer of Khoratum?"

This time, Dancer's cognizant mind could follow the tendrils' assault, the deliberate infiltration of his essence with intent to devour it, a direct assault against which he knew no defense.

He'd known the mindspeak and the patterns of the Ley almost from the time of first memory. He didn't remember learning how to shield himself against Mother's powerful thoughts or to leythiate himself between the surface world and Mother's caverns. He'd watched Mother play games with lightning, watched her use the inherent animosity between world and sky to tease storms down on Khoratum Tower, but nothing he'd experienced had prepared him for this deliberate, singularly personal, offensive use of those energies he took for granted. All he could think was to hold tight to that which was Dancer, to cower within the safety of spinning rings.

A posture doomed to failure, as his body weakened, and the assault struck once again at that infuriatingly vulnerable point, striving to enmesh him in the Dream.

But the Dream had shapechanged once more. The totality that was Love, that was Sensation . . . that was Mikhyel/Dancer . . . included now a blinding white, lightning-like blast coming out of the Mikhyel pattern alone. A blast of pure essence, a blast that drew upon the power of the Ley itself, a blast shaped by stubborn determination, a blast that could have killed.

Easily.

That blindingly-white blast mirrored now in Dancer's pattern and flashed out through the spinning rings that were his armor, striking at the threatening tendrils.

The tendrils hissed and curled back on themselves.

Then extended again.

A second time, he gathered his forces and cast, and again, the tendrils returned, this time with a soft laugh.

"Hiss all you want, little toski, I'll win in the end."

"Get *out*!" Panic filled him. He cast again and again, and screamed as the hand cradling his genitals clenched. But the hold eased and the tendrils extended, recovering ever more quickly as if having learned the pattern of the blasts and warded against them.

"You're strong, radical, but you're out of your class, this time. You play this game far too conservatively. I've several lifetimes of practice on you."

Well, boy, what is it you want? To escape? To punish? — To kill?

A lesson in back alley self-defense, a question that had filled him with revulsion: Zelin's the lesson and Zelin's the question he asked himself now.

What did he want? Every instinct urged him to run. But running was not an option. He couldn't break free physically and the tendrils would keep pursuing him until he grew too weak to resist them.

. . . you practice conservatism, not art. . . .

Mother's rebuke against holding back, of preserving some . . . that which was Mikhyel in the pattern supplied the words: trust fund against the future.

The leylight-spears he cast were born of his essence, formed by his nature and his motivations as much as what Mikhyel called Talent. By his example of one, those leylight-spears were potentially lethal. Was knowledge of that potential inhibiting him now? Disrupting his attack before it ever began? Was he afraid that to wield such power might kill him as well?

A dark chuckle vibrated the air about him. "Doubts, radical. You can't have those. Give it up. Let me in, and I can teach you to use that power. You can have all you want. dunMheric, the dance . . . whatever you want."

Let him in? Let *him* have Mikhyel?

"Chance, Rakshi-dancer. It's your god, isn't it? Take the chance. Leap now for power beyond your imagining."

And as he hesitated, those tendrils grew, weaving patterns around his rings.

Around, but not into. When they endeavored to insinuate, the spinning rings cut them off. And he radiated doubt, assumed it as an illusory cloak behind which his True Thoughts were safe. He would leap, yes, but not for the ring this composite of malignant essences flung before him. He didn't want power or anything else this Rhyys-who-was-not-Rhyys might offer. He only wanted his freedom, his and Mikhyel's.

But at the price of cold-blooded, deliberate killing?

Doubts, radical . . . This was a canny essence. It knew panic could drive him to kill instinctively, so it gave him time. Time to think himself into inaction.

Mikhyel could wield force. Mikhyel had made his peace at a very early age with the responsibility of power. Mikhyel would point out the damage this creature had already done, to him personally as well as to the Web and all the people of Khoratum. Mikhyel would say the issue was clear, the judgment made. Mikhyel would strike to destroy, even if it meant he would go down in the same flames of destruction.

Dancer did not want to die, he very much did not want to die, but if he didn't act soon, everything he held safe inside the spinning rings would die whether he wished it or not.

The tendrils surrounded him now. They interlinked on the far side of his rings, forming a sphere of corruption.

A sphere which, once complete, might be infinitely more vulnerable in its inability to retreat. If he waited, if he struck then—

"My lord, wait!" The sphere heaved, expanding as a

man's lungs would when striving to control a surge of frustration and anger.

"Not now, Mheltirin."

"Please, m'lord, you're too zealous. You'll destroy the very treasure you wish to save."

The tendrils shimmered, their organization wavered, and Dancer, in desperation, gathered his essence, absorbing even the protective rings. The tendril-web sphere triumphantly rushed in—

He struck back with that collective essence—

And his world disappeared in a flood of iridescent light.

ᕼ   ᕼ   ᕼ

Deymorin knew full well Mikhyel was awake behind his closed eyelids, but he made no attempt to reach him, knowing also that behind that thought-barrier, Mikhyel's mind was busy sorting out the myriad impressions Deymorin had received only in rebound.

The force he'd used to sever the link to Khoratum had left his younger brother's mind battered and bruised, for which he felt some guilt. He'd acted instinctively, knowing only that his brother was so enmeshed with Thyerri, he might well have been hopelessly entangled with that other force before he realized the danger.

Danger beyond that mental realm: when Deymorin had arrived in his room, Mikhyel had been ghostly-transparent, halfway to whatever hell-hole Thyerri occupied. Someone or something with the power to leythiate had wanted Mikhyel and Thyerri together.

Badly.

And Deymorin, for one, had had no desire either to lose Mikhyel to that force, or to get sucked into it in Mikhyel's wake.

{Necessary . . .} Filtered to him from Mikhyel. {No regrets . . .}

"How's he doing?" Nikki asked from behind him, and Deymorin turned.

"He'll live." He nodded toward the steaming mug Nikki held. "What's that?"

"Tea, if he's awake. Raul says it'll cure what ails him."

"He's right," Mikhyel himself answered. "Help me sit up, will you?" He groaned as they pulled him up and packed pillows at his back. "Rings, Deymio, I hope you got whoever was on the other end as well."

He transferred the mug from Nikki's hands to Mikhyel's, then said, "I fear that other end was Thyerri."

"Dancer," Mikhyel corrected quietly.

Deymorin dipped his head, acknowledging the implicit difference.

"Not only him." Mikhyel cradled the mug between hands that shook ever so slightly, sipped, and his eyes rolled back in contentment. "I don't know what you put in this, Raul, but don't ever lose the recipe."

"No concern for that, Master Khyel," Raulind said. "If that will be all?"

"Yes, Raul. Thank you. Get back to bed."

At the door, Raulind paused. "Don't keep him or yourselves up, m'lord Deymorin. There is nothing to be solved in the next four hours that can't be better solved in the following two by sleep-clear heads."

"Point taken, Raulind," he said. "We'll see you when the sun's up. Clear-headed."

As the bedroom door closed, leaving just the three of them, Mikhyel said, "I'm going to have to go to Khoratum."

Deymorin glanced up at Nikki, got a nod, and said to Mikhyel, "When do we leave?"

"You'll go with me, then?"

"Did you doubt it?"

"Not really." But the palpable release of tension in the link and the hand that went limp, threatening to spill the last of the tea belied that confidence.

He took the mostly empty mug from Mikhyel and urged him back down, willing sleep on him, reinforcing through that link whatever herb Raulind had put in that tea.

"Sleep now, brother. Raulind's right in that. We'll work out the details in the morning."

And Mikhyel's eyes hazed and closed, even as the mind behind them had begun working on those details.

"Are you sure that's wise, Deymorin?" Nikki asked from across Mikhyel's bed, and his mind was likewise closed to shared thoughts.

"Sleep? Definitely."

"Don't tease, Deymorin. Going to Khoratum. The risk. This meeting with Mauritum—"

"I agreed for the sake of momentary peace. I have every confidence that, if there's any legitimate excuse *not* to go, Mikhyel will find it by morning." He stood up and waved Nikki through the door.

But even as he closed the door, he took one final look at his brother, wondering if Kiyrstin's perceived explosion was imminent . . . or if they'd already waited too long.

SECTION
FOUR

Chapter One

Mikhyel had known for years that if it weren't for Raulind, he'd never have made it to his first majority. Other hands might have held his mangled body afloat in Barsitum's healing pools, but only Raulind could have salvaged the equally mangled mind that had entered the Barsitum caverns with that body.

That had been the first time, but not the last that the older man had helped him sort the tangled web between necessity, morality, and responsibility.

He'd never really known what had prompted Raulind to voluntarily leave his post and the priesthood to accompany child-Mikhyel to Rhomatum—had known less why Raulind had remained through the years when that fiercely private child tried so hard to push him away. But Raulind had persisted, had won that child's trust and had been at his side to lend wisdom, insight, and support through the Anheliaa years and beyond.

Even the Dancer affair had failed to drive him off.

All these years of increasing stress, the adult-Mikhyel was certain, must have strained normal bonds of loyalty beyond the breaking point; so it was no small relief to Mikhyel when his announcement, made in the midst of his morning grooming, of his plans to return immediately to Khoratum rather than prepare for the announced trip to Persitum were met with a simple:

"You'll be telling Master Deymorin, of course."

"I already have." Mikhyel's spine relaxed for the first time since Raulind had begun the morning's routine. Raulind murmured approval, and began a serious assault on the knots beneath his shoulder blades. Those knots were a constant in his life these days and half the reason (so Nikki insisted) for the muscles still stiff from his last riding session with Nikki. "Deymio's going with me," Mikhyel said into the pillow of his crossed arms. "Or at least, that was his stand last night. I trust he's of the same mind this morning. I'm quite confident our earlier problems of working together have been resolved."

He paused, waiting for commentary from his advisor, and when none was forthcoming:

"This is not a subterfuge mission. I intend to go quite openly to demand Thyerri's release."

Another pause.

"I also intend to use the mystique of the Triumvirate to its fullest advantage."

The massage continued; Mikhyel finished in a rush:

"One of us should stay here for communication with the Tower—both ways. The women are just too close to their time. Deymorin offered to go last night, and he truly is far more prepossessing than Nikki or myself. . . . But I think I must go myself. . . . Not just because of Dancer and what I owe him—and I do owe him—"

"Of that, there is no doubt, Master Khyel. Turn please, and sit."

Not a casual interjection. Such comments were never casual coming from Raulind. He obediently swung his legs over the side of the table and Raulind began to work his left shoulder in circles.

"I refuse to feel guilty, Raul."

"No one said anything about guilt, only obligation. — Ah." As something snapped in his shoulder. "There we have it. You're leaning on that shoulder again. You *must* watch the way you sit as you write. Your other reasons?"

"Whatever has Thyerri wants me, and it's using Thyerri to get to me." That much had come through all too clearly at the end last night. "What this individual wants, I don't know, but the attacks on Thyerri are not likely to end until I personally respond."

"Or until Master Thyerri dies."

"You think I haven't thought of that?"

"No. I prompt you for your reasons. You grow defensive, Khyel."

Which meant, *step back, Khyel, take a breath. Address the question.*

And it *was* a question he'd considered. At length.

"Unlikely," he said, after the requisite breath, and as Raulind's hands continued to work their magic.

"Because?"

"Thyerri is its only link to me."

Raulind's hands stopped for an almost imperceptible pause, then resumed. "Most unlikely, then." His voice did not reveal that hesitation, but it was not the answer his mentor had expected: an uncommon occurrence in their long history together. "And the third reason?"

All these years . . . and Raulind was still able to keep the Barrister on his toes. "Did I say there was another?"

"Two reasons have never been sufficient to convince you."

"Am I so predictable?"

"You're so cautious, my friend. And so clever. You can always come up with three solid reasons for something you believe in. Your instincts are generally sound, but your faith in those instincts has always been somewhat lacking."

Faith. Instincts. The concepts sat oddly in the mouth of the man who had taught him to reverence reason. "*Equity* demands I go, even if Deymorin won't go with me."

"Equity? Between whom?"

"Myself. Deymio. Since I returned from Khoratum, I've immersed myself in familiar work and ignored that business for which I am, apparently, singularly suited. Before I asked Deymorin to include the Rings in his life, I should have demanded the same of myself."

"Meaning?

"Evidence supports that of the available options, I'm the only one qualified to go, even were I not the target of this individual. Whatever is going on up in Khoratum, it involves the Ley, and the Ley . . ." He grimaced, lacking words to express his . . . instinct, as Raulind put it. "The

Ley likes me, *speaks* to me. I don't know how else to express it. Mother wanted me. Rhomatum still does. *Me*, not the Triumvirate. I stick my hand blindly, stupidly into a ley pool and get a warm welcome; Deymorin does the same in conscious and legitimate need and practically loses the hand for his efforts—well, theoretically speaking. The Ley certainly tried to convince him it was happening. The point is, I've talents I've ignored as surely as Deymorin once denied his talent for ringspinning. I can't very well expect him to acknowledge his gift without expecting the same of myself."

He paused, waiting for some indication that the comment was as arrogantly foolish as he feared, but Raulind remained silent, hands as well as voice gone still. He had no choice but to go further out on a thin structure of conjecture:

"I'm certain there are others who share this . . . affinity for the Ley. Mirym, for one. Thyerri . . . I'm certain Dancer is on an entirely different scale than any of us, but only, perhaps, because he was raised by Mother."

"Lie flat again, if you would, Master Khyel."

He did so, rested his face in the cushioned cradle, and the massage resumed, along with Raulind's probe.

"A fourth reason, then, for personally going to Khoratum would be for the sake of information?"

"Information?" He considered the matter. "I suppose. *Answers* is a more accurate word. Definitive answers."

"What is the question you seek to answer?"

"Question?" Mikhyel countered. "I said answers."

"There is always one driving force, Mikhyel. What is your question?"

Trapped. Mikhyel caught, and held, a quick breath, then made a rapid retreat. "I don't know."

"Truth, my friend."

There was no hiding from Raulind. There never had been. Not even the night he'd gone to dunHaulpin.

He confessed it, for all it sounded vaguely silly. "I want to know where I belong."

"Not here?"

Mikhyel shook his head. "I don't . . . I don't think so."

"In the Khoramali?"

"Possibly. I've certainly never felt more alive than when I was there."

"In New Khoratum? With Mirym?"

"I scarcely know the woman!"

"She bears your child. I'd say you know her quite well."

"Fornication does not constitute a lifelong bond."

"The child does."

There was no answer to that. The child *was* a life commitment for both of them, and he'd done what he could to make certain neither of them, mother or child, would want for anything. She had an open draw on funds, an open line to his office and his ear—hells, she had an open line to his head—if she'd use any of those things. Thus far, his efforts to reach her in the ordinary way had been fruitless. She either wasn't receiving his messages . . . or she was ignoring them.

He'd deny her nothing within reason, but he wouldn't, *couldn't* force himself into that partnership. He wasn't wanted and he didn't belong.

"Khoratum itself, perhaps?" Raulind asked, and in a heartbeat, undermined all the good he'd accomplished as Mikhyel's back stiffened, growing as tight as it had been when he rose from his bed. *Not* a chance question on Raulind's part, oh, no.

"With what's brewing there?" He sniped back, for all his voice caught. "Out of the question."

Raulind, as if oblivious to the very signs he'd taught Mikhyel to notice, continued his musing. "Not a place then. Perhaps the place you seek is a person. Not your brothers, for they're here. Not Mirym, who carries your child . . . Thyerri, perhaps?"

Raulind was mocking him now. Mocking his willful self-deception.

"I didn't say that."

"Ah. I mistook your argument, then. The Ley likes you. Likes him. Your minds touched in the night and required Lord Deymorin's intervention to force you apart, and now you intend to join him in a great hurry to answer the question of where you belong. Yes, I might well have read too much into your statement."

No hiding. Ever.

"Thyerri's in significant trouble—or at least, he *seems* to be in trouble, thanks to his connection to us. For that reason alone, I'd feel compelled to try to free him from whatever situation of our making in which he's gotten involved. I also have an undeniable link to Dancer, apparently as inescapable as the link with my brothers. And I *do* love him, for want of any alternative explanation for my feelings. I can't deny that any longer. I was so certain, when I left him last spring, that those feelings would ease with time, but my desire to be with Dancer, my admiration for Dancer, only increases every time I think. . . ."

He paused, having nearly forgotten the question, embarrassed in that lapse as only Raulind's presence could make him.

"Tell me, Khyel," Raulind asked, and the mockery was gone. "Why do you call him Thyerri one moment and Dancer the next?"

"I . . . don't really know."

"Of course you do. I've noticed, if you haven't. What is Thyerri to you? What is Dancer? Where has Temorii gone?"

It was not a casual question. Raulind's rarely were.

"Thyerri is . . ." He frowned into the shadows below the table. "The young man who is working for my brother is Thyerri. The boy who survived the Khoratumin alley-rats was Thyerri. Thyerri is how Dancer asked to be introduced to the Syndicate. Thyerri is . . . Thyerri is the face Dancer chooses for the world, and I'm trying to respect that choice."

"And Temorii?"

He smiled into those shadows, recalling: *It was a beautiful dress. A dance for Mikhyel* . . . Understanding came slowly, sweetly. *Temorii was only a name before Mikhyel* . . .

"Temorii is the pattern Dancer reserves for Mikhyel." An addition to Thyerri, he could at long last acknowledge, not a substitution. And in that sum, he hoped with all his heart and mind, lay the answers to that darkness within him. Thyerri's challenge would help him face it, Temorii's tempering would help him control it, Dancer's love would help him conquer it.

"And Dancer? What is Dancer?"

He lifted his head, propped his chin on his crossed arms.

"The totality of the pattern. That essence that calls to me and that I can call from the depths of hell."

Without Dancer, he would merely continue to fester inside, of that he was now convinced. And with that conviction, he saw clearly not only where Raulind would lead him, but the real path he'd been seeking:

"But Thyerri's situation, Dancer himself, is a symptom of what drives me, not the cause. I sincerely doubt that the *where* I seek is a place at all, or even a person. It's . . . an aspect of myself. A missing aspect, I think. As I couldn't deny either Thyerri or Temorii without rejecting Dancer, so must I find this . . . part of myself. My instinct says go to Khoratum—not just to Dancer. Logic supports that decision—though for quite different reasons. I think, if I ignore this instinct, I could be running away from that aspect for the rest of my life."

Raulind's massaging hands paused. "I've waited for . . . oh, quite a long while now, to hear you say that, Mikhyel dunMheric."

"What do you—" Suspicion flared. He swung up and around to face his old friend. "Rings, don't tell me you're one *of them*."

"Them?"

"Them. *Us*. Thyerri. Mirym . . ." Or worse. "*Please,* Raulind, don't tell me you're a stray piece of Barsitum web that followed me home fourteen years ago! I'd hate to have to dismiss you, but after all that's happened, I really don't think—"

But Raulind was laughing. "No, my dear boy, I'm quite human—although, I suppose, in a way, you could describe me as a part of Barsitum. I was a healer-priest for thirty years before your family delivered you to us. I lived in

Barsitum. Soaked daily in his pools. Breathed his ley-touched vapors. I suppose, in a way, I am a piece of Barsitum. But I've no claim to Talent such as yours. Nothing like your brothers', either. I suppose certain of my own instincts are, perhaps, aided, but other than that . . ."

"Thirty *years*?" Mikhyel extracted from that recital of facts that which most surprised him. "Were you born there?"

A slow smile spread across Raulind's thin face. "I'm sixty-seven years old, Mikhyel. My first pilgrimage to Barsitum was just after I reached my first majority; the sense of homecoming I felt when I went back for my second pilgrimage convinced me I was meant to spend at least some portion of my life with the brothers."

Sixty-seven. And yet, the Raulind Mikhyel recalled from childhood had at least seemed younger than Mikhyel was now. It was a mark of how thoroughly he'd accepted his Barsitumin savior as a part of his life that he'd never, in fourteen years, looked into Raulind's history. Of course, neither had Anheliaa or Deymorin or anyone else had him investigated. Perhaps Raul had simply provided an easy answer for everyone regarding the care and feeding and dressing of a thirteen-year-old boy, and no one wanted to look further.

Or perhaps Raul hadn't *wanted* them to check. Mikhyel had learned to look carefully at what *didn't* happen. When one tried to see the wind at work, one had to look at its effects, not its substance.

"The pools were good to you," he probed cautiously, not wanting suspicion to enter this most precious relationship. And yet, he couldn't afford *not* to consider the ramifications of Raulind's connections; the man had had too much influence on him over the years to let that knowledge pass without serious examination.

"As they are good to many of the priests. We never discussed such matters, yet there was one brother who made jokes about knowing Darius I." A smile twitched Raulind's mouth. "I've occasionally wondered, in the years since, if those truly were jokes."

This wasn't Dancer, wasn't someone who had blown into his life one day and shattered his world the next. Dancer affected *how* he was; Raulind affected *who* he was . . . had helped shape a broken boy into a reasoning man.

"Yet you've aged in the time I've known you," he continued. Raulind had had the shaping of him; it was important to know who and what had had the shaping of Raulind.

"I left the pools."

"Left virtual immortality to become manservant to a thirteen-year-old."

"Hardly immortality. And I hope I became more than just a manservant."

"That's what the accountant's record books call it. Why did you do it?"

"I left when that same instinct that told me to join the brothers said the child with the too-old eyes was going to need a friend."

"Instinct again." He tried to keep the censure from his voice, but he felt . . . betrayed by this uncustomary lapse into mysticism from the man who had been his primary source of rational thought.

"Instinct supported by reason. The clever man listens to both. I left because I knew this day would come."

"And that child would have power." It had to be said between them. He had to make the blunt challenge of Raulind's motives.

"Did I leave to be near that power? No. To be part of it? No. I looked toward Rhomandi House and saw that the child I'd been given could turn bitter and malevolent . . . oh, so easily. And with the power that child might one day wield, that would make him a very dangerous man. I hoped to help him become at least a wise man as well."

That much was certainly true. Many were the times these past months that he'd looked back at his life and wondered that—and sometimes *if*—he had any soul left.

"So you left Barsitum for the sake of the Syndicate and the Web."

"Only indirectly. My scope was never so large. The Barsitum Rings spin for the sake of the Web, not for the brothers, not even for what they do. The brothers don't manipulate the Ley or the healing pools. They manipulate the minds and hearts of those who would seek the Ley's help."

"To what end?"

"Only to form a bridge. So the sick can accept that help."

"And me? What did you need to manipulate in me? What . . . bridge did I require?"

"For the Ley to work its cure, nothing. And that very lack of need made me fear for the soul—*and* the heart— of the man that child would become. I realized then that the political power that was a given for the boy's future might only be a training ground for the real power he might one day wield. I didn't want that power to destroy that which had been given to me to save. Fate put you into my hands, and I've never regretted that duty. It was for your sake I left Barsitum, my boy, not the Web's, not the Syndicate's. Their benefit is only incidental."

It struck his own instinctive beliefs . . . which Raulind said he should trust. It was a dangerous ring to grab and trust forever without suspicion, but grab it he would. Raulind had never, in almost fifteen years, given him reason to believe his agenda was anything other than what he described. He owed his very ability to *form* the suspicion to Raulind's influence.

And trust, too, had to begin somewhere; if he'd learned nothing else this past year, he'd learned that trust was as essential as doubt.

"We should have had this conversation a long time ago," he said.

"We couldn't have."

"Why not?"

"Ask yourself."

Mikhyel smiled, thrown back to Raulind's earliest lessons, the earliest catechism of logic and debate. "Because I didn't ask the question. And the brothers don't force; they refine what already exists."

Raulind nodded. "Just so."

"But . . . *how* did you know?"

"Know what?"

"You said you knew this day would come. *How* did you know? Did you know about Dancer? Did you know about my brothers? Did you know all of that?"

"Oh, much more simple than that, my friend." A reminiscent smile pulled the corners of Raulind's mouth. "In thirty years, I never saw the pools glow the way they did when you were in them. Oh, yes, Mikhyel, the Ley likes you. I don't know what you're meant to do, but you won't find it sitting behind your desk. What would you like me to pack?"

Chapter Two

Mikhyel had not changed his mind. Mikhyel had, in fact, been up and out making arrangements behind an unassailable mental wall long before he asked his brothers to his room to announce his departure for Khoratum . . . while dressing for the ride out. Alone. Raulind was out executing his brother's arrangements.

Deymorin couldn't claim surprise, had in fact been making a few plans of his own. But he'd have appreciated confirmation and a timetable.

"I'm sorry, Deymio," Mikhyel said in answer to his own thoughts. "I assumed you understood."

"That you planned to go, yes," Deymorin said, and calmly adjusted his barriers: this meeting had all the earmarks of a session best left to surface exchange. "Go, yes, but not so quickly. Rings, Khyel, give it time. A day, at least. We're living crisis to crisis at the moment. Be certain that in moving on to the next crisis, you aren't leaving the last one to break loose. Everything you've worked for—everything *we've* worked for is hanging in the balance at the moment. There's personal debt, yes, but there's a debt to this city, too, and damned if I'll let you risk it all again for the sake of personal obligations!"

"Not just personal, Deymio," Nikki said quietly. "We *all* owe Dancer. You. Me. The City. We wouldn't have had Mikhyel to lose now, if it weren't for Dancer."

"Thank you, Nikki, but I can make my own arguments," Mikhyel said curtly, and Nikki started, then sat back in his chair, arms folded, chin tucked in to his chest. Mikhyel, arms and chin reflecting much the same attitude, leaned back against his dresser and said, "Let's get this out in the open right from the start. I'm *not* blind to the dangers *or* to the consequences of my actions last spring. I recognize I risked my life unnecessarily to prove some esoteric point to myself, and I realize that in doing so I caused a great deal of unnecessary concern."

Deymorin said dryly, "That's one way of looking at it, I suppose."

Mikhyel had gone into Khoratum undercover, so *Ganfrion* of all people had finally managed to explain to him, in order to prove to himself that he didn't have to sit in the background and let others do the . . . *dirty work.* In that quest for independence, he'd put himself in the way of a young dancer. Had exposed his newly aroused masculine pride to the worst of all possible temptations . . . and then tried to deny it.

And in denying, had exposed his fascination to a curious and censorious public in a way the Barrister, having a discreet, *controlled* affair, would never have done.

Mikhyel caught that thought and frowned. "It was aberrant behavior on my part. No, I didn't cause it. I couldn't stop it, either. And yes, that behavior might have played into the rebels' plans, but that behavior did not cause the rebellion. *That behavior* did not even ignite the attack. If it hadn't been the dance the rebels used for that purpose, it would have been something else. And whatever that 'something else' might have been, it *couldn't* have hurt my position any less within the City." His face took on a puzzled look. "For some reason utterly incomprehensible to me, *that behavior* seems to have strengthened my position with the Syndics and Councillors and businessmen of the Syndicate rather than hurt it."

Deymorin chuckled. "Perhaps because it was one of the most *comprehensible* things you've ever done."

"*Comprehensible?*"

"The people you've been dealing with all these years understand passion and foolishness and mistakes. It was your gods-be-damned perfection, uncompromising logic, and cold-blooded disposition of lives that set you apart."

"Perfection? Hardly."

"Damned right, perfection," Nikki muttered, and cast a dark look that included both of them. "And then they come to my office, nervous as hell . . . and exit *relieved* to discover a tongue-tied incompetent within the household."

Mikhyel's dark brows twitched.

"These are people who make mistakes every day—mistakes a whole lot worse than you made with Temorii. They laugh it off. *You*, you let it escalate into—" Nikki broke off and jerked to his feet. "Hell, Deymorin's right. Stay here. The City needs you, just as you are: perfect with just a hint of a scandalous past to prove you're human."

Mikhyel's head dropped, his loose hair veiling his face but not the black anger that seethed a cloud about him. Very slowly, that anger cooled, and when the clouds had turned to ice, Mikhyel's burning gaze lifted.

"Let me tell you something, brothers. The City doesn't need me. Since my return, since my . . . experiences . . . I've been far *less* accommodating than at any time in my career. I've spent the past few months convincing people who might well have their own answers for those problems that my way was the only way and that my hand at the helm was indispensable to the peace. I've used everything from guilt, to fear of the Triumvirate, to implications of treason to gain their agreement. All in the name of efficiency; I've pressed to get this *done.* We have certain issues resolved, but that *doesn't* mean I approve of *how* I accomplished that end. And from now on, the City doesn't need me, no. From now on, the City is damnwell better off *without* me, because I sincerely doubt I could ever retreat from this Darian position now."

Mikhyel's melancholy this time had its own internal darkness, enough to give Deymorin pause.

"You didn't actually threaten anyone, did you?"

"It wasn't necessary. Guilt supplied the threats in the minds of the guilty, and there are plenty of guilty parties in what happened in Khoratum and elsewhere. They think they get a second chance. In fact, they do. But it's their last chance. If they foul this one, they will take the full consequences. I've used every bit of leverage, burned every bridge. From here, they're on their own. The other outcome is, I *can* leave Rhomatum now with a relatively clear conscience that *should* something happen to me, the Syndicate will fall apart only through the determined efforts of the Syndics themselves. And if the Syndicate is truly that fragile, then . . . then to hell with the lot of them."

"That's a bit cold-blooded, don't you think? What about the thousands of lives that could be ruined?"

A slow silence hung between them. Not resentment. Consideration.

"You know, Deymorin, I don't particularly care."

"I don't believe that! I was there, brother, when you stopped the cab on the way home from the Crypt. I saw the look on your face when you saw what the riots and panic had done to the City, the sadness you felt."

"For the City."

"Your poor foolish Rhomatumin, wasn't that how you put it?"

"How I *thought*, as I recall. You caught that, did you? But it was damage to the City I saw. Sadness for the people as a whole, not individuals. I don't know what that says about me. To me, the City and Syndicate are a system of balancing parts. A machine. I can look at the system and repair it, I can care that it functions smoothly for the sake of the parts, but the people themselves . . . they're numbers on a sheet. The people I care about, *truly* care about—besides you and Nikki—I can count on one hand. Kiyrstin, Nethaalye, Ganfrion, and Raulind . . . beyond that, they're all faces. Obligations. Needs and wants."

"But can't you see?" Nikki said, impatiently. "*That's* what makes you so good." And then clarified, as they both turned to face him: "Hells above, if you tried to make each life important, you'd waste all your time and energy on a handful of people, wouldn't you?"

Black melancholy gave way at last. Mikhyel sat down and kicked his house shoes off. "Thanks, Nikki. I needed to hear that. I truly needed to hear that."

Under other circumstances that might be a victory. But

it wasn't, not truly, and Mikhyel had his boots in hand. He was going.

"It's all in that packet in the safe in my office, Deymorin," Mikhyel said, shaking the boots out over a convenient waste can. "Paulis has the combination. Raulind has too. Raulind could finish everything. As for Mauritum, the meeting has been delayed until further notice. No explanation. Let them wonder, dammit. They've left us hanging often enough." He leaned over to pull on his well-worn riding boots. "I've spoken with Paulis. He can write my letters better than I." He straightened. "Are you coming?"

Nikki leaned forward. "I will, if he won't."

But Mikhyel shook his head, his attention all for his right boot. Without a word, he raised that booted foot to Deymorin who grabbed the heel and pulled it free, then handed it back. Mikhyel shoved his hand down the shank, wiggling something free, and shook it again over the waste can. He leaned over again to pull it on, and said, without looking up. "If only one remains here, Nikki, it must be you. Deymorin would be at bare blades with Lidye in two days. Better if I went alone."

Abrupt, uncaring of feelings: it was Mikhyel at his most autocratic. Nikki's fingers turned white, where he gripped his chair arm: unhappy with that dismissal of his offer, as Deymorin was damned unhappy about his own summary disposition.

"Deymorin expressed the willingness to go last night." Mikhyel tossed his head back, flinging his hair out of his eyes. "If he's still of a mind—"

"I haven't said otherwise, Khyel, but—"

"How soon can you be ready?"

He raised a hand, then let it drop to the chair arm. "I could *go* now, but . . . dammit, Khyel, I . . . hell, *you* can explain to Kiyrstin!"

"Fair enough." Mikhyel sat up, with another toss of that untamed mane. "Where is she?"

"For the love of . . . I was *joking,* brother. I'll handle my own explanations, thanks all the same."

Mikhyel shrugged and stood up to shove his feet firmly

into the boots, and Deymorin heard Nikki take a deep breath, a breath just the slightest bit shaky.

Whatever permeated the air this morning, it was setting them all dangerously on edge.

"How urgent do you think it is?" Deymorin asked.

"Very."

Nikki asked, "Should you contact Rhomatum again and ask him to leyapult you there?"

"Considering the state of the Web between here and Khoratum, I can't risk it. The Tamshi are too damned unpredictable under the best of circumstances. Besides, we have no idea who is hearing what in these long-range conversations. As for involving Rhomatum at all . . . with Mother potentially at the core of the problem, considering what happened the last time those two met . . ." Mikhyel gave a twitch of his shoulders. "Besides, if Mother isn't a part of the problem and *can* be reached, she could be a surprise option I'd like to have in reserve."

"If you even need her to leyapult you in," Deymorin said pointedly.

"Of course, I do."

"Who was trying to hand you over to Rhyys last night? Or was that your doing?" And at Mikhyel's blank look. "You were going, brother. You were halfway to ghosthood when I came in your room."

"And you pulled me back?" Mikhyel asked, face blank as he stared down at them.

He nodded, and anger, frustration and questions roiled in the underneath. "Rings, Khyel, what would you have had me do? Let you go? Not knowing why or to where, or into what, or to whom?"

"No, of course not." But a part of Mikhyel, Deymorin could sense, wished logic would go away. A part of his brother wished very much he were with Thyerri that moment, fighting for freedom together. And that rejection, however slight, of the rational thought processes, was so antithetical to the Barrister, he couldn't let it slip past unremarked.

"Dammit, listen to your heart," he said, "and acknowledge its part in your judgment now. That's all I'm trying to say; you've got the bit in your teeth and are running for the finish line, forgetting about the fences! There are still questions—"

"Answers to which we won't get sitting here. I don't know what's going on or why this person wants me—"

"Khyel—*Khyel*!" he interrupted. "This is what I'm talking about. Your mind is open then closed tight. Emotions and impressions are flying, but you're not telling us what we need to know. All our reports say Rhyys is still in command. Did you get something last night to indicate he's not?"

Mikhyel took a deep breath. He could almost hear his brother's heartbeat slow.

"Thyerri thought something like *Rhyys, but not Rhyys*," Mikhyel said. "I don't know what it meant. Personally, I'm not ready to speculate on who or why, or even how many are involved up there. I'm certainly not about to stake my life on that assumption. I wouldn't have thought there was enough cognizance left in Rhyys to accomplish anything like what we experienced last night, let alone what we experienced on the mountain." He slid on a pair of gloves, flexed his fingers, then shook his head and pulled them off. "But I take nothing for granted. The courier I have standing by carries a letter to Rhyys based on your information; that doesn't mean I think it's actually Rhyys in charge."

"Courier. I suppose it's foolish to ask, but have you tried just calling to Thyerri? Have *him* inform . . . whoever, that you're coming?"

"A part of me hasn't *stopped* trying since you pulled me out last night. But I can't get through."

"Dare I suggest, would you like some help?"

Mikhyel frowned as he pulled a second pair of gloves from a top drawer. "I considered it. Then rejected it. I . . . don't like what I was picking up. If we were to break through, now, together, with Khoratum alerted . . . I'm not certain what I might drag you and Nikki into." He glanced up. "I'm not willing to risk that . . . yet. The thing is, I not only can't get through, I don't think it's Thyerri keeping me out now."

Which could account for the hint of panic that slipped past his barriers.

"Rhyys? Having alerted you, he'll let you stew?"

"Possible. But we don't even know if it's only one person or one faction. It could be some spinner from another node taking advantage of the situation, or one of Rhyys' monitors. We can't even discount the possibility of some unknown local—like Mirym—having stepped in."

"You said Mirym was in New Khoratum," Nikki protested.

"I said *like* Mirym." A trial of a second pair of gloves, also rejected. "Another hiller . . . chosen, as she claims she was chosen. Or perhaps even more than one individual—considering our own example. Another . . . triumvirate, perhaps."

Deymorin frowned. "Ringspinning is not something you just step into the Tower and start doing, Khyel."

"Says the man who just reset the Khoratum ring?"

"That was not entirely an accident, brother."

"And whoever is in there has had at least as long as you to figure things out—perhaps with Rhyys' help; perhaps with the help of some . . . ley-adept, like Mirym. Again considering our own experience: I can't be blind-sided if I don't assume I know the answer. The letter I've drafted requests Rhyys meet me to discuss the future of Khoratum, and it demands the release of *Thyerri gorMikhyel.*"

"Khyel, you can't just—"

"It's a declaration of responsibility for Thyerri. A statement of official position. Thyerri will deny it, but legally it says I'm assuming responsibility for anything he's done; more importantly, it makes him, alive and well, a piece with which to bargain. They won't throw that away."

"Aren't you *assuming* that?"

Mikhyel froze. Put the first pair of gloves with the coat laid out and waiting for him. Then said: "Hoping."

"And if whoever's there doesn't understand Rhoma-tumin law?"

"Rhyys would. Whoever receives that letter will assume I believe myself to be facing Rhyys—and, from the tone of that letter, Rhyys as I knew him, not as the person capable of last night's . . . incident. If they think I'm taken in, I'm none the worse off and they'll believe they have the advantage of surprise over me, perhaps get careless."

"But what if the new node out there gets in the way of the link between us?" Nikki asked, and his eagerness to be included in the planning, his frustration at not being part of the action, were clear—and damnably understandable. "Maybe I should go at least as far as the base, where we know I can reach the mountain."

Mikhyel, who had picked up a sheet of paper and perused its contents while Nikki spoke replied almost absently. "It didn't keep me from reaching Dancer last night, and I won't be blocking you as he was blocking me." He signed the sheet, then met Nikki's gaze. "Besides, we need you here in the capital. You're Deymorin's link to the Rings and Kiyrstin. She and Lidye are too damned close to their time. Thaalye can handle the Tower—"

"We don't know that," Deymorin objected, still seeing a man in far too great a hurry, following far too many tracks at once.

"Then stay here and tend them yourself!" At least he'd gotten Mikhyel's full attention, however enraged. "What in hell do you want from me, Deymorin? We don't know much of anything, now do we? *I know* how to make Thyerri an issue. *I know* how to negotiate. *Your presence* might conceivably lend a real importance to those negotiations— something beyond my damnably public fascination with the object in question. Beyond that, we're writing the rules as we go. *Have* been for months now."

Deymorin's clenched teeth began to ache. He *didn't* know why now, all of a sudden, the entire gambit felt wrong. Certainly the air seethed with emotion, made all the words charged and barbed, but his concerns had left that factor behind long ago. He sensed events thrust ahead by the other side, not theirs: the other side's choice of time *and* place. In negotiation, he trusted Mikhyel's judgment; in fencing with edged steel, he trusted his own.

And he wasn't the least bit certain *negotiation* would be the result of Mikhyel's headlong rush up that mountain. Mikhyel was, in Kiyrstin's words, a man very much on the edge.

"We're being pushed," he pointed out. "They want us now and not before, not after. There's a reason and we don't know it."

"Obviously." Mikhyel's arrogant chin lifted, and the wall between them thickened. "If you'd feel better staying here to man the Tower yourself, by all means do so. Far be it from me to compare instincts."

"Oh, I'm going, you hard-headed idiot," Deymorin said. "You'll not shed me that easily—our *instincts* are not that far removed. But I'd appreciate it if you'd slow up a bit, make sure you've thought it through before we make an overt move. . . ."

"'Thought it through.'" Mikhyel repeated slowly, and he leaned back against his dressing table, arms crossed. "I've done nothing but *think it through* since you told me Thyerri was doing *my dirty work* in Khoratum."

"Damn it, Khyel—"

"Call it what you will. I'm not *accusing* you. I'm not *accusing* anyone. What is, is. He was working for the Rhomandi when, for whatever reason, he felt compelled to venture into the Tower—"

"And *I* feel compelled to point out, he went in without waiting for clearance, Khyel. Without giving us time to prepare some sort of plan to get him out."

"You're the man who hand picks independent operators. Working independently—for you and because of me—he's been discovered, and damned if *I'm* willing to leave him there as long as it might take us to be absolutely certain of all your answers."

"So you'll compound the loss by going after him."

"I'll do what needs doing."

"You listen to me, Mikhyel dunMheric! You're irreplaceable at the moment. We all are! You're the one who spent the last year convincing me to accept my responsibilities. Now, dammitall, you can listen to your own advice. Send in Ganfrion, but *you* stay clear until you know the lay of the land!"

Temper boiled dangerously hot in this room, in this concentration of their presence above the Ley, and Deymorin could not but think they were all at the limit. Guilt came through in Mikhyel's anger; hurt in Nikki's reaction, anxiousness in his own. But while all those things might be a factor in Mikhyel's mind, Mikhyel was *not* one to let any of those things decide the case. If he couldn't trust that in his brother, he couldn't trust anything.

"*You've* thought it through, brother." Deymorin leaned forward on the settee, resting his elbows on his knees, hands palm up and open. "Help me see it your way. I'm not *fighting* you. I just need—no, I *want* to be as certain as you seem to be. I'm with you either way, but I'd rather be with you without reservations."

And it seemed he found the key at last; the underneath cooled abruptly. Mikhyel lifted a mollifying hand, and sat back down.

"I *did* discuss it with Ganfrion."

"Hah! That explains the temper, then."

Mikhyel's mouth twitched. "Most likely. He was, as you might imagine, of much the same opinion as you at first. He . . . has conceded the point. He's certainly willing to try, but the simple truth is, with all his talents, *he* hasn't a streetlamp's chance in lightning-blasted hell against whatever's holding Thyerri. Holding *Dancer*: think on it . . . with all that suggests. Ganfrion can't deal with the Ley. We might. I think we pose a large and potent *might*. This far away . . . I'm just casting blind, a thought as terrifying, I assure you, to me as to you. The links are so fraught with emotion and associations, sometimes they do nothing but confuse the most important and simplest facts. Up there, I'll have some confirmation of the real state of affairs. Once I know, *maybe* I can do something substantive about whatever is blocking Dancer from me. Dancer's link is with me, therefore, I, at least, must go."

"Need I remind you what happened the last time one of us tried to approach Khoratum?"

"And if the same thing does occur, we turn around and come back. I don't think there's a lightning blasted chance it will. As you say, whatever is up there is calling the timing on this, and they're ready for me, at least, to come up that mountain. I'm not crazy, Deymorin.

"All of this for one man."

"Hardly." Mikhyel shook his head. "I'm not going to Khoratum just to free Thyerri. I've an obligation to him, yes, but I've also got to stop these attacks, for my sake, and yours and for the Web. Whoever—*whatever*—has him is using him to get to me. To what end remains to be seen. Perhaps if we understood the Ley and this so-called gift we share . . . but we don't. I've waited too long. You talk about my care for the City. This threatens the mechanism. You talk about the lives of thousands of people. This could affect them. Profoundly. I shouldn't have ignored Khoratum. I *knew* something was wrong months ago. *I* should have tried contacting Mother. At the very least, we should have been actively following up on the Talent we know we possess. Should have been looking for others who share it, who might be able to go to Khoratum now."

"Someone like Thyerri."

"Someone like Thyerri—but with Ganfrion's experience."

"There's no such person."

"We don't know that, now do we? After the battle, we had Mirym and we had Dancer, in addition to our own example. I should have looked for others. Should have put it above all else. Instead, I let it slip through our fingers. I did, Deymorin, none other on this one. I was foolish and self-centered. I drove Dancer off and let others try to find Mirym. And now someone *like Rhyys but not Rhyys* is in Khoratum Tower, in possession of the Rings, possibly even in possession of a relationship with Mother, from the smell I got out of Khoratum all those months ago. This isn't good, brothers."

"No reason to think you could have done any better."

"No? The instant I tried to reach through, I succeeded.

The instant I tried to reach Mirym, I did. I *should* have tried both . . . long ago. But I didn't. I assumed I couldn't. The Barrister broke the cardinal rule of law. He *assumed* that something was true because he damnwell *wanted* it to be true; he assumed that if Nikki couldn't get through the warding up there, none of us could. If I had at the very least contacted Mirym, we might have her help now. Might have the advantage of her knowledge and experience with Mother and the Khoramali hillers. Instead, she shoved me away last night."

"Why don't you just leave her alone?" The raw pain in Nikki's voice startled them all . . . including, so the link revealed, Nikki, who rushed ahead, as stubborn as his brothers: "You've ruined Dancer's life, and Nethaalye's, must you ruin hers as well?"

Silence filled the room, broken only by Nikki's shaking breaths.

"I'm sorry, Khyel. I didn't mean that." But that link that couldn't lie implied otherwise. It was filled with raw pain, with seething anger such as he'd never associated with Nikki. Not the petulant, self-centered angst of last spring, but a need to strike back, for all there was no target. Their youngest brother had been pushed to his own edge by the raw emotions seething in the room and he and Mikhyel had no one to blame but themselves.

"Nikki, you shouldn't be the one to apologize," he began, but Nikki interrupted.

"Not the only one perhaps, but, yes, apologize, for my timing, if not my sentiment. I just wish—but, Mikhyel, you didn't even *name* Mirym amongst those you care about, and she carries your child. *How could you not name her?*"

Nikki, who had had what they'd thought an infatuation with Mirym, who in his still-green years had agreed to marry Lidye for the dynasty. But Nikki had not anticipated Mikhyel of all people would draw Mirym into his bed on his very wedding night and in one try get her with child. It was not fair, Nikki's anger shouted at them all. It was not fair how they had dealt with Mirym, whom he . . . *might have* loved.

Mikhyel stared at Nikki for a long moment more: drawn at last out of his self-absorption.

"I asked you a question on your wedding day, Nikki," he said quietly. "I doubted your answer then, and have regretted ever since not acting on my own judgment in the matter. It's still not too late. I'll do what I can to get Mirym back here, if that's what you want and provided she returns your regard."

Nikki's eyes flickered at that, but he shook his head. "Second wife to Lidye's first? I think not."

"We could make Lidye behave."

Another shuddering breath, a deeper, steadier one.

"We could, but would that be fair to Lidye? She has her own happiness, her own pride."

"So have you!" Deymorin said sharply.

"My happiness wouldn't let me go back on our agreement, and she's as much Anheliaa's pawn in this situation as any of us! Mirym . . ." Nikki took a deep heaving breath, and the air about him cooled. "I didn't love her then, Khyel. I don't love her now; I just know I can't love Lidye. I think . . . I think I want to love . . . someone. I've . . . *felt* what Deymorin feels at just the mention of Kiyrstin, I've felt what Dancer brought to you . . ."

"You can't possibly want that!"

"Yes, I do. Maybe you don't understand that, but I do, absolutely. And it's not going to happen: that's the reality of my life. Deymorin's with Kiyrstin, you'll be going to Dancer—and I *want* you to, Khyel. I *want* Dancer safe. I *want* you to work out whatever it is you need to work out and be happy. But you'll be gone, then, too, and I'll be left with—" Nikki's shoulders dropped, and he turned his back on them to face the window. "I'm sorry—both of you. I didn't mean to bring any of this up. There are more important matters facing us now. Far more important matters. My botched love life is my own problem."

Instincts honed in a lifetime of caring for Nikki protested. Deymorin inhaled to object; Mikhyel's similar intake of breath was audible, but Nikki's hand raised to stop them both.

"And *when* we have the time for such things, I'll appreciate your help and advice." Nikki turned to face them, and
his expression was well under control. "Let's look forward
to the time when such minor problems are all we have
to face."

Deymorin felt Mikhyel's mind reach out in concern, felt
Nikki's open to it, and the three-way linkage snapped into
place. Nikki had smothered the upset, pushed it far down
beneath conscious thought.

He had learned, Deymorin feared, a certain talent in
that regard.

"I'm sorry, Shepherdess." Deymorin pulled on his warm-
est coat, then paused to give her a quick kiss on his way
to his dressing room where Tonio was busily preparing a
saddle pack of necessities, a valise for the pack horse, as
well as a trunk to follow at a slower pace . . . just in case,
Mikhyel had said.

"The heavier one," Deymorin answered, in response to
a choice of dress coats. "It's damned cold up there by now,
and I doubt they've got decent—"

A disturbance in the Ley. A *profound* disturbance. He
sought the lead monitor's mind and found . . . nothing.

Damn. He wasn't used to this multi-tracking. He headed
for the door—

And met Kiyrstin head-on.

He scarcely recognized her. Her face was sickly pale, and
the whites showed around her eyes.

"Kiyrsti, what—"

"Deymorin, you *must* do something now!"

He grasped her by the arms, and fear struck him to his
heart as she collapsed in his hold. He swept her bodily into
his arms and took her to their bed and packed pillows
behind her.

"No!" she screamed and her body convulsed as if in pain.
"Damn you, Lidye!" Fury distorted her face and she
grasped his hands hard. "Stop her, Deymorin. If you have
to kill her, *make her stop*!"

"What's she talking about?" Tonio asked, but Deymorin

ignored him, ignored everything in the room, seeking the Tower and the Rings, discovered anger to match Kiyrstin's when he felt the waves emanating from those lines he'd just cleared yesterday.

"Stay with her," he commanded Tonio, and ran from the room, heading for the Tower.

{Deymorin, dammit, what's going on?} Mikhyel's voice asked in his head.

{It's Lidye,} he answered the same way as he took the stairs to the Tower three at a time. {She's trying to force her baby's birth and she's taking every baby in the Web with her!}

Chapter Three

The guards seated outside the ringchamber door just stared sightlessly at him. Dead or drugged, Deymorin didn't even stop to check: others were following. He kicked the door open.

"Get out!" Lidye's screech echoed through the ring-chamber and into the stairwell. Deymorin winced and slammed the door shut, hiding the image of the woman sprawled on Anheliaa's huge couch from any others who might come up the stairwell.

The monitors, like the guards, were frozen in their chairs, and like the guards, their condition would have to wait.

Appearing child-small on a piece of furniture made to accommodate Anheliaa's dimensions, and with only a filmy negligee for her pregnant dignity, there was nothing young or innocent in the snarling vision that greeted him.

"Give it up, Lidye."

"Damn you, I lost the rhythm!" Her eyes closed and sudden calm swept her face. "Ah, . . . there."

And here in the Tower, he felt those waves sweep his own body. Nerves tingled, muscles twitched . . . he could only guess what that suggestion did to the female bodies it encountered.

"I should never have allowed you to reopen that stair-well."

"You *allowed* nothing; you had no say in the matter. Dammit, woman, *stop what you're doing*!"

She shrugged, eyes still closed and voice distant. "You're overreacting, Rhomandi, as always."

Her only attendant in this madness was a frightened servant girl, who cowered behind the couch.

"Leave us," he said abruptly, felt immediate remorse when the girl ducked her head in like a turtle, and fear colored the very air of the Tower. "It's all right. You've done nothing wrong, and will not be held accountable. Just leave her to me."

The servant dipped a curtsy and squeezed out the door.

"Turning midwife now, Rhomandi?"

"What did you do to the guards and the monitors?"

A shadow smile drifted across her face, and she held out her hand. "Would you like to see?"

"Hardly." But he sought, now, to touch those minds of the monitors, here within the chamber itself, and discovered only too-quiet sleep.

"Coward," Lidye's tone was absentminded, and her hand drooped, releasing a long, thin needle.

"Drugged?" An answer more palatable than the more exotic options.

She didn't answer, her breath coming hard and fast. Her attention was all for those waves of nature-shifting suggestion rippling out through the Web. He could *see* that Web now, saw it as an intricate maze of glowing lines emanating from the viewing globe and extending out from the Tower, could see her suggestion shimmering out through that Web like a stone tossed into a pool. And shimmering in that Web, tiny points of light: miniature patterns within the Web, individuals sensitive to Lidye's determined efforts.

And some of the points throbbed red in time with those waves: other mothers-to-be within the City, caught in that insidious assault.

One of those was Kiyrstin.

"Shut it down!" he demanded. With the lives of mothers and possible offspring at stake, he fought the instinct that would simply wrest control of the Rings from her hands.

The body under the negligee contorted as if with pain, but the face above remained eerily unaffected.

"What's—" That gasp after breath left no mark on that too-pretty face. "What's the matter, Rhomandi? Afraid to take control? I thought as much. You're no master. You'll never *be* a master." Another panting pause. "Get out of my tower."

"You *know* I can't take the Rings. Not with this. I could kill every woman you're dragging into labor with you!"

"Coward." The epithet exploded on a sharp bark of laughter. "A true master wouldn't even stop to consider the risk."

It was a risk he wasn't willing to take. Not with his untried Talent, not with his male body. There was an indelible link between master and Rings, a link that made the flow of power an extension of the master's own body. He could sense that flow of energy, but his body could no more correctly judge the effect of those waves than it could direct a bird to fly.

"Just *do* it, JD." Kiyrstin's voice. And Kiyrstin was in the Tower, along with his brothers. "You can't be any more ham—" Her voice caught, and she finished on a snarl, "handed than that *cow*!"

He hadn't even heard them come in.

"Help?" Mikhyel asked, not chancing the link.

Tempting. So tempting, but:

"One ignorant male in the mix is bad enough. Three arguing over technique would kill them for certain." And he chanced the link to clarify the thought as only the link could, sensed both brothers' rather bemused concession to his judgment, and chanced a further: {Watch Kiyrstin!}

{I've got her.} Mikhyel, he thought, though for a moment, it was his own arms that supported Kiyrstin's uncharacteristically weak body. Then he severed the connection and built the wall between himself and his brothers, needing all his concentration to insinuate himself into those rhythmic waves originating on Anheliaa's couch.

{No!} Lidye's protest echoed through the Web, and what Dancer called her essence rippled violent red and orange through the waves. He countered that anger with cool greens and blues, and the result hissed along his nerves. But the waves subsided, becoming minor ripples by the time they reached those other points of light, those gentle, frightened entities that were part of the Web without even knowing it, whose associated bodies writhed in beds and on floors throughout the City. He saw the tiny patterns clearly now, felt the fear and caught flashes of the world through their eyes. Rather than sort and interpret those images, he simply damped the waves, absorbing the energy generated as Lidye writhed and screamed, a cancerous growth on that throbbing web of humanity.

But it wasn't enough. He knew in his head what those waves attempted to do, knew theoretically the mechanical sequence of birth, but his body, his inherent pattern, was woefully ignorant. He could absorb but he could not counter.

. . . you can only imagine . . .

Kiyrstin's words to him, and his own reply: *my imagination is pretty good.*

But not good enough. He could only feel that new life vicariously by wrapping his arms about her, or pressing his ear to her beautiful round belly. Even if he could link with her at will, as he could with his brothers, he doubted it would be enough.

And if he failed, Kiyrstin would suffer, not he.

. . . I can't promise I'll be there . . .

If Lidye's anger overcame him now, Kiyrstin could die in the backlash.

Frustration and fear dimmed the blues and greens, and the red seeped through, turning the whole a sickly mauve. Kiyrstin moaned, and somewhere in the room came the sound of sickness. He would lose her. He'd lose their son. Mikhyel's deal with Garetti, his marriage, none of it would happen, all because of one woman's arrogance.

{Marriage?} That one woman's protest struck his mind like a solid blow. And in his mind, that one woman was neither Lidye or Anheliaa, but some strange amalgam of both. {Never.}

The waves increased in amplitude, the red streaming through, carrying the taste of anger, hatred, for all things Mauritumin—including Kiyrstin.

Anger was her weapon, fear his weakness. But if he answered in anger, would he not destroy the very ones he hoped to save?

"I'm here, love," Kiyrstin's whisper infiltrated his world, "*We're* here. Feel him?"

He did feel. She was in his arms, the forced contractions rippling against his fingertips as one of those waves escaped his control altogether. Mikhyel's mind was back, hesitantly providing the body sense he'd gained from his link with Dancer: {*For what it's worth, brother . . .*} and Nikki was there as well. With them came an awareness of Kiyrstin, a blending of bodies that sent that ley-driven ripple through his own gut.

And another awareness, weak and sleepy and without form, riding the waves without thought to consequence.

His son.

"Remember Deyma, JD," Kiyrstin breathed into his ear. "You've watched her often enough."

You're not a horse, he thought, but must have said aloud, because her laughter vibrated his body.

"I'm glad you—" A gasp as another wave broke past him. He snarled and struck back, knew horror as his battle with Lidye brought another gasp from Kiyrstin, who then finished in a rush, "—noticed. But it's close enough. We're not that different."

And at a distance, through the haze of his brothers' minds, he saw Deyma and that matter of fact manner she had of lying back quietly when the birthing pains subsided, head heavy in the clean straw. Breathing. Just breathing. Long and slow. And he thought of the scent of clean straw, new-mown hay, and spring in the Khoramali. And he thought of lying back on Anheliaa's too-comfortable couch and thinking of nothing and falling quietly into deep slumber. . . .

And the ripples ebbed.

The Web's healthy iridescence returned.

The tiny patterns fluttered into varicolored stars.

{Deymio?}

He yawned . . .

"Deymio." It was a whisper this time; he felt the breath

against his ear. "You did it, brother. You can let them go now."

. . . and blinked himself awake. He was lying on the floor, a mop of red hair in front of his nose: Kiyrstin curled on the floor next to him. Quite comfortably, or so it appeared. He caressed her side as he slid his arm free, then pushed himself up off the floor. How he'd come to be lying there, he had no recollection.

The Tower was filled with a singularly quiet lot of people. Nikki sat next to his wife, his hands poised above her, ready, Deymorin realized, to hold her—or knock her cold, from the mental hints seeping out—should she awaken.

Ready, as he'd been all during that battle for control. Ruthless, as he hadn't know Nikki could be.

"We've got to get her away from here," Nikki said. "We can't risk this happening again."

Deymorin blinked again, gathering wits that still seemed inclined to drift off along that healthy Web of light.

"We could have her taken to Armayel." That was Mikhyel's suggestion, and it took a moment for the name of their nearest Outside holding to register on him, he was that deeply enmeshed in the Web. Deymorin shook his head, not in disagreement, but only to clear it.

"I doubt that will be necessary. If she refuses to stay out of the Tower, yes. But from the fight she didn't put up, I don't think she can do anything without the direct presence of the Rings. Also, considering what she just tried to do, who's to know what it will do to the pregnancy? Best she's as near the Rhomatum hospitals as possible. Not—forgive me Nikki—that I particularly care what happens to her, but that child—your child—doesn't deserve to suffer for her foolhardiness."

"No apology necessary, Deymorin. I just can't imagine what she was thinking."

"She's losing control," Mikhyel said, and held a hand to help Deymorin to his feet. "She's losing control of the Web and her body all at the same time, and she's fighting back. I imagine it's Deymorin's presence in the Tower that sent her over the edge. It's Anheliaa all over again. I warn you, brother," he said as he steadied Deymorin's wavering balance, "if you start to act like this, I'll send you to our ex-roommates in the Crypt myself."

"Don't bother." Deymorin closed his eyes and forced his head to clear. "Just take me Outside the Web and shoot me."

He knelt beside Kiyrstin, leaned over and kissed the side of her mouth. She murmured something unintelligible, then rolled over, letting her arm drop above her head, presenting the full prospect to his waiting lips.

"Oh, my." Her whisper brushed his mouth. "I want you to remember just what you did the next time junior keeps me awake all night."

"Have to move the bed up here," he whispered back.

"Laddybuck, I don't give a damn where the bed is, so long as you're in it."

"Now and forever, my lady wife."

"Which reminds me, did you remember to say thank you to Khyel?"

"Thank you to Khyel," he murmured, and sealed his promise with a kiss.

{You're welcome. Now, don't you think you should get the mother of the next Rhomandi off the floor?}

{Spoilsport.}

Chapter Four

{Dancer, if you can hear me, hold on.}

Anything was possible in this sea of Non, even promises from Mikhyel. Non-fear. Non-hope. Non-thought. Non-time.

{If you can hear me . . . Tell Rhyys if he touches you, he's a dead man. Tell him I'm coming.}

Rhyys? There was no Rhyys, no Scarface, no Dancer. Certainly no Mikhyel. Thought strove to drive him from the world of Non. To make him feel again, to make him care. But with care came fear, with awareness came pain. In the sea of Non, there was only a sense of being stretched across the world, arms, legs, head . . . all being pulled in different directions.

His rings of inner sanctuary were gone, burned to ashes in that final assault on the creature that called itself Rhyys. Rhyys had not returned; nothing had touched him since he'd returned to this non-world.

Or had it?

With that question, the world of Non rejected him. Pain lanced through his shoulders from arms stretched overhead. Darkness and cold surrounded him.

He felt battered, as if he'd fallen down a mountainside, but could recall nothing past that all-consuming flare of light. How long had it been? What had happened?

His doing, that blast. A final attempt to destroy the tendrils that were Rhyys-but-not-Rhyys, a failed attempt surely, else he'd be dead or free. Those under Rhyys would have no hesitation in taking some action against his murderer. Neither had Rhyys taken over his body—surely he

would know if his mind were not his own? And Rhyys
would hardly let himself remain hanging like tomorrow's
stew.

That Rhyys had not had him killed was not entirely surprising. Rhyys wanted Mikhyel. With him dead, Rhyys had
no bait, though he'd fight that fate with all the strength
remaining to him. And yet—

Tell Rhyys I'm coming . . .

Could it be true? Could Mikhyel be returning to Khoratum? Had Rhyys—or Vandoshin—succeeded after all?

Hunger and thirst grew with each passing breath. His
shoulders ached. His burning eyes were glued shut. He
didn't want to know with what, for he recalled an afternoon
lesson with Zelin, a lost match, and Zelin, in victory, drawing back, face averted. Zelin had said then that with his
moves and his Tamshi eyes, Thyerri needed no more help
from him.

He'd had at the time and still had no idea what Zelin
had feared, but from the feel *he* very much feared that
whatever he had just done might well have burned those
Tamshi eyes from their sockets.

He couldn't see and the only sound was the throb of the
mountain's ancient heartbeat. He sought the world of Non,
where time passed without notice.

The world of Non called to him, welcomed him into
nothingness.

And on the edge of nothing, She was waiting.

§ § §

The breath of cinnamon and cloves vanished, assuming
it had ever been there. Mikhyel let his head sink into his
crossed arms, relaxed fists he didn't remember clenching.

It was the closest he'd come to reaching Dancer and
would have to be the last attempt for a while: his head felt
disastrously close to bursting. Including his brothers in that
call might have alleviated the headache, but might also
have exposed them to whatever had Dancer. *He* had al-

ready been exposed, and so, he tried. And reached . . . something that had done nothing to ease his mind.

The familiar sounds and sights of his Rhomandi House office surrounded him, but his reality in that moment was the sights and sounds—and smells—of Sparingate Prison. Perhaps it was those memories alone that raised the gag reflex he fought to control. . . .

And perhaps that hint of spiced raspberries had been real, perhaps that gag reflex was only a reflection of some other distant, but current horror. The sights and smells not Sparingate at all, but only his mind's interpretation of the impressions that had come through as haze-obscured as the scent of spices.

The Rhomandi were not a religious family; Darius had led the Exodus out of Mauritum precisely to escape the pitfalls of deification of the ringmasters. Mikhyel had a surface understanding of all the varied religious factions throughout the Web, but for himself, only a healthy skepticism remained. Even Mother and Rhomatum, which some would willingly call gods and others magical, were to him only phenomena to be examined and understood.

At times such as this, he envied those who did believe. With his mind scoffing at him all the while, his heart called out to whatever gods might exist to allow Mikhyel dun-Mheric, not Dancer, to pay for Mikhyel dunMheric's mistakes.

And in the end, his mind won: his heart found no peace at all, only the impatience of yet one more delay.

Lidye lay sleeping in her apartments, with the physician, Diorak, at her side and guards at her door; Deymorin was in his rooms with Kiyrstin, his anxiety a constant niggling at the back of Mikhyel's head; Nikki was in the Tower with Nethaalye, an instant link to himself and to Deymorin, should Lidye prove able to affect the Rings despite all their beliefs to the contrary.

He couldn't leave, at least not until Lidye awoke. It might take all of them to control whatever had driven her to such extremes. And Deymorin might have changed his mind altogether about going. He couldn't blame him if that

were the case, but Raulind said his instincts were sound,
and the same instinct that drove him toward Khoratum
demanded Deymorin's presence as well—

Though in all good sense, he should challenge that instinct more than any other in his life. If his instincts were
not his own, drawing Deymorin, the only potential ringmaster among them, away from the Rhomatum Rings might be
the best way to weaken them.

But if the unnamed They believed that, if they counted
on that assumed weakness, they would be sorely mistaken.
Even now, with the Rings beating smoothly up in the Tower,
it took only Nikki's presence for Deymorin to feel—

He couldn't know that. He didn't, but Deymorin did.
Deymorin was similarly concerned and their thoughts
flowed one to the next near seamlessly, and he wondered
if he should be concerned.

{I'm not.} Deymorin's thought, clear and strong: deliberate communication as opposed to that subtle melding of
impressions. And from Nikki: {It's not as if it hasn't been
going on for a long time—maybe even all our lives.}

It was a curious possibility, one that could well account
for a variety of past arguments, where issues seemingly
clear suddenly became confused in his head when he was
in his brothers' vicinity.

Wry amusement filtered through from Deymorin.
{Hardly necessary, Khyel. Ask any set of brothers.}

{Perhaps all brothers share a similar link,} Nikki said.

Open laughter now. {Then may Darius protect us all.}

For his own part, he found the possibility singularly attractive. He'd prefer not to be singled out from the rest of
humanity—any more than he already was.

Pain rippled through the link—not a part of it, but disruptive of the flavor—and anger followed.

{Lidye's awake.} Deymorin. Nikki. His own thought. The
source hardly mattered.

{I'll meet you there,} he said into that shallow link, and
then let it dissolve.

§   §   §

It was Mother as Dancer had first seen her twenty years ago, rising out of Grandmother's blood. Mother as she was before there was a Dancer, when there had only been the Child. A woman delicate and beautiful, with hair long and black and sleek—like Mikhyel's. A woman in hiller clothing, who called herself Mother and the Child she had cradled in her arms she had called Dancer.

{Mother?} Dancer called to the Woman on the edge of Non. {Is that you?}

{Child?} Weak, that voice, as the image faded in and out of the inner vision. {Have you a chicken for your Mother?}

{Mother! It *is* you!} Dancer reached out with non-hands, strove to grasp that shifting image, but it slipped like shadow between non-fingers. Tears fell, iridescent drops in the shadows. {Where are you? What has happened to you?}

{It wasn't at all what I expected, Child. I was free . . . I roamed the world and beyond, following the Ley to the ends of forever, and then . . . I was gone. Where am I, Child? Who has taken you away?}

{The Rings are back up, Mother. The Ley is tainted. I don't understand . . .}

{The stench, Child. Oh, the stench.}

{Mother, I need your help!}

{I'm weak, Child.}

The image was fading.

{Please, Mother, don't go. Please, free me. Call me to you. Help me—}

{No!} And it was Mother no longer. At least, not Mother as Dancer had ever known her. It was her most reptilian form, but she glowed with an inner fire, angry and determined. {You'll not escape that way, chameleon.}

{Don't call me that!}

Anger. Distrust. This inner world reeked of it until Dancer floundered in utter confusion. Overhead, as if he were in the Tower itself, he sensed the Rings spinning now, as if they hadn't been only moments before.

{Call the rijhili for that which rules the Tower. Give the creature the pattern. What does one more or less mean to us?}

{You aren't Mother.}

{Oh, but I am. You never have understood, have you?}

{Understood what?}

{Call the rijhili. Break the Triumvirate's hold on Rhomatum forever, Child, and the world will be whole, you'll understand all . . .}

{If it means giving Mikhyel over to whatever has done this to you, the world will remain broken forever, and I'll be content in my ignorance.}

{Then I've trained/reared/nurtured a fool.}

{As you've told me before.}

{Good-bye, fool.}

The vision faded, leaving . . . nothing.

§   §   §

Deymorin arrived last, which was to be expected, his suite being the farthest physically from Lidye's, but the delay was greater than that distance between rooms would account for, and when he finally entered the sitting room where Nikki and Mikhyel were waiting for him, his stone wall was securely erected, keeping the reason for his unusually pale countenance a mystery.

"Have you spoken with her yet?" Deymorin asked, and Nikki shook his head.

"Didn't want to run any chances. Diorak said she was in great pain and has given her something to ease it, but his options are limited, with the baby and all."

"Baby or no baby," Deymorin said, with a vehemence at odds with the flavor of his mind only moments ago, "if she gives us trouble, so help me, I say we drug her to one jump short of insensibility and keep her that way."

"No, Deymorin. I won't have that." And Nikki held steady as Deymorin glowered at him. "Diorak says it's dangerous for the baby, and I won't risk *my* child that way. If that's our only option, I'll have her sent to Armayel. She can't possibly do anything from there."

"Kiyrstin woke up, too, did she?" Mikhyel asked quietly before Deymorin's anger could retort.

Deymorin's glower eased, and he nodded, then said: "You're right, Nikki. Exile before risk to the child."

But Nikki could tell a part of him wished to send Lidye to hell right now, and while he couldn't blame Deymorin for that anger, more than Lidye would suffer if that anger was allowed to rule their actions. More than Lidye, more than the child she carried.

Concern mingled with frustration, as Mikhyel's and Deymorin's barriers wavered simultaneously. Concern for Kiyrstin. Fear that the circumstances which had set their departure back a day already would not necessitate a further delay.

Nikki strove for calm, to keep his mental stream flowing smoothly through the turmoil, picturing himself sitting quietly and letting the horse balance itself beneath him before attempting to change their mutual direction.

"Don't worry, Khyel," Deymorin said, "I'll be ready to leave tomorrow. Kiyrstin is already trying to push me out the door; insists she's fine. Khuishiin checked her out—that's why I'm so late—and seems to think the contractions will stay relaxed."

"Should we have her moved to Armayel, do you think?"

"I asked her; she declined the offer. Here, with Nikki, she'll know if something happens to us. Besides, Khuishiin fears the trip might induce the contractions again."

"The same would hold true for Lidye," Mikhyel said, and looked to him for his reactions.

"Better early than drugged," Nikki maintained stubbornly. "For one thing, I suspect the mere threat of taking her away from the Tower for the birth will be sufficient to keep her in line. But if not . . .I won't let her hurt Kiyrstin, Deymorin," Nikki promised. "Even if it does take drugging her short term. I—I'd rather risk her and that child than lose all the babes in Rhomatum. I just wish I understood why she'd do such a thing in the first place."

His face grim, Deymorin pressed the door handle down and turned the key.

"What say we ask her," he said, and pushed the door open.

*   *   *

Lidye lay in her bed, propped all about with pillows: a
delicate mermaid amidst a foaming froth of lace. Her face
was pale and frightened-seeming. Having been burned too
often, Nikki steeled his heart against that apparent fragility.
Yet a part of him—the obliging part, or the hopeful, he
wasn't certain—still called this woman wife, and that part
drove him to approach the bed and to take the hand she
reached to him.

"Can you possibly forgive me?" she asked, her voice
barely above a whisper.

Nikki sensed Deymorin's bristle and raised a cautioning
hand. Somewhat to his surprise, Deymorin deferred.

Trying to keep anger from his voice, Nikki said, "To
forgive would require a trust you have never inspired in
me. Did you truly expect it?"

Her hand pulled free, and her supplicating eyes turned
away. "No." She drew a deep breath, and asked, in a remarkably stronger voice, "I didn't mean to hurt anyone,
only to rid myself of a child ready to be born. I frankly
never suspected this body had the ability to affect anyone
outside itself."

"Rather like Anheliaa overshot herself on Nikki's wedding night," Mikhyel said from the room's farthest corner,
a shadowy spot from which he would observe with almost
as great accuracy as the link might have given. "I would
have thought, madam, that you might have learned from
your predecessor's mistakes."

Lidye didn't even look at him. "You're going to bar me
from the Tower permanently, aren't you?"

"Yes."

"I can't blame you for that. I'd bar myself, were I you."

"Then why in hell did you do it?" Deymorin asked.

"Ah, a Triumvirate inquisition? Are you linked and
haunting my mind to ensure my truthfulness?"

"No," Nikki replied.

"And *I* am to trust *you*?"

"That's up to you. *I* tell you, we're not linked."

"And you don't lie well at all, do you, little Nikki?" Her

tone was soft, but held the patronizing tone he most hated in her. She shrugged. "I meant only to affect our child. I had no idea it would spread beyond." But her tone implied she didn't particularly care that it had.

"That I can well believe," Mikhyel said. "If you had suspected, you'd have waited until Deymorin and I were well on our way. You never intended to be found out."

She shrugged.

"Why do it at all? I thought you wanted this child as much as Anheliaa did."

Her face hardened. "I wanted my tower back. That brother of yours laid claim to it, then immediately made plans to run off. Fully in character, but hardly responsible."

"With Nikki monitoring for me in the Tower," Deymorin said shortly, "I might as well be here myself. He's the absolute ultimate monitor. I'll return soon enough."

"If you return at all. There's good reason ringmasters don't leave their towers."

"My death would suit you well," Deymorin returned. "You'd have the Tower to yourself. Why risk your own death?"

"It was all or nothing, Deymorin," Mikhyel answered for her. "She wanted to be certain she could be master *while* we were in Khoratum. Am I right, romNikaenor?"

She gave another shrug, refusing to meet Mikhyel's hard gaze.

"If she could induce the birth, she could put pressure on Nikki to gain access to the Tower," Mikhyel continued. "Or did you intend to treat him as you did the guards? Leave Deymorin without a link to the Rings should the need arise, and you in control of them?"

She simply glared at Mikhyel, but Nikki knew Mikhyel had the right of it, knew he meant nothing to her, that she would willing stick that toxic pin into his neck, would kill him, if it meant regaining control of the Rings that consumed her thoughts.

"And once you were in charge, you could ensure we *didn't* come back and that the need *would* arise."

Her mouth twitched. "I trained you well, Mikhyel dunMheric."

"*You* trained me?" Mikhyel snapped.

"I meant Anheliaa, of course. Sometimes she seems very much a part of me. We were . . . very close at times."

"Then I suggest, madam, if you entertain any notions of remaining in Rhomandi House, let alone ever returning to Rhomatum Tower for so much as a visit, that rather than purge yourself of your valuable offspring, you purge yourself of any taint Anheliaa may have left in your head. You're flirting with mental illness; I've seen it before. Do I make myself clear?"

"As crystal, *nephew,* as crystal."

Mikhyel's eyes narrowed. "Guards, Nikki. Four at all times. And warn them about that damned drug of hers: she may have some hidden somewhere in here. They're not to allow contact of any sort. As for this nonsense about Anheliaa, take it seriously, but not as she would have you. Anheliaa used to have similar illusions in the ringchamber, at the edge of sleep. Not speculation: I was there to hear. And the next day her temper would be out of all reason. I don't like what I'm hearing now. I don't like it at all. If she gives you any further trouble, pack her off to Armayel and let Deymorin's foaling man midwife her."

"You're the one with the illusions. And Nikki would never do such a thing," Lidye said loftily.

"In an instant, wife. In an instant. Mikhyel, it's still light out. Will you leave tonight?"

Mikhyel looked to Deymorin, who cast a worried look in the general direction of his own apartments. "We'll wait at least until tomorrow . . . until we know Kiyrstin is out of danger."

Deymorin protested that Kiyrstin would be fine, but Mikhyel shook his head.

{Tomorrow, brothers. Whatever is happening in Khoratum will happen regardless of where we are enroute.}

Common sense agreed, but Mikhyel's frustration, his need to be moving, masked even Deymorin's concern for Kiyrstin as he left the room, ending any possible argument.

Chapter Five

{Dancer, if you can hear me, hold on.}

Dancer floated in a different sea of non-pain, a sea this time filled with dreams . . . and love . . . and hope.

"Ha' ye ever seed th' like?"

{If you can hear me . . . we're coming.}

Foolish to hope. Foolish to even think of the source of that promise. Thought was a bridge and bridges led both ways. . . .

"Sick, I calls it."

Coarse valley-speak. Rijhili tones. The sounds drifted through Thyerri's head as if there were no mind to interpret them.

{Two days. I'll be there in two days. Tell that bastard. Tell him I'm coming. Tell him you're mine.}

Tell him you're mine. . . . That was silly. An outright lie perpetrated by his own desires. Dancer belonged to no one, and Mikhyel dunMheric had rejected him. Still, non-Mikhyel's whisper tempted him to return to his world of Non, and he drifted toward that nothingness willingly, having discovered only one rijhili in the world he cared to talk to.

But the whisper had fled, whisked away on a non-breeze into a shadow he could not find amongst the rest of nothing.

A moment and an eternity later, a painful, intimate invasion of his body jerked him back to the world of the harsh-voiced rijhili.

He writhed away, gasped as his abused shoulders screamed their objection.

There was laughter and more hands holding him for that

probe, twisting him for their convenience, with no thought to the rope that suspended him from hands gone utterly numb, and threatened to pull his arms from their sockets.

Pride, and a throat too dry to croak, kept him silent.

"Leave off," another voice spoke for him. "Feed 'im an' be done."

Feed him . . . and the scent of Food drifted past and pulled him entirely from his world of Non. They'd come to care for him. He wasn't to be left to die, hanging here in the dark.

" 'im? Gi' it another look, Vokhim. Better yet, feel 'er up, eh?"

" 'Er, 'im, it, I don't gives a fuck. Th' boss said keep 'im alive, 'an I don' think 'e'd put up with th' likes o' you feelin' up 'is piece, so keep yer 'ands t' yerself, leastwise when I's aroun'."

Muttered curses protested, but the hands retreated and he wanted to thank the man on the far side of eyelids glued shut, but his mouth was too dry and that man, as were the others with the cruel hands, was just a darkness in the Ley, his essence a depletion of, not an addition to the world pattern.

Keep him alive . . . That promised hope. Alive, he could at least pretend Mikhyel's promises were real.

He opened his mouth, almost eager in his renewed interest in life, but they didn't give him the option to eat; they simply forced a block into his open mouth and shoved Scarface's tube down past his gagging throat and into his stomach. He felt the tube's passage, saw the damage to his throat as a red flare at his own pattern's core, but it was all nothing compared to the sudden distension of his stomach with cold contents, like a bellyful of ice.

His essence protested. His mind protested.

And as they jerked the tube from his throat, and pulled the block, his body protested.

The first voice swore. The second muttered, *thankless bastard,* and they left him hanging, his body purging itself of their contamination as his essence purged itself of their dark malignancy.

They left him Alive. Aware. And emerging from the shadows, Mikhyel's voice fluttered again at the edge of his essence, a link, if it was real, to Khyel himself. A clear danger to Khyel, if it was real.

Tell him you're mine . . .

Dangerous to him, dangerous to Khyel to believe in Dreams.

"No . . ." he whispered to the empty room, and hope dripped from him along with the tears that washed the blood from his eyes, as with grim determination, he banished Mikhyel's voice to the shadows.

Ƨ Ƨ Ƨ

Morning fog made shadows of men and horses, the only spot of dimension and color the red feather of Truth on the shadow banner that rippled slowly on an unfelt breeze. A second banner glinting of silver and gold joined his as Mikhyel drew Nikki outside the stables to let Deymorin say his final good-byes to Kiyrstin in such privacy as ever existed among the three of them.

The residual aura—in this case a mixture of joy and sadness from Deymorin, a touch of fear mingling with regret from Nikki, who would prefer to be going with them—was simply part of their existence now.

For himself, Mikhyel was ready to be moving. His mind, and his heart, were already halfway to New Khoratum.

With each passing moment, the horses, the stone face of the Old Wall beyond them gained definition. This stable was one of the few structures remaining from the time before the Khoratum expansion. Most of the rest of this land, lost to the power umbrella and reclaimed six months ago, had been farms, farms on land that had gone sterile with the expansion. Land that for the first time in ten years showed signs of life, weeds blown in on the breeze taking eager root. Soon, the winds of winter would take them away, but they'd be back in the spring, and the farmers would return.

There was no reason to let the land go to waste, and it would be years, perhaps centuries, before New Khoratum could compare in size to the old Khoratum. And that was the standard for capping it, that was what he had argued and that was the concession he'd won.

The banners snapping in the rising breeze were a formality Mikhyel had deliberately omitted on his last venture outside the City, having preferred to travel as inconspicuously as possible, his mission one of compromise and explication. This time, he traveled from a position of legal authority and moral outrage, and he would utilize every psychologically intimidating tool available to him.

Theirs was a position fraught with ambiguity. Khoratum Tower, once owned by investors from throughout the Web, now belonged to the Rhomandi, thanks to monetary compensations they'd made to those dispossessed by the events of the spring. Until otherwise agreed, the city-state of Khoratum was still legally, if not physically, a part of the Rhomatum Web Syndicate of Nodes, and as a Syndicate member, required to account for its actions regarding Rhomatumin citizens.

It could be argued that Thyerri, never having been registered or paid taxes, was not a Rhomatumin citizen, but he was in the pay of the Princeps of Rhomatum, performing (as far as the Rhomatumin legal system would be concerned) a perfectly legal reconnaissance of a potentially hostile takeover of a Syndicate tower.

Or so he'd expressed in his letter to Rhyys, and then claimed Thyerri gorMikhyel. It was all posturing. He knew it; whoever was in charge in Khoratum would know it. All he could seriously hope for under the circumstances was to intrigue or fluster that individual long enough to get himself and Deymorin up that mountain.

"I've sent word to my sources," he told Nikki in a low voice. "I've told them to spread the rumor that we're not satisfied with the reports coming out of Khoratum. That Rhyys has ignored our attempts to reopen communications and negotiations, and that we have new information that gives us reason to suspect it is not, in fact, Rhyys who is in charge. That the new node is holding the line steady, but that the Triumvirate refuses to go into negotiations with Mauritum until the Khoratum issue is satisfactorily settled."

"That should keep the critics quiet for at least a few days," Nikki said. "Vague, but with urgency enough to make the postponement of the Mauritumin summit reasonable."

But his voice trembled along the edges, his unspoken fear that the mission before them would not be over in that handful of days, that too much remained unresolved.

"A few days should be enough," Mikhyel said firmly. "I refuse to let this drag on indefinitely. Three, perhaps four days to get up there, and then . . . well, we should know one way or the other and as soon as we know, you will. We can decide then how to slant the rumor mill."

The stable boy brought out Tharan, a long-legged bay mare Deymorin had brought in from Darhaven, and of whom he'd grown quite fond over the past months. He ran his hand along her shoulder where the once summer-slick hair was growing plush with winter.

"Paulis knows your sources?" Nikki asked, and Mikhyel nodded.

"He's at your disposal, Nikki, and he's very good. He knows everything I've been doing and everyone I've been talking to. He introduced me to half of them."

"And I supplied the other half." Ganfrion's rough voice drifted across Tharan's back, and Ganfrion himself appeared a moment later on the far side of her head. "Cutting it close, Suds."

"Tower emergency."

"Assumed as much. Earlier start than we'd have had yesterday. Stop at the *Raven,* or push on?"

"Push on, I'd say now. Ask again at noon."

Ganfrion nodded, slapped Tharan's shoulder and moved on.

Nikki held the rein as Mikhyel checked the girth and swung up. The mare moved beneath him, unusually skittish, having been roused from her warm stall early, and with a sense that this was not just one more morning ride. He swayed easily in the saddle even as it occurred to him that

Nikki would not be with him this time, that his seat and
hands, his communication with Tharan was to be completely his own for the first time.

In a moment of panic, his hands clenched on the reins,
his legs tightened and the already nervous horse danced
sideways. His balance threatened, his foot slipped in the
stirrup and she danced again.

{Relax, brother. You're thinking too much and making
yourself a stranger to her. Your body knows what it's
doing. Just get out of its way.}

You're thinking too much . . .

Temorii's words, and Raulind's, who claimed he should
trust his instincts. Now Nikki said the same.

But Nikki, at least, proved right. As his body took over,
with only the slightest reminder from Nikki, Tharan relaxed
and stood, alert but quiet, beneath him. Nikki left him with
a mental box to the ear and an admonition not to revert.

"Good luck, Khyel," Nikki said, and held up his hand.
Mikhyel leaned over and grasped it, wrist to wrist, continued to hold when Nikki would have pulled away.

{One more thing,} he reached cautiously with his mind
through that hold. {Something Lidye said yesterday got to
me. I didn't want to broach it while we were anywhere
near the Tower. I just don't know how much she hears and
what she doesn't.}

"Go on," Nikki said aloud, but low.

{She said 'this body,' referring to her own, but as if it
belonged to someone else. And there have been other
things. I called it mental illness . . . but I'm not sure that's
the name of it. At times she *feels* like Anheliaa. Darius
save us, I don't know how else to put it. Coming on the
heels of that strange composite 'image' of Rhyys that I
got from Dancer, I'm increasingly suspicious of just *what*
Lidye is.}

{You think Anheliaa might . . .} An image followed for a
concept that had no words, an image of a ghostly Anheliaa
enveloping Lidye, seeping into her through every pore.

{I just don't know,} Mikhyel replied, and released Nikki's
arm. {Just don't take any chances. The Rings can do strange

things—the Rings *do* strange things to the people who touch them. Of that much, I'm damned certain. Remember it for yourself and remind Deymorin if ever for some reason I can't. And for Lidye— If she is some unholy amalgam of who knows what all, if somehow Anheliaa *did* share her mind and *did* leave some residual taint, we don't want her anywhere near the Tower.}

"I'll kill her first, Khyel." Nikki's voice was low, but the emotion behind the words was anything but pale, for all Nikki tried to mask it. Nikki, who had dreamed not of simple *normalcy* as Mikhyel had, but, more than any of them, of the grand passion of true love: Nikki, who had been forced instead to deal with the most pragmatic of political alliances—might be pushed to such great anger.

And when he thought of that deep, hidden anger that had flared so unexpectedly earlier when Nikki argued with him and with Deymorin, he feared for Nikki. He knew all too intimately about hidden anger. Now he left Nikki to deal with this unthinkable situation alone, and he had neither the right nor the sure knowledge to intervene in Nikki's dealing with his own darkness. The possibilities were there. He had warned Nikki about all he knew: about the Rings and about his wife. Beyond that, he could only hope Nikki would find his own answers as a man. That was the search they shared, deeply; and he had no knowledge from which to give Nikki advice—only sympathy.

He gripped Nikki's shoulder, passing all of that as he could to his younger brother, then answered aloud, "Don't think of it, Nikki. There are easier ways to separate you from her, if that's what you want."

"You don't really think I'd—just for the sake of—"

There was the Nikki the world saw, the world Nikki dealt with by asking nothing more than IOUs—earnests of the world's good behavior. Performance? . . . he feared Nikki was losing all hope of it, either from himself or the world. He asked for performance, and when the world failed, when he did, found reasons for that failure and stored the disappointment, the anger, killing his own soul in the process. Mikhyel suddenly found himself in the unique position to understand that transaction.

"I think, Nikaenor, that you'll do what you feel you have to do, like any good man. I just want you to know you have options—and advisors. Good advisors I've trusted for years. If anything happens to me—"

"Dammit, Khyel, don't even suggest it."

"We must face that possibility. If anything should happen, Raulind has promised me to stay with you as long as you want him. He's been my lifeline to sanity for years. You can trust him as you would me—more. He's far wiser than I can ever be. You aren't alone. Ever."

Nikki stared at his feet and nodded. Mikhyel glanced at the nearby bodyguards, urging caution in what they said. "Don't dwell on it, Nikki. Mostly, I wanted you to be aware of the hazards in the Tower: in the Rings' influence. With Lidye, you may be dealing with something we've never mapped. I have no positive proof, only vague suspicions."

"You'll discuss them with Deymorin?"

{Of course he will.} Deymorin interrupted without warning as Deymorin appeared at the stable door. {Discuss what?}

"As soon as we're well away," Mikhyel answered both aloud and to Deymorin's mind.

Nikki nodded.

"One more thing." Mikhyel gathered his reins. "Should anything, gods forbid, go wrong—"

"Dammit, Khyel, stop talking like this."

A silent reminder got him another nod of acquiescence, though his brother's reluctance was clear.

"Promise me—if anything happens, you'll seek out Mirym."

"Khyel, I don't think—"

"Follow your own heart where it involves your personal life, Nikki, but for the sake of the Web, ask *Mirym's* help where it regards the Ley and Mother. She was not indifferent to you, once. Build on that. Get her help, and tap her resources. In knowledge lies strength and power. Gods know we've gone as far as we can without it." He backed

Tharan a step to retrieve her wandering attention from Nikki's soothing hands. "Promise me you'll at least try."

"I promise."

Deymorin's stallion sidled and hopped over to join them. "While you're making promises to sustain the universe, fry, keep Kiyrstin in line for me, will you?"

"Just make sure you get back in time to help hatch your own 'fry,' brother."

"We'll do our best," Deymorin said and Mikhyel promised:

"He'll be here, Nikki, if I have to leyapult him out of the Khoramali myself."

Chapter Six

"Cut him down! Oh, please, get him down now. Careful! Don't let him—"

The floor rose up and smashed Thyerri in the face. He groaned and tried to turn away from the stone and the dirt and his own excrement, but his entire body seemed made of granite. Heavy, immobile, formless, a mass of unrelated substances squeezed together by the weight of the ages.

"Bring him in here. Quickly. Quickly. —Oh . . . Careful, please. Set him here." The light, sweet voice drifted to him on an equally gentle essence. Strong, in its way, an essence filled with the scent of healing herbs, and only the slightest hint of raspberries. This one, who bathed his face and his wounds with sweet-scented water, had touched the Khoratum Ley, but not become one with it, not as Dancer or Mikhyel had, not even as Scarface had.

{Who . . . Mheltirin?}

Sensitivity met his cautious probe. Vague awareness of the mental touch, but lacking the capacity to respond.

"Who—" He forced sound past his swollen throat. "Who are—"

The gentle voice shushed him. "Don't try to talk, Radical. Time enough for that later. Rhyys sent me here to make you well. He told me what that evil rijhili did to you, how you had to be tied that way to keep from hurting yourself, but you won't hurt yourself now, will you? You won't hurt me? You're here, aren't you? Not in that terrible Other Place. You won't fight. You know we want only good for you?"

And that compassionate touch, all healing and concern,

brushed his essence, untutored, but instinctively sure. He doubted the owner of that essence even realized that inner touch existed. He'd known others like that; Mikhyel dun-Mheric had been the first other human he'd met who recognized it.

"You're not mad at all. Whatever the rijhili did, you're better now. Strong and beautiful, inside and out."

Mheltirin's soothing chatter continued, distraction while those gentle hands straightened and cleaned his limbs, then brought comfort to his body. The shape of the Ley was different here, the stench of his own making was gone. It was a different room, and a mat padded the stone beneath him. Hand-warmed oil slicked his back as practiced fingers worked the knots from twisted muscle, then urged him over onto his back.

A hand cupped his chin, held his face for examination while the sweet voice murmured in dismay. The warm wet sponge rested across his eyes until it began to cool, was pulled away to the sound of rinsing and returned warm and wet.

And slowly, very slowly, his eyelids began to come free.

"Ah, that's much better." The sponge began to dab, then paused. "Wait. Your eyes are not yet ready for the light." The sponge left, to the sound of scuffling feet, and what light existed beyond his lids vanished. "Careful now, Radical. Open them slowly."

As if he could have done otherwise. The lids parted, lashes still sticky and tangling, but he'd have endured far worse for the sight of Mheltirin silhouetted against the lamp on the far side of the room.

"I was afraid I was blind . . ."

Teeth showed ghostly-white in Mheltirin's shadowed face. "We'd never allow that to happen. We'll heal your body, and you'll dance again. Soon, very soon, I promise you."

Dance? The rings were down forever. Surely they wouldn't spin for that monstrous amalgam of cruelty ruling now in the Tower.

The gentle essence recoiled. "Such darkness, Radical.

You must send it away. You're safe now. We'll take care of you. My lord Rhyys will. He cares very much what happens to you."

He wanted to laugh, but couldn't find the strength.

"Lord Rhyys told me of your dance, told me how special you were. He took me in because of you."

"Because of me? I don't understand . . ."

"It was after the sacred spring turned, which I know now was after the rijhili corrupted the Ley, after they forced Lord Rhyys from the Web. I went to the spring the morning after the Ley rained from the sky, and the air about the spring had changed its taste. I tried to warn the priests, tried to warn everyone that the water had changed, but they wouldn't listen. When Master Velton died in the middle of the morning communion, they blamed me. They said I'd defiled the spring with my cursed touch and then they flung stones at me until I was senseless, because none dared touch me openly, for fear their children would be cursed as well."

"Cursed?"

The oil-slick fingers slid around his buttocks and touched his flank. "I am . . . cursed, as you are cursed, though Lord Rhyys says I'm not to think of my disfigurement that way. Seeing you, I'm not surprised at his disappointment in my pitiful self. I'm not nearly so perfect."

Disfigurement. Thyerri. Temorii. That's what he meant. Of all times to discover another like himself.

"How did you come to be with Rhyys?"

"I don't really remember. The townsfolk sold me to someone who sold me to someone, who brought me here, having heard Rhyys was looking for one such as you. But I was ill—from the stones, and . . . and from those less reluctant to touch my curse than the townsfolk. I remember very little, however, until Rhyys, and in that ignorance, I am quite content. Can you sit up?"

Scarface had saved this gentle creature, who urged him to sit up and worked a warm robe around his aching shoulders, then set pillows at his back and a tray of warm food before him. Had saved him because he'd been looking for one such as himself.

Had that search been for any Child of Rakshi? Or only one Temorii, Radical Dancer of Khoratum? Object of Mikhyel dunMheric's obsession? And in either case, why hadn't he, or one of the other men Rhomandi had combing Khoratum heard of that search?

"You're not eating?" he asked, and his dark-haired nurse lifted a shoulder.

"I'll eat later. With his lordship."

Thyerri shivered at the thought, recalling dinners of many varieties with Rhyys in either form, and his gentle nurse was filled with mistaken concern, seeking injury, fearing the food was unsatisfactory.

"It's nothing," Thyerri said. "Your name's Mheltirin, do I remember correctly?"

"Or Mheltiri. Whichever you prefer, Radical, by your leave."

Mheltiri, Mheltirin: a northern Khoramali name, the same name, man and woman. The simple stew turned to dust in his mouth. "Your name is your name and yours to leave or take."

"Mhe–Mheltiri, then, if it pleases you, my lord."

"It pleases me fine. Mine's Thyerri. You do me no favor or honor to call me otherwise."

Mheltiri drew back, hurt plain on the smooth face. "Your pardon, my lord Thyerri."

"Just Thyerri." He chewed another bite, wary of a swollen jaw. "How long have you been here?"

"Since the midsummer fest, my—"

He glared and Mheltiri's head pulled in like a turtle's. "Th–Thyerri."

"You'll get used to it. And you say you are a Child of Rakshi?"

"No, my lord. I'm not a dancer. Not at all."

As he had known and used the term until Ganfrion taught him otherwise.

"I mean . . ." He sought to phrase the question for which

he had no words, and for which he refused to use Mheltiri's. "Your . . . difference. Are you both man and woman?"

Mheltiri looked away, blushing. "I don't . . . more man than not, I think. My parents called me 'son' and 'Mheltiri,' but my lord treats me as a gentlewoman, and insists those about him do likewise."

To them, I was cursed. Zelin had said his folk, in a village on the dry, eastern face of the Khoramali, a village now gone, had honored Rakshi's Children. Zelin had spoken of his Tamshi eyes; he hadn't really understood then that Zelin might actually have been referring to his other physical differences as well. In Zelin's world, those such as he lived separately, but for honorable, respected reasons.

Here on the western face, in the lands touched by Darius' exodus, he'd have been anathema, just as this gentle Mheltiri. Growing up with Mother, he'd been spared that fate. It had taken Mikhyel to make him conscious of the difference, and Mikhyel's reaction, based at least in part in startlement and hurt, seemed somehow insignificant in comparison.

"And you?" he persisted. "What do *you* say you are?"

"I'm . . . Mheltiri. I'm . . . me. I've a gift for healing, and for the sake of that healing, the townsfolk of Oletiin overlooked my shame and granted me purpose. Man or woman, it's . . . good to be useful."

Good to be useful. A concept utterly foreign to the Dancer that was, though Dancer, too, had been both name and avocation. Dancer had never thought of man or woman, only of the Dance. But Thyerri understood that other part, that part about being *useful*. Thyerri was a creature of the world of Men, and Thyerri had reveled in each report to Rhomandi's men. Thyerri had known that information would help Mikhyel, and it had felt . . . good.

Thyerri *liked* being . . . useful.

At the moment, *Dancer* could wish Thyerri had never emerged. He was in this mess and drawing Mikhyel into it with him thanks to that urge to be . . . useful. Temorii was far more sensible and self-protective. Temorii would have pursued Mikhyel to Rhomatum and convinced him he was being a fool, and together they'd have cleansed Khoratum. Together, Temorii and Mikhyel . . .

Pride, Dancer's and Thyerri's, seemed very distant.

He set the plate aside and hugged his arms to his middle. "And now," he asked Mheltiri, "here. Have you purpose in Khoratum Tower?"

"To get you well, Radical. And to serve my lord. He has given me purpose and respect."

And treated Mheltiri as a gentlewoman.

"And how do you serve him?"

"By helping you."

"I've only just arrived."

"There have been others in need. My lord Rhyys himself is frequently in pain. He finds those whose hearts have been misshapen by the rijhili. He seeks to free them of their curse, which leaves him in pain greater than theirs, and still, he sends me to those first, and takes whatever I have left over for him. I think it very brave of him, and generous. When last I saw him, just before sending me to you, he was in great need, here." Mheltiri touched his forehead and then his heart. "Yet he said: go to the dancer and make the dancer dance once more."

He imagined Scarface's essence was in great need. If there were anything like justice, Scarface's essence would never recover from that white blast. But he stifled the retort, not wanting to estrange this gentle healer. He needed time, time to recuperate, time to observe, time to plan his escape.

And in that control of his thoughts, he became aware of a subtle intrusion, a brush of warmth, of gentle persuasion—an urging to trust Rhyys. To love Rhyys. To serve . . . Rhyys.

And knew that Rhyys-who-was-not-Rhyys was not the only danger descending the steps from Khoratum Tower.

Chapter Seven

The shadows around the node lake's perimeter road held more than trees.

The village listed in the Rhomatum record books as *New Khoratum* lay behind them, a healthy little community on the edge of the lake, with children laughing and playing in the cobbled streets—and a dearth of adult males.

Though they'd paused at the central fountain long enough to inquire of a handful of women after the needs of the village, they hadn't asked about Mirym. Mikhyel had no wish to place these quiet folk in the position of lying to the Princeps of Rhomatum.

And they would lie, of that he had no doubt. He knew she was here; he knew how to find her, should she endeavor to avoid him.

He hadn't thought to stop here. Hadn't intended to try and contact her, but the closer they'd gotten to the new node, the more certain he'd become that he had at least to try to see the woman who carried his child. He had to do what he could to set the stage for future negotiations with New Khoratum.

It was, he came to realize, the last of the node agreements. Different in execution, but the same in spirit. An acknowledgment of a combined fate, a commitment to a combined future.

That was the Barrister's interest in Mirym. Mikhyel had his own need to fill. Mirym and her child were part of his ley-legacy, part of his . . . pattern, if not his essence. If he was to understand himself, he couldn't ignore them any more than he could ignore Dancer.

"She's watching us," Mikhyel murmured to Ganfrion, riding close to his right side, and simultaneously cast the thought to Deymorin, three lengths ahead.

{You're certain?} Deymorin asked; Ganfrion only nodded acknowledgment.

As certain as he could be without actually seeing her. The nearer they'd drawn to the spring, the more powerful that internal pointer had become, and as he rode past an ancient oak, he drew Tharan to a halt.

{Hello, Mirym.} He cast the thought into the shadows.

{Ravenhair.} Acknowledgment came on a faint whiff of mountain heather. The new node's character/color/scent? Acknowledgment again.

{Will you come out and talk to me?}

{Have I a choice?}

{Ask that of Mother. *I* won't force you.}

{And yet I'm inclined to agree.} Curiosity tinged her thoughts. {Despite the fact I don't feel Mother's presence in this at all.}

{Trust me?}

{Not particularly.}

{Good. Then we begin on even ground.} He slid down from the saddle and held the reins out to Ganfrion, who swung his leg over his horse's withers and jumped down facing him.

Ganfrion ignored the reins.

"What in hell do you think you're doing?"

"What I have to. —Deymorin?"

"I 'heard,' Khyel. Are you sure?"

He shrugged. "As I am of anything."

"Take the reins, gorMikhyel," Deymorin said. "She's not likely to do anything drastic with the garrison minutes from her village."

Ganfrion scowled, but he took the reins. "Watch the suds, Khyel."

Which meant he thought there was a good chance Mikhyel was doing something extremely ill-considered.

"If she knows anything that might give me an edge up there," he jerked his head in the general direction of Khoratum, "I'll take it. She won't talk with an audience, of that I'm certain; there's a slim chance she'll talk to me alone. If she tries anything, Deymorin will know in an instant."

"By that time, you could be a half-mile underground."

"Get used to it. That's always a possibility when I'm dealing with Mother, and I'm convinced Mirym is, or at least was, deeply involved with Mother."

"Doesn't mean I have to like it," Ganfrion muttered.

"I'm not fond of the notion myself, trust me."

"Never." A half-smile pulled Ganfrion's scarred upper lip. "But I trust Rakshi, here in the Khoramali, fool that I am. And you've Rakshi's blessing, bubble-brained fool that you are."

"I hope so." He slapped Tharan on the neck as he ducked under, slid his hand along her flank as he headed, with what he trusted to be an effective air of nonchalance, into the shadows.

The woman who greeted him bore only the most superficial resemblance to the mousy little creature who had attended Anheliaa's every physical need for the final two years of his aunt's life.

A mass of fawn-colored hair, unfettered here in her woodland home, made a cloud about Mirym's face and down her back. Her clothing, dyed soft browned-blues and greens, might have been woven out of the very woodland shadows in which she stood. Round with child—his child—as she was, she appeared the very embodiment of the Earth Mother the hillers worshiped.

And unless his internal sense was mistaken, the shadows surrounding them held her congregation.

Earth Mother, Father Sky . . . the third primary of the hillers' pantheon was the Mother of the Ley. Or so Darius' chronicles had interpreted the religion of the folk he'd displaced in the valley. No one in three hundred years had expanded on that scant knowledge—at least that the clerk he'd put onto the research project had been able to find. Lack of interest on the part of Darius' descendants, or stubborn silence on the part of the few remaining hillers who still followed the old ways were equally possible explanations for that dearth.

But Darius had made intricate drawings of the statues he'd found in one of the valley shrines—before he'd ordered those statues destroyed: one of the Web's founder's more ruthless tactics for keeping his people free of the religious tyranny they'd fled—and having met the animated counterpart of the androgynous, reptilian, leythium-touched statue Darius' journals had described for that third god/ goddess, he was inclined to question even that most basic analysis.

"You look well," he said, which vastly understated her aura of health and vitality.

{As do you, Ravenhair. The hills welcomed you.}

"That they did."

{Do you fear the touching of essence, that you disturb the forest song with your voice?}

{Not particularly. Habit, I suppose.}

{And yet, you're quite facile now. And your defenses are very strong; I couldn't touch you unless you welcomed me.}

{The link with my brothers is excellent training.}

{Your elder brother is with you now.}

{By my choice,} he answered, even as Deymorin's stubborn presence informed him Deymorin wasn't about to change that status without an argument. {Did you expect otherwise?}

{No. And I can feel it is in part his presence that strengthens your barriers—his essence gave Anheliaa headaches every time she touched him. But your diversion is more subtle, I think. I think she believed she reached you when, in fact, you lay hidden. You are very Talented, son of Mheric.}

{So I begin to accept. I've very little time, Mirym, and many questions I'd like answered.}

{And if I refuse?} Surface cool, she seethed beneath with trepidation. She was no fool. She knew that, should the Princeps of Rhomatum decide she and her folk were not welcome here, they would be gone.

And she very much wanted to stay here, that came through as well.

{No one will run your people out, Mirym. Not for this.}

Palpable relief, quickly hidden as she realized he was picking up those fluctuating emotions.

{On the other hand,} he continued, {your own future might well depend on your cooperation. To say that you lived among us under false pretenses for two years is to speak conservatively. Legally, you would have little recourse, should I decide to prosecute. And while fear is not, to my mind, an effective hold over someone from whom you seek knowledge and long-term cooperation, I feel it only fair to point out that I seriously doubt there's anywhere in the Web you could hide that I couldn't, eventually, find you.}

Her face didn't shift from its quiet calm, but through the touch of their minds, he could feel the pulse quicken in her veins.

{But our lives have slipped free of the safe haven of law, haven't they?} he said.

Her brow puckered, and he continued:

{I seek understanding, Mirym, of your motives, of the rules *you* live under, that I might act in an equitable and ethical manner, not only where you're concerned, but for the Web itself. You left Kiyrstin with dark warnings but little of substance. I seek that substance.}

{And is it for substance that you race up the mountain toward the node you set free?}

{I think you know exactly why I'm "racing up the mountain."}

She shrugged.

{Will you help?}

{In what? Your mission to free the dancer? Would you squander your limited coin with me on so personal and short-sighted a goal?}

{Only indirectly. If you have knowledge that will help me now, that will be welcome. Should anything happen, should I need aid in reaching Nikki in Rhomatum, if you can supply that aid, that would be appreciated.}

{And directly?}

{To free Mother. Someone has raised the Rings. Whoever has done so, I do not believe their control is of benefit to either of us.}

{And what would I receive in exchange for this aid?}

{That remains to be seen. What have you to offer?}

{That remains to be seen.} She lifted a hand back from which the sleeve rippled in myriad small drapes, revealing a skin-hugging lace that looked more like spiderwebbing than any product of human hands. Spiderweb that glittered with rainbows. He had no doubt that closer examination would prove it to be strands of leythium thread, and considering the way that web extended independent strands down her fingertips, the hint of rainbows at her temples, he had to wonder whether or not it was actually a garment or an intrinsic part of her skin.

{I am a part of this place now,} her essence whispered, in response to that half-formed query, and her essence carried with it a sense of blending, a certainty of death should she leave this place to which she'd given herself.

She'd seen it happen. The images of that death were engraved in her mind.

{Then we must endeavor not to risk that fate,} he returned even as he thought deliberately of the ways in which she might prevent that eventuality, thoughts of cooperation and trust. Her serene brow tightened ever-so-slightly before she deliberately closed . . . then opened . . . her raised hand.

Shadows separated from shadows and faded away: her fellow hillers, there to protect her had that signal been a different one.

Her worshipers.

{After a fashion, yes. —Follow . . .} She headed deeper into the shadows. {Their world is in flux, thanks to you and your family. My child could be their savior.}

{Our child.}

She paused, turned her head slowly to look at him, up and down and back to his face. {After a fashion, yes.}

{I make no claim on him that you don't grant, Mirym— at least at this time.}

{If not now, when?}

{That remains to be seen. If I am to be portrayed to him as the destroyer of your world—}

{Your word, not mine.}

{More truthful of the underlying sentiment.}

Her steady gaze dropped away, and she continued down the shadowed pathway. {I do not think of you that way. Rhomatum, perhaps, but not you.}

{Still, I state the obvious: that the savior you propose is also the son of the man you at the very least hold responsible for the loss of the village your people had for generations.} The death of that priestess, was the underlying implication. {That child will be related to, if not a part of, the family who can—and likely someday will, if I can't find the way to prevent it—run you all away from this new node to make way for another city.}

Interest flared, and triumph, then both vanished.

Not surprising: the goal he had implied would certainly please this hiller woman, and she might well wish to disguise a desire which could be used to manipulate her. The only catch was, he hadn't considered the fate of the village before now. That the node would be allowed to exist uncapped for some unspecified time was in the deals he'd made with the rest of the Web. That it would never be capped . . . he was not exactly pleased that such a radical notion came from him first, and could not help but wonder if her desires, consciously or not, were affecting his thinking.

{I could not.} Her whisper filtered into his thoughts.

{No? Yet you also say I am barriered against you, then proceed to respond to every doubt I half consider.}

{Only what is on the surface, Mikhyel dunMheric, and only because you have granted me access.}

{So you say.}

{So I say.} A few silent steps then: {Why did you call the Child your 'son'?}

{Lidye insists Anheliaa wanted a male heir.} Though he couldn't conceive why, having been the direct recipient of his aunt's feelings regarding the male of the species. {I don't doubt the sex of any of the children conceived that night.}

{Ah. So positive, Ravenhair.} She paused beside a rock face covered in a thick coat of vines. {But Anheliaa's were not the only dreams and hopes at work that night. One learns not to assume. I should think you had learned that by now.}

The taste of the thought left no question as to her singular reference. Resentment flared, that this most private and personal error in judgment should be included in this meeting.

{Not at all. You are here because of that 'error in judgment,' if error it was.}

{Of course it was.}

{Dancer is many things that even Dancer does not yet understand. What lives above Khoratum now has woven itself into the heart of the Ley, and not, I am in full agreement with you, to good purpose. Were Dancer not involved, you might have left the wound festering until too late to lance it. How, then, could there be error involved?}

{How, indeed?}

{Ah, Ravenhair, like your younger brother, you agree for the sake of peace, not in true understanding. Come. Perhaps here you'll find the truth easier to fathom.}

The vines moved aside seemingly of their own accord to let them pass—into a world as fantastical, in its way, as the leythium caverns themselves, a world illuminated with the silver glow of leylight. Innumerable tiny waterfalls, from mere trickles to cascades, erupted from the walls, creating a web of miniature rivers leading to a luminescent, ley-touched pool that disappeared beneath a rocky shelf.

A shelf that dripped with vigorous, flowering vines: plants, of varieties he'd never seen, that glowed with leylight and apparently thrived in the spray of those falls and about the edge of the pool. Without soil, without sunlight, their only source of nutrients had to be the ley-touched water.

Plants, when tradition said nothing grew in the vicinity of the Ley.

{Because your tradition insists on holding to the past. Your tradition tried to force the new life to conform to the old. On its own, the Ley is part of the whole, these plants are the Ley's partners in the depths. But the Ley is of the earth. Your people were surface dwellers. They grew surface plants. They drew the Ley to the surface, turned its essence to their own purpose, and it drew nourishment where it could.}

{I've heard nothing about these plants. Ever.}

{Your people mine deep for the pure substance, ignoring all that lies between. They set the Rings in motion before they even build their homes. The Rings draw the Ley to a single channel. They magnify the energy. Nothing that draws its nourishment directly from the earth can survive beneath the umbrella—above or below ground.}

In and around the silent words came images flaring with passion. Images from a small child's height. Vast caverns of these plants bursting spontaneously into cold, multicolored flames, while a dozen people watched helplessly. Other images, of outside plants withering, a delicate perfect flower cradled in small hands crumpling to dust at the touch of a falling teardrop.

{When?} he asked.

{When Anheliaa set the Khoratum Rings in motion. These are the true victims of the battle for supremacy.}

{Yet some survived.}

{A handful only, in the outermost caverns. Two species were lost forever, as far as we know.}

He cradled a blossom in his fingers; it glowed and warmed where it touched his skin. {I'm sorry that your people's gardens were destroyed. Yet because of the Rings, hundreds of thousands of people lead healthy, happy, productive lives.}

Another of those measuring looks.

{If you say so.}

{What would you have us do? Destroy the Rings outright?}

{Done is done, Mikhyel dunMheric.} She sat on a stone among the plants, and drifted her fingers in the radiant pool. The lace on her arm glowed. {Your ancestors built the Rings and multiplied accordingly. Their descendants must be accounted for. We all move to a pattern not of our own making. Lives interlace, past with present, present with future. We weave our individual segments, but we must weave within strands left by others, and do our best to leave a good pattern for our descendants. Not to interlace is to drift without purpose.}

She gestured toward another seat, invisible until the vines moved aside for him. He sat, vaguely surprised when the plants closing back in around him roused not a hint of unease.

{Ask your questions, son of Mheric, but I caution you: this is a holy place. I will know if you lie to me; you will know if you lie to yourself.}

He wondered if that knowledge would come via her pet plant that even as she spoke insinuated itself around his neck, or if it would simply save time and choke him. As if insulted, the vine withdrew.

{Put your hand in the pool, Mikhyel dunMheric.}

{I didn't come here to waste time with lies,} he said.

{Then we are of a mind. Put your hand in the pool.}

That her demand was a test, he had no doubt. Whether of character or trust, he wasn't certain. More often than not, liquid leythium would eat the meat off a man's bones. Barsitum was an exception. It's eastern counterpart Hariisidum was another. He himself had touched both Rhomatum and Khoratum pools with impunity.

Defiantly, he thrust his hand into the pool—

And squeezed his eyes shut as brilliant rainbows flared all about the cavern, and he felt as much as heard Mirym's gasp.

In thirty years, I never saw the pools glow the way they did when you were in them.

He held steady, despite the heat (or was it cold?) that engulfed his hand and traveled up his arm, obstinately confident that as long as that sensation continued, the hand must still be attached to the arm, and he was damned if

he'd give her the satisfaction of pulling his arm out of the
pool—

A resolve that faltered when the lights beyond his eyelids
eased and he opened them to discover webbing similar to
Mirym's creeping up his arm. Only Anheliaa's training kept
him from jerking free of that liquid.

{What's happening?} he asked without taking his eyes
from that disturbing phenomenon. {What's it doing . . .
to . . .} Question and thought deserted him as he looked
up into her face. Anger and resentment, horror and a touch
of hatred—he read all that and more despite the cold mask
that greeted him.

I will know if you lie to me . . .

Apparently that truth went both ways.

{Mirym, talk to me. Whatever's happening, I don't want
it. Dare I take my hand out?}

She blinked, and the kaleidoscopic emotions permeating
the air dissipated leaving only a mild scorn.

{Of course. Withdraw from the touch at any time.}

{Why are you angry at me?}

{Not you, not directly. You cannot help that which you
are. I am angry at Rakshi, at the twist of fate that granted
you so much and left the rest of us with so little. You,
who cannot imagine the meaning of that which you hold
in your hands.}

{I don't understand.}

{My point, exactly. In my first month here, I spent hours
every day communing with the pool. *Hours*, Mikhyel dun-
Mheric, *days* to achieve a fraction of the pattern which you
have been granted in a single heartbeat.}

{This?} Without thinking, he pulled his hand from the
pool; a low moan filled the cavern. He jumped up, scanning
the shadows, but it was instinct that drove him. His heart
knew that moan was the Ley wanting him to return.

Oh, yes, Mikhyel: the Ley likes you. . . .

Obstinately, he remained on his feet, cradling the affected arm in his other hand.

{That. In the first day, I noticed a pale glimmer about
my fingertips. In the months since, I have bathed daily, and

each time, the pattern extends farther.} One hand still in the pool, she caressed her protruding stomach with the other. {It developed here fastest. It is, or so I believe, this Mother's way of merging with her chosen. You, obviously, are high on her list.}

{Well, she can just get behind Rhomatum, and Mother, and Barsitum, for that matter, if Raulind has the right of it, and they aren't about to have me any time soon, if I have my way. *Any* of them.}

{Again, you make my point for me. But perhaps that is your value to them. Perhaps the fact that you do not seek their favor makes you useful to them in some fashion. Tell me, do you hear her?}

{The Mother of this node?}

She nodded; he shook his head. {Only a moaning.}

{Have you listened?} she asked. {Do you dare?} And gestured again to the pool.

He slid his hand into the pool, prepared this time, though the flare of color was less.

{I hear . . . purring . . .} Like one of the Armayel barn cats.

{Content, then. She has few needs at the moment. Only a need for believers to feed her essence.}

He had an unpleasant image, then, of sacrifice and death, and Mirym frowned. {Not at all. Belief here.} She tapped her head, then pressed a hand to her chest. {And here. That is what feeds her.}

He traced the pattern on the back of his hand, knew, for all he could not see or feel it, that it extended up his arm beneath his sleeve. It had substance, was a raised pattern, but as a substance attached to the skin, not raising the skin.

{Is it permanent?}

{I wouldn't know.}

{You said you would die if you left. Am I similarly tied here?}

{Are you a believer, Mikhyel dunMheric?}

He frowned. {Do I believe this new Mother of yours is a goddess of some sort? I'm afraid not, Mirym.}

{And yet, you've met the Mother of Khoratum. You've

met the Father of Rhomatum. Do they not wield the power
of life and death? What are they, if not gods?}

What, indeed? He'd avoided asking himself that question
directly for months, for all his mind had wrestled with the
problem since he'd come face to face with Rhomatum for
the first time. And it seemed, as his hand rested in that pool
of Truth, that his months of musing gained a logical form.

{I don't think they are living creatures at all, as we know
life. I think they are the sum total of all those with Talent
that resonates with a given node.} And the logical form
found a resolution, of sorts. {A . . . manifestation, created
out of the Ley itself, of those individual wants and needs
and demands—and of the lingering purpose of all those
with Talent who came before them. I think that's why Anheliaa is able to haunt me still at times. I think that's why
Rhomatum, whose believers left centuries ago, has lain dor-
mant, and Mother, who gained all those believers as well
as those run out by Darius' people from all the other nodes,
is so active. I think that's also why Mother is so very fickle.
I think her . . . mood . . . swings with the mood of the
greatest Talent within her umbrella. That's why great ringmasters can cap a node and control it. I have no proof, of
course, but that hypothesis seems to fit what I've observed.}

{And given your Truth, is that not as sound a definition
of a god as any other?}

{You're a very strange sort of priestess.}

{I'm not a priestess, Mikhyel. I'm a voice. People believe
what they will. So long as they believe in the life-giving
aspect of the node, the Mother can flourish. The details of
that belief are irrelevant. We have our small rituals here,
but others lead those rituals, not I.}

{You said 'Not to interlace is to drift without purpose.'
What is your purpose, Mirym? What are your dreams for
these people, for this place?}

{Truth, Mikhyel dunMheric. That is a question I have
been asking myself since our essences collided. I knew you
would come here. I knew I would have to account for my
actions eventually, but once Mother was free, once Mother's needs ceased to drive my actions, my life became form-

less. I had to destroy the ring because, to use your own metaphor, there were too many Talents demanding their way. Once the actions of the Northern Crescent rebellion had caused that ring to stop, those voices weren't about to let it start again.}

{And were you one of those voices?}

She nodded. {My people were the keepers of these lives.} She swept a hand that dripped rainbows through the air. {Our pattern was simple—until Anheliaa capped Khoratum. As a child, I believed I was meant simply to speak to and for the Mother, but my world expanded beyond that simple pattern—once Anheliaa capped Khoratum. I became too much aware of the world beyond our own home. Mother took that awareness and turned it to her purpose, and that purpose took me from the world I knew, a world destroyed by the capping, and set me into your world. Once Mother's purpose was realized, I tried to return home—not because I feared Mikhyel dunMheric's justice, but because I felt my people needed me. But I returned only to find the Khoratum Rings once again in motion, and my people scattered, only a very few tending the last of the plants. We came here, have stayed here by your brother's grace, have slowly gathered our scattered folk to us. But purpose? Beyond the building of the village, beyond this—} Again, that sweeping gesture. {I don't know.} Her eyes met his. {What is yours?}

Somehow, the words he would have used a moment before to answer her did not come. Finally, he said, using Raulind's term: {Knowledge. I want to understand. I want to use what I understand to . . . expand my world. To take care of that world—which is Rhomatum and the Web, my brothers and my family, the dark areas between the lines and the Ley itself. I want . . . I want a stable, vital world pattern to bequeath to my child.}

{It is possible that I could share that goal.}

{To do it, I need to understand the Ley. I need to know its needs that I might best nourish it even as I use it. I need to understand why this place is so important to you.}

Obstinance/fear/pride: a war of emotions filled the air, foremost among them a fierce desire not to be foresworn.

{If you were sworn to secrecy, you broke that promise the moment you brought me here. Perhaps you sought Truth only, but in seeking your Truth, you have exposed your people's secrets. You can't back away from that now. I know your people use the Ley in ways we haven't imagined. Are these plants part of that? If so, capping this node . . . which will happen one day, unless you can convince me otherwise—and in ways I can carry to the Syndicate and make stick . . . will only cause a repeat of what happened with Khoratum's capping. Your plants will die again.}

Her eyes flickered in the silvery light.

{That's what you're afraid of, isn't it?}

She jerked her hand free of the pool and jumped to her feet. She wandered among the plants, the mist from the falls gathering in droplets in her curly hair, giving her a halo of multicolored stars, ley-touched, in her own way. She paused beside one plant and cupped it gently, then turned to face him, chin arrogantly lifted.

{Would you know the true irony of Khoratum's capping?} she asked, and without waiting for his answer: {*This* could have cured Anheliaa's arthritis.}

Chapter Eight

"Well, I'll be . . ." were the Rhomandi's first words in hours.

Ganfrion shook himself awake, found the Princeps' eyes focused at last on the interior of the tent rather than some otherwhere he couldn't follow.

"Back with us?" Ganfrion asked, and the Rhomandi's eyes turned to him.

"He's coming out. But we'd best . . ." The Rhomandi's eyes wandered full about, seeming to actually *see* the canvas walls surrounding him this time. "I see you already have. All the men camped?"

Ganfrion nodded. "Asleep two hours and more." He stretched to his feet, and held out a hand to help the Rhomandi. Rhomandi scowled, then after one abortive attempt to rise to his feet, gave a rueful grin and grasped the proffered hand and hauled himself up.

"How long?" he asked and Ganfrion shrugged.

"Morning now, though just barely.

"Rings. I had no idea . . . *He* hasn't." Rhomandi's face took on that glazed look for an instant, then returned. "Thought it would still be light out. We'd best get out there."

"Guard?"

"You're enough. He'll want you."

To observation, Rhomandi's head still seemed to float in and out of focus, but he followed a path through the moonshadowed woods without hesitation, and only a handful of strides past the last tents, they met Mikhyel and a young hiller woman coming to join them.

"You heard?" Mikhyel asked by way of opening, and Rhomandi nodded. "Explain to Gan, will you?" Again, Rhomandi nodded.

Ganfrion twitched. Sounded to him like Khyel was not planning on joining them back in the camp. Sounded to him like Mikhyel intended to return to the shadows with this hiller woman, who watched him and no other as they stood there in an enchanted forest beside a lake that even a ley-blind man like himself could tell reeked with power.

"It seems to be later than I thought. . . ." Mikhyel's voice held an uncommon degree of uncertainty. The gaze he cast at the star-filled sky seemed puzzled.

"Long past your bedtime, Suds," Ganfrion said.

"Strange. I could have sworn . . ." Mikhyel shook his head as if to clear it. "Never mind. I've a few more question for Mirym." An admission which did nothing to settle Ganfrion's suspicions. "But I don't know how long they'll take."

"Need I remind you we're already a day behind schedule?" Ganfrion asked, and he wasn't surprised when the hiller woman shifted her attention at last to cast him a hostile glance.

Khyel set his hand on the young woman's arm and her expression eased.

"Relax, Gan. I'll sleep in the saddle tomorrow, if I must," Mikhyel said, but Ganfrion barely heard him; that hand resting on the woman's arm glowed in the moonlight.

"What the hell's that?" Ganfrion demanded and jerked his chin toward the disfigured hand.

"Deymorin will explain," Mikhyel said, and his voice was weary, but eager.

"Dammit, Suds—" Rhomandi's vice grip on his elbow ended his protest.

"Your gorman has a point, Khyel," Rhomandi said calmly. "Sleeping in the saddle isn't a particularly viable option. Your curiosity won't be settled in a single night. Make it short, make plans for the next time, and get a few hours' sleep so you have half a chance of there *being* a next time."

The hiller woman touched Rhomandi's arm, and a short silence later, he gave a brief nod, and said: "See that you do."

More of that damned mindtalk. Ganfrion stirred, stifling a protest as Khyel and the woman returned the way they'd come.

"Ease off, gorman," Rhomandi said, though his tone held no censure. Ganfrion would wager they shared the same concerns. "Mikhyel's made his judgment call; it's not for you—or me, for that matter—to question it."

"He trusts her?"

"He trusts the hold he has over her."

"Don't give me that. He's oblivious to the way she looks at him."

Rhomandi snorted. "Most women look at him that way, in case you hadn't noticed. Always have. Whatever the man has, he should bottle it. Even Kiyrstin loses her common sense where he's concerned. No, it's not that hold I meant." He jerked his head back toward camp, and held his peace until they were safely ensconced in his tent, and sharing a bottle of whiskey. Then his voice would not have carried even to the doorflap.

"It appears that Mirym and her folk here fancy themselves the Ley Mother's gardeners, and when Anheliaa capped Khoratum, the increased flow of energy nearly destroyed those gardens. They've moved the remaining few plants to this place—a cavern somewhere down that trail."

"And your brother will make a deal not to cap for the sake of a bunch of plants?"

"If those plants can do half of what Mirym claims, he might well. She claims her people have used them in their purest form to heal everything from a toothache to arthritis to gangrene. If she's to be believed, they're damned near a cure for aging. She claims the eldest of her people are over 150 years old, though they're dying rapidly, now the reserves of their potions have run out."

"Hell, we've already got too many people."

"That will be the least of our worries for a long time. The plants themselves need to be old and well-established before they can be tapped and the potions take years to prepare. The gardens they had before the capping barely provided for a handful of villages."

Ganfrion snorted. "Going to be one hell of a rich little node here, if that's the case—at least until the chemists start refining the stuff. Name their price, they can."

"If the ignorant hounds don't run in and tear it to pieces first. No doubt about it, he's walking a delicate line. He and Mirym both want the same for the node in that sense, but he's not about to give it away."

"Hell of a time to discover it."

"But inevitable. Mirym was an unresolved question. He couldn't have headed up to Khoratum without at least trying to see her. When she explained about the plants . . ." Rhomandi stopped and stared straight ahead. "It's hard to describe what the inside of Khyel's head looked like. Fireworks, perhaps. Connections, new ideas, possibilities, dangers . . . there were no clear images, just profound relief and excitement and assurance that what had been happening, had been happening for reasons he now understood, and so he knew what he had to do now." He gave a little shake, rather like a dog coming in out of the rain. "I think I learned more about my brother in that moment then in the rest of our life together. His reaction that instant when the pattern snapped into order was . . . hell, sex pales in comparison."

"Only your brother," Ganfrion said dryly, and Rhomandi laughed.

"I can appreciate it, I can be very glad he's on our side, but I damn sure wouldn't want to be him. Most of the time, that mind is walking a knife's edge of uncertainty—he just sees too damned many options. But with what he's found here, he's set his mind at ease regarding the last major duty he feels he owes the Web and the Syndicate. He'll set the stage; we'll contact Nikki and fill him in, just in case anything should happen to us, and he can head for Khoratum clear of conscience."

"Until he gets there and discovers the dancer died while he sniffed flowers."

"That has always been a possibility ever since Thyerri was taken captive. At the moment, Thyerri's situation is unchanged."

"How can you be so damned certain?"

"Khyel is. And by his way of thinking, it would be unconscionable to set his personal fears above what his rational analysis of his available data considers a justifiable—and even necessary—delay."

"Too damned tidy, if you ask me." Ganfrion took a long pull from his glass to steady nerves gone shaky. "A man needs a bit of chaos in his life to remind him he needs to stick around for tomorrow."

Rhomandi grunted.

"Shit." He poured another glass. "I could wish this didn't stink of a suicide mission."

The long silence that followed, as Rhomandi swirled the last of the whiskey around the bottom of his glass, did nothing to ease his mind. Finally, Rhomandi tossed that last bit down his throat, and said, "Why do you think I was determined to come along?"

§   §   §

The pool welcomed Mikhyel's fingers, the web on his hand glowed, and rejuvenating energy rippled up his arm: yet again, the Ley welcomed him, healed him. One part of him could wish it had chosen someone else. Another . . . the possibilities for the future were endless. To be a part of those possibilities damned exciting.

Providing he survived the near future.

{Mirym, you know where I'm going and why, don't you?}

She shrugged, the movement setting her halo of colored droplets to shimmering. {As I need to know.}

{If anything happens to me—if I die, will you seek Nikki out? Will you show him all this, help him understand and decide together what is best and how to accomplish it? Beyond the future of this node, I mean. What we've been involved with is bound to come out. Religion is bound to flourish. Will you help him guide that movement? Help him disseminate both knowledge and faith wisely?}

{And if you do not die?}

{I would be grateful for any help you could give us under any circumstances, but it is for Nikki's sake I'm asking now.}

Leaving the question hanging heavily between them, she gathered her hair with a graceful sweep of her hands and twisted it atop her head, secured it there with some unseen aid. Then casually, as if she were quite alone, she shed her outer robe, leaving only a loose gown of some gossamer fabric, and stepped down into the pool to sit on its edge.

The garment did not float, but instead . . . merged with the pool.

It was perhaps a deliberately provocative act; he made no comment and chose to accept it at its face value: she had said she soaked daily; obviously his arrival had interrupted that routine.

{You could join me,} her voice whispered in his head, and he had a sudden vision of that webbing on the back of his hand extending to the rest of his body.

{I think not.}

She looked up at him. {I think it would be best if you did not die, Ravenhair.}

{It is a distinct possibility. Whatever has Thyerri wants me, and if it takes my life to free him, I owe him that and more.}

She frowned and refused to meet his eyes. {You owe Dancer nothing. Dancer did as Dancer chose to do—as Dancer always has.}

Dancer. Not Thyerri.

{How can you know that?} he demanded. {How do you know *anything* about Dancer?}

{I know what I need to know.} She pulled her feet out of the pool and stood up and turned her back on him. {I think it is time for you to go now. Your brother is correct: you will do no one any favor to fall asleep in the saddle tomorrow.}

He grasped her hand, gripped it tight when she tried to pull away.

{How?}

She jerked free, then sat beside him, hands folded in her lap, chin defiantly lifted.

{I knew of the dancer Mother raised. One did not merge with the Mother without knowing something of what she considered her greatest treasure.}

Her thoughts hinted of jealousy. She started, glanced about the cavern, and tipped her head. {It appears you are not the only one to be tested today, Mikhyel dunMheric. Yes, I was jealous. Dancer held a special purpose for Mother, and I became merely a part of the mechanism to achieve Dancer's purpose. As a part of the greater Khoratumin community, I could gain access to the Rings and provide a bridge for Dancer to cross.}

{The hiller girl who was scared to dance.}

And in his mind was an afternoon in the hills above Khoratum, and Temorii at his side telling him of the girl who had given Dancer her time on the rings, whose sacrifice had eventually led to Dancer's own acceptance within the ranks of the apprentice dancers.

Mirym's slender shoulders lifted in an indifferent shrug. {Hardly a sacrifice. My interests were never in the Dance.}

{Reason enough for resentment, however, and jealousy would logically follow.}

{But should not have lasted past our first meeting. Dancer's essence exceeded anything I could imagine. Dancer's Talent was beyond question.}

{Perhaps someday you'll tell me the whole story.}

{Perhaps.} But the flavor of her thoughts suggested the possibility was not likely.

{So Dancer's obsession with the Dance was another of Mother's interventions,} he said.

{Hardly. No one can create or instill in another that which makes Dancer unique. Mother saw the treasure in her hands and helped it find its way to fruition because Mother believed that through the Dance her freedom could be restored.}

{Foolish of her. The dance rings control nothing. They're mere mechanisms, for all the presence of the energy umbrella is required to elevate them.}

{You actually believe they are nothing but a machine?}

{I've seen the blueprints for them.}

{Then you are the fool, Mikhyel dunMheric. The real strength of the Ley is the minds and hearts of those who believe. By giving them Rakshi incarnate, Mother would ensure that true belief for at least one more generation. By your own definition, her believers would grow in number and their belief would become more uniformly focused.}

{I stand corrected.}

Her mouth twitched. {On the contrary, you're sitting and you're enlightened, not corrected.}

{I'm glad to see not all the Mirym I knew was sham.}

{There was no sham, Mikhyel. As with Temorii, you saw what you expected/wanted/needed to see at the time. As Dancer did, I willingly played the role for you, for my own reasons.}

{And Mother's.}

{And Mother's,} she conceded. {A role, but still part of the whole. I choose now to give to you another piece.}

{Will I ever see the entirety?}

{Why should you expect to? The Whole shifts moment to moment. To know the Whole, you must know the past and the future as well as the present in all its facets.}

{Nonetheless, it would be a fascinating journey of discovery, I'm certain.}

Her head tipped to one side, as if to study him from a different angle. {Another puzzle to solve, Mikhyel dunMheric? You do so love them, don't you? The subject doesn't matter, only the facts to be fitted into a pattern you can comprehend.}

{Of course, I—} But in the presence of that pool, he was reminded of a conversation with his brothers, and the realization that he didn't care for much of anyone. Deymorin, yes, and Nikki, for certain. Kiyrstin, for Deymorin's sake. Ganfrion and Raulind . . . But for the rest . . . most of humanity could live or die without impacting his . . .

pattern. He sought a healthy pattern for the Web and the Syndicate not for individuals, but for the satisfaction of a mechanic watching a well-oiled and balanced machine leave his shop.

Except for Dancer. More than any of those others, more even than his brothers, he knew now that if Dancer died, a part of him would as surely be gone.

{And in that, perhaps, was Mother's true triumph. Once you fought for Dancer, you fought for Mother and so for Mother's people. And with Darius' descendants on her side, her freedom was assured.}

{But we lost. The Khoratum Rings are spinning again.}

{And because you knew Dancer, because through Dancer you have accepted the reality of the Mother, your greater pattern now accepts our presence, as Anheliaa's never could. Hence, Mother wins.}

{Mother is held silent and Dancer has been taken hostage trying to reach her. I don't exactly consider that a win.}

{Of a battle, if not yet the war. And if the war is won, it will be because Dancer has drawn you beyond the pattern-that-was. The Mikhyel that was would have left things as they are, would have counted Khoratum Outside the Rhomatum pattern and therefore beyond his jurisdiction, and Dancer a loss of war. How did the dancer do it? How did Dancer breach that fascination with the puzzle and reach Mikhyel dunMheric's essence? What is it that makes you rush blindly into the face of Death for the sake of one person?}

He had no answer. His mind shifted about, seeking the arguments he'd given Raulind. But here, in this garden cavern, with his hand drifting in a pool of Truth, he could not find them.

Her hand touched his, there within the ley-touched water. {Don't hurt yourself, my friend. I seek no real answers. I only find yet one more source of envy for the dancer who has the ability to move someone like you.}

Truth permeated the air here, and on her thought came the depth of her feelings: not for Nikki, as he had always believed, but for himself.

"But . . . Nikki—" He broke off as the sound of his voice ricocheted about the cavern. {I thought . . . You said once that you loved him—}

She jerked to her feet, pulling her hand from the pool, and her emotions from the air. She turned her back on him, hiding even her carefully controlled expression.

{I said, if you recall, that I loved you all. That I could not love one without loving the other. You are part of a whole. Die, and there is nothing left. I advise you to avoid death, Mikhyel dunMheric. Do not assume your brother can carry on without you.}

"But, Mirym, I—" The pool erupted in the center at this second assault, as if from some explosion deep beneath its surface, Mirym spun about, wide-eyed, tripped on a vine and would have fallen had he not steadied her. They clung to one another as the echoes slowly faded and the pool's surface collapsed to its former unnatural mirrorlike state.

{Forgive me.} He whispered the thought, for all he would have saved her the accompanying lack of emotion on his side.

{Forgive? For what?} Her question arrived on its own, her face hidden by that cloud of fawn-colored hair. {For not loving in return? That was never in doubt. For shattering the peace of this place? That also was never in doubt. You stir pots, Mikhyel dunMheric. Your quest for understanding and truth calls substance to the surface that might have been better to have remained hidden. But that is your function within the great pattern at this time. Perhaps that will change.}

Her face lifted at last, and the naked truth of her desire shone in her eyes. But even as that look met his, he knew it was not Mikhyel dunMheric, the man, she loved, and he had no real urge to find out what part of himself she did desire.

{Do not fear that part of you, Mikhyel. There was a time I might have loved you as woman loves man, but not now. My body does not hunger for yours, though my mind treasures the memory of your touch. What you can do now, what you might someday be capable of . . . I envy the dancer who will be part of that.}

The dancer. As if that might not be Dancer. Not Thyerri. Fear shot through him, and in this place he knew beyond doubt he wanted no other.

{And if the dancer loses his wings?} Her face had gone blank; her eyes looked through him to the pool. {If his essence withers and dies, will you die as well?}

{What are you talking about? What's happening to Dancer?}

She blinked. {Dancer? I don't know. Why should I?}

Chapter Nine

Two days, if Dancer could trust his sense of time. Two days, perhaps three since Mheltiri had brought him to this place, and in all that time, only Mheltiri had entered here: of Scarface, of guards, there'd been no sign. Of guards, there were only locked doors. Of Scarface, there was only that pressure to accept. To love as Mheltiri loved.

It was enough to put anyone off their appetite.

Thyerri picked at the latest offering, a delicately spiced roasted chicken, and found his thoughts turning constantly to Mother, even as he tried to shift them away. He could feel a presence about him constantly, a presence that felt vaguely of Rhyys-who-was-not-Rhyys, and he feared to think of Mother or Mikhyel, lest his needs rouse them and pull them into that Web he felt spinning ever more densely about him.

Which left him very little to consume his increasingly long waking hours. Mheltiri came and went, sharing his life story in bits and pieces, spending long hours rubbing that scented oil into Thyerri's skin, a healing touch that approached intimate, only to back off the instant before Thyerri could bring himself to object to the seemingly innocent gesture.

And yet, not innocent. While there was no sense of the predator in the young healer's surface essence, there was an uninhibited and rather overwhelming fascination with Thyerri's body, a fascination that had moved beyond that initial reverence to an unmistakable desire. How the healer could set aside the experiences he described and still seek intimacy of any nature baffled Thyerri, who had seen such a different reaction in Mikhyel, but he recognized in that good-hearted interest his only hope, however slim, for escape, and so rather than attempt to end Mheltiri's advances altogether, tried to find it in himself to accept and use them.

But hope for escape was very slim, indeed. That Mheltiri was fully under Scarface's spell was without question, and all Thyerri's instincts warned against probing more deeply, against putting himself and all he loved into so vulnerable a position.

He closed his eyes and chewed slowly, striving to lose his thoughts in the delicate flavors, the spices that enhanced rather than disguised the native taste of . . .

Mother so very much loved chickens . . .

And drenal leaves with aphids and dewdrops . . .

The bite soured in his mouth, and he set the half-finished meal aside, tucking it well out of the way to leave as much of the small room's floor free as possible. Eat, sleep, exercise . . . and only in the exercise did he trust his mind not to drift toward those vulnerable thoughts. In exercise, there remained no room for awareness beyond the interplay of muscle and bone, the finely tuned balance, the need to protect a shoulder still weak from the wrenching it had received in the cell.

His body warmed, and he began to work that shoulder deliberately, finding in it for the first time the strength to push himself from the floor one-handed on that side. Twice, a third time, without shaking, a fourth, and once more—

{I've received a message from your precious Khyel.}

Scarface's mind invaded his, shattering his careful concentration.

His arm collapsed, and he cried out as pain shot through the shoulder.

{How careless of me. My profound apologies.} But that mind held nothing of regret, or even surprise. The wonder was that it found no apparent pleasure in his pain, only satisfaction at having caught him off-balance and thus gained a tactical advantage.

Rhyys-that-was would have reveled in the pain.

{I do not seek your discomfort, radical dancer, only your cooperation.}

He pulled himself to a sitting position and pressed his back against the wall to keep him upright against a world suddenly spinning. He rubbed the shoulder, trying to keep his mind on that injury, trying not to wonder what that message from Mikhyel dunMheric might have said.

{Your Khyel seems to think he's still dealing with Rhyys. I wonder, is he really so headblind? Or does he think to put me off my guard. What *did* you tell him, dancer?}

Dancer. Not as in who and what Dancer was, but as a function. A thing, not a person. He used the implied insult to fight the reflex that would rouse the memory of that exchange, fought against thinking of Mikhyel at all, though his heart pounded at just the suggestion of his name.

{He's coming here, you know. He's coming to personally demand your release. He's coming to rescue one Thyerri gorMikhyel. Isn't that sweet?}

Which simply confirmed his fears. GorMikhyel. Mikhyel's, as Ganfrion was Mikhyel's. Both less and more than he had been. He stifled the protest that rose, knowing it would do no good. Knowing the moment he responded, Scarface would gain greater access to his mind and the thoughts now roiling about there.

{He's bringing his big brother. He thinks to terrify Rhyys into cooperation with the power of his precious Triumvirate and his Rhomatumin law. Is it show, do you think? Or is he truly so foolish?}

Rhomandi was coming as well. Hope flared, and he buried it, but not before Scarface detected it.

{You don't actually believe they can keep me from entering the younger one's shell, do you? Ah, the sweet confidence of youth. You're good. They are. But to get you, they will have to enter my ringchamber, and there, all advantage is mine. —I'll send Mheltiri to see to that shoulder.}

And then his mind was his own again, and the shakes set in with force enough to send waves of pain from his shoulder. He concentrated on that pain, set it to the foremost in his mind, sending healing thoughts toward the strained ligaments, all the while knowing, beneath, that he must get away . . . somehow. He must not let Scarface dictate the time and the place, must not let him get Khyel into that Tower, where the one who ruled the Rings would hold such advantage.

"My lord radical?"

Mheltiri's gentle voice whispered from the doorway, and the young healer gave a soft cry and slipped into the room to kneel beside him. Mheltiri. His only means for escape.

This time, he would not repulse those gentle advances.

§   §   §

{Stay with me tonight?} Mirym's request came with the tea she handed to him across their flower-draped dinner table, and Mikhyel nearly dropped the stoneware mug. He steadied it with both hands and took a sip before answering:

{To what purpose?}

{Only to lie next to you, here, in the place that will be our child's playground. To give our child a chance to know you. His/her mind stirs to increasing awareness. I would have him/her know his/her father, and should you fail in this endeavor—}

{No.} It was unnecessarily abrupt an answer, he realized too late, and tried to soften it. {I know you mean no harm by this, Mirym, but the very idea is . . . vaguely repugnant to me. I'm sorry.}

{It is I who am repugnant to you.}

"*No.*" She flinched and he took a large swallow of the steaming tea to stop further vocal protest. {I refuse to think that I shall not know my child in the normal way. I am not going up there to die, and to spend this night as if that were the expected outcome is not acceptable to me.}

She sipped from her own mug, and refused to meet his eyes, staring out across the shimmering pool. Her chin trembled, as if she were a step short of tears. He steeled himself against the softening in his gut. He would not give in to this whim. He would not risk lying next to a woman who had professed such personal interest in him, not knowing how such interest could weaken resolve. She wanted him alive. She might well strive to keep him here, to let the dancer she envied rot in the cell to which their mutual folly had condemned him.

As if aware of her failure, her mouth tightened into a smile. {As you will.} She lifted the teapot suggestively. {Your cup is empty. Would you have more? It will help you to sleep.}

Suspicion flared. He drew back the mug he had willingly extended.

She gave her silent laugh and cast back the last of her own mug and refilled it. {Relaxing only, as any warm drink will do. Your mind is tense, filled with plans. Moonflower tea relaxes the body and frees the mind for dreaming.}

And indeed, it was just a sense of ease that drifted through his muscles and brought a long overdue yawn. Feeling rather silly in his paranoia, he held the mug to be refilled. One more, to take with him back to the tent where Deymorin would be sleeping. In the morning, they'd contact Nikki and give him the details, then they'd move on. One more night, and he'd be with Dancer again.

His essence flared as the thought of Dancer and all Dancer was rippled through him, until even the steam rising from the mug assumed the shape and color of Dancer. He drew the steam into himself, a deep inhale, and while the scent was not Dancer's scent, it was pleasant, and carried a tingle reminiscent of all he'd felt as he held and was held by Dancer.

His hands trembled as he sipped the tea, spilling small drops that fell to the table and dribbled rainbows across the stone. . . .

Rainbows?

He set the mug down; it missed the table and crashed to the floor. Rainbows chased among crumbled pieces of pottery.

Once a fool, always a fool. Would he never learn where Mirym was concerned?

He levered himself from the chair, wove a staggering path toward what he thought was the cavern's mouth, but met only stone.

{Deymorin!} He sought his brother's mind, but wallowed in a cloud of swirling colors.

Arms caught him as his knees gave way, eased him down into some soft, fragrant nest. Clothing yielded to gentle hands until skin met skin.

{Forgive me, Ravenhair. The time is now.}

Sweetness filled his mouth. A kiss, gentle and undemanding, and then his head was cradled against a full bosom, his hand directed to a taut, round belly. . . .

That glimmered rainbows in the darkness.

$$\mathfrak{S} \quad \mathfrak{S} \quad \mathfrak{S}$$

Thyerri had thought it would be easier. He'd thought it would be better this way, to bind Mheltiri however briefly to his cause by granting this simple wish rather than trying to dissuade him from his love of the man he knew as Rhyys.

And indeed, Mheltiri was an enthusiastic partner, gentle and skilled, eager to indulge his fascination with Thyerri's body.

Yet all Thyerri felt, besides embarrassment at his complete lack of skill and a vague sense of boredom, was guilt. Dancer's times with Mikhyel had been profound experiences, a mutual sharing of instinctive responses, a dance where each move generated the next. Even when anger had been present, when the loving had come, conscious thought, decisions, had been . . . unnecessary.

The only profound aspect of this meeting was the thought that, should he successfully use this young healer to escape, Mheltiri would undoubtedly suffer the consequences. That concern for an innocent nearly overwhelmed Thyerri's determination to prevent at any cost Mikhyel falling into Scarface's grasp.

Almost. Mikhyel *would* be safe. Dancer *would* escape. If Mheltiri would come with him, he would find him sanctuary with the Rhomandi. He doubted, however, that Mheltiri would come. The healer would never leave Scarface, would never be able to comprehend the danger lurking here.

That profound betrayal drifted on the horizon even as he had to think about where to put his hands, and how to shape his mouth to fit another's, and all that thinking, all for the sake of manipulating that gentle essence to his own ends somehow defeated his body. Still, because he must escape, he persevered, following Mheltiri's lead mechanically, striving to arouse some hint of passion to match that so freely displayed by his partner, who entered Temorii eagerly with the sense of fulfillment of needs long suppressed. But there was nothing in Thyerri beyond a rather distant compassion for a fellow prisoner, who hadn't the wit to see his own prison, and when Mheltiri collapsed atop him, heaving from his efforts, Thyerri held him there, hoping that compassion would suffice.

{It is because you require the blending of essence, Radical . . .}

His hands tightened around the slender body. He'd have sworn Mheltiri lacked the silent speech.

{Ah, you underestimate me, Radical.}

And indeed, that gentle essence seemed to have gained an assurance it had lacked, as if . . . as if coupling had given him some sort of power he had been missing. Thyerri shivered, all too aware, suddenly, of just how ignorant he was in matters of this mystery of sex, wondering how great an error he might just have made, in his attempt to escape as Mheltiri began anew to urge a response out of him, this time, opening his mind as well, inviting Thyerri in.

But in to what? How much had Scarface infiltrated? Was that new assurance, this new ability Scarface's doing?

{He's taught me, yes. And seeing him with you . . . I've listened, learned.} Hurt, that Thyerri would not trust, that Thyerri still feared the one Mheltiri looked on as a savior. {Why, Radical? Why do you fear him? Help me to understand. Share with me that which you believe that keeps you distant.}

Mistake or not, he was committed to this leap. If he was to win this dance, he must win Mheltiri. It was possible Thyerri could compromise that way. Possible Thyerri could risk sharing his incomplete pattern and not lose Dancer into that maze. Sending his thoughts of escape swirling away to his mind's deepest recesses, he brought up all Thy-. erri knew of Scarface, all he knew of Mikhyel and his brothers, all the arguments he might have used to sway the healer to his side honestly, then cautiously cracked the barrier he'd held about his thoughts.

Mheltiri rushed in. Mheltiri's thoughts and emotions flooded him, swirling in and around those carefully prepared arguments, consuming, processing, eager to please . . . everyone.

{Oh, poor Radical. No wonder you hover beneath such a cloud of fear . . .}

Eager kisses devoured him. Eager thoughts drew images of Mikhyel from him, reveling in the flow of love those thoughts contained, crying protest at the darker memories he sought too late to hide.

{How much he has hurt you . . .}

{No!} he protested that thought, and yet it was true. He and Mikhyel had unwittingly hurt one another deeply, and because they'd wounded, they were now in danger of losing everything. {You don't understand. He's a good man. A wise man. I must go to him. Help me get away . . .}

{Poor Radical . . .} More kisses, and he gasped as lip-padded teeth closed on a suddenly sensitive nipple. {He comes not to free you, but to use you again. To hurt you again. Stay here, Radical. Stay with those who will love and appreciate all you are.}

Caught in his own trap, he sought those memories that would counteract those negative twists Mheltiri sought to impose on Mikhyel's love: moments pure and unadulterated, of essences meeting, of the overwhelming joy Dancer found in Mikhyel's touch, mind and body.

{Yesssss . . .} The thought hissed into his swirling mind.

{And we shall have that again, radical. Come to me now, join me now, and we'll call him here together . . . in love.}

Images already roiling in emotion swirled in a new current, a whirlpool drawing him ever deeper into the morass of his own need.

{You think to escape, but there is a way so much easier. So much more pleasant . . .}

And in that instant, as Scarface's unmistakable essence swept over his head, he knew the true depths of his error.

Chapter Ten

{Khy! Khy, help me . . .}

The frantic whisper invaded Deymorin's dreams of Kiyrstin.

{Dancer?} his hazy mind formed the connection. {Dancer, what—}

Acknowledgment. Terror that Mikhyel was not there, and indeed, Deymorin could share that concern. Mikhyel's mind was hidden in a cloud of swirling color.

"Dammit," he muttered, then flung a thought to Dancer, who grasped it as a drowning man would a rope. He felt a draw on his Talent, and as he'd learned to do with his brothers, sent a flow of strength along that connection, undirected, unspecified, without question. And when, with a sigh, that connection was consciously severed from the other end, he could only assume whatever need the dancer had had had been filled.

His brother was another matter.

He dove for that cloud which every sense declared held his brother. It closed about him—and snared him like a bug on a spider web. The harder he struggled to free himself, the more firmly it held him.

And before him stood Mirym, veiled in leythium lace, head to foot.

{He patterns to his child, Deymorin Rhomandi. Leave him.}

{Hell if I will.} He fought those bonds, only to find himself held that much tighter.

{He will ride with you in the morning. Give us this moment in peace and what aid we can give will be offered freely. Continue to fight for his freedom, and you risk my child. Injure my child and your brother will not leave the cavern alive.}

{I don't like threats, woman.}

{Neither do I. But this child *needed* something only Mikhyel could supply.}

{What in hell are you talking about?}

{If I understood, I wouldn't have required such methods to achieve what had to be.}

And that thought carried with it its own confusion, a sense of need Mikhyel's arrival had roused in her, of fear that she'd ignored the child's cry for too long.

He thought of those moments, the flashes of awareness from within Kiyrstin's womb, and had to wonder just what they were bringing into the world.

§ § §

The air shimmered about the child, who huddled in a fetal position even as its form shifted from new-born infant to a step short of adulthood and back to infant.

{Why do you hate/discard/ignore me?}

The thought that formed slowly in Mikhyel's head might have been his own, once and so very long ago. First his mother, then his father, and the ultimate rejection from Deymorin. That his own child, even unborn, felt the same desertion he had felt once too often cut him to his essence. He took a step toward that distant figure and was instantly beside it, looking down into eyes that shimmered with all the colors of the Ley.

But not the eyes: it was the tears that formed but did not spill that bore the distinctive glimmer. The eyes were like his: palest gray rimmed with green. And the black lashes were his. The hair was dark and fell in deep waves about a delicate face.

He dropped to his knees beside a figure that settled into prepubescent child, and jerked away, pressing itself into some unseen corner, lips pulled back in a snarl like some cornered animal.

A gesture, an expression, he knew all too well.

He closed his eyes against the sight, fought back his own anger, anger at himself, to know he'd done this to his own child.

And yet, he hadn't. His child wasn't yet born. He was fully prepared to take responsibility for its care.

{Lies.}

The feral sprite leaped to its feet and ran, light-footed as a fawn. Stopped and spun about as he tried to follow.

{Don't pretend to me! You didn't want me. You didn't even try to find me. I disappeared. Months and months and what did you care?}

Mirym's concerns. The child had Talent and heard her even in the womb.

And his own thoughts echoed back to him: Deymorin, and Nikki, Kiyrstin for Deymorin's sake, Ganfrion and Raulind . . . And Dancer . . .

{No one else matters, do they, Father?}

{You heard that, too?}

{How could I not? You take such pride in not caring.}

Pride? No. He wasn't proud of it.

{Certainly makes life easier, doesn't it?}

{No!} But did he protest to himself or the child? Where did such thoughts come from?

The delicate mouth trembled despite teeth that cut deep enough to draw blood . . . that glimmered. Ley-touched, as was all else in this place.

{I'm trying, child. I'm trying to learn to care.}

Crossed arms and a hunched shoulder, answered him. Then a petulant eye peeked from behind tousled hair. {Try harder.}

Laughter threatened and he let it out. Not completely broken, his unborn child.

{You'll have to help me.}

He held out his arms. The sprite shuddered, took one step toward him, then drew up, chin lifted.

{You'll have to come back.}

He let his rejected hands drop, all tendency to laughter gone.

{I can't promise that.}

And in his mind was the obligation to Dancer. The sure sense that if only one survived, that one must be Dancer, whose life he had so utterly destroyed.

That small body—whose life he had helped create—tensed, the eyes filled, then blinked clear.

{Go back to your world, Mikhyel dunMheric.}

Mikhyel dunMheric . . . as he had been unable to call Mheric "Father" in years. He stumbled backward. He turned to run from that accusatory face, tripped and fell over the infant, whose cries filled the air. Helpless, unable to run away.

Vulnerable to a world it didn't yet understand, sensitive to adult fears and betrayals as no child should be, let alone one still floating in what should be the safest harbor of its life.

Security. Assurance it wasn't alone, that someone cared . . . not just someone, but those responsible for its existence in the first place. Deymorin exuded that love. It was in the very air he exhaled whenever he was near Kiyrstin, in his thoughts every time those thoughts turned toward Rhomatum. For Deymorin's child, sensitive as this child was obviously sensitive to the thoughts surrounding its small world, there had been loving security.

For his child, there had been nothing—at least not from him. At least, not until now, and now, there was only rejection.

From Mirym . . . he would no longer guess what the child might have gained from her these past months, from a mother who floated for hours in a ley-touched pool while her people worshiped her and her unborn child. Expectations . . . that was the very least.

He gathered the baby up, cradled it in his arms as he had wanted to do with the child, amazed at how small it was in his adult arms, arms that remembered what his child arms had learned with Nikki. It cried as a tired baby would cry, but it didn't struggle for freedom. Resigned. Another, all too familiar reaction to powers beyond one's control.

He couldn't promise to be back. That would be a greater cruelty should things go wrong, but he could extend one *small gift—or torment—to his child. As he'd done on instinct with Deymorin and Nikki, and later with Dancer, he did now with full conscious thought, wrapping his essence around that of his child and wove their patterns together.*

This is what I am! He cried into that void surrounding the pattern, and the babe grew, extended arms that hugged his neck, a tear-damp face that pressed into his throat, even as the child's patterns extended threads to mingle with his own. "This is your father," he whispered into the dark waves. "And you are now, and forever, a part of that pattern. I pray you don't come to hate me for that."

The fog shimmered and dissipated, the child in his arms warped, swelled to a woman's rounded belly. He blinked tears from his eyes, lifted his head to meet Mirym's calm, satisfied gaze.

"Never," she whispered softly, and brushed the hair from his eyes.

ॐ　ॐ　ॐ

Thyerri's mind was his own, when he awoke, which was vaguely surprising, his body was not, which did not surprise him at all.

He knew, even before he opened his eyes, that he was in the Khoratum tower, and lying spread-eagled on a rough stone floor, directly beneath the Rings. Nothing else would account for the intense flow of energy that seemed, from behind his closed eyelids, to fountain straight from his chest, then flare out in every direction.

He'd seen a butterfly collection once, the prize possession of one of Rhyys' endless guests. He remembered thinking at the time that he understood how those creatures must have felt as their final essence had faded from their delicate bodies, plucked from the air and spread for display.

He'd been very naive, once.

He thought at first nothing held him there except the spinning Rings, until the delicate touch of a fingertip brushed his foot without eliciting so much as a twitch, and he realized his arms and legs, even toes and fingers refused to answer his mind's commands. He could feel, he just couldn't move.

"You got help." It was Mheltiri's voice, but he knew better than to believe it was Mheltiri who spoke. "Oh, Mheltiri is here. Much more so than Rhyys, in actual fact." The voice traveled up from his feet to manifest near his head. "Your blast physically shattered that drug-infested mind; we had to do something. —Oh, your eyes."

Lips brushed his eyelids, and he was able to blink them open . . . to the dizzying whirl of the Rings directly above him. He gasped and squeezed them shut again.

"Oh, no, no, no, child." Hands cupped his face and his eyes opened without his willing it, and this time, Mheltiri's upside-down face eclipsed the Rings. "I brought you here to appreciate the view. Can't have you avoiding it, now can we?"

The face slipped to the side, as Mheltiri stretched out on the floor beside him, stroking those limbs that tingled with energy but would not move to his desires.

"We wouldn't have chosen such a sweet soul, and gentle Talent, except that you left us no choice. Ordinarily we prefer those who can appreciate the pairing."

"Not to mention someone whose Talent is somewhat more useful," Thyerri sniped back, realizing that tingling kiss had released more than his eyes.

Mheltiri/Rhyys/Scarface smiled, and gently smoothed the sweat-tangled hair from Thyerri's face.

"Oh, you don't understand at all, child. Half the excitement of living is finding the strengths and weaknesses of the new host and helping that host learn to use them. But the simple fact is, there is never any point in choosing someone that lacks real world power. Talent is not enough. You would have been ideal, with your connections to the Rhomandis as well as your obvious physical talents."

"I'm no ringspinner."

"Ah, but we are. Your other skills would have made a unique addition to the whole, but once you realized, you proved too strong and willful. Even without help—Rhomandi, wasn't it?—you'd kept us out. Too bad, really. I think you'd have been pleasantly surprised."

"I doubt it."

"Don't be like that." That sweet, velvet-covered voice chastised softly, while Mheltiri's trained hands stroked and smoothed his immobile body.

"Pleasant?" Inside, Thyerri shuddered. Inside, he struggled against the invisible bonds holding him. "Pleasant to share my body with—what, three minds? Four?"

"Oh, rather more than that, child."

For a moment, Thyerri's voice froze for reasons that had nothing to do with the Rings. "How . . . How m–many?"

Again, that gentle smile, as Mheltiri-who-wasn't lay on his side, propped on one elbow, and ran a finger down his breastbone, throat to navel. "You don't really want to know, child. Suffice to say . . . some of us knew Darius, the thief."

Darius. Mikhyel's ancestor. The man who had led an exodus out of Mauritum, to escape the ringmaster's domination.

Three hundred years ago.

Mheltiri chuckled. "I told you you didn't want to know." He rolled over onto his stomach, chin propped on crossed arms, never taking his eyes from Thyerri's, a move utterly un-Rhyys, and even further from Scarface. "Now, Thyerri of the Khoramali, the question remains, what to do with you?"

"Just let me go. You've got Mheltiri. You've got Khoratum. Be content with that."

"You jest, naturally. I've already explained to you that Mheltiri simply hasn't the power to ensure that we would keep the Rings, and without the Rings, we would ultimately die, in the natural course of time. If that was what we wanted, we'd have done it a long time ago. So, if I let you go, you'll run to dunMheric, and he and his brothers will bring their little army up the mountain and destroy my tower. No, I don't think I'd like that. No, we're back to finding us a proper shell, one that will last us a goodly while. We're getting . . . oh, quite tired, bouncing about as we've been doing. And I think Mikhyel dunMheric is the perfect choice, don't you?"

"No!"

"But the advantages are so obvious." Up again, to both elbows this time, an unholy enthusiasm shining in that young face. "He has youth, but maturity, political power, access to the Rhomatum Rings, but not the ultimate responsibility for them. He understands intimately the art of compromise, and might easily welcome this very simple opportunity to solve so many pesky little problems."

"He's stubborn and self-centered and very private. And my Talent is weak compared to his. He will blast your minds to ashes. Let me go. I'll tell him to leave Khoratum alone, to leave you alone. I won't tell him about you—"

"Oh, child, as if you could keep it from him. Besides, with what I know of dunMheric, he might delight at the prospect of adding our knowledge of Mauritum to his own pattern in this way . . . a true merger of giants. Oh, yes, talking so helps to clear one's thinking, and I have had so few to talk with these past months. Ever since leaving Garetti, you know. No one who could comprehend what I am. We were quite close, in some ways, Garetti and I. Intimate knowledge of each others' strengths . . . and weaknesses."

He didn't care about Garetti. Didn't care what this creature did, if only he would let him go. He was utterly lost in this game. It wasn't a dance, not of love or even of aggression. He couldn't see the patterns. Couldn't sense the winds or the cut of the Rings through the world pattern.

"Now, the problem is—" The velvet voice continued to caress his ears. "—if I leave you alone, somehow you *will* escape, won't you? Perhaps you'll simply vanish, the way dunMheric disappeared from Khoratum the night of your great triumph. But if you were going to do that, you'd have done so by now, so I think you don't have that particular skill. DunMheric does, though, doesn't he? Of course. He appeared out of nowhere at Boreton. I'd thought Anheliaa behind that, but considering the way he disappeared from here the night of the competition . . . perhaps it wasn't.

Interesting. That knowledge and ability should add nicely to the whole. But you . . ."

Fingers traced his, sending shocks through his system, and he couldn't move. Could not escape even that mild torment. And he couldn't help but think that it was possible, that Mikhyel might well have the ability to call on Mother, as he had before, might well be able to transport into the middle of this madness.

Mheltiri's eyes brightened.

"*Can* you bring him here? He almost was, that first night, wasn't he? Can we call him, do you think? What would it take to galvanize him? Something carnal? He loves you quite to distraction, doesn't he? I could turn you over to the guards—they offered their services to break your resistance, but that would be quite useless, now, wouldn't it? You've dealt with that aspect of your nature. You'd simply hide behind that dream of yours. But that won't be necessary. There are other ways to convince him . . . and you, that it is best he come and visit us here."

His hand began to track the contours of Thyerri's arm.

"One works within the confines of the new housing. Rhyys . . . he had potential once, I'm quite certain, but the ocarshi had nearly destroyed the body's ability to focus. I knew from the moment I was forced to escape into it that I'd have to leave it prematurely. Your rather unexpected attack compromised that house completely, and so I took this one. But it is delicate, if not exactly weak. Its talent has been . . . otherwise directed. A healer, by nature and by upbringing. It hasn't the physical strength to do much damage directly."

That delicate stroking continued.

"Ah, but *indirectly,* using this body's inborn abilities . . . it might be interesting."

Shivers filled him, spasms that could find no outlet in the body held hostage in the lines of the ley-energy.

"So much. So very much is determined by what you believe about yourself. We make decisions at the intersections of our lives and by those choices, form the pattern we must live with from then on. As the pattern is shaped, so lies the potential. Mheltirin balances her life by her cycles. She knows she is strongest then . . . or rather believes she is and so creates the reality. An ancient belief: the power of blood, you know.''

Blood on the bedsheets in a cheap inn in Lesser Khoratum, blood on the sand beneath the rings, blood in his old room, blood in Mikhyel's nightmares . . .

"Mheltirin is a healer. Rhyys was the worst sort of dreamer, a dreamer of fantasies not possibilities. You . . . you are a risk taker. Death doesn't frighten you, but you will fight it to the last. In that, you lose your value to me as a host. In taking you, I would necessarily destroy the very aspect that makes you valuable.''

Of course death frightened him. He didn't want to die, not with Mikhyel— He shied off that dream touch that might be real and might not be, and if yes, was too dangerous to even contemplate.

"DunMheric, on the other hand, is a compromiser. No deal is beyond his grasp, given sufficient motivation, and so . . . so that motivation becomes the key in our dealings with him. And what could possibly motivate such a man to release his most precious possession, his own sovereignty?''

Nothing, Thyerri thought defiantly, and Mheltiri/Rhyys/Scarface smiled faintly.

"Oh, I think you're wrong there, radical dancer. I saw his face, as you danced the night of the parade of contestants and during the contest itself. I think, no I'm quite certain, I know the answer to that. He loves you, Rakshi. But he loves your dance. Without that, you are only a fraction of yourself. I wonder, would he love part without the whole?''

Thyerri turned his head, the only part of his body that would respond to him, away from that deceptively gentle face. The words faded in and out, the hum of the Rings, the haze of their spin filled his senses. Eventually, he would break . . . or fall asleep, which might be worse. Best to try to reach Mikhyel now, while his wits were at least somewhat with him. Risk that one final contact to tell him everything, and convince him—somehow—to stay away.

And if not him, his brother. He'd reached Deymorin that last time. Perhaps Deymorin would keep his brother away.

"Part of the fascination of this procedure is the investigation of the new body's potential. For instance, this body knows the intricacies of itself to the chemistry of its smallest drop of blood, and it can sense those details in another body. She is a healer, and by nature would never strike a blow. But she heals by directing the Ley to specific areas of her body, reknitting flesh and bone. I wonder. . . ?" His touch had worked its way to Thyerri's right thigh, a tingling that reached deep, caused a twitching itch that defeated all attempts to ignore it. A sudden crack, and the itch was gone. In its place, a sense of wrong, a growing discomfort.

"Ah. I think, perhaps, you should not move, Rakshi. I think perhaps, if you do, the pain will be the least of your concerns."

Move? He couldn't move.

"You can now, child. All that holds you steady now is your own desire not to move."

Another crack.

"And yet, eventually, you must sleep, and in sleep will come movement, and with movement, a hint of sudden pain."

Crack!

"Startled, your body will jerk, and with the contraction of those beautifully honed muscles will come damage of unknown scope."

Crick!

"Perhaps irreparable damage, even for one so in harmony with the Ley."

He tried to shut the voice out of his head, tried to follow the route of the damage, pouring his body's resources to repair the damage.

"Too late, Rakshi. You know too little, and this mind is quite thoroughly versed in these patterns. It is unfortunate that such very potent knowledge is housed in so meek a mind."

Crack!

"I think, perhaps, you should call your Khy. Not to warn him, but to plead with him. Because if you do not—
Crack.

"—inch by inch, bone by bone, you're going to lose your dancing legs."

SECTION
FIVE

Chapter One

{*Dancer!*} Mikhyel's waking essence shouted, even as his mouth whispered: "Thyerri . . ."

Dancer was there and gone in an instant, leaving behind a throbbing in Mikhyel's leg and terror twisting his gut while he crouched shivering in Mirym's cave. He had now an absolute certainty that he had not had the time to delay here: his mistake, no one else's.

{*Deymio!*} he called in one direction, and in another and another: {*Nikki! Mirym!*} and without waiting for their acknowledgment, he dove after that fleeting mindtouch, and found—

Nothing.

For a moment, he feared he'd mistaken dreams for reality, worse, that the touch had been real and he'd lost it, that he'd written Thyerri's future with his arrogance and sealed Dancer's fate with his inadequacy.

Relief: a flickering thread of presence within an infinity of dark. A thread that in one instant both cast itself toward him and· jerked away, evidence of two great contrary needs—or perhaps opposing wills—nearly at equilibrium.

He held his ground in that great void and called the thread to him, striving to breaking that equilibrium, refusing this time to be denied. He felt the strength of his own demand increase tenfold as his cries for help found answer from all three to whom he had appealed.

Still that stubborn battle of Dancer's raged on, just beyond his reach.

He wrapped his three-ply lifeline about him like a dancer about to plunge into the rings, and secured by his brothers'

will and by Mirym's dove for that darting strand, caught it
and held. Despite its whipping about, its frantic attempts to
free itself, he held on. Despite the shocking, heinous evidence
flowing into him through that thread, still he would not let it
go, would not leave Dancer to face that horror alone.

{Mother!} he shouted, and threw into that cry all his
heart, mind and Talent. {Mother, *get me to him!*}

{Wait!} Instinctive objection from Deymorin weakened
his lifeline, and, at that betrayal, his hold on Dancer's
thread slipped. Deymorin's reason warred with Deymorin's
instinct, as despite the cries of instinct Deymorin strove to
reinforce his efforts to reach Mother.

But that war within his brother weakened rather than
bolstered those efforts, and Mikhyel deliberately—ruthlessly and absolutely—cut his brother out.

Mother *would* answer him. Mother *would* answer him,
would send him to Khoratum Tower, *would* help him save
her most precious—

{Maybe . . .}

Infinity imploded around him, leaving him blind and deaf
and gasping after breath.

Triumph filled him as he fell, and he called again to
Dancer, telling him to hold on, telling him he was coming.

Starved lungs finally expanded; dazzled eyes cleared . . .

On leythium lace iridescence.

And the air that filled his lungs held the peculiar taste
and vitality of the great leythium caves, not the controlled,
scented air of a ringtower, and the walls surrounding him
were billowing leythium lace. Mother had brought him not
to Dancer's side but to her World Cave, and Mother herself
loomed over him, Mother at her most alien, scaled and
armored, tail whipping, reptilian mouth bared in a snarl.

{Maybe . . .} Mother's voice whispered again in his head,
{or . . . maybe not.}

ᔕ   ᔕ   ᔕ

Khyel's presence was gone. So was Nikki's. Headblind,
Deymorin fought his way through clinging vines and burst

into the ley-cavern that moments before had held his brother.

Mirym met him at the entrance . . . alone. He looked past her, searching the place he'd seen only through his brother's eyes, foolishly hoping he might yet see Mikhyel himself, that what he'd felt in his mad dash for this place had been a dream.

{He's gone, my lord Princeps.} Mirym's voice was coldly formal, but Mirym's touch, hand and mind, informed him otherwise. {I don't quite know whether to be terrified or elated.}

"You think—" He broke off, shocked as his voice reverberated wildly, and jerked his head toward the cavern's exit: what he had to say, he would not trust to mindspeak with this woman; what he suspected the threat to be, he did not want to say here, in this ley-touched place. In that conviction he seized her by the hand and drew her outside.

Clear of ley-threads and vines, out beyond the cavern mouth, he said, "You think that—all of that just now—was Mother's doing?"

{At the last, yes, I'm quite certain of it. At first . . . I don't know.} Her mind truly was a roiling mass of conflicting emotions. {So much pain. Such fear. I can't believe she'd be party to that.} But the uncertainty lingered, a sense of unqualified trust betrayed. {You've lost contact with him as well, Lord Princeps?}

He nodded, distracted, part of him striving to track her even as a second, larger part fought to reach his brother. "Thyerri's been taken to the Tower, did you get that?"

She shook her head. {I only got that call for joining, then the draw. Nothing more.}

"Whoever has him is terrifying him." The details of that torture eluded him, only that it somehow threatened all the dancer held dear: terror more than pain had come through. Terror and hopelessness. "They're deliberately trying to provoke Mikhyel into jumping there. They don't seem to realize it's Mother's doing, not Khyel's, when he leythiates. Khyel cut me out." Damned bad timing that had been, and

he could only blame his own hard-headed caution for causing it. "Did *you* get any sense where he landed?"

Mirym shook her head. But of course she hadn't; it had
been a foolish question. *He* knew Mikhyel's goal had been
Thyerri and that meant Khoratum Tower, plain and simple.
Whether or not he'd made it there . . .

"I'm heading out immediately." He started back for his
tent. Morning light touched the eastern sky and brought
shape to the surrounding shadows; he could be on the trail
with his men in half an hour.

But it was still two days to Khoratum Tower on horseback. He wasn't like Mikhyel, able to travel that way without the Rings and without burning the hide off his back:
Mother ignored him, if she even heard him. With the best
riding he'd ever done in his life, he saw little chance he'd
get there in time to do anything but pick up the pieces—

Assuming Mikhyel was in the Tower, and not somewhere
with Mother.

He didn't know which might be worse.

{Khyel! Dammit, where are you?}

No answer. No better information. And no choice.

"We'll go straight for the Tower," he said to Mirym, who
was keeping pace at his side, "and hope to hell we can get
in without a fight, because we damnsure won't have much
left to fight with." Reluctantly pulling his mind back to last
night's events, he asked: "What about you? Are you . . .
satisfied?"

{Our child is content.}

That same morning light caught movement on the trail
ahead of them.

{I'll leave you now, Lord Princeps. May Rakshi smile
on you . . .}

And like the moonshadow, she was gone.

"The lads're up and saddling," Ganfrion said, by way of
greeting—Ganfrion, whom he'd run over on his way out
the tent door. Sometimes he wondered if Mikhyel's gorman
was as headblind as he professed. "But something else has
come up. The captain came up from the big camp last night

while you were out. We chatted a bit. Seems he's got a hiller down below demanding to see you."

"He'll damnwell have to wait." He kept walking and Ganfrion spun to join him. "Mikhyel's gone," Deymorin continued. "Left. Leyapulted gods know where. Hell with visitors. We're riding for Khoratum. Ten men—choose them yourself. The rest can follow, but we'll be cutting corners. I want to be in that Tower yesterday."

Ganfrion's scarred mouth twitched: not happy with the news—but who would be, who gave a damn about his brother as well as the men they led? And yet: "Maybe you'd better hear this visitor," Ganfrion said. "A hiller down from the mountain. Showed up yesterday morning before we arrived. Says the *barrister's Child of Rakshi* sent him."

He stopped short, spun to face the gorman.

Ganfrion continued: "Sorry to say, the lads in the camp thought he was a bit touched in the head. Put him under guard and sent a courier to Rhomatum, that being the cautious course."

A courier who necessarily took a fast and dangerous course down the mountain, not the leyroad they had followed. They'd had a message from Thyerri and it had gone to the capital while Mikhyel had gone straight into whatever it warned about.

"Says he can get us into the Tower," Ganfrion finished.

"Can he ride?" He envisioned a trip as fast as horses could bear and the last thing he wanted on his hands was a novice rider; but if this messenger had a way to get them in past all the barriers they might face, a way inside that might be their only way in and Mikhyel's only salvation . . . what could they do?

"Damned if I know," Ganfrion said. "He's a hiller."

"Tie him to the saddle if necessary, but bring him along. We'll get his story on the way."

ᛋ   ᛋ   ᛋ

Crack!

The sound of breaking bone sickened him. The flash of

cause and effect he'd already received from Dancer heightened the nausea Mikhyel felt.

But desperation focused his purpose.

"Mother?" Mikhyel whispered the word cautiously, not trusting his spinning head to form the kaleidoscopic gestalt that constituted identity in that mental realm. He knew he was here physically. He knew he stood in the World Cave below Khoratum. He knew by all previous experience he should be safe.

But he was no longer even certain that the antipathetic creature towering before him *was* the same as the ley-creature who had raised Dancer.

{Mother? And Dancer. Dancer's Mother. Naturally.} She swirled down beside him into human dimensions and cupped his chin in a painful grip, her scaled lips stretched in a travesty of a human smile. More androgynous in her form than he'd ever seen her. Larger. Almost masculine.

And recalling, in that heart-pounding instant, his discussion with Mirym about the essence of the ley-gods, he had to wonder how much of the whimsical Mother he had known could survive intact, with the defilement ruling her rings, and with Dancer's influence overwhelmed by that degrading—

Crack! . . . came from the Tower.

He flinched. Stifled a sympathetic groan.

{I suppose I should say "Welcome, child of Darius" . . . except you're *not,* you know.}

"Which, Mother?" he whispered, the answer being of some significance. "Not welcome? Or not Darius' child?"

{Questions! Always questions!} She thrust him away. Her talons ripped his cheek as he fell, and her eyes flared. Her tongue flickered from between her lips, and *hunger* filled the caverns as the leythium lace rippled a deep red.

The color of blood.

Faster than thought, she was gone, reappearing in a far recess, her eyes closed, her head twisted away from him. The sense of *hunger* dissipated, but did not vanish.

{Heal the wound, Mikhyel dunMheric! Heal it quickly!}

A retreat. A distancing from temptation. And in that

action, that restraint on her part, he discovered hope. Following that demand, the Ley beneath his hand, solid in one instant, was liquid the next. Never questioning what resource she lent him, he cupped that liquid to his throbbing cheek, but to no avail: the pain continued and the hand he pulled away dripped a sluggish red trail.

The scent of blood filled the cavern, and Mother's nostrils flared. He saw madness in her eyes.

Crack!

He closed his heart to the sound, focused on the matter of his immediate danger . . . and Mother's. Thyerri had no help, without him; he had none without Mother; Mother had been pushed to the brink of madness.

Heal the wound . . . she said, as if he must take an active part. As a child, he'd drifted in Barsitum's pools, and the Ley had responded in a way the brothers had never seen before. But he'd *done* nothing to cause it.

Mother, ravening for blood, brought him here. Yet she appealed for human intervention . . . his intervention.

Heal the wound . . . Which wound? How many needed healing beyond that in his cheek?

But the cheek did not heal with a simple touch; this time, healing would not come without effort. He was a child no longer. The brothers helped those who came to the pools to help themselves. Hadn't Raulind said he'd had a gift? And was ley-magic not a matter of wills?

At the moment, *his* will not to be eaten was pretty damned potent. He shut all thoughts of Dancer into a safe zone in his mind and lifted a second handful of liquid to his cheek, *willing* that wound healed.

Still bleeding.

{Too late, child . . . too late . . .} Mother eased toward him, her tail lashing, a sidling swish more reminiscent of a snake. The insanity grew. Her eyes held the reflection of blood-red leythium.

He ignored her, denied the fear with which she strove to distract him as he'd learned to block Anheliaa's threats from his mind while altering the wording on proposals and presenting them to the Representatives.

He scooped a third handful of ley-stuff, and crouching low, backed slowly away from her.

There was a war raging here in the caverns, a war that had little or nothing to do with his presence. The fresh scent of mountain raspberries that was Mother's signature wafted past him in one breath, but in the next instant something old and tired, like the smell of a deathbed, tainted that freshness.

And one moment, it was the Mother he'd known approaching him, an egocentric, autocratic creature, who had held Dancer gently and soothed his childhood fears. In the next, it was a predator, hungry and with prey in sight.

Crack!

I'm sorry, Thyerri . . .

And the most powerful mind affecting Mother now was the same one inflicting that unimaginable torment. A torment as yet more of the spirit than the flesh.

Madness . . . on a godly scale.

"Mother," Mikhyel whispered, and dared that silent voice, calling to that entity he'd known and Dancer had treasured, calling on her now with the full force of that kaleidoscopic image that manifested as *Mother*. {Mother, I don't know how to do this. I'm not a healer. I can't—}

Her head snapped up and back, like a snake about to strike. But:

{Do I hear *can't*? Mother would never have asked had the child not been capable! Of *course* you *can*. You must reverse the process, that is all. Undo that which was done. Simplicity incarnate!}

Starting from what was and going backward. It was not the way he had been thinking. To a mind shaped in law it made no sense at all. He pressed his back to the stone, cupped his ley-damp hand to his cheek and fiercely tried to imagine the cut of that talon through the layers of skin.

Thought of the images he'd seen in books of the structure of skin, then sought the real counterpart of those images, knitting layers of skin together, starting at the deepest point, joining the tiny capillaries . . .

Mother sidled closer. Her webbed hand raised . . . trembled . . . poised to strike . . .

Crack!

He closed his inner ear to that sound, closed his eyes to Mother's looming, taloned fingers, and willed that wound reversed.

Willed it nonexistent . . .

And the swish of Mother's tail stopped. The hand descended . . . slowly.

Talons caught and delicately lifted strands of his hair. A slight tug as they snagged in a tangle, then the locks fell free to his shoulders.

"You cut your hair!" Her petulant protest hissed in his ears rather than his head.

Startled, he snapped his eyes open—to find a hooked talon close enough to brush his eyelashes. He froze, but that talon delicately snared his finger and lifted his hand away from his cheek. A tongue flicked toward him and he squeezed his eyes shut again. But the tongue made a light exploration of his cheek and retreated.

"Very good, child of Dariuss-ss-ss . . ." It was only the scent of raspberries, pure and fresh, that met his mind and his nose, as he inhaled deeply of air and essence.

And his hand, when he opened his eyes to look, ran clear of blood, shimmering only with an opal residue of the liquid leythium.

{Mother?} he ventured.

{Of course I am, child. Now, about your hair . . .}

Hope flared. She was all Mother as he'd known her, at her most charmingly, distractingly exasperating.

{Never mind my hair! Mother, help me get to Dancer. He's in terrible trouble—}

{*About* your hair . . .} Charming and stubbornly centered on her current obsession.

Crack!

Thyerri! his heart cried out, and in his mind: {Don't you feel him, Mother? How can you let him suffer?}

{Such beautiful hair. How could you punish it so?}

He felt a tug as her talons combed through the strands,

and this time the strands landed beneath his shoulder blades, thrusting him back to another time, to another transformation in this same place: Temorii huddled at Mother's feet, her shaded hair ruthlessly chopped short by her own hands at her own choice, restored by Mother's hands . . .

"Stop it!" His shout set the leythium strands to shivering, a disturbance that in turn sent a shimmer of discordant music about the cavern. He jerked away from her and ran to the far side of the pool, then spun to face her. He didn't even know why he had run: something about independence, something about not yielding to Mother's distractions and following her into the mire in which she had sunk.

He had made that decision about his hair, *he* would decide when to change it. He was *not* a dancer, *not* a Child of Rakshi, and *Mother* did not dictate his life, *Mother's* needs would not dictate his actions.

Strangely, she hadn't moved. She could have materialized in front of him . . . had done so in the past. Running away had been instinct, not sense, on his part. But damn it, he was right. She would listen to him, not the other way around.

Crack!

His legs shook, collapsed beneath him. Dancer's weakness, not his own. He found himself on hands and knees. The hair Mother had partially restored hanging like a curtain about his face, blinding him to all but that distant battle.

Crack!

He heard Dancer's silent scream, a scream still more of terror than of pain: terror the dancer strove to keep confined . . . without complete success.

Too late for that, my love. I do hear you. He thought it, but did not send; he did neither of them any favor to bridge that distance and entwine himself further in Dancer's struggle—yet. Not before he could answer that need in truth, and with any realistic hope of escape.

That hope rested on Mother. Somehow, someway, he had to find the arguments to sway her.

Chapter Two

Crack!

Every hour on the hour; Deymorin could set his watch by that gut-twisting sound that was no sound at all.

Mikhyel's mind leaked, every time that jolt reached him. That was the only way he could account for it. And with it came impressions of the caverns where Mother-and-not-Mother had drawn him. Fleeting images supplied him details, none comforting, none assuring him Mikhyel was not dealing with leyforce run amok.

He knew by that leak that Mikhyel had not yet arrived in the Tower to stop the torture. By that leak he knew Mikhyel was in danger of his life, though not in danger from Dancer's persecutor. The taste of blood and Mother's serpent aspect arrived with the sound of breaking bone, and there was no evidence Mikhyel heard him at all.

They pushed hard, horses and men, holding still to the leyroad, that proximity to the Ley being his best chance of hearing Mikhyel, should Mikhyel call for help, but it was a mountain road, and steep enough an ascent that the pace necessarily slowed at times.

Hour after long hour, pressing the pace, stopping in mid-afternoon at—thank the gods it was still manned—an official Syndicate posting inn to change horses: not all the evidence of civilization had gone down that night leylight had coruscated above the mountains. The stable-keeper had stayed by his four-footed charges, a lowland man, glad to see authority on a road devoid of traffic all summer. The horses were well-shod, exercised, pastured-out when the grain supply had failed . . . all done because a man had stayed by his post though no one had come.

It was Mikhyel's life this man might have saved; it was their chance of reaching Khoratum in any good time. He promised the man the pay he hadn't had in six months, with interest.

And as they shifted the gear to fresh mounts, Deymorin called the hiller—Zelin, the man's name was—forward. Zelin had, he had said, left the Tower complex by way of a tunnel; left Thyerri in one hell of a mess—he'd said that, too. And thank the gods, too, Zelin was no novice on horseback: a former soldier, a man not used to the saddle, but bearing up with what was going to be a protesting, outraged body come any rest at all.

"You're certain you can find this tunnel?" he asked, and Zelin nodded.

"Took note, specially, sir. I feared the lad was in a bad way—there bein' no way he could have escaped those wolves—and reckoned as how since he sent me to you, and how it was you who sent him in there, as 't were, that you might be wanting to send a rescue party, and maybe avoid the front door, so to speak. I was on my way downcountry when I found m'self hip-deep in Rhomatumin men, an' tried to persuade 'em it was damn urgent they send for you."

"You thought correctly."

"Luck of Rakshi you were already halfway here."

"Luck had nothing to do with it. I hope to your own Rakshi we aren't still too late."

The horses were ready. He set himself at the head of the column, rode beside Ganfrion a space, but the holes in the account nagged him.

"He was with Thyerri. Both of them were going through that place together."

"That's the way it sounded."

"We haven't heard all he knows." He reined back to Zelin's side, and Ganfrion dropped back with him.

"You were with him last," Deymorin said. "Was there

anything . . . anything at all he said, during all the time you were together, that you didn't report?"

"Nonsense to me, sir. Said . . ." Zelin's brow furrowed, and his mouth pressed together.

"Yes?"

"Sorry, sir. Don't want to get this wrong, and it comes to me this was what I was most to say. He said . . . tell you that Rhyys wasn't Rhyys."

"Heard that part."

"And when I asked him who he was if he wasn't Rhyys, he said Rhyys was Scarface. Then I'm to tell you remember Mother and not to trust your eyes or ears. That Rhyys died, not romMaurii." Zelin pulled the reins between his fingers, avoiding Deymorin's eyes for a moment, then looked up, apologetically. "Lad was scared, sir. Maybe not thinking straight. Don't know what he meant. But that was before they chased us down the tunnel, and it fell clean out of my head. It was gettin' 'im out I was thinkin' of, and what he said—I damn all forgot."

"It's all right, man. I think I do understand it."

Reinforcement of the message Thyerri had sent Mikhyel, with one notable difference, this business about Mother.

Rhyys who was not Rhyys . . .

Rhyys died, not romMaurii.

Remember Mother. Don't trust your eyes.

Mother, who appeared to them in many guises, as the shapechanging Tamshi of the old tales were said to assume the shapes of loved ones who had died. Ghosts visiting the living. Ghosts and not-ghosts.

He'd seen it more than once, and not always involving the dead, not always with the green glow about the eyes that had distinguished Mother's appearances. That was an embellishment she seemed to use and not use.

Or perhaps, recalling details of childhood stories long since forgotten, not an embellishment, but a sign . . . an indication of active magic . . . of drawing on the Ley. Tamshi eyes.

And romMaurii. Vandoshin romMaurii, who should have died at Boreton. Should have died again in the fall of the

Tower. And Thyerri, to all watchers, died on the rings. Was it Vandoshin, or Rhyys, or something completely else?

"Rhyys died, not romMaurii: those were his exact words?" he asked the man Zelin.

"Aye, sir."

"And you left Thyerri . . . when?"

"Four days ago, sir."

Before Mikhyel's mental contact with Thyerri, then.

Remember Mother . . .

Rhyys died, *not* romMaurii. Not good. Even before Rhyys had exhaled what talent he had in ocarshi smoke, he was never up to ringspinning on Anheliaa's scale, but then, who in the history of the world had been? And yet Anheliaa had chosen him to warm a chair in Khoratum Tower. Harmless, had been Anheliaa's assessment of Rhyys.

Anheliaa's pawn, as Lidye was Anheliaa's pawn. It was enough, in hindsight, to seriously question Anheliaa's motives in choosing spinners.

His own assessment of Vandoshin romMaurii, who had come down out of Mauritum, Garetti's agent, and the head of the plot to peel the northern crescent out of the Rhomatum Web . . . was far, far different. Lightning had had two tries at the Maurii priest. Surely the second time . . .

. . . or not.

"You've seen Rhyys? Personally? Since the fall of the Tower?"

"Aye, sir."

"And you'd seen him before? No mistaking whom you saw."

"Aye, sir. Saw 'im clear as I'm talkin' to you, sir. And it was the same man, I swear it."

"Have you ever seen Vandoshin romMaurii?"

"Not so's I'd know."

"Thank you, Zelin. Well done. Well reported." He sent his horse up to the head of the column, and Ganfrion closed up behind him, then swung alongside.

"Not good," he said to Ganfrion.

"Didn't sound to be. Rhyys and not-Rhyys? RomMaurii and not?"

Shapechanger? Or something else? He thought about Nikki's appropriation of Mikhyel's body when they went riding and thought, perhaps, that was more plausible than the other, at least for human practitioners. Mother, according to Mikhyel, had no real body. According to Mikhyel, Mother was animated leythium, capable of changing shape at will.

And if he assumed Vandoshin was a shapeshifting Tamshi, that violated the other of their cherished speculations: that Mother could not manifest beyond the confines of her own source node.

Certainly Mother and Rhomatum, both ley-creatures, had had to meet on the neutral territory between their nodes.

As for physical form, Kiyrstin had known Vandoshin romMaurii for years. She'd come across the Kharatas Mountains with him and into the south in his company, so if romMaurii were a Mauritumin Tamshi, *other* rules would have to apply to him. He'd have to observe ley-creature boundaries, stay out of other creatures' territory.

Or was there a point it wasn't the same romMaurii? Rings, the possibilities were enough to drive a man insane.

Had the man died, or fallen by the wayside during the journey east, and was there a Tamshi from this region involved, with Kiyrstin none the wiser?

Without that stretch, it seemed to involve a manifestation of one ley-creature inside another creature's domain, which didn't seem to happen, at least on the slim evidence they had . . . and with it, it meant this romMaurii-Tamshi, if it existed, was Mother.

That made no damned sense at all, unless Mother was playing a complicated game, amusing herself on this side and on that . . . and with greater hostility than he'd felt hostility from Mother.

Though what he had seen confronting Mikhyel in that eye-blink image of sight/sound/smell/mindspeech raised the hair on the back of his neck.

Did Thyerri mean, instead, that they should remember how Mother had changed?

Was he trying to warn them, in so many words: Remember the taint in the Ley?

Or, if romMaurii was dead, had he just infiltrated Rhyys' mind so often he'd left some residual pattern that was driving Rhyys now to total madness? They had wondered how Rhyys had ever raised the damaged rings. Was it Rhyys who had done it, after all, or a dead Mauritumin priest, lingering on in Rhyys' ocarshi-hazed brain?

And was budding to account for the frightening change in Mother, or was it the sadistic madness of a Khoratum ringmaster gone right over the mental brink? Mikhyel had proposed to Mirym that the Tamshi reflected the strongest Talent. Rhyys had a personal grudge with Mikhyel; no less, romMaurii.

And putting the whole into a single stew pot, considering what Mikhyel had discussed with Mirym regarding the nature of the Ley and Mother herself . . . what if that which held Khoratum now was a Tamshi born of the infestation of the node by the influx of minds, all bent on the destruction of the Rhomandi, all concentrating their wills to that end at the very moment the Rings went down?

Gods, still so much they didn't know, still so easy to be caught watching the wrong hand . . . and Mikhyel, one way or the other, was in the midst of that madness.

"—gorMikhyel, get Zelin up here with you. Follow his directions and get us to that tunnel."

Ganfrion eyed him suspiciously. "Going to try to nap in the saddle a bit, Rhomandi?"

Yes, he was going to try to contact his brother, and no, he didn't need a watchdog. But he couldn't say that. He could only nod casually and ignore the silent question. He reined his horse back into the middle of the line, hoped he could trust the borrowed mount to do what horses generally did in the middle of a line and follow the leaders—and hoped Mikhyel's watchdog minded his own damned business and didn't make things worse than they were.

His horse found the pace and settled into stride, and he closed his eyes, blocking out as much stimulus as he could.

Mikhyel was just out of reach, as he had been ever since he'd disappeared, a mental shadow without substance. He could feel Mirym, and beyond her, Nikki, but without Mikhyel, his and Nikki's distance communication was marginal at best, and his deeper link with Mirym, without Mikhyel, was nonexistent. He tried to inform them both of this newest and troubling half-information, but he feared the message was more confusing than helpful, the sort of thing that was more apt to manifest as a vague sense of trouble than useful specifics. Not that those specifics could matter; there was nothing in the world either Nikki or Mirym could do about what was happening to Mikhyel and his dancer.

He couldn't touch Nikki's mind, yet when he reached through his brother, he could feel the Rhomatum Rings as well as if he were in the Tower himself. Nikki was spending his days in the Tower, guarding the Rings, prepared to be his bridge should he need it. He could feel the raw power. He knew it, recognized its pattern.

Seized it.

The next instant, the link with Nikki snapped tight.

The instant after that, he reached for what he truly, desperately wanted: Mikhyel's pattern. He felt resistance, and struck again, piercing the fog that surrounded his brother.

ᛋ   ᛋ   ᛋ

Crack!

Mother flinched.

{Feel him, Mother?} Mikhyel cried, desperately ignoring his brothers' sudden, distracting presence, and refusing to let that simultaneous—and painful—breakthrough detract from what was happening to Dancer. {Did you feel that?}

{Yes-ss-ss. Exquisite, don't you think?} She was the predator once more, and he found himself very thankful for the pool of blood-red leythium flaring between them.

{Exquisite?} he railed at her. {How can you say that?

How can you even think it? This is Dancer, Mother. Your
special child. This monster is destroying—}

{This is no one. Nothing to me. Gone/Deserted/Alone.
Mother's children left her. Why should Mother care at all,
who famishes for want of a chicken?}

{Dancer didn't desert you, Mother.} He courted disaster,
forcing himself up on legs that shook so that he could
barely walk. But that weakness was illusion: his own legs
were as sound as ever and he forced them to carry him
around the edge of that pool, while he kept his hands to
the wall, on lace curtains, on stalagmites, on whatever
slight, slick surface gave his fingers purchase, while Mother
slithered along the rim with a serpent's grace.

Avoiding him. Avoiding the Truth he brought her.

{Dancer loves you,} he insisted to her. {He respected your
wishes. In everything. *You* sent him to me that night—}

{Lies! You stole Dancer from me. Dancer *had* the rings.
Dancer was *one* with Mother and Dancer left—ran away from
Mother, to go mate with the offspring of the progenitor's
creature, and left Mother in the arms of another *creature*.}

Crack!

Mikhyel cried out, caught his balance against a slender
leythium pillar.

{I don't know what you're talking about! Lies? Ran away?
Creatures? You thrust him away from you, and declared your
independence from the ringmaster, from the Tower, from
Rhomatum himself! And *still* Dancer loved you. He could
have lived in Rhomatum, in comfort and safety. *Still* he returned to Khoratum to try and reach you, for all you wouldn't
speak with him, and now whatever rules in the Tower is killing him! How can you let this go on?}

{Creatures.} It was a mental mutter. {Mother *hates* creatures. And now Mother has one sitting on her because
Child-of-Darius *stole* Child-of-Mother. Mother would have
shared, but Child-of-Darius was greedy.}

{I didn't steal him!}

{Wanted/needed/demanded/contaminated.}

{He was leyapulted practically into my arms. *I* can't do
that! Who *did?*}

Mother's stance shifted again. Her scent shifted with it. Her expression became one of warm exasperation.

{Can't! Again I hear *can't*. Of course you *can*. It's *always* the child's doing, but they never understand. Surely you can grasp it. You're such a clever child.}

He gripped the pillar tighter. {What do you mean *always the child's doing*?}

Dancer had leyapulted on his own, or so he'd claimed. But without Mother's help, there had been a protective oil that prevented that devastating burning . . .

{Unnecessary. Silly crutch. The child *wanted* Mother to be necessary. Wanted to claim Mother's attention for *silly* things. Silly, silly child . . .}

Crack!

Mikhyel's knees gave, and he slipped to the smooth ley-thium floor of the cavern, arms still around the pillar, on the pool's edge; Mother's eyes closed, her mouth tightened into a fang-baring grin.

Exquisite. Exquisite, she said of that terrible sensation.

And she was what her children made her. What the "creature" sitting on her was making of her.

{Khyel?} Deymorin's voice, solid and sane. {Talk to me, brother.}

Exquisite . . .

He shuddered, horrified at anyone or anything that could actually enjoy what was happening directly above them, horrified at whatever had become of Mother. He'd thought life with Mheric had hardened him to the atrocities of the predators within his own species.

He was wrong.

{Khyel,} his brother's voice said, demanding attention. {Khyel! we've had a message from Thyerri.}

§   §   §

Deymorin swayed, nearly taking the saddle with him, and was glad enough for the watchdog's hand that caught and steadied him.

"You reached him?" The watchdog's rough voice murmured, and Deymorin nodded, then felt compelled to add:

"Nothing you haven't been doing, Captain, but I'm making it official. You know what's going on with my brothers and me. The others don't. If I begin to drift; take over."

A nod. Simple as that. No further explanation required. Ganfrion had come back in the line after him, kept him from falling down the mountain.

"Where is he?" Ganfrion asked. And with a snarling lift of his scarred lip: "Half-mile underground?"

"Actually, possibly farther than that. But down, that's certain. He's with Mother."

"She going to pop him into the Tower?"

"She's changed. It appears that whoever has Thyerri is warping *her* beyond all— "
Crack!

He swayed again, then pulled himself up, and steadied his stomach. He'd gotten his message through, but how much of the theoretical part Mikhyel had been able to absorb past the horror of his reality, he wasn't certain. The edge . . . If only Kiyrstin had known how close Mikhyel was. And now this. Madness surrounded him, madness induced by the creature Mother hated. He hadn't realized . . . hadn't remotely known the danger Mikhyel was in. And he couldn't maintain the link. He tried to put his discovery into reasoning words for Ganfrion:

"What that animal . . . Rhyys . . . romMaurii . . . whoever . . . is doing to that young man—we must get up there. Whether Mikhyel talks Mother into sending him . . . we can't let him go into the Tower alone, and he's not in any mood to wait. He *can't* wait. Mother's not what she was."

"Doing the best we can."

"The hell we are." Deymorin dug his heels into his horse's sides, and the willing animal sprang forward, taking the small company with them. He'd tried to save the horses. He didn't count that a priority now. He'd tried to maintain contact with Mikhyel: also no longer a priority.

He'd tried to warn Mikhyel. He wasn't sure, in the distraction Mother posed, whether Mikhyel had heard him, even with the Rhomatum Rings augmenting his voice. He was in Mother's territory where Rhomatum had no power. In the madness Mikhyel suspected, the Khoratum Rings whole and intact above her head might not have restrained her from striking out. But they weren't intact. They were damaged. Mother claimed her territory, and an erratic rule above her hadn't improved her moods or her stability.

The Ley, for whatever reason, wouldn't let him through. He had no wish to press with Rhomatum's power and provoke another pyrotechnic confrontation of Mother with Rhomatum, either, not with his brother in Mother's grip.

He had to go the hard way.

§   §   §

"Is he coming, dancer?" Scarface's velvet tones reached new heights from Mheltiri's throat, but they still roused memories of a dark and chilling power emanating from a cloaked and hooded figure.

Thyerri's breath caught on a sob. He was frightened as he'd never been before. He didn't dare retreat to his inner haven, couldn't risk even the comfort of sleep, for all the sunlight through the ceiling had come and gone and come again since this torment began.

Best for everyone if he could somehow die, but even that was not an option. His body was too strong, his heart's desire to live and his spirit's urge to hope more potent than his mind's assessment of probabilities. And in that strength, in that desire, lay his ultimate fate. He'd fall asleep, fall unconscious, shift . . . relax . . . and be crippled for life. A living death, from which Mother would not, this time, save him.

And still, Mikhyel would come. Mikhyel would compromise with Mheltiri for his dancer's freedom, because therein lay his duty, even though the Dancer he loved was nothing without legs and without Mikhyel.

Mikhyel would come, and the amalgam within Mheltiri

would consume that which was Mikhyel dunMheric. The darkness that Mikhyel feared in himself would be as nothing to the darkness that would manifest in him once it found this willing partner, this scarfaced partner who avoided the sweet and gentle Mheltiri's soul and sought a soul instead who could appreciate the advantages of such an unholy alliance, someone who would understand the anger and the violence.

For Mikhyel, that descent into his own darkness would be another kind of living death. Strong as Mikhyel's desire to avoid that descent might be, he could not possibly offset so deep a darkness as that which Scarface brought with him. It was a fate worse, far worse, than any other he could have given Mikhyel.

And Thyerri saw no way to prevent it. Mikhyel was coming. Mikhyel would come.

Mheltirin's velvet-fingered touch stroked lightly down his left leg, inside and out, sending a near-unbearable tingling between the two hands.

"Ah, there's the spot."

Crack!

The touch withdrew, the tingling ended, and the dull throb resumed. So very little real damage done thus far: just a weakening of bone. He sent his own energy to the spot, trying to repair, knowing even as he tried to keep pace with the damage that it would be too little.

Healing had never been a large part of his world. Mending ley-burn, a simple break in a single bone . . . that he'd learned to do before he could remember. But bending the Ley to a specific task required practice. Like a muscle underused, the strength to counteract Mheltirin's actions simply wasn't there.

Besides, the Ley here answered to Scarface. Some small part of it still resonated to his call, a small part that seemed to be growing, but perhaps that was only his imagination. Even so, it was only a small part, a very small trickle of a powerful river, far different from the collapse of the flow when the line between Khoratum and Rhomatum had been damaged. The Ley flow then had been weakened and intermittent, but unchanged and pure. The stream that flowed steadily through his gut and fountained from his chest was tainted with Scarface's perverted essence.

"Get your lover here, dancer, and I'll repair the damage. Won't that please him? Isn't that what you want?"

Lies. Scarface would take Mikhyel's body, and Mikhyel's body hadn't Mheltiri's healing Talent, and Thyerri would be left crippled, inside and out; Dancer would, in every sense, be dead.

"Not at all," Scarface said through Mheltiri's lips. "I'll repair the damage before the joining. He simply has to promise not to leave." The velvet stroke resumed, but without the probing tingle. "He's an honorable man. If he gives his word for your release, he'll stick by it, the more fool he. He'll learn better once he's joined us. But you're no good to me crippled, dancer. The possibilities of the love you two *almost* share is most intriguing, intellectually and sensually quite appealing."

As if what this creature would make of his Khy would have anything in common with the Khy he loved. The patterns of what had been pure changed in the foulness this creature exuded; the creature admitted as much.

"Not that much." The hand slipped up to his chest and rested there, as Mheltiri's slight body slithered closer to him, there beneath those corrupted rings. "Call him, dancer. Call him to us."

Never.

"Too bad."

Pain stabbed through his chest, sudden and startling. He screamed, jerked, and bones shifted.

Chapter Three

For a moment, he was thirteen and huddled, battered and broken, in the nursery closet at Darhaven. Mikhyel pressed against the pillar, eyes closed, and held in the screams that ripped him apart inside, even as he fought to break free of the past, of all the painful memories and past needs into which Dancer's current torment had thrust him.

"Why didn't you call me, Khyel?" It was Deymorin's voice, and Deymorin knelt beside him, there in the Khoratum World Cave, and laid a hand, large and strong on his shoulder. "You should have called me, told me everything that was going on. You should have let me help. . . ."

But it wasn't Deymorin. It was Mother . . . gentle and understanding, and in Deymorin's form . . . because that was what he needed.

Mirym had said, *what is a god but belief given form*? Whoever, whatever lay behind Thyerri's torture, the *creature* Dancer's Mother so vehemently condemned, drew on the Ley to do it; Dancer, Mirym, all those who joined their cause now and in the past, *they* were the essence of the Mother he acknowledged.

But they were not all of Mother, nor was this predatory side of her altogether new.

Her followers had always had that in them, the fight, the will to survive, the single-minded determination to hold their ground in the face of opposition.

But it was stronger, more coldly vicious than before, and yes, far more predatory.

That was the war within her, the war that made her first one thing, then another . . . a war being waged at a distance, the Dancers and Miryms on the one side—and on the other, the perverted force within Khoratum Tower supplemented by the Khoratum Rings.

But *he* was part of that equation as well, and he was here in person. He had the advantage of seeing the result of that warfare firsthand.

And for that reason he had both the risk and the chance to directly influence her, if he could only find the means to move that pendulum-stroke of gentle healing and blood-seeking destruction to his own purpose.

He twisted away from the pillar and committed himself on the pool's hazardous edge, gripped the illusion of Deymorin's broad shoulders, discovering it a very solid illusion.

{Mother, *listen* to me. You *gave* him the dance, you gave your people—your *children*—Rakshi incarnate, and now . . . and now Rakshi's legs are gone! Destroyed by that black essence that taints your world. We can't leave him alone, can't let this continue. *Help me!* Help Rakshi dance again, or where is Chance and Whimsy to have a place in the world?}

Deymorin pulled away, his form shifting, turning fluid and reforming into the reptilian goddess.

{Mother helps no one who will not help himself.}

{Not help! Mother, for the sake of your children, *feel* his draw. He's trying to fight and losing the battle. He needs help. He needs *us.*}

{So—help. Go away!}

"I can't go away. Not without your help."

{Nonsense. Go away!}

Another *crack!* as if his own leg twisted and warped. He grabbed at her, used her to pull himself to his feet, held himself upright with a grip on her shoulders.

"Dammit, help me get to him!"

Her eyes flamed, and with a sweep of her arm, she flung him across the pool. He slid into the solid wall and her entire body flared now with the prismatic leythium flames. "I told you! Never make Mother angry!"

Mikhyel staggered to his feet, spread them wide against waves of vertigo, and shouted back at her. "You say I

should help myself! You say I can go to him if I help myself! *How?*"

As if his defiance were water to her flames, she was back
to her old form, reptilian, graceful, with a hint of very non-
reptilian, human female curves.

{I've raised a pack of idiots. *You* should have called your
brother. *Dancer* should call you. You cannot go where you
are not welcome. Going and coming, the Ley must receive
as well as reject. I've done with you!}

And with that damnation still ringing in his mind . . . she
was gone.

He caught himself against the stone, staring at where she
had been.

Trapped.

Or was he?

The Ley must receive as well as reject . . .

Leyapult, Nikki had called it. Leythiate was Dancer's
term. Not an easy equation; perhaps not even the same
equation. Anheliaa had thrown people from her tower, had
used her power like a slingshot, throwing human bodies and
souls into a void to fall to earth . . . seemingly at random.

Or did they?

While there were many factors not known—yet—and
while Mother was inclined to speak in absolutes where
there were an infinity of nuances, the Barrister, never comfortable with notions of *chance,* less so with *coincidence,*
seized on the notion that none of the events of the past
year had been either of those.

Anheliaa had thrown Deymorin from the Tower in the
fall; he'd fallen into Kiyrstin's suspicious but ultimately welcoming arms in a Persitumin sheep-pond. *They* had never
met, but perhaps the Ley had known: soul match, some
would call what they had found. Had the Ley, in fact,
sensed "receiver" in Kiyrstin?

And Kiyrstin had carried as a matter of course a burn
ointment that had been *proven* against the flesh-consuming
ley-burns. An ointment that was something of a require-
ment among the band of ne'er-do-wells with whom she had

been traveling, a few of whom, according to Deymorin, had been Anheliaa's previous victims.

Had Anheliaa tossed Rhomatum's rejects toward her personal nemesis, Garetti, only for them to find a place amongst similarly-minded Mauritumin rejects?

Receive and reject. Easy to try and force a pattern. Easy to *want* an answer that much.

But he himself had flown from Rhomatum Tower to the Boreton road *because Nikki had needed him.* Nikki had *called* him. Nikki had called and because he had wanted beyond life to save Nikki, in the blink of an eye and a crack of thunder he had wound up in Nikki's lap, not damn much use to anyone, but precisely where he wanted to be.

A bit singed, yes, but there had been anger in the air that day, Anheliaa's, his own, Vandoshin romMaurii's. There'd been a battle waging between the Ley and the encapsulator, and a second battle for his location: *Anheliaa* had tried to force him to stay in the Tower. *His* need had proven greater.

As there had been a battle between Deymorin and Anheliaa the day she leyapulted him to Kiyrstin.

When he had moved unharmed between the surface world and the leythium caverns, it had been as a willing participant in the process . . . albeit the need was sometimes subconscious on his part.

When Mother had sent him into Khoratum, it had been to Thyerri's alley. Thyerri, who by his own admission had already discovered a deep desire for Mikhyel dunMheric. Mikhyel had wanted to be in Khoratum. Thyerri, in Khoratum, had wanted Mikhyel. Two needs, two patterns, come together.

Patterns. Did it all come down to patterns? Patterns of conscious choice intersecting with those essential patterns, the patterns of *Self,* of which he'd become so conscious in the past months.

Deymorin had declared, just before his ejection from Rhomatum Tower that *he'd rather a shepherdess* than a woman of Anheliaa's choosing, and he'd landed in the direction of Mauritum: Anheliaa's choice, in a shepherd's pond: Deymorin's, and virtually in Kiyrstin's lap. Kiyrstin, who desperately to meet with the Princeps of Rhomatum, for her sake and for Alizants. Deymorin's pattern and Kiyrstin's obviously resonated from the moment they met: wishes and patterns. At that time, Deymorin and Kiyrstin's patterns were . . . sympathetic, perhaps. Enough to attract, but not for a . . . safe arrival.

His and Dancer's had been a pattern already begun.

Not an easy equation. Not a simple question of rejection and acceptance, but one involving the wishes of those being moved about, as well as the needs of the essences and patterns involved.

Perhaps there were other means of transport through the Ley. Perhaps only *safe* transportation depended on a receiving party.

Perhaps it all meant nothing.

Easy to create a rationale, given a premise; easy to *create* a mental pattern to match observed events, given the ultimate intertwining of lives that had occurred. How that rationale translated to real cause and effect, he couldn't imagine—yet—and couldn't afford to care—yet.

He had to act now. Assuming that that rationale *did* have substance, that rationale might just provide the means of his escape from this place and Dancer's salvation. *If* he could get to Khoratum Tower, he and Dancer *might* be able to escape the same way.

Belief was the key . . . belief was always the key to the Ley. The key . . . and the controlling force.

If Mother was, as he *believed* her to be, a reflection of the wants and needs of the Talented within her umbrella of effect, Mother . . . the node itself, would reject or accept as the Talented in question required.

Even if it were not that simple, Mother had surely rejected him a moment ago, the one condition—while Dancer . . . surely . . . would receive him: the other. And for the rest, nothing could deny the affinity of pattern, nothing could be more potent than his desire to *be* with Dancer at that moment.

{Dancer!} he called, and made that demand to the totality, the essence that was more than Thyerri alone, determined not to be denied: {Dancer, answer me. Don't be afraid. Let me come to you.}

Denial. Sense of danger. Thyerri alone: a purposely incomplete pattern: Dancer's defense against Mikhyel. Dancer was *using* that self-imposed bifurcation to keep Mikhyel at a distance.

{I have no other way out, Dancer!}

{Call to your brother!} There one instant, darting off in the next: an equally determined refusal, filled with fear for Mikhyel.

{*Dancer!*} He made the name a demand for the pattern.

A fluttering, near involuntary acknowledgment; an equally determined refusal.

A silent scream.

Acceptance, fleeting and nearly imperceptible. Desire for Mikhyel's touch, for Mikhyel's support, for Mikhyel's love overwhelmed all else.

Taking ruthless advantage of that instant of weakness, Mikhyel reached for Dancer's essence, and wove their patterns together, *willing* himself gone from Mother's caverns and at Thyerri's side.

Quick as the crack of a whip, he was falling . . . falling . . . aware of time passing, of fear, as Deymorin's six months' suspension loomed in his mind.

He had wished instantaneous speed, and nothing of the like happened.

Chapter Four

They kept the horses going. Two pulled up lame and their riders dropped behind, unwillingly; but there was no time for argument, and none was made. They had done the best they could, had cut hours off even Raulind's downhill ley-road time, but in the end, they'd fallen victim to a miscalculation. A wrong branch trail taken on the edge of darkness, and by the time the mistake had been realized—at the head of a steep and dangerous descent—it was spend two hours backtracking to the easier, but longer way into the mountain valley, or stop and spend that same time sleeping and dare the descent in the light of day.

So close. So damned close . . .

Six hours and more sleeping on hard, cold ground. Time wasted, to an anxious brother's distracted way of thinking, but the Rhomandi knew they'd be no use to Mikhyel fainting from exhaustion, or falling off a cliff unseen in the darkness of night.

At least, Deymorin hoped, as they made that steep descent in the first light of dawn, the men had slept. He had lain awake, his mind seeking his brother, his body twisting to find a position that didn't offend a leg aching from too long in the saddle and too distant from both Kiyrstin's and the Rings' soothing effects.

The occasional glimpse of Khoratum the short descent provided proved as eerie as all the reports had claimed: living ruins, with a clear demarcation between Lower and Upper, a ridge of piled stone, not a proper wall, but accumulated rubble from the clearing of Lower Khoratum. A clearing created and inhabited by an influx of hillers, so reports claimed, hillers tacitly declaring their independence from the weakened and apparently disinterested Tower glowing fitfully above them.

And not so tacitly, according to Zelin, who gave details, in their dark and cold camp, of his meeting with Thyerri. Hillers moving in, attempting the Tower: rebellion was in the air and in the Ley.

It was all part of the turbulence he'd felt when he'd touched Mikhyel.

Lake Khoratum stretched pure and serene, to the southwest of the ruins, the scars of last spring's occupying forces reduced to the occasional fire-trace. The forests ruled here, the first signs of growth already showing along the edges of Lower Khoratum. To do its will, the force in charge here had focused the energy of the Rings into a very small umbrella indeed.

The trail eased as they entered those trees, and the Tower, at eye-level when they began that descent, now loomed above them as they forged ahead, only to have a trail of blood necessitate yet another delay as they paused to check the horses for injury resulting from that steep and rocky trail.

There was only one, a clean slice deep into the frog of one hoof, bleeding profusely: yet one more lost from their party, Deymorin thought in an agony of concern that extended to these men who trusted him, bodyguards who were willing to die for him because he claimed this mission worth dying for. Men who, in a starting force of fifteen and from the situation Zelin had described might have stood a good chance against those underground guards. With each man lost, the odds grew more grim.

"Not far now, m'lord," Zelin said, coming up beside him. And as if he realized the dilemma in Deymorin's mind: "And a stream right near where he can stand th' horse. Maybe stop the bleeding. But can't take th' horses in th' tunnel anyway."

Deymorin forced a smile. "What it needs, certainly, Zelin." And to the man, who had heard all Zelin said: "Follow, but don't push him."

The soldier nodded, and relief showed on his face, not to have been left out of the action. Deymorin turned from that look and urged his borrowed mount into action, leaving that devotion to duty behind.

Gods, he was playing with lives. For the sake of two, he was risking ten. Where was the equity in that? Where the morality? The army made sense, preparation against invasion. Protection of homes. This action had nothing to do with anything so obviously valid.

Ten for two. But the two in question . . . Would he commit these men if the two in question were not his brother and his brother's lover?

"Turn off here, sir," Zelin said, into the steady rattle-thud of shod hooves on soil-covered stone. And the hiller pointed upslope, a route, not a trail.

Deymorin eyed it dubiously. "You're certain a horse can make it?"

"Not far, sir, but yes."

Ganfrion said, "Wait here," and set his horse at the slope, several hard thrusts, the last of which sent dirt down on their heads. A few moments later: "A flat up here. Grass. Room for all the horses. Sound familiar, Zelin?"

"That's it, sir," Zelin said to him.

Deymorin eyed that slope. Ten for two. Ten for two, who between them might hold the keys to all their future understanding of the Ley. In love, yes. Foolish . . . what lovers weren't at times? Actions leading to their current dilemma unfounded? Not in the least.

Deymorin waved his hand. "Up we go, lads."

⑨   ⑨   ⑨

But half an hour later, with the horses grazing quietly on that small flat, he stared into the dark pit that had swallowed Zelin and began to revise the decision to follow Zelin's path. To hell with shortcuts. Get back to the leyroad and meet the rest of the men coming up from New Khoratum.

"This is the one." Zelin's voice preceded the hiller out of the hole. A hand was next, and Deymorin grabbed it, helping the man worm his way back to the surface.

"You're certain," he said, eyeing the hole, hoping for error. He'd have to strip and grease himself to squeeze through that opening, with a good possibility he still wouldn't make it.

To his distress, Zelin nodded emphatically. "Aye, sir."

"Damn. How far is it like this? How far till it widens?"

"Make it though that, sir, and maybe three, four lengths of crawl, then it's standing room the rest of the way."

His still-chancy leg, the old injury, throbbed just looking at the damn hole: the eye of the needle, for sure. "Well, there's nothing for it." He shrugged his coat off. "We'll have to send weapons through separately and—*Yes*, gorMikhyel?"

Ganfrion, who had momentarily been headfirst into the hole, then noisily scraping at the edges, had lifted his hand like a child in grammar school. "If it's all the same to you, Rhomandi, I'd as soon knock this rock out and save the skin on my shoulders."

"Why don't we just blow the whole opening, while we're at it? Because we've been traveling the Ley, man! We don't have any explosives with us and that's solid—"

Ganfrion stood upright and shook his head vigorously, sending dirt flying. "Been a slide sometime—not too long ago. This one's ready to move." He kicked at its base. "Scrape a bit there, lever it here—"

"And bring the mountain down on the whole damn opening! Then where will we be?"

"I don't think it will. And it's that, or the smaller men go on into the snake's nest without us, and you and I, and half these men, head for the front door to knock and ask politely. We aren't fitting through, Rhomandi. No way in hell. You try it, we'd better attach a rope, because you'll stick like a cork in a bottle, and so will I."

He bent. He looked, wiggled a dust-mortared rock, and considered what the old injury tended to do with him when he set himself in the wrong position.

Divide their forces—or stay behind himself, when he had the nagging, though as yet unconfirmed, fear that Mikhyel was no longer under this mountain, but up in that Tower at last.

They had camp shovels in their packs: required equipment: small and light, but effective. They had axes.

"You're right," he said, reluctant though he was, and knowing he had already compromised the leg, waved a signal to the younger men. "Get digging. Get deadfall to brace as we hollow it out. And for the gods' sakes, don't bring it down."

§   §   §

The first thing Mikhyel noticed as his vision cleared was the skin on the arm that bent beneath his head: smooth and clear, save for the scratch left by a wayward branch on the trail. And beneath the arm, the rough stone and rubble floor of the Khoratum Tower, a sight just as familiar to him, though his only source of information was Thyerri's impressions of his current prison.

They'd done it, he and Dancer. He was in Khoratum Tower.

But *when* had he done it? He'd had the impression of time passing, which he'd not had before.

And where was Thyerri? How long ago was Thyerri?

He let his head drop back onto his arm, more drained than these jumps had ever left him. He'd worked harder than necessary, he could see, now the attempt had been successful, had thrown too much into the wanting and needing on both sides of the jump. Without the need to simultaneously convince his receiver, the transit might even prove effortless.

He was strangely unfocused, now the immediate goal had been achieved. His senses took in that floor, a hum that was, almost certainly, the Khoratum Rings. That other sense told him, on his next widening breath and even without his directly contacting his brother, that Deymorin was practically underneath him, below and radiating concern for him.

Two days, then, his mind drifted through the calculation, two days more or less since he'd shared tea with Mirym. So much time passed, and for him, only moments. But thank the gods it was not more time. Thank the gods he had not burned himself to incapacity.

Two days.

Or so it had seemed. Lying here now, his body felt as if it had indeed been two days awake.

And Thyerri had had to hold out two more days against the master of this Tower.

A door creaked, and a draft wafted into the chamber.

"Well, hello there."

Smooth voice. Soft as velvet. A stranger's voice.

He wondered, lying there in a slowly dissipating mental fog, if that two-day delay was yet another need manifesting, whether Deymorin's presence just below at this precise moment was coincidence or effect. Deymorin would have been waiting all along for just such a coincidence.

And Deymorin had Rhomatum's Rings behind him.

Dancer had been alive when the leythiation had begun. Now . . .

He lifted his head, forced himself up onto an elbow, and then to his shaking knees, visually seeking that which had drawn him here.

Visually, because that inner sense of *Dancer* remained ominously silent.

"Lovely as you are . . ." It was a gentle voice, a voice that somehow fit the slender individual who drifted into view, coming between him and the Rings spinning a dark cloud at the edge of his vision. Hiller. Like Thyerri, but not: that much his mind could manage. "Perhaps you'll be more comfortable . . ." And warmth enshrouded him, easing a chill, masking a nudity of which, in Mother's caverns, he hadn't even been conscious. He fumbled with numb fingers for the edges of the blanket, and pulled it closed, shaking his head to clear the fog from his thinking.

Two days. What had happened?

His eyes stung from the passage, his cheeks burned with tears. The unknown hiller knelt before him and brushed his hair back, then cupped his face in both hands, and with smooth thumbs wiped away those cleansing tears.

Smooth. Uncallused. A gentlewoman's hands. Hands given to stitching and other nondestructive tasks.

Still, he doubted, seeing that slight masculine cast to the jaw, that gentlewoman quite described the individual beside him.

"Who are you?" Mikhyel asked, past the spinning in his head, that question seeming somehow more useful than *Where am I*? and far less volatile than an immediate, collected: *What have you done with Thyerri*?

Details came to his clearing vision, details that cast doubt on his location. Logically it had to be Khoratum Tower. This rough floor was ingrained in the impressions he'd received from Thyerri, as was the dark cloud of spinning rings. But the stark, white-plastered wall he discovered supporting his shoulder had no place in his single memory of the Khoratum ringchamber, as the huge nest of brightly colored pillows just to his left had none.

The Rings spinning just beyond the hiller were black, dull and lifeless, unlike the shining ley-touched silver of all the Rings he knew. He'd thought that image from last summer's attack had somehow only been indicative of the tainted nature of the Rings, and not of their leythium-coated substance. That blackened surface implied a compromise to their very structure, which meant to the leythium component, which in turn roused memories of the catastrophic demise of Rhomatum's Khoratum/Persitum ring.

He had to wonder how they'd ever been raised without shattering.

But they were undeniably up and aligned and their hum filled the room, his ears and his head, adding to his wit-wandering confusion. Until he conquered his own mind, he could be no help whatsoever to Thyerri—wherever Thyerri was.

He couldn't feel him. Where Dancer's essence should have been, there was only humming.

{Oh, Khy, how can you be so cruel?} Brush of thought that accompanied a brush of lips to his cheek. {Don't you know me?}

Raspberries, cinnamon, and clove.

He slammed the wall down between them, and pulled away sharply enough to topple his delicate balance. He caught at the wall, hooked a hand in a simple window sill above his head, and pulled himself to his wavering feet.

Hands caught and held him, carrying that scent to him in profusion, a scent that bore a hint of recognition with it.

His mind roiled with thoughts of Nikki and merging minds. But it wasn't Dancer beside him, touching him. It couldn't be Dancer looking at him through this stranger's eyes. Dancer would never allow—

"But I did, Khy. I had to."

"No!" It wasn't even one of Mother's shapechanging masquerades: this person looked nothing at all like Dancer, *felt* nothing like Dancer. His body knew the touch of that body. His mind would have known the moment Dancer touched him.

"My body died, Khy, along with that pattern. I had to take refuge in this one. I had to be here to meet you. My legs were gone."

He shook his head.

"But it's true, Khy. This is Mheltiri. Another Child of Rakshi. He helped me, for hate of what was done to me."

"What *who* did to you?"

"Rhyys. RomMaurii. All of them, but mostly, it was Rhyys."

He blinked. His head buzzing, the words crazed enough to make sense.

"Where are you?"

Smooth hands stroked his cheek, the slender body pressed close at his back, and a whisper in his ear said: "When someone dies, near the Rings, when two patterns are joined, and death comes . . . both can live. One can live in the other. But this body doesn't love me, doesn't want me, detests my presence, begrudges me the dance. Oh, Khy, you take me. Please. Let our spirits be one within your body."

Alarms went off: Dancer never spoke of spirits. And for Dancer, his essence was one with his body, his essence linked to the dance only that body could create. Dancer could not be Dancer without both Dancer's essence and Dancer's body.

"But you said this . . . body accepted you. Is a dancer." Which was a lie. Slender and graceful for certain . . . but it hadn't the moves.

"Not a dancer, Khy, a Child of Rakshi. Mheltiri didn't understand. Mheltiri's mind was willing, his heart was, his pattern was not." The too-smooth hands slid around his shoulders, smoothing the blanket, pulling it tight around him . . . restricting his arms. One hand slid beneath to rest against bare skin. One hand glinting silver and gold: the missing Rhomandi ring. "It is not a happy joining. Ours would be . . . exquisite. Please, Khy, bring me into you. All you have to do is open to me, welcome me . . . love . . . me . . . I'll do all the rest."

One has to reject, the other accept . . .

But rejection here, according to Mheltiri, was death.

And Mheltiri wore a ring that had been stolen from Nikki and had last graced the hand of Vandoshin romMaurii . . .

Whose body was thrown out of the Tower six months ago.

"You said . . . when two patterns are joined and one body dies . . . must death be part of your joining me?"

"Trust me, Khy." And cinnamon-scented breath filled his mouth.

Acceptance . . . nothing in him acknowledged this hiller as Dancer. Were that hand resting against his bare flesh Thyerri's, he'd be overwhelmed with the desire to fling the blanket from him and take the hand's owner into his arms. Were that mouth Dancer's, nothing could stop him from devouring it, so great was his need.

Yet his body remained numb. His mind distant and unmoved.

Dancer would never opt for life in a body not his. And if somehow forced into such a transaction, Dancer would never propose to escape by any means that included death—anyone's death, not even the villain who forced him into partnership. It was, perhaps, Dancer's greatest vulnerability: that he could not conceive of killing another human being.

Beyond all else, Dancer would never suggest he fling his mind wide open in this place.

"No!" He pushed to his feet, away from those hands, forced his own legs to obey him, and knew by their very shaking uncertainty that Dancer was still alive, that the essence he loved had not somehow taken up residence in this stranger's sound body. And foreknowing the answer, called, to Dancer's pattern: {Are you there?}

A touch, quickly stifled. *Not* from the hiller.

"Where is he?" {Speak to my mind. Speak in his voice, with his essence. Then I'll know you are what you say.} He flung the thought at the hiller, at the . . . essence of non-Dancer that had come to him through that kiss, that hint of raspberries, yes, but mixed with herbs.

"Clever." A slow smile stretched the hiller's thin face, and that overwhelming scent of cinnamon disappeared in favor of the herbs. "You mean you don't know? You don't hear him at this moment?" That velvet-soft voice held a hint of mockery. "We've overestimated your gift, Mikhyel dunMheric. More, we overestimated your love. We're disappointed. Quite, quite disappointed."

We? There was no one in the room. Just himself and this pretend-Dancer. He could barely hear himself think, the buzz was so loud here.

And growing louder. At the edge of his vision, the Rings' motion made him so ill he couldn't bear to look at them.

Couldn't . . . look. *Do I hear can't . . .*

Damned if it wasn't Anheliaa all over again. Or Mother: in that sense, they were equally intolerant.

Defying that stomach-churning reluctance, he forced

himself to look squarely toward the Rings. And there beneath their dark, spinning blur, his body hidden beneath a plain brown blanket, eyes closed and, to a headblind eye, relaxed in sleep, was Dancer.

Not asleep, however, to a guarded mental probe, once he knew precisely where to direct it. Dancer was thoroughly awake, though exhausted, and deliberately, determinedly blocking Mikhyel from his mind, keeping a distance Mikhyel feared to bridge by putting himself closer to the Rings. Dancer fought to keep his body still, he knew that from the handful of times their minds had touched. Fought to protect legs now so terrifyingly fragile even the weight of that blanket endangered their integrity.

He longed to touch Dancer's mind, to reassure Dancer that help was coming, that Deymorin was near—but he was foolhardy even to think about that fact, not knowing how much "Mheltiri" was picking up. And he did not after all know for certain how near Deymorin might be: information was constrained to a steady trickle of hazy images, a sense of direction he always had for his brothers. Anything further and here in this enemy Tower, any mental exchange might well be intercepted by the young hiller, who was, it seemed obvious, Thyerri's "Rhyys-but-not-Rhyys." A man far more dangerous than his slight body would indicate.

He fought the buzz, strove to fit this hiller into the information given him by Deymorin's last fleeting message. Not Vandoshin romMaurii, for all the message from Deymorin had suggested as much. Not romMaurii, but perhaps someone romMaurii had trained. A hiller who perhaps had shared minds with Rhyys and been tainted, as Lidye had been tainted with Anheliaa: a sane mind driven mad by another's drug-polluted essence.

He could almost pity the hiller-who-had-been.

Until he looked at that beloved figure lying beneath the Rings.

"Who are you?" he asked, and received an innocuous, pleasant smile.

"Our name's Mheltiri."

Our name: a world of speculation in that one word, and

he had a plummeting fear that perhaps the invitation hadn't been simply to get him to lower his defenses against an assault on his mind. He began to fear that there was indeed an amalgam of souls, of Dancer's "essences" here, in this slim body.

An amalgam wrought by the Rings.

Mother's *creature*.

And it wanted . . . him. Perhaps that assault was meant precisely to claim his body. To make Mikhyel dunMheric, among other things, Thyerri's tormentor.

His stomach churned; he threw a hand out to catch a wall and steady his balance.

Mheltiri's smile broadened; the buzz in Mikhyel's head grew. The buzz, Mikhyel thought to himself, was a childish trick, the least of Anheliaa's means of annoying unwanted guests to the Tower. He was well used to it, as he was used to ringchambers.

He faced the Rings squarely, found their rhythms, and isolated that gods-be-damned hum. Then at a stroke he blocked both dizzying sight and mind-numbing sound out of his conscious awareness.

Mheltiri failed to react. Reserving a modicum of awareness to his enemy, Mikhyel moved closer to the Rings.

He knelt then beside Dancer's still form and without touching Dancer himself—which would prove his own undoing—he lifted the blanket free of Dancers's legs, granting him that small relief from threat.

Beautiful legs. Legs that, to all appearances, could even now test the dance rings.

"Curious," he commented to his enemy, steeling himself to the sight, "I'd expected to find the legs shattered. It felt as if they had, at the last."

"They had." The hiller moved to his side. "We repaired the damage . . . this time. As we will fix the whole . . . if you cooperate."

"Ah, is that it? Threaten him with permanent disability to lure me here, blackmail me with his recuperation. Interesting stratagem you have."

"I take that as a compliment."

"As you wish. A proper invitation through the mails might have been easier on all parties involved, don't you think?"

"Somehow we doubt very much that you would have come."

"Perhaps you underestimate your attraction. Now, you'll never know, will you? It's a curious way you have of speaking of yourself. Is that a Mauritumin royal or literal 'we'? And where's the rest of your—triumvirate? That's the Rhomandi ring you wear, *stolen* from my brother. What else has Vandoshin romMaurii stolen? Is *he* here? Is Rhyys?"

The hiller's answer was a gentle smile.

Mikhyel shrugged, and taking a tuck in his own blanket to draw it clear of the floor, made a slow circuit of the room, dragging his fingers along rough-plastered walls, staring out mismatched, differently-painted windows . . . windowpanes and frames alike no doubt gleaned from buildings that had survived the battle. It was a room of rapid salvage and necessity, not style.

He looked at the ravaged complex and darkened node city, filling his head with the visual images, making those impressions available, should Deymorin seek them from his passive mind.

Mheltiri, Rhyys, or Vandoshin romMaurii, this hiller manipulated the Ley and had reached into the mental web that was growing daily between him and his brothers, extending out to include those whose Talent they touched. How far those tendrils extended into his mind and his link with his brothers remained to be seen. He didn't feel Mheltiri's presence, he didn't think the subliminal activity of his inward thoughts reached outside himself even here in the ringchamber, but he wasn't about to risk drawing attention to Deymorin by actively reaching for his brother for the sake of a few architectural details of the potential battleground.

But if that trickling awareness of stone and ley-lit dark that told him Deymorin was drawing closer did go both ways—please the gods it didn't reach his enemy—and if it reached Deymorin, he was sure his brother might find such information useful.

The chamber itself was little larger than the Rings—about half the size it had been—and but for the fact the complex was built on the highest point geographically, would be shorter than many of the buildings visible outside those windows.

"They say Rhyys raised the Rings in the open air."

Mheltiri didn't answer, but Mikhyel knew the hiller's gray-green eyes never left him in his movements, and he made a point not to openly avoid looking at Dancer, but to let his eyes slip across Thyerri's still form as if it were of no more significance than one of the pillows piled in a corner.

There was no other furniture in the room. Just those pillows and a brazier above which a teapot warmed.

"Rings spinning outside. That must have been interesting. I've never heard of unprotected Rings, other than the dance rings. Are they physically damaged? They certainly look to be."

"They do their job."

"But are we in danger from them?"

"Always. You're dealing with life and death. That's the nature of the Ley."

Interesting way to avoid answering his question. Mikhyel nodded acknowledgment. "As I understand it, you—or rather, Rhyys—raised the Rings, then had the workmen build around them." Throwing his head back to examine the timbered ceiling: "Hard to imagine how they managed that roof."

Poorly, it appeared, from the leak stains about the uneven floor and the joints between the slats up there.

As for entry, there was one: a stairwell that looked narrow and steep, a darkness up from which scents more in keeping with caverns than a tower complex wafted. He took special note of that even as he leaned casually against a plastered corner.

"Where is he, by the way?" he asked.

"He?"

"Rhyys."

The hiller shook his head ever so slightly as if in disbelief.

"I must admit, dunMheric, your reputation's quite well deserved. Cold as ice, aren't you? I thought you more enamored of the dancer."

He turned to face the hiller, who had moved with him, keeping that physical barrier between himself and Thyerri.

"All an act, was it?" the hiller continued. "Make them all believe Mikhyel dunMheric had lost all his common sense and wit over a dancer?"

"Something like that."

"I'm impressed. You certainly had us fooled at the competition."

"Oh, I'm fond enough of the creature," Mikhyel said coolly, "or at least I was. But it's served his purpose now, hasn't he?"

"And what purpose was that?"

"Why, to help me incite the riot, of course. To undermine the rebellion. And afterward, once that troublesome break occurred between Rhomatum and Khoratum, to get me into this Tower, in my own time and under my own terms."

Thyerri's eyes opened at that, his head turned, and the doubt, the pain that filled them nearly proved his undoing. He raised a brow and turned from that look. In his mind, he kept the picture of Thyerri, his brother's spy, in the forefront of his thinking. Thyerri, who might well be sacrificed, an unfortunate but necessary casualty of war.

"And you expect me to believe that these are *your* terms?"

"Believe what you like. I didn't, as you may have noticed, come in through the front door."

"I did, indeed . . . notice." For all Mheltiri tried to hide it, there was lust behind that phrase: Mheltiri wanted to know how he'd done it. Mheltiri wanted that secret . . . badly. "And will you be leaving the same way?"

He shrugged. "Depends, doesn't it?" He leaned calmly against a window. "After Nikki's experience, I've been feeling my way carefully, to say the least. Thyerri proved able to reach Khoratum without notice, proved he could infiltrate the Tower. I required his presence here to make the jump in. Now I'm here. To get out . . ." He shrugged, deliberately leaving that statement incomplete, but able to exude confidence knowing that, should he want to leave, he could, at any time. And it might be true. Nikki would welcome him. Mirym would. Deymorin would.

But who, here, would reject him?

Certainly not Mheltiri. Thyerri would try, but the pull of their pattern was too strong. He could wish himself out . . .

Thyerri's eyes left him, and his face hardened. Though it was painful to hurt him, Mikhyel welcomed Thyerri's uncertainty of him; if even Thyerri had begun to doubt his motives, it would only strengthen his position.

. . . but that, of course, was the ultimate catch to his escape. Nothing short of Thyerri's death would induce him to leave this place without the dancer, and if this hiller stuck by his offer, they were at least at stalemate. But he didn't allow that limitation more than a passing thought, and turned his shoulder on Thyerri's unnerving, accusatory look.

"I must admit," he said to Mheltiri, "I was expecting someone . . . taller . . . more . . . impressive. Who *are* you? I mean, beyond your name. Where did you come from? And what happened to Rhyys, beyond the obvious, the leylightning? Or was it Vandoshin romMaurii who died? I'm really quite puzzled now."

"And here I thought the dancer had told you everything."

"Not at all. He's often poetic but scarcely informative. Rather a failure as a spy, I regret to say. Please. Enlighten me."

"Your letter said your brother would be coming with you. Will he be appearing next? Do we expect him?"

Tempting to claim otherwise, but outright lies were dangerous foundations on which to build an argument under any circumstances. With the added factor of mental touch passing unknown limits, outright lies became impossible. And he trusted Deymorin not to be a fool.

"Eventually," he acknowledged. "For now, it's only you and me."

"*And* the dancer."

"You . . . and me."

"Ah, another feint."

Mikhyel shrugged. "The dancer's good health is your only negotiating piece. I suggest you restore him and prove you can deliver anything you claim. So far you're a grand illusion. Beyond that . . . let's see if there's substance."

"Such a hurry. We've plenty of time. Your brother is still some distance away. Besides, my men will take care of his little party."

Not as he read the pattern of the world around him, but far be it from him to disabuse this individual of his— convenient for them—delusions.

"You were wise not to lie about his coming. I felt him on the leyroad this morning. I feel him now . . . close, as you think him; but not as close as he thinks; it's a maze, that place: he could wander for hours. But please, let's be comfortable." The hiller waved toward the nest of pillows with that hand that glinted gold and silver, and settled himself in the middle with a flourish of his outer robe, a shining movement of hair, dark brown, like Dancer's where the ley-passage hadn't affected it. "You're not going anywhere, are you?"

Mikhyel nodded toward Thyerri's limp form. "You've made quite certain of that, haven't you?" He eased down onto a pillow, propped a second between his back and the wall, and arranged the blanket around him.

"Have I? I did hope so, but you have me wondering now. Does his fate actually matter to you? Certainly he cares for you, but in return . . . I wonder. Another wonder: what is to keep you from simply jumping out the same way you jumped in and taking him with you?"

"And risk those precious legs? I think not—unless, of course, you give me no choice." He cast the hiller a sideways glance. "You have your argument. Let's hear a proposal I like."

A momentary pause as Mheltiri poured tea from the pot waiting above the warming brazier.

Calmly, as if Deymorin were no concern at all. And that last had shaken him more than he cared to admit. *Was* Deymorin lost?

Legs or no legs, a part of him wanted to do exactly as "Mheltiri" suggested, to grab Thyerri and run however he could. A part of him longed to reach to Deymorin and try to jump Deymorin's whole lot into the Tower. But the uncertainties were too many, the risks too great. He'd made it here, but damned if he could trust doing anything more.

Besides, the hints from his brother did not indicate confusion, whatever Mheltiri chose to believe. The hints indicated a rising adrenaline, of imminent confrontation. Best to stay the course, to trust his own sense of his brother's position and status.

Beyond all else, he was here to do more than simply rescue his brother's spy in any condition he could. For all rescuing Thyerri was Mikhyel's idea—with all his heart it was his idea, his responsibility, his desire at any cost—Mikhyel dunMheric was also a Rhomandi, and the *Rhomandi* in him wanted answers to this enigma, this amalgam of living and dead Mheltiri claimed to be.

This . . . had profound implications for what they were dealing with: implications for the triumvirate, for three brothers that had begun to live their lives inside each others' heads, brothers for whom the lines of personality and self had become just the least disturbing bit blurred.

This . . . had profound implications for the behaviors he had ascribed to mental illness in Lidye.

"You say you won't risk the dancer's legs." Mheltiri handed him a steaming cup. "Yet I find myself asking: is that the answer you truly believe, or is it the answer which you think will convince me I have it within my power to move you? What if you don't care about the dancer at all?"

Mikhyel smiled, just enough to keep that one question in the forefront of this hiller's mind.

The hiller laughed, light, musical laughter disturbingly reminiscent of Thyerri's own, and gaily at odds with the horrors this creature had inflicted on Thyerri, and for all he knew, countless others before him.

"He's here, you know," the creature said through the steam rising from the mug he handed Mikhyel.

"He?"

"Rhyys. RomMaurii. A host of others I trust you'll find most interesting. *My* name, as I said, is Mheltiri."

"*Rhyys* is here? *And* romMaurii? Who died, then?"

A slow, slow smile. "You truly don't understand. How disappointing in you. They're here, I say." He tapped his temple, then his chest. "And here."

"Madness." He challenged, goading the creature into time-wasting explanation. "You've been spending too much time with the Rings. Getting too much in each others' heads."

"Hardly madness. And far more than a sharing of minds. We live on, through Mheltiri."

"You're telling me you're—all—body thieves?"

The hiller blinked, his nose wrinkled in distaste. "Such an ugly term. Besides, *I* am hardly a thief. I was born in this shell. My village's healer. It will be my hands, my knowledge, that will restore the dancer."

"You are Mheltiri."

"I am Mheltiri."

"And Rhyys. How? How did you . . ." he sought the words from that initial exchange, "join patterns? By force?" It was not a ringdancer's body, but it was far, far more perfect than Rhyys at his best. He didn't believe he was speaking in any sense to the rightful occupant, taunt the creature as he did. He couldn't believe a healer capable of such acts as this creature had perpetrated on Thyerri, far less enjoying them.

Mheltiri seemed to give his question of force sober consideration as he poured a second mug for himself. "No. Not force. Not thievery. We are . . . a cooperative. Negotiated settlements. I . . . *we* have stolen nothing. Ever."

"That ring you wear is stolen."

"Is it?" Mheltiri raised his hand to look at that ring, and his brow puckered. "From whom?"

"My brother." Mikhyel raised his own hand, the ring all that had come through the dual leythiation with him, as if, somehow, it was part of his essential pattern, at least in his own mind. Essential to his being as clothes, evidently, were not.

"Oh, dear . . ." Mheltiri pulled the ring off his finger—no hard task: it was very loose—and handed it to Mikhyel. "Please, give it back?"

And in that simple, ingenuous act, the hiller rocked Mikhyel's notions about the amalgam that ruled the body.

Mikhyel slipped the finger-warmed metal over his middle finger, and closed his fist to hold it on. A ring sized to a man Deymorin's size, not his and not Mheltiri's. When he looked again at Mheltiri, a variety of emotions seethed on the otherwise deceptively innocent face.

The war raged for only a moment, then Mheltiri's eyes brightened, reminiscent of Temorii's in their eager innocence. "I've returned your ring. Now it's my turn. How did you get in here? How did you escape Khoratum the night of the competition? I assume it *was* the same means."

"I was under the impression you wanted me here, so I came."

"Just like that."

"Just like that."

"You don't intend to explain, do you?"

Mikhyel shrugged. "I might, if I could. I can't. It just . . . happens. Rakshi's will, don't you know?"

"Religious naivete does not become you, dunMheric."

"Then *you* enlighten *me*. Why *am* I here? Truly, why am I here?"

"Out of turn, Barrister. Satisfy my curiosity. How did you get in here? It's plagued me ever since you fell from the sky into my cart. Even before that, I had to wonder how your brother came to fall on my lover's head."

His blindside ploy to shake Mikhyel's calm—or perhaps to rouse a reaction from Deymorin, in case Deymorin was with him—nearly worked: the business about the cart and that about the pond were both things very few individuals knew. But in an instant's review of who had known, he realized. "Say I believe your story. Say I believe you . . . harbor all those you claim. Kiyrstin was not your—not *Vandoshin's* lover."

"No? And who is in a better position to know the truth of that?"

He gave a practiced laugh, feigning surprise. "Certainly neither of us, hiller." And followed it with a sardonic smile. "But Deymorin saw Vandoshin romMaurii and Kiyrstin together. What Deymorin saw, what Deymorin *felt*, I have seen and felt. My brother holds love in great esteem and quite . . . sacred. Kiyrstin and romMaurii might have had sex. That they were lovers . . . never. Besides . . ." He paused, raising his cup to his mouth as if drinking. "Kiyrstin has better taste."

A twitch of upper lip indicated a score, however small. Vandoshin romMaurii had been a vain man. As Rhyys had been. He was curious how much of those attitudes resonated in this marred mind.

Past the horror of its manifestation, the concept of the creature was actually quite . . . fascinating.

Mheltiri's eyes brightened. "*Fascinating?* I was certain you'd find it so."

A chill passed through him. He immediately threw more effort into his barriers, wondering how much else this creature had picked up, here in its own lair, beside the Rings it ruled.

"Don't work *too* hard, dunMheric. That thought alone resonated with that which I hoped to hear."

"And I'm to assume the rest of my mind is sacrosanct? And you're helping me? I think not."

"I've no gain at all in lying to you, dunMheric. I told you. I don't steal. Consent is my rule. We've had it the other way, and we aren't interested. But if I were, I'd simply plunder that which I want to know right now. You lack the strength to stop me. It would, however, leave something of a mess behind, and I'd rather avoid that. So tell me, how *did* you do it? How did you come here, and more to the point, why aren't you seared like so much beefsteak?"

There was a peculiar intensity to the question, a bitterness that recalled a man scarred almost beyond the recognition of his closest associates.

"This is more than just curiosity, isn't it, romMaurii," Mikhyel asked softly. "Have a sudden trip out of Boreton, did you? Arrive a trifle early on Rhyys' doorstep? Have a bit of trouble en route?"

"How?"

"Sorry, can't help you."

"I'm beginning not to care what I leave behind, dunMheric."

"And I'm not here simply for mutual enlightenment. Explain your real position, and I'll consider explaining what happened to you that day."

"Either way, I'll find out."

"Perhaps. And if you overestimate yourself? Would you live your life not knowing?"

"You *do* know why you're here, then."

"I suspect. Enlighten me."

"This body is . . . inadequate to our needs. Yours would suit us quite well."

"And so we come to it. We're not talking an exchange merely of information here, are we, Mheltiri?"

"Of course not."

"So what are we talking about?"

Mheltiri leaned forward, propping one elbow on the pillows, cupping his chin in his hand. "I've brought you here to do what you do best, Mikhyel dunMheric. Negotiate."

§   §   §

The tunnel was blacker than the blackest night. The Khoratumin bulbs they'd brought for the trail lamps glowed fitfully at best, the Rhomatumin bulb, which should work on any Rhomatumin satellite, glowed not at all: Deymorin's most concrete evidence yet of the shift in the essential nature of the node.

"How in the name of Darius did *you* find your way through here?" Deymorin asked, and Zelin's voice answered from just ahead:

"The lad . . . made it glow, sir."

"Made it . . ." And at the thought, he became aware of
a faint tracing in the stone against which he leaned. A
thread of leythium, similar in size to the filaments grown
for the bulbs. The walls were permeated with such tiny
threads. The filaments in the bulbs had to be aligned with
the ley-flow in order to glow. For these stationary threads
to . . . glow, as Zelin said they had, the energy would
have to flow from the Tower and along this tunnel like an
underground stream—

He jerked his hand away as that stone flared with warmth
and light, nearly blinding him. Men cried out, the oil lamp
at the front of the line crashed to the tunnel floor and
shattered, leaving them in darkness all the deeper for the
momentary flare.

It was too easy . . . too damned easy.

Deymorin spread his hand on the wall again and more
cautiously wished for light, visualized that flow as a trickle
rather than a river . . . A gentle glow, that was all he
needed/wanted.

Resistance. A sense of . . . indignity that the previous
answer to his request had been rejected. The Ley sulked.

He laughed at his own interpretation of that response
and tried again.

Light spread from his hand, pulsing—like blood through
veins—working farther along the tunnel in both directions
with each wave. But it wasn't a shift in the flow this time:
those individual crystals were shifting, moving to his will as
the Rings shifted in their orbits.

And only now did the red outline of veinwork fade from
what had seared itself into his night-accustomed eyes.

"Just chock full of surprises, aren't you, Rhomandi?"
Ganfrion murmured, standing just behind him.

"Just say thank you and shut your yapper, crypt-bait."

" 'Thank you and shut your yapper, crypt-bait.' Can we
move now?"

Deymorin choked on a reluctant laugh. Sometimes the
mad commonalities with this uncommon man were too
great for his own peace of mind. "Touché, gorMikhyel,"

he muttered out of the corner of his mouth, and aloud: "Well, lads, shall we move on?"

Move on, they did. With a muttered awe, and renewed confidence in the man who led them. He sensed that confidence and hoped it was not misplaced.

The glow filled the tunnel and lighted their way; it would also alert any guards.

He damned sure hadn't expected a reaction like that, especially here. It was the Rhomatum Rings he'd commanded. By all he understood, he should have no effect at all here—certainly not without at least as much work as he'd put into connecting to Rhomatum. Certainly some ringmasters must be able to violate those boundaries, otherwise, they'd never be able to cap a foreign node, but controlling the Rings was fundamentally different from affecting the . . . living leythium. Mikhyel, perhaps, might have; his brother had a proven affinity for a variety of leythium sources. If he were in contact with Mikhyel, he might suppose Mikhyel working through him as he worked the Rhomatum Rings through Nikki, but he hadn't reached for his brother. Hadn't wanted to draw attention to their presence . . .

Yet as he thought to look for it, there the link was: a faint stream between them, a flow of images and vague impressions—and knew he hadn't been alone in those few moments, even as his brother's images of the ringchamber above became part of his conscious pattern of this place.

. . . of the ringchamber above.

Damn!

He tapped Ganfrion's shoulder, got a profiled nod.

"Khyel's up there," he murmured.

Ganfrion started. "Already?"

He nodded.

Ganfrion cursed then called out, "Let's hurry it up, lads!"

Chapter Five

"What you're saying," Mikhyel said, "is that if I let . . ." He traced a circle in the air. ". . . all of you . . . cohabit my body, you'll . . . repair the damage you've done and Thyerri will be free to go."

It was, at best, a surreal conversation, in a setting of whirling rings and bright pillows.

"As will *you*, dunMheric. You know *you'll* repair it. That's your guarantee it will happen. Your mind will be your own. Your life, yours. You'll have the power, the *wisdom*, of any number of great ringmasters. Do as you please. We will simply be . . . an advisory committee."

At its worst, the blackest comedy, reeking of death and cruelty.

"Yet you refer to yourself in the plural. To whom am I speaking now? Where is Mheltiri?"

"Here, with the rest of us. But he is . . . quite shy. He holds you in no little awe, and so asks us to speak for him."

"I see. Poor overawed fellow. And with an equal vote?"

A faint pull of the smooth brow, a nervous pull of a sparkling tassel. "It's not a matter of votes, dunMheric. I thought you realized that. If he wished, he'd do exactly as he pleased. He . . . pleases to defer to those of us with greater experience. The position of greatest strength lies within the host. The host's preferences rule unless the host wishes otherwise."

"How many of you are there?"

"That's difficult to say. It's simply more expedient to think of ourselves as the current host. To do otherwise can compromise the whole. I *am* Mheltiri. *We* are Mheltiri."

Mikhyel rose to his feet, pulled the blanket up over his shoulders, and moved to where he could look down at Thyerri.

Thyerri's eyes were open, staring at the Rings spinning directly over his head.

They didn't even flicker in his direction. And Thyerri's thoughts were equally silent, not the least hint of emotion seeping past his solid barriers.

He pulled the blanket a degree tighter. "And this sorry scene? Was this Mheltiri's concept of how to lure me in?"

A stir in the pillows, a brush of fabric against fabric, a voice, soft and apologetic, at his side: Mheltiri had joined him, side by side looking down at Thyerri. "I told you. Mheltiri has abdicated to those with greater experience. We have made errors of judgment in acquisitions in the past. I fear Rhyys was one such. His mind is weak, but his corrosive influence had not yet been brought under control when we began to call you in. After the process was begun, to abort in the middle would have negated all we had gained."

"I see. And how often have you had to fight this . . . corrosive influence?"

"You fear what you invite into your mind." A light hand touched his blanket-protected arm, stroked inward, slipping beneath the blanket to the bare skin of his chest. "Why don't you . . . come in for a visit? Just a visit, to set your mind at ease."

"I don't fear you. *Any* of you." He moved out from under that hand. "On the contrary: it is you who should beware what you invite into your cooperative."

"We doubt that. Join with us, just the surface thoughts. Let us examine one another for compatibility."

"Not yet. I want to make certain you have anything truly to bargain with."

Deymorin was coming. At any moment, he might be required to move Thyerri, or at least to take some firm action. He had to know just how bad those legs were.

Keeping the incomplete pattern of Thyerri foremost, throwing all his strength into his own barriers to keep his mind from merging too deeply with Thyerri's the moment he touched the dancer's smooth skin, he knelt beside that stubbornly averted head and freed his left hand from beneath the blanket.

Mheltiri's body came snakelike between them, his hand intercepting Mikhyel's wrist, holding it with a heretofore hidden strength.

"Not yet," Mheltiri whispered in his ear, too close, too familiar, too damned intimate, as all Mheltiri's actions had been.

Red anger flared, smothering rational thought, and it required every pain-wracked lesson of Anheliaa's schooling to keep him from thrusting that light body into the spinning rings, killing it *and* the abomination it contained.

Soft laughter warmed his ear. "Oh, no, dunMheric. You don't want to do that, I assure you. Kill me and the Rings come down. The Rings come down and your lover is dead. If he's lucky. Just think of all that weight coming down on him—assuming of course the Rings survive the shock, and don't riddle him with a million and one tiny arrows."

"Damn you," Mikhyel hissed, and the façade between them, his carefully cultivated indifference, ruptured.

Laughter, not the least bit soft, rang throughout the small room, setting up harmonics in the hum of the Rings themselves.

"*That's* the essence we felt!" Fists buried in the blanket drawing him forward, that smooth face thrust close to his. "You hide well, but the anger, the killer instinct is there. *Yes,* damn me. Damn me, damn Garetti, damn Anheliaa, damn your brother. And who will do it, dunMheric? *Who* will damn us? There are no gods, you know that. I very much do. The people believe *we're* gods in Mauritum, and they live secure in that thought. We order their lives, and they are content."

The voice was chilling, without a hint of Mheltiri's breathy tones. He could almost believe it was a Mauritumin orator speaking. The ancestral, aristocratic accent came through.

"Darius is a hypocrite. He encourages his people to believe what they will—anything so long as they don't trouble him with godhood—then leaves them to rule themselves, while the great Darius lives as a god and plays games with their lives without them even knowing it!"

Mikhyel's anger froze cold as logic, and this time he reached out and seized Mheltiri's arm, so that now it was he who kept Mheltiri from pulling away.

"What do you mean, 'Darius *lives*?'"

§   §   §

"There's trouble ahead," Deymorin said to Ganfrion, keeping his voice low, "side tunnel. Coming in from the right."

Ganfrion eyed him suspiciously a moment, then tapped his temple. Deymorin nodded. He didn't know how he knew, but that pulsing light that veined the walls brought back a sense of living entities, and no few of them.

Moments later, Zelin stopped and waved Deymorin to him. "Near the finished tunnels, now, m'lord. Guards'll be about."

"Do you know the way through the tunnels to the Tower?"

"Like the back of my hand, m'lord. Helped reconstruct the passageways—part of the brute labor."

"Good enough. Naimii, Morok, take the lead. Zelin, keep to the rear until we clear the tunnel, then center—"

"I'm a fightin' man, sir. Rather hold my own place."

"And our only guide." Besides that mental lodestone in his head that pointed inexorably toward Mikhyel, that was true. But there could be many a twist of passage between himself and that goal. "Keep to the center of the line and don't take chances. We can't lose you. We've still got to get out of here."

"Mind your own advice, Rhomandi," Ganfrion muttered in his ear, and Deymorin, without looking back, nodded.

"I'm no fool, gorMikhyel."

And with that utterance, he entrusted his back to a man he'd once vowed to kill.

The scent of smoke reached them first: the oily stench of
torches. Naimii turned a corner, then backed quickly, hand
raised. Deymorin pressed his hand to the wall, sensed . . .
heartbeats. ·

"Five of them," he said softly, and the word passed
ahead, giving him back looks of doubt mixed with awe.
"Put them out fast and hard, enough to keep them that
way."

Zelin had said Rhyys had all his people marked . . .
including Zelin himself. He feared Zelin's presence might
well alert Rhyys' suspicions.

But Deymorin was betting Rhyys didn't hear his people's
thoughts or even track them all continually. Mikhyel insisted Anheliaa had been able to track the whereabouts of
a great many people, but that she'd had to consciously find
and follow them, and that meant suspecting they were up
to something.

Besides, at the moment, he was banking on Mikhyel
keeping Rhyys well occupied.

ॐ   ॐ   ॐ

"Darius is dead," Mikhyel said flatly. "Two hundred and
fifty years dead."

Mheltiri's laughter achieved the shrill note of madness,
but Mikhyel no longer found refuge in that explanation.
Don't assume . . . yet he had, over and over again, in the
name of his *own* sanity.

Sanity which was currently under direct attack.

"Darius knew the secret of immortality," Mheltiri insisted. "He created the means there in Rhomatum. Do you
honestly believe he died like a common laborer?"

"Of course he's dead." Yet even as he spoke, thoughts
of Anheliaa and her continued interference in his life after
her death mocked him. But . . . that was different. With or
without the link such as he had with his brothers, Anheliaa
had contaminated *his* pattern since he was a child. That she
had influenced the essential Rhomatum node pattern was
utterly conceivable.

Surely his own lifelong obsession with serving her was enough to help her manifest in his room. His own fears intersecting with some . . . predeath wish of her own . . . surely that was only his own nature haunting him, until Deymorin purged his memory in the Outside burial of her corpse.

But what Mheltiri suggested had nothing to do with immortality of the body.

Amalgam. Like what was in front of him.

Suddenly, Anheliaa's obsession to create the perfect ring-master took an even darker twist. There had been so few Rhomandi in the course of time. Not that the Rhomandi didn't breed . . . the children just rarely survived. Three hundred years, and the legitimate bloodline ran no farther than the three of them. None of them had proven adequate to Anheliaa's purposes, or perhaps more importantly, in retrospect, *pliable* enough.

So she'd gone outside the family to get her heir. To *make* one that would be conceived, born, and raised to *her* specifications.

But why? he asked himself, still holding Mheltiri. If she— if Darius—could shift bodies at will, why stay with Anheliaa's? Why the farce of an heir?

Linkage came through that grip, an uneasy sense of contact. "Because, dear boy, there are only a handful of methods for blending patterns. The easiest is quite pleasurable to most people, but Darius was repulsed by that from the start. Using the Rings to force entrance into an unwilling mind is unpleasant for both sides and can result in a most unstable final pattern . . . rebellion, constant rebellion. Negotiation is possible, with both sides seeing the value of the cooperative and working for the same end, both desirous of power . . . for whatever reason. But without direct cooperation, one requires a physical similarity to achieve a stable union. The blending of patterns already similar through physical relationship and years of association—that makes the blending relatively simple, without any need of active cooperation on the receiving side. Preferable, possibly even after all these years, to the Darius we knew."

The Darius we knew . . .

"It's madness."

"Is it? Yet, what did you tell your brother, just before you left Rhomatum?"

"How do you know anything about that?"

More laughter. "Because you're thinking about it right now, you silly child. Of course you've suspected something of the sort. You're a smart child. A clever child. And we can make you very, very clever indeed. We can rule here, your brother in Rhomatum . . . and naturally Darius will join your brother, if he hasn't already."

"Never!"

"You think too much, dunMheric. I doubt very much that anyone other than Darius has *ever* ruled in Rhomatum. But why does that bother you? Can't you see the beauty of the pattern? You'll have the wisdom of a thousand years at your fingertips. You'll heal your dancer. You'll have all the power you want. All the knowledge."

"Knowlege . . . perhaps, but not wisdom. And I fear I still find your premise difficult to accept."

"Then I repeat my offer: let us touch minds. See for yourself whether or not I tell the truth."

"And invite madness on myself? I think not."

"Oh, I'm quite certain." Mheltiri knelt beside Thyerri, laid a hand on his arm, and an audible snap cut through the hum of the Rings. Thyerri cried out, and where Mheltiri's hand had been, the arm bent. Deep bruising rushed to the skin, spreading outward.

"Stop it!" Mikhyel took a step forward, froze as that hand settled around Thyerri's throat.

{Let him, Khy.} Dancer's silence broke at last, and his eyes, when he turned his head to face Mikhyel, were tired and pained.

{I can't let him.}

{You must. He's not lying. I've seen the patterns. His pattern is a world pattern unto itself. Can't you see it's better this way? He's done too much damage. Mother's gone. *I* can't fight . . . You won't. If I'm dead, he can't use me against you.}

{Dancer, I didn't mean what I said. I didn't—}

Gentle laughter, horribly out of place on Thyerri's pale lips. {Of course you didn't, Barrister. You said/did/felt what you needed to.}

{This is all very touching.} A thought that was no longer that false spiced raspberry, but rather a sickening mixture of scents, like an overspiced stew, cut between them. {But you'd best make up your mind, *Barrister.*}

"Then get the fuck out of it while I do!"

A half smile. The sickening brew slid away . . . completely—and for the first time, he now realized, since he'd jumped into the Tower.

"Heal the arm," he demanded.

"I'll do no such thing."

"Heal the damned arm! You've proven you can hurt—many times over. *Prove* to me you can make him well!"

The Rings' spin increased to a blur. The very air about the wound pulsed in time with the Cardinal ring's passing. How long it took, he had no idea, but when Mheltiri's hand again pulled away, the bruising had vanished and the arm itself was no longer twisted at an unnatural angle.

He'd lost. He'd thought he'd find a way out of this, but there was none.

He'd hoped Deymorin would get here and tip the balance, but he had not.

He had assumed he was dealing with madness, easily put off for whatever time Deymorin needed: but he was not. More, it was not confined to this room. It was back in Rhomatum Tower at the heart of everything. It was in Lidye, mothering Nikki's child. If there was a hope in hell of his doing anything to protect anyone he loved, it was in taking this amalgam into himself and fighting to maintain dominance.

He had no illusions. If this creature joined him in his body, he was up against experienced, centuries-old theft, by master ringspinners one after the other. There'd be little or nothing of Mikhyel left. Even should his mind rule the decisions, even should he influence the whole sufficiently to live the life he had intended, the very fact of surrendering would change him forever. If he were any other man, if he were not Mheric's and Anheliaa's . . . and gods knew . . . through her, Darius' . . . he might have had a remote chance. But he was dark inside. If he did this . . .

The darkness within him would win. Ultimately it would win.

And in contaminating himself, he contaminated his brothers, who were linked to him. They might fall, one by one, through him.

Yet if he refused that contamination, Deymorin would never find out what had happened here.

If he refused that contamination, Dancer would die—he would; he had no doubt that if Dancer died, a part of him would die as well, and the will to escape would go with it.

And perhaps, just perhaps, that would be better for both of them.

ᔕ   ᔕ   ᔕ

"That's the stairs to the Tower," Zelin murmured, pointing across the stony ledge and through the catwalk's grid to a dark opening on the far side of the large room. It was a single, open floor some fifteen feet below, a room better guarded than the rest of the place had been.

Ten men, as he counted them. Maybe two more, from the sounds in a hidden corner.

Eight large rings lay at its center: Tower rings in their final cooling stages. The stone ledge came and went about the circumference, supported a catwalk and track from which the hoist for moving the molds about could be operated.

Zelin pointed to the right. "Ledge ends over there, behind that walk. There's a path down from there."

Ganfrion nodded, then drew the old soldier back from the verge, scuttling back to the wall and into the workman's crawl, a shortcut that thank the gods the old man had known, or they'd still be wandering the tunnels trying to find this room.

But just the two of them had come back. The Rhomandi lingered, there at the edge, on his stomach, staring down into the room, like he hadn't better sense. Fearing he was caught in one of his communications with his brother, Ganfrion edged back out to pull him to his senses, but found full cognizance in the man.

"Planning a whole new set," Rhomandi muttered as they lay side by side on their bellies staring down at those rings. "Must've fried the lot of them."

"Thought the secret process for casting the rings was kept in a safe in Rhomandi House." Ganfrion said.

"It is."

"When did you start a lending library?"

"I haven't."

"Wishful thinking, then?"

Slow shake of the head. "Don't you see the glow?"

"Nope." And glad he was for the blindness.

"Damn."

The Rhomandi's soft curse, his uneasy glance toward the blank arch of stone overhead did nothing to ease Ganfrion's growing concerns. He had that distracted look that said he was chatting with his brother.

"Problems?" Ganfrion asked, when that unhappy gaze met his, but Rhomandi shook his head.

"Nothing I can do anything more about—not until I get there." A jerk of the head, and they retreated to where they could stand out of sight of those guards. Just short of the men, Rhomandi continued, "Can't get specifics, but I think, at least at the moment, this Mheltiri doesn't know we're here—or at least, doesn't know we're this close."

"Mheltiri?"

"The one in charge up there. And don't look at me like that. That's all I—*damn*!"

"Translation: We get you up there—now?" Ganfrion asked and even before the single, pained nod of the head, Ganfrion was naming names and setting them to Rhomandi's defense.

"All right, let's move. Sergeant, Anrikhiim, Khranis, Rosh and Zelin—you stay with me. Naiimi, you, Morok and Trenik take the Rhomandi down Zelin's path to the right, keep behind those crates down there. The way the light's reflecting, you should be able to get all the way through to the far side. We're going across the 'walk. When you're in place, we'll drop in noisily on our friends down below. While we've got the lot distracted, you three get across to that stairwell and then get him the fuck up to the Tower any way you can.

§ § §

"All right," Mikhyel said. "You get your deal."

{Khyel, no!}

He ignored the protest from Dancer. Where there was life, there were options. There was a point past which you acquiesced and found a different winning condition. He'd learned that basic rule years ago. Twice, he'd broken it, twice someone had been there to pick up the pieces.

This time, it was Dancer's life he gambled with, and he wasn't about to risk it, to which end, he waved off Mheltiri's eager approach.

"One condition. Heal Thyerri first."

Mheltiri frowned. "I couldn't possibly. Your demand to heal the arm exhausted me."

"Then we wait. I won't agree until he's able to leave safely."

"Don't be ridiculous. I'd have no hold on you."

"You'd have my word."

"There is that. Of course, by then, your brother will have arrived, and all deals will be off. I think not."

"I've told you, heal him, and I'll cooperate. Besides, if you haven't the energy to heal him, you couldn't possible have the energy to make this . . . transfer, and *I* won't have it afterward to heal him. So let's put things in the right order. Heal him. Now. Or no deal."

"On the contrary . . . which you haven't learned, yours is the vitality necessary for that. All that is required of this shell of mine . . . is to deal death."

"You said nothing of death."

"How else do you suppose the transaction is sealed? Of course, there is the slightest problem. There are no weapons in here." Mheltiri walked a slow circle around him, trailing fingers on the blanket. Those fingers slid upward and caressed his neck. "Just think, dunMheric: there's the chance, the absolute, slightest chance that you can break my neck instead, before my hold is firm. Then you and your love will be free."

He stilled the instinct that longed to catch those fingers and snap them.

"Of course," Mheltiri added, "there is one slight problem were I the one to die. Snap my neck, and the Rings fail. There's even the chance they might explode. You will have noted their color, I'm sure. They're very fragile at the moment. The battle last spring was not kind to them. Either way, your love would be free but quite, quite dead. So I think perhaps you won't kill me."

"And once the . . . composite soul . . . is confined to this body? I'm no healer. What if I *can't* heal myself? If it's Mheltiri's 'shell' that generates the healing . . . what about Thyerri's legs?"

"We'll manage." The intrusive hand slipped up through his hair and combed the strands back to cup his skull. "The knowledge and the patterns will be here, in this head."

"And if not?"

"If not, why, we can use the ability to travel that this rather bony shell of yours has already displayed. We can transfer the dear boy to one of your hospital nodes—jump him right into one of the pools, if that's your fancy, I should suppose. That Talent you do have."

"It's not that simple."

"I wouldn't know that . . . yet."

"And what about the Rings? Mheltiri is of Khoratum. So was Rhyys. I'm *not*. I can't hold them anyway. They'll come down, or explode, and we'll all die."

"We're safe to the moment of this shell's death. At that time, you'll have the pattern from the Rhyys-self as if you were born to this node, and you can quite naturally hold the Rings."

"I don't believe you. I *won't* take the chance with Thyerri's life. I think we'll wait until the Mheltiri-self can fix what you damnwell broke."

"And give your dear brother time to get here? I think not. I suspect my guards will be able to deal with him, but if not . . . by the time he gets here, it's *going* to be too late."

"No."

Mheltiri spun and dropped to his knees beside Thyerri in a dancer's liquid move, hand poised over Thyerri's throat.

"I said I hadn't sufficient left to heal his legs; I've *plenty* to kill. Weaken the tissue of the windpipe, and the weight of his own chin will choke him while you argue."

"Damn you." He'd lost the gamble. Deymorin wasn't going to make it in time. He was going to have to fight from the inside. "What do I do?"

"Simple, really. As I said, the most pleasurable joining of patterns you've already tried." Mheltiri held out his free hand, the one still poised above Dancer's throat.

"This is a sick joke."

"Hardly. Lie here beside me. I'll do the rest."

"Dammit, *no*."

"You do pick the oddest sticking points, dunMheric. It's not as if you haven't prostituted yourself before."

"I said, no."

"Very well, then just sit here."

Seeing no other course open, he sat, obstinately choosing the side opposite Mheltiri's free hand, the side from which he could see Thyerri's face.

There were tears in his eyes.

"I want to kiss him."

"There will be plenty of time for that later."

"Just *me*, dammit!"

"There is a limit to my patience, dunMheric!"

He said nothing, but ignored Mheltiri's outstretched hand.

"I let you kiss him and you bolt and run!" Mheltiri shouted. "Damned if I'll allow it!"

"I told you, it's not that easy to do."

A lightning-fast strike captured his wrist, and the scent of the amalgam, focused now into a dark and deadly poisonous brew, invaded his mind, seeking confirmation of its objections. He winced, allowed just enough truth through to satisfy, and, from the smile on Mheltiri's face, to make Mheltiri believe he'd truly broken through his last defenses.

"But of course, my dear. Love's final kiss. So romantic. So silly. Soon you'll realize how silly. But go ahead."

Mikhyel turned his back to Mheltiri and saw only Thyerri. He ignored the tug as the hiller pulled the blanket from his body, ignored as well the hiller's hands on his back, the brush of air as the Rings spun above his head, ignored everything except the feel of Dancer's smooth skin beneath his fingers as he cupped that beloved face.

{Don't do this, Khy. We'll have nothing.}

{You'll be alive.}

{*You* won't be.}

He smiled gently, and leaned to press his lips against Dancer's trembling mouth. His Dancer was so tired. So very, very tired. Two days he'd lain here, unable to sleep, unable to relax his vigilance even for a moment. To move was to destroy himself.

{Don't count me out, love,} Mikhyel whispered, seeking that pattern they shared, preparing a lifeline to future sanity. {But I'll need you. *I'll need you!* Hold on. *Stay with me!*}

{Enough.} Again, Mheltiri tried to come between them, and desperation colored his inner voice. His hand stretched again to Dancer's throat.

Mikhyel thrust the hiller aside easily, body and mind, let him feel at last the full strength of his resolve, let him know beyond doubt that only the threat to Dancer had won the day. Mheltiri slithered away, leaving them alone again.

{Trust me.} A final brush of his lips, and he ducked back from under the spinning rings. But Dancer grabbed his hand. Desperation came through that touch.

{I've seen what it does.}

{So have I. It's what drove Anheliaa mad, I'm willing to bet, and what's driving Lidye mad even now.}

{You're next.}

{Very likely.}

{Then why—}

{Because there's a chance I can win. Anheliaa was a damned efficient teacher. Others have tried to rule me all my life. So far, I'm still my own man.}

{You're such an arrogant bastard.}

He chuckled, oddly relaxed, now that the moment had come. He'd made his own decision. "I love you," he whispered aloud, and Dancer's eyes widened, stared without blinking a long moment, then squeezed shut, and his mind cut itself off from Mikhyel's touch.

Another body reared up between them, thrusting Mikhyel back into the pillows, holding him there as the poisonous stench invaded his mind.

This time, he made no attempt to fight it off.

Chapter Six

There was no shortage of death this time. Ganfrion pulled his blade from the last of the guards, and fell back against the stairs, sinking slowly. Khranis was down. So was Captain Polkirri, though Anrikhiim knelt at Polkirri's side, pulling away clothing to staunch a copious bloodflow. Only Zelin, who had done more with his feet and hands than the sword he carried, had come through unscathed; all the rest nursed significant injuries.

Not a good outcome. And they were deep in hostile territory.

"Stay with him," Ganfrion said to Anrikhiim, and used the sword to lever himself back onto his feet. "Get out of sight. We'll be back for you."

If they survived. He didn't like the sounds that had come down those stairs from Rhomandi's retreating backside. Zelin at his back, he staggered up the stairs, overtaking Naiimi and Morok, stopped at the first level, taking on men while the Rhomandi moved on. A sweep of his bloodied sword, a snap of Zelin's heel, and they were through. With three at his back, he pushed onward, legs growing more leaden with each stride.

Two more bodies blocked his path: clean kills, no doubt of it. Rhomandi was efficient in that as well.

And still . . .

His legs faltered. Magic. They were slogging through invisible mud. Naiimi collapsed behind him. Moments later, Morok gave a cry of frustration and had to stop. Only Zelin, small and tough, continued to fight that strength-sapping mire though he fell behind.

Whatever had Mikhyel dunMheric in its grip damnwell didn't want to be interrupted, and he'd bet his life on that assumption.

He was about to lay a counter-bet: that it wasn't going to stop him.

He snarled and bent to the task, defied the strain on his knees, and made the next step. He'd make it to the Tower if he had to crawl there.

And once he got there, if it turned out it was Mikhyel dunMheric making his life this living hell, he'd kill the bastard himself.

§　　§　　§

Mikhyel wallowed in a kaleidoscopic nightmare of memories. Flashes of a dozen lives and more, all clamoring for the right to attach to his pattern first. Lives battling one another, tearing at him, mind and body, fighting for the right to *become* Mikhyel dunMheric.

Years of training held him back in his private room, let the wolves rip at one another outside the door, encouraged them by noticing first one, then another, acknowledging, then backing away from the latch, about to make a fatal choice . . . then not.

It was, in actual fact, quite fascinating. The minds he encountered were almost universally clever, and he had to wonder how Rhyys had ever been included in that number. It certainly didn't recommend the collective intellect.

{We wouldn't have taken him into the fold, had we had an option,} a voice whispered to him through the door, a tone reminiscent of Thyerri's Scarface, but not. {You and your brothers left us little choice. To retain the Rings here at all, we had to sacrifice the Vandoshin shell, which loss plagued us with this monster—}

The monster in question flared, and that other shadow enveloped the fire, snuffed it in a casual twist of darkness.

{Unfortunately, there are those within who share some of his less . . . savory . . . tendencies. Being a person of refined taste, you will help us curb those, I'm certain.}

{Are you the oldest?} Mikhyel asked.

{I—no.} An image of iridescent fire, of leythium lace and glowing pools more reminiscent of Mother's caverns than of a ringtower. He pushed the latch . . . opened the door cautiously. Had an impression of many individuals, men and women, standing in line, each awaiting their turn. {I was strong in talent, but equally strong in my unwillingness to cooperate with the priests. I had no interest in eternal life either, Mikhyel dunMheric, not at the price. I was sorry, afterward, that I had fought so hard. I've seen . . . so much . . .}

A gentle stroke of a shadow hand, with it, a sense of . . .

{You were a woman?}

{Does it matter?}

{I . . . suppose not.}

{Join with me?} Stroking shadow hands sent shockwaves through his own shadow essence. A softer, more subtle attempt to be first among the wolves.

{Not yet.} He pulled away.

Disappointment. A drifting apart.

He caught a shadowy hand before she escaped entirely. {Stay?}

A sigh of content, a curling closer and interlacing of fingers. There were so few, he sensed, that she had wanted to include, that she had held back, always content to be on the edges of the pattern.

{Who else?} He whispered through that touch, and as they drifted among the shadows and the memories, she pulled one, then another to them. Four in all. A coalition of sanity, he began to think of them, and she laughed delightedly and spun closer around him.

In a far recess, a quiet shadow huddled in on itself and made no attempt to attract his attention. His shadow companions stretched shadow hands toward it, and the loner slid gratefully in among them.

Mheltiri. Gentle healer that he was. Lonely and aching for acceptance. So vulnerable to the offer that had been extended him, so overwhelmed by what he had just been party to.

{I didn't want to hurt him. I tried so hard . . .}

The woman gathered him close and kissed him . . . and they made love, those two shadows, as if they were alone

I didn't want to hurt him . . .

It appeared more individuality remained within the amalgam than he'd been led to expect from outward appearances. *Information* seemed confined here. He touched minds and won from the shadowy pieces only a sense of their own lives, their own memories.

{I should be first.} A large shadow loomed before him. {I'm the one who knew his ancestor. Who helped him escape Mauritum.}

{Darius? You knew Darius?} Mikhyel asked.

{Naturally.}

{What do you mean, you helped him escape?}

{He left the fold because Brodriiani demanded his cooperation. Surely you knew that.}

An image, then, of a face he knew well from the many busts and painted renditions of his illustrious ancestor. A face in this memory all twisted in pain and fear—and anger.

Laughter. An insinuating whisper: {Why do you *think* Anheliaa is so set on Brodriiani/Garetti's destruction?}

{Garetti is *another*?}

{Of course. Don't be naive, child. Simplicity doesn't become you.}

Yet another accused him of naïveté.

And his ancestor had left Mauritum at least in part because Garetti's former self had tried to rape Darius' pattern as well as his body.

Interesting. Not particularly happy news in his own position.

{Khy?} Music on a breeze of spiced raspberries. A darting ribbon of rainbow.

Shadows swarmed.

The ribbon danced free, and he held out his hand, avoiding naming names, avoiding patterns of any sort that might bridge to that essence, trusting it to know him. The ribbon rippled to him, wound about his hand.

Then cupping that ribbon in both hands, he inhaled deeply of the spices—

And the ribbon vanished, to curl safely in his gut, like a child in a womb, part of his pattern already. The first to join him.

The shadows milled, then scattered, the ribbon forgotten.

{Rhyys, Khy! Rhyys holds the pattern of the Rings!} Reminder from the spiced raspberries filling him from within.

And the uncharacteristic fear was gone. Excitement ruled. Hope ruled. Jump for the next ring and damn the consequences!

Death was one thing. To give up? Never. Not when Dancer was part of the pattern.

{Where's Rhyys?} he asked, and his shadow-friends, his coalition of sanity, objected to that request.

{Join with us first. Let us be united against him.}

{Where is he?}

With a scent of reluctance, they drifted through the cacophony of voices, and came to a shadow that was wildly, fiercely bringing itself to a climax. They waited patiently for the short performance to be over, then touched its shoulder.

The shadow spun about, saw him and with a formless mental shout, leapt at him, an attack so sudden, so mindlessly frantic that he was down before he realized he was under assault.

The coalition that had formed of the loners stepped between them, grabbing shadow arms and legs, holding the writhing creature until he could gather his wits and approach it.

{Hello, Rhyys.}

{Not Rhyys. Mheltiri. Ah, such a wealth of feeling . . .}

More writhing.

{You wish me to be the first?} Eagerness, triumph and a sense of unquenched and unquenchable desire.

{Possibly I do. Will you allow me a sampling?}

{Free me . . .}

{Not yet.} His partners held Rhyys, exuding a certain joy in their united opposition to an obviously unpopular addi-

tion to the union. And while they held him, Mikhyel
touched the shadow face, then leaned to inhale the fetid,
ocarshi-laden breath, the scent of rotted teeth. Strange that
real world senses retained any meaning here . . . yet he
supposed sane minds needed that association to remain
sane . . .

He willed that sense of smell away, set his barriers
against his own pattern and pressed his lips to the shadow
lips, seeking . . .

And finding.

Worlds within worlds. Patterns within patterns. Disgusting, revolting source, but of all the shadows, only Rhyys
and Vandoshin had touched and held the Khoratum Rings.

And Vandoshin was far too clever to have let him gather
part without demanding the whole.

{Thank you, Rhyys,} he whispered, then willed himself
to the far side of his tiny coalition. {You can let him go
now. I . . . have what I want.} Without dwelling on time
and place, he dropped all barriers and shouted:

{Deymorin!}

⑨   ⑨   ⑨

Mikhyel's call exploded in Deymorin's mind even as he
rounded the final curve of the staircase and burst into the
ringchamber. The sight that met his eyes was madness incarnate. Thyerri lying silent beneath the Rings, one hand
clenched on Mikhyel's while Mikhyel himself lay limp beneath the humping body of a total stranger.

But the mind that invaded his was anything but defeated.
It invaded, and withdrew, a darting presence that left in its
wake a pattern.

{*The Rings,* Deymorin! Can you hold them?}

{Hell if I know! Mikhyel, what—}

{Hold them and kill the bastard!} And in the wake of
Mikhyel's thought, was the fear that should this stranger
die, the Rings would fall, crushing the delicate form lying
prone beneath them.

He felt the pattern, sensed the flow of energy as he had sensed it with Rhomatum, but this flow fought him.

{I can't . . .}

Like a wolf above its prey, the creature devouring his brother's mouth lifted its head and feral eyes glared at him through a fall of dark hair.

{Of course you can't. You're *of* Rhomatum.}

{Try, Deymorin. Dammit, you must.} And that was Nikki, all guards down, the link in full flower.

{Can't? Like *hell* I can't!} He drew on Nikki, pouring his energy into that pattern Mikhyel had given him, making it his own, stealing it from its weakened master. The creature screamed and writhed.

{Kill him, Deymio! Kill him now!} And on that darting thought rode a disorienting sense of his brother's wavering control, of minds assaulting him.

"I can't!"

"Kill him!" Mikhyel screamed aloud, and the edge of terror in his brother's voice chilled him to the core. Images broke through in a flood: child-Mikhyel and Pausri dun-Haulpin, a night in Sparingate with the prisoners descending on him.

But while his temper flared, he steadied his hold and refused to give in to it. It was all in Khyel's mind, and Khyel was fighting for his sanity. He felt the draw on the power that came flooding from Nikki, gave that to Mikhyel, and felt the shadows assaulting his brother weaken.

And in the lull he created, other shadows slipped in, coming not between Mikhyel and himself, but between Mikhyel and those shadow attackers.

Support from within. That would have to be enough.

{Gods, Deymio . . .} Weak. Exhausted.

"I *can't*, Khyel!" It was not morality. It was one physical act or the other. Hold the Rings, or—

"I can," a gravelly voice snarled, and with an audible snap, the battle for control ended.

Chapter Seven

They'd won.

His mind was his own. The stench had vanished, leaving only the faintest hint of herbs and spring flowers and sun-warmed oranges: his tiny coalition of sanity, whose intervention had saved him in the end.

For a moment, Mikhyel didn't even try to move, the weight holding him on his back beyond his remaining strength to shrug off. Then someone else rolled the weight away, and he levered himself up on one elbow to stare into those sightless eyes in a face lying at an unnatural angle to the rest of the slender body.

He thought perhaps, he should feel something more, pity, perhaps, for the young hiller, but his only inclination was to close those eyes and adjust the body to a more natural orientation. Not even the grating sound as he turned the head moved him or disgusted him. Done was done. In truth, the young hiller had been murdered long before any of them had entered the Tower.

A big hand hooked his arm and levered him to his feet. Ganfrion. And it was Ganfrion who held out the robe Mheltiri had shed during the encounter.

Mind-numb, he slipped into the garment, balanced with one hand to the wall as Ganfrion lapped the front and tied a careless knot in the cummerbund sash to hold it in place. When Ganfrion was done, he pressed Gan's arm as he moved past.

"Thank you," he found the breath somewhere to say, for all it was too shallow a gesture for what he owed his gor-man, not to mention his brother who stood steadfastly still, holding those many times cursed, blackened rings stable in their orbits.

But they would have to wait. He fell to his knees beside Dancer, that part of the business still unresolved.

"Khyel . . ." Deymorin's hoarse voice brought him around. Mikhyel swayed as the room swirled around him. "Khyel, I can't hold them."

He tried to reach Deymorin, to add his strength to his brother's, but his own disorientation and a sudden strange shift in Deymorin's pattern held him off. {Nikki!} he called, recognizing the source of that shift of center.

The answer was faint. All Nikki's energy was pouring into Deymorin.

{You've got to move him!} Nikki sent. {Pull him out now—get *out* of there! The hiller was right. There's something wrong about the Rings . . . they're going to explode. Don't try to move Deymorin. He can escape! Just get Dancer away from him!}

That was what Deymorin was trying to tell him.

Mikhyel swayed back to Dancer, who reached to grab his hand. {Just pull me out, Khy. Never mind the legs.}

Mikhyel shook his head, swallowed hard against the nausea that threatened. {I can jump us out. I know . . .}

{Oil. In my bags . . .}

"Not necessary," he whispered, the mental touch sickening him further. He called to Mother, seeking a bridge . . . but she wasn't there to receive them. That same sense of *wrong* that surrounded Deymorin plunged deep into the heart of the node.

"Rings," he muttered and cast further. Nikki was too absorbed, and Deymorin's bridge to Deymorin's source of strength. Barsitum would be ideal, but there was no link, no one to draw them there, no one to receive—

{Here, Ravenhair,} Mirym's thoughts brushed his, a soothing sense of welcome and stability. {Bring him here . . .} and the image that formed in his mind, the haven for Dancer's delicate bones, was the garden cavern pool.

{If it rejects him?}

{Kill or cure, Ravenhair. I believe it will welcome him, as it did you.}

He was suddenly all the way back in the Tower. "Trust me?" he whispered, and Dancer reached up an arm, hooking his neck to pull him down for the deep kiss they'd been denied.

{Mirym?} he called, and she was there, as at the end of a long tunnel, hands outstretched in welcome. One arm locked around Dancer's shoulders, he reached the other toward her. Fingers touched, and this time, the transition seemed endless, a gentle drift toward . . .

Sanctuary.

Chapter Eight

The moment his brother vanished from the room leaving only a pile of colorful robe mingling with Thyerri's blanket, Deymorin hissed, "Get the men clear!"

Ganfrion shouted down the stairwell and shoved Zelin, who had arrived in Ganfrion's wake, out the door.

All the while, Deymorin could *feel* the pulse of the Rings, a multilevel vibration increasingly out of synch with itself. He held them spinning to the pattern he'd received from Mikhyel, but his head was spinning with them. The pulse had caught his heartbeat and threatened to pull it into the same arrhythmic state.

"Now you," he ordered Ganfrion when the men were clear, but Ganfrion didn't leave. "Dammit, gorMikhyel, get the fuck out of here!"

But Ganfrion ignored him. Ganfrion grabbed up a pillow and threw it out the door, a second followed. "Back up, toward the door."

"You're mad!"

A third pillow and another and another.

"And you've a woman and child waiting for you. Not to mention a brother—somewhere—who will have my hide if you don't make it home safe. *Back the fuck up!*"

He backed, there being nothing left in him to argue with. He was half conscious of Ganfrion kicking obstacles from his path behind him, then:

"Hold."

A last shuffling beside him, a tasseled corner teasing his peripheral vision.

"On count of three," Ganfrion said, "Fall back and let the damn things go. —One."

But they'd delayed too long. His heartbeat was following the Rings, painfully.

"Two."

He was caught in their self-destruction.

"Fuck it!"

Something large and heavy hit him in the gut and his hold on the Rings shattered. The world erupted around him as he skidded on his back and headfirst down the stairwell, sliding along a carpet of pillows, Ganfrion's large body plummeting after.

He came up hard against the wall of the first landing, shaken, battered, blinded—temporarily, he hoped—but alive. He lay there, heaving after breath, waiting for his heartbeat to stabilize, and on his first reliable thought queried: {Khyel?}

{Safe, brother.} Crystal clear. An image of that underground garden, a sense of Dancer, safe and asleep, drifting on the surface of the pool, his body held steady by loving hands and mind, a sense of following. And Nikki, in distant Rhomatum, sighed with relief . . . having just told the wisest and hardest lie of his life—he'd told one brother the other could escape . . . to avoid losing them both—and was relieved, ever so relieved it had turned out to be the truth.

Deymorin kept that link open, needing that sense of his brothers more than ever, his assurance of life beyond the darkness that surrounded him.

And on his first reliable breath, he queried, "Ganfrion?"

No answer.

He cast blindly about, found the gorman's body twisted around that damned pillow. Found a pulse, and finally, with his fumbling at it, roused a groan.

"Keep your bloody hands to yourself, Rhomandi," Ganfrion's gravel-voice snarled, and he gladly retreated.

"Lord Rhomandi?" The query floated up the stairwell, and a light, an oily Outsider torch, preceded Zelin's square face. "Thank the . . ." Zelin's eyes widened as his gaze followed a trail up the stairwell.

Feathers. The damned stairwell was a trail of pillows, shattered by their passage. And in Ganfrion's hands was the most telling of them all: the huge soft shield he'd held between them and the Rings, ripped and shredded, filled with bits of metal that would have similarly shredded their skin if not for that pillow.

He raised a brow at the gorman. "Fast thinking."

Ganfrion tipped his head. "You're welcome."

Deymorin pushed himself to his feet, reached a hand to haul Ganfrion up beside him.

"Let's go home."

Chapter Nine

The baby was coming, and Deymorin hadn't made it back.

Kiyrstin swallowed her disappointment and welcomed Nikki's heartfelt surrogacy, as much for his sake as for hers. Nikki, banned from his own child's birthing bed, deprived all along of the intimacy she and Deymorin had shared, needed to be included in some part of this next major transition beyond conception.

For all the arrival was early, doctors and midwives agreed that everything was proceeding quite normally. The contractions came regularly now, and Nikki's hand on hers provided a link, she knew beyond doubt, directly to Deymorin.

She could almost hear him cursing with every powerful stride of the horse beneath him.

Riding through the night, while she lay in splendor in the huge Princeps suite in Rhomandi House, her every need supplied, her pangs timed by the best doctors.

And all she really wanted was his big beautiful body coming through those—

"Ah!" She gasped as the contraction came sooner than she'd expected.

"Breathe deeply, Lady Kiyrstin," the midwife murmured, and: "Time to move her to the birth chair, Master Nikaenor."

He nodded and gripped her hand, his face a crazed mixture of excitement, joy, and concern.

"Carry you?" he asked. "Or do it yourself?"

But there was mischief behind those eyes as well. She eyed him suspiciously. "Going to drop me?"

"Wouldn't dare." He held out his hands, she chuckled and wrapped her arms around his neck.

"Unhand my woman, you ungrateful brat!" Deymorin's voice filled the room, and in the next moment, Deymorin filled her arms, filthy, sweaty, horse-smelling, and oh, so real. "Told you I'd make it." His whisper in her ear was all she needed to make her world perfect.

§　§　§

Nikki closed the door silently behind him. For all he was with Deymorin in a way he couldn't avoid here in Rhomandi House, he didn't need to intrude further on this exquisitely personal moment.

He'd known how close to the room Deymorin was. Had conspired silently with him for a moment that had proved more than worth the effort. Now, it was only right for them to complete the moment together.

He followed the serpentine route to the wing that contained his wife's chambers. Within her room, a similarly early delivery went on, a delivery from which he had long since been banned. He wouldn't risk his child by insisting, but he feared on a level beyond rational thought for the child's safety on completely different grounds.

Mikhyel had shared his experience with them, had remembered, in such detail as only Mikhyel could manage, the conversation with Mheltiri. The three of them had agreed not to reveal their suspicions regarding Lidye, but to observe and act with the knowledge that they might be dealing with a dangerously unbalanced conglomerate of individuals.

And that conglomerate was even now giving birth to his child.

He longed to reach out with hands and mind to that vulnerable entity striving to escape the womb in which it had drifted for so many months. But he didn't dare. Whoever Lidye was, she would know that intrusion, and take steps to eliminate his presence.

So he sat outside the chambers, like those fathers he despised, those who refused to stand with their partner at this vital moment in their child's life. As his own father had remained distant from his mother, the night of his own violent birth . . .

How, he wondered, did he know that? Then he recognized it for a thought drifting to him from Mikhyel, still in New Khoratum with Dancer and his own soon-to-be-born child.

"Nikki?" Jerrik's voice came from the shadowed hallway that led to his own rooms. "Want company?"

"Always," he said, and held out his hand to welcome his friend. Friend, as Raulind, en route even now to Mikhyel's side, was Mikhyel's friend and confidante. Jerrik, with whom he'd shared all his dreams, once so long ago.

"It'll work out, Nikki," Jerrik said, into the silence that grew between them. A comfortable silence. A silence of trust grown out of the years of being together. "What Lidye is or is not, that's your baby, too, and that's got to count for something."

Nikki nodded . . . and the silence settled around them.

§   §   §

{You were right, as always, Mirym,} Mikhyel said as he cradled the child in his arms, immersing it in the pool to cleanse it before releasing it to her waiting arms. {I was wrong to anticipate. I leave the problem of finding a name to you.}

He took the tiny hand and touched it with his lips, then rose to join his own Child of Rakshi, free of the pool for the first time, standing on legs uncertain from disuse, but sound again of bone and muscle.

Dancer's arm slid around him and pulled him close, and Dancer's breath brushed Mikhyel's ear.

{How does it feel to be a papa?}
{Strange. Very strange.}
{Would you be willing to make another?}

He turned to find Dancer's wide eyes fixed on mother and child. With a chuckle, he cupped Temorii's face with his hand and turned those wide eyes to him. {Rein in your hormones, love. There's a lot more than making babies in our near future.}

A slow smile answered him, and the look in those Tamshi eyes shifted, the mischievous demon he loved so very dearly rising to the surface. Thyerri's fingers tangled in his hair and pulled his face in to a deep, deep kiss.

And somewhere, deep inside him, Mheltiri sighed.

§ § §

"Guess," Deymorin said, holding the child close while the blood cleared the umbilical cord.

"Oh, stuff it, Rags," Kiyrstin whispered, tired, but deliriously happy, "and hand me our son."

"You peeked."

"Hardly."

He laughed and set their daughter on her mother's breast. "How do you feel about the name Temorii, Shepherdess?"

§ § §

Lidye's cries and curses had gone silent an hour ago. There was a great deal of rushing about within the chamber, but no one answered when Nikki rang the bell.

He swallowed the wine Jerrik handed him and stared at the door, waiting for that distinctive cry that said his child was safe. Jerri sat at his side, hand on his knee. But there was nothing he could say. Nothing anyone could say, except . . .

The door opened, and Diorak slipped out carrying a silent bundle. The physician looked up, met his gaze, and shook his head.

Nikki rose slowly to his feet, stunned.

"I'm sorry, Master Nikaenor," Diorak said in a low voice

as he crossed the room. "We did everything we could, but . . . it was an unnatural birth from the start. Too early. Too strained. We couldn't save her."

"Her?" Nikki tried to make sense of the words. "Lidye was so certain it would be a boy."

The physician stopped short. "And indeed it is. Your *wife,* Master Nikaenor, is dead."

And from the depths of the blanket, his son stared up at him with old, old eyes.

Coda

The dance rings of Khoratum lay silent in the windswept sand. Behind them, the stands of the amphitheater rose silent and empty, as the city beyond them was empty, gone cold and dark with the destruction of the tower rings.

The sky was heavy with the year's first snow, though it wouldn't fall for hours yet.

Footprints in the sand, seemingly aimless at first, began, as Mikhyel knew they would, to form a pattern. With far less thought, bits of clothing, designed to warm a body against winter's chill, littered the pattern.

Dancer's muscles were warm now, his body strong and sure, and physically unable to remain still in this place where the heartbeat of the mountain, the music of the wind rang so loudly even Mikhyel could hear them. And clothing, for a dancer, merely restricted the body's intercourse with the music.

They'd avoided the place since returning to Khoratum, not because of the memories it held, Mikhyel realized now, but because Thyerri had known that a Dancer could not enter it and ignore that music. And once the Dance began in his lover, the Dance ruled, not the limitations of his body.

Mikhyel understood that now, and accepted it. Accepted Dancer's judgment that the body he treasured was strong enough to meet the mountain's challenge.

So he gathered that scattered clothing that would be welcomed again when the Dance was finished. He settled in the center of one circle, the first, which Dancer had placed around him, careful not to disrupt the pattern, as he had carefully followed it in collecting the clothing.

Such things were important.

They were at once at their closest and most distant when the Dance took over. He felt the exquisite stretch and pull of muscle as Dancer swayed and twisted and tumbled to the music that rang clear and true within that shared awareness. Warmth filled him even as the chill of the ground crept through his own clothing.

He put Thyerri's coat on under his own, for added warmth and to keep it warm . . . and for the touch of that which still held Thyerri's warmth.

The Dance held a new dimension for him, roused feelings at once intense and soothing. They made love with increasing ease these days, working steadily past his own entrenched inhibitions against intimacy · of all kinds. Nightmares came . . . and went, now that he had Thyerri/Temorii/Dancer to help conquer them. The secrets that haunted them both rose to the surface . . . and were secrets no more.

There were arguments, and many of them. There were fights, and occasionally, Mikhyel won.

Raulind had returned, first to New Khoratum, and then here, where with his household staff he had created a place of comfort—a haven, despite the lack of ley-power.

He'd learned to appreciate a warm fire last winter, and this year that warm fire held the added attraction of a warm Dancer.

In response to that fleeting image . . . or perhaps he had conjured it . . . the Dance flickered and flowed an undulating path that leaped and tumbled and slithered back to him, curling around him, brushing his lips, then darting away again on a breeze.

He laughed.

The mountain and the empty seats of the amphitheater echoed his unadulterated joy.

Mother remained silent, though her scent ran clean and fresh, as it hadn't, Dancer maintained, since he was a youth.

As it hadn't, in truth, since the rings had been raised.

Hillers returned to the village that had been. The spring that had been the center of their worship had been freed of the tower complex and made available to their needs.

Since the birth of his child, he'd returned once to Rhomatum, jumped there, in part as a test to make certain he could, in part to see his brothers and his niece and nephew—and to return the Rhomandi ring at last to its rightful owner.

He hadn't even visited his offices.

The process he had set in motion was sound. The men he'd put into power with that process were proving capable, and he was content. How long his vacation would last depended in part on a future he could not yet predict.

A future he had not as yet even tried to predict.

The Dance had arrived at those fallen rings and achieved a sorrow that cut Mikhyel to the core. The radical wove among the inanimate steel, and with his passage the steel itself sent a minor scaled wail into the Song.

Tears threatened and fell. Without the Tower, without the umbrella of energy, the rings would not rise, and the Dance of Khoratum would never again be that meeting ground of past and present.

And in Dancer's head was the memory of flying among the rings. Mikhyel shared that joy, the sorrow of loss, the wish that it could be different. Nikki and Deymorin, busy in their own lives, far distant, caught that sorrow and sent sympathetic support.

But something flared in him, a sense of . . . injustice. Dancer had given so much, suffered so much, lost—so very much. He deserved . . . more. He was a Child of Rakshi, Rakshi incarnate, some said. The rings were gone for him, but the leythium caverns still lived. That flitting dance among the living strands was his by right.

{Mother!} Mikhyel called, but gently, slipping it past Dancer's exquisitely balanced concentration. And he included in that call his sense of injustice, his proposal for retribution . . .

Laughter: faint, but without question, the essence of Mother at her most deliciously wicked. And a thought drifted up, lacking strength and form, but full of confidence

{You still have much to learn, child . . .}

The sand about his supporting hands vibrated.

The singing of the steel shifted, a smooth transition from that minor wail to the sound of blades clashing in the salle

And as twilight closed about him, the rings began to rise

Without questioning, without energy wasted, Dancer leaped joyously among them, darting between honed edges as they scissored past one another, challenging the rings to try and end the Dance even before it began in earnest.

A Dance of life, as it had always been. A challenge between the Dancer and Rakshi, between logic and fate.

And as the rings sorted themselves in the air, Dancer put them into motion, leaping one to the next, making them spin to his own whimsy, adding their harmonies to the music of the mountain. The final notes of the symphony came from the pipes of the organ, whose symbiotic link to the rings was one of the engineer's secrets.

At its worst, it was cacophony. At its best . . .

Mikhyel was on his feet, never aware of having risen. And he swayed to those rhythms, as captive to them as Dancer himself.

Even the ground undulated.

Laughter filled him, his own and Dancer's. Perhaps the mountain itself laughed.

And from the undulating sand came a hint of iridescence quickly hidden . . . like Dancer playing with the audience from the entrance to the arena. Teasing. Rousing a sense of anticipation as it caught the glow of . . . starlight.

The clouds were gone.

That playful essence darted, dancing just beneath the surface of the sand—until, he suddenly realized, it was certain he was watching.

Then it burst forth, a ribbon of pure leythium, swirling twisting—

And darting into the rings.

The chase was on. Radical dancer against radical streamer. A dance without precedent. A dance for its audience of one, who stood, transfixed . . .

. . . as the lights within the city began to glow.

IRENE RADFORD

THE DRAGON NIMBUS HISTORY

☐ **THE DRAGON'S TOUCHSTONE (Book One)**
0-88677-744-5—$6.99

☐ **THE LAST BATTLEMAGE (Book Two)** 0-88677-774-7—$6.99

☐ **THE RENEGADE DRAGON (Book Three)** 0-88677-855-7—$6.99
The great magical wars have come to an end. But in bringing peace, Nimbulan, the last Battlemage, has lost his powers. Dragon magic is the only magic legal to practice. And the kingdom's only hope against dangerous technology lies in the one place to which no dragon will fly . . .

THE DRAGON NIMBUS TRILOGY

☐ **THE GLASS DRAGON (Book One)** 0-88677-634-1—$6.99

☐ **THE PERFECT PRINCESS (Book Two)** 0-88677-678-3—$6.99

☐ **THE LONELIEST MAGICIAN (Book Three)**
0-88677-709-7—$6.99

Prices slightly higher in Canada **DAW: 188**